Girls Burn Brighter

ALSO BY SHOBHA RAO

An Unrestored Woman

Girls Burn Brighter

Shobha Rao

FLATIRON
BOOKS
NEW YORK

GIRLS BURN BRIGHTER. Copyright © 2018 by Shobha Rao. All rights reserved. Printed in the United States of America. For information, address Flatiron Books, 175 Fifth Avenue, New York, N.Y. 10010.

www.flatironbooks.com

Designed by Kathryn Parise

The Library of Congress Cataloging-in-Publication Data is available upon request.

ISBN 978-1-250-07425-6 (hardcover)
ISBN 978-1-250-07426-3 (ebook)

Our books may be purchased in bulk for promotional, educational, or business use. Please contact your local bookseller or the Macmillan Corporate and Premium Sales Department at 1-800-221-7945, extension 5442, or by email at MacmillanSpecialMarkets@macmillan.com.

First Edition: March 2018

10 9 8 7 6 5 4 3 2 1

For Leigh Ann Morlock

Indravalli

The most striking thing about the temple near the village of Indravalli was not readily apparent. No, one had to first climb the mountain and come close; one had to take a long, thoughtful look at the entrance. At the door. Not at its carved panels, or its fine graining, but at how the door stood so brave and so luminous and so alone. How it seemed to stand strong and tall, as if still a tree. It was the wood, lumbered from a grove of trees northwest of Indravalli. The grove was cultivated by an old woman—they said more than a hundred years old—who was childless. She and her husband had been farmers, and when she'd come to understand that she would never have children she'd started planting trees as a way to care for something, as a way to nurture something fragile and lovely. Her husband had surrounded the young saplings with thorny bushes to keep out wild animals, and it being a dry region, she'd had to carry water from many kilometers away to water them. Their grove now boasted hundreds of trees. All of them steady and swaying in the dry wind.

A journalist from a local newspaper once went to interview the old woman. He arrived at teatime, and he and the old woman sat in the shade of one of the trees, its wide leaves rustling high above them. They sipped their tea soundlessly; even the journalist, forgetting all his questions, was overcome by the quiet green beauty of the place. He had heard of her childlessness and her recently dead husband, and so, to be delicate, he said, "They must keep you company. The trees."

The old woman's gray eyes smiled, and she said, "Oh, yes. I'm never lonely. I have hundreds of children."

The journalist saw an opportunity. "So you see them as children?"

"Don't you?"

There was silence. The journalist took a long, deep look into the grove of trees, their thick trunks, their strength, despite drought and disease and insects and floods and famine, and yet shining with gold-green light. Radiant even in the heat and heaviness of afternoon. "You're a fortunate woman," he said, "to have so many sons."

The old woman looked up at him, her eyes on fire, her wrinkled face taking on the glow of her girlhood. "I am fortunate," she said, "but you're mistaken, young man. These aren't my sons. Not one. These," she said, "are my daughters."

1

Poornima never once noticed the door of the temple. Neither did Savitha. But the temple watched them closely, perched as it was on the mountain that towered over Indravalli. The village itself was near the banks of the Krishna River, a hundred or so kilometers inland from the Bay of Bengal. Though it was situated in a level valley, the hamlet was shadowed by one of the largest mountains in Andhra Pradesh, called Indravalli Konda, with the temple halfway up its eastern face. It was painted a brilliant white and looked to Savitha like a big boll of cotton. To Poornima, the temple looked like the full moon, perpetually embraced by the sky and the branches of the surrounding trees.

Poornima was ten years old when she stood outside her family's hut, staring at the temple; she turned to her father, who was seated on the hemprope cot behind her, and asked, "Why did you and Amma name me after the full moon?" Her mother was sitting at the loom, working, so Poornima didn't want to bother her with the question. But she might've—she might've thought nothing at all of bothering her, of clinging to her neck, of breathing in every last trace of her scent—had she known her mother would be dead in another five years. But her father didn't even look up when she asked

him. He just went on rolling his tobacco. Maybe he hadn't heard. So Poornima began again. "Nanna, why did you—"

"Is dinner ready?"

"Almost."

"How many times do I have to tell you to have it ready when I come
in?"

"Was it because I was born on a full moon night?"

He shrugged. "I don't think so."

Poornima then imagined the face of a baby, and she said, "Was my face
round like the moon?"

He sighed. He finally said, "Your mother had a dream, a few days after
you were born. A sadhu came to her in the dream, and he said if we named
you Poornima, we'd have a boy next."

Poornima looked at him as he lit his tobacco, and then she went back
inside the hut. She never again asked about her name. On full moon nights,
she tried her hardest to not even look up. It's just a stone, she decided, a
big gray stone in the sky. But it was hard to forget, wasn't it? That conversation. It would pop up out of nowhere at times, seemingly out of nothing.
While she tasted for salt in a pot of sambar, for instance, or while she
served her father tea. The sadhu had been right, of course: she had three
little brothers. So what was there to be sad about? Nothing, nothing at all.
She even felt pride at times, and said to herself, I was their hope and I came
true. Imagine not coming true. Imagine not having hope.

At fifteen, Poornima came of marriageable age, and she stopped going to
the convent school. She began to sit at the spinning wheel, the charkha, in
her free time to help the household. Each spool of thread she completed—
the thread sometimes red, sometimes blue, sometimes silver—earned her
two rupees, and this seemed like a fortune to her. And in some ways, it was:
when she'd begun menstruating at the age of thirteen, she was gifted the
most expensive piece of clothing she'd ever worn, a silk langa costing a hun-

dred rupees. I can earn that in less than two months, she thought breathlessly. Besides: that she, a girl, could earn anything, anything at all, lent her such a deep and abiding feeling of importance—of *worth*—that she sat at the charkha every chance she got. She woke early in the morning to spin, then spun after the breakfast dishes were washed, after lunch was prepared and served, and then again after dinner. Their hut had no electricity, so her spinning was a race against the sun. Full moon nights were also bright enough to continue, but they only came around once a month. So on most nights, once the sun went down, she'd put her charkha away, look impatiently at the crescent moon or the half-moon or the gibbous moon, and complain, "Why can't you always be full?"

But sunlight and moonlight weren't Poornima's only considerations. The other one, *the main one*, was that her mother was ill. Cancer, as far as the doctor at the American hospital in Tenali could tell. Medicine was expensive, and the doctor put her on a diet of fruits and nuts—also expensive. Her father, who made the homespun cotton saris that their region of Guntur district was famous for, could barely keep his wife and five children fed on government-rationed rice and lentils, let alone the luxury of fruits and nuts. But Poornima didn't mind. She relished—no, not just relished, but delighted, actually *savored*—the food she was able to buy for her mother every day: two bananas, a tiny apple, and a handful of cashews. By savoring, it was not that she actually ate any of the fruit or nuts. Never did she take even a single bite, though her mother did, once, coax her into accepting a cashew, which, when her mother turned away for an instant, Poornima placed back on the pile. No, by savoring, what Poornima did was watch her mother slowly eating the banana, even chewing such a soft thing exhausting her, but Poornima watched her with such conviction, such hope, that she thought she could actually *see* her mother getting stronger. As if strength were a seed. And all she had to do was add her two rupees' worth of food and watch it grow.

It got so that Poornima almost made as much as her father. Here is what she did: she'd get loops of raw thread, undivided and in thick bundles, and by using the charkha, her job was to spin the thread so that it separated, and as it did, wound around a metal canister. She once looked at the thread wound around the canister and thought it looked just like a tiny wooden barrel, nearly the size of her littlest brother's head. This thread would then eventually end up on the loom where her father made the saris. It was treated further before it got to the loom, but Poornima always thought she could spot the lengths of thread that she had spun. The canisters that she had wound it around. Anyone would've laughed if she'd told them this—they all look the same, they'd have said—but that wasn't true. Her hands had felt the canister, known the places it was dented, the contours of its body, the patterns of its rust. She had held them, and it seemed to her that anything a person has held is a thing they never really let go. Like the small wind-up clock her teacher had given her when she'd left school. It had a round blue face, four little legs, and two bells that chimed every hour. When her teacher, an old and embittered Catholic nun, had given it to her, she'd said, "I suppose they'll get you married now. With a child a year for the next ten. Hold this. Hold *on* to this. You won't know what I mean now, but you might one day." Then she'd wound up the clock and let it chime. "That sound," she'd said. "Remember: that sound is yours. No one else's but yours." Poornima had no idea what the old nun was talking about, but she thought the chiming of the clock was the most exquisite sound she'd ever heard.

She began carrying the clock everywhere. She put it next to her charkha while she worked. She placed it beside her plate when she ate. She put it by her mat when she slept. Until one day, just like that, the clock stopped chiming, and her father exclaimed, "Finally. I thought that thing would never stop."

A few months after the clock stopped chiming Poornima's mother died. Poornima had just turned sixteen—she was the eldest of the five children—and watching her mother die was like watching a fine blue morning turn to gray. What she missed most about her mother was her voice. It was soft and mellifluous and warm against the rat-chewed walls of the small hut. It pleased Poornima that such a lovely voice should reach for her, that it should cut through the long hours, when all those hours really amounted to were two bananas, an apple, and a handful of cashews. Her mother's was a voice that could make even those few things seem like the ransom of kings. And now Poornima had lost both her mother and the clock.

With her mother dead, Poornima slowed her charkha; she put it away sometimes even in the middle of the day, and she would stare at the walls of the hut and think, I'll forget her voice. Maybe that's what that old nun had meant, that you forget a sound you don't hear every day. I don't think I will now, but I will. And then I'll have lost everything. Once she thought this, she knew she had to remember more than a voice, she had to remember a moment, and this is the one that came to her: In the course of her mother's illness, she had been well enough one morning to comb Poornima's hair. It had been bright and sunny outside and the brush strokes had been so gentle and light that Poornima had felt as if the person holding the comb were not a person at all but a small bird perched on its handle. After three or four strokes her mother had stopped suddenly. She'd rested her hand on her daughter's head for a moment, and Poornima turned to find her mother's eyes filled with tears. Her mother had looked back at her and with a sadness that had seemed old and endless, she'd said, "Poornima, I'm too tired. I'm so tired."

How long after that had she died?

Three, maybe four months later, Poornima guessed. They'd woken up one morning and her eyes had been open and empty and lifeless. Poornima hadn't been able to cry, though. Not when she'd helped bathe and dress her mother's body. Not when her father and brothers had carried her, jasmine-laden, through the streets of the village. Not even as the funeral pyre had burned down to a cold ash. Nor when she'd strung the last chrysanthemum on the garland that hung from the framed portrait of her mother. Only later, when she'd walked out into the season's first cool autumn morning, had she cried. Or tried to cry. The tears, she recalled, had been paltry. At the time, she'd felt like a bad daughter for not crying, for not *weeping*, but no matter how sad she'd felt, how profound her sorrow, she'd only managed to squeeze out one or two tears. A vague reddening of the eyes. "Amma," she'd said, looking up at the sky, "forgive me. It's not that I don't love you. Or miss you. I don't understand; everyone *else* is crying. Buckets. But tears aren't the only measure, are they?"

Still, what she had imagined came true: as the months wore on she forgot her mother's voice. But what she *did* remember, the only thing that truly stayed with her, was that for a short time—while combing her hair—her mother had rested her hand on her. It was the slightest of gestures, and yet Poornima felt it, always: the weight of her mother's hand. A weight so delicate and fine, it was like the spatter of raindrops after a hot summer's day. A weight so small and tired, but with strength enough to muscle through her veins like blood.

In the end, she decided, it was the most beautiful weight.

Once a month, Poornima went to the temple on Indravalli Konda to offer prayers for her mother. She stood in the incense-choked anteroom and watched the priest, hoping the gods would speak to her, would tell her amma was with them, though what she truly yearned to reach was the deepa, more a small lantern, that was perched at the very summit of the mountain. Sometimes she'd stand outside their hut and look up, on a Sunday or a festival day, and it would glow, distant and yellow and blinking, like a star. "Who lights it?" she once asked her father.

"Lights what?"

"The deepa, on the summit."

Her father, sitting outside the hut after dinner, his arms fatigued, his body hunched, glanced at Indravalli Konda and said, "Some priest, probably. Some kid."

Poornima was quiet for a moment, and then she said, "I think Amma lights it."

Her father looked at her. His look was dark, ravaged, as if he'd just walked out of a burning building. Then he asked for his tea. When she handed it to him, he said, "Another ten months."

"Ten months?"

"Till her one-year ceremony."

Now Poornima understood what he was saying. After a family death, it was inauspicious to have a celebration of any sort, let alone a wedding, for a full year. It had been two months since her mother's death. In another ten—her father was saying—she would be married.

"I've already talked to Ramayya. There's a farmer near here. A few acres of his own, and a good worker. Two buffalo, a cow, some goats. He doesn't want to wait, though. He needs the money right now. And he's worried you won't take to being a farmer's wife. I told Ramayya, I told him, Look at her. Just look at her. Strong as an ox, she *is* an ox. Forget the oxen, *she* could plow the fields."

Poornima nodded and went back inside the hut. The only mirror they owned was a handheld mirror; she couldn't even see her entire face unless she held it at arm's length, but she held it up to her face, saw an eye, a nose, and then she moved it down to her neck and breasts and hips. An ox? She was overcome with a sudden sadness. Why, she couldn't say. It didn't matter why. It was childish to be sad for no reason at all. She only knew that had her mother been alive, she would've probably already been married. Maybe even pregnant, or with a baby. That was no cause for sadness either. She was concerned about this farmer, though. What if he *did* make her pull the plow? What if her mother-in-law was cruel? What if all she had were girls? Then she heard her amma speak. None of those things has even happened yet, she heard her say. And then she said, Everything is already written in the stars, Poornima. By the gods. We can't alter a thing. So what does it matter? Why worry?

She was right, of course. But when she lay on her mat that night, Poornima thought about the farmer, she thought about the deepa on top of Indravalli Konda, she thought about beauty. If her skin had been lighter, her hair thicker, or if her eyes had been bigger, her father might've found a better match for her: someone who wanted a wife, not an ox. She'd once heard Ramayya saying, when he'd come to see her father, "Your Poornima's a good worker, but you know these boys today, they want a *modern* girl. They want fashion." Fashion? Then she thought about her mother; she thought about her last days, spent writhing in pain; she thought about the weight of her mother's hand on her head; and then she thought about the two bananas, the apple, and the handful of cashews, and as if *this* were the moment her heart had been waiting for, it broke, and out poured so many tears that she thought they would never stop. She cried silently, hoping her sleeping father and brothers and sister wouldn't hear, the mat she lay on soaked so thoroughly that she smelled the wet earth underneath, as if after a rainfall, and at the end of it, her body was so wracked with sobs, so drained of feeling, so exquisitely empty, that she actually smiled, and then fell into a deep and dreamless sleep.

2

It was around this time, around the time of the death of Poornima's mother, when Savitha's mother—much older than Poornima's mother would've been, far poorer, and yet who hadn't been ill a single day of her life—came to Savitha, her eldest daughter, of seventeen or so, and confessed that they had no food for that night's dinner. "No food?" Savitha said, surprised. "What about the twenty rupees I got for the bundles yesterday?" By bundles, she meant the bundles of discarded paper and plastic she'd collected at the garbage heaps outside of town, next to the Christian cemetery. It had taken her three days of crawling over stinking and rotting and putrid scraps, fighting off the other garbage pickers, along with the pigs and the dogs, to make the twenty rupees.

"Bhima took it."

"He *took* it?"

"We still owe him thirty."

Savitha sighed, and though the sigh was slow and diffuse, her mind was alert and racing. She thought of her three younger sisters, who also scoured the garbage heaps; her mother, who cleaned houses; and her father, who, after years of drinking, had finally given it up when his rheumatoid arthritis had gotten so bad that he could no longer hold a glass in his hand. He might get a handout from the priests at the temple, where he begged most days, but it would hardly be enough for him, let alone his wife and four daughters. She also had two older brothers, both of whom had gone to Hyderabad looking for work, with promises of sending money home, but there had not even been a letter from either in the two years since they'd gone.

She stood in the middle of their meager hut and tallied all the ways in which she could make money: she could collect garbage, which clearly wasn't bringing in enough; she could cook and clean, as her mother did, though there were hardly any families rich enough in Indravalli to keep even her mother employed; she could work the charkha and the loom—she did belong to the caste of weavers, after all—but money from making cotton saris was dwindling each year, and given how little each sari brought in, if a family owned a charkha or a loom, they kept the work within the family, to keep the money there as well. Savitha looked at their charkha, broken, draped with cobwebs, slumped in the corner of their hut like a heap of firewood waiting for a match. For five years now, they hadn't had the money to get it fixed. If only it were fixed, she thought, I could make us more money. She was, of course, aware of the absurdity of the thought: she needed money to make money.

But thread! To hold it again between her fingers.

She still remembered clutching a boll of cotton in her tiny hands when she'd been a little girl and being amazed that such a bit of silly fluff, filled with dark and stubborn seeds, could become something as lovely and smooth and flat and soft as a sari.

From boll to loom to cloth to sari, she thought.

She left the dark hut, the broken charkha, and her mother, staring list-lessly at the empty pots and pans, and wandered into the village. She walked past the huts of the laundresses and past the train station and past the to-bacco shop and the dry goods shop and the sari shop and the tailoring shop and past even the Hanuman temple, in the middle of Indravalli, and found herself in front of the small gated opening to the weaving collective. She heard voices and the whirring of a fan. And just there, if she put her face to the gate, she could smell the faint aroma of new cloth, a mingling of freshly cooked rice and spring rain and teakwood and something of those hard seeds, so unwilling to let go. More captivating to her—this slight scent, lost so soon in the wind—than the most fragrant flower.

With hardly a thought, she opened the creaking gate with a firm grip and went inside.

Poornima's father owned two looms. One was where he worked, and the other was where her mother had worked. They'd each taken two or three days to complete a sari, but now, with only one person at the loom, there were only half the number of saris. That meant half the money. Poornima was too busy with her charkha and the household chores to take over the second loom, her brothers and sister too small to reach the treadles, so her father began looking for help. He asked everyone he knew, he inquired at the tea shop he frequented in the evenings, he went to the weaving collective and announced he was willing to offer a quarter of the proceeds of every sari that was made, along with meals. There were no takers. Indravalli was a village composed mainly of sari makers, and most of the young men were busy helping their own families. The village was purportedly founded in the time of the Ikshvakus, and ever since, had been weaving cloth—in ancient times, clothing for the royal courts, but now simply the cotton saris worn by the peasantry and, occasionally, the intellectual elite. The Quit India Movement, along with the image of Gandhi sitting at his charkha, spinning, and his inception of the homespun ideal, had improved Indravalli's prospects considerably, especially in the years leading up to independence. But now it was 2001, a new century, and the young men of Indravalli, those who were born into the caste of weavers, to which Poornima and her family also belonged, were struggling to feed their own families. In fact, many had abandoned weaving and taken up other occupations.

"Weaving is dying. It's death," her father said. "I heard they have fancy machines now." Poornima knew that was why her father was looking to marry her off to the farmer. He laughed bitterly and said, "They may have invented a machine to make cloth, but let's see them invent a machine to grow food."

Poornima laughed, too. But she was hardly listening to him. She was thinking that if she could get her father to buy more kerosene, she could weave at night, by lantern light, and then he wouldn't have to hire someone.

But the following week, a girl leaned into the doorway of the hut. Poornima looked up from her cooking. She couldn't see the girl's face—the sun was behind her—but by the curve of her body, by the way it bent into the low doorway with the grace of a strong and swaying palm, she knew she was young. Her voice confirmed it, though it was more gentle, and older, than she expected. "Your father?"

She could obviously see Poornima. "Come back in the evening," she said, squinting. "He'll be home before dark." She turned away and reached to take the lid off the pot of rice; as she did, the edge of it burned her finger. She snatched the hand away—the finger was already turning red—and put it in her mouth. When she looked up again, the girl was still there. She hesitated, and the image of the palm came back: but now it seemed like a young palm tree, just a sapling, one that wasn't quite sure which way to bend, which way the sun would rise and set, which way it was *expected* to grow. "Yes?" Poornima said, taken aback that she was still there.

The girl shook her head, or seemed to, and then she left. Poornima stared at the place she had just been. Where did she go? Poornima nearly jumped up and followed her. Her leaving seemed to empty them in some way—the entrance to the hut, and the hut itself. But *how?* Who was she? Poornima didn't know; she didn't recognize her from the well where she went to draw water, or as one of the girls in the neighborhood. She guessed she was from the temple, come to ask for donations, or maybe just a peddler, come to sell vegetables. Then she smelled the rice burning, and forgot all about her.

A week later the girl was seated at her mother's loom. Poornima knew it was her because the room filled again. She'd forgotten it was even empty.

Filled, not with a body or a scent or a presence: that was her father, seated at the other loom. No, *she* filled it with a sudden awareness, a feeling of waking, though it had been light for hours. Poornima set a cup of tea down next to her father's loom. He glanced at her and said, "Set another plate for lunch."

Poornima turned to go. She was now standing behind her. The girl was wearing a cheap cotton sari; her blouse was threadbare, though still a vivid blue, the color of the Krishna at the hour of twilight. There was a large round birthmark on her right forearm, on the inside of her wrist. Striking because it was at the exact point where her veins seemed to meet, before they spilled into her hand. The birthmark seemed to actually gather them up—the veins—as if it were ribbon that tied together a bouquet. A bouquet? A birthmark? Poornima looked away, embarrassed. As she hurried past, the strange girl pulled the picking stick of the loom out toward her, and in that moment, Poornima couldn't help it: she saw her hand. Much too big for her thin body, more like a man's, but gentle, just as her voice had been gentle; though what truly struck Poornima was that her hand gripped the picking stick with such force, such solidity, that it seemed she might never let go. The pivot of her entire body seemed to be pulling the picking stick. To hold it tight. Poornima was astonished. She'd never known a hand could do that: contain so much purpose.

That night, after dinner, was when her father first mentioned her. The deepa on Indravalli Konda was dark, and Poornima was putting her siblings to bed. Her youngest brother was only seven years old, her sister was eleven, and she had a set of twin brothers, twelve. They were relatively good children, but sometimes Poornima thought her mother might've died from tiredness. She was unrolling their sleeping mats and telling one of the twins to stop pulling his sister's hair, when her father, rolling tobacco, said, "You eat with her. Make sure she doesn't take more than her share."

Poornima turned. "Who?"

"Savitha."

So that was her name.

Poornima stood still, a mat half unrolled. "She's all I could find," her father said, lying back on his hemp-rope bed, smoking. "The weaving collective said I should be happy. As if my wages are low. Besides, she should be grateful. That father of hers, old Subbudu, can hardly feed himself, let alone that miserable wife and those four daughters." He yawned. "I hope she's not as weak as she looks."

But Poornima, smiling into the dark, knew she wasn't.

Savitha was quiet around Poornima at first. She was a year or two older, Poornima guessed, though neither truly knew their exact ages. Only the birthdates of the boys were recorded in the village. Still, when Poornima asked, over lunch one day, Savitha told her just what her mother had told her: that she was born on the day of a solar eclipse. Her mother had said that while in labor with her, she'd looked out the window and seen the sky darken in midday, and was paralyzed by it. She was convinced she was about to give birth to a rakshasa. She'd told Savitha that in that moment, all her labor pains had subsided and were replaced by fear. What if she *was* giving birth to a demon? Her mother began to pray and pray, and then she began to tremble, wishing her new baby dead. Wondering if she should kill it herself. That was better, she'd told Savitha, than unleashing evil into the world. Anyone would do the same, she'd told Savitha. But then the eclipse had ended, and her baby was born, and it was just a regular, cooing little baby.

"Your mother must've been relieved," Poornima said.

"Not really. I was still a girl."

Poornima nodded. She watched her while she ate. Savitha had a healthy appetite, but no more than anyone else who sat at the loom for twelve hours a day.

"That's why she named me Savitha."

"What does it mean?"

"What do you think? She thought that if she named me after the sun, it wouldn't go away again."

She licked her fingers of rasam, the birthmark on her wrist swaying between her mouth and the plate like a hammock, and then she asked for another helping of rice to eat with yogurt.

"Do you want salt?" Poornima asked.

"I like it sweet. To tell you the truth, what I love with yogurt rice is a banana. I squish it up and mix it in with the rice. Don't make that face. Not until you try it. It tastes like the sweetest, loveliest sunrise. And I'm not just saying that because of my name. It just does; you should try it."

"But bananas," Poornima said, thinking now of her own mother and the two bananas she'd bought for her every day, and how, in the end, they hadn't made a bit of difference.

"I know. Expensive. But that's the thing, Poori—do you mind if I call you that?—you *shouldn't* eat it at every meal. It's too good. Too perfect. Would you want to see the sun rise every morning? You'd get used to it; the colors, I mean. You'd get so you'd just turn away."

"And that's the same with too much yogurt rice and bananas? I'd just turn away?"

"No. You'd still eat it. You just wouldn't think of it."

Think of it?

No, she wasn't quiet anymore, Poornima thought. Not at all. And she was strangely obsessed with food: the thing with the bananas and yogurt rice, calling her Poori, the way she licked her fingers, as if she would never eat another meal. Poornima's father had said her family was poor, poorer even than they were, which was hard to imagine. Six children in all, her father had told her, old Subbudu so frail that he'd long ago given up sitting at the loom, her mother cleaning, cooking for other families, no better than a common *servant*, he'd said derisively, and her older brothers moved to Hyderabad, promising to send money home, though the family hadn't yet received a single paisa. And with four daughters unmarried. "Four," her father had exclaimed, shaking his head. "The old man's done for," he'd said. "He might be better off finding four big rocks and a rope and leading them to the nearest well."

"Which one is Savitha?"

"Oldest. Of the girls. Not even enough for *her* dowry." So her marriage was delayed, too, just like Poornima's. Her father narrowed his eyes then and looked at her. "Not eating too much, is she? Tucking a little away for her sisters?"

"No," Poornima said. "Hardly anything."

What Poornima liked most about Savitha—in addition to her hands—was her clarity. She had never known anyone—not her father, not a teacher, not the temple priest—to be as certain as Savitha was. But certain about what? she asked herself. About bananas in yogurt rice? About sunrises? Yes, but about more than that. About her grip on the picking stick, about her stride, about the way her sari was knotted around her waist. About everything, Poornima realized, that she herself was *unsure* about. As the weeks went by, Savitha began to linger a little longer over her lunch; she came earlier to help with the morning chores, though she must've had chores to do at her own house beforehand. She and Poornima also began to go to the well together for water.

On one of these trips, as they were walking back together, the clay pots of water balanced on their hips, they came across a crowd of young men about their age. There were four of them, clustered around the beedie shop, smoking, when one of them, a boy of about twenty or twenty-two, thin as a reed but with a thick shock of hair, noticed Poornima and Savitha and pointed.

"Look over there," he called to the other men. "Look at those hips. Those curves. Such fine examples of the Indian landscape."

Then another of the men whistled, and another, or maybe the same, said, "Not even Gandhiji could've resisted." They all laughed. "Which one do you want, boys," he continued, "the yellow or the blue?"

Poornima discovered he was talking about the color of their saris.

"The blue!"

"The yellow," another yelled.

"*I* want to be the clay pot," another said, and they all laughed again.

There was no way to get around them, they realized. The men came closer and surrounded them. The circle they formed was porous but menacing. Poornima looked at Savitha, but she was looking straight past them, as if the men weren't even there. "What do we *do*?" Poornima whispered.

"Walk," she said, her voice firm, steady and as solid as the temple on Indravalli Konda, the one on which Savitha's gaze seemed to be fixed.

Poornima glanced at her and then she glanced at her feet.

"Don't look down," Savitha said. "Look up."

She lifted her gaze slowly and saw that the men were now in a tight huddle. They were jumping up and down like crickets; one grabbed Savitha's pallu and yanked it. She slapped his hand away. This brought out a long howl from them, and more dancing and laughter, as if the slap had been an invitation. Poornima was mildly aware of other women, standing at the entrance to their huts. Boys, they would be thinking, shaking their heads. Poornima felt a rising panic; this was a common occurrence in the village, but the men usually left them alone after a little teasing, a few winks. *These* men were following them. And there were four of them. She looked at Savitha. Her face was as determined as before, staring ahead of her, straight at the temple and Indravalli Konda as if she could bore a hole through both. The men seemed to sense something in her, something like defiance—and this defiance, its *audacity* seemed to enliven them even more. "Darling baby," they said in English, and then in Telugu, "why don't *you* choose." They were talking to Savitha.

And this. This was the signal she was waiting for.

She set down her pot of water, straightened her back, and stood still. Absolutely still. And with her stillness came an even greater stillness. The people standing at the entrances to their huts, the bend of the street leading to Indravalli Konda, the fields of rice all around, and even the clacking of the looms, ubiquitous in the village at all hours, were strangely quieted. They could almost hear the Krishna, a few kilometers away—the lapping of its waters, the flapping of the wings of water birds.

"I know who I want," Savitha said.

The first man, the thin one with the abundant hair, whooped and hollered and skipped around the circle like a child. "She knows. She knows. Sorry, boys, better luck next time."

"Which one? Which one?" they chirped.

Savitha looked at each of them in turn, met their eyes, and then she walked a step or two in each of their directions, as if taunting them with her choice, and then she smiled—her flash of teeth as gleaming and virtuous as the white of the distant temple—stepped toward Poornima, took her hand, and said, "I choose her." With these words, she picked up her pot of water, tugged at Poornima's arm, and pulled her out of the circle. The men let them go but hissed and growled. *"Her?"* they groaned. "She's uglier than you are."

When they got home, Poornima was trembling.

"Don't," Savitha told her. "It's no good."

"I can't help it."

"Don't you see? I could've chosen a tree. A dog."

"Yeah, but they could've hurt us."

"I wouldn't have let them," she said.

And so, there they were: those five words. They were a song, an incantation. Poornima felt a weight, an awful and terrifying weight, erode. Had the weight been borne from her mother's death? Or from being an ox? Or was it from something less obvious, like the passage of time, or the endless spinning of her charkha? Though, when she thought about it, they were the same thing, weren't they? It hardly mattered. She and Savitha became such close friends that neither could eat a single meal without wondering if the other would've preferred more salt, or if she liked brinjal with potatoes. Breakfast was suddenly their least favorite meal, and Sunday their least favorite day. Poornima even saved a paisa here and there and began to buy bananas whenever she could. The first time she did, she presented one to Savitha at lunch, when she served her the buttermilk. There had not been enough money for yogurt that morning. Savitha didn't seem to mind. She mixed her watery buttermilk and rice with as much relish as if it were the thickest, creamiest yogurt she'd ever eaten. Poornima watched her, and then she held out the banana.

Savitha gasped. "Are you sure?"

"Of course. I bought it especially for you."

She was so delighted that she became curiously shy. "My mother says if I'd eaten fewer bananas in my life, they would have had the money for my dowry."

Poornima smiled and looked down.

Savitha stopped eating. "When did she die?"

"Four months ago."

Savitha mixed the banana into her rice. First she took off the entire peel then mushed it with her thumb and fingers into the rice. The banana ended up in unsightly lumps, strewn across the carpet of rice like wading bandicoots. It was all a gloppy, unappetizing mess.

"You *like* that?"

"Try some." She raised a handful toward Poornima. Poornima shook her head vigorously. Savitha shrugged and ate the rice-and-banana concoction with great relish, closing her eyes as she chewed.

"You know what's even better than this?"

Poornima wrinkled her nose. "Most things, I would imagine."

Savitha ignored her. She leaned toward Poornima, as if revealing a secret. "I don't know for sure, I've only heard, but there's supposed to be this rare fruit. Unbearable, Poori. Pink inside, almost buttery, but with the sweetness of candy. Sweeter. Better even than bananas, better even than sapota. I know, I know, you wouldn't think it possible, but I heard an old woman talking about it in the marketplace. Years ago. She said it only grew on some island. On the Brahmaputra. Even the way she described the island was lovely. She looked at me, right at me, and she said, 'You know how Krishna plays the flute for his Radha, wooing her at twilight, just as the cows are coming home? It is that sound. That is the sound of the island. Flute song. Everywhere you go there are the fruit, and there is flute song. Following you like a lover."

"That's what she said?"

"Yes."

"Like flute song?"

"Yes."

Poornima was silent. "What's the name of the island?"

"Majuli."

"Majuli," Poornima said out loud, slowly, as if tasting the word on her tongue. "And you believed her?"

"Of course I believed her," Savitha said. "Some of the crowd didn't, but I did. They said she was senile and had never been north of the abandoned train depot, let alone to the Brahmaputra. But you should've seen her face, Poori. How could you *not* believe her? Lit up like a star."

Poornima thought for a moment, perplexed. "But how can an island be like flute song? Did she mean she loved the island? Like Krishna loves Radha?"

"No. I don't think so."

"What then? It's a song of love, after all."

"Yes," Savitha said, "but it's also a song of hunger."

Now Poornima was even more confused. "Hunger?"

"Maybe what she meant was that the island was the end of hunger. Or the beginning of it. Or maybe that hunger has no beginning. Or end. Like the sound of Krishna's flute."

"But what about love?"

"What is love, Poori?" Savitha said. "What is love if not a hunger?"

3

The following week, Savitha invited Poornima to her house. It was a Sunday. Her father didn't mind as long as she first cooked and fed her brothers and sister and laid his tobacco and mat out for his afternoon nap. The day was hot; it was March, though already they had to keep to the shade—Savitha ahead, Poornima following close behind her—skidding along under the trees and the overhanging thatched roofs of the huts to keep out of the sun. Savitha lived on the other side of the village, farther from Indravalli Konda but closer to the Krishna. Many of those belonging to the caste of laundresses lived on that side of town, because of its proximity to the water. There were also—discovered on that side of the village—inscriptions dating back to the time of the Cholas, though, being close to the railroad tracks, it was also the village's primary bathroom, and the inscriptions mostly ignored. Still, the majority who lived there belonged to the caste of weavers, Savitha's family among them.

Their hut was on a small ridge. The road—more a dirt path—leading to it was lined with scrubs, their leaves and branches already withered and gray from the heat. When Poornima reached down and touched one, a silky film of gray came off the leaf, and she realized it was ash, from the wood fires that were built outside the huts along the path—they being too poor to have even a cooking area inside their huts. Piles of trash also lined the huts, sniffed occasionally by a stray dog or a pig hungry enough to withstand the heat. It was almost time for tiffin, four in the afternoon, but no one seemed to be home. By now, the sky was white, glowing like a brass pot lit from within. Beads of sweat dripped down Poornima's back. Clung like mist to her scalp.

When they reached the hut, Poornima realized her family was wealthy compared to Savitha's. They couldn't even afford palm fronds for the roof of their hut; it was a discarded sheet of corrugated tin. The outside walls of the hut were plastered with cow dung, and a small area of dirt was cleared in front of the scrubs, though it was still scattered with trash—bits of old yellowed newspaper, disintegrating, blackened rags, vegetable skins too rotted even for the tiny piglets that roamed freely from hut to hut. Poornima stepped over these, and when she followed Savitha into the hut, the first thing that overcame her was the smell. It smelled like old, unwashed clothes and sweat and pickled food. It smelled like manure, woodsmoke, dirt. It smelled like poverty. And despair. It smelled like her mother dying.

"We don't have any milk for tea," Savitha said. "Do you want one of these?" She held out a tin of biscuits that were clearly meant only for company. Poornima bit into one; it was stale and crumbled into a soft yellow paste in her mouth. "Where is your mother? Your sisters?"

"My mother cooks today. For the family that owns that big house, the one near the market. My sisters go collecting in the afternoons," Savitha said.

"Collecting what?"

She shrugged. "I usually go with them."

"Where?"

"Edge of town. By the Christian cemetery."

Poornima knew that was where the garbage dumps were. Not the small heaps that dotted the village, practically on every doorstep, but the massive ones, three or four in all, where the small heaps were eventually deposited. Poornima had seen them only from a distance—a far mountain range on the southern horizon that only the poorest climbed. Seeking discarded cloth or paper or scraps of metal, food, plastic. Usually children, she knew, but sometimes adults. But always the poorest. She remembered her mother saying once, as they passed them, "Don't look," and Poornima had not known whether she meant at the cemetery or at the children scrambling up the heaps. But now, standing in Savitha's impoverished hut, and with her mother long dead, she thought she understood. Her mother had said don't look and she'd meant don't look at either the cemetery or the garbage heaps. She'd meant, don't look at death, don't look at poverty, don't look at how they crawl through life, how they wait for you, stalk you, before they end you.

"*You* go?"

"Not anymore. Not since I started working for your father."

Poornima looked out the one window of the hut. It looked out onto Indravalli Konda, and she looked at the temple and felt pride for the first time toward her father; he'd given Savitha a livelihood and led her away from the garbage heaps. She had never thought of him as generous, but she realized generosity could be a quality that was hidden, obscured, veiled as if by ash, like the true color of the leaves on the scrubs outside Savitha's hut. "But how did you learn to weave?" she asked.

"My parents used to. My mother still has her old charkha," she said, pointing to a pile of wood in a corner. Pinned above it was a calendar with Shiva and Parvati, with Ganesha and Kartikeya seated on their laps. Next to the broken charkha was a large bundle wrapped in an old sheet, maybe a shawl. A few dented aluminum pots and pans lay in another corner, below a hanging vegetable basket that contained a stray piece of garlic, a distended onion, and a round orange squash. Poornima saw a leftover clump of rice swarming with flies. A frayed bamboo mat leaned next to them. "We used to have a loom. But my father drank it away. A small beedie shop. Not here. In the center of town. He drank that away, too."

Poornima had never heard of such a thing. The word for alcohol in Telugu was *mundhoo*, which could mean medicine, or poison. It was considered taboo to even mention the word, and never around women and children.

Drinkers were spoken of in hushed voices and considered leprous, or worse.
To be standing in the *home* of a drinker—Poornima shuddered. "Where is
he now?"

Her eyes turned to the window. "Up there, probably."

Poornima followed her gaze. There was Indravalli Konda, the temple,
sky. "The temple?"

"He goes and begs for handouts. Usually the priests feel sorry for him
and give him half a coconut, a laddoo if he's lucky." She said it so offhand-
edly that Poornima was amazed. "It's enough to keep him."

They both stood, looking out at the temple. The story—not a myth; it
couldn't be a myth because it actually happened, Poornima had seen it—
was that once a year, inexplicably, nectar would run from the mouth of the
deity. A sweet, thick nectar flowing freely. No one knew where it came from,
why it started, or why it stopped, but Poornima looked around at Savitha's
hut, at the one clove of garlic and the rotting onion and the squash that she
knew was the entirety of their provisions, maybe for the week, and thought,
It should run all the time. If we are truly God's children, like the priests say,
then why doesn't it run all the time?

"I won't give him my earnings. He thinks I'm saving for my own dowry.
But I'm not. I'm saving it for my sisters' dowries." Savitha looked at Poornima. "I'm not getting married, not until they are."

"No?"

Savitha looked past her, as if into a cave, and said, "No."

The farmer was no longer interested. He sent word to Poornima's father. He
said he couldn't wait the remaining eight months, and besides, he said, he
had heard his daughter was as dark as a tamarind. Poornima's father was
crestfallen. He prodded Ramayya, who'd brought the news, with question
after question. "What else did he say? Any chance he'll change his mind? A
tamarind? Really? She's hardly as dark as a tamarind. Do you think she is?

It's a curse: daughters, darkness. What if I buy him another goat? A few chickens?"

Ramayya swung his head and said it was hopeless. He took a sip of his tea and said, "We'll find her another. I already have a lead."

Poornima's father's eyes lit up. "Who?"

It was a young man who lived in Repalle. He had passed his tenth-class exams and was now apprenticed at a sari shop. His parents were both weavers, but with their son working, and in anticipation of a daughter-in-law who would bring in a dowry and hopefully extra income with a charkha, they were slowing down and focusing on getting him married. "There's a younger daughter, too, so it's unclear," Ramayya said. He was referring, of course, to the fact that the young man couldn't get married until his sister was married and settled. But, according to Ramayya, the younger daughter's marriage was already fixed. Only the muhurthum—the most auspicious date and time of the wedding—remained to be arranged. Poornima's father was delighted. "Plenty of time, then," he said, smiling. "And what about the dowry?"

Ramayya finished his tea. "Within our range. He's still an apprentice, after all. But one thing at a time."

The next afternoon, Poornima told Savitha what she'd overheard. She'd come in for lunch. They always ate after Poornima's father, and he'd asked for a second helping of capsicum curry, leaving Poornima and Savitha with only a small spoonful to share. They ate their rice mainly with pickle. "Where did you say?"

"Repalle."

Savitha was silent for a moment. "That's too far."

"Where is it?"

"It's past Tenali. It's by the ocean."

"The ocean?" Poornima had never seen the ocean, and she imagined it to be just like a field—a field of rice, she thought—with ships in the distance instead of mountains, blue instead of green, and as for waves, she'd discussed them with a classmate once, when she was in the third class. "But what *are* they? What do they look like?" The other girl—who'd also never seen the ocean—said they were the water burping, and they looked like a cat when it's stretching. A cat? Stretching? Poornima was skeptical. "Will you visit me?" *

"I told you. It's too far."

"But, a train."

Savitha laughed out loud. She held up a bit of capsicum. "You see this? You see *this*?" she said, indicating her full plate of rice and a fingertip's worth of last year's tomato pickle. "This is a feast. How do you think I will ever afford a train ticket?"

That night, Poornima lay on her mat and thought about Savitha. It was vaguely unsettling, but it seemed to her that she couldn't possibly marry a man who lived too far away for Savitha to visit. So that, essentially, *Savitha* was more important than the man she would marry. Could that be true? How had this happened? Poornima couldn't say. She thought about the fierceness that sometimes flooded Savitha's eyes. She thought about the view of the temple from the window of her hut. She thought about her mixing rice and buttermilk with banana, and how, when she'd finally asked her for a bite, Savitha, with a wide grin, had rolled a bit of dripping rice into a ball between her fingers, and instead of handing it to her, she'd fed her. Raised the bite to Poornima's mouth, so that she'd touched the very tip of her fingers with her tongue. As if she were a child. As Amma might've done. But with Savitha, there was no illness to mar the gesture, no dying; she was alive, more alive than anyone she'd ever known. She made even the smallest of life seem grand, and for Poornima, who had always ached for something more than the memory of a comb in her hair, more than the chiming of a blue clock, or a voice that she tried so often to conjure, watching Savitha, watching her *delight*, was like cultivating her own. And even in her daily duties—cooking, going to the well for water, washing dishes, scrubbing clothes, sitting for endless hours at the charkha—she found a sudden and glimmering satisfaction. Perhaps even joy. Though what surprised her most was that she could no longer imagine her life without her. Who had she talked to at meals before Savitha? What had she done on Sundays? Who had she cooked for? Her father, who was slow to notice most things, had said the previous evening, "That Savitha seems like a good girl. She's a hard worker, that's for sure." Then he'd turned back to his tobacco and said, "Shouldn't let a girl like that run around. Should get her married. How old is she? Too old to run around, I'd say. No telling."

No telling, Poornima repeated to herself. No telling what?

Her father looked at her. "They'll be here tomorrow. Probably in the afternoon."

"Who?"

"The boy from Repalle. His family."

"Tomorrow?"

"Here." Her father handed her a few rupees. "Send your brother out for snacks in the morning. Pakoras, maybe." Poornima stared at him. "Don't just stand there. Take it."

In the morning, when Poornima told her, Savitha only smiled. "It'll come to nothing," she said.

"How do you know?"

"Because these things always do."

"What things?"

Savitha pointed at the sky. "Things that are not ordained. That are broken before they ever begin."

"But—they're on their way. Gopi is out buying pakoras."

She smiled again. "A few mornings ago, I was on my way to your house. I was crossing Old Tenali Road, you know, where all the lorries pass on their way to the highway. As I was crossing by the paan shop, I heard a thump. More like a quick thud. I didn't think much of it. But I did turn around to look, and when I did, I saw an owl on the road. It had obviously been hit. One of its wings looked wrong, just *wrong.* Do you know what I mean? It looked dead. Or sleeping. But no, it was awake, Poori. *Awake.* More awake than anything I've ever seen. It was not making a sound. No calling, no whimpering. Do birds whimper? Anyway, none of that. It was just sitting there, fallen there, in the middle of the road. With all the bicycles and people and lorries whisking by it. One lorry even went right over it. But the owl just sat there. Its eye—the one facing me—like a marble. A perfect black-and-gold marble. Reflecting everything. I was now close, you see, bending over it, wondering what I could do to help it. But what could I do? Its shattered wing was awful. Like a lonesome day. Like hunger. But as I looked at it, I realized it was *saying* something to me. It was trying to tell me something. I swear. And you know what it was? What it was trying to say?"

Poornima said nothing.

"Owl things. Things I couldn't possibly understand. They were dying words, the words of the dying, but spoken in an another language. A silent one. But it was also saying something else, something to me. It was saying, The man from Repalle doesn't matter. You'll be together. (He was talking about you and me, of course.) That's the way it is: If two people want to be together, they'll find a way. They'll *forge* a way. It may seem ludicrous, even stupid, to work so hard at something that is, truly, a matter of chance, completely arbitrary, such as staying *with* someone—as if 'with' and 'apart' have meaning in and of themselves—but, the owl said (and by now, Savitha added, the owl was sighing, maybe wheezing, nearing death), But that's the thing with you humans. You think too much, don't you?"

"Wait," Poornima said. "The owl said all this to you?"

"Yes."

"So, it knows me? It knows you? It knows the man from Repalle?"

"Knew. It's probably dead by now."

"Okay. Knew."

"Yes."

"Yes?"

Savitha returned her gaze, unblinking, and said, "Yes."

The marriage viewing took place that evening. They arrived a little after six o'clock. There was the groom, who was apprenticed in the sari shop, along with his mother, father, Ramayya, and an uncle and aunt. Though the uncle and aunt could have been an older cousin and his wife. It was hard to tell, and Poornima never found out for sure. She was in the weaving hut, where the looms were located, when they arrived. Her father's sister was helping her with her sari—cream-colored cotton with a green border, which had belonged to her mother—and tying a garland of jasmine to her hair. Poornima had oiled it that morning, the coconut still scenting her fingertips, and the kumkum leaving a thin film of powder on them as if she'd caught a red butterfly. Her aunt yanked at her hair as she braided it, pulling the strands with such force that Poornima squealed in pain.

"Shush," her aunt scolded. "One boy already fallen through. The shame. How do you think it looks for a girl? Huh? Thank the Lord Vishnu he never laid eyes on you. That would've been the end. Your poor father. First he loses a wife, five kids on his own, and now *this*. Working his fingers to the bone. But this one will work out. You'll see." She lathered Poornima's face with a thick coating of talcum powder. She reapplied the kumkum and kajal. And then she took the gold bangles off her own wrists and squeezed them onto Poornima's. "There," her aunt said, taking a step or two back. "Now, keep your eyes down, and only speak when spoken to. Don't get frisky. Just answer their questions. And try to sing. If they ask you, sing something. A devotional ballad is good. Simple, so you don't mess it up."

Poornima nodded.

Her aunt then led her out of the weaving hut, around the back of the main hut, and into the front, where they were all seated. She nudged Poornima onto the straw mat, on which were also seated the groom's mother and aunt or cousin. The groom's father was seated in the chair, while all the other men were seated on the edge of the hemp-rope bed. Pleasantries were exchanged with Poornima's aunt, whom the aunt or cousin seemed to be acquainted with. Then the groom's mother reached over and touched the gold bangles. "Not very thick," she said.

"Yes, well," Ramayya said lightheartedly, "all that can be discussed later."

The woman smiled, let go of the bangles reluctantly, and said, "What's your name, dear?"

Poornima lifted her gaze to the woman she assumed would be her future mother-in-law. She was fat, well-fed, her stomach above the waistline of her sari rested as round and moist as a clay pot. Her nails and teeth were yellow. "Poornima," she replied. She liked that she'd called her dear. But she disliked the timbre in her voice, was suspicious of it; it'd gone too easily between the thickness of the gold bangles and her name, as if they were one and the same, as if they were part of the same inquiry, the same pursuit.

"Ask her, Ravi," the groom's aunt or cousin said. "Ask her something."

The groom was sitting on the edge of the bed; Poornima saw only his shoes (brown sandals) and the cuff of his pants (gray, with pinstripes). His ankles—the only part of his body that was in her view—were dark, the hair on them wiry and thick. "Can you sing?" he said.

She cleared her throat. A devotional song, she told herself. Think of a devotional song. But then her mind drew a blank. Not a blank, not exactly. What she thought of was the owl. The dying owl that had spoken to Savitha. What had it said? Something about finding a way, forging it. What would she do in Repalle, alone, without Savitha? That question seemed greater than any other question she'd ever been asked. Greater than all other questions put together. "I can't," she said. "I can't sing."

Her aunt gasped. "Of course you can," she said, laughing nervously. "Remember that one. That one we sing at the temple. About Rama and Sita and—"

"I remember it. I remember it perfectly. I just can't sing it. Like I said, I can't sing."

Ramayya rose a little, his eyes wide. "Shy. That's all. Such a shy girl."

The groom cleared his throat. The aunt or the cousin said, "Well, that's all right. Singing's not all that important. She can cook, right? How many canisters can you spin on the charkha per day?"

"Four, five."

"Now, see," the woman said, "that's not bad."

"Swapna can spin eight," the groom's mother said. "And that's *with* the baby."

The conversation went on like that. They finished their tea, all the pakoras, and most of the jilebi, leaving only bits of sugar syrup on the plate. They talked about the lack of rain, and about how the trains from Repalle were always late, they talked about the price of peanuts and mangoes and rice, and then they talked about the new government, and how prices had been cheaper, and the quality of the produce better, when the Congress party had been in power. Her aunt then led Poornima out of the room. She was scolded, as she knew she would be. "You fool," her aunt said. "Who'll marry some-one like you? Who'll marry someone so wicked? Thank the Lord Vishnu your mother wasn't here. It would've killed her. A daughter so terrible. Don't you see? It has nothing to *do* with whether you can sing, you fool. They just want to make certain that you will *listen*. That you'll be obedient. And now they know. They know you're wicked."

When Poornima told Savitha the next day, she laughed. "That's it! That's how we do it." Then she pushed a strand of hair that had fallen across Poorn-ima's face and said, "That's it. We're safe."

4

A heat wave settled into Indravalli in the days after the marriage viewing. Poornima began getting up in the dark to do the morning chores. Getting water at the well, cooking for the day, sweeping and washing—all of it had to be done before the sun came up. Once the sun touched the horizon, licked even the mere tip of it, the earth burned as if lit on fire. The air, through the mornings and afternoons, was still and hot, searing; a thin breeze drifted along in the evenings, but that too was hardly a whimper. Poornima sat at the charkha in the afternoons, spinning listlessly, and waited for dinnertime. She couldn't visit Savitha during the day, while she was at the loom: her father was in the weaving hut, too, watching them from his own loom. In the afternoons, she took their tea to them, but she and Savitha hardly exchanged a glance. Besides, Poornima's father was furious. The Repalle family was now demanding an even larger dowry, *double* what had previously been discussed. "Double," her father hissed, "for your insolence." They'd also asked for a set of gold bangles for their daughter, the groom's younger sister. "*Gold*," her father repeated, "gold, gold, gold. Do you understand? Gold. How do you suppose I get the money to buy gold?" His eyes, already bloodshot and inflamed from the heat, gaped at his daughter. "And I've got another one after you. In what? Two or three years? And that friend of yours. Savitha. What do you think she asked me the other day? She asked me if she could use the loom, after work. Come in early, leave later. *My* loom. And she asked, just like that, as if I owed it to her." He shook his head, swiping at a mosquito on his arm. "It's your audacity," he said. "It's the audacity of you girls, you modern girls, that will be your ruin. That will be *my* ruin."

"Why?" Poornima asked.

"Why what?"

"Why does she want to come in extra?"

"How should I know?" her father said. "Why don't you ask her?" Poornima stood looking at him. He slapped at another mosquito. "Well, don't just stand there. Get me the swatter."

She asked Savitha the next day at lunch. The air in the hut was liquid; it throbbed white and raw with heat. Flies buzzed listlessly, lifting a little off the ground and then settling back, as if exhausted from the effort. Savitha was sweating from sitting at the loom. Beads of perspiration stood at her hairline, studded her collarbone. Poornima could smell the scent of her body: jungled, musky. Not the slightest whiff of laundry cake or a bit of sandalwood soap or even talcum powder. Animal: that was her scent.

Savitha stopped eating and listened as Poornima told her about the Repalle people, and how they were asking for more dowry. "Can your father give it to them?"

"I don't think so. He can barely afford the dowry he's offering now."

"So it's done."

Poornima shrugged. "Maybe. Everyone is furious, though."

"Because you wouldn't *sing*? What are we? Trained monkeys?"

Poornima didn't answer. Instead, she said, "Why do you want to work longer at the loom? Why did you ask my father if you could?"

Savitha took a bite of her rice and sambar. Her eyes twinkled. "I'm making you something. I'm making you a sari. That's why I asked your father if I could use the loom. Do you think he'll let me?"

"A sari? But how? Where will you get the thread? How will you make two saris at once? You can't."

"That's why I wanted to come in extra. I'll finish the sari for your father by working after hours. And then, when that's done, I can start yours on a Saturday night, work all day Sunday, and have it done by Monday morning. And the threads? I got those from the collective. They had extra. Apparently somebody dyed them the wrong color. Indigo. They can't dye over it, or they don't want to. Either way, they gave it to me for cheap."

"A sari in *one* day?"

"Two, if I work day and night."

"That's ridiculous. You can't work without sleeping for two days. Besides, why? Why do you want to make me a sari?"

"It'll be my wedding present to you. You will eventually get married, you know. Not to this guy in Repalle, I hope. I hope it's somebody in Indravalli. But when you do, I can't afford to give you anything else. Besides, look at this," she said, holding up a handful of rice. "No one has ever cooked for me. My mother must've, but I don't remember it. As long as I can remember, I've cooked for myself, and for my parents and brothers and sisters. And the bananas. I know you save your money to buy them for me. But it's not just the cooking. It's everything. Everything. From the way you sit and spin the charkha, as if you weren't spinning thread at all, but as if you were spinning the strangest stories, the loveliest dreams. And the way you set the tea down next to me when I'm at the loom. And the way you hold the pot of water when we're walking back from the well, as if nothing, nothing in the world, could match the finery, the fineness, of that pot of water. Don't you see, Poori? Everything else is so bland, so colorless, except you. But that indigo." She smiled. "The least I can do is make you a sari. I *know* how to do that. And a few sleepless nights won't matter. Imagine when I see it on you."

Poornima wanted to get up, pull Savitha up from her plate, and embrace her. No one—not ever—had thought to *make* something for her. Her mother, of course, but she was dead. And the weight of her mother's hand, holding the comb in her hair, was all she had left of her. At times, many times, she gripped that memory, that weight, as if it alone could guide her through dark and savage forest paths, and eventually, she hoped, into a clearing, but it wasn't true. It couldn't. All that memory could do was give small solace. One drop after another after another, like the glucose drip that had punctured and bled her mother's arm when she'd been in the hospital. It had been nothing. Not really. Sugar. They had dripped sugar into her. "To keep her strength up," the doctors had said. As if sugar were a stand against cancer. But *Savitha*, Savitha wanted to make her a sari. A sari she could wind around her body and hold to her face. Not a memory, not a scent, not a thing that drifts away. But a sari. She could take that sari and weep into it, she could stretch it across a rooftop, a hot sand, wear it to the Krishna and wade into its waters, she could wrap herself in its folds, cocoon herself against the night, she could sleep, she could dream.

5

The owl was right: negotiations with the family from Repalle fell apart. They refused to budge from their dowry demands, though Ramayya did get them to agree to accept one gold bangle for the sister instead of two. "One, two. What does it matter? I can't afford half a gold bangle. Let alone the dowry," her father said.

"They've seen her. That's the thing," Ramayya said. When Poornima brought Ramayya his tea, he looked at her with such distaste that she thought he might fling the tea back in her face. She moved away. "Shy," he said with disgust. "You're not shy. You're rude. You and your father are lucky I'm still willing to help. Word's gotten around, you know. Everyone between here and the Godavari knows about you. Who would want you now?"

When Ramayya left, Poornima's father slapped her, hard. Then he grabbed her by the hair. He said, "You see this? You see what you've done?" His grip on her hair tightened and he said, "The next time somebody asks you to sing, what're you going to do?"

Poornima blinked. She held back tears. Her scalp burned, hairs snapped like electric wires. Her brothers and sister crowded around the door of the hut to see. "What?" he growled. "What will you do? Say it. *Say it.*"

"Sing," she whispered, wincing in pain. "I'm going to sing."

He let go with a shove, and Poornima fell forward. She knocked against the steel cups in which she'd served the tea, and her hand split open. One of her brothers ran to get a rag, and she tied it around her hand. The blood soaked through, and there was still dinner to prepare. She sent them out to play and leaned against the wall of the hut. It was the eastern wall. Across from her was a high window. Through it, beyond Indravalli Konda, she could see the setting sun. Not the sun itself, but pink and yellow and orange clouds, thin, their ends sharp as knives, rushing toward the mountain as if they meant to bring it to its knees. How delusional, she thought: as if those useless bits of fluff could maim a mountain.

She closed her eyes. The pain in her hand, her scalp, her face where he'd slapped her, none of them she even noticed. They were still there, but she could no longer feel them. Her body swam, slowly, as if through a thick and sedimental sea. It's the heat, she thought, but the heat wave had passed. It was April, and though the temperatures had lessened some—although stepping outside in the afternoons was still unwise—the heat would not completely abate, not until July when the monsoons arrived. Until then, the air was stifling. The hut was stifling. Poornima could hardly breathe. She wanted to cry, but her body felt as dry as a coconut husk. The heat having sapped everything, even tears.

And it was only April.

Savitha saw the cut on her hand, the bruise on her face when she came in for lunch the next afternoon, and was livid. "Don't you worry," she said, fuming.

"Worry about what?" Poornima asked.

"Nothing. Don't you worry about a thing." Then she laid Poornima's head in her lap, she brushed the hair from her face, and she said, "Do you want to hear a story?"

Poornima nodded.

"What kind of story?"

"You're the one who asked."

"All right, but an old story or a new one?"

"A new one."

"Why?"

Poornima thought for a moment. Savitha's lap was warm, though a little uneven, like sleeping on a lumpy bed. "Because I'm sick of old things. Like Ramayya. And this hut." She raised her hand to her face, the cut still open on her palm. Curved, like a clay pot. "I want something new."

"In that case, once upon a time," Savitha began, "though not very long ago, since you want a new story—once upon a time, an elephant and the rain had an argument. The elephant was proud. It walked proudly around the forest. It ate whatever it wanted, reaching high into the trees, scaring away all the other animals. It was so proud that one day the elephant looked up, saw the rain, and declared, 'I don't need you. You don't nourish me. I don't need you at all.' The rain, after hearing this, looked sadly back at the elephant and said, 'I will go away, and then you will see.' So the rain went away. The elephant watched it go and had an idea. He saw a nearby lagoon filled with water and he knew that without rain, it would soon dry up." Here, Savitha stopped. Poornima lifted her head from her lap and sat up.

"So what was it? What was his idea?" Poornima asked.

Savitha turned to face her. She smiled. "The elephant, you see, saw a poor old crow walking along the forest path, looking for grubs, and ordered him to guard the lagoon. 'Only *I* may drink from the lagoon,' he told the crow. So the old crow sat and sat and guarded the lagoon. Eventually there came a monkey and said, 'Give me water!' and the crow answered, 'The water belongs to elephant.' The monkey shook its head and went away.

"Then came a hyena and said, 'Give me water!' and the crow answered, 'The water belongs to elephant.'

"Along came a cobra and said, 'Give me water!' and the crow answered, 'The water belongs to elephant.'

"Then came a jungle cat and said, 'Give me water!' and the crow answered, 'The water belongs to elephant.'

"Then came a bear and a crocodile and a deer. They all asked for water and the old crow always gave the same answer. Finally, there came a lion. The lion said, 'Give me water!' and the crow answered, 'The water belongs to elephant.' When the lion heard this he roared; he grabbed the poor crow by the neck and beat him. Then he took a long, refreshing drink from the lagoon and walked away into the forest.

"When the elephant returned, he saw that the lagoon had dried up. 'Crow,' he said, 'Where is the water?' The old crow looked down sadly and said, 'Lion drank it.' The elephant was enraged. He said angrily, 'I told you not to let anybody else drink from the lagoon. As punishment, shall I chew you up, or simply swallow you whole?'

" 'Swallow me whole, if you please,' the crow said.

"So the elephant swallowed the crow. But once the crow entered the elephant's body, the crow—our little crow—tore at the elephant's liver and kidneys and heart until the elephant died, writhing in pain. Then the crow simply emerged from the elephant's body and walked away."

Savitha was silent.

Poornima looked at her. "What about the rain?" she said.

"The rain?"

"Did it come back? Did it fill the lagoon again?"

"The rain doesn't matter."

"No?"

"No."

"But what about—"

"That doesn't matter either."

"It doesn't?"

"No," Savitha said. "Here's what matters. Understand this, Poornima: that it's better to be swallowed whole than in pieces. Only then can you win. No elephant can be too big. Only then no elephant can do you harm."

They grew silent.

Savitha went back to her loom, and Poornima, washing up after lunch, looked at the wound on her hand, open again now from scrubbing dishes, and she thought about her father, she thought about the old crow, and then she thought, Please, Nanna. If you swallow me, swallow me whole.

6

Savitha began working longer hours. She was fast, but orders for the wedding season were even larger than expected. She came in early in the morning and left late at night, working harder than any man Poornima's father had known. Sometimes, Savitha caught him eyeing her greedily—as if he were already counting the coins she was minting for him. She didn't mind. "He's paying me extra," she said to Poornima. "Besides, once the rush ends, I'll be able to make yours." She was trying to cheer her, but Poornima only looked back at her sadly. Ramayya arrived every evening at teatime and proclaimed defeat. One night, she told Savitha, she'd stood behind the door of the hut and listened. "No one will have her. No one," he declared to her father. "They've all heard. The minute they hear her name, *your* name, they shake their heads and say they're not interested. And dark, on top of it. Word travels, after all. No, we might have to increase the dowry. *Some* poor fool will need the money."

Savitha said to her, "Come over tomorrow. I want to show you something." When she did, Savitha showed her the bales of indigo thread for her sari. "It's not completely paid for, but the collective gave me credit." She held it against Poornima's skin. "Like the night sky," she said, smiling. "And you the full moon." Poornima, too, managed a smile. She offered her tea, and when Poornima refused, Savitha turned to a corner of the hut and said, "Nanna, do you want some?"

Poornima swung around. There was an old man sitting in the corner of the room. Huddled. He'd been quiet all this time, invisible. There seemed to be movement, and Poornima thought to say, No, please don't get up on my account, but then she saw that he was trembling. Then there came a grunt, maybe the broken half of a word, and, as if in response, Savitha poured out some tea into a steel cup. She went over to her father and cradled his head as she held the cup to his lips. He caught Poornima's eye. He said, in a hoarse whisper, but strong, stronger than Poornima would've thought possible in a man who looked so weak, "You see that? You see the temple?" He was pointing out of the small window, at Indravalli Konda. "They can see us, just as we can see them. I've looked. I've stood on the steps of the temple and looked. The door of this shithole looks just as mysterious, just as inviting as that door does from here."

"Drink," Savitha said.

The old man—too old to be Savitha's father; he looked more like her grandfather—said, "I did too much of that. Too much, don't you think?"

Savitha tipped the glass. A drop of tea dribbled out. He pulled his hand out from under the blanket, instinctively, and Poornima stepped back in horror. It was a bundle of broken twigs, the fingers smooth but twisted. Savitha saw the look on Poornima's face. "Joint disease," she said.

"That's not right. Not joint disease. That's too easy. You see this here?" He raised his hand into the air and sunlight touched its very tip, like the top branches of a tree. "This is freedom. This is the human spirit, perfected. If we were all born like this there would be no war. We would live like brothers, afraid to touch each other. Do you know, Savitha, what I saw the other day? And what is your name?" When Poornima told him, he said, "Do you know there are some places in the world where people's names have no meanings? It's true. Can you imagine? What kind of places are they? Empty, that's what I say. Empty and sad. A name without *meaning*, it's like having night without day. There are places like that, too, I've heard. Now, what was I saying? Savitha, the tea's cold," he said, laughing. "You see. I talk too much. Far too much. Mondhoo kept me quiet. Mondhoo kept the words quiet, chained to a tree. Oh, yes! What I saw the other day. Why, now I can't remember." He laughed, copiously and happily, like a child.

Poornima liked him. She didn't care what he'd meant to say, nor did she have any idea what he meant by words being chained to a tree, but she liked him because he was so unlike her own father. Unlike Ramayya, unlike any man she'd ever met. She forgot, then, and for the entire walk home, that she was dark, that she was unmarriageable, that there was not enough money for her dowry, that there was a poverty even greater than her own.

Ramayya was jubilant when he came over the following week. He nearly danced through the door. It was the beginning of May. The wells were dry. The streams were choked with dust. The level of the Krishna was so low that laundresses from either shore walked to the middle of the river to share gossip. After two weeks, and after a few children had died of dysentery, the municipal government brought in water in massive tanks. Lines formed around the tanks—sometimes a hundred, two hundred people long. People watched the sky for the slightest hint of a cloud. Even a thin one, the most trivial strip, would have them holding their breath, waiting for rain. Everyone knew the monsoons wouldn't come until June or July, but someone had heard of a bit of rainfall in Vizag, just enough to fill the streams. Maybe it would come down the coast.

But Ramayya seemed unconcerned. "Poornima," he yelled out as soon as he was within earshot, "bring me a glass of water, would you? My throat is parched. And for my feet. Enough to wash my feet. Look at all this dust. I practically ran here."

Water? Poornima wondered. She looked into each of the empty clay water pots and scraped the bottom of one to fill a small glass. When she took it to him, he was already engrossed in conversation with her father. "He's perfect. I haven't talked to the family yet, but he's perfect."

"Who's perfect?" Poornima asked.

"Who do you think? Go do something. Go find something to do."

Poornima walked back into the hut and stood just inside the door.

"Would you believe it? I didn't even have to go very far. Just to Namburu. The boy's grandparents were weavers. Did well, it seems. Bought up a sizable chunk of land around Namburu. They were farmers, before independence, but now they've sold most of it. Made plenty, too. He has two younger sisters. They're looking for matches for the older one, our Poornima's age, but seems she's a bit picky. Well, they can afford it."

Poornima heard her father say, "What does the boy do?"

"An accountant!" Ramayya said jubilantly. "He studied. There's no money in weaving. You know that. None at all."

"How much do they want?"

"That's just it—they're within our range. Well, almost. But I've heard we might be able to talk them down."

"Talk them down?"

Here, Poornima heard shuffling. When Ramayya finally spoke, his voice was lowered. "There's nothing *wrong* with him. Nothing like that." More shuffling, a further drop.

"But what *is* it?" Poornima's father's voice rose with suspicion.

"Our girl's no catch, you know. So no need to be so dubious. Just a small affectation. An *idiosyncrasy*. Nothing to worry about. That's just what I heard, mind you, and really, who knows."

Savitha squealed with delight. She took Poornima in her arms. "So you're getting married! *And* he lives in Namburu. That's not far at all. It's right here. I could *walk* there."

"Yes," Poornima said. "Maybe." Then she was silent. Then she asked, "What does *idiosyncrasy* mean?"

Poornima stood outside her hut and looked at the palm trees. They caught the breeze, a slight one, just enough to rustle the topmost fronds. The other plants that surrounded the hut— a neem tree, a struggling guava, a vine of winter squash—all looked exhausted. They drooped. They sulked hopelessly in the heat. There had been no rain—it was absurd to think there would be. It was only mid-May. The temperature hovered somewhere near thirty-nine degrees Celsius in the mornings, rising to forty-one or forty-two in the afternoons. Shade—that elusive place—was without meaning. The hut broiled like it was set on a frying pan.

Information, as Ramayya learned of it, trickled in. He'd talked to the parents and they had said their son would not be ready to marry for another two months; exams, they'd said. The timing was perfect. That would be just after Poornima's mother's one-year death ceremony. The son's name was Kishore. He was twenty-two years old. "I haven't met him yet," Ramayya said, "but there's no condition that *they* mentioned. He seemed perfectly fine. College. An accountant. What else could our Poornima possibly hope for?"

"Do they want to see the girl? They must. Don't they?" Poornima's father asked.

"Of course. Of course," Ramayya assured him. "No telling when the boy will be able to come, though. Like I said, exams."

"And the dowry?"

"Settled."

It was decided that they—the parents, at least—would come at the end of May. If the visit went smoothly, there would be a full month to plan the wedding, and then, at the end of June, would be the ceremony. June! "But it's so *soon*," Poornima said.

Savitha was already busy with plans. "Exactly. That's just it. I hardly have time to finish all the saris. And I still have to make yours. What do you think of a red border? I think red would be nice with the indigo. I can hardly wait! You. Married. Do you mind if I spend the night sometimes? That would make things easier. I could stay at the loom as long as I wanted."

Poornima asked her father later that evening, and he said, "Fine, fine," hardly hearing her as he rolled his evening tobacco.

And so Savitha began spending nights. They slept together on the same mat—they had none to spare. Despite the sweltering nights, Poornima liked the feel of Savitha's body close to hers. She liked how Savitha seemed to savor everything, even the most mundane. "Look at the sky!" she would exclaim. "Have you ever seen so many stars?"

"It's too hot to look at the sky."

Savitha would then take Poornima's hand and squeeze it. "My amma said we might have enough money by next year. For my sister's dowry. Two more after her, but that's *something*, don't you think?"

Poornima nodded into the dark. She thought then she might tell Savitha about her mother, and the chiming clock with the blue face, but she didn't. Her father might hear. She lay still and listened to the breathing of her brothers and sister, and it occurred to her that she might've never met Savitha had her mother been alive. She saw no betrayal in it: her mother had died, and here was Savitha. But what she did wonder about was Kishore, her future husband. They had sent a photograph. Ramayya had brought it and showed it to them. But it was of him as a boy, maybe eight or nine. He was standing in a row with his sisters, one on either side. They were posed in front of a photographer's canvas of a glowing white palace and fountains and gardens. Above them was a crescent moon. Clouds approached the moon, wispy and romantic. Poornima stared intently at the little boy's face. It was a perfect oval. The mouth a small almond. One of his hands hung listlessly at his side, as if his fingers ached for the toys or the marbles or the toffee he'd been forced to set aside. The other hand was behind his back. His face was the most childlike. Soft, with the features of a baby still clinging to it. Poornima liked that. She then studied his eyes, trying to see into them, or at least see something *in* them, but they were empty. Barren. As if he were looking into an abyss. A strange land. "It's a *photo*," Savitha scolded. "What *do* you expect to see? His heart?"

Yes, Poornima wanted to reply. I want to see his heart.

This time, during the viewing, Poornima was allowed no mistakes. She understood—dressed again in the same silk sari belonging to her mother, though the blooms of jasmine were different, garlanded this time with an alternating row of orange kankabaram—that she was absolutely being monitored. Her aunt sat closer to her. Instead of being led out by the elbow, like the previous viewing, her aunt placed one hand on her braid, as if prepared to yank it at any moment. When she sat down on the mat, her father smiled at her. Smiled. But it was not a smile of encouragement or love or paternal feeling. The smile said only one thing: I'm watching. I'm watching, and the first sign of defiance—the first glimmer in your eyes *leading* to defiance—will be acted upon. Acted upon how? Poornima bent her head and shuddered to think.

Still, she had no plans of ruining this viewing. The groom wasn't there—studying for exams, his father said—but his parents, the middle sister, and a distant cousin who lived in Indravalli were there. Poornima raised her eyes just enough, after looking at her father, to see that *his* father seemed small next to hers, shy and hesitant. The mother, seated across from Poornima, was fat and boorish, maybe from the heat or the bus ride from Namburu to Indravalli, though her eyes were flinty and exacting. The sister, who sat to Poornima's side, looked at her askance and hardly said a word. Her gaze was like her mother's: scrutinizing, vain and impatient, cold. But they were both plump, and Poornima liked that; fatness indicated to her a certain jolliness or abandon, certainly a richness. The sister reached out and took Poornima's hand and rubbed the fingers roughly, one after another, as if counting them. Then she let go and smiled coolly. The men continued to chat, and Poornima, silent and awkward for the remainder of the viewing, nearly embraced her future mother-in-law when, just before they were to leave, she took Poornima's chin in her hand—not gently; no, she couldn't say it was gentle, but it was with what Poornima thought was genuine feeling—and said, "No, you're not nearly as dark as they said."

The sister snorted, or was it a guffaw? Then they left.

She told Savitha about the viewing that night. Savitha had gone home to help her mother with the cooking and had returned before dark. She sat at the loom for another hour, and when she came in for her dinner, Poornima already had her plate ready. She'd made roti, with potato curry. There was a bit of yogurt and leftover rice from lunch. "But they didn't ask you to *sing*," Savitha said. "I like them already. Is there any pickle?" When Poornima rose to get it, she said, "And what about the groom? What about him?"

"Exams," Poornima said. Then she grew quiet. "What if we have nothing to talk about? I mean, he's in *college*, after all. He'll think I'm stupid, won't he? He'll think I'm just a villager. A bumpkin. And what *is* accounting? That thing he's studying?"

"Numbers," Savitha said. "It's numbers. Your father gives you money, doesn't he? To buy food. And you go to the market, don't you, and get change. And you keep a log. I've seen it. A log of all the expenses, so you can show them to your father every week? That's accounting. That's all it is. Besides, Namburu is smaller than Indravalli. He's more of a villager than we are."

Poornima was unconvinced. That couldn't be *all* it was.

The wedding preparations began. There were still details of the dowry and wedding gifts to work out, but Ramayya was confident he could convince them to lower their demands. Savitha raced to finish the sari orders so she would have enough time to make Poornima's. Kishore, her groom, was scheduled to take his exams at the end of the month. But first, there was Poornima's mother's one-year death ceremony. It was set for the beginning of June. It included a day of feasting. A goat would be slaughtered, and the priest would conduct a puja. Her father would perform a ritualistic lighting of a funeral pyre. During the days that followed, Poornima watched her father anxiously: his mood darkened. She guessed it was from the memory of her mother's death, or the dowry demands. He said it was because they were falling behind on the sari orders. "Doesn't she know we have work to do?" he'd say if Savitha went home for even an hour or two in the evenings. "Tell her I'll pay her extra for staying longer. I can't afford much. Hardly any to spare. But some," he said.

The day of the ceremony, when it arrived, brought a drop in temperature along the entire coast of Andhra Pradesh. Poornima woke that morning and realized there was a breeze. Not a cool breeze, not really, but she rejoiced. Her mother must be watching. She must be speaking. She must be saying, Poornima, I'm happy. Your marriage will be a good one. She must be saying, I miss you, too. And that comb, she must be saying, I hold it still.

The young goat to be slaughtered was tethered to a pole outside the hut. It was brown and white; the white in bands, one around its midsection, around each hoof, and another patch dropping down its head and between its eyes. Poornima tried to feed it some dry, dead grass she'd plucked outside the hut. The goat sniffed it and then looked at her. Its eyes were dark globes, and its gaze curious—to see if she had any other food—but when it saw that she didn't, it looked away. Poornima knew she shouldn't look at it for too long, that looking would only increase her sympathy for the doomed goat, but its smell was what kept her there: urine and wilderness and hay.

She thought of its smell when she watched it being slaughtered. The knife—clearly not sharp enough—had to be run back and forth across its neck as if it were a loaf of tough bread. In order to hold it down, they forced the goat onto its side, and one man sat on the hind part of its body, while two others each held a pair of legs. Another man held a bucket under its neck. But there was no need to have done all that. The goat, struggling at first, and then seeing the knife, or perhaps *sensing* the knife, let its body go limp. Losing hope, Poornima thought, or maybe losing nerve. The first slice of the knife left it bucking in pain, one quick surge that ran the length of its body and then came to rest. The knife drove deeper, but the goat still blinked, looking now into a grayness, Poornima guessed, a falling darkness, the globes now losing their light. Its tail wagged one last time, the muscles no longer beholden to their master, and the man who was sawing its neck put his thumb into the mouth of the young goat. Poornima wondered whether he meant to do it, to give the goat one last comfort, one last suckling, or whether it was simply accidental. The goat was dead a moment after. First its body, then its blinking. But something of it seemed to Poornima to go on for a moment longer, an energy, a feeling of life; and then that, too, went away.

The smell—the urine and wilderness and hay scent of the goat—was drowned out by the scent of copper and other metals Poornima couldn't exactly name: the smell of her hands after she'd lifted the bucket at the well, the smell of the freshly scrubbed pots, the smell of river water and silt. It was also hot, the scent, and flies gathered around the goat in great armies. They drank and drank, as armies do, and then they settled on the flesh.

That night, Poornima lay awake for a long while. She thought she would be kept awake by images of the goat, the globes of its eyes, but she wasn't. She was instead thinking of her mother. They had, when she was nine or ten, set out to visit Poornima's maternal grandparents' village. Kaza was a two-hour bus ride away, and she and her mother had started early, hoping to be back by nightfall. Her mother had woken her while it was still dark and washed Poornima's hair, then scrubbed her with a cleansing powder that left her skin red and tender. Then she'd had Poornima put on her best langa, red bangles, and silver anklets, which had been part of her mother's dowry; on the way to the bus stop, her mother had splurged on two pink roses, one for each of their braids. The bus ride had started a little after seven A.M. It was packed with people. They sat in the front, in the women's section, with the back reserved for men. Poornima stepped over chickens, over bundles of produce and kindling that cluttered the aisle; babies wailed and fussed. She sat next to her mother and looked out the window. She'd rarely been on a bus, and the speed with which the fields spun past her window delighted her. She looked out and tried to count all the dogs and the pigs and the goats they passed. But there were so many she lost count, and started over with huts, and when even those became too many, she laughed and thought, Mountains, I'll count mountains.

But then, with a loud clank and a screech, the bus came to a halt. Everyone looked at everyone else. A few of the men in the back yelled out. The bus driver, seated calmly, upright, with a neat mustache and a freshly pressed khaki uniform, turned the engine. It ground but didn't catch. The voices in the back rose. "Aré, aré, maybe the RTC will send a car." "Sure they will," someone yelled back, "its name is Gowri and she runs on grass." The driver told them to shut up.

The bus driver got out—along with most of the men—and looked under the hood. Poornima heard the sound of a wrench or a metal pick clanging against the engine, maybe, and then it went still. The bus dropped. Actually sagged, as if it were suddenly too exhausted to go on. The women, too, exited the bus. The babies quiet now, alert.

The day was cool, late in October, and the morning chill still hung in the air.

Poornima got down with her mother. She'd brought a shawl with her and this she wrapped around Poornima. Most of the mothers had already settled on the side of the road, their children running or playing in the dirt. The men huddled around the open hood.

Poornima looked up and down the road. There was a bullock cart in the far distance, almost a haze, coming toward them. Women in colorful saris tucked between their legs dotted the fields, bent over the flooded rice paddies. There was a small temple, white against the emerald stalks of rice. She thought of that temple, and of the black carved deity inside, and the simple offering of a flower—maybe a pink rose, the kind that was in her hair—left at its feet. She settled, then, beside her mother. The men were now smoking their beedies, spitting, laughing, and the women minded the children. Another bus was due to go past in an hour or two, and they would all pile into that one, space allowing. Some would probably have to climb on top of the bus, or hang by the bar on the door. But for now, everyone seemed perfectly content to sit there by the side of the road. The sun like a small yellow bird, fluttering awake.

Poornima turned to her mother. She had never been alone with her; her father or brothers or sister had always been nearby, or just outside the hut. She was sent on errands for her mother, but never *with* her mother, and when they'd traveled to her grandparents' house in the past, one or more of her siblings had always been with them. In a kind of revelation—in the morning light, sitting on the red dirt by the side of the road—she saw that her mother was beautiful. Even with all the other young mothers crowded around, and the blossoming adolescent girls, youthful and lovely, giggling among themselves, her mother was still the most beautiful. Her eyes were deep black pools, with tiny silver fish gleaming in them when she laughed. Her hair curled at the nape of her neck in ringlets, and her lips were the pink of the rose. Even the dark circles under her eyes had a certain prettiness, as if they were gray crescents, moonlit, pulling in the light.

"Are you hungry?" her mother asked, opening the bundle of last night's rice and spiced yogurt and the dollop of mango pickle she'd brought from home.

"Yes," Poornima said.

And her mother, unthinkingly, her gaze not even on Poornima, but on the distant horizon, watching for the second bus, perhaps, or maybe the approaching bullock cart, took handfuls of rice, rolled them into balls in her palm, and—as she had when Poornima had been a small child—fed them to her. Poornima chewed. The rice, having been cradled in her mother's hand, tasted better than anything she'd ever eaten; she couldn't imagine a greater food. Her mother, though, still paid her no attention. Her thoughts were elsewhere. On her husband, maybe, or the children she'd left behind, or the chores she'd left undone. But for now, for these few moments, Poornima thought her mother's body was enough. It was more than she could ever ask for. To be fed by her hand, to sit next to her, so close she could feel the warmth of her skin in the chill of an October morning, and to know that life, its crowds, would soon separate them. But not now. For now, just until the next bus, her body belonged to Poornima. And when her mother finally noticed the tears brimming in her daughter's eyes, she stopped, looked at her quizzically, and then she smiled. "The bus will *be* here. Any minute now. There's no need to cry, is there? We won't be out here for much longer."

Poornima nodded, the rice having caught in her throat.

7

Savitha shook her awake early the next morning, while it was still dark. "Will you make tea?"

Poornima rolled off their mat. She folded the blankets, placed them on top of her pillow, and stacked them in the corner of the hut. Her father and brothers and sister were asleep.

"So early," she said, yawning, gathering her hair into a knot. "Why are you up so early?"

"That sari isn't going to make itself. Besides, your father said I could make extra if I finished six by your wedding day."

"*Six*? That's one sari every three days."

"Seven. I still have to make yours."

Poornima shook her head. She cut a branch off the neem tree and chewed on it. By the time Savitha was settled at her loom, Poornima brought in the tea. Savitha took a sip. She took another. "No sugar?"

"My father's saving everything for the wedding."

"Has he even seen you yet?"

Poornima shrugged. "I told you. He has exams."

"Exams, Poori? How can he dream of you if he hasn't seen you?"

Poornima blushed. And then she was confused. Her mother's one-year death ceremony had kept her occupied, for a time, but now she was back to wondering. It was not uncommon to marry someone without first seeing them, or hearing their voice, but it struck her as strange that Kishore, her groom, showed no *interest* in meeting her. His parents had already come twice to handle the dowry negotiations, the Indravalli cousin had stopped by last week for evening tea, and her father and Ramayya were going to Guntur in a few days to shop for the wedding, and yet he had never arrived, not even on his way home to Namburu from college. Not once. He actually had to pass *through* Indravalli to get there! She shook her head. It would be nice, she thought, to see him, but she couldn't insist. Insist to *whom*? Besides, it was a good match, as everyone said. A college-educated match; Poornima couldn't hope for more. And that idiosyncrasy that Ramayya had alluded to: no one had mentioned it again. It was probably nothing.

Poornima looked around her. Savitha had finished her tea; the empty cup rested on the dirt floor of the hut. She was working away at her loom. Sunlight flooded in, through the open eastern end of the hut, and Poornima wondered what he was doing this very instant, her groom. Was he watching the sun rise? Was he thinking of her?

She also wondered, at times, whether her father would miss her when she married and moved to Namburu, or wherever her new husband would find a job. Because it occurred to her, despite what Savitha said, that she could possibly move farther away than Namburu. Maybe to Guntur. Maybe as far away as Vizag. Regardless, she would no longer be here. Would her brothers and sister miss her? Her sister was now old enough to cook and clean; she was twelve, and she could perhaps, after a time, begin working on the charkha. At least for two or three years, until she, too, got married. Family—the thing that she and her father and her siblings were bound by— suddenly seemed strange to her. What had collected them like seashells on a beach? And placed them together, on a windowsill?

She thought, in the weeks leading to her wedding, that she would ask her father. Not whether he would miss her—*that* she obviously couldn't ask—but whether he would miss her mango pickle, say, or the stuffed egg-plant she made, his favorite. But then, Poornima thought, she didn't have to; she already knew the answer. It had come to her when she'd overheard him and Ramayya talking, and her father had told him a story Poornima had never heard before.

The story was about when she was little, just over a year old, and she and her parents had gone to the temple in Vijayawada. It had been raining all morning. It had been the day of her mundan, the offering of a baby's hair to the gods, and afterward, they'd found a covered spot, a fisherman's palm-frond shelter, on the shores of the Krishna. Poornima's mother had laid out the food for their lunch. By this time, the rain had slowed, he told Ramayya, but it was still gray, the mist still hovering over the river, which was only a few yards away. According to her father, while they had been busy laying out the lunch, Poornima had squirmed away. "Straight into the water," her father said. "Probably she followed a boat or some other kid into the water. She did that a lot. Followed whatever caught her eye." Within seconds, he continued, she was up to her neck. "Her mother panicked. I jumped up and ran as fast as I could. It was only a few steps, but it seemed to take ages. Ages. I held her in my sight, I willed her to stay right there. If I even said, if I even whispered, 'Don't move!' I was afraid she would move. Fall. Be taken by the river. So I didn't say anything. I just looked at her and willed her to be still." And she was, he told Ramayya, she was as still as a statue. Her newly shorn head gleaming under a break in the clouds.

When I got near the waterline though, he said, I stopped. I know I should've plucked her up and given her a slap, but I couldn't. You see, he said, she looked like she was nothing. Just a piece of debris. In that mist, in that gray, in that vast, slippery rush of water, she looked like nothing. Maybe the head of a fish tossed back in the water. Or a piece of driftwood, not even very big. I looked at her, he said, I looked and I looked, and I could hear her mother shouting, running toward me, but I couldn't move. I was standing there, and I was thinking. I was thinking: She's just a girl. Let her go. By then, her mother had come up from behind me, and she'd snatched her out. Poornima was crying, he said, her mother was crying, too. Maybe they both knew what I had thought. Maybe it was written on my face, he told Ramayya. And then her father had let out a little laugh. "That's the thing with girls, isn't it?" he'd said. "Whenever they stand on the edge of something, you can't help it, you can't. You think, Push. That's all it would take. Just one little push."

A week before the wedding, Ramayya brought an urgent message from Namburu. "What is it? What is it?" Poornima's father asked him, sitting on the edge of the hemp bed, holding a cup of weak, unsweetened tea, his eyebrows raised.

"It's the dowry," Ramayya said, shaking his head. "They want twenty thousand more." Ramayya's tea was sweetened, but he still looked up at Poornima as if she were the reason for this sudden demand.

"Twenty thousand! But *why*?"

"They must've heard. Something. Maybe from the Repalle people. Who knows what they've heard. But they know it's too late. You've committed, and you'll have to pay up."

Her father gave Poornima a look of such loathing that she backed into the hut. She thought of the mother from Namburu, and how her kind words had turned so quickly to dust; she thought of the resignation in the father's eyes, the sister's laugh. But where was *he*? she wondered. Where was the groom? And what had he to say about this sudden, inexplicable demand?

The next morning, Savitha announced with a smile, "I'm starting it this afternoon."

"Don't bother," Poornima said gloomily. Then she told her about the increased dowry demand, and how her father had said that even if he sold both of his looms, he'd still barely have enough.

"What will he do?"

Poornima shrugged and looked out at the blazing light of late morning.

The heat—after a slight cooling—had risen again like a wounded beast. Dripping, thrusting, moving across the plains of Andhra Pradesh with a hatred so intense it had killed more than three hundred people the previous week. Anytime after midmorning was far too hot to work; by afternoon, everyone slept from exhaustion, waking with sweat pooled around their bodies. Even so, and even with the heat, just as she'd said she would, Savitha began making the sari that afternoon. After lunch, while everyone else spread out their mats, she strung the loom with the indigo thread, with red thread along the border. "Sit with me," she said to Poornima. "Bring your mat in here." Poornima sat against one of the wooden poles until her eyes nearly closed, and then she dragged her mat inside.

They talked; Poornima stayed awake as long as she could, until her eyelids, in the searing heat of midday, closed like lead. Mostly, she listened to Savitha talk. She told Poornima that her father was sick. Sicker than he had been. She said most of the extra money she'd made over the past few weeks had gone toward his medicines. "But we may still have enough by next year," she said. Her face soft and ochered against the surrounding bright white of the sun, her braid pulled into a knot at the back of her head. Concentrated now, focused on the working of the loom.

Poornima heard it clattering, repetitive, and yet so like a lullaby. The swooshing of the shuttle felt like water washing over her, and Poornima closed her eyes. Savitha was telling her something. Something about one of her sisters, and how she'd scorched a pot of milk. And then she heard her saying that they were building a cinema hall in Indravalli. Maybe we can go to a cinema when you come to visit, she was saying. Floor seats, of course. But imagine, Poori, a cinema!

Poornima felt herself sink, sink like a stone. She knew she was asleep, but she could still hear Savitha's voice. It seemed to go on and on. Like the murmuring of wind, the fall of rain. And she heard her say, Don't forget a thing. Not one thing. If you forget, it's like you've joined the stone at the bottom of the sea. The one we're all tied to. So remember everything. Press it. Press it between the folds of your heart like a flower. And when you want to look, *really* want to look, Poori, hold it up against the light.

That night, Savitha let Poornima sleep. She sat at the loom alone. She adjusted her lantern so that the light fell on the sari, half done nearly. The indigo thread was simply the night, weaving itself into the sky, the stars. Her hands and her feet merely the day, watching it fall.

Her mind wandered. The clacking of the loom led her away. Back to her childhood. Back to what she had pressed into the folds of her own heart. What she now held up against the light.

And it was this: She was three, maybe four. Her father was doing odd jobs at the time, and on some days he would take her along, whenever her mother was busy cleaning or collecting. On this day, he was working for a rich family whose daughter was getting married. Her father's job was to make the tiny sugar molds shaped like birds. Savitha had no idea what the birds, hardly bigger than her hand, would be used for (decoration, her father told her, but how *could* they, she wondered, when they looked so tasty), so she sat quietly and watched the pot, and then the molds, hoping some of the sugar would dribble out. Her father had only been given a dozen molds, so the pot was left to simmer while they waited for each batch to harden. Once they set, he carefully lifted out each of the white sugar birds, their wings outstretched, and placed them in the sun to dry. She wondered whether she could lick one, just once, without anyone noticing, but when she looked over, her father was watching her. By now, he'd made nearly a hundred or so. She sat hunched by the birds for some minutes when she heard her father gasp; his eyes grew wide when she turned to him. He pointed. "Look. Look at that one. Its little wing is broken."

Savitha followed his finger. There! One of the birds, drying in the middle of the grid of birds, *did* have a wing that had broken off. She jumped up, alarmed. "What will we do, Nanna? Will they make us pay for that bird?"

Her father shook his head solemnly. "No, I don't think so. But we'd better eat it, just to be sure."

Savitha thought about that statement, and then she smiled. Laughed. "I'll get it, Nanna. I'll get the bird." She ran to the edge of its row and leaned over, carefully, carefully, but she lost her footing and fell, crushing all but one or two of the birds beneath her. Savitha lay for a moment on the broken birds. Her eyes flooded with tears. She knew she was in for a scolding, maybe even a beating, and what was more: her father would have to make all those birds all over again. She finally got up, gingerly, her arms and legs and frock and even her face studded with splintered pieces of sugar. Her cheeks hot with tears. She was afraid to look at her father, afraid to raise her gaze, but when she did, to her surprise, he was laughing. His eyes were shining. She couldn't understand it. "But Nanna, you'll have to make them all over again." Her father still laughed. Now he pointed at her. "And I thought you were sweet before," he said.

It took her a moment to understand, and when she did, she flew into his arms; he laughed some more and hugged her close and lifted her off the ground. "Forget those birds," he said. "You, you, girl of mine, *you're* the one with wings."

Sitting at the loom now, on a hot June night, she considered those two wonders: a girl bejeweled with sugar and the words *you're the one with wings*.

A darkness fell over the lantern light.

Savitha turned and saw Poornima's father. He smiled, and she thought, But he's never smiled. And then he said, "Come with me."

8

Poornima was asleep. A sound reached her. Cut through her dreams. She thought the sound might be an animal, a stray dog or a pig. Poornima listened. Then it came again. A cry.

From where? From where?

The weaving hut.

Poornima jumped up. She ran.

The weaving hut, she saw, was dimmed by shadows. A lantern burned. "Savitha?" she whispered.

At first only silence, except heavy, as if it had grown viscous in the heat, the dark. And then a low moan.

"Savitha?" She walked toward the sound. From the corner of the hut. Her eyes adjusted, and she saw a bundle, a shadow deeper than the surrounding shadows. She passed both looms. They looked massive, sinister in the dark, as if they were giants, hunched and full of hunger. But the bundle—she could see now that it was weeping, this bundle, sobbing so quietly, so achingly, that Poornima wondered if it was human, if the creature before her was born with anything besides this weeping.

She stumbled. She bent down.

Then she stilled. For a single moment, fleeting, she thought, Maybe I'm dreaming. Maybe my eyes will open. But when she reached out her hand, she touched bare skin. Hot, heat like sunburned earth. Like desert sand. It was then that she saw Savitha's clothes, ripped. Some on, some off. Lying around her like torn sails. "Savitha. What is it? What's happened?"

The sobbing stopped.

Poornima knelt and took her shoulders. She felt the bones, the sharpness of them. The bones of a small animal. The hull of a tiny ship. Savitha shrank away. As she did, Poornima saw the part in her hair. The lantern lighting a river. Her braid undone, her long hair in disarray, but her part untouched. Silver. Waters pulsing through a mountain pass.

It was then that her grip on Savitha's shoulders loosened. "Who?"

Savitha—whose head was bent over her knees, let out a wail. Low and tender and broken.

"Who?"

Her eyes filled with tears.

Savitha shook so violently that Poornima held her body against her own. She clasped her head to her chest and they rocked like that. Poornima thought she should get help, rouse her father, the neighbors. But when she made a move, the slightest stirring, Savitha gripped her hand. Gripped it so tightly that Poornima looked at her in astonishment.

"Who?"

Their eyes met.

"Poori," she murmured.

And it was then that she understood. It was then that Poornima knew.

She let out a scream so loud that no less than ten people came running. By now, Savitha had shrunk. Retreated like a wounded animal. Scraps of her blouse fell from her shoulders. Her shoulders brown and denuded like distant hills. They stood around them; the questions and gasps and exclamations singing past Poornima like arrows. She dropped to her knees. A neighbor stood over her and said, "What is it? What? What's wrong with you girls?"

"Bring a sheet," someone yelled, trying to lift her up, but Poornima refused, covering Savitha's body with her own. What other use could it have, she thought, this body of mine? What other use?

The sky the next morning was white with fever. The air so thick and hot it tasted of smoke. Poornima blinked awake, her eyelids wretched and unbelieving. Savitha was seated just as she had been, the sheet thrown over her, and Poornima eyed her desperately, thinking, No, this is no dream. Why couldn't it be a dream? A moment later, Poornima's brother sidled past the door, averted his eyes, and said, "Nanna wants his tea."

Poornima looked at her brother, and then, when he'd gone, she looked at the empty doorway.

"Nanna wants his tea," she parroted in a whisper, as if not only those words but all of language were a stranger to her.

She sat with those words, thinking through each one, and then slowly rose to her feet. Savitha didn't move. She didn't even seem to be awake, though her eyes were open.

Poornima moved through the heat, dazzled by the light, dizzied, from the weaving hut into the main hut, and set the water to boil. She added the milk, the sugar, the tea powder. She watched the blaze. It didn't seem possible: it didn't seem possible that she could make tea, make something as ordinary as tea. The world had reordered itself in the night, and to make tea, *tea*, for her father, seemed, in some way, a more fundamental offense than the one he had committed. She watched it with disgust, first simmering, then boiling, and then held the cup away from her, as though the wound he had opened, induced, was already festering, maggoted; as though she held that wound in her hand.

He was seated on the hemp-rope bed, just outside the hut. The elders were some distance away, and she could see that he was straining to hear them. When he saw her, he straightened his back and held out his hand, callous in its reach. A hot venom shot through her; she recoiled. She took steps toward him but her feet didn't seem to be striking anything solid, anything sturdy. The ground is so soft, she thought, so like cotton. But then the venom turned to nausea, the heat, the glare of morning made her sway, her vision suddenly swam with iridescent dots, flashes of lurid light.

She was only a step or two away from him when her body gave out, gave in to the vertigo, the pull of the earth. She stumbled, a drop or two of tea splattered, her other arm reached to break her fall, and it was this arm that her father caught. It was this arm—the one he had never before touched, never in her memory—that he touched now. She felt the sizzle of his skin. The serpent curl of its claws, tongues, fingers. Scales like burning coals. She pulled away with a kind of violence, horror, and fled back to the weaving hut.

Back to Savitha.

She huddled against her, burrowed against her body, as if she had been the one who had been wronged. Wronged? It was a father, steadying his daughter. And yet, to steady her in this way, at this time, with its sickening glint of kindness, seemed to Poornima a greater affront than if he'd simply let her float away on the Krishna, all those years ago. Why, she wanted to ask, Why didn't you?

It was then that Savitha's father arrived. His hands—those gnarled fingers, bent and misshapen—no longer hidden. But held out in front of him, as if beseeching. Begging. Waving before him like wild branches. Twisted by lightning strikes, bugs, disease. But his face, his face, Poornima saw, was frozen. Such despair as she had never seen.

"My girl," he said simply, his eyes red, shattered. His voice in ruins.

He tried to lift Savitha—to take her with him—but she gripped

Poornima's arm. "Leave her," someone yelled through the door. He tried lifting her once more, but Savitha gripped harder, and finally, watching his struggle, Poornima looked at him as she would at an empty field, and said, "She wants to be left."

The afternoon brought swirls of chaos and maddening commotion. Neighbors, elders, onlookers, children hushed and sent away, men, everywhere men. But Savitha—Savitha remained still. Not since she'd gripped Poornima's arm had she so much as turned her head. She'd simply pulled the sheet up to her neck, blinked once, and then stayed sitting, stonelike, exactly as she was. Poornima sat beside her and at one point, panicked and unnerved by her stillness, held her fingers under her nose for a moment to make sure she was still breathing. The dewy warmth of her exhalation, its delicacy, countered all the voices, the noise, the endless *people*.

Hands, sometime in the afternoon, tried to pull Poornima away. Tried to pry her away from Savitha. But this time, Poornima clung to *her* with a kind of madness, frenzy. She heard someone say, not even in a whisper, "It'll taint her. These things always do. And so close to her marriage being settled." Another said, "A dung heap is a dung heap. If you step in it—"

Poornima, though, felt like a blade of grass bent viciously by wind. She spoke to the wind. Please, she said to it softly, please stop. But when it did, just for a moment, she was stunned by the silence. Afraid. Afraid it would reach through the smoke, the heat, the numbness, and swallow them, she and Savitha, piece by piece.

The day wore on. The heat still savage. Clawing. Invading everything. Even Poornima's tongue and her ears and her scalp were coated in a layer of dust. She paid it no attention; evening drew to a close. She listened. She heard everything. The village elders were still gathered outside the hut, debating what to do. Late in the evening, Savitha's father joined them, and every now and then, Poornima heard shouting, and they seemed to her the shrieks of strange and startled birds, caught in nets.

"*You*," a voice said.

Poornima looked up. Standing in the doorway of the weaving hut was a woman she didn't recognize. But she seemed to know her.

"You," she seethed. "It's *your* fault."

Poornima shrunk farther into her corner. The wall behind her hard and rough and unforgiving. She knew now: Savitha's mother.

"Your fault. Your fault."

"I—"

"If it wasn't for you, if it wasn't for your *friendship*, my Savitha would've never come here. She would've never stayed here. In this house of demons. In this house. Never. You're a demon. Your house is demonic. And that sari." The tears began; her voice failed. She slid to the ground. She clutched at the doorpost. She crawled toward Poornima like an animal. "That sari. That sari. That she was making for *you*. This would've never happened otherwise." Now she had crept so close that Poornima felt her breath against her face. Hot, rancid, poisoned. "My child. My *child*, you understand? No. No, you don't. You couldn't, you demon."

Someone came in. They saw her. They pulled her away. She screamed— wretchedly, without form, as if a stake were being driven into her heart. She kicked as she was dragged away. Dust flew into Poornima's eyes. She blinked. In the quiet that followed, a pall descended over the hut. Over Savitha and Poornima. A great and unendurable silence. As if Savitha's mother had opened a portal, and air had rushed in. It was then that the tears started. And once they started, Poornima saw, they had no end. They came in great and uncontrollable sobs. If her mother's death had brought a storm, *this* could drown the earth and everyone with it.

No one paid her any attention. They went in and out of the weaving hut. All manner of people. Late in the evening, a child—a little boy—peeped through the doorway, and one of the village elders grabbed his arm and pulled him away. He admonished him. "What is there to see?" Poornima heard him say. "Spoiled fruit is spoiled fruit."

The tears kept coming.

At one point Poornima choked with her weeping, and when she did, she realized she'd forgotten to breathe. Forgotten that there was such a thing as air. That there was anything other than pain.

She took Savitha's limp hand and held it in hers—and youth and middle age and senescence passed before her like the cinema she had never seen, like the cinema Savitha had delighted in one day seeing.

"Savitha?"

Nothing.

"Savitha?"

Not the slightest movement. Not a twitch or a breath or a blink.

"Say something."

Deep into that night, the village elders came to a decision: Poornima's father was to marry Savitha. They all agreed: it was to be his punishment, and it was just.

No one bothered to tell Savitha the decision. Poornima only heard of it when Ramayya walked by the door of the hut and hissed, "She'll get married before you. The trash picker. And without even having to give your father a dowry."

Poornima stared at him. She turned from the doorway only when she felt movement; Savitha had blinked. For the duration of the second night, Savitha sat again, motionless. "Savitha," Poornima tried one more time, shaking her, pleading once more for so much as a word, a gesture, before falling finally into a disturbed and plagued sleep. Mostly by dreams, nightmares, visions, and premonitions, but once by Savitha's voice.

"Do you remember?" her voice said.

Poornima rolled her head in her sleep; she mumbled, "What?"

"About Majuli. About flute song. And that perfect fruit. Do you remember?"

"Yes."

There was silence. Poornima shifted again in her sleep, felt for Savitha's hunched body but found only air.

"I'll be many things, Poori, but I won't be your stepmother."

"Okay."

A shuffling.

"Poornima?"

"Yes?"

"I'm the one with wings."

In the morning, Poornima woke to screams and clamoring and calls for a search party; she looked around the weaving hut and found it empty. Savitha was gone.

Poornima

1

Poornima's wedding was postponed indefinitely. The groom's side wouldn't budge from their demand for twenty thousand more rupees. Especially now with rumors swirling as to the fouled runaway girl, her friendship with Poornima, and suggestions—by people whom Poornima had never even met, by people not even from Indravalli—that Poornima had helped her to run away. And what could be said about a girl like that? they said. What good would she be as a wife?

Not only that, but every day, more details dribbled in from Namburu confirming their hesitation. The father sent word that his son—in addition to the twenty thousand—would need a watch and a motorcycle. The older of the groom's sisters, whose name was Aruna, wondered aloud, in the company of some of the other village women in Namburu, whether it wouldn't be difficult for her to have a sister-in-law so clearly beneath her. Beneath you? one of them had asked. Beneath you how? Supposedly, the sister had looked at her gravely and said, "Beneath me in the way a monkey is beneath me."

Still, it was the mother's comment that most agitated Poornima. She'd told one of Poornima's distant cousins, while bemoaning her college-educated son's marriage to a village girl, "What can one do? That's the thing with a successful son: you either have to get him married to a modern college girl who'll ruin him with her excesses and demands, demands of makeup and fashionable saris and jewelry every time she so much as passes gas, or the village bumpkin who is as dark as a mustard seed, with the social graces of a mama pig in mud." But hadn't she said Poornima was not as dark as she'd thought? Hadn't she taken Poornima's chin in her hand?

She wished Savitha were here, so she could talk to her about it. Savitha? Her heart blazed with pain. And then gave out like a candle.

She had been gone for a month now. Thirty-three days. The search party that had gone to look for her—made up of a group of young men from Indravalli (there had also been a local police constable in the beginning, but he'd returned within two hours of starting the search and declared, wiping his brow in the heat, "The last time I spent more than an hour looking for a girl was the daughter of an MLA. We ended up finding her at the bottom of a well, not two hundred yards from the MLA's house. It's always the same; take my word for it. In this heat, I give it a day or two. Maybe three. And there she'll be, floating, puffed up like a puri.")—had gone as far as Amravati to the west, Gudivada to the east, Guntur to the south, and Nuzividu to the north. Nothing. They'd come back without so much as a rumor as to her whereabouts. Where could she have gone? the women in Indravalli wondered. Where is there to disappear to?

Poornima looked in the direction of the Krishna, east, and wondered the same thing.

After two months of back and forth, Ramayya and Poornima's father finally reached a compromise with the Namburu family. Poornima's father would add an extra ten thousand to the dowry, paying out five thousand now and five thousand within a year of the marriage, along with a scooter instead of a motorcycle—Ramayya suggesting to them that a scooter would be more convenient as Poornima began having children (sons, he was careful to add). The Namburu family, after a tense week of silence, finally agreed, grumblingly, bemoaning the generosity of their discount. Ramayya was overjoyed that the match had finally been settled, but Poornima's father was miserable. "But you won't have to sell the looms," Ramayya said, trying to cheer him. "And just think, you only have one more to go." Poornima's father raised his dark gaze to her, when she handed him his tea, and eyed her with contempt. And Poornima, surprising even herself, eyed him right back.

The wedding was set for the following month. Poornima spent most of that month inside the hut. It was considered gauche for a girl to be seen out and about in the village after her betrothal, and there was also the matter of the evil gaze of the other villagers, putting a hex on Poornima, envious of her good fortune in marrying a college-educated boy. "Besides," her aunt said, staying with them for the month to help with the preparations, "we don't need you getting any darker." It didn't matter either way to Poornima: light and dark, inside and outside, hope and hopelessness slowly started to lose meaning for her.

Sometimes, while sitting listlessly at her charkha, or combing her sister's hair, she would look up through the open door of the hut and wonder, What is that shining thing out there? What is it, so painful, so bright? People, too, lost their place in her mind; they were no longer moored to anything Poornima recognized or controlled or even understood as *herself*. Once, early in the month, her younger brother ran inside with a cut on his arm. He held it up to her, crying, waiting to be bandaged, but Poornima only looked down at him and smiled kindly, distractedly. She handed him a fifty-paisa coin and nudged him back out the door, drops of blood trailing him, and said, "Go. A banana. Quick. Savitha's on her way." Later in the month, her aunt asked her to put rice on the stove for dinner, and Poornima looked up from the corner where she was seated, stared at her aunt, and with her eyes as empty as an open field, she asked, "Who are you?" Twice, maybe three times, Poornima felt a flash, a stab of something she couldn't name. Something akin to a shard of bitter cold, or blinding heat. What was it? What was it?

She thought that it might be illness, that she had caught something. Malaria, maybe. But then it settled. It settled in her chest, on the left side, just above her heart. At first it was only a sprinkling, like a few grains of rice that might've spilled onto a stone floor. And all she had to do was bend to pick them up, one by one. But then the sprinkling of rice grew into a weight. A density. It became a *mound* of rice. She tried to press her palm against her chest, in an attempt to soothe it away. But it wouldn't slacken, it wouldn't loosen; it simply sat there, tight as a fist. She thought of the weight of her mother's hand, resting against her hair, and now, in her chest this time, was yet another weight. But this one ravaged, conjuring no memory, no longing, no lost childhood or honeyed voice or a hand raised to feed her, conjuring nothing, nothing at all except the two words: *she's gone.*

2

More aunts and uncles and cousins started arriving the week before the wedding. The hut was bustling. A tent was erected, blue and red and green and gold. Mango leaves had been bought and garlanded together, strung across the doorway to the hut and all along its edges. Various items for the ceremony—turmeric, kumkum, coconuts, rice and dals, packets of camphor and incense and oils—came in every few minutes. It all had to be stored, put away. And then there was the cooking. All those relatives, there must've been more than thirty by Poornima's last count. They all had to be fed, bright green banana leaves spread before them as plates, the dirty ones collected and thrown to the pigs. Her aunts and cousins helped, but every few minutes someone would turn to Poornima—usually one of her young cousins—and say, Where do you keep the salt? or, Imagine, you'll be the wife of a fancy man, or, What is it, why are looking at me like that? To which, to all of which, Poornima would place her hand above her heart, and wonder at the hardness, and the ache.

The days passed.

When the morning of the wedding came, it came like an invader. The sun rose in a clamor of paint strokes—pink and purple and orange and green—then rested angrily against the horizon, waiting for land, women, villages on fire. Early in the day, all her female relatives gathered around Poornima, along with her future sisters-in-law and a few neighbor women, for the bridal ceremony. They oiled her hair and then they rubbed turmeric over her body. Each one, in turn, then blessed her with rice soaked in turmeric and kumkum and sandalwood. With the older women, Poornima rose and bent to touch their feet. Aruna, the sister who'd compared Poornima to a monkey, stood a little apart, watching, as if she were bored by it all. When her turn came to bless Poornima and sprinkle her bowed head with turmeric-soaked rice, it felt to Poornima that the grains landed on her head with a kind of jab, like hail, but they also served to wake her up, and, as if she were coming out of a long and complex dream—so convincing it was, so utterly irrefutable, that the waking world, the one in which she was surrounded by twenty women, all smiling, all with yellow teeth, seemed to her the fraudulent one—she blinked and bowed her head lower, saw the throw of rice, and thought, Rice. Is there anything else in the world besides rice?

The muhurthum—the exact time the marriage ceremony would start, based on the bride's and groom's horoscopes—was set for that evening at 8:16 P.M. It was a little after seven P.M. and Poornima was seated on the veranda with the priest—without the groom—conducting the Gauri Puja. It wasn't until *after* this that she would be led to the mandapam, the wedding dais, and seated next to Kishore in order to go through more pujas, and then have him tie the wedding necklace, the mangalsutra, around her neck. Poornima sat listening to the priest, following his instructions, but everything still felt to her like a mirage, a distant and unreachable place. She listened to the drone of the priest's voice; she stared into her lap—her head bent, just as a bride's should be—her hands folded in prayer.

She was wearing a red-and-green sari, made of heavy silk. She wore a few jewels, mostly fake or borrowed, the row of bangles on each wrist glittering in the camphor flame. The henna crawled up her arms and her feet like moss, smothering and airless.

Everything—everything from the bridal ceremony to the dressing in the shadows of the hut, helped by her aunts, the pujas, the young priest yawning as he incanted them, and the constant rush of color and noise and people—all of these were things Poornima could in no way feel, only see, as if she were peering through a window.

Through this window, the priest looked at Poornima, who was squirming a little, incense smoke choking her, and said, "Pay attention." Then he said, "Get up." It was time to go to the mandapam, where her groom was waiting.

Her father waited beside her, to lead her to the dais. Poornima looked at him, his face set hard against her, or maybe against her dowry-raising in-laws, or maybe his own frailty—although she saw none of it; she saw only madness, her own—and he said, "Let's go," and she said, "Where?"

The sun was beginning to set by now, the western sky blazed green and orange and red. The line of the eastern horizon was once again white with heat. Where am I being led to? Poornima wondered. Wherever it was, she didn't mind. Not really. She noticed the sunset, with wonder, and thought, It is such a lovely evening, and such a lovely sari I am wearing. It delighted her. That window she was peering through: so much loveliness behind it. And yet, somewhere deeper, she thought, No, I don't want this sari. I don't want this day. I don't want this father. What do I want—what do I want? She was not able to answer, and so all of it remained, and she walked on, pretending to be delighted.

Her head was down, of course. She didn't look up, but she knew she was nearing the tent when the heat, the air around her, grew heavier. Her father didn't seem to notice; he seemed entirely focused on the dais, leading her to it. But the air was stifling, no longer lovely, and Poornima felt a rising panic. She tried to stop him, she tried to buck him off, but he kept his grip on her elbow and steered her toward the dais.

"I want to stop," she said to her father.

Her father tightened his hold on Poornima's elbow. He said, "Don't be stupid."

Don't be stupid, Poornima thought, and the words seemed decent enough. And so that's what Poornima chanted to herself, Don't be stupid. Don't be stupid. Don't be stupid. Don't be stupid. Don't be stupid. Don't be stupid. Don't be stupid. Don't be stupid. And she kept chanting this, over and over and over again, until she arrived at the mandapam, climbed the two steps, and was seated next to her groom.

Don't be stupid, she told herself.

Her father placed Poornima's hand in the groom's. She didn't look. Why look? Who was this strange man? He barely held it, anyway. More pujas. The priest handed her two bananas and an apple. Two bananas and an apple. Poornima looked at them. They seemed so familiar. So enticing. As if she'd waited her whole life to be handed this exact number and variety of fruit.

Why?

She wanted to ask the man sitting next to her. He might know. She was about to turn and do exactly that when the priest, impatiently, as if he'd already told her many times, said, "Ammai, can't you hear? I said, give him the fruit." And so Poornima decided she would ask later, after handing him the fruit. His hand came closer, closer and closer, and this time, Poornima raised her eyes. Just enough. She gasped. His right hand: it wasn't whole. He was missing two fingers. His middle and most of his index. The nub of his index finger looked like dry shredded meat, still pink, and the end of where his middle finger should have been was closed up, turned inward, like the mouth of a toothless old man. She shrank away.

So this, she thought with disgust, this is what they meant by idiosyncrasy. She recalled that she'd once known someone else with these hands, with hands just as grotesque (someone's father, but whose?). And then she thought, But who is *this* man? And why am I to hand him these two bananas and an apple? They're mine. These fruits. I don't want to place them in that hand, she thought; I don't want to place them in a hand so harmed.

It was not the fruit. Or perhaps it was the fruit. Either way, by the time Kishore had tied the mangalsutra around her neck and they'd walked the seven steps around the fire—her five fingers held in his three (and a half)—she understood. And that window? She understood now that there was no window. There never had been. Or, if there had been, it had broken, a rock had crashed through it: and here she was, staring at the rock, the shards, the air rushing in. She understood, in that moment, that she was married.

3

Her husband's home, in Namburu, was not at all a hut. It was a real *house*, made with concrete and with two floors. It had four rooms on the first floor and one large room on the top floor, with the remainder of the flat roof serving as a terrace. Here, laundry was hung, and on the hottest summer nights, everyone brought their mats up and slept under the stars. But not anymore. Here was where Kishore and Poornima would live, and here was where Poornima was escorted for their first night together. Poornima's young cousin accompanied her, serving as a chaperone, and her new mother-in-law and sisters-in-law greeted them at the door with a glowing aarthi. Poornima looked down at her toes.

They played a game, she and her new husband, while all the relations cheered them on. It was a game that had been played since ancient times: the same game, in the same way. Water was poured into a brass vessel, narrow at the top. A ring was dropped in. Plop. Into the water. They were to reach their right hands, only their right, into the vessel, and whoever came up holding the ring was the winner. The narrow opening was the key—their hands were meant to touch. The fingers meant to interlock. The foreplay—between these two strangers—meant to lead to sex. The first sex. Poornima reached her hand in and felt an immediate disgust. Instead of five, she felt three fingers. The thumb and pinkie hardly fingers, so that left only one. And this one rubbing against hers, the nub of the other—the index, the one that was minced—like moist, undercooked meat. And then nothing. The middle finger just an absence. An omission. She smiled shyly, trying to hide her revulsion. This is your new husband, she told herself. This is your new life. And then she looked up. Her new husband was looking right back at her. At her? Maybe through her. But he had a peculiar look in his eyes. Poornima recognized the look; what was it? She went through all the recollections of her youth, and her girlhood, the whole of her life, really, and it seemed to her that it was not at all peculiar, or unfamiliar. It was, in fact, the most familiar look of all. It was the look of a man: undressing her, teasing off her clothes, her innocence, ripping it with his teeth, biting at the tender heart of it, and then laughing and cruel, savoring the completeness of his incursion, its terror and its desire, and here she was, already half spent, half spoiled, half naked.

And here she was: already half swallowed.

And it was then that the tears started—before she could stop them, while her fingers still searched for the ring, but not really, because she already knew he would win; or rather, that she would lose—but they didn't matter, because hardly anyone noticed, and if they did, they mistook them for tears of joy.

That evening, after the afternoon filled with games and gentle teasing of the bride and groom ended, Poornima was bathed and dressed in a white sari and her hair adorned with blooming jasmine. She was handed a glass of warm milk for her new husband, scented with saffron, and she climbed the steps to the rooftop room. Slowly. So slowly that her young cousin, who accompanied her up the stairs, along with a few of Kishore's female relations, looked at Poornima and thought she might cry again. This young cousin, named Malli, knew nothing of what had happened back in Indravalli—only that there was a strange hush over the ceremony, one that she guessed was associated with the crazy-looking woman curled up in the weaving hut all those weeks ago, nestled under Poornima's arms, the one she'd only gotten a glimpse of, though a boy cousin, who'd gotten a better look, had told her she was a rakshasi come to devour new babies. "But why new babies?" she'd asked him. "Because, stupid, they're the tenderest." That seemed to make sense. "So we're too tough?" He'd looked at her and sighed impatiently. "*I* am. I don't know about you. Let me see." He'd squeezed her arm, and said, "Probably you're all right." Still, Malli was happy to join Poornima on her journey to Namburu. It was the custom—a young female relative joining the bride to her new home, a way to ease the journey to the strange, unfamiliar place—and Malli had jumped at the chance. But now that she was here, climbing the stairs beside Poornima, a cousin she barely knew but who struck her as being in an awful, pounding sort of pain, Malli wondered whether it wouldn't have been better to take her chances with the rakshasi.

Outside the door to the room, Malli and the other relations left her, giggling as they hurried away.

Poornima watched them go.

She looked at the doorway. There was a garland of young green mango leaves strung across the top of the doorframe. The door itself had a fresh coat of green paint and was blessed with dots of red kumkum and turmeric. She stood against it and listened. Not for sounds of her new husband, who, she knew, waited beyond, but for something else, something she could not name. Maybe a voice leading her away, maybe to the edge of the roof, maybe to its very edge. But there was nothing. The glass of milk in her hands grew cool. She looked down and saw the layer of skin on its surface. It had appeared out of nowhere: thin and creased and floating. Cunning. How did milk do that, how did it *know* to do that? she wondered. To protect itself? How, she thought, could it be so strong?

She set the glass down next to the door and walked to the center of the terrace. The concrete burned her bare feet, but she hardly noticed. She saw something shining toward the middle of the roof, but when she reached it, she saw that it was only a piece of wrapper, for a toffee. What had she thought it was? A coin? A jewel? Poornima didn't know, but she was so disappointed that she sat down, right next to the wrapper, and stared at it. "You could've been a diamond," she said to it. Then she said, "You could've been anything." The wrapper stared back. It was nearly dark by now. It had cooled some, but the afternoons were still hot, in the high thirties, and the concrete that Poornima sat on held the heat. She didn't mind. What she minded was that when she was small, three or four years old, one of her earliest memories, she'd gone with her mother to the market to buy vegetables. While they were walking back home, her mother had stopped in a dry goods shop to buy a gram of cloves. Poornima looked at all the tins on the counter of the shop, filled with chocolate candies and biscuits and toffees, and asked her mother to buy her one. Her mother hardly looked at her. She said, "No. We don't have the money."

Poornima waited, watching the tins.

Another customer—a fat lady with her fat son—came into the store. The boy—even to Poornima's young gaze—struck her as spoiled. He was older than her but seemed slower, as if he'd been fed all his life on butter and praise. *He* didn't even ask for a candy. He simply pointed at the toffee he wanted and yanked on his fat mother's pallu. The owner obliged him by opening the tin, and then, laughing obsequiously, he said, "Take as many as you want, Mr. Ramana-garu." The boy grabbed a handful and walked away. The owner was busy helping the mother, and so he, too, walked away. Poornima's mother was bent over the jars of spices, examining a handful of cloves. Poornima turned back to the tin.

Its lid was still open.

She didn't eat it until she got home. She'd clutched the toffee in her little fist all along the walk home and then she'd waited until she was alone—while her mother was making dinner and her brothers were playing—and then she'd slowly unwrapped it, the red toffee in the middle of her palm nearly as *big* as her palm, and sparkling like a gem, a smooth and sugary gem. She licked it, once, twice, until she could no longer stand it. Then she popped it into her mouth. She'd had toffee before, but never a whole one; her mother had always broken them into pieces so she could share them with her brothers. The worst part of it was the shattering, Poornima thought: to take a perfectly luscious round gem and to break it into shards. It was indecent. She resented her mother even more than her brothers. But *this*, this one was whole. She sucked on it and sucked on it until the sweetness flooded her mouth, tickled her throat. It was down to nothing, barely a sliver, when she heard her mother calling for her. She swallowed it down, and when she went to the back of the hut, where her mother was cooking, she started to cough from the woodsmoke.

"What is that?" her mother said.

Poornima looked at her.

"Come here," her mother said.

Poornima took a small step toward her mother. She grabbed her daughter's cheeks and squeezed. Poornima puckered her mouth like a fish. "Open up," her mother said. "Don't think I don't see you."

Poornima finally opened up, a little, and then when her mother squeezed harder, her entire mouth gaped open, red and shining and slippery like the inside of a pomegranate.

"Did you steal it?" her mother asked.

Poornima said nothing, and then she nodded.

Her mother sighed. She said, "Stealing is wrong. You know that, don't you, Poornima. You should never, ever do it." Poornima looked at her mother and nodded again. "You've already eaten it, so we'll have to go tomorrow and give him money. I won't tell your father, you understand, but it wasn't yours. Remember that, Poornima: never take what isn't yours. Can you remember that?"

Poornima remembered, but she no longer agreed. Sitting in the middle of the terrace, on the evening of her wedding night, she looked at the wrapper and she thought about her mother. She thought about the red toffee; she could taste it still on her tongue, feel the sweetness, still, traveling down her throat. But she didn't agree. Amma, she said to the wrapper, if only I *had* taken what wasn't mine. If only I had taken a moment to insist, insist on meeting him before the wedding, I could've counted his fingers like they counted mine. If only I'd refused. Refused it all: to let you die, to let the goat die, to let that blue clock stop chiming. If only I'd said, *You* are flute song. She picked up the wrapper. She said, Don't you see, Amma, if only I had taken the things I wasn't meant to take. If only I'd had the courage.

She dropped the wrapper and watched it blow away.

She walked to the door, behind which her new husband was waiting, probably asleep by this time, and picked up the glass of now cold milk. She saw on its surface specks of dust that had blown in, sailing on the wrinkled layer of milk. She looked at them, the specks, and decided to let them convince her: hold fast, they said, stay on the surface, and these waters, these creamy, sumptuous white waters, let them carry you. Where would they take her? She had no idea, but behind that door was a man who was not her father. And to whom she now belonged. That seemed an improvement; that alone was a better place.

Inside the room was a bed, a wooden armoire with a long mirror fringed with a design of berries dangling from curling vines, a desk, and a television. A television! No one in Indravalli had a television. Kishore saw her staring at it, and said, "Don't get excited. It doesn't work." Her eyes left the television and returned to the glass of milk in her hand. He took it and placed it on a small round table beside the bed. The thin yellow sheet on the bed was covered with rose petals arranged in the shape of a heart, and Poornima wondered who'd done that: shaped them into a heart. It was a gesture so enchanting, so unexpected, that she wanted to sit on the edge of the bed—gingerly, so as not to disturb the petals—and look at it. Just look at it. But Kishore seemed not at all interested in the heart, because without prelude, he pulled her onto the bed, tugged at the folds of her sari, and burrowed his head, his wet lips, into the dip of her blouse, his fingers stabbing at her breasts like the ends of a potato. In the ensuing confusion, Poornima missed whatever it was that lanced into her. She let out a whimper, too scared to scream, but by now, Kishore was grunting away on top of her. She couldn't decide—as she watched his face, its grimace, its shudderings—what hurt more: the thing coming in or the thing going out. But then it ended. Just like that. After one final push, Kishore looked down at her and smiled. A true smile. And she thought, Yes, after all, yes, you are the one I belong to now. Then he rolled off her, and in the dark, just as Poornima felt for the first time the velvet of the rose petals against her back, cool and forgiving like rain, he said sleepily, "I like two cups of coffee. One first thing, when I wake up, and one with tiffin. Do you understand?"

She nodded into the dark. And tried her very hardest to understand.

4

At the end of their first month of marriage, on a Sunday, Kishore took Poornima and his sister Aruna, seventeen and younger than Kishore by six years, to Vijayawada. His other sister, Divya, who Poornima saw for the first time at the wedding, was ten years younger than him, and studious. She was quiet, the opposite of Aruna, and didn't want to come along to Vijayawada because she had exams. So Poornima and Kishore and Aruna set out after breakfast. Poornima wore her best sari, an orange one with a pink border that she'd gotten as a wedding gift. They ate masala dosas at a restaurant near the bus station. Aruna and Kishore didn't enjoy their dosas—Aruna said the curry was flavorless and that the waiter was insolent; Kishore added that the restaurants near the company where he worked, on Annie Besant Road, were far better—but Poornima had nothing to compare hers to; she'd never been to a restaurant before. Afterward, Kishore took them to the cinema.

This was also a first for Poornima.

Her eyes warmed with tears as she and Aruna waited for Kishore to buy the tickets, wishing she were here with Savitha, as they'd once planned, but Poornima gasped and forgot all about her when she entered through the balcony doors. She'd never seen a room so big. It was like entering an enormous cave, but one that was chiseled and glamorously lit. She stood in awe—looking at the red plush seats, some of them ripped but still luxurious, and the droplets of golden light along the walls where the lamps were hung, and the crowds of people, rushing to find seats. Kishore and Aruna must've been to this theater before because they pushed past Poornima to a row of seats in the middle of the balcony.

Then the curtain parted, the screen filled with light, and Poornima was astonished again. The people were huge! They seemed to be bearing down on her, ready to lunge. Her eyes grew wide, a little afraid, but when she looked anxiously at Kishore and Aruna, they were already engrossed in the film—a sad tale of two lovers separated by the disapproval of their parents, especially the girl's parents, because the boy was penniless, and he had no job (as far as Poornima could tell), but he was strikingly handsome, and he had a handsome motorcycle, even though he was poor. The girl's parents, in an effort to keep them apart, went so far as to lock her up in a remote mountain home. It was sad, but there were song and dance sequences of the lovers in Kashmir, and Shimla, and Rishikesh, dancing and frolicking in the snow. The actress was wearing only a shimmering, diaphanous blue sari against the white of the snow, and Poornima leaned over and asked Kishore, "Isn't she cold? Isn't snow supposed to be cold?" He ignored her, or maybe he didn't hear.

At the end of the movie, the hero won over the girl's parents by rescuing their family business from a greedy relative who was plotting to overtake it and throw them out of their mansion. If the hero hadn't exposed him, and if he hadn't held the bad relative at gunpoint, the girl's family would have lost everything—money, jewels, cars—and would've been left homeless. The girl's parents, in that instant, recognized the boy's cleverness and quick-wittedness, and the movie ended with the girl's parents placing their daughter's hand in his.

Poornima was so touched by the radiant faces of the hero and heroine, by all they'd had to overcome, that she began to cry. Kishore and Aruna looked over at her and laughed. "It wasn't even that good," Aruna said. Poornima didn't agree; and on the way home, as the bus wound through the darkening paddies of rice and the fading fields of cotton and peanuts that lined the road from Vijayawada to Namburu, and as the outlines of the distant hills bled into the night sky, she realized she wasn't crying because of the film, she was crying because she *hadn't* forgotten. Not for an instant. Savitha had been there, seated next to her, in some way. In some way more essential than even Kishore and Aruna had been there. She could picture it: Savitha would've grasped her hand when the hero pulled out the gun, and she would've liked him, the hero, because he was poor like they were, and because he loved the heroine with such sweetness, such guileless longing. Imagine, Poori, she would've said, shaking her head, imagine how cold that poor girl must've been, in that thin sari. All that snow, she would've said, it looked just like yogurt rice, don't you think?

In the days and weeks after going to the cinema, Poornima thought more and more about it. Not the film itself. Not exactly. What she thought about were the faces of the other people in the theater, especially Kishore's and Aruna's. She'd never seen such a thing: lights flashing, changing colors, illuminating the rapt faces of people in an audience. She'd not even seen the lights of a television shining and shifting, let alone the lights of a movie screen. It seemed to her, as the months wore on, that the quality of that light, distant yet penetrating, menacing yet harmless, was how the events of her own life felt.

For instance, one evening, while she was cooking dinner for the family, her mother-in-law walked into the kitchen (which was actually a separate room, much to Poornima's astonishment) and demanded to know where her garnet earrings were, the ones in the shape of a flower; she wanted to wear them to the temple, she said. Poornima, who hadn't even known her mother-in-law owned a pair of garnet earrings, said she didn't know, and went back to making the eggplant-and-potato curry on the stove. Her mother-in-law, watching closely as Poornima added salt to the curry, sighed loudly and muttered, "The poor. You never know around them." Poornima put down the spoon, watched her mother-in-law leave the kitchen, and wondered, You never know what?

But then the lights of the cinema moved closer, became more menacing.

This time, it was while the family was having tea and pakora on a Sunday afternoon. Poornima had just sat down to drink her tea when Aruna eyed her closely, turned to her mother, and said, "*Somebody* discolored my silk shalwar. Amma, do you know who it could've been?" It had been a delicate pink, but was now apparently splotched with blue and purple. They both turned to Poornima. Their gaze took on a kind of hatred, sudden and smoky. "You soaked it with something blue, didn't you? Was it that blue towel? I bet you soaked it with that towel. Amma, can you believe it? You're jealous, aren't you? It's impossible to have nice things around some people. I know you soaked it with that towel. How can you be so stupid?"

Poornima opened her mouth to protest, but she honestly couldn't remember. She did the entire family's laundry, so maybe she had soaked it with the blue towel. But not on purpose, and certainly not because she was jealous. She looked at Kishore, but he was busy chewing an onion pakora. She turned to her father-in-law, who rarely said anything in front of his wife, and had a habit of slinking off whenever a discussion became heated or turned to him. Today he simply sat with his hands folded, staring into them as if into a deep well. Only Divya was an ally—a serious girl who Poornima had grown to like, but who had no voice, being the youngest, and was often shouted down.

But before Poornima could even turn to Divya, her mother-in-law was at her side, yanking her head back by her braid. "Ask forgiveness," she growled. "Ask." Poornima was so surprised she couldn't get any words out, not even a scream. Her mother-in-law finally let go, and Poornima did ask forgiveness, but then, that night, as she was falling asleep, she thought, It was absurd of me. It was cowardly of me. I should've never asked for forgiveness when I'm not even sure I had anything to do with it. I don't remember ever even seeing that silk shalwar. What did it mean to ask forgiveness, she wondered, not knowing the crime, or who committed it. It meant nothing, she realized. Nothing at all. And so she decided in that moment—decided, yes, decided, astonished that she could even do such a thing as *decide*—that she would never again ask forgiveness for a thing she didn't do, for crimes she could in no way recall committing. And so she fell asleep smiling, and drifted into a dream.

After six months of marriage, the days took an even darker turn. Poornima's father had been able to give them the first five thousand rupees at the wedding. He'd taken a loan from the weaving collective, at an exorbitant interest rate, but had been able to keep both of his looms, and even hired a boy—young, hardly able to reach the treadles—to work the second loom. But he still hadn't managed to buy Kishore a scooter, nor had he any way to pay the remaining five thousand. Poornima would've known nothing about this, since she hardly had any contact with her father, had it not been for the fact that her in-laws began to mention it more and more. *Mention?* That wasn't quite the right word. *Hound* was a better word. They began to hound her about it.

At first, Poornima didn't even know they were talking about the five thousand. They were circumspect, and they would say things like, Some people. Some people are just too lazy to pay their debts, or, You can't trust anyone, especially not the poor, the ones with daughters. Why should their bad luck cost *us* money? or, Liars—if there's one thing I can't stand, it's a liar. But after a few weeks, the grumbling became more pointed. While Poornima was eating dinner one night, after all the others had finished—first Kishore and her father-in-law, and then her mother-in-law and Aruna and Divya had to be served—her mother-in-law walked into the kitchen, where Poornima was sitting on the floor and eating, and said, "Did you get enough to eat, my dear?"

Poornima looked up at her in astonishment. My dear?

"It's just as well," she continued. "Eat your fill. *You* can live off of us. But who are we going to live off of?"

Poornima tried to talk to Kishore about it. She brought it up one night, after they'd climbed to their upstairs room. The nights were cooler now. It was January, and they'd had to switch out the thin sheets for the woolen blanket. The sky was a deep and distant blue; winter stars pierced it with cold indifference. Poornima stood on the terrace for a moment, looking out at the other houses in Namburu, most of them only thatched-roof huts like the one she'd grown up in. Golden lantern light spilled onto the dirt passageways between the huts, and there was the smell of woodsmoke, cooking fires setting rice to boil, round wheat pulkas browning directly over the flames. Poornima looked in the direction of Indravalli and knew this same cold night air must hang over Indravalli, too, this exact night air, probably, and yet she felt no kinship with it. No affection. It was as if the winter had turned the season of her heart, too, and left it filled only with smoke and distant, frozen stars.

Kishore asked her to come to the bed when she entered. He was lying on top of the covers. "Take off your blouse," he said. Poornima took off her blouse and wrapped her pallu around her shoulders, though the shadowed curves of her breasts, her thin arms, could still be guessed through the fabric of her sari. "No," he said, "take that off, too." She did so reluctantly, shy, unaware, even after six months of marriage, and even with Kishore on top of her practically every night, of her adolescent body, and of the crude brutality it could inspire. "Massage my feet," he said. She moved to the end of the bed. Her fingers, though they'd already been rough in Indravalli from the charkha and the housework, were now calloused and cracking from the constant work, her hands the only part of her that seemed to absorb the daily disgraces, the accusations, the domesticity of everyday cruelty. When she lifted her eyes, she saw that Kishore's were closed, and though her bare chest was cold, she didn't dare to cover it again. She thought he might've fallen asleep, but when she slowed the massage a bit, he called out, "Keep going. Who told you to stop?" She heard him snore lightly, or maybe he grunted, and then, after a moment, he said, "Come here." He took her while she was on her back first, and then he turned her over onto her stomach and took her again. When he finally came, he collapsed on top of her and lay there for so long that Poornima watched as three different mosquitoes bit her and flew away, drugged, heavy and bloated with her blood.

She waited a moment, once he rolled off, and then she took a deep breath. She said, "I can't help it. I can't help it if my father doesn't have the money."

Silence. She slapped away another mosquito, the room now thick with them, attracted by the heat of their bodies.

"Yes, you can," he said.

Poornima stopped. She stared at him in the dark. "I can?"

His voice grew cold. The room, too, grew suddenly cold. All the mosquitoes wandered off. "Tell him there's worse to come," he said, "unless he pays up."

"Worse? Worse how?"

But Kishore didn't say anything, and after a moment, he was snoring. Fast asleep. Poornima lay awake, the returning mosquitoes now a welcome distraction, the loss of blood an offering.

It wasn't that conversation. Or maybe it was. Regardless, Poornima, a few weeks after that night, began to sneak upstairs between her chores, or race to finish them, or find any excuse to leave the main part of the house and climb to the second floor, close the door to their room, and sit on the edge of the bed. She never lay down; lying down reminded her of Kishore, and she didn't want to be reminded of him. She didn't want to be reminded of Savitha, either, so she didn't close her eyes.

Instead, she studied the room. The walls were painted a pale green. There were watermarks on two of the walls, but none on the third and fourth. Two windows on either side of the door looked out onto the terrace, and these had bars and shutters across them, to keep out thieves. There was a lot to steal, Poornima thought: the wooden armoire was handsome; nothing in their hut in Indravalli was as handsome as the armoire. Inside it were mostly Kishore's work clothes, along with her wedding sari, some papers and jewelry and cash that Kishore kept in a locked metal box, and a doll that was wrapped in crinkly plastic, which a distant relative had brought back from America. There was also, in the armoire, a bronze statuette Kishore had gotten for being the best student at his college each of his four years there, and this he kept especially protected, in a designated place nestled between some clothes. Tucked in between everything were mothballs. Against the other wall were the television and the desk. The television still didn't work—Poornima wondered whether it ever had—but the room felt rich for having it there, a piece of muslin cloth covering it to keep out the dust.

Next to the television was the desk, and on the desk were Kishore's papers. These papers were different than the papers in the armoire, he'd told her. These papers were just his work papers, he'd said, while the ones in the armoire were government papers and bankbooks. Poornima looked at them, and seeing that they were in disarray, she got up from the bed and went to the desk to straighten them. As she did, she saw that they were filled with columns—six of them, with many, many rows underneath filled with lots of numbers and scribbles that she couldn't possibly understand, so she laid them back down on the desk. But something caught her eye: she saw that the first row on the topmost page *did* make sense. It was simply the numbers in the second, third, fourth, and fifth columns added up, and listed in the sixth column. The first column was just a date. That was easy enough; she'd learned addition well before the fifth class, which was the last year she'd attended school. Then she checked the remaining rows, and they, too, were the same: simple addition, that was it.

Was *this* what Kishore did at work all day? She nearly laughed out loud. Asking for foot massages, demanding that she press his shirts every morning, yelling for a glass of water as soon as he walked in the door: as if he'd crossed a desert, as if his labors had utterly parched him, when all he was really doing was adding up numbers! But then she checked the other sheets of paper, and it wasn't true. Those columns weren't added up; something different was happening in those columns.

Poornima sighed and went back downstairs. There were the lunch dishes to wash and dinner to prepare. Her mother-in-law and Aruna liked their tea at four o'clock, and it was already ten past. Poornima hurried to the kitchen. But as she boiled the water and milk, and raced to add the tea powder, and brought down the sugar things, she wondered about those other pages. What *were* those columns doing? Maybe Savitha had been right, she thought. Maybe, in the end, accounting was not much more complicated than when her father gave her money to go to the market, hardly any money at all, and she'd still had to buy enough vegetables and rice for all of them, and even so, he'd demanded that she bring back change, along with a full rendition of all she'd spent and where. If she'd bought a kilo of potatoes for five rupees, he'd say, "I could've gotten them for four," and if she did get them for four, he'd say, "They're small. Pockmarked. No wonder."

Still, as she was scooping the sugar into the cups, Poornima suddenly put down the spoon. She put it down and looked up. She was amazed. She'd just thought of Savitha, and yet she had felt none of the usual blunt, dreary pain or confusion or longing that she always felt, nor even the gleaming, sharp hatred toward her father. None of it. She'd simply, and without suffering, thought of Savitha. It was the first time she'd done so, and the feeling was like being handed a kite in a strong wind. Poornima smiled. But then the smile immediately fell. Because in the moment right afterward, it all rose up again: the desperate sorrow, the disorder, the mystery of her whereabouts that drove her, on some nights, to huddle in a corner of the terrace and weep under the waning or waxing moon, the watching stars.

But she'd been free for a moment, and besides, those columns couldn't possibly be all that difficult: those two things she knew. Those two things she was certain she knew.

5

The first time Poornima talked back to her mother-in-law was on the morning of a marriage viewing for Aruna. She was six months older than Poornima and yet still not married. The problem, according to Aruna and her mother, was the boys. They were never good enough. One had a good job, high-paying, in Hyderabad, but he was balding. Another, tall and handsome, had a father who was keeping a woman even though his wife was still alive—and who knew if bigamy had a genetic component? Yet another was perfect in every way—job, hairline, family reputation—but he was the exact same height as Aruna, and she liked to wear a little heel whenever she went to the cinema or out to eat. "What am I supposed to do," she said, pouting, "wear chapals everywhere? Like a common villager?"

The boy coming today was from Guntur; he worked for Tata Consulting and had been to America on a project, and might even have the chance to go again. He was an only son, so the entirety of his family's inheritance would go only to him, *and* he looked like a film hero. At least, that's what one of his neighbors told the matchmaker, when he went around to inquire. "Which hero?" Poornima asked. "Is it the one in the film we saw?" Aruna scowled and shook her head. "No. Not *that* one, you pakshi. A hero in a good film."

It didn't matter which film. The house in Namburu had been aflutter since four in the morning. The stone floors in every room were washed and mopped. All the furniture was dusted, the cushions on the sofa and chairs aired out. A small puja was conducted—as soon as Aruna had washed her hair and dressed, she made an offering to Lakshmi Devi and lit incense. They were arriving at three in the afternoon but had said nothing about staying for dinner—which meant that Poornima had to make enough sambar and curries in case they did, along with pulao rice and bhajis. She was cutting strips of eggplant for the bhajis, the oil already heating on the stove, when her mother-in-law came in, yelling for her to hurry up, the milkman had arrived, and there was the milk to boil and the yogurt to set. Poornima turned down the oil and got up to get the milk pan, when her mother-in-law looked at her, up and down, and said, "When they arrive, don't show your face. Stay upstairs. We'll make up something. We'll tell them you had to go back to Indravalli for the day. Something. Just don't make a sound."

Poornima turned from the stove. "Why? Why would I stay upstairs?"

Her mother-in-law sighed loudly. "You're not—well, we don't want to bring Aruna's status down, do we? Besides, six months, seven months, and you're still not pregnant? I don't want you to rub off on my Aruna. On *her* chances. Barren women are a bad omen, and I don't want you down here."

There was silence. Poornima listened. She strained her ears and found that there was only the small, quiet sound of the oil beginning to boil, though this, too, magnified the other silence, the greater one. "How do you know?" she said. "How do you know your son isn't the one who's barren?"

The slap that followed was so powerful that it knocked Poornima backward, reeling, crashing into the stove. The milk wasn't on the burner yet, but the oil was. It splattered across the wall, dripped off the granite counter, and landed in thick, hot drops on the floor. A few drops flew onto Poornima's arm, and she could feel their sizzle, spreading like papad, hissing like snakes.

Her mother-in-law eyed her with real hatred, and then she said, "Keep acting up. Go ahead. There'll be worse. Just keep it up."

Worse? There would be worse? Kishore had said the same thing: Was it a coincidence? Or wasn't it?

That afternoon, when the boy's family arrived, Poornima was relegated to the upstairs and told not to come down until they called for her. She didn't mind. She sat in the middle of the terrace for a few minutes, away from the edge so no one would see her. It was after four o'clock when the boy's family arrived, the hour when flower vendors walked through the village, shouting and singing out the kinds of flowers they had for sale. Poornima could hear the song of the old man who sold the garlands of jasmine, plump as pillows, and just beginning to open, releasing a fragrance so intoxicating that she was certain she caught their scent on the terrace, two, maybe three streets away.

Her mother-in-law sometimes bought a long strand, cutting off the longest lengths—as long as her forearm—for Aruna and Divya (who didn't even like wearing jasmine in her hair and took it off as soon as her mother turned her head); she took a short one for her own, puny bun and gave the remainder to Poornima. Poornima, whose father, after her mother had died, had never once given her money for flowers, would rush to oil and braid her hair, wash her face, then reapply talcum powder to her face and neck, draw kajal around her eyes, and paint on a fresh bottu. And only then, only after she'd made herself worthy of the flowers, their sweetness, their beauty, would she finally put them in her hair. On those nights, after Kishore took her—not once commenting on the flowers in her hair; did he even notice them? Poornima wondered—she'd lie back on her pillow, and their scent would drift up toward her like mist, like drizzle, like the unbearable sadness of that upstairs room, her husband turned away from her, the shutters closed against burglars, but still a mild breeze sneaking in, rustling the edges of the sheet, and Poornima, lying there in the dark, her eyes open, warm, inundated by the fragrance of flowers.

The voice of the old man selling the garlands of jasmine faded, and

Poornima got up and walked across the terrace. She went into the upstairs room and closed the door. The papers were still on the desk. They were the same stack, sitting in the same place, and had been for the past two weeks. She moved aside the top page, the one with simple addition, and looked at the next one. This one had more numbers, but it also had a heading at the top of the page. The heading was in English, which Poornima couldn't read, but there were other details in Telugu. For instance, the first column had a listing of various machines, such as cars (6), lorries (3), tractors (2), combines (2), and so forth. Each machine had an amount next to it. Judging by how high the numbers were, and how all the numbers in a group—such as the group of cars—were approximately the same, Poornima guessed each number corresponded to the value of the listed machine. Next to one car, she saw it read "Dented," and was valued less than the others. The lorries, on the other hand, were all valued far more than the cars. Poornima shuffled to the next page. She was doing this out of boredom, she realized, but it was also fun, in a way. She couldn't say why, only that figuring out what the numbers meant, what the columns stood for, gave her a sense of accomplishment, of gain. The feeling itself was unfamiliar, and she wondered at it: Why hadn't she felt it when she'd worked at her charkha, or when she made a particularly tasty sambar, or even when she'd bought the two bananas, an apple, and the handful of cashews for her mother? Well, one reason was obvious: her mother died, the sambar got eaten, and the charkha, well, the charkha spun and it spun and it never stopped spinning. But *this*? This stack of papers? It was leading to something; she could sense it. She left that page and turned to the next.

The nagging from Poornima's mother-in-law and Kishore escalated. Aruna's marriage to the boy from Guntur was nearly fixed; it was just a matter of a little more haggling over the dowry and the amount of jewelry (measured in ounces of gold) each side would give the bride. Aruna's family had the dowry money, though they had to sell a small farm they owned outside Kaza for the gold. But the farm didn't bring in enough, and so every time Poornima entered a room, or left one, her mother-in law yelled after her, "That no-good father of yours said within the year. All five thousand. Well, the year's come and gone. And here we are, feeding you three times a day, without even a grandchild to show for it. No-good fathers beget no-good daughters, that's what I say. And here's my poor son, a prince, stuck with you. We should've never married into such a family." Poornima snuck a look at Kishore's mangled fingers and wondered, Who is stuck with whom?

Kishore's mode of escalation was more subtle, though also more painful: the sex became rougher. Violent. He'd grab her hair, yank her around the bed by it, slam into her with such force that her head would hit the wall behind the bed. The next day, bruises bloomed across her body, green and blue and gray and black, growing like nests, as if tiny birds were coming in the night to build them, one feather and branch and twig at a time. At the end of two weeks, Poornima could no longer see the true color of the skin on her legs and arms, and she wondered—bracing every evening for Kishore's return from work, serving dinner with as much care and slowness as she could manage without being told to hurry up, washing the dishes even more deliberately, and then climbing the stairs one by one, knowing he was upstairs, knowing what the night would hold, and even, once or twice, closing her eyes when she reached the top step, praying, hoping, that when she opened them, Savitha would be there, standing on the terrace, laughing, saying, Let's go—but wondering, wondering, she couldn't help wondering if *this* is what they meant by worse.

Kishore's work pages took on a kind of poetry for Poornima. She could've gazed at them for hours, days, were it not for chores, and for the simple fact that she didn't know what they actually *meant*. Individually, she knew what they meant, but not together: the first page was simply various payments made to Kishore's company over the past three months, added up. The second page—the one with the listing of cars and lorries—was a listing of the company's assets. The third page, Poornima realized without much trouble—based on the columns of other company names and an amount beside each name, some getting smaller, some getting higher—were the company's debts. But what did they *mean*, when taken together? Why was Kishore always shuffling them around, punching numbers into some small machine, grumbling about this or that outstanding payment? Loans. Debts. It didn't make sense. Poornima wandered through her chores in a daze for a full week, until one afternoon, while she was hanging up the laundry to dry, one of Aruna's shalwar tops was whipped to the ground by the wind, and Aruna ran up behind her, caught Poornima's arm in a grip, and swung her around to face her. "Do you know whose this is? Do you know what it's worth?" Poornima looked at her, and then she couldn't help smiling. It was so simple. Of course. That must be it. All those papers, stacked on the desk: they added up to something. They added up to what the company was worth.

And so as the stacks kept changing—with Kishore taking stacks back to work, bringing new ones, all the while completely unaware that Poornima was studying them, that she was *learning* from them—she began to see the world differently; she began to see it with a kind of clarity: there was what you owed, and there was what you could sell to pay off what you owed, and whatever was left (if there was anything left) was all that you could say was truly yours, all that you could truly love.

6

By the middle of the second year of Poornima's marriage, the nagging grew into outright hostility. She couldn't recall a single day when she hadn't been slapped or screamed at or forced to ask for forgiveness (for the smallest things, like when she dripped a few drops of tea onto the stone floor). The five thousand rupees was still outstanding, and her mother-in-law and Kishore reminded her of it every time she put a bite of food in her mouth, or drank a glass of water. "You think it's free?" her mother-in-law hissed. "You think that water's free? That pump we installed cost three thousand rupees. So *you* wouldn't have to go to the well. And where do you think we got that three thousand rupees? Where? Not from your father, not from him. That's for sure, the thief. Both of you. Thieves." But the water pump was installed the year *before* I came to Namburu, Poornima wanted to say, but didn't. Not because she was afraid; fear began to lose meaning in her life— fear was a thing she'd felt for so long, first with her father and then with her mother-in-law and Aruna and Kishore, that it took on a monotony, an everydayness that struck Poornima as being just as boring as washing dishes, or ironing clothes. Why should she be afraid? She'd left her father's house and nothing had changed. Maybe nothing ever did. She understood now that Savitha had been right to run away. She'd been right to leave. Fear was no good, but neither was the monotony of fear.

But then, all of a sudden, everything changed. It simply stopped.

There was no more yelling, no more demands, no more violence. Poornima went about her chores and they simply ignored her. Sometimes, she'd catch one or another watching her, waiting, it seemed. But for what? She didn't know, but she did know one thing: she had to get pregnant soon. She'd heard of barren women being replaced by second wives. She wouldn't mind that much—she might actually prefer it—but she thought they might send her back to Indravalli once the second wife arrived. She sometimes dreamed that they had, and when she walked into the weaving hut, Savitha was seated at the loom, waiting for her. But that wasn't true; only her father was there, and Poornima refused to see him. Even during festival days, when daughters were expected to return home, Poornima wouldn't go. Why should she? "No," she said with finality, "I won't go," and her mother-in-law cursed her under her breath, mumbling, "No. No, you wouldn't. That would save us a week's food, so why would you?"

Aruna's marriage was finally fixed—with the man from Guntur—for the end of August. The family was overjoyed. It was now July, and preparations began in earnest. There was shopping to do, invitations to send out, the marriage hall to book. Aruna was beside herself. She grabbed Divya by the arms and spun in circles, laughing. "He's so handsome, Divi, and so rich, and we'll have to live in America. That's what his father told Nanna, that he would have to go back soon on another project. Oh, Divi! Can you imagine? Me, in America. I need clothes. Amma, I need clothes. Not these ugly shalwars, but modern clothes. Amma, did you hear me?" She went on and on in this way, and Poornima was glad she would soon be out of the house.

Preparations intensified in the middle of July, but on a windless day, late in the afternoon, during tea, the matchmaker, whose name was Balaji, arrived at their door. He was invited in with great aplomb, but Poornima's mother-in-law took one look at his face and put down her teacup. "What is it?" she said. "What's wrong?"

The matchmaker looked at the nearly empty teacups, and then at Poornima. "Don't just stand there. Tea. Bring us some tea."

By the time Poornima returned, Aruna was crying.

"*Off?* But why?" her mother-in-law wailed.

Balaji wouldn't say. Only that they'd had a change of heart.

"Change of heart? But why? Why? We gave them everything they asked for."

He sipped his tea and looked at Aruna sadly. "She's a fine girl. We'll find another match."

"Another match? You fool. What happened to this one? How does it look? Practically on the altar, and *then* they cancel. Why?"

She got no more out of him, only that it was better to leave it all behind. Move forward, he told Poornima's mother-in-law. The way forward is the only way, he said.

But rumors trickled down.

The main one was that somebody had told the Guntur family that Kishore's mangled hand was a genetic condition, and any children Aruna would have might also be disfigured.

"That's ridiculous," Kishore said, infuriated. "They're idiots. Dongalu."

Poornima was serving him dinner. She scooped some rice onto his plate, and then she said, "Is it?"

"Is it what?"

"Is it a genetic condition?"

Kishore blanched; he got up from the table and left the room without a word.

"Get out!" her mother-in-law screamed. "Get out of this house. It's you. It's because of you they canceled the wedding. You're a curse on this family. It's all because of you."

Am I a curse? Poornima wondered vaguely, climbing the stairs to the second floor. She didn't go into the bedroom, where she knew Kishore would be. Instead, she stood on the terrace and looked out at the palm trees swaying in the distance, and the thatched-roof huts huddled beneath them, and then she turned to the west and watched the last rays of the sun leave the sky, as if they had no use for it anymore, and Poornima wanted to follow it, follow the sun, and she thought, What has my life added up to? What's been taken, what's been left? What's it worth? Then she heard footsteps. She thought it must be Kishore, and braced for what would come, but it was Divya, holding out a plate of rice. "You didn't get to eat," she said.

Poornima nearly cried out with gratitude.

Divya turned and went back down the steps.

Poornima idled on the terrace well into the night, and then snuck noiselessly into the bedroom. Kishore was turned toward the wall, and she thought he must be sleeping, but no, his breathing was ragged, uneven. He was awake, and he was angry. She could feel his fury. She edged to the opposite end of the bed and waited, expecting the worst, but he seemed to eventually fall asleep. Or maybe she did.

The next morning, too, was strangely quiet. Divya went to school; nowadays, Aruna nearly always stayed in the bedroom she and Divya shared. Kishore stayed home from work. He said he was feeling ill, but instead of resting, he and his mother locked themselves away in the upstairs bedroom. Midafternoon, Poornima's mother-in-law came downstairs. She looked at Poornima sweetly and said, "My dear, how about some bhajis for tea today? I feel like eating bhajis. Would you mind?"

Poornima stared at her. She'd never once heard this voice before.

There was only one potato in the house, and some onions, so she cut those up and put the oil on to heat. Her mother-in-law lingered in the kitchen and even offered to help with the chopping, but Poornima said it was all right; she would make them. The oil began to pop, and then to slightly smoke. Poornima dipped an onion into the batter. Just then, Kishore walked into the kitchen. Poornima was startled—never once, not once, had Kishore come into the kitchen.

He, too, smiled sweetly.

No, she thought in that instant. No.

None of it made sense, and yet it did.

She dropped the onion back into the batter and stepped away from them, and away from the stove. In that instant, both of them lurched: one body toward her, and the other toward the stove.

Poornima's vision blurred. She didn't know who it was that grabbed her, but she pushed them away so hard that she fell backward. She was on the floor, and they were both now by the stove.

Why are they standing there? She had just enough time to think, Why are they standing by the stove? before an arm swept something off it, and Kishore and her mother-in-law sprang away and raced to the other end of the kitchen.

She turned her head to follow them, and that was why, when the oil landed, it splattered across the left side of her face, down her neck, and caught her upper arm and shoulder. Poornima felt a fire, and then the fire, and everything with it, went out.

7

Kishore and her mother-in-law refused to pay the hospital bills, so Poornima was discharged on her second day. Only her father-in-law and Divya came to get her; when she sat down in the autorickshaw, the bandages still on her face and neck and arm and shoulder, she felt so small, so placental, that she shivered in the midday heat. Her father-in-law said, "You can stay for a day or two, but then you have to leave. It's no good for you in Namburu. It's no good. I'll go tonight and buy you a ticket to Indravalli."

Poornima nodded imperceptibly, and that slight nod sent a shattering pain up the left side of her face.

When they reached the house, her mother-in-law and Kishore were in the sitting room, and they watched her with contempt. Divya led her up the stairs, and when they reached the terrace, Poornima had her go in first and cover the mirror on the armoire. Only then did she enter. She lay down on the bed. Divya left, and then she came back that evening with a plate of food. Poornima looked at the plate of food and started to cry. Divya left again and came back with a glass of milk, and this she forced Poornima to drink.

The next day was the same. Only Divya came and went. But this time, she brought her books with her, and opened one of them, and began to study. Poornima made a sound, a squeak. Divya looked up from her book. "It's my Telugu primer," she said.

The primer was from the British era, she told Poornima; the small village school in Namburu never having had the money to buy new ones. Poornima opened her mouth slightly, the slightest amount, in an attempt to speak, but the pain shot through her like a cannon.

"Do you want me to read aloud to you?"

Poornima blinked.

The story Divya read was told from the perspective of a man on a ship in the early 1900s. The man's name was Kirby. Divya paused and said, "It doesn't say if it's his family name or his given name." Then she continued reading.

In the story, this man Kirby was traveling on a ship from Pondicherry to Africa. While traveling, he met another man, also on the ship, who was a Portuguese army colonel. The colonel, according to Kirby, was traveling to his family's estate in Mozambique. They grew sisal, the colonel told Kirby, and went on endlessly about how sisal looked (like a Mexican agave, Kirby wrote, though neither Poornima nor Divya, even with a footnoted explanation, had any idea what that was either), how it was grown and then harvested. He said the blades of the sisal plant could cut deeper than a sword. Kirby then asked the colonel, But how do you handle it?

Oh, we don't, the colonel said. The Negroes do all that.

On his last night on the ship, before he was due to disembark the next morning at Lourenço Marques, the old colonel told Kirby this story:

It happened one winter, the colonel began, when I was stationed at Wellington, near Madras. Years ago. Our cantonment, quite suddenly, was overrun with rats. Hundreds and hundreds of them. They got into the food, the beds, the artillery. And not just any kind of rat, he said, and here he cupped his hands so that they were as big around as a dinner plate. They were enormous. Well, no one knew how to get rid of them. We tried poison and traps and we even had this tribal shaman come down from the mountains, some sort of expert on rodents and scorpions and such. None of it did any good, you see. The rats went right on eating and shitting everywhere. (Here there was inserted another footnote indicating that the colonel had meant to say *defecating*.)

After about a month of this, the colonel continued, one of the young soldiers noticed that after he'd spit on the ground, a rat came around, sniffed his sputum, and looked up at him with the kindest, most concerned eyes the man had ever seen. The soldier told us about it at dinner that evening, almost joking, you see. But I could tell the young man was a bit shaken. The camp doctor heard this, and that very night he diagnosed him with early-stage tuberculosis.

Kirby noted that here, the colonel took a sip of his champagne (again, Poornima and Divya shrugged, not knowing what that was). Rats, you see, he said, putting down his glass of champagne, can detect tuberculosis well before modern medicine can. That damn rat very nearly saved the camp from an epidemic. Amazing, isn't it?

Kirby, apparently, then asked the colonel, What about the rats? What happened to them?

That's the thing. One day they all just left. Picked up and disappeared. It was as if their sole purpose was to warn us. To save the thing that was trying to destroy them.

At this point, Kirby, writing this account, said he laughed out loud but that the colonel only closed his eyes. At the end of the story in the Telugu primer, Kirby wrote that early the next morning, when the ship had docked in Lourenço Marques, they went to wake the colonel, but he was dead. Kirby wrote that laying on his narrow ship's bed, the colonel was pallid, his skin nearly translucent, and that he could almost see the blood drifting away from the colonel's heart.

That was the end of the story, and when Divya stopped reading, Poornima looked at her. A young girl, the same age she and Savitha had been when they'd first met. She then looked down at Divya's neck—brown like bark, a vein throbbing, pulsing steadily, a lighthouse beneath her skin— and then

Poornima thought about the poor colonel, and the rats, and Mozambique, wherever that was, and she didn't have to wonder what it looked like, blood drifting away from the heart.

The next day was a Sunday. Everyone was at home. Poornima could hear them moving downstairs, talking, laughing, and the vendors, mostly vegetable sellers, stopping at various doors, yelling out their wares, eggplant and beans and peppers plucked just that morning. The dew still clinging to their skins. The Krishna didn't flow past Namburu, but Poornima thought she caught its scent on the wind, could see the fishing nets flung into its waters, twirling like langas. When she closed her eyes, there were the saris drying on the opposite shore. Every color, fluttering in the river breeze, fields of wildflowers.

Her eyes, now, were often closed. She stayed in the room all day, only going downstairs to use the latrine. She hadn't bathed since the spill, and her musk and animal smell, mingled with the smell of her sweat, of rotting bandages, of copper (Had she gotten her period? Maybe. She didn't care to look.), and burned flesh, always the smell of burned flesh, assaulted her as she tried to sleep. She didn't mean to sleep. She meant to stay awake, all night, if needed. Her father-in-law had come upstairs the previous night and handed her a train ticket to Indravalli. Second class, instead of third, so she could travel in relative comfort. He hadn't looked her in the eye, but she knew he was sorry. She knew so little about him, but she knew suddenly that his life was lived in regret. He stood at the door for a moment, before leaving, and she was lying on the bed, and she thought they must look like two wounded animals, circling in a dark cave.

After he left, Poornima stared at the ticket, and then she put it under her pillow. It was the twice-daily passenger train, leaving Namburu at 2:30 P.M. and arriving in Indravalli at 2:55 P.M. Twenty-five minutes. That's all there had ever been.

She thought Kishore might come upstairs, if only to ensure that she was leaving, but only Divya came in the evening, bringing Poornima's dinner of rice and pappu, the rice cooked soft so that she wouldn't have to chew very much. After she left, Poornima closed her eyes again. It was dark when she opened them. There was a gibbous moon, so when she studied the shadowed room, she saw the shapes of the furniture, the gleam of the stone floor, the pattern of flowers on the sheet that covered her. She looked at the desk; she saw, even in the moonlight, the stack of papers, the accounting papers that had given her such pleasure to decipher, such a sense of accomplishment and purpose. It was nothing, she realized, her heart breaking. All of it was nothing. It was nothing in the face of something as simple as hot oil, and the slightest evil.

She then rose heavily, into the silver moonlight, and stepped onto the terrace. She would miss the terrace; she realized it was the only thing, along with Divya, that she *would* miss from her two years in Namburu. She walked to the edge of the terrace and looked at the first stars, and she thought of the many years she had left to live. Or maybe she had none at all. It was impossible to know. But if she didn't die tonight, if she didn't die within the amount of time a human being can readily foresee, can honestly imagine (a day? a week?), What, she wondered, will I do with all those years? All those many years? To look forward, Poornima realized, was to also look back. And so she saw her mother, as she had once been: young and alive. Sitting at the loom by lantern light, or bending over a steaming pot, or tending to one of Poornima's brothers or her sister, wiping their faces or bathing them or pushing the hair from their eyes. That's all she could recall her mother ever doing: something for someone else. Even Poornima's most tender memories—of being fed by her mother's hand on the bus trip to see her grandparents, or the weight of it against her hair while she'd been combing it—had all of them to do with her mother doing something for her child, never for herself. Is that how she'd meant to spend her life? Is that how lives were meant to be spent?

Now, Poornima looked to the future. She saw herself going back to Indravalli. At 2:55 P.M. the next day, she would step off the passenger train, walk to her father's house, and enter it. She could see him clearly, sitting on the veranda, on the hemp-rope bed, smoking his tobacco and watching her. Just as she was watching him. Perhaps her siblings would be there, perhaps they wouldn't. But what the future held most clearly—more clearly even than the image of her father—was the image of a battlefield. And no battlefield, in all the histories of man, could compare with the one Poornima now saw: blood-soaked, and littered—littered with what? She moved closer, she knelt to see, her eyes widened: it was herself. It was littered with her limbs, her organs, her feet, her hands, her scalped hair, and even her skin, shredded, mangled as if by dogs.

Poornima blinked, but it wasn't tears she blinked back. What was it? She didn't know, but she could see it—floating in the air around her, suffocating, spinning like ash.

She walked back into the upstairs room, took out the train ticket from under her pillow, and ripped it in half, then quarters, then eighths, and then she let the tiny pieces fall to the floor like confetti. She watched them fall with a certain delight, and then she turned to the armoire, opened it, and took out the locked box. There was no key that she could see; probably her mother-in-law had the key on the key ring she always kept tucked into the waistband of her sari. Calmly, Poornima gripped the statuette—the one that had been presented to Kishore for being first in his college—and slammed it against the lock. The lock broke, but so did the statuette, at the point where the figurine (of a bird taking flight from a branch) was cauterized to the engraved base. She threw both pieces of the statuette back into the armoire. The papers in the box were of no interest to Poornima, but the jewelry—only a thin gold chain and two bangles; the rest Kishore kept in a safe-deposit box at the bank—she tied into a pouch at the end of her pallu and slipped it into the waistband of her own sari; the cash (a little over five hundred rupees) she placed into her blouse, next to her left breast. Then the box, too, she tossed back into the armoire, closed the door, and stood in front of it.

The mirror was still covered with a sheet, and Poornima stood looking at the sheet, as if it held an answer. A sign. But it held nothing; it was just a sheet. She ripped it off the mirror with such force that the wind in the room shifted; her hair flew up and around her face as if she were staring out to sea. But Poornima felt none of it, none of the wind and none of the sea. She stood perfectly still in front of the mirror—it was the most she'd ever seen of herself. The mirror in Indravalli had only been a hand mirror, and while in Namburu, though she'd been living here for almost two years, she'd never really stood in front of this mirror. Or any other. But now, she stood. She saw that she was no longer a girl. And if she had ever been pretty, she certainly wasn't anymore. She stepped closer, and then she raised her hands to her face and removed the bandages, one by one. The left side of her face and neck were just as she imagined them, or worse: flaming red, blistered, gray and black on the edges of the wide burn, the left cheek hollow, pink, silvery, and wet, as if it'd been turned inside out. Her left arm and shoulder, though, were not as bad as she'd thought. They had only been splattered by droplets of oil, rather than splashed, and the splatters already seemed to be healing. But the face and neck she knew she had to keep from getting infected, which meant she needed clean bandages and iodine. With the bandages off, she looked even more grotesque than she did with them on. She recalled the doctor saying, while she was in a morphine haze, "You're lucky it didn't get you below the neck."

She'd turned her sleepy gaze to him.

"Your husband won't leave you. As long as you have proper breasts, a man won't leave you."

She'd wanted to say—had she not been in an opiate haze, had she not been content to simply close her eyes—Then I wish it'd gotten the breasts, too.

Poornima lay back on the bed and waited. She waited until the darkest part of the night, then changed into a fresh sari, drank the glass of water that Divya had left for her, and snuck downstairs, out of the house, and out of Namburu, and all of this she did with a shocking stealth and precision and cold-bloodedness, because of course she knew exactly what she was going to do, no matter how long it took her, no matter how difficult the journey, and she knew exactly where all of this had always been leading, always.

She was going to find Savitha.

8

Poornima made a rough calculation and decided that Savitha had left at around four in the morning. She guessed this because, as she recalled, on that last night, she'd gone to sleep with her arm around her, and when she'd woken up, with the sun, Savitha was gone. When did the sun rise? Maybe six thirty or seven? If that was the case, then Savitha had to have left much earlier, to avoid detection, so probably she left at four or five in the morning. Closer to four, Poornima guessed. But why not earlier? Say at two or three in the morning? It was possible, Poornima thought, but where would she go? None of the buses or trains ran at that hour, and trying to catch a ride on a lorry on the highway would've been too risky. Besides, if she'd done that, if she'd gotten into a random lorry on the Tenali Road, then she could be anywhere by now. She could be in Assam or Kerala or Rajasthan or Kashmir. Or anywhere in between. Anywhere at all. And *that*, Poornima refused to consider.

She also refused to consider the nearly two years that had passed since Savitha had left, and that that amount of time, too, could have taken her anywhere. But this Poornima chose to ignore. After all, she told herself, time was simple. Time was no kind of mystery. It was naked and unblinking; it was like the buffalo she saw plowing the fields. All it did was plod along, never wavering and without a thought in its head. Time was all her days in Namburu, and all the days before that. But geography? Now, geography Poornima considered a mystery. Its mountains, its rivers, its vast and end-less plains, its seas that she had never seen. Geography was the unknown.

So it was decided: if she had left at four A.M. or thereabouts, she could've taken only one of two buses. Only two buses ran at that time of morning. One went south, to Tirupati, and the other went north, to Vijayawada. Now, here was another geographic mystery: Which one would she have taken?

Poornima considered the question, and then something floated back to her. Something so fine, so like gossamer, that it could hardly be considered a thought, or even a fragment of a thought, but it was there, she was certain it was there, and she brushed at it as if it were a spider's web, caught in the deep recesses of her mind. Poornima was by now on the outskirts of Nam-buru. She was going to the bus depot that was on the highway, rather than the one in Namburu, so that no one would see her. As she approached it, she saw an advertisement for amla oil. On the advertisement was the green amla fruit, with sparkling oil, lit by the sun, dripping out of it and straight into a pale green bottle. Next to the bottle was a photograph of a woman with thick, lustrous hair, taken as she spun her head, her hair fanning out toward the viewer as she turned. Presumably, the amla oil had made her hair so lustrous and thick. Poornima stared at the advertisement—she stud-ied the perfect amla fruit, and the drops of oil, and the woman—and then she looked again at the amla. *The perfect fruit.* She waved aside the gossa-mer web, and then she knew. She knew where Savitha had gone: she'd gone to Majuli. She had to have.

Poornima smiled; her entire face burst into pain, but she smiled anyway. And where was Majuli? She recalled her saying it was on the Brahmaputra, and Poornima knew this much about geography: she knew the Brahmaputra was north, and so, twenty minutes later, Poornima flagged down the bus to Vijayawada, going north, and she didn't even notice when the driver and the conductor and the old woman she sat down next to gave her strange

looks, revolted looks, as they stared at her face, her burns, no longer covered, but raw and pink like the sunrise.

When she got to Vijayawada, the first thing she did was go to a medical shop and buy bandages and iodine. She learned how to wrap the burns and apply the iodine from the man who was working there—an old man with glasses, who asked no questions at all about how she'd gotten the burns, as if he saw women with this exact injury every day, which Poornima figured he probably did. The only question in his mind, she guessed, was whether it was oil or acid. But even that he didn't ask, though she thought he might've been able to tell just by looking at them. Regardless, she liked him; she liked how gentle he was when he showed her how to wrap the bandage around her neck and over her cheek, and then to tie it so it was snug but not too tight. He said, "It needs air," referring to the burn, and then he said, "What else do you need?"

Poornima said she needed directions to the train station, and he nodded. This, too, he seemed to expect.

The walk, he said, was long, so it was better to take the bus. But Poornima decided to walk anyway, and along the way, she bought a packet of idlis, because they were all that she could manage to chew. Then she drank a cup of tea, standing next to the tea stall, with the men gathered around staring openly, or surreptitiously, but all of them with disgust—knowing what was beneath her bandages—and maybe a few, one or two, with shame.

When Poornima reached the train station, after an hour of walking, the sky was just beginning to lighten. The white marble floors, strewn with sleeping bodies, still shone between the array of arms and legs draped over the very old and the very young. She stepped gingerly between them, entered the vestibule, and studied the listing of trains. Obviously, Majuli wouldn't be listed, since it was an island, so Poornima looked for all northbound trains. There were none. At least, none that left from Vijayawada.

She stared and stared at the listings, thinking she must be mistaken, but not one was going anywhere beyond Eluru. She turned and went to the ladies' counter. It wasn't open yet, and it wouldn't be for another two hours. At this, Poornima considered waiting in the vestibule, but then she thought she might be able to find out more information on the platform.

She paid five rupees for the platform ticket, and when she walked through, the entire length of the first platform was bustling. An overnight train from Chennai had just arrived. The coffee and tea stalls were steaming, the puri wallah yelled through the windows of the train, running up and down its length, vada and idli packets were piled nearly to the rafters, and even the magazine and cigarette and biscuit shops were open, along with the sugar-cane juicer shop across from it, already thronged with people. When she passed the water fountain, it was ten deep, with everyone pushing and trying to get to one of the six taps.

Poornima had never seen so many people. She stood for a moment, disoriented, and then realized she should be looking for someone to ask about the northern trains. There were hundreds of porters, everywhere it seemed, in their brick-colored shirts, but they paid her no attention, and in fact pushed her aside once or twice to make way. Poornima edged toward the wall, away from the train, and waited. Finally, after twenty minutes, the train pulled away, and everything, all of a sudden, stopped. Now the porters, the ones who hadn't been hired, were standing around, listless, drinking a cup of tea or coffee, and waiting for the next train. Poornima pulled her pallu over her head and approached a group of three who were standing near one of the wide girders. They weren't talking to one another, but they were definitely standing together.

"Do you know anything about the northern trains?" Poornima asked.

The slightest one, hardly older than an adolescent, looked her up and down and stopped just before her face. He said, "Do I look like the information booth?"

"It's closed."

"Then wait," another one of them said.

"But there's not a single one going north. Nothing past Eluru. Do you know anything about it?" she said, turning to the third man, older, with a graying mustache and a thick shock of salt-and-pepper hair.

He, too, looked at Poornima, mostly at her bandaged face, which she was trying unsuccessfully to obscure, and said, "The Naxals. They blew up the tracks past Eluru."

"So there are *no* trains?"

"Did you hear me?"

"But no trains? None? How can that be?"

The young man laughed. "Take it up with Indian Railways. I'm sure they'll be happy to explain."

Poornima walked away from the porters and back to her spot by the wall. She slid to the ground.

How long would five hundred rupees last her? Not very long. And it was too soon to sell the jewelry. She decided to stay at the train station, sleep in the vestibule, with the others, or on one of the platforms, maybe the farthest one from the signaling office, until the northern tracks were fixed, or until they kicked her out. She could wash at the taps, eat from the stalls, and as for the latrines, well, the latrines were just the tracks, anyway. Why didn't I bring a blanket? she thought, annoyed with herself.

Still, once she decided to stay, the first thing she did was buy a small water jug, for the purpose of washing up, and then she sat down, next to the Higginbotham's bookstore stall, and tried to look like she belonged there, like she was waiting for a train, or for someone—someone dear to her, someone *on* a train—to arrive. The stall had a niche, behind a stand of magazines and comic books, and Poornima found that she fit perfectly into this niche, as long as her legs were pulled to her chest and wouldn't be seen. From this vantage point, looking up, she was amazed by how few people looked down. None, as far as she could tell during her first few hours in the niche.

After a time, she got up to stretch her legs and walked up and down the bridge that stretched over the platforms, with stairs leading down to each. From here, she could see the long sinews of the trains coming and going, the roofs over each of the platforms, and the tracks—how many were there?

Maybe twenty, maybe more; she'd never seen such a thing, she'd never even known that so much commerce, so many people, and so much travel existed in the world—stretching in every which direction like the lines on the palm of a hand.

This was her daily schedule: sleep on one of the platforms, or the vestibule, check the train departures first thing every morning for anything going past Eluru, and if there were none, buy herself a packet of idlis and a cup of coffee or tea, depending on her mood, and then walk or huddle in the niche behind Higginbotham's.

It wasn't until the beginning of her second week that she met Rishi. He was a slim boy about her age, maybe a little younger. She had noticed him before, lurking on the platforms, at their very edges, and studying everyone who passed him. He studied them so keenly that she wondered if he wanted to draw them, or rob them. But he never did, at least not that she could see. He was there every day, just as she was. He'd studied her, too, once or twice, though she'd ignored him and had kept walking. Still, he must've known she was mostly living behind Higginbotham's because one afternoon, he came over and began to examine the stand of magazines and comic books. He picked up a *Panchatantra* and flipped through it. Then he picked up a film magazine that had a woman in a red dress on the cover. When he put that one back on the stand, somebody Poornima couldn't see yelled out, "Hey. Hey! You. Either buy it, or don't. But don't get your mother's hair grease all over it." The boy backed away from the stand—Poornima could see his sandaled feet take a step back—but then he swung his head and looked right at her.

Poornima jumped. Her heart stopped. Was he the police?

"What happened to your face?" he said.

Poornima pulled her pallu down over her forehead, nearly over her eyes, and didn't say anything.

"Are you deaf?"

She shrugged.

"Let me see." He came toward her; Poornima pushed deeper into the wall. He knelt a little, but gently, with a kind of grace. He wasn't the police; that much Poornima knew, though she kept her face lowered and raised only her eyes. He looked in them, and then he said, "Your neck, too? Your father or your husband?"

Poornima was quiet for a moment, as if she was trying to decide, and she said, "No one. It was an accident."

The boy nodded, and then he said, "It always is. My name's Rishi. What's yours?"

Why was he talking to her? What did he want? She clearly had no money, but he didn't seem frightening. He seemed more like a brother than anything else. Still, she didn't respond, and after lingering a few moments, he shrugged and walked away. She watched him: he walked forward, still where Poornima could see him, and then he went and talked to somebody unloading burlap sacks from a goods train, and then he bought himself a cup of tea. He looked in Poornima's direction once or twice, as if making sure she was still there, and then, when he'd finished his tea, he waved at her, as if he'd known her all his life, as if she were an old friend he was seeing off at the train station, and then he walked right past her, out of the vestibule and into the world.

But he was back again the next day. And the next. And the next. And each time, he waved at Poornima when he came in the mornings and waved again when he left at night. She began, surprisingly, to look forward to seeing him. If he happened to pass her in the middle of the day, as he often did, seeing as they both wandered the same ten platforms, then he didn't wave; he didn't even look at her. They nearly bumped into each other once, on the passenger bridge over one of the platforms, and yet he didn't so much as acknowledge her. How odd, she thought. That evening—after they'd bumped into each other on the bridge—she sprang up when she saw him approaching the exit, on his way to wherever he went every night, and she said, "Poornima."

He looked at her and smiled, and she felt a rush of relief and warmth.

After that, they walked and talked together almost every day. She told him about Kishore, and her mother-in-law, and even about Indravalli, and a little about her father. Then she said, "Where do you go every night?"

He straightened his back, and his voice grew serious. "I have a very important job."

"Oh? But you're here all day. Is it a night job?"

He seemed to consider this for a moment, and he finally said, "I work here. I'm working now. I go in the evenings to report back to my boss."

"You're *working*? But all you do is walk around."

"It just looks like that. You don't know anything."

Maybe I don't, Poornima thought, but she knew when someone was working, and Rishi certainly wasn't. "What is it that you do?"

"I find people."

"Like who? Like lost people?"

He shrugged. "How long are you going to stay there? Behind Higginbotham's?"

"Till the northern trains start running."

"The Naxals blew up the tracks."

"Why do you think I'm still here?"

"Do you have someone up north? Someone waiting for you?" he asked, his voice taking on a strange curiosity.

"Yes. In a way."

"The tracks could take weeks, months. Why don't you just go around?"

That had never occurred to Poornima. Why hadn't it ever occurred to her? Something so simple.

"You're lying."

"I'm not lying. About what?" she said.

"You don't have someone waiting for you. I can tell. I can tell you're alone."

Poornima scratched at her bandages. The itchiness had begun, and she could hardly sleep or eat or do anything for how maddening it was to not scratch. "How can you tell?"

"I help girls just like you," he said. "Girls who are alone. I help them be safe and make money. Just until they're ready to leave. Like when the tracks are fixed, for instance. But most never leave, they like it so much." He asked Poornima if she wanted a cup of tea, and she said yes.

"What do they do?"

"Office work. Like a secretary. Or they work in a fancy shop. Or sometimes in a sari store. Things like that. Easy work."

"And you've helped lots of girls?"

Rishi nodded. "Oh yes. Hundreds. Probably more. I know every single girl who walks through this train station. I have one of those memories, you see. I know them all. And I know which ones could use a job like that."

Poornima was silent, and then she said, "Every one?"

"Not a single girl gets on or off any train in this station without me knowing. I remember their faces. I never forget their faces. Sometimes, I talk to them, just like I'm talking to you, and then they take the jobs and they always make a point to come and find me and thank me."

"I've never seen any girl thanking you."

He sighed loudly. And then he said, "Why would you? Sitting like a mole behind Higginbotham's. Anyway, I have work to do. I can't stand here and talk to you all day. Take the glass back when you're done," he said, referring to her teacup. He turned away, but not very convincingly. He started to walk down the platform.

"Wait," Poornima yelled after him. He stopped a yard or two away from her, and she thought he might be smiling, but she couldn't be sure. It was just a sense she had. Though why would he be smiling?

When he turned to look at her, his face was serious. He said, "What? I have things to do."

"Every girl?"

"Yes. That's what I said."

"How long have you been here? At the train station?"

"Why?"

"Just curious."

He thought for a moment. "Maybe three years. Four."

Poornima felt a shiver go through her, and she thought, What if he did? What if he *did* see her? "Did you happen to see a girl, not quite two years ago? She would've been a little taller than me. And wearing a blue sari, patterned with peacocks. A beautiful smile. From Indravalli?"

Rishi considered for a long moment. His eyes began to spark. "What else?"

"She was thin, but not as thin as me. Straight hair, but with small ringlets at her forehead. Probably she was going north, too."

"Did she have pretty lips? And did you say the sari was blue?"

Poornima's eyes also lit up. "Yes! And her name was Savitha. Did you see her?"

"Savitha? Did you say Savitha?" Rishi smiled—a wide smile that plumped up his thin face, as if his cheeks had sprouted for just that smile. "Why didn't you say so earlier? Of course I know Savitha."

"You *do*?"

"Yes, it must've been two years ago. Now I remember. And she was from Indravalli. Are you from there, too?"

"What did she say? Where did she go?"

"Not north. Where did you get the idea she would go north? She's right here. In Vijayawada. I got her a job."

"Here? In Vijayawada?"

"Yes. Right here. Come on, I'll take you to her." He smiled again, and this time Poornima noticed that one of his teeth was discolored: one of the lower ones, in the front. She looked at it and wondered if he was lying.

9

They left the station by the same way Poornima had come in, nearly two weeks earlier. They walked for what seemed like hours, through the Green Park Colony and Chittinagar, and then they entered an area with run-down homes and shacks. The tea stalls seemed dirtier, and the eyes of the men followed them, rimmed with red. They saw Poornima's bandages and turned quickly away.

"Do you have to have those?" he said.

"Have what?"

"Those bandages."

Poornima felt the need to scratch again, the moment she thought about them. "Well, yes, of course I do."

"Savitha might mind them."

"Why would she?"

They walked on. By now, there were no more run-down houses, but only empty lots. Poornima could tell they were getting farther away from the Krishna. The wide-open lots were inhabited only by pigs and feral dogs and heaps of trash. At the edge of one of these garbage-strewn fields was a massive house, much bigger than anything else in the area, and much better maintained, too. They turned into the drive. "Savitha is *here*? She works here?"

"Sort of," he said enigmatically.

Rishi didn't ring the bell; they walked right in. As soon as they did, Poornima heard shuffling coming from the second floor. She looked up into the open balcony and saw maybe five or six girls, her age and even younger, milling for a moment, and then turning and walking away. She didn't see Savitha, though. Rishi said, "Come on," and led her deeper down the first-floor hallway. At its end was a door, and when they entered it—knocking this time—a thin man with large spectacles was sitting behind a desk. He had skin the texture of jackfruit, maybe from a childhood disease, Poornima thought. He looked up and eyed her, and his expression of boredom turned to distaste. But the edge of his gaze held more than distaste, and Poornima nearly stepped back and fled, to see such bold and ready ruthlessness.

"What is that?" he said, not looking at Rishi but clearly addressing him.

"Train station, Guru."

"Are you stupid?"

"You said we were short, Guru. So I thought maybe—"

"Is that right? Is that what you thought?"

Rishi lowered his head and nodded.

"Well, take it back," the man growled. "She's ugly. And those bandages. Who'd pay for that? Don't you have any sense? No one does. That's the problem. And guess what that Samuel did? Left without a word. Took one of the girls with him. Now what am I supposed to do? Nobody to do the books and one less girl. And you. Bringing *that* around. Get rid of it."

Poornima looked from Rishi to the man behind the desk. She thought of her money, and her jewelry, and she thought she might never have another chance. "Do you know my friend? From my village. Rishi said—" she began.

The man was scribbling in a book, a logbook of some sort, and when

Poornima spoke, he looked up at her as if he was amazed, perplexed that she had a voice. He made a slow fist. "I said, get her out of here."

"He said you did."

He put down his pen, and she could see the anger rising. Constricting his mouth, his nose, and finally his eyes into pinpoints of rage. "You know, I've seen monkeys more attractive than you."

Rishi grabbed her arm, as if to pull her out of the room. Poornima shook him off. She thought of the weaving hut, the morning after Savitha left, and she thought of how she must've walked out, all alone, into the night. She wondered whether she had turned around, just before leaving, and stood at the door, searching for a reason to stay, and yet hadn't found one. Nothing, not ever, would be emptier for Poornima than that thought. "I can do books," she said.

The man looked at her.

"I can do books. Accounting. I've learned."

The man laughed. He said, "Since when do village girls learn accounting? Where did you say you were from?"

"I can. I'll show you."

The man looked at Rishi and Rishi looked back at him. Then they both looked at Poornima. The man then turned the logbook around to face Poornima and said, "Go ahead."

Poornima studied it. They just seemed a jumble of numbers at first, with letters heading most of the columns, with what had to be dates on the leftmost column. But the longer she looked at them, the more she realized there was a pattern: the numbers under some of the letters were always bigger. And the dates, she saw, were the previous month's dates. Then she realized what the letters were; they were initials. Three of them were *S*, followed by a number. Cold dripped down her spine. "Wouldn't it be better if you knew more? Like, if it was the same man, over and over again? And what days he was coming. And whether for the same girl. If you tracked that, you could charge more."

There was silence. A dog barked. "So you can," the man said. He looked at her, as if for the first time. "What else can you do?"

"I can cook, and I can clean, and I can work on the charkha."

Guru signaled with a wave of his hand for Rishi to leave the room. Once he'd gone, he looked at her with sudden interest, but interest laced with cruelty, with calculation.

"Guru," he said. "That's my name. We have more of these. Six others. You have to do all of them. Where are you staying?"

"At the train station."

"There's a room in back. You can stay there. Nothing in the room will belong to you, but we can try it for a few days. Are you willing to try it for a few days?" His tone sharpened, pointed at her like a dagger, and Poornima realized he was no longer talking about the books, or account keeping. She nodded.

Then he said, "What happened to your face?"

"Nothing," Poornima said. "I had an accident."

Guru smiled, horribly. Then he sat back in his chair and said, "Oil? Or acid?"

She was given a windowless room in the back, on the first floor. There was a cot on the floor, a framed picture of Ganesha over the door, and a small refrigerator in one corner. There was an attached bathroom with a latrine and a sink with running water and a high strip of window, which Poornima couldn't reach. She stood and stared at the unreachable rectangle of light. Then she examined the bathroom; she'd never been in a room with an attached latrine or running water. She hid the money and jewelry under the cot and then went to take a bucket bath.

When she came out and tried to open the outer door, she found that it was locked. She pushed on it, banged and yelled, but there was no sound on the other side. She stepped back and stared at the door. Maybe it had locked by accident? But it couldn't have; she'd seen the metal rod on the door handle, and how it had to be pushed into a set of grooves to lock. What did that mean? Were they imprisoning her? *Were* they? The thought pushed a scream out of her throat so loud that the frame of Ganesha fell off the wall. She flung herself at the door. She grew hoarse from yelling and crying; her hands stung from pounding on the door. Nothing. Not a sound from outside. She slumped against it and closed her eyes. When she opened them, she saw the refrigerator on the other side of the room. She rose unsteadily and looked inside. There were two bottles of water and a bowl of glistening fruit: guavas and apples and sapota and grapes. She closed the refrigerator and banged on the door again. Still, nothing. When she'd exhausted herself, she went and lay down on the cot and forced herself to sleep.

She had no idea how much time had passed when she woke up. For a moment, she was afraid. Afraid of what? she asked herself. Being locked in a room? The door never opening again? The door opening? Suddenly, none of it felt much different from the years she'd spent in Namburu, so she went to the refrigerator again and took a hesitant sip from one of the bottles of water. Then she took another, longer sip. She was hungry, so she reached for one of the fruits, but then her hand, of its own accord, simply stopped. Paused. Just as she reached for an apple. She held it there, motionless, wondering why, and that's when they came back to her, Guru's words: Nothing in the room will belong to you. Why had he said that? It seemed—with her hand still hovering near the fruit—a strange thing to say. But was it? Maybe this is a test, she thought, with sudden clarity. Maybe he wants to test whether I'll take any of the fruit. It seemed a perfectly reasonable test for an accountant: to see if they would steal from their employer. Take what had been clearly stated didn't belong to them. But she was hungry, and she thought for a moment she would take the fruit anyway, but then she thought, If Savitha *is* here, eating an apple—an apple—might spoil my one chance of finding her.

She closed the refrigerator door.

She sat in the room for three days without eating. At first, she felt a slow, growing hunger that soon gnawed at her stomach. Doubled her over in pain.

And then weakness. The hunger was a beast, and she willed it to be still, restricting herself to the cot as if chained, drinking great gulps of water. She slept fitfully but stayed in bed well into late morning. By the middle of the second day, her skin was hot and feverish. The water did no good. She wondered if she was ill. She seriously considered eating the fruit—what if they never opened the door?—but then she thought of Savitha. She was here. Poornima only needed to pass this test; she was here. She settled back on the cot and thought about food. That did no good. So then she thought about hunger. In Indravalli, there had been plenty of days when she'd gone hungry, giving her share to her brothers and sister, but there had always been a little for her, even if it was only a handful of rice and pickle. But *this* hunger: this hunger was a ravaged land.

The weakness spread. She was tired from the exertion of going to the bathroom, of lifting the water bottle. On the third day, her skin ceased to function. A drop of water landed on her arm, and her entire body convulsed from the impact. It was as if she no longer had skin, and the water had landed on raw, exposed tissue. She didn't take a bucket bath on the third day. She could hardly stand. But her body began to emit an odor. She thought her burns might be infected, or the bandages were rotting, but it was neither: it was her pores. It was not her usual sweat; that smell she knew. This was more piquant, intense, and absinthal. The sheet on the cot was sticky with it, and yet the peculiar scent of her famished body, every one of her limbs afire, felt to Poornima as if hunger were the most natural state, the truest one. She hardly even wanted food; food became an abstract thing, a memory for which she felt mostly apathy, and sometimes hatred.

On the morning of the fourth day, the door opened.

Still on the cot, Poornima opened her eyes and didn't bother to get up. It was Guru. He looked at her, visibly disgusted, and said, "What is that *smell*?"

She continued looking at him, and then she closed her eyes. She said, "I didn't eat them."

He went to the refrigerator, looked inside, and said, "So you didn't," and then he turned to her. "I wouldn't have cared if you had."

She opened her eyes again.

"Is that what you thought I was after? To see if you'd eat the fruits?" He laughed. "You village girls are all so amusingly stupid. They wouldn't have lasted past the first day, anyway. No," he said. "No, what I wanted to show you, what I wanted you to *appreciate* is what I own." Poornima began to sit up, confused, but he said, "No, no, don't sit up on my account. In fact, lie back down, and turn over." She lay down again, but remained on her back, watching him. "If you're going to work for me then I need you to understand what I own. I own *you*," he began. "I own the food you eat. I own your sweat, your stink. I own your weakness. But most of all, I own your hunger." He was standing above her, looking down. "Do you understand? I own your hunger. Now," he said, unbuckling his belt, "turn over. I don't like faces. Especially not yours."

She began working for him the following day. Her desk was next to his, but smaller, so he could watch over her. But he was rarely there. She was usually alone, and she left the door open, looking up at every girl who passed by it.

None of them was Savitha. At least, none at this location. Poornima wasn't allowed to talk to them—Guru watched her keenly when he was there, and when he wasn't, the cook, named Raju, watched her—but every time one of the girls came downstairs, Poornima nodded or smiled. They mostly ignored her. Some of the younger ones, or newer ones, would look back at her sadly, or bravely, and then they would go back upstairs. There were thirteen girls. But *were* they girls? Poornima wondered. Of course they were. None of them was probably older than sixteen. But there was something missing in them; some essence of girlhood had left them. What was it? Poornima thought about it every day during her first few weeks at the brothel. Innocence, certainly. That was obvious. And they were damaged. That, too, was obvious. But there was something else. Something finer.

And then she had it. It came to her while she was watching one of the girls trudge through the house midafternoon, just after she'd woken up, on her way to the latrines. She was rubbing her eyes, and her face was swollen with sleep, or maybe fatigue. Her gaze was even, and indifferent, as she stood at the back door, looking out. And it was when Poornima saw this gaze, this indifference, that she understood: the girl had lost her sense of light. It was all the same to her, to all the girls, really: light and dark, morning and night. But it wasn't an outside light they'd lost a sense of, Poornima realized. It was an interior one. And so *that* was the aspect of girlhood they'd lost: a sense of their own light.

Poornima thought of light, and then she thought of Savitha. There were six books she had to track and balance and audit against the money that was coming in. They'd even given her one of those little adding machines Kishore had used. The machine made everything much, much quicker. Even so, she worked diligently, all the while trying to figure out a way to go to the other brothels, to see the other girls. By now, she knew Rishi had been lying, back at the train station when he'd said he knew Savitha, but Guru ran nearly all the brothels in Vijayawada, and Poornima decided she couldn't make her way north until she knew for sure. And so she stayed, and she waited.

By her ninth month working at the brothel, Poornima had only managed to visit two of the other locations, asking to go along with Guru when he collected. "I'm not one of the girls," she said. "I want to drive around a little." He agreed reluctantly, though she sensed that he'd come to trust her. She never stole money, she never asked for money, and she never made a mistake in the books. He came to confide in her at times and even began giving her a small salary. She realized it was because of her scar that he trusted her, in the small way that he did. It was odd, but it was true. She was no longer wearing bandages, but the burn had healed and left scar tissue that was shiny and wide and blisteringly pink. It made her look damaged, harmless, and, most important, pathetic.

One day, Guru came in complaining of the cost of buying food and clothing and sundries for the nearly hundred women and girls in the brothels. "Thousands of rupees I spend per month. Thousands. All they do is eat."

Poornima didn't say anything. She knew for a fact that he made over one hundred thousand rupees a month off the girls. In some months, he made two lakhs.

"For instance, just the other day, a girl tells me it's her birthday, and could I buy her a sweet. Her birthday! I said, You'll get a sweet when you do ten men in one night. That's when you'll get a sweet."

Poornima nodded.

"Every day. Every day they eat and eat."

She went back to her work; it was common for Guru to complain, and she'd grown used to it.

"And the audacity. One time, this one girl says to me, I want a banana. So I say, I buy you rice. Go eat that. And you know what she says?"

"No. What?" Poornima hardly looked up.

"She says, But I like to eat bananas with my rice. With my yogurt rice. Can you believe that? A banana! The audacity."

Poornima's head shot up. She stilled her thoughts, she evened her voice. "Oh," she said. Then she said, "What happened to that girl? The one who asked for the banana?"

Guru shrugged. "We sold her."

"Sold her? To whom?"

Guru looked up. His eyes narrowed. He said, "You think all we have are these shitty brothels? You think you're doing *all* the books? Our main income is from selling girls. To rich men. To men in Saudi. Dubai."

Poornima took a breath. She told herself, Don't let him see. He won't tell you if you let him see. "But that one," she said lightly, "the one who wanted the banana. Where did she go?"

"I think she was part of that big shipment we made. A year ago? Some rich man in America. Get this: he wanted girls to clean apartments. Apparently, over there it costs serious money to hire people to clean. To *clean.*

Common Dalits. It was cheaper for him to *buy* them. He owned hundreds of them. Apartments, I mean. Some place called Seetle, Sattle. I don't know. But he paid good money for them."

Poornima could feel the air around her cooling. She could feel a great wooden door creaking open. "How do you get there?"

Guru started to laugh. He started to howl with laughter. "It's far. It's far, far away. You'll never get there."

Poornima laughed with him, but she knew she would.

Savitha

1

Savitha knew she wouldn't get the banana, not at first, at least. But what would it take to get something as simple, as small, as a banana?

She'd find out.

Savitha also knew she had to deal with the leader of the ring, named Guru. No one else. He came around occasionally to check on his goods, as he called the girls. The first time was within a few weeks of her arrival. She'd left Indravalli in the early hours of the morning, on the same day she was to marry Poornima's father. Her body hurt. She'd been crouched in the corner of the weaving hut for three days. She hadn't wept, she hadn't blinked (not that she was aware of), she hadn't hoped or prayed or felt pain, nor had she had a single thought. Not one. Well, maybe one. Her only thought had been, Which is better? This? Or being dead? Or are they one and the same? Before leaving the weaving hut, and the sleeping Poornima, she'd untied all the tiny knots of the sari she'd been making for her, not yet even half completed, stretched out on the loom like a shroud, and folded it into eighths, and then tucked the cloth into the inside of her blouse, against her flat chest.

Then she left Indravalli, knowing it was forever.

When she got to the bus stop—out on the highway, not the one in town—the first bus that pulled up was the one to Vijayawada. It was empty, except for the conductor. Not even the farmers were headed to market yet. Savitha didn't have any money, not a single paisa, so when the door of the bus opened, she looked up at the driver, not at all pleading, but with a look that was stern, deliberate, and she said, "No one will possibly find out if you give me a ride."

The bus driver looked at her, up and down, and then he laughed and closed the door and drove away. A lorry was her only chance. She waited a few more minutes until one came into view. It drove off, not even slowing, as did four others, ignoring her utterly, until the sixth one. The sixth one was painted intricately, a Ganesha on top of the windshield, in the middle, with a scene of a tranquil lake with a hut and cows on one side and a bouquet of roses on the other. Two fresh limes dangled from its front bumper, for good fortune. Along the inside top of the windshield was draped a length of red streamers, sparkling even without the sun. Savitha hailed the driver, stepping onto the edge of the road, and when he slowed, she saw that he was young, hardly older than her. Closer up, once she'd climbed into the cabin, she saw that his teeth were the most brilliant white she had ever seen, whiter even than the temple on Indravalli Konda, though his eyes were bleary, red, maybe from the lack of sleep or dust or drink.

"Where are you headed?"

"Depends," she said. "How far are you going?"

"To Pune."

"Then that's where I'm going."

He smiled, and this time, Savitha wasn't so sure of the brilliance of his teeth. Their whiteness, yes, but not their brilliance.

It took less than ten minutes, bumping along on the Trunk Road, past the shuttered roadside tea shops, and the dark huts, and the dewy fields of rice, and the sleeping dogs, for the driver's hand to leave the steering wheel. It didn't inch along the seat, as Savitha might've expected, but simply took flight and landed on her thigh. "I'm in no hurry," he said. "Are you?"

Savitha took a breath.

She understood, in that very instant, that a door had been opened. Not today, but three days ago. What was this door? she wondered. Why hadn't she ever known it was there? She had no answer. Or maybe she hadn't wanted to know the answer. Regardless, it was now open, and she was through it. Poornima's father, of course, had been the one to open it, the one to push her through, and she felt rage, an intense and terrible rage toward him—for no other reason than that he hadn't asked her what *she* wanted. He hadn't said, There is a door. Do you see it? Do you want me to open it? Do you want to see what's on the other side? But now it was done. And now, she realized, that's all she'd ever be in the eyes of men: a thing to enter, to inhabit for a time, and then to leave.

They drove on. The lorry driver's hand inched up her thigh. They drove across the Krishna and turned onto the national highway.

Well, if that were true, then something else also had to be true. She didn't have to think long on it to figure out what it was; it was like it had been waiting there all along, alongside the road. And it was this: there was yet another door. A smaller door, a more formidable one. A hidden one. But through this other door, she knew, lay the real treasures: her love for Poornima, her love for her parents and her sisters. *These* treasures gleamed: the feel of cloth, the one against her chest, yes, but really, all cloth. How it lay like a hand (not the lorry driver's, but a tender one, wanting nothing) against your skin, protecting you, softening with time. They shone through the night, these treasures: the memory (already a memory) of her father's hands, the way they reached with such fear, such longing, the taste of yogurt rice with banana, the way it was creamy and sweet, both at once, the fill of her heart, the way it swelled but never broke.

"Stop here," she said.

The lorry driver's hand paused, nearly at her crotch.

"Here?"

"Right here."

"But we're hardly past Vijayawada. You said Pune."

She looked at him, at his dark lips, the top one nearly completely curtained by his mustache. Then he smiled, as if she might smile back. But she only looked some more, at the red of his eyes and the white of his teeth. He slowed the lorry but didn't stop. Savitha looked out the window. A mangy dog lay next to a garbage heap; farther down, a chicken scratched at the dirt. He'd swerve to avoid *them*, she thought. Anybody would. And then she thought, I hold the key.

She lifted his hand from her thigh and wrenched it, hard, at the wrist. He gasped, slammed on the brakes. The lorry tilted and then screeched to a halt.

"You bitch. Pakshi. Get out."

When she did, the lorry pulled away with a loud squeal and a cloud of dust. Savitha stood on the national highway and looked to the east and to the west. Toward the east were the outskirts of Vijayawada. They'd mostly skirted the city, but it would be easy enough to go back. Back. That didn't seem very smart. To the west were Hyderabad and then Karnataka and then Maharashtra and then the Arabian Sea. Not that Savitha knew any of this; she knew only that Pune was to the west, and beyond was a sea. She sat right down, on the dirt, on the edge of the highway, and wondered what to do. There were more vehicles now, mostly lorries. She could hail another one, hope for a better man. Most any one of them would take her to Pune, if Pune was where she wanted to go. What did they speak there? Marathi, of course. Which, of course, she had no idea *how* to speak. What if she asked them to take her to Bangalore? They spoke Kannada there. Close to Telugu, but not quite. She turned her head and looked toward Vijayawada again. It was wiser to go back, she decided. It was better to first make some money, and to make money it was best to stay where she knew the language. And really, if anyone in Indravalli went looking for her, which she doubted they would, somewhere as obvious as Vijayawada would be the last place they'd look. Or so she guessed. But this she knew: it was better to be wise than to be smart.

Everyone called him Boss, or Guru, but his real name was probably some-thing different. He was thin, with huge spectacles, and wiry, and seemed weak, but his physical aspect was a foil. This Savitha could see plainly in his eyes. His eyes: boring through her as if through rock, through mountain, through the Himalayas, looking not for metals or minerals or gems, but for *girls*, poor but pretty girls, which she came to understand was just another word for profit.

The first time he came around Savitha was still drugged. She'd made it so simple for them; it was almost laughable. She'd walked back into Vijayawada. For three weeks she'd gone to various tailoring shops and seamstresses, looking for work, and in the nights, she'd slept next to a gutter in the goldsmiths district, scented by the coal braziers used to filigree the shining yellow metal during the day, teeming with rats and pigs at night. One rat had tried to nibble on her ear as she slept. She'd eaten whatever she could find: the insides of discarded banana peels, a half-gnawed roti, a slice of coconut from the Kanaka Durga Temple. Toward the end of her first month, she'd gone to a tea stall, on a narrow alley off Annie Besant Road, and stood on the edge of a group of men, looking up at the soot-grimed walls of the close buildings, the narrow strip of sky, glowing with sunrise, and the clotheslines, crisscrossing between the buildings, slicing open the morning sky. She wondered what to do. A man came up behind her, one she hadn't even noticed in the huddled group of men, and he offered her a cup of tea. Savitha looked from the steaming, sugary cup of tea to his face. He was middle-aged, well dressed in clean pants and a shirt; his hair was neatly oiled and combed.

"Go on. Take it."

She hesitated.

"Are you waiting for someone?"

"Yes. My husband."

"Where's your mangalsutra?"

She shrugged, and he laughed. And it was then that she realized her mistake: her hands should've instinctively gone to her neck. But he only laughed some more, good-naturedly, and said, "Go on. This stall serves the best tea in the city."

She took a sip, and then another, and then another. Then she drained the glass. She felt light-headed at first, which she took to be from the lack of food, but then when she opened her eyes, she was tied to a hemp-rope bed in a damp-smelling concrete room with no windows. She was tied at the wrists and the ankles. And no matter how much she strained and screamed, no one came; the rope didn't give. After what seemed like days, someone entered the room, a boy, she thought, but couldn't be sure because it was dark inside the room and dark outside the room. He ran his hand over the bed, then over her face. When he found it, he pinched her nose shut until she opened her mouth, then he threw another bitter liquid into it, this time without the benefit of tea.

She dropped again into a deep sleep.

Three or four or five days later, or maybe a month later, the door opened for a second time. This time, a thin yellow light seeped in from outside the door, and Savitha saw that it was a little girl. She was lugging a bucket, far too heavy for her, splashing water on the floor and over the front of her torn frock. Savitha was still hazy in her thoughts, her body still limp, but she told herself, Talk to her. Talk to this girl. Tell her you'll do anything, anything. Her mouth opened, or so she assumed, but nothing came out. Savitha willed harder, she closed her eyes, she focused on the fog, the heaviness, she told herself, Speak. "Untie me," she finally managed to whisper. "Please."

The girl seemed not to hear. She went about raising a wet cloth to Savitha's legs, her crotch, her underarms, her chest. My chest, Savitha thought. Was the strip of Poornima's sari still there? Was it? "The cloth," she croaked. "Is it?" By now the girl had found it. She raised it to her face, seemed to sniff it once, then threw it into the corner. Savitha let out a long wail. Animal. Wounded. The girl still paid her no attention. She went about her work, the damp cloth now wiping down Savitha's neck, her arms. When she reached for her hands, Savitha grabbed the girl's forearm. She yanked her closer, so she could see the child's face in the dim light of the half-open door. She looked into the girl's eyes; they returned her gaze, but they were unmoved, blank, gray, as if the concrete of the room had blown like sediment and settled into them. Savitha's alarm pushed through layers of confusion, rage, incoherence, and flame, and she said, "Can't you hear me?"

The girl let out her own wail, though hers was even more animal, more wounded. And it was then, at *that* sound, when Savitha truly began to understand her bondage, her imprisonment, the totality of its vision, the completeness of her fate. And that she'd been neither smart nor wise: the girl was a deaf-mute, and the boy had been blind.

She flailed. She strained at her wrists and ankles, managing only to tighten their grip. She beat her head against the hemp, she screamed, she wept. She bit and snapped against the rope with her teeth. Too far away for her to cut through, but the ends she caught and gnawed until her gums bled. She tasted copper and thought, Good. And then she thought, How long will it take to bleed to death? Out of my gums? The drugs she spit out, gagged on, retched every time the boy poured them in. That's when he started injecting it—mostly by plunging the needle into her stomach, but if she squirmed too much, straight into the side of her buttocks. But even in her haze, her bafflement, Savitha could see clearly the edges of the bed, the dark corners of the room, and in the dank of the windowless walls, the beauty she'd lost: sunlight, wind, water.

In between bouts of sleeping, sweating, waking, and vomiting, there were other memories, floating in and out, above and beyond, like breath. There was the shimmer of the temple on Indravalli Konda, the perfume of freshly cooked rice, the shouts of flower vendors, spilling petals on the streets, there were the words of an owl, there was the feel of the loom, the feel of thread, the feel of form, taking shape, *becoming* something. She could've woven a river; she could've woven a sea. Why was she lying here? Why?

The door opened, soon after the girl had cleaned her again. This time it was a man she'd not seen before. Although, in truth, she was bleary-eyed, weak, sodden, and high, her limbs long ago gone numb, so really, it could've been her father.

But it wasn't her father.

This man—who she learned in time was the one called Guru—let the light spill in. Savitha squinted. He approached the bed with a small smile. Then he laid a knife at the edge of the bed, just beyond her reach. Despite her frailness, a sliver of something feral, a shard of some lucidity, sliced through her consciousness. Savitha lurched for it, nearly tipping the bed over. She rocked violently from side to side, side to side, until the knife fell to the floor with a clang. Guru ignored her. He walked to the corner of the room, where Poornima's half-made sari still lay, and nudged it with the tip of his shoe. He bent a little, taking a closer look. He held his face away from the cloth, as if it were rotting meat, and then he smiled and said, "I know this weave. So distinctive. You're from Indravalli, aren't you?" Savitha said nothing. He walked back to the bed. His smile widened. She looked up at him, called him names, she begged; she sensed what was to come. "You stink," he said placidly. Then he said, "There's nothing worse than a woman who stinks." He picked up the knife. He studied the blade intently. After a long moment, he said, "Maybe there is one thing. Just one. And that's a woman who won't listen." He lowered the blade and ran the tip of it along her cheek, her neck. He yanked back the folds of her sari; her blouse fell away in tatters. He traced the edge of the knife against her breasts, under them, between. "Not much to them, is there," he said, looking down, and then he said, "You'll listen, won't you? Won't you, my dear?" He looked into her eyes, almost kindly, and then he spit in her face. The spit, in the midst of her grogginess, her fear, just as she turned her head to avoid it, landed at the edge of her mouth and on her cheek. Guru rubbed it over more of her face. "A smudge, you see," he said lightly, and then got up and left.

The thick glob of spit dried and puckered on Savitha's cheek. He'd been chewing betelnut; she could smell it for hours.

They untied the rope but kept her locked in the room. They made sure she was hooked—if the boy with the needle was even a few minutes late, she pounded on the door, shivering and beseeching and mad, skin alight, on fire—and then, when she was good and hooked, they made her go through withdrawal. When they finally let her out (a month later, two?), Savitha had lost nearly ten kilograms, and her face was gaunt and gray. Large clumps of hair had fallen out. She was bruised, her ankles and wrists inflamed and red, not having yet healed. The madam took one look at her and clucked with disapproval, as if Savitha were a child being naughty, misbehaving, come home late for supper.

Savitha bent her head, believing she was that child.

Her first customer was a middle-aged man, maybe forty or forty-five. He worked in an office; Savitha could tell just by looking at him, slacks and a neat shirt, a gold watch, clean toes. There was a faded strip of ash across his forehead—had he conducted the puja that morning, or had it been his wife?

The man was furtive at first, but then he sat down next to her, on the edge of the bed, and said, "Will you give me a kiss?"

Savitha looked up at him. "I don't know how," she said. The statement so guileless that the man seemed to almost wilt when he heard it. "Here," he said finally, "let me show you."

After that, the mechanics of it all became routine: the five to six customers she had per day, the constant clucking and recriminations from the madam, the talking and laughing and teasing and silence of the other girls, whose names Savitha tried to remember but couldn't, as if her mind had jellied, relented, forfeited. Relinquished something essential—kingdom, subjects, throne—while even the blood in her veins collapsed, not wanting, any longer, to carry the enormity of memory, the sorrow of new names.

But something remained, a constant, a comfort, and it was this: the cloth on which she lay. While the men pushed into her, pressed her face into the sheet—rough, cheap, bought at one of the tawdry stalls on Governorpet—Savitha closed her eyes and pressed her face, her back, her knees, her palms, deeper and deeper and deeper. The scent of woven cloth, threadbare with use, with semen, filled her nostrils. She held back tears. She held back thoughts of Poornima. She held back her girlhood, squandered on heaps of garbage. She held back her father, her mother, her sisters, her lost brothers. She held back the loamy scent of the Krishna, the laundresses laughing, the temple deepa quivering, the dark of the weaving hut, forever mourning. Though what she did let loose, let soar like a bird out of a cage, was the flight of her hands, weaving.

She allowed herself to recall that one thing.

Once, while still a small child, she'd gone to the cotton fields outside Indravalli, on the way to Guntur. Her mother had worked for a summer in the fields, and Savitha had trotted behind her, jumping for the bolls, wanting to help. She'd been far too short, but one had floated down from her mother's hands and Savitha had caught it and squealed with delight, as if she'd caught a piece of a crumbling cloud. When she'd yanked her mother's pallu and held it up like a prize, her mother had barely looked at her; instead she'd said, "Keep it. It's what your frock is made from." At those words, Savitha had stood still in the middle of the cotton field, hot under the summer sun, and had looked down at the boll in her hand, soft, full of seeds, and then she'd gazed up at the rows and rows of them, round white moons held aloft to the sky, so exquisite, so out of reach. Then she'd looked down at her frock, a faded pink, frayed at the hem, dirty, but still a frock. But how? she'd wondered. How could this little piece of fluff with the little brown seeds become my frock? She'd thought it was a secret, a secret kept by the adults. Or magic, more likely. But a mystery. Always a mystery, even after she grew up and began sitting at the charkha and then sitting at the loom and then sitting next to Poornima, eating dinner together, which, by her weaving, at least in some part, the purchase of food, *food*, had been made possible. So, an even greater mystery: from boll to cloth to food to friend.

And this mystery remained with her. All through the years. From then until now. She held it close while at the brothel, tucked away inside her pillow. Along with Poornima's half-made sari (she'd screamed for it in one of her drug-fueled rages, and someone had—not out of kindness but to shut her up—found it lodged in a corner of the concrete room, lifted it with their toes, and flung it at her face).

There, then: the mystery of cloth, and the cloth itself. She felt both, burning—as mysteries do—inside her pillow.

2

The second time she saw Guru was a few months later. One of the girls was sick from an infection. A customer had given it to her, and she lay in bed with a scalding fever, a wide, blistering rash on her thighs and crotch, unable to swallow even a single sip of buttermilk. The girls crowded around her. A doctor, one of them yelled. There was a scampering. The madam pushed her way to the front. "It's a Sunday," she said, without much regret. "There'll be a surcharge."

A Sunday.

There is such a thing as days, Savitha suddenly realized. There is such a thing as time.

Her mind pricked. Something small, behind the eyes, grew rigid.

Guru arrived later that afternoon. The madam had phoned him and asked him to come. The girls gathered around again. This time, Savitha noticed that his shoes had a slight heel, and that the betelnut had colored his teeth orange. "You call me for *this*," he said.

The madam kneaded her hands. "It's the worst I've seen."

He studied the girl's wan face, her lips split and bleeding from fever. "Was she one of the popular ones?"

"She is," the madam said.

Guru then studied her some more, turned on his elevated heels, walked to the door, and said, "Let her die."

Savitha watched him leave the room. The girl whimpered in her sleep, as if she'd heard the words. Though she couldn't possibly have. Not through all those layers of heat and withering and waste. Let her die. The words hung in the air for a moment, and then they began another journey, this time snaking through Savitha's own layers of heat and wither and waste. Her eyes grew wide; they ached with new light. There was a door, she remembered, a hidden one. Where all her treasures lay. And it remained closed, through the tea stall and the concrete room and the drugs, through the men and the men and the men. And it was through this door that the words found their way.

She looked around the room.

It seemed to her, looking now, that they were all simply children, waiting to die. And in the next instant, she thought, No. No, we're all old. Old, old women, ravaged by time, and waiting to die.

And it was this thought that brought the others. An avalanche of others—not in their number, but in their precision.

The first one was this: she couldn't stay here. It wasn't an obvious thought, not to her. Since Poornima's father had raped her, she'd floundered in something like life, but not life itself. A veil had fallen when he'd held his hand over her mouth. A fadedness, too, had fallen, when he'd pried her legs open. A branch had snapped—a branch from which all things grew, from which every banana, every hope, every laugh sprouted—when she'd looked into his face, and, in a small way, seen her friend's. After that, what did it matter where she lived, or ate, or breathed her lesser breaths? What difference would it ever make? So that now, when the thought came to her that she needed to leave, that she *must* leave, she realized, with surprise, that she was beginning to live again. That it *did* matter. That this again was life.

Her second thought: in order to leave, she had to get past Guru. She recalled, a few months ago, that one of the customers had wanted to use a wooden pestle, and when Savitha had run out of the room, horrified, the madam had yanked her back inside and said, "It would be a shame if someone snapped your father's fingers off, wouldn't it? Or if your sisters ended up where you are?" The madam hadn't gathered those things on her own. Guru had. That much she knew. And yes, she'd been barely conscious for the past few months, but she'd been conscious enough to notice that this was no singular house or madam or undertaking. Not at all. It had its leader—Guru—and it had its lieutenants, like the madam, and it had its foot soldiers, like the man who'd offered her the tea, and the boy who'd injected her, and the girl who'd cleaned her, and the one who'd gone to Indravalli, asked around, and had made sure that no one would come looking for her, or at least that no one had the money or the power or the pull (all three, one and the same) to look for her.

Her third and final thought was this: she needed an advantage. There were only a few clear advantages in the world. She obviously had no money, her only skill was weaving, and she could barely read or write. That left only one thing: her body. My body, my body, she thought, looking down at the now used-up husk of the girl she'd once been, the chest still flat, the hands still big, the skin still dark. She moved then to the mirror—a small round mirror, framed by green plastic, hanging by a nail on a wall opposite the bed. She'd not once looked into it, not once, but now she took it down and studied her face. Her eyes, her lips, her nose. The curve of her cheeks, the sweep of her lashes. She moved the mirror closer, then farther. She tilted it; she straightened it. She looked. And there, just there. What was that? "Stop," she said out loud, into the emptiness of the room. "Hold it there." And so she held it there. And that was when she saw it. Had it always been there? That lamp glowing from within. How had it survived all these previous months? How had it held on? No matter, it was greater than her body, it was greater than all else. She laughed, for perhaps the first time since the night in the weaving hut, to see it there. To know it was hers.

Over the next few days, she watched the other girls in the brothel; she stared into their faces, their eyes, five who'd been there longer than Savitha, one who had arrived only the previous month. And none of them had it. Not one. Theirs had been extinguished. But hers, hers.

So now she had two advantages: she had her body, and she had her light.

She bided her time. On every full moon night, she looked up at the sky.

It took the better part of a year, but one winter evening, when Guru came to check the account books, she waited outside the madam's door. He was saying something about having hired a new accountant, someone trustworthy, he thought, and then he laughed, and then the rest of the conversation was muffled. When he came out, Savitha stepped in front of him. Guru was taken aback, or so she guessed by the slight quiver she saw at the edge of his lips, though he said and did nothing more to indicate his surprise.

"Do I know you?"

So that's how many girls he had: more than he could remember.

"Savitha."

"Savitha?"

"I'm the one you spit on."

He seemed to consider the statement, the words themselves, and the fact that they'd been spoken. *To him.*

"I'd like a banana," she said.

By now, the madam had come to the door. Her eyes blazed. She laughed nervously. "A joker. It's nice when one of the girls is funny."

Savitha braced her feet to the floor. She willed her body taut. Her eyes blazed back. Guru seemed amused. He rocked on his elevated shoes, eye to eye with Savitha, and said, "You get enough rice."

"I do. But I'd like a banana to eat *with* my rice. My yogurt rice."

He laughed out loud, for a long while. And when he finished, his voice dropped; it settled like stone. "Come with me," he said. "Let me show you how you can get that banana."

She followed him inside. He sent the madam down the hall and closed the door behind her. Then he walked to the desk in the center of the room and opened one of the large books stacked in a far corner. Savitha had never seen a book that big, the pages filled with lines and columns and numbers and all manner of scribbles. "You see this," he said, pointing to a row in the middle of a page. She leaned over. No, she didn't see. It looked to her like random markings. "This is how much you make in a month. And you see these? These numbers here are what you cost me. The difference is my profit. You see?"

Savitha nodded.

"Very good. Then you must also see that for every banana you want, all you have to do is take on one more customer. One banana, one customer. You see?" He looked at her.

Savitha looked back. "I see. I'd also like to know how to leave here," she said.

He sat down on the chair behind the desk. He folded his hands. His look was one of sorrow, or maybe sweetness. "Forget what I said about a woman who won't listen. The worst thing is a woman who knows what she wants." He rose slowly and came around the desk. His heels clicked on the stone floor. "Let's start here," he said, and led her to a cot in the corner of the room. Savitha lay down on her back, but he turned her over and took her that way. "I don't like faces," he said.

Over the next months, Guru sought her out whenever he came to the brothel. It wasn't very often; usually he had the books delivered to the main house, where the accounts were kept. Somewhere outside of town, Savitha was told.

He'd asked for her by name.

Each time, he'd ask her how many bananas she'd earned that month. Six, she'd say, or five. You like them that much? he'd ask. They keep me from forgetting, she'd say. Forgetting what? Savitha would only smile and burn brighter.

In the spring of that year, Guru summoned Savitha into his office. It had been nearly two years since she'd left Indravalli. This time, as she looked around the room, she saw that the books were gone; there was only him, behind the desk, waiting. "Sit down," he said. And when she did, he said, "There's a Saudi prince."

"Saudi?"

"It's a country."

"Is this a story?"

"Sort of. Yes, yes, it is. He wants to buy a girl. Young, not too young. You might be just right."

Savitha listened.

"A lakh rupees. We'll split it two ways. A year or two over there, and you'll be free."

Savitha's eyes widened. Fifty thousand rupees! She could get all her sisters married; she could buy her parents a house, a castle! But wait. Why would he share the money with her? Why would he give her a single paisa?

"The thing is . . ." Guru continued, hesitating, though Savitha had never before seen him hesitate. "The thing is, he has interesting tastes."

"What kind of tastes?"

"He likes amputees."

"What's an amputee?"

"Someone who's missing a limb."

Savitha shook her head, confused. "But I'm not missing a limb."

He looked at her. A long, cruel look.

"No." She laughed, chilled by the realization of what Guru was suggesting. "Never."

But he continued looking. He waited. She jumped up, breathed with effort. "You're worth about a quarter of that to me," he said. "Twenty-five, let's say. Do you know how long it will take you to buy your way out of here?"

Savitha thought of the book, the markings, the figures. She thought about what a banana cost. "I don't care. I'm not—"

"So the question is," Guru said, interrupting her, "do you want to be worth what you are, or do you want to be worth more?"

There seemed no greater question in the world.

Savitha looked down at her hands, and as if prophetic in her gaze, when she asked, "Which limb?" he said, "Any limb. A hand, let's say. Either one. You choose."

The operation was scheduled to take place two days later, but was then moved up to the next day. Less time to change my mind, Savitha thought. Regardless, she lay in bed all the night before, cradling her left hand, letting it wander over the ridges of her body. How can they take a hand? How can a hand be taken? she wondered. The palm, the fingers, the crescent moons at their tips. The warmth of blood beneath the skin, already curtailed, lost. The ends of a body as beautiful as its beating center. She decided in that moment, resolutely, lying in bed, No, I won't do this, I won't let them. But then she gazed into the dark of the room, into the dark oblivion of her waiting sisters, their waiting dowries, and knew she would. Knew she had to. She would let them buy it—her hand; she had nothing left to sell.

3

It was called a general anesthetic, but it felt to Savitha as if a light had been turned off, as if night had crashed through her like an anvil. When she woke up, the stub of her left arm was bandaged. The doctor beamed with pride and said, "Cleanest one ever. It looks almost pretty." When the bandage came off, Savitha sat in her room and stared at it. What did they do with my hand? she wondered. Where did they take it? If someone paid for a stub, then maybe someone else paid for a hand?

Regardless, in the end, she realized, it *had* come down to the body.

She held back tears. She could never again sit at the loom, or the charkha, but why would she need to? With fifty thousand rupees she could buy all the cloth in the world. Silks and chiffons and gold-bordered pottu saris. Saris she could've never before imagined, but now could buy as gifts for her sisters on their wedding days. With that thought, she searched in her pillow and took out Poornima's half-made one. She held it to her chest; she buried her head in its folds. What reason was there to be sad? It was just a hand. Imagine Nanna's surprise, she thought. Imagine his delight. All that money. And yet, and yet the scrap of a sari she held now, she knew—the knowledge grottoed in her heart, hidden in a cove, reached only by the darker waters, the quieter ones—was the truest offering. What did they matter, the ones to come? What did they matter to her? What mattered was that once, long ago, a line of indigo thread had met a line of red, and out had poured a thing of beauty. A thing of bravery.

She lifted her head and noticed a dampness. She was crying. And the cotton, as cotton will, had soaked up the tears.

Savitha waited for her ticket to Saudi to arrive. She tried to find a map, but she couldn't. When she asked the madam where it was, she said, "In the desert." So it was near Rajasthan. That wasn't so far. Though it did occur to her that far might be the best place to be. She had been wrong to turn back, to come to Vijayawada, where she could still, in a certain wind, scent the waters of the Krishna. And that scent would then plunge her into a terrifying and quarried understanding of how little she'd managed, how corrupt her fate: she'd come all of twenty kilometers from Indravalli. What would've happened if I had gone to Pune? she wondered. She looked at the space at the end of her left arm and thought, Would I still have you? But now she was going even farther, and to go far, and then to return, *with money*, was, she decided, what the crow had told her that long-ago day: Let them eat you, let them, but be sure to eat them back.

Money. Money let you eat them back.

She was no longer considered one of the regular prostitutes, but one of the special ones. What did that mean? Savitha wasn't quite sure. She didn't have to take as many customers, that was one thing, because mostly, as it turned out, the fetish for an amputee wasn't all that common; most of the men preferred one of the girls with both hands intact. Though the customers she *did* have paid more, and were much more talkative than they had been, as if her missing hand were an expensive conversation piece, as if it lent her an added ability to understand their deepest selves, their darkest fears. Savitha was happy to listen. In fact, she became such a good listener that she could sense a man's sorrow—the *source* of it—the minute he entered the room. It was easy. A man with a nagging wife held his head unnaturally high when he entered. A man who'd been unloved as a child waited for her to speak first. A man who had no money—who was perhaps spending the last of it on her—held on to the doorknob for longer than he should.

She once had a customer who confessed to having been in jail. For killing my brother, he said, though he said nothing more about it. But he went on to tell her that after his third year in jail, he'd escaped and lived as a fugitive for more than twenty years. In Meghalaya, he said, in the forests. He said he'd been the pampered eldest son of a wealthy family. Wheat merchants. I had no idea how to cook even rice, he said, let alone live in the wilderness. But he learned to make his way in the forests, he told her, and he began to realize certain things.

"What things?" Savitha asked.

But at that point in the story, he stopped. Savitha waited. She watched him. He didn't *look* like a fugitive, though she had no idea what one would look like. She'd expect them to at least be wild-looking, haunted in some way, but this man looked quite serene, contented even, as if he'd just had a refreshing bath and a nice breakfast.

At last, after almost ten minutes of sitting in silence, the man, with graying hair and dark eyes, by turn tunnels and then becoming the smooth faces of cliffs, said, "By my fifth year in the forest, I realized I could no longer feel. Not just that I couldn't feel pain or loneliness or lust. Not just those things, but that I could no longer even feel my own heart. Do you understand? It was beating, but it might as well have been a stone, beating against another stone."

By his eleventh or twelfth year, he said, he was no longer human. He said, "I'd catch an animal, in a trap or with a crude bow and arrow, and kill it without a thought. Strangle it, snap its neck, while I looked into its eyes, and not feel the slightest thing. Not even victory. I would bash its head in with my bare hand, and it felt like I was cracking a nut." As he neared the twentieth year, he said, he could recall no other life than that of a fugitive. He had memories, he told her, of the time before he was a fugitive. Vague memories of being in jail, even vaguer of being a son, a brother. "It was as if," he said, "it was what I was born to be: a fugitive. Not just that. But that I was *born* a fugitive. Do you understand?"

This time, Savitha did, a little.

"Every so often, I met other fugitives. Sometimes tribals. But they generally left me alone. They asked no questions. Questions are for the living, and they could very clearly see that I was dead. At the start of my twenty-fourth year," he said, "I began talking to the universe. Not just talking to it, but commanding it. I could make clouds part. I could make fish swim to me, swim into my hand with nothing in the hand besides desire. I could make wind stop blowing. I remember one night, deep in the forest—I couldn't ever be near a ranger station, or a village, even the smallest—I was asleep, and was awoken by a strange rustling. When I sat up and looked around me, there was a cobra, staring straight back. I'd fashioned a kind of hatchet, so I reached for it. But the cobra was faster. It caught my hand just as I touched the hatchet, and it said, 'You can't kill me twice,' which is when I knew it was my brother. And then the cobra said, 'Find out something for me.' I waited. I thought he, it, would ask me to find out whether our parents were all right, or whether fate and chance were in battle or in collusion, or whether our cycle of suffering would ever truly end, but instead, the cobra said, 'Find out for me the depth of the forest floor.'

" 'The depth?' I said.

" 'Yes. I've tried, you see. I've tried to snake my way all the way down; that's what we do, after all, we snakes. But I can't seem to find its floor. It's as if I could keep going and going and going. That maybe there is no end. But there has to be. Maybe it goes to the core of the earth, or maybe somewhere even darker. Or hotter. Don't you think?'

" 'No, I don't,' I said.

" 'Neither do I,' the cobra said, and slithered away into the forest."

Here, the man—who was clearly no longer a fugitive, as he was sitting in Savitha's room—looked at her, maybe for the first time, and said, "That's when I walked out of the forest. The very next morning. Because you see, the cobra didn't want an answer; it didn't want anything, certainly not to know the depth of the forest floor. What it wanted was to reveal to me that there is no end to guilt, no end to the prices we pay, that we are the forest, and our conscience, our hell, is the forest floor."

He looked at her. She thought he might be waiting for her to say something, but no, he was just looking at her.

"I went to the nearest ranger station that morning. That very morning. Walked right through the doors and told them who I was and what I'd done. At first they didn't believe me. Some guy who was saying he'd lived in the forest for twenty-five years—why would they? They didn't even think it was possible. But after some discussion among them, they drove me to the police station in Shillong. And there, they *had* to call it in. So they called the police station in Guntur, but they said that the old courthouse, where all the criminal case files would have been kept, had burned down long ago, years ago, and that their own files from that time, kept in boxes in a musty back room, had been chewed through by rats, so really, there was no record of me at all. Anywhere. The constable put down the receiver, looked at me, and explained everything the Guntur police had told him, almost apologetically. And then he said I was free to go."

"What did you do then?" she asked.

"I came home," he said. "But by then, both my parents had died. From heartache, some said. But that's what people want to believe. It's more romantic that way. If I had to guess, I'd say my father died from rage and my mother from boredom. They were childless at the end of their lives, it's true, even after having had two sons. I wish I could've apologized to them for that. I wish for many things. But they must've searched, too, for the forest floor."

And with that, the former fugitive, who was now a customer, and yet had not once touched Savitha, his face as placid as the surface of a still lake, said, "So how did you lose your hand?"

4

The ticket for Saudi never arrived. Guru called her into his office three months after her operation and said the prince had found somebody more suitable. More suitable? Savitha asked. What's more suitable?

"Apparently, a missing leg."

"He told you that?"

"*He* didn't tell me anything. His people did."

Her left hand—the phantom one she'd been feeling over the past few weeks—clenched. It drew phantom blood. "What about the money?"

"Forget about that measly one lakh. I have a better deal."

Savitha was seated in front of his desk, but she still slumped. She was tired. She was tired of deals. Every moment in a woman's life was a deal, a deal for her body: first for its blooming and then for its wilting; first for her bleeding and then for her virginity and then for her bearing (counting only the sons) and then for her widowing.

"Farther away, though," he said, twirling a pen in his hand.

She waited for her exhaustion, her despair, to pass. Then she said, "Farther is better."

"A temporary visa first. Then they'll figure out a way for you to stay. Or you can come back, if you want."

"What do they want me for?" she asked, afraid of the answer.

"To clean houses. Flats. Apparently, they have to pay maids so much over there, it's cheaper to buy them from here."

"But how will I—" she began, but Guru, before she could finish, said, "I told them you'd work twice as fast."

"Where?"

"America. Someplace called Sattle. Good money, too."

Unlike Saudi, *America* she knew. Everyone knew America. And it was indeed far away. Far, far away. On the other side of the earth, she'd once heard someone say.

"How much?" she asked.

"Twenty thousand. Ten for you, ten for me."

"That's hardly anything! You said yourself I was worth more than that."

Guru put down the pen. He leaned back in his chair and smiled. "Dollars, my dear. Dollars."

But why would Guru split the money with me? Why would he ever have? That was the first thing that passed through Savitha's mind, sitting across from him, watching the avarice glow in his eyes. The second was, He won't, of course. Still, what bothered her was not that he was lying, which didn't really matter, nor that she had been so slow to see it, but that she, *she*, had said the word *worth*.

It was a Telugu man who'd bought her, Savitha learned. In this town in America, she was told, he owned hundreds of apartments and a handful of restaurants and even a cinema hall. Maybe I'll finally get to see a cinema, she thought, not with excitement or bitterness, but with a kind of shame. She'd always have to sit to Poornima's left, she realized, so that they could hold hands during the scary parts. The man in America had two sons and a daughter. The daughter was married to a doctor, a famous doctor, the kind who made women's breasts bigger or their noses smaller. Savitha had never heard of such a thing, had never known there were doctors who did such things, but wondered whether the extra nose bits went to the same place her hand had gone, and whether the extra breast bits came from that same place. The two sons helped the father run his many businesses, and Savitha didn't know whether they were married. The man in America had a wife who was from Vijayawada, which is how they'd come to know of Guru, and she was exceedingly devout. She was involved in good works all over the city, giving money to the poor and the sick, and every year, she donated ten lakh rupees to the Kanaka Durga Temple, along with a new set of gold ornaments for the deity.

Then she learned of a thing called the exchange rate.

Guru, out of this deal, would make over thirteen lakh rupees. That was a sum Savitha couldn't even imagine, and she smiled with him when he said, "We could *buy* Indravalli, you and I." After a moment, she asked him why her, why someone with only one hand, why not one of the other girls, one of the ones with both hands; they would certainly agree to go to America, and they would also clearly make better maids. Guru's eyes sparkled. "That's the beauty of it," he said. "Only *you* can go." Apparently, this all had to do with something Guru had mentioned earlier, something called a visa. There were visas to do different types of things, such as one to visit a place, and another to work in a place, and another to study in that place. And then there was one to get treatment.

"What kind of treatment?" Savitha asked.

"The kind you're going to get," Guru said. "At least, that's what they'll tell him. To whatever official." Then he nodded at the stub of her left arm, resting on her lap. "They'll say you need to enter America for a special operation, one only they can perform. One doctor here, a doctor there—their son-in-law, maybe—will vouch for your need for *American* medical treatment. And once you're there, well, the rest is easy."

"But will I get the operation? Will they give me a new hand?"

He looked at her with something like incomprehension, maybe even a trace of contempt. "Of course not, you fool. There *is* no operation. You're going to clean houses."

So she was going to clean houses. That was fine. That was better than sleeping with men. But something Guru had said kept echoing inside of her. No, *echo* would indicate it was his voice she heard. It was not. It was her own, and it repeated, over and over and over again: Only you can go.

Only you can go. What did those words mean? They meant that of all the girls in all of Guru's houses, only she could go. And why was that? Because she was the only one with a hand missing—the others might be prettier or stronger or sweeter; they might be lighter skinned or bigger breasted or have longer and thicker hair, plumper and rounder hips; but only she could go.

But what did that *mean*?

Savitha smiled.

It meant that she had leverage. It meant that she had power.

"I won't go," she said to Guru a week later.

His eyes widened in alarm. He laughed nervously. "What do you mean, you won't go? Think of all the money."

"I am."

He was an animal in the dark, she thought. His eyes scanned the night forest for movement, sound. "You're afraid I won't give it to you? How could you? It's just that I won't get the money until after you're there. Upon receipt. It's like goods, you see."

It wasn't *like* goods, she thought.

"I'll go on one condition," she said.

He relaxed into his chair. He lifted his arm in munificence.

"My little sisters. I want you to give my parents enough money for their dowries. I want you to give them enough money for a new house. I want you to give them enough money to last the rest of their lives."

He roared with laughter. She sat very still. He looked at her face, then at the strength of the one hand resting on her lap, and he stopped. "All right."

"I want you to do it before I leave. And I don't want them to know it had anything to do with me."

He nodded.

"And one other thing," she said. "I want you to loan me a car."

"Why?"

"Because once you say it's done, I want to make sure it is."

She went in the middle of the night. She asked the driver to go up Old Tenali Road, and then told him to stop a few hundred yards from her parents' hut. How will I know? she wondered. How will I know if he gave them the money? I'll know, she thought, just from looking at the hanging vegetable basket. She walked up the stinking hill, keeping off the main path, so she wouldn't be seen, and along the backs of the huts.

Indravalli Konda loomed in the distance. The temple floated at its center, a lone and beating heart. Its colors changing in the moonlight, according to her glimpses of it: buttermilk and pumice, then mother-of-pearl, then the froth of the sea. The deepa wasn't lit, and so the rest of the mountain, its contours, was lost to the sky. When she passed by one hut, a sleeping dog woke at the sound of her footsteps and barked into the night. An emaciated goat, tethered to an emaciated tree, stiffened with fear.

The moon was high, and when she finally came upon her parents' hut— the one she'd been born in, and all her brothers and sisters—she crept along the back of it quietly, meaning only to peek inside, but there was no need: it was empty. Only a dried gourd and a rat-chewed blanket in one corner.

She, too, stiffened and ran. Down the hill, her breath a fist through her body. All manner of thoughts, as she ran, all of them culminating in the one: they're dead, he's killed them to get out of paying.

She slammed into the side of the car. The driver jerked awake. "Ask. Go ask," she hissed. "Ask them what happened."

He cursed his luck for being on duty tonight, and then drove around until they reached the highway. There, a tea stall was still open. Inside, behind a false door, was whiskey and moonshine. "Crazy bitch," he muttered, and partook, asked a few questions, and then came back outside.

She was slouched in the backseat so no one would see, but sprang to attention like a coil. "What did they say? *What?*"

"They've moved," he said, the scent of whiskey filling the front seat and then the back. He started the car. They drove again, this time away from Old Tenali Road, to the other side of the village. Hardly five minutes away, but the houses richer, bigger, no longer thatch but concrete. He stopped at the end of a road Savitha had only walked by, not ever having known anyone wealthy enough to live in one of the dhaba houses. "That one," said the driver, pointing to the third house on the left, painted pink and green and yellow, with still-green mango leaves stretched across the front door. There was a gate, locked, and she stood outside of it and saw a figure sleeping on the veranda, on a hemp-rope cot, a thin blanket over them. Through an open door, three more figures slept on beds. Beds!

When she came back to the car, she said, "It isn't them. There are only four people in that house."

"One of your sisters is already married. Last week."

"She *is?*"

She told him to wait a moment more and went back and stood at the gate. She studied the dim interior of the veranda, the rich moonlit marble floor, the sleeping bodies—still skeptical. A breeze swept past her and into the house, and with a rustle, the figure on the veranda threw off the sheet. And in that moment, she saw the fingers, gnarled and noble and lovely, more beautiful than broken. And then she knew.

The driver turned toward Vijayawada, but she said no, there was one more place she needed to go. He sighed loudly and turned the car around again.

Poornima was married by now, of that Savitha was certain. She thought vaguely of asking the driver to take her to Namburu, but *where* in Namburu, and was that even the boy she married?

That hut was the same. The same thatched roof, the same dirt floor, the same dusty and stunted trees. Four small figures were asleep on the ground, on the same mats, under the same thin sheets, with forlorn faces peeking above them, impoverished even in the moonlight. Another, larger figure was asleep on the hemp-rope bed, and from him, Savitha averted her eyes, allowing them to rest, just for a moment, on the nearer structure, the weaving hut. She gazed at it with sudden emotion, maybe even longing, for what she had left inside, for what she had been, and then she turned to the driver and said, "Let's go."

5

She left for America two months later. All of the necessary documents had been witnessed, notarized, fingerprinted, and all manner of other words Savitha had never heard before. Guru took her to Chennai on the train, and from there, she was to be accompanied by an older woman who was to pretend to be Savitha's mother. The older woman was indeed probably her mother's age, maybe a little older. Savitha never quite understood who she was, how she was related to the people in America, or why she'd agreed to accompany her, but she was, in her way, the perfect choice: she was grave, her sari was simple yet impressively well woven, humble to look at, and she wore round spectacles, which gave her an air of seriousness, and more important, gave her an air of concern—which was exactly what she should feel for a beloved daughter about to travel halfway around the world for hand surgery.

In Chennai, Savitha put on a cast, so no one could see that her stub had completely healed, and then they boarded a plane. Guru had explained it to Savitha—that she would travel to America on a long bus that could fly through the air. She had been confused, and still was, even as the plane taxied down the runway. And then: it lifted into the air. The old woman—the one who was supposed to be her mother—sat beside her. She had hardly spoken to Savitha, merely nodded when they met, and now, once they were on the plane, she'd inserted what looked like tiny cotton balls into her ears, with wires coming out of them, and seemed completely absorbed or asleep or maybe just unwell; her eyes closed the moment they sat down. Savitha thought that she might have an ear infection. One of her little sisters, who was prone to ear infections as a baby, had always needed to have cotton balls, dipped in coconut oil, stuffed in her ears to ease the ache and her crying. But now, as the plane lifted off the ground, Savitha grabbed the woman's hand and stared frantically from her to the window and then back again. The plane climbed higher and higher; Savitha swallowed back her racing heart. The woman opened her eyes, looked down at her hand, took out one of the cotton balls with the other hand, and shook Savitha off as if she were a fly. Then she said, speaking Telugu with a Tamilian accent, and without a trace of a smile, "This is the best part. Enjoy it."

What did she mean by that? Did she mean that this was the best part of the plane ride, or that this was the best part of all that was to come? Maybe she meant this was the best part of all of it: the plane ride, what was to come, and all that had come before.

Regardless, after an hour or so, after Savitha had stared, unblinking, at every cloud that floated by her oval window, she leaned back in her seat and fell into a deep sleep.

When they landed at Heathrow, the first thing Savitha noticed was that it smelled like nothing, absolutely nothing—as if not a single animal had passed through here, nor a single flower bloomed—and then she noticed that it was cold. So cold that it seemed to be spilling out of the walls, climbing out of the floor. She asked the woman if they were in America. The woman said, No, we're in England. Why did we stop here? she asked. Because it's halfway between India and America, the woman said. They sat in the transfer lounge, which Savitha only registered as a long, crowded room with row after row of orange chairs. There were also a few shops, which were so brightly lit that they scared her away. She sat in one of the orange chairs and looked at the other people in the lounge. They, too, scared her. She noticed a few Indians, but mostly, the people around her—sleeping or eating or reading or talking—seemed to her like giants. Tall and unwieldy and oily. Some of them pale giants, some of them burnt, crisp giants, but all of them towering over her, even over the woman who was supposed to be her mother. Where had they all come from? Where were they all going? It felt to Savitha as if the world was full of them, these giants, suddenly, and that she and the old woman and Indravalli and Vijayawada were all merely their playthings, kept locked in a box in a hotter part of the world.

After that, after boarding another plane and after more hours upon hours had passed, during which, whenever Savitha woke and blinked into the dark of the plane and into the dark of the world beyond, she thought that maybe she was dead, and that this was the afterlife: all of them headed in a long bus to whatever was next, and around and beyond them was only stillness, and stars, and below, far, far below, only some gigantic moving mass, by turns white and then gray and then only black, reflecting the stars but darker, angrier than any night sky, and when she pointed to it and asked the woman, in alarm, What is that? the woman hardly even glanced at it, never even took out her cotton balls, and as she closed her eyes again, she said, "Water."

The next morning, or what Savitha presumed was morning because the woman said, "Go brush your teeth," they landed again. This time, when Savitha said, Is this America? the woman said, Yes.

They were at JFK.

They stood in one long line and then another. Then they sat down in another transit lounge. This one had blue chairs. Otherwise, it was just the same: the same lack of scent, the same cold, the same giants. "What city are we in?" Savitha asked. "Are we in Sattle?" No, the woman said, New

York. And then she told her to sit right there, don't move, and went off to make a telephone call. Savitha could see her in the distance, standing at a pole with a telephone attached to it. The woman put something into the telephone and pressed some buttons and started talking.

Savitha was nauseated, or maybe just lonely, so she closed her eyes and tried to think of Poornima, of her sisters, of her father, of anything that had perfume that she could inhale. Her mind swirled, but she was so tired, so depleted of memory, that nothing came to her. Not one thing. So she leaned down and opened the suitcase that Guru had given her to pack her few things, and she took out Poornima's half-made sari and held it to her nose. She breathed. And there, even after coming all this way, to the other side of the earth, there was the scent of the loom. The scent of its picking stick. The scent of the rice starch used to dampen the thread and the scent of the charkha and the scent of the fingers that had wound it on the charkha, perfumed with turmeric and salt and mustard seed, and there, just there, was the scent of Indravalli Konda, and the deepa, the oil burning low, drenching the cotton wick as if with rain, with typhoon; she buried her face deeper and out rose the scent of the Krishna, winding its way through the mountains and valleys and into the sea.

When she raised her head, the woman seated across from her was watching her.

Savitha averted her eyes, but the woman kept looking.

The woman who was supposed to be her mother seemed to be saying her good-byes. Savitha wished she would come back quickly, but then the conversation seemed to take another turn, and the old woman began talking animatedly again. Savitha looked over, and when she did, the strange woman across from her, one of the giants, her hair the color of jilebi, and with round spots on her face like a ripe banana, leaned across toward Savitha, gazed at the cast on her arm and then into her eyes, and said, "Are you okay? Do you need help?" Savitha had no idea what she'd said, so she only shook her head, and then nodded, and then waited, hoping the jilebi-haired woman was satisfied and would leave her alone. She considered getting up and going to the woman who was supposed to be her mother, but she'd specifically told Savitha to stay put and watch their bags.

"Do you understand English?"

Savitha smiled and nodded again.

The woman smiled back. And it was then—when the woman smiled, when she revealed her tiny teeth, not at all giant, but dazzling, pearls, the most luminescent pearls, as if the oyster who'd made them had been in love during their making—that Savitha saw how gentle the jilebi-haired lady was, how concerned. Gentler and more concerned than anyone she'd met in a long, long time. Maybe ever. And Savitha thought, Maybe I've come far enough away. Maybe I'm in a good country. Maybe I'm in a kind one. Just then, a loud announcement came over the PA system and Savitha jumped, but the woman seemed unafraid; she reached inside her purse and took out a small white rectangle of paper and held it out to Savitha. Savitha took it, not knowing what else to do, and then the woman picked up her purse and her bag and walked into the mass of people that had gathered when they'd heard the announcement. Savitha watched the woman, inexplicably sad at her departure, and then she looked at the card. It had letters, maybe her name, and then more letters. She stared at it and stared at it, and when she looked up, the woman who was supposed to be her mother was walking toward her. Savitha had no idea what the letters spelled, but she knew enough to slip the card into the inside of her cast.

6

When they landed in Seattle, a man came to collect them. On the plane from New York, Savitha had looked out the window and seen the sky in front of her brushed with strokes of deep orange and rose and rust, but when she turned around, so was the other side. Though ahead of her it was brighter, the reds fiercer. West. They were heading west.

Savitha stepped through the sliding doors into the open air (after what felt like a lifetime) and saw that it was midday. The sun was high and warm. Lines of cars, shiny and silent, drifted by her; a few were stopped and had one or two people standing next to them, loading luggage or embracing or standing expectantly. One couple even kissed, and Savitha looked away in embarrassment. A few were standing at a far end, smoking. Otherwise, it was empty. There was no noise or clamor or porters or horns. There was not one policeman blowing his whistle, shouting for people to keep moving, nor a single person haggling with a taxi driver or laughing or eating from a cone of peanuts, dropping their shells on the ground, birds pecking among them for food, dogs sniffing at blowing wrappers and the discarded rinds of an orange or a mango, not even idle young men, standing in groups and watching the women and smoking beedies and spitting betelnut. Waiting for life. Here, there was nothing but a silent, ordered sleekness.

She looked up at the sun again.

It, too, was quiet. Not blazing and insolent and angry and rowdy, like it was in Indravalli, but tempered, emasculated. She didn't know if she liked this sun. She doubted it was even the same one.

It was then that a black car, the windows so spotless they shone like a mirror, pulled next to her and the woman who was supposed to be her mother. The man who'd come to collect them, named Mohan, stepped out. He was older than Savitha, maybe thirty, though she couldn't be sure, because he, too, was a giant. The first Indian giant she'd ever met. He was not exactly fat or puffy, though certainly there was something cherubic about his face. He was muscular, though, like the images of the cinema heroes Savitha had seen on posters, when she'd passed a handful of times along the Apsara or the Alankar. She saw them again now, those heroic muscles, curved, firm, rising from Mohan's arms, his chest, while his neck and his hands held taut with their power, their magnificence, nearly discomfited by their rising and falling. Savitha found it disconcerting: this well-fed, well-tended extravagance, this health.

Nevertheless, what struck her most about Mohan was his melancholy. Eyes and lips turned by some sorrow, some blunder, the sad slope of his stride as he came around the car, reached for their few bags. His gaze paused at Savitha's cast and then continued up her stomach and breasts to her face.

"Is that all?" he asked in Telugu. The old woman nodded, and they climbed into the car.

It smelled like a lemon.

Below the scent of lemon was the smell of coffee. Both thick and bitter, Savitha thought, and then she searched the car and saw a white cup with a white lid. Mohan's hand hovered near it even as he drove: first on a curved road out of the airport and then down a wide road that was the blackest one Savitha had ever seen, with more cars than she had ever seen. They drove in silence—with the old woman sitting next to Mohan and Savitha behind her. After a few minutes, Mohan turned on the radio. It was a kind of music Savitha had never heard before; it had no words. At times, the music soared to a lofty peak, like being on the top of Indravalli Konda, and at other times it was gentle, yet controlled, like lapping water. She wanted to ask what it was, but the silence in the car, too, seemed controlled and inflexible.

After twenty minutes or so, Mohan pulled off the many-laned road to a smaller one. On this road, Savitha noticed low, flat buildings; there were cars parked along this street, and the storefronts (or so she guessed by the genteel window displays) were not at all like the storefronts in India. In India, they were choked with colorful streamers and the windows piled high with merchandise and the whole crowded with people yelling and pushing and shoving. Here, they seemed hardly occupied. Only their lighted interiors revealed a few customers, any sign of life. Halfway down the street, Mohan stopped the car in front of a long building, lined with doors, and he and the old woman got out. She leaned into the car—as Mohan was getting her bags—and said, "Stay here," and then she seemed to waver, or sway with a kind of discomfort, or guilt, and added, "Be careful."

Be careful of what? Savitha wondered.

She watched them. What is this place, she puzzled, with its series of doors, though the old lady and Mohan ignored these and instead entered the only glass door, more prominent than the others. They were inside for maybe ten minutes, and then Mohan walked the old lady to one of the regular doors and said, "See you tomorrow." When he returned to the car he looked at Savitha shyly and said, "Come to the front if you'd like." She got into the front passenger seat, and now, now she felt the true enormity of this new country. It could only be felt from the front seat, she realized, only from the wide window and the unobstructed light.

The music came on again.

They drove over a bridge, though from Savitha's seat, it looked to her more like a bolt of unfurled silk over a layer of mist. Above Savitha, from the little mirror Mohan had looked into earlier to take fleeting glances at her, dangled a thin yellow tree-shaped decoration. Lemon! So that's where it was coming from. Then the road curved, and suddenly, before Savitha, were the tallest and shiniest buildings she'd ever seen and the bluest stretch of water and the greenest mountains. "Is this Sattle?" she asked.

"*See*-attle," he corrected her.

They neared the buildings, rising out of the earth like blazing rectangles, reflecting the sun, and then cut along their right-hand flank and went down another black road with many lanes, for quiet mile after quiet mile, until Mohan said, "Are you hungry? We can stop."

"Yes."

"Not for long. There's a McDonald's, Taco Bell up there."

Savitha looked where he was pointing. He saw the expression on her face, and he said, "No, not Indian food, but it's not bad."

She turned to him and said, "Do you have bananas here?"

He was startled by the question, she thought, because he slowed the car, and then he met her gaze. He was unused to looking at women. Maybe not all women, she thought after a moment, maybe just women with a certain openness, a kind of curiosity, perhaps even that radiance she had glimpsed long ago, bearing itself up behind her eyes like a crumbling fort, an embattled army. They stopped at a massive building with many parked cars, and he went inside, and when he came out again, he handed her a bag.

Inside the bag were bananas.

There were six of them. The biggest bananas she'd ever seen, worthy of giants. She took one and tried to give the remaining five back to him. "They're yours," he said.

In all her life, Savitha had never possessed this many bananas at once.

That first one she ate in the car. With only one hand, she'd learned to use her teeth to rip open the end of the banana, opposite the stem, and as she did, she felt Mohan watching her. She offered him one, but he said no. She was about to eat a second one, with a vague sense of bafflement, awe, repletion at the thought that she even *could*, when Mohan stopped the car. He parked in front of a building that was four stories tall, cream-colored with chipped brown windowsills and a brown roof. Many of the windows were open, and from them fluttered all colors of curtains. Some seemed to be sheets, torn in places, tie-dyed, others were flags; a few had broken blinds. A small tattered awning over a sagging door in the center of the building indicated the entrance. Next to the front door were three rows of cubbyholes, some with bent or rusted metal flaps. "What are these?" Savitha asked.

He looked at her curiously. "Mailboxes," he said in English.

"What are they for?"

"Letters."

She studied them, many bursting with browned envelopes that seemed to have been set out in the sun and rain for weeks, months. "But why don't they take their letters? Don't they want to read them?"

"No. Not these kind of letters."

What kind were they? she wondered. Savitha had not once gotten a letter (From whom would she get one, and why? She could hardly read.), but she thought if she did, she wouldn't leave it out in the sun and rain, she would tear it open and stare at it, relish the slant of the letters, the way they'd written her name (*that* she'd known how to read and write since she was three years old), the feel of the paper, which she knew would be very different from the paper scraps she'd collected from the garbage heap, and the color and the beauty of ink. But when they went inside, Savitha's reverie ended. They climbed a musty stair and then walked down a musty hallway. Mohan carried her one suitcase—though it was practically empty; what was there to put in it?—and Savitha carried the bag of bananas. At the end of the hallway, Mohan opened a door, with the assurance of knowing it would be open, as if he lived there, and inside the small room was another man, also Indian but older. He was watching something on television, holding a glass—the chair on which he was sitting, the glass, a small table to hold the glass, and the television being the only four things in the room. He looked up when they entered, at Savitha with barely conccaled contempt, and then he said, in Telugu (was *everyone* in this country Telugu?), "A stub to clean houses. I suppose next he'll buy a one-legged man to ride a bicycle."

Mohan stammered something in embarrassment and glanced at her once, for a moment that felt to Savitha as if he were at war, or had just returned, and then he left. She didn't see him again for three months.

7

The older man took her up another flight of stairs. He'd taken one look at her suitcase and her bag of bananas, and then had looked away without a word. Savitha carried the suitcase in her right hand and the bananas in the crook of her left arm. At the top of the stairs, the man opened a door that led into a room smaller than his own. On the floor of this room, laid out on the mildewed and stale-smelling beige carpet, were three cots. He pointed to the farthest one, on the side of the room opposite from the door, and said, "That's yours," and then he said, "That's *all* that's yours." He closed the door behind her.

Savitha took two steps into the center of the room—still holding her suitcase and her bag of five bananas (and the peel of the one she'd eaten)—and saw that there was a tiny kitchenette in one corner of the room and a door to the bathroom in the other. She looked at the cots. They were positioned in the shape of a U, with the one in the middle beneath the only window in the room, one behind her, against the wall with the front door, and hers, next to the bathroom door. The cot by the front door was neatly made, with the pillow fluffed and centered and a small, cheap suitcase like her own resting at the foot. The sheets of the one in the middle were in complete disarray, the pillow half flung, and there was no suitcase in sight, only clothes and toiletries and hair things tossed in every which direction as if it were the wreckage of a ship, and the beige carpet a sea.

The first thing she did was to take out Poornima's half-made sari from her suitcase and look at it. From boll to thread to loom to this, she thought. And then she thought, I made you. She tucked the cloth into the inside of her pillowcase. Then she slid off her cast and placed the little white rectangular card back inside its hollow. She placed them against the wall. After a time— during which Savitha tried to take a bucket bath, but there was no bucket in sight, only a long white rectangular hole (was everything in this country white and rectangular?)—she washed her face and drank a glass of water and ate another banana. She lay down on her cot, but as soon as she did, there was a sound at the door. A girl entered, and she said, "Who are you?"

The girl's name was Geeta, short for Geetanjali, and she was talkative.

"I'm named after the film," she began, in Telugu. "Did you see it?"

Savitha shook her head.

"My amma saw it a few months before I was born. It was the first movie she'd ever seen. She said she didn't really follow the story, not really—she was only thirteen or fourteen—but she said that when she came out of the cinema theater, back into the world, it felt new. Polished. Like it was a different world, and that anything could happen. She said she practically skipped home. Back to the little hut she lived in with my nanna, on the edge of a jute field, neither of which they owned. She said she felt the same way when I was born, that the world was somehow new. That I'd made it new. So she named me Geetanjali. Isn't that nice?"

Savitha had to agree.

Then Geeta laughed. A tinkling laugh that cut through Savitha's fatigue, the fog of the long plane ride. "It's funny, though, isn't it? It's still the same old world. They're still in that same hut, leasing that same farm. And here I am, just a housecleaner and a whore."

Savitha blinked. She got up from her cot, her legs unsteady.

A whore?

"Didn't they tell you? Maybe they didn't. Anyway, it rains a lot here. Rain is the only sound in this country. If *you* make any others, if you talk to anyone, if you even open your mouth to speak, they'll come for you."

"Who'll come for me?"

"Who brought you here?"

"Mohan."

"No wonder," Geeta said knowingly, laughing again. "You're lucky. He's the nice one."

Geeta told her that Mohan was the younger of the two sons. The older one was named Suresh, and he was more like his father, cruel, slapping them around to show them who was boss, as if they didn't know; he worked them long hours, sometimes through the night if an apartment or office building needed to be cleaned by morning, so they wouldn't have to go even one day without collecting rent on it, as if they didn't have tens of thousands, maybe even lakhs of dollars in the bank, Geeta said; Suresh came around whenever he wanted, he had his favorites, of course, she added, but he'll come around at least once, try you out. She glanced at the stub and then the cast, and said, Well, maybe not you.

Then she told her a story. The story was about Mohan and Padma.

"Who's Padma?" Savitha said.

Geeta nodded toward the third cot, the unkempt one. "She says they make her clean other people's toilets, but they can't make her clean her own. But she's the prettiest. She could've been a film star." This Padma, as it turned out, was in love with Mohan. "Stupid. Idiotic. What chance does she have with him? With the son of the man who *owns* us."

"What's his name?"

"Whose?"

"The father's."

"Gopalraju. Are you going to let me finish?"

It was about six months ago. Geeta had just arrived. From where? Savitha wanted to ask, but thought she would wait. Padma had already been here for more than a year and had already fallen completely and utterly in love with Mohan. The problem (other than the obvious ones of caste, class, ownership, enslavement, and opportunity) was this: Mohan refused to sleep with her. The father and the older son had already been by, but the younger wouldn't even look at her. But why? But *why*, Padma kept lamenting. Geeta said Padma tried everything: she borrowed Geeta's new hair clips, the ones her mother had given her before she'd left for America; she tore the sleeves off her blouses and sewed up the ends, to show off her pretty arms; she tried to wear her hair down like the American girls they saw on the streets as they were being driven to and from the cleaning jobs, but they had no shampoo, and they were forbidden to go to the store, or anywhere for that matter, so her hair hung like the greasy ends of a scruffy broom, and no one noticed, least of all Mohan, but she kept it that way, hoping, until Vasu (the man from downstairs, who managed the building, but mostly managed the girls) said, Unless you're going to mop with it, put it up. It went on like this, with Padma trying to lure him more and more desperately, dropping things on the floor and bending to pick them up slowly, ridiculously slowly, in low-cut blouses, or wearing a horrid bright orange lipstick that they'd found left behind in one of the apartments. It made her look like an orangutan, Geeta said, laughing. None of it worked, you see, she said, until one day, he came by the apartment drunk. He was only there to pick us up and take us to a cleaning job. Usually he waited for us in the car, but that night, he came to the apartment, he took one long look at us, from one to the other, and then he stumbled to my cot, lay down, and began to cry.

"Cry?" Savitha asked.

"Cry. Actually *cry*, more like sobbing," Geeta said.

When he'd finished sobbing—during which time Geeta and Padma began to panic, wondering if they'd been at fault, and if so, if Gopalraju would go and demand the money their parents had been paid for them, money, as they both knew, which was long gone by now, used already to pay off debts, or to pay the dowries of their other daughters—he sat up and asked them for a glass of water. Padma ran to get it. He drank it down, and then he said, Do you have any vodka?

What's that? they asked, and he said, Never mind.

Here, Geeta paused.

"So what happened?" Savitha asked.

"Nothing," Geeta said. "Nothing, until we got to the building we were supposed to clean. It was the middle of the night, you see. And he gave me the key, and he said, Go on up. So I did. But I watched for Padma, wondering what was happening, but also knowing, and when she finally came up, disheveled, maybe twenty minutes later, I said, What happened? And she said, He took me. In the back of the car. But she didn't look altogether happy when she said it.

"I mean," Geeta said, "I know he forced her, I know he didn't make *love* to her, but I thought she'd be happier. So I asked her. I said, I thought you wanted him to. Yes, but it was cramped, she said, and his breath was awful. He reeked. And then she said, And here's the other thing: When he was done, he dragged me out of the car; I'd barely had a chance to put my clothes on again. He dragged me out, and he pushed me to the ground, and he stood staring down at me. I thought he would kick me, but instead he dropped to his knees, right next to where I was sprawled, but he wouldn't look at me, he wouldn't, he looked only at the ground next to me, and then somewhere into the dark, and then he reached up to where I was lying on the grass, and he took each of the buttons of my shirt, open, because I hadn't had time to do more than pull up my pants, and he buttoned them. One by one. Gently, like they weren't buttons at all, but beads of rain. Not even my mother, she said, was ever that gentle."

And then what happened? Savitha asked.

Nothing, Geeta said. Then we went back to cleaning.

What about Padma? Savitha said. Does she still love him?

Geeta laughed, and then she said, She loves him even more.

When Padma came in late that night, dropped off after a cleaning job in Redmond, she looked over at Savitha and said, "New girl?" Savitha nodded.

She was indeed pretty. But she knew it, and she said, "Oh," and then went into the bathroom and closed the door.

The next morning, just as Geeta had said, it was raining. Savitha was picked up with the others. When she'd come out of the bathroom (Geeta had showed her how to work the shower and explained that there was so much water in this country that no one took a bucket bath) wearing one of the two saris she'd brought along, Padma had laughed, and Geeta had said, "They don't want us wearing those. We stick out too much," and lent her a pair of black polyester pants and a gray-and-pink checkered shirt. The shirt, Savitha noticed, was cotton and felt good against her skin. She checked the threading, even though it was clearly machine made. When they handed her a pair of old sneakers to wear, Savitha looked at them and then at Geeta and Padma. They stared back. "She can't tie them," Padma announced glee-fully, as if she'd solved a riddle. Geeta tied them for her and told her she'd find her Velcro ones. "What's that?" Savitha asked. "You'll see. You'll be able to tie your shoes with your teeth," Geeta said, laughing. My teeth, Savitha thought, and wondered how tying a shoe could be like peeling a banana.

They were dropped off, and each of them went to clean different apart-ments. Padma and Geeta first showed her how to use the various mops and brooms and brushes, the sprays, the vacuum cleaner. None of it was difficult—running the vacuum cleaner was even fun—but it was hard to do with just one hand. She was slow. When Padma and Geeta came for her an hour later, she'd hardly even started. But within a week, she was almost as fast as they were. At the end of two weeks, recalling what Guru had said, that all she had to do was work twice as fast, Savitha sometimes finished before them.

The apartments were always empty. That made it easier. The tenant who'd moved out, usually a student at the university, would've been gone for only a day, sometimes only a matter of hours, and Savitha always, upon enter-ing, stopped at the threshold of the apartment. She stood still and smelled the room. The houses in Indravalli never had a smell, because the windows and doors and verandas were open to the world, and every scent in the world was a scent of theirs, and the small windowless huts always smelled of the same thing, poverty. But here, the smells were subtler. Was it a boy or a girl who'd lived here? That was easy enough to tell. But underneath. Underneath, there was so much more. What did they eat, how often were they home, how often did they bathe, did they like flowers, did they like rain. She could sometimes even tell what they had been studying. She thought one boy might've been studying the stars, because they were drawn in great detail on his walls, at the height he must've been. He liked milk, cheese, dairy, she guessed, and he didn't bathe very often. Another girl was probably studying the arts, she thought, by the scent of paints and oils, and she must've liked rain and sun, because every window had been thrown open.

All this within minutes of entering the apartments.

By the end of the month, she was cleaning almost a dozen of them a day, but she no longer took any great pleasure from guessing at the previous occupants. There was always another to clean, and then home to a plate of rice and pickle, maybe pappu if one of them had the energy to make it, her only hand trembling from exhaustion, unable to lift even a bite of rice to her mouth, and then to sleep. Walking now into the empty apartments, she scanned them quickly, assessing in the first sweep how much work needed to be done. She saw—on the carpets and the walls, sometimes on a shelf—the places where furniture or picture frames or potted plants or books had once been, and once removed, had left the square or the circle or rectangle brighter, untouched by feet and dirt and damage, more luminous than the space around it. Savitha stared at the spot of brightness in the middle of a dull, gray room and wished she were that space, the protected one. Instead, at the end of a few weeks, at the end of many apartments, she understood she was the pallid part, the discolored one. She was what absorbed the dirt and the distress. What was fatigued by sun. What lay, like a hand, over brightness.

8

She'd been in Seattle for two months, but she'd never before seen the man who came to pick her up—in a bright red car—one Saturday night in December. Only Vasu had ever driven them, picked them up. And with each passing day, the walls of the apartments closed in; the air grew thinner. She ran to open windows, and stuck her head out, starved for cold, for feeling, for the fall of rain.

Unlike Vasu, the man in the bright red car was tall, a few silver hairs at his temples. He had the beginnings of a belly, and though not nearly as muscular, he was clearly Mohan's brother. He said, "Get in," in Telugu, and then drove her to a low building on a side street. Savitha had been trying to learn her letters, studying street names and signs, but she couldn't see any, it being too dark or the area too industrial. A flickering white light seeped from a distant streetlight. The area was deserted, and when Suresh turned off the headlights, they were plunged into a deep darkness. Her eyes adjusted and she saw that the building he'd parked in front of had a thin line of light at the seam of the door and the sidewalk. It glistened in the dark like a knife.

Inside, they passed through an area lined with boxes to a door at the back and to the left. Suresh knocked, and a voice said to come in, and even

before she saw him, Savitha knew it was the father, Gopalraju, the one
who'd bought her. He was not as old as she'd expected him to be, his hair
unnaturally blue-black, clearly colored, but his face wide and alert, flushed
with the same peculiar raw, cold light that came with success, wealth, that
she'd seen in Guru, except Gopalraju's face was even sharper, more calculating. He looked at her for a long moment, and then, with false tenderness,
he said, "Getting along all right?" She nodded, though she knew it wasn't
truly a question. Not really, not in a concerned sense. More precisely, she
knew it was a statement, followed by a *different* question entirely. The statement was this: You *will* get along all right. And beneath that statement, just
as Geeta had said, was this: If, perchance, you don't get along all right, if,
perchance, you feel like talking, like telling, like running, like shouting,
if, perchance, you feel coming upon you any kind of despair, distaste, if
you feel the need to find a phone, to stop a person on the street, to scan the
sidewalks for a policeman, and if, perchance, you feel descending upon you
breathlessness, madness, a desire for revelation, then you will no longer be
all right. And so this, in turn, was the true question: Do you understand?
he was asking. Do you?

Then he saw her stub.

His lips curled up, ever so slightly, in what she knew was disgust, and he
closed his eyes, just for a moment, and in that moment, he looked almost
ecclesiastic, almost beatific, and Savitha thought they would simply let her
go, back to her empty cot, her pillowcase tucked with a half-made sari, a
small rectangle of paper, back to the apartment where Padma and Geeta
were sleeping, dreaming.

"Be careful. Might poke your eye out," he finally said, still looking at
Savitha, but clearly talking to Suresh. She turned to him, and he was laughing, and it was then that she saw she wouldn't be led back, that what lay
ahead was another door, behind Gopalraju, and it was through this door
that Suresh pushed her. It was dark inside, and when he turned on the light,
there was only a roughly made bed, a squat fridge, and some bottles strewn
on a corner table. There was a small bathroom on one side. The smell of

stale beer, which Savitha didn't recognize, hung in the windowless room, though the other smells she did recognize: unwashed sheets, shit, semen, salt, sweat, cigarettes, a kind of anguish, a kind of listlessness, a kind of gloom, all of which had a scent, all of which had a shape, all of which sat hunched in the corners of the little room.

He told her to get on the bed. And then he did, too. When she lay on her back, he said, No, you'll do the other thing. And so she turned, but he said, No, no, that's not what I mean. Savitha looked at him, confused, and then he showed her what to do. He had a bottle of something clear that he smeared over her stub, and then he showed her. He said, Like this, and then he got on the bed. On all fours. He told her to go in and out, and when she did, he said, Oh, yeah, like that, like that. A pain hit somewhere behind her eyes, and she turned away. But the pain was thunder, it broke and it broke. And he said, Yeah, oh yeah, yes, just like that. And she began to cry, willing it to end. Praying that it would. But he said, Keep going. And so she did, and so it broke.

She closed the door of the small bathroom. The light made her dizzy so she turned it off. She felt her way to the sink and washed up, scrubbed and scrubbed with a little cake of soap, her brown skin reddening all the way up to her shoulder. Then she turned off the water and was about to leave, when she heard something. What was that? She listened. It was coming from the toilet; it seemed to be humming. She leaned closer and listened, and it was. The toilet was humming! Just for her. It was humming a simple song, a child's song, but it was humming it for her. Savitha smiled into the dark, and then she knelt next to the toilet and she gave it a hug. She hummed along. Such a simple song, such simple notes, and yet so exquisite. She knelt and she hummed. The cool of the porcelain and its song; the cool of a river and its gurgle.

He was lying on the bed and smoking. Her legs were weak, and maybe he could see that, because he said, in Telugu, "Come here. Sit down." So she walked to the end of the bed and sat at its edge. He looked at her for a long while, and then he said, in English, as if she could understand, "I wasn't raised here, you know. I was raised in Ohio. You know where that is? I was on the track team. You know what they called me? Curry in a Hurry. Mohan was on the wrestling team, and they called him Curry Up. They didn't think anything of it, the kids. And I would laugh along. There was so much to laugh about back then. But I wanted to punch them. Every time someone said it, and they laughed, I'd laugh, too, and stare at their mouth, and I'd imagine grabbing its edges and ripping it open. Nice and wide."

He took a sip from a bottle that had been resting on the corner table. He sank deeper into the bed with a contented sigh, and he said, again in English, "How'd you lose that hand, anyway?"

He closed his eyes for a moment, and when he opened them, he sat bolt upright. His eyes widened, and he said in Telugu, "Hey. Hey, watch this."

There was a fly on the table. It jerked here and there. He was watching it intently. Savitha too. He took the cigarette out of his mouth. He held it poised above the table, not near the fly, but a little away, as if he knew where the fly would veer. And it did. It inched right toward his hand, which was still as a statue. Savitha had never known a man to be so still. To wait so patiently. For what? She didn't know, but his stillness seemed to her a state of fallen grace. A form of dark worship. Then, in a flash, his hand swept down and he caught it: he trapped the fly under the burning cigarette. Savitha blinked. He couldn't have. She looked again, and sure enough: there was the fly, a slight sizzle, a flailing of this or that limb, and then it was still. As still as Suresh's hand had been.

He laughed out loud. "No one else can do that. No one. I've been able to do it since I was five." He looked at her. "The key is: your hand has to move before your mind even tells it to move. That's the only way to kill a fly."

He lifted the cigarette, the fly still caught on its end, its body no longer distinguishable from it, and dropped the butt into the ashtray. His smile, too, dropped, and he said, "Let's go." When he pulled up to her building, he said, "I'll be back in a week or two."

When she got back to the apartment, she stood for a moment and looked at Padma's and Geeta's sleeping faces.

We were once children, she thought; we were once little girls. We once played in the dirt under the shade of a tree.

Then she turned away, the nausea rising in her throat. She showered. She smelled burning flesh, though was there enough to a fly to be called flesh? She didn't know, and she stopped wondering. After her shower, she drank a glass of water, went to her cot, and took out Poornima's half-made sari. She looked at it, she looked at it hard, and she thought, In a week or two. He'll be back in a week or two. And then she thought, but of course there was enough to it. There had to be. There was enough to everything to be called flesh. Even the smallest creature. The poorest. The most alone. And yet. And yet, he'd be back in a week or two. She looked at the fragment of sari in her hand, and she thought, I am not that girl in that room. I am not. I am this; I am indigo and red. And to be here in a week or two, and a week or two after that, and a week or two after that, was to surrender to what the crow had warned against, had always been warning against, it was to surrender to being eaten piece by piece.

She didn't sleep that night, thinking. And she stayed thinking all the next day: while she cleaned apartments and one floor of an office building and a few rooms of a residential hotel. When she got back to the apartment, late that night, she ate, thinking. Padma came home after her. Still pretty after a day of cleaning, Savitha thought, but all that prettiness came to nothing. Just a made-up girl wearing orange lipstick, heavy kajal, cleaning the houses of strangers, and waiting for a man who would never come.

Savitha was quiet, and Padma must've noticed, because she said, "What's with you?"

Savitha looked at her as if she'd never seen her before. "What keeps you from leaving?"

"Where would I go?"

"Back to India."

"Where would I get the money? Besides, India's no prize. Nothing there. My father used the money he got for me to buy a motorcycle."

Savitha was silent.

"Why? Are you thinking about it?"

"No, but you. You're just so pretty."

That made her smile, touch her fingers to her hair, and Savitha smiled back, imagining Padma believed her.

She was wrong.

The next time she took out Poornima's half-made sari, a few days later, she gasped: a long swath was ripped from it. Torn, the weaving mutilated, the tear uneven. Who'd done such a thing? She looked inside her pillowcase and then in her cot. She looked at the remaining piece, a third of it missing. Gone. She sat for a moment, and then she jumped up and scoured the entire apartment: the kitchen cabinets, the bathroom, the hall closet, Geeta's and Padma's things. Padma! She must've told someone Savitha had been asking about India, about leaving. And they'd . . . they'd what? She slumped again on her cot. They'd taken a piece of the only thing that meant anything to her. And why would they do that? Why wouldn't they take the whole thing? "Why," she said to the walls. But the walls said nothing back.

I have to be more careful, she decided. Much more careful. The sky seemed to agree: the rain came harder; the air grew heavier.

9

Over the next weeks, she lay in bed every night and thought about the journey from India to Seattle. She dissected every moment, every document. When she and the woman who was supposed to be her mother had first arrived at the airport, in Chennai, the old woman had taken out two strips of paper and two small blue books and handed them to the lady at the counter. The strips must've been their tickets, because the lady at the counter had stamped them and handed them back. The blue books she'd only glanced at before handing them back. Then what? Then nothing, until they'd arrived in New York. Here, the whole process had been reversed. Here, Savitha recalled, they'd stood in a long line, and this time, the old woman had shown the tickets and the two small blue books to a man. The man had stamped the blue books but not the tickets. What were those books? Savitha had no idea, but she knew she needed one: the blue book. She also knew she needed a ticket. And for both of those? She knew she needed money.

Her heart sank.

Because she realized that even with money and a ticket and the blue book, she obviously still couldn't leave. Not at all. They knew her family, they knew they were in Indravalli, and if she left, well, anything could happen to them. Gopalraju had paid a lot of money for her, more than she could imagine— she was an *investment*, something Savitha knew only in terms of cows and goats and chickens. And why would anyone let their cow or goat or chicken simply walk away? They wouldn't. Never. And as for her family: they could be killed. She knew that, she knew that as she knew her love for them: in her gut. So she would stay.

Toward the end of her three months in Seattle, there was a knock on the door. Savitha panicked. Vasu usually barged right in, using his key, so it wasn't him. It was a Wednesday night, and Padma and Geeta weren't home yet. What if it was Suresh? But he usually picked her up at one of the buildings, and took her to the room, and handed her the tube with the clear liquid. Those were the nights she came home well after Padma and Geeta were asleep. A few times, afterward, she'd vomited on the sidewalk when he'd pulled his car away; one time she'd held her stub over a flame.

Another knock. Who could it be?

She stood by the door and listened. Nothing. Then a shuffling of feet. Not going away, not yet. She waited. There was no peephole, though in some of the apartments she'd cleaned, she'd noticed the hole in the door. Now she wished she had one.

On the third knock, she turned the knob silently, as quietly as possible, and peeked through the crack.

It was Mohan.

She opened it wide, and he stood there sheepishly, not moving. She waited at the open door, wondering if he, too, had come to take her to the room.

He smiled shyly, maybe even sadly, and then he handed her a brown paper bag. When she opened it, there were six bananas inside. The bananas, the sight of them—their smooth yellow skins, their defiant firmness, their subtle beauty—made her laugh with pleasure. She looked at them and she looked at them, and when she finally looked up, Mohan was looking back at her.

"In America, they cut them lengthwise and put ice cream in the middle," he said.

She tried to imagine that and couldn't. "I like them with yogurt rice," she said.

They stood for a moment, and she invited him inside (though she felt funny about the invitation; it was his father's building, after all). He said, No, maybe another time. Maybe next week, he said, and then he left.

That night, Savitha had two helpings of rice and yogurt and banana. The first helping so sweet and creamy and divine that tears streamed down her face. Geeta laughed, and let her have a little of her portion of rice. The second helping—Geeta's kindness, Mohan's kindness—made her think of Poornima, and more tears came to her eyes, though these, she knew, were for different reasons.

"Let's go," Mohan said.

He'd come to an apartment she was cleaning, and he stood by the door, as if the carpet were wet, which it wasn't, or as if there were other people inside, which there weren't.

"But I'm not done," Savitha said.

He looked around the lit room once, let his gaze pass perfunctorily from one end of the room to the other, and then he said, "It's fine."

She climbed into the same car in which he'd picked up her and the old woman from the airport. It was still flooded with the scent of lemon. She didn't know where he was taking her, but he'd turned away from the direction of her apartment. He was quiet, almost morose, but she hardly noticed. She was looking out the window, at the nighttime streets. She'd only ever been driven from cleaning jobs to her apartment and back again, ten, twenty minutes at a time, but now, she sensed, they were *drifting*, a word she'd never associated with her life, never associated *with* life, life being only a constant doing; doing so that there could be eating and sleeping and surviving. But now, now, on a wide street, and on a wide and drizzly night, to glide under the traffic lights and to watch people sitting in brightly lit rooms and to imagine the smell of those rooms, the warmth, the chatter of the people inside or of the television or of nothing at all, just the silence, but to imagine it, sitting in a fancy, lemon-scented car, and with nothing ahead, and nothing, not really, behind, it was enough to make Savitha's heart swell, enough to make it ache with something like happiness.

They eventually turned off the wide main street and started to go up a hill. They wound through dark streets. The wind picked up, and she asked if she could open the window, and when Mohan didn't respond, or maybe didn't hear, she fidgeted with some buttons on her door until the window rolled down, with a smooth, thrilling ease, and the breeze lifted her loose hair (with only one hand, she could no longer wear her hair in a braid), and the drizzle sprayed her face, set her shivering with delight, and the shadowed leaves swayed above her and beside her as they drove past, moving as if wedded to the night, as if dancing with the wind.

No, she couldn't remember a night so wondrous, here or anywhere, and when she turned to Mohan, nearly laughing, she saw that he was unscrewing the cap of a small bottle, lifting it to his mouth, and it was then, when she saw the gold liquid in the bottle, tipping, when she saw his face wince with the first sip, it was then that she knew she was mistaken. None of this was true. Not in the least. This night, this drizzle, this uphill climb. None of it was her own. It was his. He *owned* her, and that was the only true thing.

She rolled her window back up; the walls closed in again; she closed her eyes.

When she opened them, the streets were even darker, and they were still climbing. Eventually he pulled the car onto a small embankment, off the side of the road, and he turned the engine off. He took a long pull from the bottle, and when he saw her watching, he held it out to her. Savitha thought about her father, then she thought about Poornima's father, and then she took the bottle. It went down like fire—her first taste of whiskey—and she coughed and sputtered until Mohan laughed and took the bottle back. She thought then that he must be unused to laughter, or at least unused to laughter not tinged with sorrow. The whiskey reached her stomach, and then her eyes floated and bobbed along on a warm sea. When they focused she saw that they were on a high ridge, and below them and beyond them, all the way to the dark horizon, was a field of lights. The lights spilled like beads on black velvet. "Which way are we facing?" she asked.

"West."

West, west.

She studied the lights, and she thought that somewhere below, just below, must be her apartment. Beyond the lights, in the distance, was a strip of solid black. "What is that band without lights?"

He looked up, clearly drunk by the way his head wobbled, and he said, Where? She pointed into the distance. He followed her arm and said, "Water. That's water." She remembered the bridge they'd gone over and yet, in her three months in Seattle, had forgotten they were so close to water. All she knew were walls. Even on sunny days, the light was gray, slanting dolorously into dirty apartments. The dust motes spun in place, having nowhere to go. She stared into the black mass before her, that strip of dark, and though she knew all about washing machines now, she wondered if that black mass had ever had laundresses on its shores, if saris had ever fluttered there like flags.

"You know when I had my first drink?" he asked into the dark, in Telugu. She took another drink from the bottle.

"I was eleven. Almost twelve. Behind the carousel at the state fair." Now he was switching between Telugu and English, and Savitha struggled to understand. "Went with my friend Robbie and his dad. His dad thought it was time, so he bought us beers." Then he was silent for a long moment. "We moved the next year. Nanna sold the motel, bought another two. I'll build us an empire, he said. An empire!" He looked at Savitha, and he said, "I guess you're it. I guess you're the empire."

The whiskey was gone. Mohan flung the bottle into the backseat and leaned his seat back. How did he do that? Savitha wondered, pushing against her seat to get it to lean.

"Open that," he said, pointing to the glove box.

She fiddled with it, and when it popped open, there was another bottle inside. She handed it to him, and he held it close, without opening it, as if it were a talisman, an object of great beauty.

Into the silence of the car, he said, "I stopped wrestling at sixteen. Just stopped. Suresh must've asked me a million times. Still does. Why, he'll say. Why'd you stop? You were good, Mo, really good. You could've made it to the state finals. The nationals." He stopped and looked at Savitha. He asked in Telugu, "Do you understand any English?"

She shook her head no.

He continued, this time only in English. "He picked me up after school one time. Just that once. There was a girl sitting in the backseat, about my age. I looked at her, and then I asked, 'Who is she?' He didn't even turn his head. Said, 'Just go in there, Mo. Just go with her, wait for her to be done, and come back out. Nothing fancy.' By then, he'd pulled the car up to a clinic, and we just sat there in the parking lot. The three of us. By then I understood. I said, 'Why can't you go?' He waited. I didn't think he'd answer, but then he said, 'They might recognize me.' So I took the girl in there and talked to the nurse. I knew what she was thinking, the way she looked at me. She gave me pamphlets on contraception and abstinence and all that. I must've turned beet red.

"When the girl came back out, she was carrying the same pamphlets. Couldn't speak a word of English, but she clutched those pamphlets as if they were a hand. Wouldn't look at me. Wouldn't raise her head. I didn't know what to say. I was a kid. We both were. I finally stammered something about getting her some water, and she said, 'No, thank you, sir.' Can you imagine that? Sixteen, and she calls me sir."

He laughed.

"After we dropped her off, I said, 'Who the fuck is she? What's she doing in our building? What'd you do to her?' He looked at me, long and hard, and he said, 'What do you *think* she's doing in our building? Huh? What do you think we do, Mo? How do you think we make it in this country? Make it big. You think Dad got us where we are *without* girls like her?' "

The drizzle turned to rain.

"Girls like her," he repeated, and then he grew quiet. In Telugu he asked, "What did you understand?"

Savitha said, truthfully, "I understood the word *girls*."

He looked at her with what she thought was real longing, or real loneliness, and then he ran his fingers slowly down the side of her face, and he said, in English, "You are an empire. You're more than an empire."

Savitha looked at him and she wanted in that moment to tell him everything, absolutely everything, but instead she took the bottle from his hands, saw the liquid tilt against the raindrops, the distant lights, drank as her father would've drunk, and then she smiled.

It was the following week. He came to another apartment, on Brooklyn Avenue, and without a word he lay her down on the carpet. He kissed her arm and then her throat and then her mouth, and even though she had been kissed many times before, she thought, So this is what it's like to be kissed. The give of the carpet was on her back, and he pushed the hair from her face, and then he unfastened her blouse. It didn't fall completely open, only to one side, and on this side he took her breast into his mouth. She cradled his head in her hand, and Savitha saw, in the quiet black of his hair, his first coarse gray. A window swayed above their heads and then a thick cloud shifted and light flooded in, fell onto her face. He took off her pants, her underwear, both a size too big because they had to share clothes and Geeta was bigger than her, but he seemed not to notice, nor to care, because he was kissing her stomach. He laid his head against it, as if listening for voices, and she cradled his head again, keening to him, wanting him to continue, but no, he wouldn't. Not yet, he said. She felt first impatience and then despair. Please, she almost said, in English, in Telugu: *please*. But he waited, held himself above her, looking down. No, he said again, no, I want to look at you first. The full fiery brown gleam of you. She rolled her head back, and he held her away like that, poised above her, poised perfectly, heartlessly, and the light beyond her shivered, nectared and alive.

They sat together afterward in the fading light. Under the window, on the floor, their legs outstretched and touching. Neither spoke. Savitha wanted to take his hand, but he was sitting to her left. She looked at her stump, resting on her thigh, though Mohan hardly ever seemed to notice it. Instead, he reached for his pants, took out his wallet, and said, "Here. I want to show you something."

It was a small photograph, and though it was creased and yellowed, she saw immediately that it was Mohan and Suresh, as boys. "How old were you?"

"Eight and fourteen."

She studied them: the too-long hair, the round eyes, the expression of irrepressible wonder on Mohan's face, tilted half toward his older brother, half toward the camera, his smile unabashed and absolute, and Suresh not smiling at all, but with an adolescent seriousness, or maybe an adolescent stubbornness, but still with his arm around his little brother, holding him close, though not too close. "Where's your sister?"

"She took it. We were on vacation. The only vacation we ever took. My dad wanted to show us Mount Rushmore. This was back when we lived in Ohio. '*That* is greatness, kids,' he said, 'when your face is chiseled onto the side of a mountain.' I don't much remember it. Mount Rushmore, I mean. But what I do remember is that place," he said, nodding at the photograph.

Savitha looked deeper into it, past Mohan and Suresh, and at the stand of trees behind them, and maybe a river or a lake in the near distance. "What is it?"

"Spearfish Canyon. We just drove through, but I remember it was perfect. It was the most perfect place I have ever been."

She stared some more. It didn't look like much; it didn't look half as awe-inspiring as Indravalli Konda. "Perfect how?"

He was silent. And then he shifted his arm and wrapped the fingers of his right hand around her stump, as completely and as naturally as if she, too, had a hand. "There is no way," he said. "There is no way to explain a thing that is perfect."

Savitha considered the photograph. "Was it like flute song?"

"What?"

"This place. Was it like flute song?"

A small smile played at the edge of his lips. "Yes. In a way, it was." Then he said, "I never thought of it that way. But yes, it was flute song."

"What is it called again?"

"Spearfish Canyon."

She broke the words down into parts and said them to herself. Spear. Fish. Can. Yon. Then she said them out loud. "How do you spell it?"

"Other side," he said. And when she turned the photograph over, there it was: written in blue ink: S-P-E-A-R-F-I-S-H C-A-N-Y-O-N. When she handed it back to him, he said, "Maybe we can go one day," and she nearly laughed. Why, she didn't know, couldn't say; only that she felt no joy.

10

She had been in Seattle for over a year. Sometimes, when Vasu drove her from apartment to apartment, they would pass the university, and Savitha would look out the window of his old beige car, at the waiting or the walking or the laughing students, and she would look especially at the girls. They were her age, sometimes older, and she looked at their skin, the fall of their hair, the slope of their shoulders, both of their hands, and she would think, What is your name? Where do you live? Do you live in an apartment I've cleaned?

If Mohan knew about Suresh and the room and the bottle of clear liquid, he didn't let on. He was usually silent, or he would tell her stories in English, or he would make love to her and then he would make her coffee. Even if they were in an empty apartment, with not a pot or pan in sight, he would run down to the corner store, buy instant coffee, boil water in the microwave, and then settle on the floor with her, drinking weak coffee out of a Styrofoam cup he'd found in his car.

Once, he had neither a pot nor cups, but the previous tenant had left a small plastic flowerpot on one of the windowsills. Savitha saw Mohan look-ing at it, and she said, No, that's disgusting. But he cleaned it out in the sink, and boiled water, and they passed it back and forth, the slight scent of dirt mixing with the strong scent of coffee.

Of course, she didn't tell Geeta or Padma about either Mohan or Suresh. None of them talked much about the brothers. But one night, after they'd found a bag of half-rotting capsicum at their door, probably left by Vasu, Geeta cut out the inedible bits and made a curry of capsicum and potato. They had it with rice, and then they had yogurt with rice, and as Savitha was peeling her banana, Padma said, "Where did you get that?"

She couldn't tell her the truth, and so she said, "Outside the door. Just like the capsicum."

They ate in silence, and after they'd washed up, they lay on their cots and Savitha heard a distant bellowing, and she said, "What is that?"

"It's for the fog. It's to warn the ships."

"Fog?"

A thick mist, they told her. Ships can lose their way. Savitha remembered the early-morning mist over the Krishna; she could've ladled it out like sambar. And then she thought about ships. There must be a port nearby, she guessed, and there must be sailors and captains and passengers and wonderful things from all over the world coming to that port. Like spices, maybe, or gold.

"Mohan came by earlier," Geeta said to Savitha. "He said he needed to take you to a job in Ravenna. I told him I could go, but he said no, it could wait."

Savitha was quiet, but Padma sighed into the dark.

"You should tell him," Geeta said, giggling as if she were a schoolgirl.

Padma turned in her cot, sighing again, humorless.

Their breaths deepened, and into the dark, Geeta said, her voice now serious, "What are you afraid of? I mean, hasn't the worst thing already happened?"

There was silence. Savitha felt for Poornima's half-made sari, wondering over and over whether she should hide it before she left in the mornings. Wondering *why*.

Padma and Geeta finally seemed collapsed into a restive sleep. But Savitha lay awake. Geeta's words broke through her thoughts; they held like a weight over the room. The night, too, was a weight. She wondered for a time whether she felt jealous, not of Padma, obviously, but of what was to come. Suresh, she'd learned, was married, but Mohan wasn't. She knew he would be, one day soon, to some appropriate girl from some appropriately wealthy family. She would be Telugu, and she would be charming. That, too, she knew. But she wasn't jealous. She'd known the conditions of their affection all along. Affection? No, not affection; but was it love? Maybe it *was* love, and that thought, as she lay on her cot on the floor of a run-down studio, was the one that saddened her. She turned away then, *physically* turned away from the thought, and faced the wall.

She thought of a story her father had told her, long ago. She'd been just a girl, and all day she'd played among the stunted trees near their hut, watched as the laundresses passed by, bundles of folded clothes balanced on their heads. It had been evening, and the chores had been done, and even her amma had come and sat on the ground, at the foot of her husband's bed, oiling Savitha's hair (there weren't any other daughters yet). In the story, Nanna had been Savitha's age, maybe even younger, and being the youngest and too small to start on the loom or the charkha, he was instead sent every morning to the milkman's house. Now, the milkman's house, her father told her, was almost four kilometers away, and there was no money for a rickshaw or a bus, so he had to walk.

"I was sleepy, always sleepy and stumbling along," he said, "but my favorite part was to greet the cows. They always stood waiting for me, their wet noses against their pens, and just then, just then the sun would come up and the tops of their fuzzy, funny ears would be all aglow, as if they were little hills, lit from behind. During the day," he continued, "it was a pleasant walk. Through the fields and toward the river. But in the morning, early morning, while it was still dark, maybe three in the morning, maybe four—so he could get the choicest curds, discounted for him because the milkman felt sorry for him, felt sorry that so little a boy had to come so far—the fields were awful. They were awful and frightening."

"But why?" Savitha asked, the scent of coconut oil mingling with the night air.

"Because I was just a boy," her father said, "and because it was dark, and because that's when all the fears come out: when you're a boy—or a girl," he said, patting her head, "and when it's dark. So anyway," he went on, "one morning I was on my way to the milkman's house when I stopped in my tracks. Just stopped, right in the middle of the path. You know why I stopped?" he asked Savitha.

She shook her head, her eyes wide.

"Because I saw a bear. Or a tiger. I couldn't tell, you see. It was dark, as I said, and even though I could almost reach out and touch it, even with my child's arm, I didn't dare. Who would? But it held me, it held me in its gaze. Its eyes were yellow, I could see them, and they didn't blink, or they blinked in the exact same moments that I blinked. At any rate, in that gaze, I was frozen. Absolutely terrified. And as I stood there, not moving, it stood there, too, not moving. Just stood there, gazing at me. Waiting to eat me."

Savitha gasped. "What happened, Nanna?"

"Well," her father said, "we stood looking at each other, breathing, unmoving, its yellow eyes slowly turning red. Orange and then red. And then more and more red. By this point, I'd found a small hollow near me, just a few steps away, and so I backed away from the bear or the tiger, ever so quietly, and I settled into this hollow. I would wait till sunrise, I decided, and then make a run for it. Or more likely, I hoped, it would leave and go back to the forest or the jungle or wherever it had come from. Besides, by then, I figured, the farmers would start coming out to their fields, and maybe one of them would have a stick to scare it away. Well, these were the thoughts going through my head, but mostly, there were no thoughts, just fear."

And then, much to Savitha's surprise, her father laughed out loud. "And you know what happened next?"

Savitha stared up at him.

"The sun came up. That's what happened. And then you know what happened after that? I saw that that big bear or tiger or whatever other monster I'd imagined was nothing but a tree. A tree! It was just a tree. A dead tree." He laughed some more. "It was the dark, you see. It was my imagination."

"So there was no bear? There was no tiger?" Savitha asked, a little disappointed.

"No, my ladoo," he said. "It was just a tree. Like most fears, it was nothing. Nothing."

Savitha lay in the dark and thought about that story. She hadn't thought about it in many years, but she thought about it now and realized: But my fears aren't nothing. My fears for my family, for their well-being, are real. They *are* a bear. A tiger. And if I were to leave—well, she couldn't even finish that thought. But why did I think of the story about fear on the very heels of thinking about love? she wondered. Was it obvious? Of course it was. She'd never known one without the other: she'd always feared for her father's health, his drinking, her sisters' marriages, her mother's endless days. And with Mohan. Well, with Mohan, it was even clearer—there could be no love *without* fear. The two had always been bound for her, she realized, fear and love, always, but just there, floating on the edge of wake and sleep, another thought drifted up, as if from the cloth that was tucked into her pillow: the thought that maybe there had been one exception. Maybe once, just for a short time, in her girlhood, they had been separate. For a short time (she was already snoring, beginning to dream), she had loved Poornima, and in that love, she had felt no fear.

Suresh came and took her to the room and then Mohan came and then Suresh came. Then Mohan came and they had sex in an empty apartment, and once in an office building. This pattern followed her around like a lost dog. Months went by. She once sat on the edge of the bed and watched

Suresh open a bottle of beer, and she said, "Can I have one?" He looked at her, astonished—perhaps that she had spoken at all, something she avoided, broken as she still was by him and the room and the bottle of clear liquid and the act—and handed her one. And so, yet another pattern: beer with Suresh, coffee or whiskey with Mohan. She found herself alone one night, in the studio, and could hardly sit still. She went from the window to the kitchen to the bathroom and back, and realized that what she really wanted was a drink. The thought stopped her cold. She stood at the window and thought about her father, about his destruction, and then she thought about the blind boy, and how she'd lain in her cot and stared at the locked door, waiting for him to arrive with the needle. She swore it off in that moment. All of it. And never again touched the beer or whiskey she was offered.

At the end of July, on a warm and cloudy afternoon, Mohan came to pick her up and said, "I have a surprise." They drove on a wide road again, this one next to the water, and then he parked on a busy street, between a blue car and a red car. She would always remember that: that he'd parked his black car between a blue car and a red car. The restaurant he took her to was the most colorful room Savitha had ever seen. The booths were bright red, cinema posters lined the walls, and the counter was blue. Blue and red again, she thought. When they sat down—Savitha still bewildered because he had never brought her to a public place before, and what was more, she'd never actually *been* in a restaurant before, ever, with or without Mohan— she looked around her at the other patrons, laughing and chatting, utterly at ease, and slid into the corner of her seat. She surreptitiously tucked in her blouse so no one would see how loose it was and concealed her stub under the table, and then she watched the happenings in the restaurant, the clatter and the conversation and the steaming plates of food going past their table, all with a kind of reverence, a wide-eyed wonder.

When the waitress came to take their order, she looked at Savitha with what seemed to her like ridicule, or maybe pity, and then she turned to Mohan. He ordered something Savitha couldn't understand, and when it arrived, the waitress set the shallow oval bowl down in the center of the table, between them.

Savitha looked at it. "What is it?"

"Don't you remember? I told you about it. It's called a banana split."

She looked at it, and there it was! A banana! "But what is that?"

"Ice cream."

"No, on top."

"Chocolate. And that's whipped cream."

"And that?"

"Strawberry sauce."

"Those look like bits of peanut."

"Yes."

"What about the thing on the very top?"

"It's a cherry. Have you ever eaten a cherry?"

Savitha shook her head, and so he insisted that she eat that first, and when she did, she decided it was the strangest thing she'd ever tasted. The texture like a lychee, but the taste more a sweet, syrupy alcohol. Then she took a bite of the banana with a bit of ice cream and chocolate and dipped the tip of her spoon into the strawberry sauce so she could taste all of them together. She also got a bit of the white, fluffy weightless substance, and it all took a moment, but then she closed her eyes. It was the best thing she'd ever tasted. Was it better than banana with yogurt rice? No, but it was more extravagant. It was hard to even think about both of them together. Yogurt rice with a banana was like life, simple, straightforward, with a beginning and an end, while the other—the banana split—was like death, complex, infused with a kind of mystery that was beyond Savitha's comprehension, and every bite, like every death, dumbfounding.

Mohan watched her intently, taking only a bite or two, and then he said, "It's hard to leave you, at times like this."

"Times like what?"

He didn't respond. He instead reached over and wiped a bit of chocolate from her cheek, and he said, "I have to go to the airport soon."

"Oh," Savitha said, hardly listening, focused on the banana split.

"Another girl."

Savitha looked up. She was listening now.

"A cleft lip, I think."

So another medical visa.

"Where is she from?"

"How should I know?"

"I mean, is she Telugu?"

"Probably. But we make a point not to know."

Savitha felt a rush of cold air. She held the spoon steady. "I don't understand. You make a point *not* to know?"

He lowered his voice to a whisper, though Savitha saw that there was no one seated near them. Besides, they were speaking in Telugu. Who could possibly understand them? "Otherwise," he said, "well, otherwise, in case of trouble—" He stopped, and then he said, "Not here."

So she finished the banana split and he paid the bill, and when they got back to the car, she said, "Are you saying—"

"Just that, in case of trouble, no one knows any of the other parties. No one can rat anyone out."

"So you don't know where—where this girl is coming from? Her village?"

"No."

"Her family?"

"No."

"How did your father get her, then?"

"There are middlemen. The world is full of middlemen."

"What about that old lady? The one who pretended to be my mother?"

"Not even her," he said. "Least of all her."

Savitha sat back in her seat.

Her thoughts whirled: I'll need money; where do I get money; and how, how will I leave; the little blue book; the little blue book; medical visas;

stupid, stupid, why didn't I pay more attention to signs, to roads, to English; a girl with a cleft lip; Nanna, you're safe; Nanna, you were right, it wasn't a bear, it wasn't a tiger, it was all in my head; should I tell Padma and Geeta, I can't, I can't; cleft lip; I remember someone with a cleft lip, that girl, the daughter of one of the laundresses, she crawled and fell down the well by accident, or did she; airport, should I go to the airport; banana split; death, being here will be death; the little blue book; idiot, why didn't you plan better; but Nanna, I didn't know, I didn't know it wasn't a bear, a tiger, not until now, not until sunrise, not until this moment, I didn't know.

Her thoughts whirled and whirled, spun in great gusts, and at their center, in their precise and perfect center, there was absolute quiet, and in that quiet, there was only one thought: I can leave.

11

She waited. She stilled her mind, and she waited.

The next time she saw Mohan was two weeks later. He came to an apartment she was cleaning, a studio like hers but much prettier, with fine wood floors and shining white cabinets. He made her coffee. She took a sip, waited, took another sip, and said, "Did you pick them up?"

"Pick who up?" He was distracted, fiddling with a loose faucet in the kitchen. She couldn't see his face, but she could see his hands, and she focused on them. "The girl. The one with the cleft lip."

"Not yet. Postponed. Some issue with the visa."

She watched his hands, and then she looked around the apartment. "This place is nice, isn't it? I wish I could live here."

Mohan turned to face her. He said, "I could try to get you in here. I could talk to Nanna."

Savitha nearly went to him. She nearly cried out. It is love, she thought, it is love.

Only a few days later, after she'd gotten home and was heating up rice, there was a knock on the door. She put the rice back in the pot, washed her hand, and went to answer it. Suresh. A pain stabbed her middle. When they got to the warehouse, Savitha looked again at the desk where Gopalraju had been sitting the first time she'd been here. This time the chair was empty, pushed in, and all the papers were piled neatly next to a big computer. The desk, she saw, had three drawers down one side of it. None of them had a lock.

When they entered the room, he kissed her roughly and then handed her the bottle of clear liquid. She rubbed it over her stub, and then she closed her eyes. She'd done this so many times that she could do it by feel. But behind her closed eyelids, there was a different vision. And in this vision, she saw a collapsed building. She couldn't see what had made it collapse, but she saw that not only that building, but all the surrounding buildings, and all the houses around the surrounding buildings, they were also collapsed. And it went on: beyond the houses, there were slums, and these, too, were rubble. And then followed the factories and the garbage dumps and the fields: flattened. She didn't know what had caused this collapse, all the way to the horizon; she didn't need to. She only needed to see the ruin, *know* the ruin, know it would never end.

When Suresh went to the bathroom, she slipped out of the room and rifled through the first drawer of the desk. And then the second. And then the third. Nothing. No little blue books. Where could they be? Anyplace. A million other places. Probably not even in the warehouse. She ran back inside, and when she did, Suresh was coming out of the bathroom. He looked at her, and then at the open door. "Where'd you go?" he said, his voice even.

"I heard a sound."

He raced past her and checked the warehouse and then outside. He came back and said, "Nothing." He eyed her suspiciously, sternly, and then he took two steps, to where she was standing, and slapped her, hard, and said, "Next time there's a sound, *I'll* check."

When she got back to the apartment, she sat on her cot for a long while. She listened to the night sounds: Padma's and Geeta's breathing, the swoosh of cars, the rustle of leaves, the burning of stars. Then she took out the remaining strip of Poornima's half-made sari and brought it to her face. She cried out.

Geeta sat straight up. "What? What is it?"

Savitha whisked it behind her. "Nothing. A bad dream." Padma didn't wake. She looked from her to Geeta, who'd fallen back on her pillow, and then brought it out again: even in the dark it was plain to see: Another piece. Gone. Now it was hardly the size of a towel. *Now* she understood. Now she knew. The pieces were a warning. They were a message. The pieces said: Stop. But how? How did they know? And how many pieces were left? How many till the last?

She looked at the cloth, as if for an answer. "From boll to thread to loom to now," she whispered into it. And then, "We're leaving, you and I."

She waited. She wondered about the blue book.

She asked Geeta in a whisper one morning, after Padma had left, "You need it to go places? What places?"

"How should I know?"

"You mean if Vasu can't pick me up. If I take the bus."

"*No*, not like that. You need it to get on a plane. To go to another country."

Savitha was astonished. Relieved. She looked at Geeta. "How long have you been here?"

"Five years."

"How old were you?"

"Seventeen," she said.

Savitha nodded. Around the same age I was when I met Poornima, she thought. And then she thought, But where will I go? Certainly not back to India; she didn't have the money. Or the blue book. But she didn't know anyone here. No one. Except—there was that one lady, the jilebi-haired lady, the one with the teeth of pearls. It was something, at least; *someone*. When Geeta went to take a shower, Savitha took out the white rectangle of paper and looked at it. Her name was Katie, Katie something. And under her name was a string of letters. No phone number, but there was an address: New York, New York. Twice. And to the east.

A few days later, she saw a young woman, with a kind face, coming out of one of the apartments, and she pointed to the string of letters. "What, please," she said.

The young woman looked at her, perplexed. "Excuse me?"

"What this?"

The young woman looked at it. "That's an e-mail address."

It was Savitha's turn to look perplexed.

"Do you have a computer?"

Ah. Savitha nodded, and thanked her.

A computer.

Well, she didn't have a computer, and she couldn't head west; Mohan said there was only the ocean to the west. And north, south? What was there to the north and south? She had no idea. But east. It would have to be east.

She began carrying Poornima's half-made sari with her. Every day. Mohan noticed it once, on a clear, cold day in mid-September. "What is that?" he asked.

"Nothing," she said, stuffing it back into her pocket. "Just something someone left in one of the apartments."

He looked at her, hurried into his clothes, and said, "I have to go. Pick them up."

"Who?"

"The girl with the cleft lip."

Savitha nodded. After he left for the airport, she took out the half-made sari, folded and refolded it, smoothed it with her one hand. She was now even more careful. Clutching it in her hand as she slept, never letting it leave her sight, even while she was in the shower. Still: nothing. Nothing. But she knew it would have to be soon.

On a Thursday evening, by now late in September, Mohan came for her again. He took her back to the park, the one overlooking the lights, the beads, and the band of water, and then he asked her what apartments she'd cleaned that day and took her to the one on Phinney Ridge. By now, she'd taught herself some of the street names and had learned to read a few signs, like Stop and Exit and Merge. Merge—she liked the sound of that one best. She'd also learned her numbers and how to write her name in English letters, and she'd asked Mohan how to spell his, and then she'd asked him how to spell Seattle. They hadn't gotten much farther than that.

She watched him now, in the kitchen, making coffee. She remembered the first time she'd seen him, and how he'd gazed at her cast, knowing it was false, but still with genuine concern and curiosity. And how he'd bought her her first American bananas. And how he'd wooed her, in his fashion, in this place. In the intervening years, though there was so little she knew about him—since most of his stories were told to her in English—she'd come to sense that there fluttered in him some fragile being, some lone and broken creature, beating its wings against some lone and broken heart. And if she had to guess, she would say he had no idea what to do with her either, with *this*. But that, too, was as it should be. There was no answer. He was raised for different things. Different ends. Things maybe even he didn't understand. But she? She knew what she was raised for, even with one hand, she knew: she was raised for the loom, the cloth, the magic of thread, the magnificence of making a thing, of wrapping it, like a lover, around your body.

And so it was—with hardly any hesitation—that she reached over and took out his wallet from the pocket of his pants. Why wait any longer? There was a little more than a hundred dollars, $112. Over six thousand rupees! It would certainly get her to New York. It would have to.

Just as she tucked the stack of bills into her pocket, she noticed lodged between them the photograph he'd shown her, the one of Spearfish Canyon. She considered it for only an instant before ripping it in two and stuffing the half with Suresh back into his pocket. And the half with Mohan, along with the money, into her own.

He dropped her off. Not this time, and never before, did they kiss good-bye.

She had to leave *that* night, that very night, before Mohan opened his wallet, before her love for him stopped her.

And so she did. She crept out of the apartment—after she was sure Geeta and Padma were asleep—and eased down the stairs. Nearing Vasu's apartment, she saw the crack under his door was dark. Still, she trembled as she passed it; her left foot landed. Her right. A creak.

The lights came on.

Savitha stopped; she held her breath. Footsteps. Go—go now. She bolted down the remaining stairs. She opened the front door with a crash.

She knew east. East, she knew. She ran.

Poornima

1

It wasn't easy for Poornima to get to shepherd the cleft-lipped girl to Seattle. That was what the Telugu word for it meant, *shepherd*. No, it was extraordinarily difficult. And required such meticulous planning, persuasion, and sheer ingenuity that she'd laugh to herself at times; with the effort I put into it, she'd think, I could've laid railroad tracks across a mountainous country, or built bridges across a watery one.

Most of the two years it took felt to Poornima like she was wasting time, precious time, time she counted out in minutes, seconds, but she knew she had to be still. It was stillness, she learned, that at times was the greatest movement. She would find Savitha, she knew that much, but she also knew that it would take enormous amounts of patience to understand what she *didn't* know. For instance, all she really knew was that Savitha had been sold to some rich man in America, in a city called Seattle. She didn't know where Seattle was, or how she would get there, or even what was required to travel to a place like America.

How *did* one cross the borders of a country?

Once Guru had revealed to her Savitha's whereabouts, Poornima did nothing. She waited. She knew that if she raised any suspicion in Guru's cruel mind—that she knew Savitha, or was looking for her—Poornima was certain he would sabotage every link to her and would turn Poornima out of the brothel immediately. So she waited a good three months—long, frustrating months—and then, very casually, on a hot, languid yellow morning, when even the fan seemed to stumble with fatigue, she looked up from her accounting books and her calculator, and she said, "A new cinema came out at the Alankar. I saw it last night. The crowd was a hundred thick. I saw one woman get pushed to the ground."

Guru barely nodded. He was chewing betelnut and reading a newspaper. "Another woman had her blouse torn off. The animals."

Guru looked up from his paper. He cringed, subtly, as he did every time he saw Poornima's face. No one ever got used to it, she noticed, not even she. It had healed completely, but the half that had been splashed by the oil was still bright pink, and against her brown skin, her face looked like a rotting flower. The entire left side was misshapen, hollowed out like a mine, revealing something too raw, too naked. But it wasn't just the pink, edged with an island border of white, the center cratered, dark, as if small animals lived inside; there was another aspect that was far uncannier. Poornima thought it might be her smile, and how it twisted her face grotesquely—children paused in their play and looked at her in fright—and so she stopped smiling altogether, but it wasn't that.

It was something else entirely: it was something beneath the face. Or rather, it was something *raging* beneath the face. It was a light, a fire. And it burned. Even as the hot oil on the surface of her skin cooled, capitulated, the fire within grew brighter. And that was what was truly uncanny, untoward. It was tragic to be a burn victim—oil, acid, dowry disputes, cruel in-laws, all that—though what was expected next was a humble, pained exit, feminine in its sorrow, in its sense of proportion. In other words, what was expected was invisibility. For the woman to disappear. But Poornima refused, or rather, she never even considered it. She walked down the street, she held her head high, she wore no mangalsutra, she had no male escort, she was iron in her purpose, imperial in her poise. And what was more, and what was uncanniest of all, was that all this, all this fire, began raging *after* she was attacked with hot oil.

Of course, Guru saw none of this. He saw only the burn, and the deformed face, and squirmed with discomfort.

"They filmed the songs in Switzerland," Poornima continued. "Switzerland! In the snow. That poor heroine, dressed in that tiny bit of cloth, having to dance and sing in the snow and cold."

"What did you say the name of the movie was?" he asked.

"I'd like to go there one day," Poornima said, sighing. "Wouldn't you?"

"To Switzerland? Why? Plenty of mountains here. I've heard there's some mountains two hours north of Delhi."

"I know. I know. But the mountains in Switzerland are different. Don't you think?"

"No."

She paused. "How would I get there, anyway?"

He turned back to his paper. "Switzerland? I guess you'd get a visa and a plane ticket, like everywhere else."

"A visa?"

"It lets you travel out of the country."

"How do you get one?"

"Well, you'd have to start with a passport first."

"A passport? What's that?"

Guru crumpled the paper down so that she could see his eyes, and he said, "Like anyone would let you into their country with a face like that."

"Just to visit. Just to see the mountains."

He groaned loudly, and then he explained to her what a passport was, and about the Indian government, and then about the visa, and about the Swiss consulate ("Wherever that is," he said. "Good luck finding it."), and then about how all this took inordinate amounts of time and documentation and photo-taking and fingerprinting and "Money! Most of all money. And that's *before* you buy the plane ticket, before you even get there. And from what I hear, Switzerland isn't exactly cheap," he added.

Well, Poornima thought, I'm not going to Switzerland.

Still, she was undeterred. And as Guru had said, she started by applying for a passport.

The months wore on. Poornima paid them no mind. She did her work and by then had rented a room a little away from the brothel, but on the bus route. Sometimes, she walked the five kilometers to work, and on the hottest days, or the wettest, she treated herself to an autorickshaw. She ate simple meals that she cooked on a small gas stove, shopping for the evening's vegetables on the way home and buying packets of milk, which she stored in her landlady's refrigerator. She used just enough oil to fry up the vegetables, never more. On Sundays, she walked around Vijayawada, looking into shop windows or drifting toward the Prakasam Barrage, or climbing up to the Kanaka Durga Temple. She never went inside. She once splurged and agreed to twenty rupees to take a boat ride on the Krishna. The boatswain was a lithe young man, not yet twenty, with coppery-bronze skin and the blackest and thickest head of hair she'd ever seen. He ran up to her as she walked along the shore, and said, "Look at her. Just look at her. Don't you want to sail on her? Doesn't she look like what life should've been?" He was pointing to the river, and with its sparkling waters, the sparkle even mightier because there were clouds darkening the waters downriver, the Krishna did indeed glitter like a gem, like a promise.

She talked him down from thirty rupees to twenty and climbed onto his rickety boat. "Did you build this yourself?" she said.

He laughed. She liked his smile. She liked that he looked right into her face and didn't once flinch.

He navigated to the middle of the river, and here the water suddenly turned choppy. She held on to the sides of the boat, while the boy pushed back toward shore with his long pole for an oar. The clouds were now racing upriver, and she watched as the billowing gray masses crowded above them, colliding and roaring like lions, and she said, "Hurry," and the boy only laughed, and said, "Are you scared?"

Yes, she thought, yes, I am scared.

The water now tossed them like a coin, and they landed with a thud, and then the first raindrop landed. On her arm, and as big as an apple. There was nothing else for a moment, the briefest pause, and then, as if the heavens had tired of playing, of flirting, they opened with a vengeance so sudden and so powerful that Poornima was thrown against the lee of the boat. She caught the sides, scraping her hands. The boy was now struggling against the pitch of the waters. His pole so curved against the current that Poornima thought it might snap in two. She saw his muscles, wet and taut. She saw his hair, dripping like a forest around his face. And both of their clothes, soaked through. She thought of her father in that moment, and she nearly laughed: I might drown in the Krishna after all, Nanna, she said to him. Just twenty years too late for you.

The boy finally heaved them out of the middle of the river and then pushed them toward shore. The rain seemed to abate, just a little, though there was no longer any distinction: her skin was as wet as the river that was as wet as the storm that was as wet as the sky. When they reached water shallow enough to see sand, she jumped out. She waited for the boy to drag his boat to higher ground and found that her fear had left an exhilaration, a lightness of body she had never before felt, and she tilted her face to the sky. The rain, the rest of her years.

She paid the boy twenty-five rupees, and his smile grew even wider, impossibly alluring, and she walked back through the wet streets, jubilant, though she never again took another boat ride.

Her passport arrived. She'd taken the blank forms to a local scribe, near the courts, and he'd filled them out for her. He'd then told her she needed to get photos taken and instructed her on where to submit the forms and the photos. She went back to the courts, months later, passport in hand, and searched the crowd of scribes for the same one who'd helped her before. "Now," she said to him, "how do I go to America?"

A visa, then. That's what she needed. The scribe had explained it to her, much more clearly than Guru had, and so she went back to her flat, deep in thought. She cooked herself some rice and plain pappu and had it with a bit of tomato pickle, then she had yogurt rice, washed up the few dishes, and sat down by the window. Her second-floor flat looked out onto a peepal tree, and beyond that, a man had set up an ironing stall. He was there on most days—thin, with a tired face, graying hair, his iron steaming with red coals, his long fingers dipping into a bowl of water, sprinkling it on the creases of shirts and trousers to crisp them, the edges of saris to smooth them. Poornima had watched him on occasion, but today was the first time she *noticed* him, how rapt he was, how completely consumed he was by the ironing—of what? What was that? A child's frock. It was a child's frock, and it utterly engrossed him. She watched him a little longer, watched him fold the frock, ever so gently, and then place it on a pile of already ironed clothes. He took up the next item. A man's shirt. Poornima then looked up and down the street. There was a cow at one end and a stray dog picking at some greasy newspaper thrown on the ground on the other; a rickshaw wallah was taking a nap on the opposite side of the street. A cool evening wind was rustling the leaves of the peepal tree, and there was the scent of something frying, maybe pakora, from one of the nearby houses. The sky was yellow, thick like ghee, as it cooled into evening, into night's blue mood, and Poornima came finally to see the unavoidable: that she didn't have the money for a visa. She'd used all the money and jewelry she'd stolen from the armoire to pay for the passport. She didn't even have enough for a tourist visa, and she knew no one in America who could sponsor her. That left Guru. And though she was infuriated, she saw no other option: she was far more dependent on Guru than she had imagined, than she would've liked, but she needed him now more than she ever had before.

She obviously couldn't tell him she *needed* his help; he would never give it to her. She had to appeal to the only thing he loved, and she lacked: money. Her opportunity came a few weeks later. She was checking a list of expenses for the previous month—routine odds and ends, like a new hot-water geyser for one of the brothels, the cost of repairing a gate that had rusted, and official payments like the one for a new phone line, and unofficial ones, like the bribe that had been paid to the telephone company administrator to nudge their application for the new telephone line—when she came across an expense that was huge, eight lakh rupees to be exact, but had nothing listed beside it. No name or company or even the initials of a name or a company. Poornima guessed it was a bribe to a politician; only that would explain the extraordinary amount and the fact that it was left blank and untraceable. When next she saw Guru, she asked, "That eight lakh rupees. From last month. Do you know who it was paid out to?"

He had come to check up on a new girl who'd just arrived. A farmer's daughter. The farmer had committed suicide, and the mother had sold the daughter to pay off debts. Poornima saw her only in passing, sitting alone in a room, hardly more than twelve or thirteen. Her face was round, and she wore a glittering nose ring. Poornima imagined that the mother had given her that small piece of jewelry, and that she'd said, Remember me by this, remember your father. But probably it was only a cheap ornament, a tawdry carnival item that had been bought for a few rupees. Though the glitter was real, and it made her face, in the dark room, glow like banked embers.

Guru was on his way to see her when Poornima asked him. He stood at her door, his teeth and lips orange from the betelnet, and said, "Oh, *that* money? Fucking Kuwaitis. They wouldn't pay a single paisa for the shepherd. Made me pay, the rich bastards."

"A shepherd? A shepherd for what?"

"For the girl."

Poornima looked at him. "What girl?"

"Look, can't sit here talking to you all day. You don't need to know."

"But I need to balance the books. Know expenses."

He glanced in the direction of the farmer's daughter's room and said, "On my way out." When he came back, twenty minutes later, his face was calm, and he smiled and said, "Usually, we split the cost with the buyer, but they wouldn't split."

By now, Poornima had figured out most of it: a young village girl, bought by some foreigner, certainly couldn't travel alone. She would clearly need a shepherd, someone to deliver her. But who were these shepherds? "Middlemen find them for us," Guru said. "Someone who knows English, obviously. Airports and all that."

"That's it? Someone who knows English, and they get eight lakh rupees for two days' work?"

Guru shook his head in disgust. "It's thievery, plain and simple. But you're not just buying two days' work, or English, what you're buying for eight lakhs is discretion. Or, shall we say, a bad memory."

Poornima shook her head right along with him. But her thoughts were elsewhere. English, she was thinking. English.

That very night, she rode the bus to Governorpet and asked around. There was a good English school on Eluru Road, the college kids told her, and so she got on another bus to Divine Nagar. She enrolled in a conversational English class starting the following week.

She thought about all the English words she knew, which were the same ones everyone knew: *hello, good-bye, serial,* and *cinema.* She knew the words *battery* and *blue* and *paste* and *auto* and *bus* and *train.* She also knew the word *radio.* Those wouldn't help her much. She knew the words *penal code section*, also from the movies, the ones with courtroom scenes. Those certainly wouldn't help her. She knew the words *please* and *thank you*. They might.

The class met three times a week, from seven to nine P.M. During the first class, they covered most of the words Poornima already knew, and some she didn't, and they learned simple sentences, like "My name is" and "How are you?" and "I live in Vijayawada." Those were all fine and good, but by the end of the week, they hadn't learned a single thing that would help her while traveling, in airports, or to function, even for one or two days, in a new country. When she asked the teacher about this, about when they would learn things like asking directions or reading signs in an airport or interacting with the officials at passport control (which the scribe had also explained to her), the teacher—a young woman who was a newlywed; Poornima could tell this because she wore a fresh, fragrant garland of jasmine in her hair every evening, and she looked at her watch constantly, and as it neared nine P.M., she would be flush with what could be only expectation, joy, newness—looked at Poornima curiously, averting her eyes from the scar, and said, "This is a conversational English class. You want the one for businesspeople."

"Businesspeople? Why?"

"Because they're the ones who travel," she said.

So Poornima transferred into the class for businesspeople. This class had five men in it, and Poornima. The teacher was a middle-aged man, maybe forty, with a prominent nose and an excitable manner. He would leap around the class like a grasshopper, explaining various words and their meanings and engaging them in conversation. By the end of the fourth week, Poornima was elated. She was able to have this conversation:

"What is your name, madam?"

"Poornima."

"What is your business?"

"I am accountant."

"I am *an* accountant," the teacher corrected her.

"Yes, yes," she said. "I am an accountant."

"How was your flight, madam?"

"Very good, sir."

"Did you fly from Delhi or Mumbai?"

"I fly from Delhi."

"I *flew*," he said.

"Yes, yes. I *flew* from Delhi," she said smiling, resplendent, unaware of the five other men in the class, staring at her face in horror.

The course was four months long. At the end of the four months, Poornima knew the names of major airports (Heathrow, Frankfurt, JFK), and she knew the words *gate, transit, business, pleasure, no, nothing to declare*, and lots of other business phrases she hadn't even imagined, like "In for a penny, in for a pound" and "Let's seal the deal" and "Bon voyage" (which wasn't even English!). She would walk home after class, or ride the bus, and speak to the passing scenes. She'd say, "Bird. Hello. I am learning English." Or she'd say, "Tree. Do you know English?" Once she saw a cat prowling around an alley near her flat, and she said, "Cat. You are looking thin. Drink milk." On the last day, the teacher gave Poornima a pocket-size Telugu-English dictionary for being the best student in the class. She received it in front of the other students—all of them still unused to the burn scars on her face— folded her hands, and said, "Thank you, sir. With me, I will take it America."

Once the class was finished, there was nothing more to be done. Poornima considered taking another class, an advanced class for businesspeople, but she didn't have the money to enroll, so she waited, saved most of her salary each month, and carried the Telugu-English dictionary with her everywhere, as if it were an amulet, a charm that would take her to Savitha faster. It did nothing of the sort. In fact, she had to wait half a year before she saw an-

other large payout. This one was for five lakh rupees. No name, no notations. She seized the opportunity. She said to Guru, "Another shepherd?"

He groaned. "They'll finish me, with their prices."

"How much do you make on the girls?"

"None of your business," he said, looking her squarely in the eyes, as
warning, as admonishment. The funds were kept separately, Poornima had
noticed, off the books.

"I was just thinking," she said, ignoring his look, "that I could go. Take
the girls. You'd only have to pay for the ticket."

"*You*," he said, and laughed, "with that face? And not a lick of English?"

"But I do know English."

"What?"

"I learned in school. In diploma college. When I learned accounting."

"Where are you from again?"

"Ask me. Ask me anything."

Guru didn't know enough English to ask her anything beyond "What
is your name?" and "What is your caste?" but the next day, he brought in an
English-language newspaper, *The Times of India*, and said, Read that. She
did, and explained that it was about two tribals in Jharkhand who'd been
beaten to death for being Christian. He looked at her, amazed. Apparently,
he'd already had someone, an acquaintance or a man at the newsstand, read
the article and tell him what it was about. "Diploma college, you say?"

Poornima nodded.

He was still skeptical, until Poornima started speaking to him exclusively
in English, convincingly enough for Guru, who hardly knew it, until he finally said, "There is this one girl. Going to Dubai. But you'll have to get a
passport."

Poornima jumped at the chance, hiding from him the fact that she already had one.

He warned her: This is unorthodox, he said. And then he corrected
himself: Actually, he said, it's not done. He took a deep breath. "We're
supposed to keep everything separate. So no one knows anything, all the

way up the line. But do this one, let's see." He chewed his betelnut. "Don't talk to her. Don't answer her. Don't have a *conversation* with her, you understand? You don't know her. And you especially don't know me. Who am I?"

"Who?"

"Exactly." And then he said, "I'm a stranger. The girl's a stranger."

"Okay, but who is she?"

"The farmer's daughter," he said.

2

They left the following month. The girl's name was Kumari and she was wearing a new sari, a fancy one that was yellow with a green border. Poornima noticed that she'd washed and oiled her hair that morning, powdered her face with talcum, and still wore the nose ring, still glittering against the russet of her skin. She looked like a doll, one that Poornima would see in the shop windows during her walks.

The story was that they were sisters, going to visit relatives, though with her scarred face, it was nearly impossible to tell Poornima's age. "I never even thought of it before now," Guru exclaimed, joyous at the prospect of saving the five or six lakhs he would've had to pay another shepherd. "You're perfect. Perfect. And you're so ugly, they might not be able to look at you long enough to ask all those questions."

Poornima hoped so.

Then he said, "You mention me, you utter the first syllable of my name, and I will kill you myself."

She nodded.

Guru even saved money on the train trip to Chennai, as he simply had his driver take Kumari and Poornima to the train station in Vijayawada and drop them off. Naturally, Poornima knew everything there was to know about the Vijayawada station. She bought the girl a chocolate bar at the Higginbotham's, glanced at the niche behind the magazine rack, and then boarded an overnight train to Hyderabad. From there, they took an airplane to Mumbai, barely a two-hour flight. Even so, it was the first time on a plane for both of them, and when they hit turbulence midway, Kumari looked over at Poornima, stricken, green like the green ends of her sari, and said, "Will we fall out of the sky?" Poornima looked back at her, thought of Guru's orders not to speak, and thought, What could it hurt? And though she, too, was terrified, she said, "Of course not. Planes are like birds. They never fall out of the sky."

In Mumbai, they boarded another two-hour flight to Dubai. When they passed through customs and immigration, their passports stamped with barely a glance, barely any questions, there was a man waiting for them in the arrivals meeting area—he was Indian, and humorless. He said there was a car waiting and led Kumari away. But just as the girl turned, the sun struck her face, shone against the nose ring, setting it ablaze. And it was then, with the small jewel spinning like a sun, that she turned to Poornima, and said, "Birds do. Sometimes."

"What?"

"Fall out of the sky."

Poornima watched her go, her eyes warming with tears. So that's how it can hurt, she thought.

She spent a few days in Dubai, at a cheap hostel, so that passport control in India wouldn't start asking questions. What questions, she didn't know, but Guru had given her dirhams and said, "Stay there. And don't talk to anyone." No one talked to *her*, so it was easy, and three months after she returned to Vijayawada, she took another girl to Dubai. Two months after that, she took a girl to Singapore. She also finally saved up enough money to register for the advanced English class for businesspeople. It was taught by a different teacher, another middle-aged man she didn't like as much, but she liked that there was another woman in the class this time, a stylish woman who wore skirts and jeans and who'd already been to many places, like England and America, on business. "What kind of business?" Poornima asked. "Computers," the woman said. Poornima had never seen a computer, or heard the word, but she was too embarrassed to ask any more questions.

Finally, toward the middle of the year, it happened.

Poornima, when Guru told her, sat speechless. She sat without blinking. She stared at him, her body suddenly weightless, exhilarated, and she thought of the night after the boat ride.

"Did you hear me? I know it's not Switzerland," he said, laughing. "But you might like it. Everyone else does."

America. Seattle.

They needed another girl. The girl they'd bought last time, Guru told her, was the hardest worker they'd ever seen. "And get this: the hardest worker, and she only has one hand," he exclaimed. Poornima nodded, hardly listening. She was going to America. She was going to Seattle.

"Savitha," she said that night, into the dark of her room, "Savitha, I'm coming."

3

The preparations for this trip were far more complicated than for the other trips. Much stronger rules, Guru told her. The girl Poornima would shepherd, Madhavi, had a cleft lip. Another medical visa, he added. Then he laughed and said, You two might as well be on a billboard for medical visas. Still, it took months to gather all the documentation, witness them, and submit them, and then to travel back and forth from the American consulate in Chennai. Even so, they rejected Poornima's visa initially, and she had to reapply for a tourist visa, which they delayed again, at the last minute, after they'd bought their plane tickets, so that now Guru had to pay change fees and a bribe to a consulate official, and he grumbled incessantly, but she knew it was still lucrative for him, even after all these expenses.

While they waited for the visas, Poornima slowly began selling away her things. She didn't have much, only a cot and the stove, some dishes, and a small suitcase she'd bought to store her clothes. She sold the cot for a hundred rupees and slept on the mat that had been underneath. She kept the stove for the time being but promised it to her landlady when she left. The suitcase, made of a flimsy, dented plastic, which she'd bought for sixty rupees at Maidan Bazaar, she threw out, and bought herself a new one. "Made for foreign," the man at the shop said, slapping the side of the suitcase. She carried it home, filled it with her few clothes, took out all the money she had in the bank—everything she'd saved since paying for the passport—hardly adding up to a thousand dollars, once converted, and put that, too, into a secret side pocket of her new suitcase, and then she waited.

On the morning of their flight, there was one final delay: Madhavi. She refused to come out of her room. There was no lock on the inside, but she had shoved a broom or a stick into the handle of the door, and rebuffed all their pleas to come out, or to let them in. Guru waited, cursing her mother and father, all the way to her great-great-grandparents, and when Poornima asked to talk to her, he said, "No. No, you don't talk to her. Your only job is to deliver her." But when, after five minutes, she still hadn't opened the door, he relented. "Fine. Talk to her. Tell her another five minutes before we break it open." As it was, Madhavi hadn't offered a word of explanation to the madam or the other girls, but when Poornima leaned into the door and said, "Madhavi, open the door. Open it. Don't you want to go to America? Everybody wants to go to America."

There was a slight shuffling, and then a whimper. And then a thin voice said, "I do."

"Then what is it? Come out."

"I'm afraid."

Poornima stepped back. Of course she was. She had no idea what awaited her in America. "Don't be afraid. I'll be there with you."

"But that's what I'm afraid of," she said.

"What?"

"You."

"Me?"

"Your face. It scares me. I had a dream, when I was little, and I saw a face just like yours."

Poornima laughed out loud. And then she grew silent. She said, "Madhavi," and then she stopped. She felt something rise inside of her, something bitter, something angry, and she spit out, "You fool." She heard the girl back away from the door. "You fool," she cried again, and heard the girl whimper. What a fool you are, she thought, fuming. What fools we all are. We girls. Afraid of the wrong things, at the wrong times. Afraid of a burned face, when outside, outside waiting for you are fires you cannot imagine. Men, holding matches up to your gasoline eyes. Flames, flames all around you, licking at your just-born breasts, your just-bled body. And infernos. Infernos as wide as the world. Waiting to impoverish you, make you ash, and even the wind, even the wind. Even the wind, my dear, she thought, watching you burn, willing it, passing over you, and through you. Scattering you, because you are a girl, and because you are ash.

And you're afraid of *me*?

She went to where Guru was waiting and said, "Break it down." When he looked at her uncomprehendingly, she said, "The door. Break it down."

They left in the afternoon, in mid-September. Chennai to Mumbai to Doha to Frankfurt. In Frankfurt, they waited five hours in a busy transit lounge. So far, Madhavi had avoided her entirely, wedged into the corner of her window seat and hardly speaking. She hadn't eaten on the plane, only picked at the food. When Poornima told her to eat, she said, "I don't like it." In Frankfurt, Poornima watched people coming and going. Travelers from all different places, hurrying home or away from home. The transit lounge had no windows, but Poornima raised her face to the ceiling and thought she could scent the mountains of Switzerland, she was so close. She then looked over and saw that Madhavi was staring at a display of pastries at the coffee shop near where they were sitting. She said, "Wait here," and went and bought one for her.

She watched the girl eat.

It was as deeply satisfying as if she were her mother, watching the way her eyes glistened when she reached for the pastry, how she broke off the sugary dough piece by piece, wanting it to last, and then nibbled the pieces with such pure and ravenous delight that Poornima nearly took her head in her hands, held it to her chest.

They flew into JFK in the dark early-morning hours, and just before they landed, Poornima leaned over Madhavi, sleeping now, and looked down. She saw a field of thick stars and she thought the plane must be upside down; how else could there be stars below them? But then she realized they weren't stars, they were lights, and her breath caught in her throat, her chest ached, to think a country could be so alight, so dense and dazzling. Once they landed, though, they were herded into a long line for immigration, and when Poornima reached the border control agent, all her English left her. She stammered through her responses, barely understanding the man's accent. She wondered if she'd even learned the right kind of English. He hardly seemed to notice her responses, though. He was bald, with the thickest shoulders Poornima had ever seen, and a stern face, and skin so white that Poornima could see the little pink pinpricks in his nose, and the blue and purple capillaries in his cheeks. He had the dainty rose lips of a baby, and Poornima thought his voice might be soft, but it was harsh, and deep, and he said, "How long are you staying?"

"Three weeks," Poornima said.

"Where you headed?"

Headed? "Pardon me, please?"

"Where are you traveling?"

"Seattle, sir."

He studied her face, and Poornima dared not look away, but she was suddenly conscious of her scars in a way she had never been in India. He stamped their passports and waved them through. The man at customs was the opposite of the man at immigration. He was so black he shone. Poornima could see the gleam of the fluorescent lights reflected in his face. He avoided her face, though, and said, "Anything to declare?"

This, Poornima understood. "No, nothing to declare," she said triumphantly.

They took a small train, and then, as they were walking toward their next gate, jostled and harried, people brushing past them rudely, Poornima slowed to study the gate numbers. The crowds and the newness and the enormity of glass and light and sound were overwhelming, but just as they neared their gate, Poornima stopped in her tracks. Madhavi bumped into her from behind, and some man in a suit gave them a dirty look. "What," Madhavi said. "What is it?"

But Poornima didn't hear. She was looking at a glass case. Overcome, broken, by the bowl of fruits on top. One of them a banana.

She stared at it. Could hardly believe its beauty. The perfect yellow of the sun. The biggest banana she'd ever seen, and yet flawless in posture. Arced like a bow, her gaze an arrow.

She spoke.

Look where I am, she said to the banana. Look how far I've come. We were in Indravalli once. Do you remember? We were so young, you and I. And the words of a crow were our mother and our father. Look where I am. For you. For you, I've come this far. I've lost no hope. I take this girl from slaughter to slaughter—because of that hope. Because it's made me cruel. But I have not lost it. Do you remember? We were children, you and I. And look at you now, unbendable and strong. Shaped like a machete, pointed at my heart.

She would've stood like that for days, but Madhavi nudged her, and two hours later, they boarded the last plane, the one bound for Seattle.

They landed in Seattle midafternoon. When they came out of the airport, Poornima took a deep breath and felt as if it were her first one in days. And though they had not been outside of the airport in New York, the air here felt colder and brighter. A car waited for them. Black and sleek.

Out stepped a man who glanced at each of them perfunctorily and then lifted their bags into the open trunk. He was handsome, Poornima thought, and though he was clearly Indian, he seemed unlike any Indian man she'd ever known. Too brawny, she thought, too sad. Though against his stature, his vigor, she imagined that she, with her burned face, and Madhavi, with her cleft lip, must look like circus performers, or carnival acts. And he their keeper.

They entered a wide road, and it reminded her of the road leading out of the airport in Singapore, and she realized, with something like awakening, like freedom, that this was the last road, the one that would take her to Savitha.

4

W hat's your name?" the man asked Poornima in Telugu, out of the silence. But no, it wasn't silence. Poornima realized in that moment that music was playing, from the car's radio, but the music had no words. It could've been a hum, carried on the wind.

"Poornima," she said. "And she's Madhavi."

He nodded, or so Poornima guessed, or maybe he was just hanging his head with that awful sadness he seemed to carry in his eyes, around his neck. "What's yours?"

His hand reached for the radio, and as he turned up the music, she saw in it such strength, such wholeness, that she almost took it. Held it in her own. And he seemed to sense it, because he looked over at her, and she saw in his face a fineness, a fallenness, that of great ruins, and he said, "My name is Mohan."

Immediately, Poornima could tell two things about him. The first was that Mohan was an alcoholic. The signs were all there: the eyes rimmed with red, the barely submerged anguish, just beneath the skin, the hands that fluttered, or hung limp and useless, not knowing their purpose without a bottle in their grip, the gray skin, the gray gaze, the gray, celestial waiting—for the next drink, for the next clink of bottle against glass, for the next ethereal rising. The second thing she knew was that his heart was broken.

And these two things, she realized, were her best weapons.

Besides, she understood, in this new country, that she had to confide in someone, and Guru had mentioned only three people, and even then, only vaguely. The first was Gopalraju, the patriarch, but Poornima doubted that the man who commanded this vast network of apartments and money and girls would in any way lead her to Savitha. In fact, he would most likely do quite the opposite. She'd also once heard a brother mentioned. But who was he? What was his name? Would he be beneficial? It was impossible to know.

And so she chose Mohan. They hadn't spoken any further on the drive from the airport; he'd driven her to a motel, brought her suitcase around to the passenger side, and said, "You'll stay here until your return flight."

Poornima remained in the car. "What a strange city," she said, peering out the windshield. "From the plane, the islands looked like floating banana leaves, waiting for rice."

He eyed her impatiently. "You coming?"

She turned her gaze to him, shook her head.

"You're not leaving *today*, are you?"

"No, my flight's in three weeks."

"Three *weeks*," he said, running his hand through his hair. "The shepherds usually leave in a day or two."

She watched his hands, the sorrow he held in them, as surely and as firmly as he would a glass, a lover. "They've been asking more questions. At border control," she said.

"On the Indian side?"

"Both," she lied. "But I have a thousand dollars. Is that enough for this place?"

He sighed heavily, marched to the back of the car, threw her suitcase into the trunk again, and dropped into the driver's seat. He looked at Madhavi in the rearview mirror—Poornima had hardly heard her breathe since they'd climbed into the car—and then he looked at Poornima. She couldn't quite decipher his expression. A mixture of curiosity, maybe, but also a vague protectiveness, she thought, perhaps from her scarred face and neck. She tilted her face imperceptibly to the left, to reveal the center of the burn. He studied her face some more, but he didn't seem at all to be pitying her, which she'd come to expect. Nor did he seem disgusted, to which she'd also become accustomed.

"I'm still monitoring you. Every day for those three weeks. Don't think I won't," he said, and drove them to a small, one-room flat in a different part of town, more residential, with peeks of dark blue water between some of the buildings. He and Poornima took an elevator to a flat filled with light, even though clouds were gathering to the west, which was the direction the apartment faced; it had wood floors and spotless white cabinets. She looked around the room and said, "Here? We can stay here," knowing Madhavi would never be allowed to remain with her.

"The girl comes with me."

"Where will she stay?"

"This is your first time being a shepherd, isn't it?"

She wanted to smile, but knowing her face contorted grotesquely, she only nodded.

"You'll need food," he said, looking around the empty apartment. "I'll get you a blanket, some dishes."

"Rice and pickle will be fine."

"There's a small store two blocks from here. Don't go any farther than that. They'll have rice. No pickle. You have to go to an Indian grocery store for that." He seemed to be considering that statement, and Poornima wanted to ask him where the Indian store was, but she knew he wouldn't tell her; her burned face was far too conspicuous to frequent a small store where the Indian community probably gathered and most likely gossiped. Who is she? they'd ask, and then look around for an answer. "Do you know English?" he asked after a moment.

"Yes," she said proudly, lifting her head, "I know English."

He seemed unimpressed, and said back to her in English, "I'll bring them over tonight."

What surprised Poornima was that there was no snow. It was the middle of September and she was in Seattle, and yet there was no snow. She'd heard endless stories over the years about how cold it was in America, and how the snow reached to your waist, and how the cars just went along anyway, slipping and sliding on the snow and ice. She had to admit that she was a little disappointed. Not only was there no snow, it was actually *hot*. Not as hot as Indravalli or Vijayawada, certainly, but it must be over thirty, she thought, opening the two windows of her one-room flat, fanning herself, taking off the thick brown men's socks she'd bought in Vijayawada, specifically for the trip, in anticipation of a cold country.

She was also surprised, by the time she returned from the corner store—with a small packet of rice and some vegetables and salt and chili pepper and a container of yogurt and a few pieces of fruit, along with a bar of soap and a small bottle of shampoo—that the country was so empty. In the two blocks to the store, she'd seen a few cars drive past and a plane overhead, and heard a distant honk, but there hadn't been a single person on the streets. Not one. Where were they? Did anyone even live here? she wondered. Did they all go to another city to work or to school or to shop? And where were the children? She'd passed a small park, but that, too, had been empty. It frightened her a little, the quiet, the emptiness, the loneliness of the streets and the sidewalks and the houses, standing so abandoned, built for people who never passed or never stayed. It wasn't till that evening, while she waited for Mohan, that she saw a few lights come on inside the neighboring houses, and every now and then saw a figure pass in front of a window; Poornima nearly whooped with joy to see them.

All through that first afternoon, though, she held herself back. She clenched her fists and kept herself from bursting out of the door and running up and down the streets looking for Savitha. Yelling out her name. What good would that do? None. She had to be systematic, and for that she needed Mohan.

He returned that evening with a sleeping bag (which he had to show Poornima how to use), a pillow, and a bag containing a pot, a pan, a few utensils, and some plastic plates and cups. Poornima looked at them, piled on the kitchen counter, and said, "How is the girl? Madhavi?"

He eyed her sternly. "Why?"

"I traveled halfway around the world with her."

"You no longer have anything to do with her," he said. "Forget it." He turned and walked to the front door. When he reached it, Poornima forced her voice to thicken, to break, and said, "They're loved, you know. You think they're not, because they're poor, or because they were sold, or because they have a cleft lip, but somebody loves these girls. Somebody longs for them. Do you understand? They're loved. You can't possibly know that kind of love."

He glared at her with what seemed to her like murder, and she blanched, falling silent, but then his gaze seemed to ebb in some way, and he said, his voice disquieted, "She's fine."

"Then show me where she lives. What could it hurt? Take me now, in the dark. She can't be far, can she? I just want to see."

She held her breath. She thought he would refuse again, but he looked at her for a long moment. "This once. Just this once. After this, shut up about it."

She didn't think it possible, but the streets were even quieter than they had been during the day. She rolled down her window, better to see the street names, but she couldn't make out a single one in the dark, or else Mohan drove so fast past them that she didn't have a chance to read them. The ones she did glimpse—with her limited English—just looked to her like a jumble of letters. So she began focusing instead on the turns he was making, the number of streets between each turn, and the slope of the streets and the look of the houses and the reach of the trees. Even flowerpots, on the edge of porches, she memorized.

Finally, after ten or so minutes of driving, they reached a narrow street that was long and lined with what looked like cheap apartment houses. He drove to the middle of the street, eleven houses in, on the left, pointed to a window on the second floor, and said, "There. See? The light's on. She's fine." Poornima, in the few seconds before he sped up again, noted every feature she could of the shadowed building: the tattered brown awning over the front door, the lighted windows, six across and each hung with cheap curtains, a tree with flat, dark green leaves at the edge of the building, one of its branches angled toward the window that Mohan had pointed out, Savitha's window, maybe, the branch twisted, trying to reach inside. Would it look the same during the day, or was it a trick of the light? She needed more. She looked for a star, any star, but the sky was now completely smeared with clouds. They were waiting at a traffic light, at the end of the street.

"Are the stars here the same as in India?"

"More or less," he said.

"So the North Star," she said, her voice relaxed, as if only mildly curious, making conversation, "it's behind us?"

"No, it would be there," he said, pointing ahead of them.

She said, Oh, as casually as she could manage, and smiled into the dark.

That night Poornima tried to sleep. She said to herself, You can't go out in the dark, in a strange town, in a country not even your own, in which you arrived all of ten hours ago, looking for one particular building and for one particular person in that building. So she tried to sleep. But she couldn't. She was jet-lagged, and the time difference between India and Seattle was twelve and a half hours, so basically, night was day and day was night, though Poornima didn't know any of this. She only tossed and turned in the sleeping bag, rolling some along the smooth wooden floor. Around three or four A.M., she began to doze, but she was jolted awake. She felt a sudden chill. What if Savitha had already been sold to another ring? In another city? What if the trail was dead? What if this was the end, and she'd lost her scent forever?

Her breathing became ragged; she got up and drank a glass of water. She went to the window. It was raining; streaks of water maundered down the glass. She remembered then, looking into the dark, the rain, something that had happened long ago, a few months after she and Savitha had met.

It had been the monsoon season. She and Savitha had gone to the market. It had been a Sunday, and most of the shops were closed, but the tobacco shop was open. Poornima's father had rolled the last of his leaves the previous evening, and so, before lying down for his nap, he'd told her to go to the market and fetch him two rupees' worth of tobacco. Savitha had arrived just as Poornima had been getting ready to leave, though both of them, of course, had been barefoot—Savitha because she had no shoes, and Poornima because her flimsy sandals (passed down from her mother) would've been useless if it started to rain, getting caught, or ripped, in the muddy sludge. Still, they had taken their time walking through the market— the sky overhead had been overcast, but there was no rain. Not yet.

Poornima remembered that they had stopped and peered into the window of the bangle shop, with its row after row of colorful glass bangles, a color to match every shade of sari. "Can you imagine," Poornima had said, breathless, "having ones to go with *every* sari?" Savitha had only laughed, and had led her past the paan shop and the dry goods store and the grain mill, all of them closed.

They'd entered the produce market, and the vendors had eyed them sleepily. They squatted on the ground, bits of dirty plastic tarp held at the ready, for the coming rain, to cover their heads and their capsicums and their squashes and their cilantro. They'd been able to tell that Poornima and Savitha had no money to spend—vendors always could. At one turning—as they'd followed behind a bullock cart hauling unsold produce back to the farm—a tiny round eggplant had fallen out of the cart. Savitha had squealed with delight and run and picked it up. "Look, Poori! What luck."

Yes, Poornima had thought, what luck.

They'd been nearly home when the rain had started. Poornima had thought they should run for it, but Savitha had pointed to a nearby sandalwood tree. She'd said, "No, let's wait under there." And so they'd huddled together under the tree's branches and watched the downpour. It had been a squall, and Poornima had known it would soon pass, but she'd hoped—in the way she'd once hoped that a handful of fruits and cashews would save her mother from cancer, from death—that the rain would last the rest of the days of her life. Why? She couldn't say. It hadn't made sense. But it was true: Even as they'd both shivered with cold. Even as their hair and their clothes had dripped with rain. Even as her father had waited, and she'd known he'd be furious when he saw the damp tobacco.

There had been a gust of wind then, and the leaves of the sandalwood tree had shuddered, and cold, fat raindrops had splashed down their necks and backs. Tickled their scalps. They'd laughed and laughed and laughed.

The rain had poured harder. Come down in relentless sheets. Savitha had put out her arm and drawn Poornima deeper under the tree. To protect her from the rain. At the time, Poornima had shivered and felt it to be true: she *did* feel protected, she felt safe.

But now, standing at the window of an empty apartment, in Seattle, holding an empty glass, Poornima laughed, half mocking, her lips trembling, her eyes growing hot, and she thought, How foolish. How foolish we were, how foolish *you* were, she bristled, to think you could protect me from rain. Against such a thing as rain. As if rain were a knife, as if it were a battle. And you, my shield. How foolish you were, how stupid you are, Poornima thought, nearly weeping with rage. With anger at Savitha's ignorance, her infuriating innocence. To find herself in this place, passed like a beedie between the hands of men. Don't you see, we were never safe. Not against rain, not against anything. And you, she railed, all you thought to do was huddle under that indifferent tree. As if, against rain, against my father, against what remained, all we had to do was stand closer. Stand together. As if, against rain, against fate, against war, two bodies—the bodies of two *girls*—were greater than one.

"You fool," she cried into the dark, and bolted out of the apartment into the night.

5

It took her more than five hours to find the building Mohan had showed her. She was soaked. She'd left her apartment a little before a muddled sunrise, and now it was nearly eleven o'clock. It had stopped raining, but she and her clothes were still damp, cold; she settled on the stoop of the building and waited. Of course, she knew Mohan would come to check on her, but her only strategy was to blink her eyes and proclaim innocence. "Oh," she planned to say coyly, "I didn't know I *had* to be here. It's my first time shepherding, after all."

In the first hour, only two people came out of the building, neither of them Indian. After the first person came out, she slipped in through the swinging door and considered knocking on every apartment, but when she snuck up to the top of the first flight of stairs, she peeked around the corner and saw an old Indian man sitting in a drab room, his chair tilted toward the half-open door. He was seemingly absorbed in the television show, but Poornima knew better—he was policing the stairwell. She abandoned her plan and went outside again. In the second hour, a man parked a small lorry in front of the building and came to the door holding a box in his hands.

He pushed one of the buttons and said, "Package," into the wall, and the door began to buzz. He went inside.

Poornima tried the same. She avoided the button that read 1B, as that was what the door of the Indian man's apartment had read, but she pressed the buttons to the other apartments. Most of them didn't answer or weren't home. One did answer, and Poornima, in her accented English, said, "Are you Indian, please?" The other end was silent for a moment, and then a woman's voice said, "What is this about? I just got a package."

Poornima sat back down on the stoop.

She waited until five o'clock in the evening and then started on the hour's walk home, made even longer because she got lost twice. She showered when she got back to the apartment and made rice, and when she heard the knock on the door, she knew it was Mohan, come to check on her. He hardly stayed five minutes; he scanned the room, and then her face, and then he left.

The next day, she was smarter: she took a packet of rice for lunch and got to the building at seven in the morning. She did this for three days, and finally, on the fourth, she realized she must be there during the wrong times, and so on the fourth day, she got there midafternoon and stayed late into the night. This time, she knew for certain that she would miss Mohan, and that simply pleading ignorance might not be enough; she decided she'd buy something on her way home, something she'd desperately needed, to show for her absence. She hoped it would be enough.

A car slowed in front of the building. Poornima crept into the shadows, away from the streetlights and the ones spilling from windows, and waited. She couldn't see the driver, but someone got out of the car, and as they approached the building, Poornima saw that it was Madhavi. She walked slowly up the drive, bent somehow from the last time she'd seen her. Poornima waited until the car pulled away, and when she revealed herself, feigning concern and delight, she saw that Madhavi's expression was grayer, more tired under the sallow bulb hanging over the entranceway, or maybe from the long day of cleaning. When she noticed Poornima, Madhavi's eyes widened. "Akka! What are you doing here?"

Big sister. She'd never called her big sister before. "How are you? Are they treating you well? Are you getting enough to eat?"

Madhavi shrugged. "Why are you here?"

"Come," Poornima said, hoping there was a back way, "let's talk inside. Have some tea."

Her face darkened. Her voice grew panicked. "No. No, you can't. No one is allowed inside. They warned us."

Poornima made her eyes go kind. She nearly smiled. "It's me, after all. Mohan showed me where you lived, just so I could visit you."

"He *did*?"

"Didn't he tell you? Anyway, how are you getting along? Do you live with other girls? Are they nice to you?"

She shrugged again. "They're all right."

"Are they Telugu? What are their names?"

Madhavi looked around and behind her. "I'm not supposed to tell."

"You act like I'm a stranger," Poornima said gaily. A car drove past, and they watched its red taillights disappear down the street. Poornima's vision burned with that red; she felt Madhavi shivering beside her. "Is one of them named Savitha?" she asked.

"No."

Poornima searched her face. "Are you sure?"

"I'm cold, Akka. I'm so cold. I want to go inside."

Poornima gripped her arm. "I'm no stranger; you know that, right? I may be the *only* one who's not a stranger."

Madhavi nodded and ducked into the building.

When she got home, after stopping at the corner store, Mohan was waiting for her. He was making coffee. "Where were you?"

"Coffee? This late?"

"Where were you?"

"How long have you been here?" she asked.

"Where? At this hour?"

"I needed these," she said, holding out a packet of sanitary pads.

"It doesn't take an hour to go two blocks."

"I stopped to rest at the children's park. Cramps." She grinned sheepishly, tilting her face just enough.

"No more going out," he said, pouring the coffee into a strange metal cup with a lid. "I'll pick up what you need from now on." He asked for the keys—both for the front entrance and the door to the apartment—and pocketed them. He then pointed to the pot on the stove. "There's some left. If you want."

There was enough for nearly a full cup of coffee, but Poornima saw, after he'd gone, that he'd also left his coat. When she lifted it, a small book fell out. She went through the other pockets and found only change, a few receipts. She looked again at the book. It was odd—unlike any she'd ever seen. After her wide, flat accounting books, this one was minuscule, hardly bigger than her hand. When she opened it, she found that none of the lines went to the edge of the page; they all stopped short, and each was spaced differently. How strange, she thought. Was it the Gita? No: this one had an author, and an English title. It was tattered, clearly read through many times, but one page in particular was especially frayed, dog-eared and worn.

Poornima turned to this one and began to read.

The next morning, after a long night's sleep—even after drinking the coffee—Poornima considered her options. She hadn't learned much during her time in Seattle, but she'd learned this: Savitha was not living in the same apartment as Madhavi. Madhavi had been scared, undeniably, but she hadn't been lying. So where was Savitha? She pondered that question; she'd pondered it for years. Mohan, too, she'd learned something about: she'd convinced him to show her where Madhavi lived, certainly, but she knew, just as she knew Savitha was here, *here*, that she could never—no matter how many lies she told, no matter how pathetic she looked—convince him to show her where any of the other girls lived.

And there was one other thing she'd learned about Mohan: she'd learned that he liked poetry.

She studied the dog-eared poem—called "The Love Song of J. Alfred Prufrock"—a few times and decided that she hated it. Or at least, she hated what she understood of it. The first few lines didn't even seem to be in English, though the letters were the same. And though she had no idea who Michelangelo or Lazarus or Hamlet were, the person writing the poem—presumably the man with the unpronounceable name in the title—seemed weak to her. Utterly feeble. Why was he writing the poem? Why bother? Why not just come right out and ask his question, whatever it was? Then no one would have to drown at the end. Regardless, she read it with great interest, wondering what Mohan saw in it.

When he came to check on her that evening, she held it out to him, along with his coat. "You left them here last night," she said.

He took them, seeming bewildered, and stuffed the book back into one of the pockets of the coat. Poornima waited for him to reach the door, and then she said, "It's about regret, isn't it?"

"What?"

"That 'Love Song' poem. The one you like so much."

He half turned; Poornima saw his grip on the doorknob loosen. "You read it?"

"Why not? I like poetry."

"You do?"

"I'm starting to."

He turned to face her; he took a step deeper into the apartment. "Somewhat. But it's also about courage," he said, after some hesitation. "It's about the struggle to find courage."

"And if we don't? What happens? We drown?"

He smiled. "In a way."

"You don't think this, this Puffrock is weak?"

In that moment, Mohan's eyes flashed with a sadness so intense, so violent that Poornima felt it—the sadness, the violence—flare against the back of her own eyes. Then it receded just as quickly as it had come. "I think he's just like you and me," he finally said.

Poornima looked at him. No, she thought, you're wrong. You're wrong. He's nothing like me.

6

Madhavi might still be able to help her.

That was what Poornima considered that night, after Mohan left. She couldn't be certain, but Madhavi, isolated as she was, as all the girls must be, might still have been taken to a different location initially—as a kind of holding cell, until space opened up in her current flat—or maybe the girls sometimes rode together, and she'd seen one or another being dropped off at various other apartment houses, or maybe the girls talked, or one of them mentioned a street, a neighborhood, *anything*.

It was her only chance.

She waited all the next day. Since she no longer had keys, she surveyed her own building and found an unlocked back way, by the trash bins, and she had to leave the door to her apartment open. She estimated that Mohan nearly always arrived between four and eight P.M. What did he do during the day? How many shepherds did he monitor? How many girls did they own? Did *he* know Savitha? She had answers to none of these questions; she knew only that she had to wait until after eight, after his departure, before setting out for Madhavi's.

He was late that evening. He arrived near nine o'clock, offering no explanation for his delay, and yet, in some way, he seemed more conscious of her, softer in the way he studied the room, her face, the disarray of the sleeping bag, her few things spread across the floor. It was as if their conversation about the poem had awakened in him the *possibility* of Poornima, the possibility of her existing as anything other than a purveyor of girls.

"Need anything?" he asked.

"Vegetables."

"I'll bring some when I come tomorrow."

"Stay for dinner."

His gaze darkened, perhaps with revulsion at the request, perhaps in surprise, though Poornima understood suddenly, very distinctly, as though after a clarifying rain, that here was a man who was very alone, who knew very little beyond that aloneness. He left soon afterward without a word.

It was after midnight when Madhavi was dropped off at her flat. Poornima waited again in the bushes, at the border of the apartment house in which Madhavi lived and the one next to it, to the north. This time, the girl seemed unfazed by Poornima's abrupt appearance as she passed through the thin light of the entranceway. Poornima looked at her and saw that there was no point in asking how she was doing; it was obvious that she had hardened. That in the space of a week, she had reached a slow and stoic resignation. A week. How little time it takes to sever the spirit, Poornima thought, if the spirit is disposed to severing. Above them, clouds obscured the moon, the stars; a nearby streetlight flickered.

Madhavi sighed. "Are you here about that girl again?"

"You met her? Do you know something?"

"Please, Akka, stop coming around. If anybody sees us—"

"Look, just tell me if you know where the other girls live. Any of them."

"I *don't*."

"They've never dropped someone off at another apartment house? You've never ridden with another girl? *Talked* to another girl? They've never taken you to another location?"

Madhavi shrugged and looked away.

"You have, haven't you? Who? Where does she live? What did she say?"

"Not another girl. Just . . ." Here Madhavi trailed off, and Poornima nearly burst; she clenched her fists to keep from shaking it out of her.

"Just what?" she asked gently, steadying her voice.

"Well, he took me to a room once. Different from the ones we clean."

"Where was this room? Were there other girls in it? Other people?"

"No."

"Who took you?"

"Suresh."

Who was that? Poornima wondered. The brother? They stood silent for a time, Madhavi avoiding her eyes. "Where was it?"

"I don't know. I don't know."

"Was it close to here?"

"No."

"Close to the airport?"

"No."

Poornima searched her mind for other landmarks, other sights that Madhavi might know. "Was it near that tower? That thin one? Was it near water? Or was it in the middle of the tall buildings? How about the college? Did you notice a college?"

"Akka, *please.*"

"Anything? Do you remember anything?"

Someone on a bicycle passed without seeing them. Wind rustled the leaves of the nearby tree. Poornima heard a dim and distant moan, coming from the direction of the sea. "There was something round nearby," Madhavi said slowly, forlornly, into the dark.

"Round?"

"Like a cricket stadium. But bigger. Much bigger."

How did this girl know about cricket stadiums? "And what else?"

"There were not many people. None. It was empty."

"This entire country is empty."

"And the buildings had no windows."

Poornima nodded. She would've smiled, but she didn't want to scare the girl. Instead she looked into the hushed shadows: the low clouds, unmoving, the streetlight, now gone out, the silent streets, the wearied face, the lifeless body. She recalled then the delight in Madhavi's eyes as she'd eaten the pastry—on that day in a wholly different life—the sugary dough crumbling between her fingers. Poornima took a deep breath, a deep American breath, and she thought, Such a quiet country, and yet so much to cry for. She could think of nothing more to say, and so, before leaving, before walking into the night, she said, "Be careful," knowing that care had already been squandered, that care—for this girl, for her journey—had already, long ago, been scattered and spent.

Poornima started early the following morning. She arrived at Third and Seneca, after asking no less than a dozen people how to get to the stadium, and waited for the 21 line. She took it to where she was within sight of the stadium, and then, not knowing where else to start, walked back to Third Avenue. On one side of the street were warehouses, and on the other were railroad tracks. She looked at the warehouses: no windows, and not a single person. But Madhavi had not mentioned railroad tracks, which Poornima guessed she would have had she noticed them. So she walked deeper into the rows of long, single-story buildings, all of them painted either gray or beige. She took her time, slowly reading the few signs on the outsides of some of the buildings, peering into the windowed garage doors. She kept close to the sides of the buildings, studied every car parked along them, and scanned around each corner. She knew she was conspicuous, even with her western clothing and a scarf draped over the side of her face to hide the scarring, but only Mohan knew her face—that was her biggest advantage. Besides, she concealed herself the best she could

when the few cars drove past her, knowing she could spot his car a kilo-
meter away.

She walked for hours. The maze of warehouses went on and on. Some of
the alleys between the buildings had no names, so Poornima would reach
the same warehouses from the other side, having walked in a wide circle.
She lost her sense of direction, so when she came into a clearing, she looked
for the tops of the downtown buildings to indicate true north. Two men
slowed—one in a pickup truck and another in a blue sedan—and asked if
she needed help. Poornima pulled the scarf higher across her face and shook
her head. She heard a freight train go by and thought suddenly of the train
she hadn't gotten on in Namburu. She thought of the torn pieces of the
ticket, fluttering to the ground. What if I *had* gotten on that train? she wondered. What would I have become? She was unused to such a thought—a
thought that had no end—and so she shuttered it, slammed it closed, as if
it were the door to a house that was haunted.

She left when the sun swung to the west. She was hungry and tired
on her bus ride back. It was possible she wasn't even in the right place, she
considered; it was possible Madhavi had meant another neighborhood
entirely, but it had now been a week since she'd arrived, and she had only
two left. She returned to the warehouses the following day, and every day
for the next four. It wasn't until the fifth afternoon, after walking for hours
through an increasingly heavy rain, that she turned a corner—along a gray
building advertising radial tires and other car parts—and saw it: she saw
the black car. It was Mohan's, that much she knew immediately, but from
where she was standing, she couldn't quite see the entrance to the building.
She walked the long way, around the massive warehouse that faced Mohan's
car, and emerged on the other side, hiding against one wall. She was now
closer to the door but farther from his car. There was one other car, red,
parked in front of Mohan's, and this, she guessed, belonged to either the
brother or the father.

She waited, shivering, in the cold rain, but not a single girl came out of
the warehouse or went in. At three o'clock, she returned to the bus stop,

knowing it was an hour's ride home. The rain picked up in the evening, after Mohan left, so she waited until the next morning—she bought a flashlight and thicker socks, and when she arrived, she saw that this time neither car was parked in front of the building. She tiptoed to its entrance and squinted to see through the darkened glass door. Nothing. She tried the flashlight and saw a few meters into what she guessed was a vast room, piled with boxes, and with the outlines of maybe a desk at the far end. There were no other rooms that she could see. She walked around the building, looking for an unlocked back way, or a loading dock, like she'd seen in so many of the other warehouses, but this one was only metal siding on all sides; she listened for sounds, voices; she thought she might try to break open the lock on the door, but as she stood examining it, a car passed along the adjoining alley.

If Savitha *did* live here, it occurred to Poornima, crouched against the side of the building, why would she be here during the day? She would be cleaning houses during the day.

That night, when she returned, the warehouse was even darker and quieter than it had been during the day. She knocked on the door, waiting for a light to go on. She walked around the building, slamming her fists against the sides. She tried to break open the heavy lock, and then the glass of the door, but it was reinforced, and neither the plastic flashlight nor the weight of her body did any good. Where was she? Where was she? Poornima stared at the door, gave it one last kick, said to the dark, unbreakable glass, "Not here," and left.

On the bus ride home, after midnight, she looked down at her bruised arms, her gashed elbows and hands, her broken flashlight, and realized the thing she had known all along: Mohan was her only hope.

She bought a bottle of whiskey—the most expensive she could find at the corner store—and then she spent the afternoon making rice and dal and eggplant curry (the fattest eggplants she had ever seen, and which cooked nothing like the ones in India) and potato cutlets, though the hot oil frightened her so much that she made just enough for Mohan and turned off the stove. But even with the scents of the food and the bottle of whiskey set out on the counter Mohan refused to stay for dinner. He left without a word, before she could think of anything more to convince him.

Poornima grew desperate.

She paced the small room, looking out of the window, up and down the street, every minute or so. She remembered, back on her street in Vijayawada, the man who'd been ironing the child's frock, and the sleeping rickshaw wallah, and the cows and the dogs poking among the small garbage heaps, and the vendors calling through the streets, and she was struck by a sudden and violent homesickness. She nearly bent over with it, but straightened her back at once. For what, she admonished herself, angry with herself for even this slight moment of weakness. For brothels and charkhas and men and mothers-in-law? Is that what you're homesick for? She smoothed down her blouse and jeans, unused to wearing them, and which, again, she'd bought in Vijayawada specifically for her trip to America, and took a deep breath: she recalled suddenly the one thing that had made his eyes flicker, the only thing, in the two weeks that she had known him, that had given him pause.

She left the whiskey on the counter, and when he arrived the next night, she said, "I won't drink it. You might as well take it with you."

He looked at the bottle and hesitated, and when he did, she said, "Who is Lazarus?"

"What?"

"Lazarus. From that poem. The one you like. Puffrock said something about being Lazarus."

His face softened. Or maybe it was only his lips that seemed to lose something of their severity, their density. "You remember that?"

"I've been wondering."

"He's from the Bible. Jesus brought him back to life, after he died. After four days, I think."

"Was he being tested? Like Sita?"

"No, I think it was Jesus who was being tested. Or maybe his believers. But not Lazarus."

Poornima looked at him. "Why do you like it? Because you think Puff-rock is like you and me?"

"*Proof*rock. And yes, and because it's such a lonely poem."

"You should open it," she said, nodding toward the whiskey.

This time, there was no hesitation. He poured himself a half glass of whiskey, the gold-brown liquid sending up the strong scent of deep forests and woodsmoke and something Poornima couldn't name, but recalled, maybe that thunderstorm, she thought, the one that had caught her on the Krishna. He settled under the window and placed the glass in front of him. He took a sip.

Poornima watched him. She thought he might leave after finishing the first glass, but he poured himself another. She said to herself, Wait till he finishes this one. Wait till the end.

When he did, she said, "Your days must be long."

His head was leaned back against the wall. He seemed to nod, or maybe she only imagined it.

"Are there other shepherds? What do you do after leaving here?"

"Homework."

"Homework?"

He avoided her gaze. "I take classes. At the university." He raised the bottle again and studied the label. "Where did you get this? I thought I told you not to leave the apartment?"

"For what? What are you studying?"

He laughed, poured another glass. "That Puffrock poem. Other poems, too."

"But—"

This he drank in one great gulp. "You can tell a lot about a parent from what makes them laugh. When I told him, middle of high school, that I wanted to study literature, he laughed for three days, and then he said,

'Engineering or medicine. You pick.' That's the best part of being an Indian kid," he said. "We get to pick." Then he looked at her sternly. "He doesn't know about the classes. No one does."

They sat in silence then, he against the window, she against the wall by the kitchen. Nothing stirred, not inside, not outside. Poornima shut her eyes. She could sense him watching her.

"These," he said into the dark, "these are my favorite lines from the poem: 'And indeed there will be time / To wonder, "Do I dare?" and, "Do I dare?" / Time to turn back and descend the stair'."

He went on to explain each of the lines, each of the *words* in meticulous detail, and about when the poem was written, and about how the time it was written related to the forces of fear and boredom and modernity, just before World War I, and he even told her about the author himself, and how he had been an immigrant, too, except to England, and Poornima wanted to ask about Michelangelo and Hamlet, but instead, she said, "What else made him laugh?"

There was silence again, and she thought he might be annoyed by her question, but when she opened her eyes, Mohan was asleep, the glass still clasped in his hand.

She had one week left.

Savitha

1

The bus was in the mountains when Savitha opened her eyes. She had
been dreaming of Mohan. Nothing in particular, nothing she could
name, not even in the moments after she woke up, but she had a sense that
he'd drifted through her dreams, without touching them, like a ghost, or a
scent. But then she was jolted from half sleep, and she looked around her
frantically, seeing clearly the road, the mountains, the strange faces. The
flight. Had there been footsteps behind her? She hadn't looked. She'd run
wildly from bus stop to bus stop, hailing buses just as they'd pulled away;
the third local bus that passed her opened its doors; Savitha said, breathless,
"New York?" and the driver had laughed and said, "Not quite. You want the
Greyhound. I'm going past the station, though. Get on!" At the bus station
in downtown Seattle, she'd stood and stared at a map of the United States.
She'd found Seattle, knowing there was only water to its west, and then
she'd looked for New York. Her gaze had traveled east and east and east.
Where could it be? She thought she'd missed it and started again. This time
she didn't stop, and there it was, on the other side, with only water to its
east. She'd said to the man at the ticket counter, "How much New York?"

He'd said, "Lady, first you gotta go to Spokane, and then you gotta get on another bus to New York." And then he'd said, "Thirty dollars."

She hadn't understood the first part of what he'd said, but she'd understood that the ticket to New York was thirty dollars. All that way for only thirty dollars!

She'd glanced at the doors to the station, clutched her ticket in her hand, and seated herself in a chair farthest from the entrance; her eyes never left it.

How long would it take her to get there? And what would she do when she did? How would she even begin to look for the jilebi-haired lady with the pearlescent teeth? None of these questions had answers, not yet, but once she was on the bus, pointed away from Seattle, and the fear and the adrenaline had stopped racing, and her heart had stopped pounding, she realized, looking out at the silhouettes of the pine trees and into the dark of the mountains, the road a bolt of cloth draped over them, that sometimes *leaving* was also a direction, the only one remaining.

They went over Snoqualmie Pass, though Savitha had closed her eyes again by then. Just before she did, the swing of the bus's headlights caught a clump of purple wildflowers at the base of one lone pine, as if it were an umbrella over the shivering blooms. They passed a long stretch of water on her side of the bus, but the water went on for so long that Savitha thought she might be imagining it in her disorientation, her near delirium. When she woke finally, near sunrise, the mountains were dark, blanketed with trees and farther away. The sky was steel-gray and thick with clouds. There was just enough predawn light that Savitha saw the young pine saplings all along the road, gray-green clumps that held close together and seemed to spin like dervishes in the early-morning songs of birds and wind and even the swoosh of the bus as it sped past them.

Savitha shifted in her seat, her muscles stiff, and she realized with a start that there was a woman seated next to her. Where had she gotten on? She couldn't recall the bus stopping, but maybe she had switched seats in the night. Savitha looked at her. She was fast asleep, her head lolling toward

Savitha's shoulder. She was as young as Savitha, maybe younger, with fingers littered with silver rings, all except one thumb and one pinkie. There was a tattoo in the triangle between her right thumb and index finger, a symbol Savitha didn't recognize, but it was a faint tattoo, a watery blue-green, and Savitha sensed, looking at the young woman's sleeping face, the fine lines around the eyes and the lips already forming, that she hadn't intended it that way, that she'd intended the tattoo to be a rich blue, a blue with density, depth, the ocean at night, but that it hadn't worked out that way. Nothing had.

The bus stopped near sunrise, and all the sleeping passengers were herded off. Savitha's first thought was that maybe they'd already arrived in New York. She'd gotten on at one in the morning, and it was now a little after six. Could it be? But then she looked at the sign above the main door: S-P-O-K-A-N-E. She went to the map again and saw that she wasn't even out of the state, let alone in New York. A profound tiredness enveloped her. At this rate, it would take her months to get there! She rubbed her bleary eyes and wanted to ask about the bus to New York, but the ticket counter was closed until eight. On the signboard, it listed only two departure times: one to Seattle and the other to a town called Missoula. She checked the map again; Missoula was to the east, Savitha saw, not by much, but east, and was scheduled to leave in two hours. Maybe she would have to take that bus and transfer again? She didn't know. She wanted to wait at the bus station for the ticket counter to open, but she saw that the coffee stall inside the station was also closed, and she was hungry. When she walked outside, she looked up and down, and then at every car in the parking lot; she looked for a red car and a black car and a beige car. The streets were dry and cold. It was a mountainous cold, one Savitha had never grown used to, and she pulled her sweater tighter around her shoulders. She'd stolen it, the sweater, from Padma, along with the small plastic knapsack, where she kept her remaining eighty-two dollars, the ripped photograph, a change of clothes, the white rectangle of paper, and what remained of Poornima's half-made sari. The fragment she'd wrapped gently in old newspaper and placed at the bottom of her sack. The bus station was a two-story redbrick building; outside was a row of trees like the trees that had blanketed the mountains all along the highway, and beyond the trees were some buildings, tall but not nearly as tall as they had been in Seattle. It was not yet seven A.M., but Savitha still saw a few people wandering around, not as if they were going anywhere, but simply wandering. That struck her as odd for such an hour, but they paid her no attention, almost as if she were invisible, and continued on their way.

In the parking lot of the bus station, to the right of the row of trees, a man leaned against a yellow car, smoking. There was a woman sitting inside the car, smoking as well, her arm resting on the open window, but neither talked nor looked at the other, like strangers, in fact, though Savitha could see that his thigh was touching the tip of her elbow. Another man was standing against the eastern wall of the bus station, squinting at a newspaper. She stood and watched the light of the sun emerge from behind the distant mountains and bathe him in its glow, his pale white skin turning a burnished gold. She crossed the street and walked in the direction of the buildings until she saw a restaurant. Savitha went inside and sat down in one of the booths. There was a menu resting on the table, filled with pictures, and when the waitress came, Savitha pointed to the one that looked like three little dosas, all in a row. She took a sip of her water and waited. When the plate arrived and she took a bite (with the spoon, fumbling, not knowing how to use either the fork or the spoon), she realized that they weren't dosas, not in the least. They were sweet! And inside them, instead of potato curry, was the same white fluffy, weightless substance that had been *on* the banana split. How odd. What a mysterious country, she thought, how small for all its vastness. But they were good, and she was hungry.

Before she left the diner, she bought a bag of chips, a bottle of water, and a package of what looked like little cakes.

She walked back to the bus station and sat on a bench outside, facing the row of trees but with a view of the street and the parking lot. It was fifteen minutes to eight, and she tried to stay awake until the ticket counter opened. She watched the drift of the low, round clouds rising out of the edge of the earth with the sun. To the west, the mountains, caressed now by morning light, turned pink and green and charcoal, the clouds above them also low, seeming to gather and gaze at those hills as if they were children. Savitha looked at the mountains and the clouds and thought, This is the most I've seen of this country. This is my widest view. And then she thought again of Mohan. A pain blossomed in her stomach and spread, thin and blue as ink, to her chest. She focused again on the mountains, the clouds, but they were distant and preoccupied. She concentrated instead on the street and the parking lot. At one point, a tiny swirl of tumbleweed rose into the air, spinning like birds. It was nearly transparent, whirling in the gust, carried by its own buoyancy and the slightest exhalation of wind. Savitha closed her eyes—just for a moment, she told herself—and fell into a light sleep.

She was woken by a car horn, or maybe a voice, and saw that it was a little after eight. She jumped up, cursing herself for falling asleep when they could be here, *here*, and ran inside, clasping her ticket stub. She went to the counter, held out her ticket, and said, "Hello, madam. When is bus to New York?"

The ticket lady, a black woman with crimson lipstick and silver glitter on her eyelashes, blinked, as if orbiting her two moons, and then she looked at Savitha's ticket. She said something Savitha couldn't understand. "Pardon me?"

The lady turned away and then brought out a chit of paper. On it, she wrote, *$109*. "But I have ticket," Savitha said.

The lady shook her head and said, "That's only to Spokane. *This* is the cost of a ticket to New York." She pushed the chit of paper toward Savitha, and she took it. Another small white rectangle of paper.

She walked out of the bus station.

Along the side of the bus station was a curved road, and beyond it, another parking lot. And beyond even that were yet more buildings and yet more parking lots. Savitha looked and looked at the endless, unbroken pattern, despairing, and then she noticed that she was still clutching the chit of paper in her hand, dampening it with the sweat of her palm. She threw it into a trash bin. The clouds, since the early morning, had fattened, and scuttled lazily eastward; Savitha watched them with envy. She walked with a lurch to the southern end of the station, and then to the northern. She sat again on the bench outside, listless, wondering what to do. Then she got up and walked again.

She walked for some minutes until she reached the edge of a river. Here she sat down on another bench and tried to keep herself from crying. She hugged her knapsack to her chest, as if it were the only hope left to her, and she realized, with something nearing heartbreak, that it was. She had no idea what to do, how to get more money. She'd clearly misunderstood the man who'd sold her the ticket in Seattle, and now she thought, Even if I hadn't eaten the sweet dosas in the restaurant, I still wouldn't have enough money. I never did. She felt a stabbing pain at the end of her stub, a phantom pain she had not felt in many months. She shook out her arm and considered walking some more, but her tiredness returned, more parched, depleted, so she merely sat and looked at the river.

As it neared midafternoon, more people arrived at the river. There was a jogger or two; one man was peeling an orange; a few mothers stood in a group, watching their children at play.

Savitha blinked as if waking from a deep sleep. She was hungry, but she thought she should save her chips and cakes. She didn't dare spend the money she had remaining. She drank water from a fountain and walked back southward, though away from the bus station; that was the first place they would look for her. She turned the corner. There was a long street, leading into a cluster of buildings. Cars were parked along the street, and as she drifted toward the buildings, she caught sight of the license plate of one of the parked cars. Savitha stopped in her tracks. She glanced up and down the empty street, then she bent down and read it again slowly. She was not mistaken: the letters added up to the words *New York*. She sat down, right there on the curb next to the car. What was she doing? She was waiting. What was she waiting for? Anything, she thought, I'm waiting for anything.

Her stomach growled. She succumbed and ate the chips and the two tiny cakes.

After an hour or so, an elderly couple came walking toward her. The woman was wearing pink pants, just past her knees, and a yellow shirt that read *New Mexico, Land of Enchantment*. All Savitha could read was the word *New*, and she counted it as a good sign. The woman's silver hair was curly and cut close to her head. She wore pink lipstick that she'd tried to match with her pants, but clearly hadn't, in a gauche way, and Savitha thought she must've always been so, even as a young woman, on the edges of beauty, at the very walls of prettiness, but never quite inside. The man was wearing a baseball cap and jeans and a checkered shirt, and they were obviously married. And had been for many years, since their youth, Savitha thought, noticing the familiarity, the distance, the dull ache between them. When they reached Savitha, they looked at her inquisitively for a polite moment, and then they saw her stub; they turned, suddenly self-conscious, hesitant, to their car. The New York car. The man took out a set of keys.

Savitha jumped up. "Pardon me, sir, madam. New York? You go to New York?"

They both looked at her again, befuddled, and then the woman let out a small whoop, and she said, "Oh, honey, this is a rental car. We're not going to New York. We're heading down to Salt Lake."

Savitha stood there and watched them.

"Show her, hon," the woman said. "Show her on the map."

The man brought out something from the glove compartment and unfolded it into a wide piece of paper. He laid it out on the trunk of the car, and all three of them bent over it. "Here," he said. "This is where we are." Then his finger traveled south and east, and he said, "And this is Salt Lake City. This is where we're headed." He looked at Savitha; Savitha looked back at him. She held her stub away, behind her back. But he seemed to no longer see her stub. He seemed instead to sense how confused she was, how crest-fallen, and, as if it would comfort her, he trailed his finger to the very edge of the map and said, "And this is New York."

They all turned back to the map, and by now Savitha had realized the couple was headed mainly south, not east. But she didn't want them to leave; she liked them. She could tell they were parents, that they knew a kind of love that was limitless and hopeless, both at once. She grew desperate; she considered, at the very least, asking them for some money, but was shy, em-barrassed, and didn't know how. And then, again with a rare kindness, the woman looked at Savitha for a long while, and said, "Maybe she can ride with us, Jacob. Come over to Butte with us."

He shook his head. "That's all mixed up, Mill. She'll be a tad closer, but Spokane's a better spot for her." He stopped and said, "What's your name, anyway?"

Savitha nodded and smiled.

He pointed at himself and said, "Jacob." He pointed at his wife and said, "Millie." Then he pointed at Savitha.

She smiled again, wider, and said, "Savitha."

"Saveeta," he said.

Savitha looked at the mountains in the distance, standing like sentinels, like guards against the east. The old man followed her gaze and said, "A tad closer is a tad closer, I guess; come along if you want to."

She turned to them. First to him, to decipher what he'd just said, and then to the woman. She was smiling. A little of the pink lipstick on her teeth. "Come on now," she said, "get in," and motioned to the rear door. Savitha stood for a moment, unsure what to do. She understood by now that they weren't going to New York, despite their license plate. She also understood, in that moment, her piercing aloneness, her billowing sorrow—she had no money, no food, and no road behind her.

She climbed into the backseat.

The couple chatted between themselves for some time. At one point, the woman said, "Where you from, honey?"

Savitha didn't understand what she'd asked, so she said, "Yes, yes."

The woman opened a bag of peanuts and offered them to Savitha. She could've easily eaten the whole bag, but Savitha politely took one and said, "Thank you, madam."

"Call me Millie," the woman said, and then leaned her head back and was asleep a few minutes later. Savitha heard her softly snoring.

The man drove in silence for a long while. They were in Idaho now, and the clouds grew thicker, huddled close against the horizon, and were laddered against the distant mountains, now to the east and to the west. The mountains themselves, Savitha noticed, were streaked with tendrils of blue and red. The valley between the bowl of mountains, the one they were passing through, was green and fertile and reminded her of the fields around Indravalli, fed by the Krishna.

The man popped a peanut into his mouth. He raised his eyes to the rear-view mirror. "Spent many of my days out here," he said, clearly talking to Savitha, though she had no idea what he was saying. "Fishing. The Bitterroot, Salmon, every little creek and stream. Spent most of my twenties and thirties back there in Coeur d'Alene." He pointed out the passenger side window. "Right there, right down there is Trapper's Peak. Spiked, like this." He showed her with his hands, his elbows guiding the steering wheel. "Can't look at it too long, though. It'll break you up inside. That's how some mountains are."

His eyes in the mirror were watching hers.

"What is your story, anyways? How'd you end up on that damn sidewalk? And how in God's name did you lose that hand?"

She met his gaze and then looked down. She liked his voice. She liked the way it summoned her, summoned even the uncomprehending, the wandering parts of her.

"I couldn't even take a guess. Not one. And what are you? All of twenty?"

She wanted to tell him something, maybe something about Poornima or her father or Indravalli, but there was nothing she could piece together that would've made sense to him, and so she was quiet, listening.

"Well, I know accidents happen. I know all about that. I've had my share. I could tell you stories. Boy." He stopped; he shook his head. Savitha's eyes lit up. She understood that word: *boy*. She began to listen even more carefully. "I got one," the man said, his voice rising. "I got a story for you. It's about a little boy. Little. I'll say he was about four. He and his mama and daddy lived in Montana. Just them. Just the three of them. His father was a ranch hand. One of those cattle ranches with hundreds and hundreds of heads. One of those ranches where you could spend an entire year just fixing the fences, let alone calving and vaccinating and culling and weaning. A big place. You get the idea. Well, one day, when this boy was four, his mama up and ran off. With some traveling salesman that came around, maybe, or a heavy machinery salesman. Hard to say, because immediately, before the boy could say boo, he was sent to live with his grandparents in Arizona. Tucson. His daddy put him on a bus, by himself, and sent him down to the desert. And you know what happened? I'll tell you what happened: the boy found his spot. He loved it, the desert. His grandparents lived in a little house surrounded by dirt and sand and cactus, no fences, and with a yard that ended far away, in a low range of blue and purple and orange mountains. Well, the boy couldn't get enough of it. He'd play, but mostly he'd sit and watch those mountains. He'd watch them so close it was as if he expected his mother to walk right out of them. Walk out, take his hand, and lead him away. Not back to Montana, mind you, but deeper into the desert.

"Some time after the boy moved to Arizona, his grandparents hired another boy to work for them. Older. A teenager. Just someone to come around and help with the chores. For instance, they had a detached shed that needed to be cleaned out. Out back. And they wanted help with building a porch. The sides would be braided thistle, to keep the sun out during the day, but open to the west, facing into the mountains and the sunset. They joked with their grandson. They watched him staring into the mountains—coming in only for the hottest part of the day, when the sun was directly overhead—and they laughed and they said to him, When that porch is built, we'll never see you again.

"Well, the teenage boy—let's call him Freddie—began with the porch. He built it in a couple of weeks, and then he moved over to the shed and started in on that. He must've seen the grandson dozens of times, talked with him, even answered a question or two the little boy had for him, but he'd never shown any particular *interest* in him. He was a teenage boy, after all, and the grandparents thought having a bit of company must've been nice for their grandson.

"And it was. It was. But the third week in, Freddie called the little boy over to him. It was just about sunset. The boy's grandparents had finished their dinners, and they were sitting out on their new porch with iced teas and smoking. When the boy walked into the shed, hardly any light coming through the door, Freddie coaxed him into a corner, took the boy's arm, and he said, Shhh.

"Well, you can imagine what happened next. And it kept happening almost every day for the next month. And during all that time, the boy heeded Freddie's words. He never made a sound, not one, but in the evenings, in the desert quiet, he could hear his grandparents, sitting just a few feet away on the porch. They'd laugh, they'd bicker, but mostly, they'd just talk of this and that. The weather, for instance. Or the cactus out front that had bloomed last year, but not this year. Or their small aches and pains, the ones that come with age. And the boy, from the shed, as Freddie did what he did, would listen with all his might. He'd listen to the voices of his grandparents. Although, to tell you the truth, they ceased to be his grandparents. They were just voices now, voices that he listened to with such intention, such *intensity*, that he slowly lost his own power of speech. He spoke less and less, and one day, toward the end of the month, he stopped speaking altogether. His grandparents were mystified; they never understood why. They thought it was from his mother leaving him and the move to the desert. But the boy knew why. Maybe not at the age of four, but later. He came to understand why: he came to understand that the most magical words, the only words that mattered, were the ones spoken by his grandparents. While they sat out on the porch—grown old now, their concern for the bloomless cactus, or the clouds, or the pain in their knees filling the night sky. Filling it like stars. You see, the boy knew, *knew*, even at the age of four, that he would never in his life sit on a porch as his grandparents did. He would never sit with another person and speak of small things. Or great things. Or even the most effortless things. And that *that* was what Freddie had taken from him. The boy knew this; the boy knew this as he knew those mountains, as he knew his mother would never come out of them."

There was silence. A silence so deep that when Savitha closed her eyes, she felt a warm wind brush against her face. Why is there a wind, she wondered, in a closed car?

"And you know what's most interesting," the man continued. "It's not what happened to the little four-year-old boy. No. He just grew up like the rest of us. A grown man by now." He paused; he seemed to Savitha to be studying the road. "Living somewhere, I guess. Mostly unhappy, like the rest of us, but mostly getting by. But you know what's most interesting? What's most interesting is what happened to Freddie. The boy who built the porch. He went off to college eventually—using the money he'd saved up from his odd jobs—and then, in one of his college classes, he met a pretty gal by the name of Myra, and they got married. After graduating, they moved to Albuquerque, and then to Houston. Freddie got a job at an oil company, paid good money, and he and Myra had three children, two boys and a girl. Before you know it, they had a five-bedroom house in the suburbs, and two cars, and eventually, even an in-ground pool."

The old woman let out a little snort, adjusted in her seat, and went right on sleeping. The man looked over at his wife and, as if he were talking to her, as if she were awake, he said, "Now, as I was saying, Freddie had three kids. Two boys first, and then a little girl. Freddie Jr. was the oldest boy, and he was his namesake, all right. Took after his dad, and did everything with him: they went hunting and fishing, threw the ball around. In fact,

Freddie Jr. got so good that his Little League team went to Williamsport one year. Well, one summer, the two boys, Freddie Sr.'s two boys, went to stay with their grandfather, Freddie's dad, and his new wife back in Tucson. He'd been widowed, you see, and had married a woman he met while golfing in Palm Springs. He still lived out in Tucson, and besides, it was only for a couple of weeks. So the two boys got on a plane, just the two of them, and headed to the desert. Sound familiar?" He let out a laugh, and then he said, "As you can imagine, it was boring at first for them. They sat around the house and watched television or played video games. Their grandfather, you see, had a large plot of land just west of town, but unlike the first little boy, these boys weren't at all interested. They found it dull. But eventually, a few days in, a boy about their age, a neighbor of the grandfather's, came over and the three became fast friends. He showed them how to have *fun* in the desert: how to hunt for Gila monsters and go sand sliding and dig for whiptail eggs. The neighbor boy only went home for dinner, and sometimes not even that. In fact, toward the end of the two weeks, Freddie Jr. and his brother didn't even want to go back to Houston.

"Well, on their last day in the desert, the neighbor boy came over, as he always did, and they wandered around out back. The grandfather and his wife were inside, making sandwiches for lunch. And right then—right when the grandfather was putting mustard on the slices of bread—they heard a huge explosion. I mean, massive. It rocked the house; it knocked the butter knife out of his hand. Frames fell off the walls; the lights swung from the ceiling. They thought it was an earthquake, or a bomb of some sort. But it wasn't that. It wasn't that at all. When the grandfather ran outside, he saw a huge plume of smoke rising from the edge of his property. The very edge, and he also saw flames. He ran at top speed, which, given his age, was remarkably fast. But they say that, don't they? They say in times of incredible strain, emergency, in times that require great acts, the human being is strangely capable of them: these great acts. But he wasn't fast enough. You see, the three boys had been playing with matches, and they had been near a propane tank. I don't want to be overly graphic, you understand, but they weren't near it anymore. The neighbor boy had second-degree burns; Freddie Jr.'s younger brother was also burned, but not as bad. But Freddie Jr. Now, Freddie Jr. had third-degree burns. The explosion burned away every layer of skin he had, and then it reached into his bloodstream, damaged organs. He was in the hospital for over two weeks, suffered terribly, and finally died of sepsis. He was thirteen. And his father, Freddie Sr., he was at his son's bedside every one of those days. He refused to leave, I mean *refused* to leave: even after the boy died, he just went right on sitting. He went into some sort of shock, they say. His hair turned completely gray in the two weeks he was at the hospital, and when he punched a hole in one of the hospital mirrors, a shard sliced a major nerve and he was never able to fully lift his right arm again. Of course, the grandfather was broken, too. He blamed himself, naturally. He died a few years later, but he'd died long before then. The surviving brother was never the same either. He refused to speak for the first couple of months after his brother died—does *that* sound familiar?—and when he finally did start talking, it was mostly to buy drugs."

The man was quiet again, in a way Savitha had never known: the silence a substance, water, the air in the car a lake of light.

The man smiled into the rearview mirror, but he didn't say anything for a moment. Then he said, "What is your name again? Saveeta? Well, Saveeta, I'm not a mulling man, but don't this strike you as—oh, I don't know—unnerving? All right, sure, sure, you could say these things were random, not at all linked, that life isn't *poetic* like that. Hell, maybe it was all the mother's fault. The one who ran away with the traveling salesman. But I've got my money on poetry. On its symmetry, sure, but also on its *inadequacy*. Its meanness. Its slaughter of lambs along with the lions. Everything of value. Don't you agree?" And then he stopped, and then he smiled again. "You're a pretty one, you know that? You're Indian, aren't you? You all brown up real nice in the sun. I've noticed that. Real nice. Yes, you do. Don't they, Mill?"

His wife woke with a start and said, "Huh? What was that?"

He laughed a little and ate another handful of peanuts.

2

They dropped Savitha off in the main section of Butte, Montana. The old man said, "Stay on the ninety. You got that? Ninety. That should get you over to New York or thereabouts." Then they each embraced her, the old man and the old woman, and they wished her well and gave her the remainder of the bag of peanuts. The woman waved as they pulled away. "Good luck," she said, the last of her hand out of the window waving like a flag. Where were they going? What was their hurry? They'd told her, certainly, but Savitha hadn't known what they were saying. She'd wanted to say to them, Maybe I can come with you, just for a while, but that, too, she hadn't had the words to speak. Where they'd left her was in downtown Butte.

She thought, They won't come *this* far, will they?

The town was ringed by mountains. She was on the corner of a sloping street, sloping down to the south and the west, and sloping up toward the north. To the east, which was where Savitha focused her gaze, there was another huge mountain. But this one, unlike the others, wasn't whole. Its face had been mined, skinned from the nose down, and all that remained was pink, exposed flesh, throbbing in the coming twilight. She turned away and looked along the sloped streets and saw that most of the brick buildings around her were shuttered. Her heart sank.

She ate one peanut at a time, trying to make them last, and wandered up and down the streets. She couldn't have known this, but many of the streets in downtown Butte were named after gems, minerals, metals, some shining thing that had once been hidden deep in the bodies of the surrounding mountains. She walked from Porphyry Street up to Silver. At Mercury, she turned and stood in front of another brick building, this one lighted. Inside, people sat on high stools and laughed and talked, and Savitha felt such a pang that her eyes watered. She saw plates of food, and tall glasses shot through with golden light, as if they, too, were mined from the hills. But standing outside, despite the heaping plates of nachos and buffalo wings and french fries, all she smelled was stale beer: cutting through the brick and the glass and the slope of the street, the stand and measure of her body, and reaching inside of her, through her. Suresh and the room and the bottle of clear liquid. She wanted to cry out, put her fist through the window, but instead she swallowed, pushed back bile, let out a smaller sound—that of an animal trapped in a distant cave, a faraway hollow—and hurried down the street.

At its base, she saw a sign. *Rooms, $10.*

It was musty, the sheets grayish and rumpled, not very clean. But there was a shared bathroom at the end of the hallway, and the shower was hot. She washed the clothes she'd been wearing in the sink. She hung them to dry by the tiny, dirty window in her room. She saw, in the falling light, that the mountains looked higher, closer, more sinister. There was something white and shining at the top of one, and she wondered if it was a deepa. When she slept, her sleep was dreamless, and she held the knapsack to her chest all through the night.

In the morning, she understood.

She understood that she had sixty dollars remaining. She further understood that sixty dollars would either get her six nights in a dingy room in Butte, hardly a third of the way to New York, or back to Seattle.

She took the room for another night, and then another.

At a coffee shop on the third morning, she sat down without a word on the round stool at the counter. She'd only eaten a prepackaged sandwich and a stolen apple on the previous day, and felt weak with hunger. The waitress passed by her a dozen times, though, without even a glance, until Savitha finally motioned to her, and then pointed to a little girl's plate of eggs and toast and sliced banana. When she returned with a glass of water and utensils, Savitha said, "Coffee, please, madam."

The man sitting beside her laughed. "I thought you was mute," he said, "and then out you pop with 'coffee, please.'" He laughed some more.

He paid his bill and left. The seat was empty until Savitha was almost finished with her toast, saving the banana for last, when another man sat down next to her. This one looked more stoic, she thought. He was old and black and his woolly hair was gray at the temples, balding on top. Savitha had never been this close to a black person before, and with each of their arms resting on the counter, she saw that they were nearly the same shade of brown. Her skin more yellowish-brown, and his more reddish-brown. The thought was a comfort to her, though why should it be? He saw her looking but said nothing.

He was eating from a plate stacked with what looked like uthapams, though these were only dough, without the onions and green chilies and tomato and cilantro. He poured a brown syrup on them, and when he caught her looking again, he pointed to her banana slices and said, "Sometimes I like some of them on top. Chocolate chips, if I'm feeling frisky. But not today. Today I'm feeling simple."

His voice was deep, with a slight, subterranean roar to it, somehow pained but mostly good-natured. He seemed to sense her pleasure at the sound of his voice. He said, "We're two fish out of water, aren't we? Out here. A black man, and what? Indian? Out here. Where you headed?"

She understood the word *Indian*. She smiled and nodded.

"You speak English? Enough to order you some breakfast, I know that much. Excuse me, excuse me, young lady," he said to the waitress as she walked by. "Can we get more coffee over here?" The waitress poured them more coffee, and Savitha was delighted, not realizing she could get another cup, grateful that he'd had hers filled along with his. "Rapid City. That's where I'm headed. You know Rapid City? I have a daughter out there. About your age. Nothing but a mess. A mess and a half. How did I raise such a mess? Her mother's white. Maybe that's what it is, but I don't know. She was just born a mess."

No, Savitha thought, not at all stoic.

"I'll tell you what, though. Not much else out there, but that Spearfish Canyon is nice. Only been once. She's not one to stay in a place long. But I'll tell you what: that Spearfish Canyon is something else. You understand me? I'm headed down on the ninety. You?"

Savitha's head shot up.

The man seemed startled. "You too? Where, though? Where to?"

"New York," she said, hardly listening. She knew those words; she knew the words *Spearfish Canyon.*

"New York," he guffawed. After some thought, he said, "Might be better off on the eighty, but this'll get you there eventually, I suppose."

Savitha nodded vaguely. The perfect place, Mohan had said.

"You got a car? Are you driving?" He motioned with his hands, as if positioned on a steering wheel.

Savitha shook her head. "Bus," she said, rummaging in her sack.

"Bus! Sweetheart, there's no buses to New York from Butte. Who told you there was?"

Savitha looked up; she sensed a crisis. And where was that photo? Where? She watched the man's face, wondering if hers, too, flushed darker with heat. She delved again into the sack.

"Might do better in Rapid City. You might. At least you're headed the right way. Might be able to connect up through Chicago. Eventually. Who told you anyway?"

There! There it was.

Savitha looked at him again, and it struck her that there was nothing as concerned as this man, not just for her, but for all girls of a certain age, maybe, or for those with a certain ache. She held the ripped photograph out to him and pointed to the back.

His eyes grew wide. He flipped it to the front, and then stared again at the back. "You know Spearfish Canyon too?" he asked. "You got people there? Why didn't you say so? I thought you said New York. Hell, Spearfish Canyon is on my *way* to Rapid." Then he looked, for the first time, or so Savitha thought, at her stub. His gaze didn't linger, nor did it turn away too soon. He handed the photograph back to her, took a sip of his coffee, smiled real wide, handed the waitress a twenty, indicating both their checks, and said, "Want to come along?"

Come? Yes, she nodded, yes.

On the drive out of Butte, stone spires rose up out of the mountains. Trees grew from sheer rock. Beyond, the mountains stretched out, flattened. The road curved past vast ranches and farms, and bales of hay dotted the land. Sunlight sparkled off the wheatgrass, lighting the very tips like candles.

"No," the man was saying, "no, I can't tell her anything. Not a thing. She knows it all, or thinks she does. Has since the age of two weeks, give or take. Half of her family is white. But the other half is black. And I say to her, I say, Look. Look what we've endured. What we've survived. You are a part of that survival. That endurance. I say, Your great-great-grandparents were slaves. They picked cotton in—"

"Cotton," Savitha said, smiling wide, suddenly listening.

"Don't smile like that," the man said. "Don't smile. It ain't shit. Anybody, and I mean *anybody*, says the words *cotton* or *plantation*, or hell, the word *ship*, you run the other way. You hear? You think you're not black, but when it comes down to it, when it comes down to cotton, you are. Everybody who isn't white is black. You understand? Now, like I was saying—"

Savitha looked out the window and watched the fields and the mountains and the sky. The ridges first softened as they drove east—the valleys like bowls of golden light—and then the peaks rose up again, muscled and towering. There is no way to explain a thing that is perfect, he'd said.

Toward midafternoon, the man stopped in one of the towns and split cheese sandwiches with her out of a cooler he had in the backseat. He handed her a soda, and then he unfolded a paper napkin and filled it with potato chips. She took it and began eating the chips one by one, but he signaled to her and said, "Like this." She watched as he disassembled his sandwich and placed a thick layer of potato chips over the slice of cheese, and then replaced the bread on top, and then bit into it with a loud crunch. Savitha did the same and after her first bite decided she'd never again eat a sandwich without potato chips tucked inside.

They were in Spearfish by late afternoon. The man stopped at a gas station, and he seemed sad. He said, "You don't have an address? A phone number? They'll pick you up, won't they? This is as good a place as any, I guess. Pay phone over there. Maybe your people can find you somebody going east. Maybe not *New York*, but east. You'll get there. You'll be all right, won't you?"

Savitha looked at him.

He took out his wallet and handed her a ten-dollar bill. "Get you something to eat," he said, and then he left.

It was not yet dark. She stood, undecided, at the gas station for a few minutes. No one pulled in or out, and so she walked to the corner and looked up and down the street. On the opposite side was a car dealership. There was a liquor store next door. There were low hills in the distance, dotted with clumps of trees and dry grass. Was *that* the canyon? On the opposite side, to the southwest, was more of the town, and so she headed toward it. There were brick buildings here as well, just as in Butte, but these were all open and unshuttered. Better maintained. Some of the buildings were freshly painted, she could see, and people roamed around among them, families, some of them pushing strollers or with older children running ahead of them. It seemed a nice town, one where night fell slowly and comfortably. She thought of staying in one of the hotels, seeking out the canyon in the morning, but they all looked expensive. One had a blinking sign out front that advertised rooms for $79.99.

She only had fifty dollars left.

Savitha turned away from the closed doors of the warm rooms. She was not yet hungry, but she knew she soon would be. With the ten dollars the man had given her, she went into a small shop and bought a banana, an apple, a loaf of sliced bread, and a bag of potato chips. She put her purchases into her knapsack and walked back toward the gas station, hoping to get back on Interstate 90 and to the next big town with a bus station. On her way, she passed a bank and a restaurant and a hardware store. She stood at the window of an art gallery and looked at each of the paintings. There was a sculpture in the center of the gallery of a bird about to take flight; Savitha compared it to the only other sculpted birds she'd ever seen, the sugar birds, and decided that they had been prettier. On the next block there was another art gallery; this one had a display of native Sioux quilts in the window. She studied these even more carefully—the thread, the bold colors, the integrity of the weaving, the patterns and the workings of the loom. So different from the saris made in Indravalli, she thought, and yet cloth just the same. She wondered who'd made them and how far the quilts had traveled to be in this window.

At a nearby park, she stopped at a wooden bench and carefully assembled her potato chip sandwich, making sure there were two even layers of chips, and then she pressed the bread down around the edges so the chips wouldn't fall out. She ate her banana next. She saved her apple for later.

There was more traffic back at the gas station. She didn't run up to any of the cars; she waited by the door, a little away, and spoke only to those who smiled or looked kindly in her direction. One woman, her short dark hair neatly cut, rummaged in her purse and then looked up at Savitha, smiling. Savitha smiled back and said, "You go canyon, madam? You go ninety?" The woman seemed to panic and slipped quickly into the gas station without a word. A few minutes later, another woman emerged from the station, herding her two children. The children were holding candy bars, and all three were laughing. "Pardon me, madam," she said. "Canyon? New York?" All three of them—the woman and the two children—stood and stared at Savitha's face, and then, all of them, all at once, lowered their gazes and gawped at her stub. Finally the woman said, "Sorry. I don't have any spare change," and hurried the children away.

Savitha thought she might have better luck with a man, so she picked an old man, his hair white, his face wrinkled and friendly. He looked at her and held the door open, thinking Savitha meant to go inside. "No, sir. No. You go canyon? I come?" The man's face was confused for a moment, and then closed in some way, Savitha thought, somehow slammed shut, and he said, "Do your business somewhere else, for god's sakes. Families come through here."

There was no one else for a long while. It was getting darker. She went inside and asked to use the bathroom. The large man behind the counter, with gray eyes and a suspicious stare, looked at Savitha for a moment, brought up a large block of wood with a key attached to it from under the counter, and said, "Out back," and then, "You Mexican?" Savitha smiled and took the key. When she came back, the man was busy with a customer, so she set the key on the counter, by the cash register, and left.

Now, along with the falling light, the wind had picked up. It wasn't particularly cold, but it whipped her hair, her loose clothes pulled taut in the gusts. She stood undecided, watching the road, which was empty, and the hills to the northeast, which no longer seemed low, but towering and severe. A truck pulled into the parking lot, but no one got out. She looked up and saw the first stars; beyond the pools of the gas station lights, there was only cold, unnerving night. She decided it was best to walk back into town and at least find cover in the small park. She gathered her knapsack and started past the gas pumps. The door of the truck opened. Two men got out. Savitha didn't particularly notice them, only saw that there were two of them as she walked past; she was chilled suddenly, Padma's sweater hardly thick enough to hold back the night. She'd cleared the farthest pump when she heard footsteps running up behind her.

She turned; she'd nearly passed through the last pool of light, but she turned.

3

The baby-faced one smiled first. His smile so genuine and carefree, his approach so guileless, that Savitha thought he might embrace her, as if they were long-lost friends. "Don't go," he yelled out. "Hey, where you going? Don't go."

"Let her go, Charlie," came a bored voice. Savitha then saw the second man, behind the baby-faced Charlie. The second man was bony, with a thin face and long hair, stringy and to his shoulders, and dark hollows for eyes. They came toward her slowly, but with an electric charge in their walk; she had the sudden impulse to run, and she nearly did.

But then, in the next moment, the baby-faced one was beside her. She smelled the alcohol, even before he grabbed her arm. "Don't go," he said, the words no longer a request but an order. Savitha tried to squirm out of his grip, but he tightened it and smiled again. "Look at her, Sal. She's a pretty little thing. You a lot lizard? Whoa, now. My, my. Feisty. My uncle Buck gave me a hamster just like you. When I was five. Shot himself in the head. Uncle Buck, I mean, not the hamster." And then he laughed, and then the man named Sal came up beside them, into the pool of light, and it was only now that Savitha saw it was not just alcohol, it was something else that drove them, that seemed a ruthless engine inside them.

"What's your name?" the baby-faced one asked.

Savitha understood the question, but was too panicked to answer.

"Where you from?"

Savitha shook her head. "No English," she said.

She realized instantly that it was the wrong thing to say.

Charlie's smile widened, though his face took on a quieter, sinister quality. "Is that right? No English? Hey, Sal, did you hear that? No English."

They all three stood like that, looking at one another, and Savitha, for the flash of the tiniest moment, thought the baby-faced one would simply let go of her arm, and she would continue on into town, back to the small park. But it wasn't true: something glimmered in Sal's eyes. He said, "Hold on, now. What do we have here," and then he said, "Lift up that arm, Charlie." It was her left arm, her stub, and when Charlie twisted it up toward the night sky, they both howled with laughter. "Who was it? Who bit your hand off?" Sal asked.

"I bet it was a tiger," Charlie said, still laughing, still painfully gripping her arm. "Don't you all have tigers over there?"

"Shut up, Charlie," Sal said, his face suddenly serious. "Come on. Get her over to the truck."

Charlie yanked on Savitha's arm. She jerked forward; her eyes snapped to the empty road, to the inside of the gas station, the counter. The large man who'd given her the key was turned away. She opened her mouth to shout, but Charlie was quicker: he slapped his hand over her face. Her head came to his chest, and his hand was so big that it covered her mouth and most of her eyes. He pushed her against the truck, and when the long-haired one opened the door, she thought they would force her inside, but instead, he yanked the knapsack from her shoulder. He rummaged until he found the money, then threw the knapsack into the cab of the truck. He then reached for something she couldn't see, closed the door, and said, "Come on."

"Where to?"

"You want Mel to call the cops?"

"But the truck."

"We won't be long. Let's go."

They dragged her to the back of the gas station. By now, Savitha couldn't breathe. She twisted her head this way and that, until a gap between his fingers let in air. She tried to bite and got the inside of a finger, but he yelled, "Goddammit," and clobbered the side of her head. Savitha's ears rang. "Will you shut up," Sal said, and led them to a clump of cottonwoods, a little distance behind the station. They entered the thickets, and within three or four steps came to a small clearing. Beer cans shone in the moonlight; a fire had once been built—she saw even in the low light that they'd been here many times before. "Let me see it," Sal said.

"What you going to do, Sal?"

"I said, pass her over."

It was now Sal who clenched her left arm with his own left arm, bony and cold compared to the baby-faced one's arm. He didn't bother with the hand over her mouth. Instead, he reached somewhere under his shirt, and there, in the moonlight, was something black and gleaming. He held the gun to her face. "You make a noise. One fucking noise. You understand that?"

Savitha stared at him, her thoughts stilled, her eyes wide. She was looking into it, but inside her—inside *her* was the long and dark tunnel.

"I said, do you understand?"

No, no, she didn't understand, but evil had its own vocabulary, its own language. She nodded.

"And you try to run. You try to take a fucking step."

She understood.

He let go of her arm; she stumbled back and fell to the ground. She hadn't even known he was holding her up. "Get up," he said, and when she did, he said, "Now go ahead. Put it in your mouth."

She looked at him, no longer understanding, and then she looked at the baby-faced one. And they stood like that, neither truly understanding.

"I said, put it in your mouth."

When she still stood, unmoving, not knowing what he wanted, he grabbed her arm again and shoved her stub against her mouth. It knocked her teeth into her bottom lip, drawing blood, but he kept shoving. What did he *want*? "Open it," he seethed into her face, his acrid breath greater than air. "Open it, and put it in." He pushed the gun up to her face, between her eyes, and she heard a click. "Put it in."

Now she understood. The whole night now a violence of understanding. The stars blazing like bullets.

He let go of her arm and took a step back. He waited.

She opened her mouth. She wrapped her lips around the stub.

The baby-faced one whooped with delight, but the long-haired one only watched. He nodded. His bony face white against the black of the gun, still held at the ready, pointed at her face.

After a moment, he lurched with irritation. "Not like that," he said. "Bitch, not that. You know better." And he reached over, grabbed her by the hair, and rammed her face into the stub. She choked on her own arm. Tears filled her eyes. He then pulled her head back up, and then back down, and then back up. "Like that," he said.

And so she did.

By now, the baby-faced one had unzipped his pants and was moaning at the edge of Savitha's blurred vision. She saw the movement of his hand.

But the gun. The gun didn't move. It was motionless in the moonlight, black, lustrous, untroubled, its feathers unruffled. It laughed.

You're alive, Savitha said.

The crow watched her, still laughing, in the silver and starry night. Its beak rose into the air, and there it stayed, its stillness mocking her movement.

They've taken you, haven't they? the crow said. They've taken you piece by piece. And this—*this* is the last piece. Now, in this clearing, with these strangers. I warned you, it said. I warned you all those years ago. In Indravalli. I said, Make sure they take you whole. But you didn't listen. You didn't listen. And now look at you. You are nothing. You are a girl. You are a girl in a clearing.

The baby-faced one let out a long groan, and the bony-faced one laughed, and the crow pulled back, opened its wings, and flew up and away, and Savitha followed it with her eyes, but the rest of her dropped to her knees.

And so it was: that the fabric of something she'd never understood, had never even tried to understand, was what had enclosed her heart, what had held it with its soft and wrinkled and cottony hands; it was *this* cloth that was now ripped wide open. The two men left her there, in the clearing, and she heard the turning of the truck's ignition and then the sound of the engine going up the road, becoming, at last, only the night. Silent and unforgiving.

But how was I to know? she thought, lying on the ground. How was I to know: that it was always this: always the boll to the loom to the cloth, and then, finally, and with such fragility, to the heart.

4

There was lightning to the west. She raised her head, and at first she smiled, thinking it a gathering of fireflies, synchronized in their mirth. But when she stood up, she saw the dark clouds racing toward her. Toward Spearfish. It was not as dark as she remembered. Was it morning? The thunder rumbled. It spoke. And then one drop, and then two. She lifted herself up, saw the discarded beer cans, the old circle of fire, and she wondered, Which way is east?

She straightened her clothes, but when she took a step, she crashed to the ground in a heap. Her legs were numb. And her mind was terribly empty.

Had she fallen asleep?

The storm was coming fast now. The thunderclouds racing across the prairie, over the Black Hills, into the Dakotas. She watched them with such interest, such longing, that they seemed as if they might bend down to her, the clouds, low and rushing, and carry her off in their embrace. But they paid her no attention and gathered ominously, growing darker and heavier with deluge. The lightning now struck from the west and the south, some from the north. Savitha watched it; the lightning her father's hands, reaching for her. Nanna, she said, was I ever the one with wings? But then the thunder crashed, and she stumbled out of the clearing, around the back of the gas station—the wind whipping around her, swirling with the strength of a sea—holding on to the walls, blinded as she was by wind, by rain, by sudden storm.

There was no one behind the counter. The key was where she'd left it.

She opened the door of the bathroom, saw her reflection in the mirror, in the light through the open door, and slammed it closed as she crumpled to the floor. And here, then: another clearing. Her money was gone. Her clothes were gone. The photo and the small white rectangle of paper were gone. Even the remaining loaf of bread and the potato chips and the apple were gone. But of all the things that were gone, that they had taken, it was Poornima's half-made sari that pinned her to the floor.

The rain started. She could hear it, clambering like little feet over the metal roof, hurrying on their way. To where?

East, she thought, east.

And what was there to the east? Nothing. Just as there had been nothing to the west.

She began to sob, and the sobs became a wail, and the wail became a low and gentle hum. She looked over, humming. Another toilet. It, too, was humming. She crawled over to it and put her arms around the cool porcelain. She smiled. But then the strong stench of urine reached into her head, cut her reverie with a knife, and it snapped her back—or was it the jiggling of the door handle that snapped her back? She didn't know, but she saw now that there was so little to be done. The single naked bulb above her ached, in its lonely, buzzing way. Her skin, illuminated by the bulb, shrieked with sorrow. Her thoughts folded and unfolded in pain. For it was here, under this white light and in this horrible stench, that Savitha realized how lost she was. How mislaid. How all the beacons of the world, standing all in a row, couldn't save her.

Poornima

1

It came down to this: her only chance of finding Savitha was to invoke her. Talking about poetry was well and good, but Poornima was running out of time, and what was the worst Mohan could do? Ignore her? Throw her out of the apartment? Deny knowing Savitha? Put her on an earlier flight back to India? Quarantine her until that flight?

None of those was worse than neglecting to use the last and only weapon she had.

That evening, she dispensed with preparing dinner, and when Mohan arrived, she simply handed him a glass. She waited for him to take his first sip of whiskey, pushed her gaze toward him, and said, "I became a shepherd for one reason. And one reason alone. To find someone."

Mohan studied her, nonplussed. He gestured toward her face. "Him? The guy who did that to you?"

Poornima hardly heard him. She spoke out into the room, dauntless now, insentient, and as if she were alone. "He doesn't exist for me. No, the person I'm looking for is my friend. Her name is Savitha. That's who I'm looking for, why I'm here."

Mohan seemed to shudder at something she didn't understand, and though his face was lost in the gray gloom of the far wall, Poornima felt his shudder through the floor, suspended in the air between them. Into that air, he said, "How do you know her?"

Poornima looked up. "She's from my village. The last time I saw her was four years ago."

He held his face against the light, away from it, as if they were locked in battle.

"Do *you*?"

"No," he said, and Poornima knew he did.

"I have to find her," she continued. "I need your help."

He swirled the whiskey in his glass. His body stiffened. He looked at the floor. "She left."

"What?"

"Two days ago."

"Two days?" Poornima felt a scream, a hot pulsing pain, rise to her throat. Two days! "Where? Where did she go?"

Silence.

"You have to know *something*."

"She took a bus. That's my guess."

"But to *where*? Where? These, these girls—they don't know anybody, any other places. They don't even know English. Where *could* she go? And without money."

Silence again.

Poornima's mind raced. Her plane ticket was through JFK. In one week's time. What was better, to stay here or to go to New York? What if Mohan didn't let her stay? What was the *point* of staying? When Savitha was gone? She knew, she knew already: if he made her go, she would simply walk out of the airport when she got to New York. And she would keep walking. Would anybody stop her? Could they? And even if they didn't, what then? Where would she go? How would she begin? Such a big country— how long would a thousand dollars last? No matter: she would meet her from the other end. And then she thought, enraged, She was here. She was here the whole time and I didn't find her. I was looking in the wrong places, walking the wrong streets. For *two weeks*.

"Money, she had."

She looked up at him, as if waking from a deep sleep and surprised to find him there. What was he talking about?

"What money?"

"She took it. From my wallet. Not much. Won't get her very far."

"But how far? Where?"

"And half a photograph."

"Where would it get her? Tell me."

"I don't know why she took *that*," he said.

"A photograph? Of what?"

"Some place I told her about. Me as a kid."

"What place?"

"Spearfish Canyon."

"Is that a city?"

"Near a city. In South Dakota."

"Where is that?"

"Midway. Not quite."

Poornima looked away, and then she looked back at him. "What did you tell her about it?"

Mohan shrugged. He said shyly, "I don't know. Nothing much. Just what I remembered. That it was a perfect place. That's how I remember it from when I was a kid. That it was perfect. That's what I told her. But then—but then she asked me the strangest thing."

"What?"

"She asked me whether it was like flute song."

"Flute song?"

Poornima's voice trailed off. Her face hardened into a kind of resolve, a purpose, a slow cooling, as of lava, a firming, as of the desert after a rain. And so it was: her face took on the characteristics of landscape, of natural forces, of tectonic plates and pressure and finding of place, of settling into a destiny. It no longer mattered: the logic of a thing. What mattered was the conviction in the pit of her stomach, burning its way through her body: Savitha was there. If she wasn't there, she was nowhere. And that Poornima could not abide. She had traveled half the circumference of the earth, and traveled all these many, many years. And for what? To miss her by two days? No. No, *that* she would not abide. Out of the darkness, she said to him, "I have one week left here. And then I get on a plane to New York. And you will never see me again. But I will pay you. I will give you my entire savings. Will you take me? Will you take me to this Spearfish Canyon? You don't have to, I know that. But will you?"

Mohan began to chuckle, but then his face pulled back. He was quiet. He eyed her with disbelief, but also with a kind of awe. "I can't. I have to be here. You know that. You're talking about leaving in a few days. I couldn't possibly."

"Not a few days. Tomorrow. Tonight, if you can manage it."

Now he did laugh out loud. But it was a sad person's laugh, not very deep, as thin and unconvincing as pond ice in spring. Afterward, there was silence again. They sat on the floor, facing each other, in a silence that was heavy, that hung like mercury. "You're not serious," he finally said.

She'd been wrong: She had one weapon left. She had the poem.

"These are the stairs, Mohan. She's two days gone. There is no time. There is no time."

The room spun. It spun like a charkha. He rose unsteadily, took his car keys from where he'd placed them on the counter. He said, "Twenty hours, give or take. Pack a bag."

2

They left the next morning. He picked her up at seven o'clock and they drove east. Poornima packed not just a bag but all her few things, as if she was leaving for good. They took Interstate 90, and Mohan explained the numbering of the interstates to Poornima, though they couldn't find much else to talk about. They drove toward Mercer Island, and Poornima thought they must be going the wrong way, going as they were over water, but Mohan told her it was right, it was east, toward South Dakota. They then drove over the dense, green Cascades, on through Cle Elum and George and Moses Lake, and then came into the eastern part of the state, the hills now spread before them like immense reclining women. At Coeur d'Alene, there were more mountains, these not as lofty as the Cascades, but sloping gently, forested on either side of the highway. The sky now, Poornima noticed, opened like a curtain, stretched endless and blue. Silver-tinged clouds, wispy at their edges, dense and gray at their centers, floated eastward. She pointed up toward them and said "Maybe rain." Then she said, "Lolo. That's a funny name."

Mohan seemed deep in thought, and the wordless music in his car, the same kind of music she'd heard when he'd picked them up at the airport, played on and on, and she grew drowsy.

They passed through Missoula and Deer Lodge and Butte and Bozeman. At Livingston, they stopped for coffee. Without ever discussing it, they both understood they would drive through the night. The sky clouded over some more, but Poornima looked into the horizon and thought she could see to the ends of the earth, its curving unto itself, feminine and aching. Cattle grazed in the far, far distance, sprinkled on the golden and green rolling grasses like strewn mustard seeds. Ranch houses and trailers dotted the hills at long intervals, set deep into the tapestry, and she thought them lonely, though defiant in their small conquering. They'd bought sandwiches at a gas station in Garrison for lunch, but for dinner, Mohan said they should stop, and pulled into a roadside restaurant outside Crow Agency. They ordered coffees, which were hot and had a thick, mineral taste. After she asked what various items on the menu were, never having seen the words *steak* or *meatloaf* or *burger*, Poornima ordered a grilled cheese sandwich and mashed potatoes. Mohan ordered a cheeseburger and french fries. They ate to classic cowboy songs playing on the restaurant's jukebox, and though Poornima was grateful to finally hear music with words, she couldn't understand a single one. They filled up again after dinner and drove on as the sky behind them bruised pink and orange and gray. Before them, the blue deepened, widened like water.

It was only then, once they left 90 and got onto the 212, that Mohan mentioned Savitha again. He didn't look at Poornima but spoke into the dark of the road. "What if she's not there?" he asked.

It was such a simple question, yet she had no answer. She could feel the fury moving up her throat. The frustration that she'd pushed back these last few days. All this way, and for what? Two days. Two days. She grimaced. What *if* she wasn't there? What then? She looked for her all along the highway, as they passed through towns, into the hills and the vast ranches, as if life granted such a thing. As if life granted such a thing so lovely and effortless and miraculous as seeing Savitha standing on the crest of a hill, or ambling along the street in one of those small towns. "I don't know," she said, and she didn't know: in this whole wide world, after all this searching, she no longer had a place to begin.

She began to cry then. She hadn't cried in years, but now she began to cry. As if all the ravening of all her years had, in that moment, come down upon her. She choked for breath, sobbed. "I don't know," she said, unable to stop the tears, and buried her head in her hands. She felt Mohan's hand on her arm, and he held it like that until she raised her head, wiped her tears.

"She couldn't have gone much farther," he said.

"How do you know?"

He paused, still staring unblinking at the road. "Because I only had about a hundred dollars in my wallet."

Poornima looked at him. She wiped away tears. The wind, howling past the car, ceased.

"And she had to have gone east."

"Why?"

"Or south."

"What about the others?"

"Puget Sound is to the west. Maybe there, but probably not. Water is too uncertain. And Canada's difficult without a passport."

She didn't take her eyes from him. "You've given this some thought."

"No," he said, smiling weakly. "None at all."

After the Crow and the Northern Cheyenne reservations, the road veered south-southeast toward a town called Broadus. They were nearly there. Hardly two more hours, Mohan said. "We'll wait till morning," he added, "to go to the canyon."

Poornima turned. "Morning? No, as soon as we get there."

"What's the point? It'll be dark."

"Dark is the past four years," she said.

Mohan shook his head. The first stars blinked awake, though Poornima only glimpsed them through passing clouds, gathering heavily to the east and south. There was a flash of lightning far to the south. It was after midnight when they neared Spearfish. "Are we almost there?" she said, needing to use the bathroom.

"Just a few more miles," he said.

When they reached the outskirts of Spearfish, she saw a gas station. "There," she said. "Stop there."

The lights of the town shone in the distance. And then, she knew, was the canyon.

He pulled in, and Poornima jumped out of the car. A storm was coming. The lightning was close now. There were no more stars. She felt the gray dense weight of the clouds, hanging above yet close to the earth. For now, they held their rain, crouched in place.

She glanced up again and then sprinted into the gas station. The man behind the counter rested his thick forearms on the counter. His left one had a tattoo of a woman in a short dress, kicking up her long legs, reclined in a martini glass. Poornima looked at it, and then at his gold chain. She scanned the room. She didn't see a bathroom. "Pardon me, please."

"Around back," he said, turning away, clearly disgusted by her face. "Might want to wait, though. Some Mexican gal's in there now."

Poornima understood that the bathroom was outside the building and raced out of the door. "And bring that key back," he yelled after her. When she got outside, she tried the handle, but it was locked. She looked around, waiting. She could no longer see Mohan or the car, but she heard it idling. Across the street was an auto repair shop. Next door to the gas station seemed to be some sort of warehouse. The storm clouds were overhead now. The wind lifted her hair, swirled the strands in great and roguish kites. A drop of rain landed near her foot, and then another on her head.

She jiggled the handle some more.

There was a flash of lightning. The gas station went white, bright as bone, and then, as if a light had been switched off: black.

Car lights swung like a cradle. She squinted when they swept over her.

She shivered, to be so exhausted, so alive. A car pulled up. It was Mohan. He rolled down the window and yelled out, "Looked at the map. We're close."

"How close?"

"Just southeast of here." He smiled. "You've been waiting this whole time?"

The clouds thundered. They both looked up at the boom. Then, in that instant, the clouds broke, and the rain poured down. She raised her face to it, cooling all the fires.

"All this time?"

She nodded. She looked at Mohan. He was shaking his head and laughing. The world felt so slick, as though it had washed over and out of her: time, the organs weighted with hunger, the memory of a slippery hand, holding yogurt rice and banana to her starved lips. Finally the handle of the bathroom door turned. She smiled, suddenly shy, as if she and Mohan were two lovers, come upon each other in a grove, in a garden, under summer showers.

"Not much longer," she said.

Acknowledgments

My gratitude to:

Amy Einhorn, Caroline Bleeke, Sandra Dijkstra, Elise Capron, Amelia Possanza, Conor Mintzer, Ursula Doyle, Rhiannon Smith, Rick Simonson, Charlie Jane Anders, Nancy Jo Hart, Theresa Schaefer, Nichole Hasbrouck, Sierra Golden, Mad V. Dog, Dena Afrasiabi, Jim Ambrose, Sharon Vinick, Arie Grossman, Elizabeth Colen, Hedgebrook, the Helene Wurlitzer Foundation, Lakshmi and Ramarao Inguva, Sridevi, Venkat, Siriveena, and Sami Nandam, Kamala and Singiresu S. Rao, and the ones who stood with me on the prairie: Abraham Smith, Srinivas Inguva, and Number 194.

My deepest gratitude to:

Barbara and Adam Bad Wound, for the Badlands.

Recommend *Girls Burn Brighter* for your next book club!

Reading Group Guide available at

www.readinggroupgold.com

W9-BRX-291

MCSD
Self-Paced Training Kit

ANALYZING REQUIREMENTS AND DEFINING
MICROSOFT® .NET
SOLUTION ARCHITECTURES

Exam 70-300

PUBLISHED BY
Microsoft Press
A Division of Microsoft Corporation
One Microsoft Way
Redmond, Washington 98052-6399

Library of Congress Cataloging-in-Publication Data pending.

Printed and bound in the United States of America.

1 2 3 4 5 6 7 8 9   QWT   8 7 6 5 4 3

Distributed in Canada by H.B. Fenn and Company Ltd.

A CIP catalogue record for this book is available from the British Library.

Microsoft Press books are available through booksellers and distributors worldwide. For further information about international editions, contact your local Microsoft Corporation office or contact Microsoft Press International directly at fax (425) 936-7329. Visit our Web site at www.microsoft.com/mspress. Send comments to *tkinput@microsoft.com*.

Acquisitions Editor: Kathy Harding
Project Editor: Karen Szall

Body Part No. X09-35331

Contents

About This Book

Welcome to *MCSD Self-Paced Training Kit: Analyzing Requirements and Defining Microsoft .NET Solution Architectures*, Exam 70-300. By completing the chapters and the associated activities in this course, you will acquire the knowledge and skills necessary to prepare for the Microsoft Certified Solution Developer (MCSD) Exam 70-300. This self-paced course provides content that supports the skills measured by this exam. Answer the questions at the end of each chapter to review what you have learned and help you prepare more thoroughly. The course also includes solution documents that provide you with examples of the outputs of each phase in the Microsoft Solutions Framework (MSF) development process.

Note For more information about becoming a Microsoft Certified Professional, see the section titled "The Microsoft Certified Professional Program" later in this introduction.

Each chapter in this book is divided into lessons. Most lessons include hands-on procedures that allow you to practice or demonstrate a particular concept or skill. Each chapter ends with a short summary of all chapter lessons and a set of review questions to test your knowledge of the chapter material.

The "Getting Started" section of this introduction provides important setup instructions that describe the hardware and software requirements to complete the procedures in this course. It also provides information about the networking configuration necessary to complete some of the hands-on procedures. Read through this section thoroughly before you start the lessons.

Intended Audience

This book was developed for information technology (IT) professionals who plan to take the related Microsoft Certified Professional exam 70-300, Analyzing Requirements and Defining Microsoft .NET Solution Architectures, as well as IT professionals who design, develop, and implement software solutions for Microsoft Windows–based environments using Microsoft tools and technologies.

Prerequisites

This training kit requires that students meet the following prerequisites:

- A general understanding of the software development life cycle.
- Practical working knowledge of Microsoft .NET development technologies.
- Familiarity with the MSF Process Model.
- Basic familiarity with object modeling and data modeling methodologies.
- Experience working with Microsoft Visio Professional 2000.
- One year experience as part of a software development team.

Reference Materials

You might find the following reference materials useful:

- MSF Process Model white paper on the Microsoft Solutions Framework Web site at *http://www.microsoft.com/msf/*
- Unified Modeling Language (UML) modeling techniques from the following resources:
  - Booch, Grady, Ivar Jacobson, and James Rumbaugh. *The Unified Modeling Language User Guide* (Addison-Wesley, 1999)
  - Rosenberg, Doug, with Kendall Scott. *Use Case Driven Object Modeling with UML: A Practical Approach* (Addison-Wesley, 1999)

About the CD-ROM

For your use, this book includes a Supplemental Course Materials CD-ROM. This CD-ROM contains a variety of informational aids to complement the book content:

- An electronic version of this book (eBook). For information about using the eBook, see the section "Setup Instructions" later in this introduction.
- Files you will need to perform the hands-on procedures. Also included are sample solution documents.
- A practice test that contains 100 questions. Use the questions to practice taking a certification exam and to help you assess your understanding of the concepts presented in this book.

For additional support information regarding this book and the CD-ROM (including answers to commonly asked questions about installation and use), visit the Microsoft Press Technical Support Web site at *http://www.microsoft.com/mspress /support/*. Note that product support is not offered through this Web site. For information about Microsoft software support options connect to *http://www.microsoft.com /support/*. You can also e-mail tkinput@microsoft.com or send a letter to Microsoft Press, Attention: Microsoft Press Technical Support, One Microsoft Way, Redmond, WA 98052-6399.

Features of This Book

Each chapter opens with a "Before You Begin" section, which prepares you for completing the chapter. The chapters are then broken into lessons. At the end of each chapter is an activity made up of one or more exercises. These activities give you an opportunity to use the skills being presented or explore the concepts being described.

The "Review" section at the end of the chapter allows you to test what you have learned in the chapter's lessons. Appendix A, "Questions and Answers," contains all of the book's questions and corresponding answers.

Notes

Several types of notes appear throughout the lessons.

Tip   These boxes contain explanations of possible results or alternative methods.

Important   These boxes contain information that is essential to completing a task.

Note   Notes generally contain supplemental information.

Caution   These warnings contain critical information about the possible loss of data.

More Info   References to other sources of information are offered throughout the book.

Planning   Hints and useful information will help you plan implementation in your environment.

Conventions

The following conventions are used throughout this book.

Notational Conventions

- Characters or commands that you type appear in **bold** type.
- *Italic* in syntax statements indicates placeholders for variable information. *Italic* is also used for book titles.
- Names of files and folders appear in Title caps, except when you are to type them directly. Unless otherwise indicated, you can use all lowercase letters when you type a file name in a dialog box or at a command prompt.
- File name extensions appear in all lowercase.
- Acronyms and abbreviations appear in all uppercase.
- Monospace type represents code samples, examples of screen text, or entries that you might type at a command prompt or in initialization files.
- Square brackets [ ] are used in syntax statements to enclose optional items. For example, [*filename*] in command syntax indicates that you can choose to type a file name with the command. Type only the information within the brackets, not the brackets themselves.
- Braces { } are used in syntax statements to enclose required items. Type only the information within the braces, not the braces themselves.

Keyboard Conventions

- A plus sign (+) between two key names means that you must press those keys at the same time. For example, "Press ALT+TAB" means that you hold down ALT while you press TAB.
- A comma (,) between two or more key names means that you must press each of the keys consecutively, not together. For example, "Press ALT, F, X" means that you press and release each key in sequence. "Press ALT+W, L" means that you first press ALT and W at the same time, and then release them and press L.
- You can choose menu commands with the keyboard. Press the ALT key to activate the menu bar, and then sequentially press the keys that correspond to the highlighted or underlined letter of the menu name and the command name. For some commands, you can also press a key combination listed in the menu.
- You can select or clear check boxes or option buttons in dialog boxes with the keyboard. Press the ALT key, and then press the key that corresponds to the underlined letter of the option name. Or you can press TAB until the option is highlighted, and then press the spacebar to select or clear the check box or option button.
- You can cancel the display of a dialog box by pressing the ESC key.

Chapter and Appendix Overview

This self-paced training kit combines notes, hands-on procedures, and review questions to teach you about designing solutions architecture in a Microsoft .NET environment. It is designed to be completed from beginning to end, but you can choose a customized track and complete only the sections that interest you.

The book is divided into the following sections:

- "About This Book" contains a self-paced training overview and introduces the components of this training. Read this section thoroughly to get the greatest educational value from this self-paced training and to plan which lessons you will complete.

- Chapter 1, "Introduction to Designing Business Solutions," describes the Microsoft Solutions Framework (MSF). It begins with an overview of the MSF Process Model and its various phases. The chapter also describes the key activities performed in designing an application and the deliverables associated with those activities. In addition, the chapter describes the case study that is used in the course. All the practices and solution documents are created for the case study.

- Chapter 2, "Gathering and Analyzing Information," describes the process of gathering and analyzing information for designing a business solution. The chapter begins by describing the types of information that you need to gather, sources of information, and some techniques, such as interviews, shadowing, and prototyping that can be used for gathering information. The chapter then describes how to analyze all the information that is gathered from interviews and other gathering techniques. The chapter discusses use cases, usage scenarios, and other techniques that can be used for analyzing information.

- Chapter 3, "Envisioning the Solution," discusses the envisioning phase of the MSF development process. The chapter begins by describing the purpose of the envisioning phase in application design. It then describes the roles and responsibilities of team members during this phase. It also discusses the major tasks of the envisioning phases. Finally, the chapter describes how to define the vision of the project and analyze risks associated with the project.

- Chapter 4, "Creating the Conceptual Design," describes the conceptual design process of the planning phase in the MSF development process. The chapter first discusses the purpose of the planning phase and provides an overview of the three design processes that occur during the planning phase: conceptual, logical, and physical design. The chapter also explains the purpose and benefits of functional specification. The chapter then describes the conceptual design process in detail, and discusses the three steps of conceptual design: research, analysis, and optimization.

- Chapter 5, "Creating the Logical Design," explains the logical design process of the planning phase. The chapter begins with an overview of the purpose and benefits of logical design, and then describes the team composition and the roles of each member during this process. The chapter then describes in detail how to create the logical design for a business solution. It also discusses the various tools and techniques that can be used for documenting the outputs of logical design. Finally, the chapter describes how to optimize the logical design. Validating against requirements is recommended as the best strategy for optimizing the logical design in this chapter.

- Chapter 6, "Creating the Physical Design," describes the physical design process of the planning phase. The chapter first discusses the purpose of physical design. The chapter also discusses the deliverables of physical design. The chapter then describes in detail the tasks involved in completing the physical design process: research, analysis, rationalization, and implementation.

- Chapter 7, "Designing the Presentation Layer," discusses how to design the presentation layer of an application. The chapter begins with an overview of the presentation layer and its two components: user interface and user process. The chapter then describes how to design the user interface and user process components of an application and also recommends some guidelines for the design process.

- Chapter 8, "Designing the Data Layer," describes how to design the data layer for an application. The chapter also discusses how to optimize data access and implement data validation in an application.

- Chapter 9, "Designing Security Specifications," describes the design guidelines for creating security specifications for an application. The chapter recommends some tools and methods for assessing the threats to an application and the mitigation techniques that can be used for resolving the threats. The chapter also describes some security features of Microsoft .NET technologies. Finally, the chapter discusses the steps and the guidelines that can be followed for designing authentication, authorization, and auditing for an application.

- Chapter 10, "Completing the Planning Phase," describes the tasks and plans on which the project team works to complete the planning phase of the project. This chapter describes the guidelines and recommended practices for designing for scalability, availability, reliability, performance, interoperability, and globalization and localization. The chapter discusses how to plan for administrative features such as monitoring, data migration, and licensing specifications. In addition, the chapter discusses the development plan, the test plan, the pilot plan, the deployment plan, and the migration plan. The chapter also discusses the purpose and contents of a technical specification document.

- Chapter 11, "Stabilizing and Deploying the Solution," describes the tasks involved in stabilizing and deploying a solution. The chapter first discusses the stabilizing phase and explains in detail the various types of testing that can be performed to stabilize a solution. The chapter also describes the tasks involved in conducting a pilot. Next, the chapter describes the process of deployment. The chapter discusses how to plan for deployment, and the various strategies that can be used for deploying a solution.

- Appendix A, "Questions and Answers," lists all of the review questions from the book showing the page number where the question appears and the suggested answer.

- The glossary provides definitions for many of the terms and concepts presented in this training kit.

Where to Find Specific Skills in This Book

The following tables provide a list of the skills measured by certification exam 70-300, Analyzing Requirements and Defining Microsoft .NET Solution Architectures. The table specifies the skill and the location in this book where you can find the lesson relating to that skill.

Note Exam skills are subject to change without prior notice and at the sole discretion of Microsoft.

Envisioning the Solution

Skill Being Measured	Location in Book
Develop a solution concept.	Chapter 3, Lesson 2
Analyze the feasibility of the solution.	Chapter 3, Lesson 2
• Analyze the business feasibility of the solution.	
• Analyze the technical feasibility of the solution.	
• Analyze available organizational skills and resources.	
Analyze and refine the scope of the solution project.	Chapter 3, Lesson 2
Identify key project risks.	Chapter 3, Lesson 4

Gathering and Analyzing Business Requirements

Skill Being Measured	Location in Book
Gather and analyze business requirements. • Analyze the current business state. • Analyze business requirements for the solution.	Chapter 2, Lessons 1 and 2, and Chapter 4, Lesson 4
Gather and analyze user requirements. • Identify use cases. • Identify globalization requirements. • Identify localization requirements. • Identify accessibility requirements.	Chapter 2, Lessons 1 and 2, and Chapter 4, Lesson 4
Gather and analyze operational requirements. • Identify maintainability requirements. • Identify scalability requirements. • Identify availability requirements. • Identify reliability requirements. • Identify deployment requirements. • Identify security requirements.	Chapter 2, Lessons 1 and 2, and Chapter 4, Lesson 4
Gather and analyze requirements for hardware, software, and network infrastructure. • Identify integration requirements. • Analyze the IT environment, including current and projected applications and current projected hardware, software, and network infrastructure. • Analyze the impact of the solution on the IT environment.	Chapter 2, Lessons 1 and 2, and Chapter 4, Lesson 4

Developing Specifications

Skill Being Measured	Location in Book
Transform requirements into functional specifications. Considerations include performance, maintainability, extensibility, scalability, availability, deployability, security, and accessibility.	Chapter 4, all lessons; Chapter 6, Lesson 3; and Chapter 10, Lesson 1
Transform functional specifications into technical specifications. Considerations include performance, maintainability, extensibility, scalability, availability, deployability, security, and accessibility.	Chapter 10, Lesson 4

- Select a development strategy.
- Select a deployment strategy.
- Select a security strategy.
- Select an operations strategy.
- Create a test plan.
- Create a user education plan.

Creating the Conceptual Design

Skill Being Measured	Location in Book
Create a conceptual model of business requirements or data requirements. Methods include Object Role Modeling (ORM).	Chapter 4, all lessons and Chapter 2, Lesson 3

- Transform external information into elementary facts.
- Apply a population check to fact types.
- Identify primitive entity types in the conceptual model.
- Apply uniqueness constraints to the conceptual model.
- Apply mandatory role constraints to the conceptual model.
- Add value constraints, set-comparison constraints, and subtype constraints to the conceptual model.
- Add ring constraints to the conceptual model.

Creating the Logical Design

Skill Being Measured	Location in Book
Create the logical design for the solution.	Chapter 5, all lessons

- Create the logical design for auditing and logging.
- Create the logical design for error handling.
- Create the logical design for integration.
- Create the logical design for globalization.
- Create the logical design for localization.
- Create the logical design for security.
- Include constraints in the logical design to support business rules.
- Create the logical design for the presentation layer, including the user interface (UI).
- Create the logical design for services and components.
- Create the logical design for state management.
- Create the logical design for synchronous or asynchronous architecture.

Create the logical data model.	Chapter 5, Lesson 3

- Define tables and columns.
- Normalize tables.
- Define relationships.
- Define primary and foreign keys.
- Define the XML schema.

Validate the proposed logical design.	Chapter 5, Lesson 4

- Review the effectiveness of the proposed logical design in meeting business requirements. Business requirements include performance, maintainability, extensibility, scalability, availability, deployability, security, and accessibility.
- Validate the proposed logical design against usage scenarios.
- Create a proof of concept for the proposed logical design.

Creating the Physical Design

Skill Being Measured	Location in Book
Select the appropriate technologies for the physical design of the solution.	Chapter 5, Lesson 2
Create the physical design for the solution. • Create specifications for auditing and logging. • Create specifications for error handling. • Create specifications for physical integration. • Create specifications for security. • Include constraints in the physical design to support business rules. • Design the presentation layer, including the UI and online user assistance. • Design services and components. • Design state management.	Chapter 6, all lessons; Chapter 7 all lessons; Chapter 9, Lesson 3
Create the physical design for deployment. • Create deployment specifications, which can include coexistence and distribution. • Create licensing specifications. • Create data migration specifications. • Design the upgrade path.	Chapter 10, Lesson 2
Create the physical design for maintenance. • Design application monitoring.	Chapter 10, Lesson 2
Create the physical design for the data model. • Create an indexing specification. • Partition data. • Denormalize tables.	Chapter 8, Lesson 2
Validate the physical design. • Review the effectiveness of the proposed physical design in meeting the business requirements. Business requirements include performance, maintainability, extensibility, scalability, availability, deployability, security, and accessibility. • Validate use cases, scenario walk-throughs, and sequence diagrams. • Create a proof of concept for the proposed physical design.	Chapter 6, Lessons 3 and 4

Creating Standards and Processes

Skill Being Measured	Location in Book
Establish standards. Standards can apply to development documentation, coding, code review, UI, and testing.	Chapter 11, Lesson 2
Establish processes. Processes include reviewing development documentation, reviewing code, creating builds, tracking issues, managing source code, managing change, managing release, and establishing maintenance tasks. Methods include Microsoft Visual Studio .NET Enterprise Templates.	Chapter 11, Lesson 2
Establish quality and performance metrics to evaluate project control, organizational performance, and return on investment.	Chapter 11, Lessons 1 and 2

Getting Started

This self-paced training course contains hands-on procedures to help you learn about building solution architecture in a Microsoft .NET environment.

Hardware Requirements

Each computer must have the following minimum configuration. All hardware should be on the Microsoft Windows 2000 Professional Hardware Compatibility List.

- Pentium II, 266 MHz or faster
- 128 MB RAM
- 4-GB hard drive
- CD-ROM drive
- Microsoft Mouse or compatible pointing device

Software Requirements

The following minimum software is required to complete the procedures in this course.

- Microsoft Windows 2000 Professional with Service Pack 3, or Microsoft Windows XP Professional
- Microsoft Office 2000 Professional with Service Pack 3 or later
- Microsoft Visio 2000 Professional or later

Setup Instructions

Set up your computer according to the manufacturer's instructions.

The Solution Documents

The Supplemental Course Materials CD-ROM contains a set of files that you will need to copy to your hard disk to complete many of the exercises in this book. To access the Solution Documents folder:

1. Insert the Supplemental Course Materials CD-ROM into your CD-ROM drive.

   Note If Autorun is disabled on your machine, run StartCD.exe in the root directory of the CD-ROM or refer to the Readme.txt file.

2. Select Solution Documents on the user interface menu, and then browse to the chapter folder you want to view.

The eBook

The CD-ROM also includes a fully searchable electronic version of the book. To view the eBook, you must have Microsoft Internet Explorer 5.01 or later and the corresponding HTML Help components on your system. If your system does not meet these requirements, you can install Internet Explorer 6 SP1 from the CD-ROM prior to installing the eBook.

To use the eBook

1. Insert the Supplemental Course Materials CD-ROM into your CD-ROM drive.

   Note If AutoRun is disabled on your machine, refer to the Readme.txt file on the CD-ROM.

2. Click eBook on the user interface menu and follow the prompts.

   Note You must have the Supplemental Course Materials CD-ROM inserted in your CD-ROM drive to run the eBook.

The Microsoft Certified Professional Program

The Microsoft Certified Professional (MCP) program provides the best method to prove your command of current Microsoft products and technologies. Microsoft, an industry leader in certification, is on the forefront of testing methodology. The exams and corresponding certifications are intended to validate your mastery of critical competencies as you design and develop, or implement and support, solutions with Microsoft products and technologies. Computer professionals who become Microsoft certified are recognized as experts and are sought industry-wide.

The Microsoft Certified Professional program offers multiple certifications, based on specific areas of technical expertise:

- *Microsoft Certified Professional (MCP).* Demonstrated in-depth knowledge of at least one Microsoft Windows operating system or architecturally significant platform. An MCP is qualified to implement a Microsoft product or technology as part of a business solution for an organization.

- *Microsoft Certified Solution Developer (MCSD).* Professional developers qualified to analyze, design, and develop enterprise business solutions with Microsoft development tools and technologies including the Microsoft .NET Framework.

- *Microsoft Certified Application Developer (MCAD).* Professional developers qualified to develop, test, deploy, and maintain powerful applications using Microsoft tools and technologies including Microsoft Visual Studio .NET and XML Web services.

- *Microsoft Certified Systems Engineer (MCSE).* Qualified to effectively analyze the business requirements, and design and implement the infrastructure for business solutions based on the Microsoft Windows and Microsoft Server 2003 operating system.

- *Microsoft Certified Systems Administrator (MCSA).* Individuals with the skills to manage and troubleshoot existing network and system environments based on the Microsoft Windows and Microsoft Server 2003 operating systems.

- *Microsoft Certified Database Administrator (MCDBA).* Individuals who design, implement, and administer Microsoft SQL Server databases.

- *Microsoft Certified Trainer (MCT).* Instructionally and technically qualified to deliver Microsoft Official Curriculum through a Microsoft Certified Technical Education Center (CTEC).

Microsoft Certification Benefits

Microsoft certification, one of the most comprehensive certification programs available for assessing and maintaining software-related skills, is a valuable measure of an individual's knowledge and expertise. Microsoft certification is awarded to individuals who have successfully demonstrated their ability to perform specific tasks and implement solutions with Microsoft products. Certification brings a variety of benefits to the individual and to employers and organizations.

Microsoft Certification Benefits for Individuals

As a Microsoft Certified Professional, you receive many benefits:

- Industry recognition of your knowledge and proficiency with Microsoft products and technologies.

- A Microsoft Developer Network subscription. MCPs receive rebates or discounts on a one-year subscription to the Microsoft Developer Network (*http://msdn.microsoft.com/subscriptions/*) during the first year of certification. (Fulfillment details will vary, depending on your location; please see your Welcome Kit.)

- Access to technical and product information direct from Microsoft through a secured area of the MCP Web site (go to *http://www.microsoft.com/traincert /mcp/mcpsecure.asp*).

- Access to exclusive discounts on products and services from selected companies. Individuals who are currently certified can learn more about exclusive discounts by visiting the MCP secured Web site (go to *http://www.microsoft.com /traincert/mcp/mcpsecure.asp*, log in, and select the "Other Benefits" link).

- MCP logo, certificate, transcript, wallet card, and lapel pin to identify you as a Microsoft Certified Professional (MCP) to colleagues and clients. Electronic files of logos and transcript can be downloaded from the MCP secured Web site (go to *http://www.microsoft.com/traincert/mcp/mcpsecure.asp*) upon certification.

- Invitations to Microsoft conferences, technical training sessions, and special events.

- Free access to *Microsoft Certified Professional Magazine Online,* a career and professional development magazine. Secured content on the *Microsoft Certified Professional Magazine Online* Web site includes the current issue (available only to MCPs), additional online-only content and columns, an MCP-only database, and regular chats with Microsoft and other technical experts.

- Discount on membership to PASS (for MCPs only), the Professional Association for SQL Server. In addition to playing a key role in the only worldwide, user-run SQL Server user group endorsed by Microsoft, members enjoy unique access to a world of educational opportunities (go to *http://www.microsoft.com /traincert/mcp/mcpsecure.asp*).

An additional benefit is received by Microsoft Certified System Engineers (MCSEs):

- A 50 percent rebate or discount on a one-year subscription to *TechNet* or *Tech-Net Plus* during the first year of certification. (Fulfillment details will vary, depending on your location. Please see your Welcome Kit.) A *TechNet* subscription provides MCSEs with a portable IT survival kit that is updated monthly. It includes the complete Microsoft Knowledge Base as well as service packs and kits.

An additional benefit is received by Microsoft Certified System Database Administrators (MCDBAs):

- A 50 percent rebate or discount on a one-year subscription to TechNet or Tech-Net Plus during the first year of certification. (Fulfillment details will vary, depending on your location. Please see your Welcome Kit.) A *TechNet* subscription provides MCSEs with a portable IT survival kit that is updated monthly. It includes the complete Microsoft Knowledge Base as well as service packs and kits.
- A one-year subscription to *SQL Server Magazine*. Written by industry experts, the magazine contains technical and how-to tips and advice—a must for anyone working with SQL Server.

A list of benefits for Microsoft Certified Trainers (MCTs) can be found at *http://www.microsoft.com/traincert/mcp/mct/benefits.asp*.

Microsoft Certification Benefits for Employers and Organizations

Through certification, computer professionals can maximize the return on investment in Microsoft technology. Research shows that Microsoft certification provides organizations with:

- Excellent return on training and certification investments by providing a standard method of determining training needs and measuring results.
- Increased customer satisfaction and decreased support costs through improved service, increased productivity and greater technical self-sufficiency.
- Reliable benchmark for hiring, promoting, and career planning.
- Recognition and rewards for productive employees by validating their expertise.
- Retraining options for existing employees so they can work effectively with new technologies.
- Assurance of quality when outsourcing computer services.

Requirements for Becoming a Microsoft Certified Professional

The certification requirements differ for each certification and are specific to the products and job functions addressed by the certification.

To become a Microsoft Certified Professional, you must pass rigorous certification exams that provide a valid and reliable measure of technical proficiency and expertise. These exams are designed to test your expertise and ability to perform a role or task with a product, and are developed with the input of professionals in the industry. Questions in the exams reflect how Microsoft products are used in actual organizations, giving them "real-world" relevance.

- Microsoft Certified Product (MCP) candidates are required to pass one current Microsoft certification exam. Candidates can pass additional Microsoft certification exams to further qualify their skills with other Microsoft products, development tools, or desktop applications.
- Microsoft Certified Solution Developers (MCSDs) are required to pass three core exams and one elective exam. (MCSD for Microsoft .NET candidates are required to pass four core exams and one elective.)
- Microsoft Certified Application Developers (MCADs) are required to pass two core exams and one elective exam in an area of specialization.
- Microsoft Certified Systems Engineers (MCSEs) are required to pass five core exams and two elective exams.
- Microsoft Certified Systems Administrators (MCSAs) are required to pass three core exams and one elective exam that provide a valid and reliable measure of technical proficiency and expertise.
- Microsoft Certified Database Administrators (MCDBAs) are required to pass three core exams and one elective exam that provide a valid and reliable measure of technical proficiency and expertise.
- Microsoft Certified Trainers (MCTs) are required to meet instructional and technical requirements specific to each Microsoft Official Curriculum course they are certified to deliver. The MCT program requires ongoing training to meet the requirements for the annual renewal of certification. For more information about becoming a Microsoft Certified Trainer, visit *http://www.microsoft.com/traincert/mcp/mct/* or contact a regional service center near you.

Technical Training for Computer Professionals

Technical training is available in a variety of ways, with instructor-led classes, online instruction, or self-paced training available at thousands of locations worldwide.

Self-Paced Training

For motivated learners who are ready for the challenge, self-paced instruction is the most flexible, cost-effective way to increase your knowledge and skills.

A full line of self-paced print and computer-based training materials is available direct from the source—Microsoft Press. Microsoft Official Curriculum courseware kits from Microsoft Press are designed for advanced computer system professionals and are available from Microsoft Press and the Microsoft Developer Division. Self-paced training kits from Microsoft Press feature print-based instructional materials, along with CD-ROM–based product software, multimedia presentations, lab exercises, and practice files.

Microsoft Certified Technical Education Centers

Microsoft Certified Technical Education Centers (CTECs) are the best source for instructor-led training that can help you prepare to become a Microsoft Certified Professional. The Microsoft CTEC program is a worldwide network of qualified technical training organizations that provide authorized delivery of Microsoft Official Curriculum courses by Microsoft Certified Trainers to computer professionals.

For a listing of CTEC locations in the United States and Canada, visit the Web site at *http://www.microsoft.com/traincert/ctec/*.

Technical Support

Every effort has been made to ensure the accuracy of this book and the contents of the companion disc. If you have comments, questions, or ideas regarding this book or the companion disc, please send them to Microsoft Press using either of the following methods:

E-mail:

tkinput@microsoft.com

Postal Mail:

Microsoft Press
Attn: MCSD Self-Paced Training Kit: Analyzing Requirements and Defining Microsoft .NET Solution Architectures, Editor
One Microsoft Way
Redmond, WA 98052-6399

For additional support information regarding this book and the CD-ROM (including answers to commonly asked questions about installation and use), visit the Microsoft Press Technical Support Web site at *http://www.microsoft.com /mspress/support/*. To connect directly to the Microsoft Press Knowledge Base and enter a query, visit *http://www.microsoft.com/mspress/support/search.asp*. For support information regarding Microsoft software, please connect to *http://www.microsoft.com/support.*

C H A P T E R   1

Introduction to Designing Business Solutions

About This Chapter

In this introduction to designing business solutions, you will learn about
Microsoft® Solutions Framework (MSF), a set of models, principles, and guidelines for designing applications. You will learn about the MSF Process Model and
its various phases. You will also learn about the key activities that you perform in
designing an application, and about the deliverables associated with those activities. In addition, you will be introduced to the case study that illustrates the concepts and practices that you will learn.

Before You Begin

To complete the lessons in this chapter, you must have

- A general understanding of the software development life cycle.
- General knowledge of Microsoft technologies.

Lesson 1: Overview of Microsoft Solutions Framework

MSF provides a set of models, principles, and guidelines for designing and developing enterprise solutions in a way that ensures that all elements of a project, such as people, processes, and tools, can be successfully managed. MSF also provides proven practices for planning, designing, developing, and deploying successful enterprise solutions. In this lesson, you will learn about the process model and team model that MSF provides.

After this lesson, you will be able to

- Describe the phases in the MSF Process Model.
- Describe the roles in the MSF Team Model.
- Describe the MSF disciplines: risk management, readiness management, and project management.
- Describe how managing tradeoffs helps to ensure the success of an enterprise project.
- Describe the purpose of iteration in an enterprise project.
- Describe the waterfall model and the spiral model.

Estimated lesson time: 15 minutes

What Are Process Models?

To maximize the success of enterprise projects, Microsoft has made available packaged guidance for effectively designing, developing, deploying, operating, and supporting solutions, including those created with Microsoft technologies. This knowledge is derived from the experience gained within Microsoft and from customers and vendors about large-scale software development and service operation projects, the experience of Microsoft's consultants in conducting projects for enterprise customers, and the best knowledge from the worldwide Information Technology (IT) industry.

A process model guides the order of project activities and represents the life cycle of a project. Historically, some process models are static and others do not allow checkpoints. Two such process models are the waterfall model and the spiral model.

Waterfall and spiral models

Figure 1.1 shows the waterfall model's cascading checkpoints and the spiral model's circular approach to process.

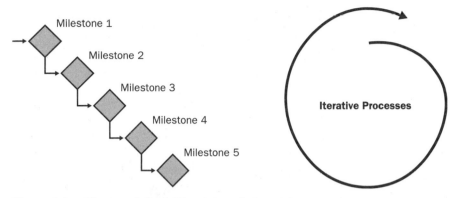

Figure 1.1.   The waterfall model and the spiral model

These models provide two different approaches to the project life cycle. The preceding illustration shows the waterfall model's cascading checkpoints and the spiral model's circular approach to process.

- *Waterfall model.* This model uses milestones as transition and assessment points. When using the waterfall model, you need to complete each set of tasks in one phase before moving on to the next phase. The waterfall model works best for projects in which the project requirements can be clearly defined and are not liable to modifications in the future. Because this model has fixed transition points between phases, you can easily monitor schedules and assign clear responsibilities and accountability.

- *Spiral model.* This model is based on the continual need to refine the requirements and estimates for a project. The spiral model is effective when used for rapid application development of very small projects. This approach can generate great synergy between the development team and the customer because the customer is involved in all stages by providing feedback and approval. However, the spiral model does not incorporate clear checkpoints. Consequently, the development process might become chaotic.

How the MSF Process Model Works

The MSF Process Model describes a generalized sequence of activities for building and deploying enterprise solutions. This process is flexible and can accommodate the design and development of a broad range of enterprise projects. The MSF Process Model is a phase-based, milestone-driven, and iterative model that can be applied to developing and deploying traditional applications, enterprise solutions for e-commerce, and Web-distributed applications.

MSF Process Model

The MSF Process Model combines the best principles of the waterfall and spiral models. It combines the waterfall model's milestone-based planning and resulting predictability with the spiral model's benefits of feedback and creativity.

Figure 1.2 shows the MSF Process Model.

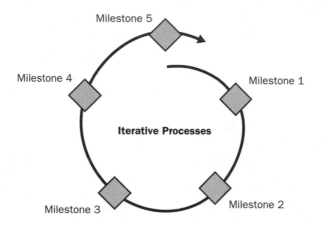

Figure 1.2.   The MSF Process Model

Phases of the MSF Process Model

The MSF Process Model consists of five distinct phases:

- Envisioning
- Planning
- Developing
- Stabilizing
- Deploying

Each phase culminates in a milestone. Figure 1.3 illustrates the phases and milestones of the MSF Process Model. You will learn about these phases in detail in Lesson 2.

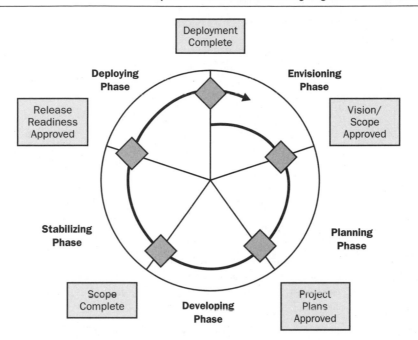

Figure 1.3.   Phases and milestones of the MSF Process Model

How to Organize Project Teams

Along with the MSF Process Model, MSF provides the MSF Team Model for organizing project teams. The MSF Team Model emphasizes the importance of clear
roles, responsibilities, and goals of individual members to the success of the
project. This model also increases the accountability of each team member. The
flexibility of the MSF Team Model helps you to adapt it to the scope of the project,
the size of the team, and the skills of the team members. This model forms the
basis of creating effective, resilient, and successful project teams.

Roles in the MSF Team Model

In an enterprise solution project, a large number of activities must be performed,
and the project must be viewed from several perspectives. To accommodate these
needs, the MSF Team Model specifies six distinct roles, and each role has clearly
defined responsibilities and goals.

Important   The team works toward a single vision, and team members operate as
peers. Within the team, each role contributes to and is equally responsible for the
success of the project.

The roles in the MSF Team Model are as follows:

- *Product management.* Responsible for managing customer communications and expectations. During the design phase, product management gathers customer requirements and ensures that business needs are met. Product management also works on project communication plans such as briefings to the customers, marketing to users, demonstrations, and product launches.

- *Program management.* Responsible for the development process and for delivering the solution to the customer within the project constraints.

- *Development.* Responsible for developing the technology solution according to the specifications provided by the program management role.

- *Testing.* Responsible for identifying and addressing all product quality issues and approving the solution for release. This role evaluates and validates design functionality and consistency with project vision and scope.

- *Release management.* Responsible for smooth deployment and operations of the solution. Release management validates the infrastructure implications of the solution to ensure that it can be deployed and supported.

- *User experience.* Analyzes performance needs and support issues of the users and considers the product implications of meeting those needs.

In a small project, individuals on the project team can take on more than one role. Note that combining roles on a project introduces risk to the project. Therefore, it is important to assign appropriate roles to the members. For example, it is not recommended that an individual be assigned to both the program management role and the development role.

To help minimize risks, use Table 1.1 as a guide in determining which roles can be combined and which ones should not be combined.

Table 1.1.   Combining Roles Within a Team

Role	Product management	Program management	Development	Testing	User experience	Release management
Product management		N	N	P	P	U
Program management	N		N	U	U	P
Development	N	N		N	N	N
Test	P	U	N		P	P
User experience	P	U	N	P		U

Table 1.1.   Combining Roles Within a Team *(continued)*

Role	Product management	Program management	Development	Testing	User experience	Release management
Release management	U	P	N	P	U	

Legend:

P: Possible

U: Unlikely

N: Not recommended

Additional team members

In addition to the roles defined previously, the project team also includes the project stakeholders, though they are not part of the MSF Team Model. These stakeholders include the following roles:

- *Project sponsor.* One or more individuals initiating and approving the project and its result.
- *Customer (or business sponsor).* One or more individuals who expect to gain business value from the solution.
- *End user.* One or more individuals or systems that interact directly with the solution.
- *Operations.* The organization responsible for the ongoing operation of the solution after delivery.

MSF Disciplines

MSF guidance includes disciplines for managing the people, processes, and technology elements that most projects encounter. The three key MSF disciplines are risk management, readiness management, and project management.

MSF risk management process

The MSF risk management discipline advocates proactive risk management, continuous risk assessment, and decision making throughout the project life cycle. The team continuously assesses, monitors, and actively manages risks until they are either resolved or turn into problems to be handled as such.

The MSF risk management process defines six logical steps through which the team manages current risks, plans and executes risk management strategies, and documents knowledge for the enterprise.

1. *Risk identification* allows individuals to identify risks so that the team becomes aware of any potential problems.

2. *Risk analysis* transforms the estimates or data about specific project risks that emerges during risk identification into a form the team can use to make decisions about prioritization.

3. *Risk planning* uses the information obtained from risk analysis to formulate strategies, plans, and actions.

4. *Risk tracking* monitors the status of specific risks and documents the progress in their respective action plans.

5. *Risk control* is the process of executing risk action plans and their associated status reporting.

6. *Risk learning* formalizes the lessons learned and relevant project documents and tools, and records that knowledge in reusable form for use within the team and by the enterprise.

More Info   You will learn more about MSF risk management in Chapter 3, "Envisioning the Solution."

MSF readiness management process

The MSF readiness management discipline includes a process to help you develop the knowledge, skills, and abilities (KSAs) needed to create and manage projects and solutions. Figure 1.4 illustrates the four steps of the readiness management process: define, assess, change, and evaluate.

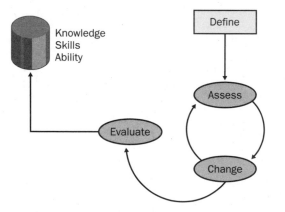

Figure 1.4.   MSF readiness management

Each step of the process includes a series of tasks to help reach the next milestone.

- *Define.* During this step, the team identifies the scenarios, competencies, and proficiency levels needed to successfully plan, create, and manage the solution. This is also the time to determine which competencies and corresponding proficiency levels are required for each role in the organization. The assigned role determines whether an individual needs to be proficient in one or many of the defined competencies.

- *Assess.* It is during this step that the team begins analysis of the current competencies as they relate to the various job roles. The purpose of this analysis is to determine the skills of individuals within each of these roles. The team then compares the competencies identified in the previous step to the current competencies. Comparing current skill levels to required skill levels is necessary to develop a learning plan, so that team members can reach the necessary competency levels.

- *Change.* During this step, team members begin to improve their skills by means of structured learning to raise current proficiency levels to the desired levels. This step consists of:

  - *Training.* The learning and mentoring that occurs according to what was outlined in the learning plan.

  - *Tracking progress.* The tracking of progress that enables individual or overall readiness to be determined at any time during the life cycle. This tracking enables the team members to make necessary adjustments to the learning plan.

- *Evaluate.* During this step, the team determines whether the learning plans were effective and whether the lessons learned are being successfully implemented on the job.

The MSF readiness management process is an ongoing, iterative approach to readiness. The process is adaptable for both large and small projects. Following the steps in the process helps manage the various tasks required to align individual, project team, and organizational KSAs.

MSF project management process

To deliver a solution within project constraints, strong project management skills are essential. Project management is a process that combines a set of skills and techniques to address the following tasks:

- Integrate planning and conduct change control
- Define and manage the scope of the project
- Prepare a budget and manage costs
- Prepare and track schedules
- Ensure that the right resources are allocated to the project
- Manage contracts and vendors and procure project resources
- Facilitate team and external communications
- Facilitate the risk management process
- Document and monitor the team's quality management process

The MSF Team Model does not contain a project manager role; however, most project management functions are conducted by the MSF program management role.

The differentiating factor of the MSF approach to project management is that the project management job function and activities do not form a hierarchical structure in the decision-making process. MSF advocates *against* a rigid, dictatorial style of project management. This rigid style hinders the development of an effective team of peers, which is a key success factor of MSF.

In MSF, all team roles fulfill a specific goal, all of which are considered equally important. Major decisions are made by consensus of the core team. If that consensus cannot be achieved, the program management role makes the final decision on the issue by transitioning into the role of decision leader to enable the project to continue. Program management makes the decision with the goal of meeting the customer's requirements and delivering the solution within the constraints. After the decision is made, the team returns to operating as a team of peers.

How to Manage Tradeoffs

Projects frequently fail, are completed late, or exceed the planned budget. Ambiguous project scope can contribute to or be the cause of each of these problems. The *scope* of a project specifies what the solution will and will not do. To effectively define and manage the scope, you need to:

- Identify project constraints
- Manage tradeoffs
- Establish change control
- Monitor project progress

In the process of identifying and managing tradeoffs, you are not necessarily reducing the features of a solution, but identifying tradeoffs might result in a reduction of features. Managing tradeoffs provides a structured way to balance all parts of the project while realizing that you cannot attain all of your goals at the same time. Both the team and the customer must review the tradeoffs and be prepared to make difficult choices.

The tradeoff triangle and the project tradeoff matrix are two of the tools that MSF uses for managing tradeoffs.

Tradeoff triangle

In projects, there is a clear relationship between such project variables as resources, schedule, and features of the project. The relationship between these variables is illustrated in Figure 1.5.

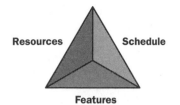

Figure 1.5.   The tradeoff triangle

As illustrated by the triangle, any change to any one of the components implies that a corresponding change might need to be made to the other components. The key to developing a solution that meets the customer requirements is to determine and maintain the correct balance between resources, deployment date, and features.

Often, project teams are reluctant to reduce the number of features in the solution. The tradeoff triangle helps to explain the constraints and present the options for tradeoffs.

Note   If you add quality as a fourth dimension to the tradeoff triangle, the triangle transforms into a tetrahedron. By reducing the quality requirements, you could simultaneously reduce resources, shorten the schedule, and increase the number of features, but this strategy is the worst approach for developing a solution.

Project tradeoff matrix

The *project tradeoff matrix* is a tool that the team and the customer can use when making tradeoff decisions. These decisions are made early in the project.

Figure 1.6 is an example of a project tradeoff matrix.

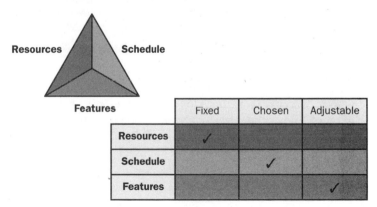

	Fixed	Chosen	Adjustable
Resources	✓		
Schedule		✓	
Features			✓

Figure 1.6.   A project tradeoff matrix

The tradeoff matrix helps identify the project features that are considered essential, the features that are not essential but that would be good to include, and the features that can be eliminated or added to the next version to accommodate the other two variables. To understand how the tradeoff matrix works, the variables of resources, schedule, and features can be inserted into the blanks of the following sentence:

Given fixed _____, we will choose a _____ and adjust _____ if necessary.

The following are the various logical possibilities:

- Given fixed resources, we will choose a schedule and adjust the feature set if necessary.
- Given fixed resources, we will choose a feature set and adjust the schedule if necessary.
- Given a fixed feature set, we will choose appropriate resources and adjust the schedule if necessary.
- Given a fixed feature set, we will choose a schedule and adjust resources if necessary.
- Given a fixed schedule, we will choose appropriate resources and adjust features if necessary.
- Given a fixed schedule, we will choose a feature set and adjust resources if necessary.

Important   For the tradeoff process to work effectively, both the team and the customer must agree to and formally approve the tradeoff matrix for the project. This approval process is also referred to as *signing off*.

How to Use Iteration in Projects

While development of the solution continues through its phases, each iteration of the process brings the solution closer to its final release. Iterations are continued within a specific phase until the goal for the phase has been reached. In addition, an iteration allows the project to be developed in smaller steps, with future iterations being based on the success or failure of an earlier step. Deliverables such as the vision/scope document and other documents, code, designs, and plans are developed in an iterative manner. Instances of iteration in a project life cycle include:

- Creating versioned releases
- Creating living documents
- Creating periodic builds (weekly or daily)

Versioned releases

When using MSF, a team develops solutions by building, testing, and deploying a core of functionality, and then adding sets of features to the solution in every release. This is known as a *version release strategy*.

Figure 1.7 illustrates how functionality develops during the creation of many versions of a solution. The time between versions depends on the size and scope of the project.

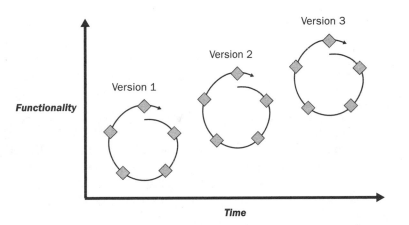

Figure 1.7.   Functionality of versioned releases

Versioned releases improve the team's relationship with the customer and ensure that the best ideas are reflected in the solution. Customers will be more receptive to deferring features until a later release if they trust the team to deliver the initial and subsequent solution releases on time. Several guidelines facilitate the adoption of versioned releases:

- *Create a multiple version release plan.* Thinking beyond the current version enhances a team's ability to make good decisions about what to create now and what to defer. This allows the team to make the best use of the available resources and schedule. In addition, you can prevent unwanted expansion of scope by providing a timetable for future feature development.
- *Work through iterations rapidly.* A significant benefit of versioning is that it delivers usable solutions to the customer quickly and improves them incrementally over time. Maintain a manageable scope so that iterations are achievable within acceptable time frames.
- *Deliver core functionality first.* Delivering a basic solution that is solid and usable is more effective than developing a solution that the customer cannot use for weeks or months. Delivering core functionality first enables developers to incorporate customer feedback that will motivate feature development in subsequent iterations.

■   *Create high-risk features first.* During risk assessment, the team identifies the riskiest features. Schedule these features for proof-of-concept testing first. If you encounter any problems that require major changes to the architecture, you can implement the changes earlier in the project and minimize the impact to schedule and budget.

Living documents

To ensure that you do not spend too much time refining the early phases of the project, you need to create *living documents*—that is, documentation that changes as the project changes. Living documents allow teams to make modifications to any aspect of the project design and development when there is a change in requirements. This process ensures that the completed solution meets the final requirements and not just the initial set of requirements. MSF project documents are developed iteratively.

For example, the MSF Process Model recommends that planning documents start out as generalized documents without extensive details. They are submitted for review by the team and stakeholders during the initial stages of the project. As the solution progresses through different phases, the documents are developed into detailed plans. These plans are once again reviewed and modified iteratively. The type and number of these plans depends on the size of the project.

Daily builds

MSF recommends the preparation of frequent builds of the components of a solution for testing and review. This approach applies to developing code in addition to builds of hardware and software components. By creating daily builds, you can ensure that you understand the stability of the total solution and have accumulated ample test data before releasing the solution.

Using the daily build approach is particularly effective for larger, complex projects that are divided into smaller subsystems. Separate teams develop and test these subsystems and then consolidate them into a single solution. Developers complete core functionality of the solution or product first, and add additional features later. Development and testing occur continuously and simultaneously. Creating daily builds ensures that all code is compatible and allows the various subteams to continue their development and testing iterations.

Lesson 2: Phases in the MSF Process Model

As stated in Lesson 1, the MSF Process Model is milestone based and consists of five phases: envisioning, planning, developing, stabilizing, and deploying. During each phase, the project team performs a distinct set of activities. In this lesson, you will learn about the various phases in detail. You will also learn about the milestones and deliverables of each phase.

After this lesson, you will be able to

- Describe the tasks, milestones, and deliverables of the envisioning, planning, developing, stabilizing, and deploying phases of the MSF Process Model.

Estimated lesson time: 30 minutes

What Is the Envisioning Phase?

The MSF process begins with the envisioning phase. *Envisioning* can be defined as creating a broad description of the goals and constraints of the project. In this phase, you identify the team and what the team must accomplish for the customer. The purpose of the envisioning phase is to build a shared vision of the project among all the key stakeholders of the project.

During the envisioning phase, the program management team identifies the tasks and deliverables that address the requirements and goals of the project. This phase culminates in a *vision/scope approved* milestone. This milestone indicates that the customer and the team agree about the purpose and direction of the project.

Envisioning process

The team performs the following key tasks during the envisioning phase:

- *Setting up the team.* Creation of a project team that represents all roles of the MSF Team Model. (The person who creates this team is usually identified by senior management.) When setting up a team, it is important to consider the skills, experience, and performance level of the team members. In addition, there are practical considerations such as availability of resources and project budget.
- *Defining the project structure.* Identification of an administrative structure for the project team and the standards for managing the project.
- *Defining the business goals.* Analysis of the business problem and opportunities in order to identify the objectives for the solution.
- *Assessing the current situation.* Evaluation of the current situation and analysis of the difference between the current and expected situation. The purpose of this evaluation is to create the problem statement and identify the direction of the project.

- *Creating a vision statement and defining the scope of the project.* Creation of a vision statement that communicates the long-term direction for guiding the team toward its business goals. Identification of the scope of the project defines what will and will not be included in the solution.

Note   A shared and clearly articulated vision is fundamental to the success of the project.

- *Defining requirements and user profiles.* Identification of the stakeholders, end users, and sponsors for the project and documentation of their requirements for the solution. This information helps to evaluate the vision/scope of the project and to create a solution concept.
- *Developing a solution concept.* Creation of a baseline solution concept, that is, the outlining of the approach that the team will take to create the solution. This concept is created by using the requirements that have been identified.
- *Assessing risk.* Identification and assessment of the risks to the project, and creation of a risk mitigation plan. This is an iterative step that is conducted during all stages of the product life cycle.
- *Closing the envisioning phase.* End of the envisioning phase. Accomplished when the vision/scope document is formally approved by all stakeholders and the project team.

Milestones of the envisioning phase

Each phase in the MSF Process Model has interim milestones and a major milestone. *Interim milestones* are associated with the various activities that are performed in a phase, such as creating a team and creating a vision/scope document. The *major milestone* indicates that the team can progress to the next phase in the MSF Process Model. For example, the major milestone of the envisioning phase is the vision/scope approved milestone. When the team reaches this milestone, the team can progress to the planning phase of the MSF Process Model.

The interim milestones of the envisioning phase are as follows:

- *Core team organized.* The key members of the team have been identified. The team might not be completely assembled at this time. A project structure document specifies the roles and responsibilities of each member of the team. This document also outlines the hierarchy of accountability in the team, the points of contact with the customer, and the structure of the team.
- *Vision/scope created.* The first version of the vision/scope document is completed and is distributed among the team, customers, and stakeholders for review. During the review cycle, the document undergoes iterations of feedback, discussions, and corresponding modifications.

The envisioning phase culminates with the *vision/scope approved* milestone. At this stage, the project team and the customer have agreed on the direction for the project, the scope of the solution, and a general timetable for delivering the solution.

Deliverables of the envisioning phase

The team creates deliverables for each task in the envisioning phase. Together, these deliverables provide context and direction for the team for the remainder of the project, and communicate the project vision and scope to the customer. The deliverables that the team creates during the envisioning phase include:

- Vision/scope
    - Problem statements and business objectives
    - A review of the existing processes
    - A broad definition of user requirements
    - User profiles identifying who will benefit from the solution
    - A vision statement and scope definition
    - The solution concept outlining the approach the team will take to plan the project
    - Solution design strategies
- Project structure
    - A description of all MSF team roles and a list of corresponding team members
    - A project structure and process standards for the team to follow
- Risk assessment
    - A preliminary risk assessment
    - A list of the primary identified risks
    - Plans for mitigating or eliminating the identified risks

What Is the Planning Phase?

During the planning phase, the team determines what to develop and plans how to create the solution. The team prepares the functional specification, creates a design of the solution, and prepares work plans, cost estimates, and schedules for the various deliverables.

The planning phase involves the analysis of requirements. These requirements can be categorized as business requirements, user requirements, operational requirements, and system requirements. These requirements are used to design the solution and its features and to validate the correctness of the design.

After gathering and analyzing the requirements, the team creates the design of the solution. The team creates *user profiles* that specify the various users of the solution and their roles and responsibilities. The team then creates a series of usage scenarios. A *usage scenario* specifies the activity performed by a particular type of user. Therefore, the team needs to create usage scenarios for all user profiles. After creating usage scenarios, the team creates use cases for the usage scenarios. A *use case* specifies the sequence of steps that a user will perform in a usage scenario.

Design stages

The three design stages are:

- *Conceptual design,* in which you view the problem from the perspective of the users and business requirements and define the problem and solution in terms of usage scenarios.
- *Logical design,* in which you view the solution from the perspective of the project team and define the solution as a set of services.
- *Physical design,* in which you view the solution from the perspective of the developers and define the technologies, component interfaces, and services of the solution.

You document the solution design in the functional specification. The functional specification describes the behavior and appearance of each feature of the solution. It also describes the architecture and the design for all features.

Design process

The team performs the following key tasks during the planning phase:

- *Developing the solution design and architecture.* Identification of business requirements, user requirements, and technologies and the use of this information to design a proposed application model.
- *Creating the functional specification.* Creation of a functional specification that describes the requirements that must be met by the solution.
- *Developing project plans.* Identification of and planning for the tasks that will be performed by the project team, and the consolidation of these plans into a master project plan. The master project plan also includes items such as the approach, dependencies, and assumptions for the solution.
- *Creating project schedules.* Creation of the master project schedule. This schedule consists of milestone-based schedules for each of the team roles in the project team.
- *Creating the development, testing, and staging environments.* Creation of a separate environment in which to develop and test the solution. This environment is independent of the environment in which the solution will finally be deployed.
- *Closing the planning phase.* Completion of the milestone approval process. Documentation of the results of completing the tasks performed during the planning phase.

Milestones of the planning phase

During the planning phase, the team performs multiple tasks. The interim milestones of the planning phase are as follows:

- *Technology validation complete.* During technology validation, the team evaluates the products and technologies that will be used to create or deploy the solution. The team also audits the customer's current production environment. This includes server configurations, network, desktop software, and all relevant hardware.

- *Functional specification complete.* At this milestone, the functional specification is completed and submitted for review to the customers and stakeholders. Remember that the design document is different from the functional specification. The design document is written for the project team and describes the internal workings of the solution.

- *Master plan complete.* The master plan is a combination of the plans of various roles on the team. Its length and complexity depends on the size of the project.

- *Master project schedule complete.* The master project schedule includes all detailed project schedules and the solution release date. Like the master project plan, the master project schedule combines and integrates information from each of the roles on the team, in this case scheduling information.

- *Development and test environments set up.* A working environment allows proper development and testing of the solution and avoids any negative impact on systems to which the solution will eventually be deployed. This is also the environment in which the infrastructure components, such as server configurations, deployment automation tools, and hardware, are identified and configured.

The major milestone of the planning phase is the *project plan approved* milestone. At this milestone, the project team and key project stakeholders agree that interim milestones have been met, that due dates are realistic, that project roles and responsibilities are well defined, that everyone agrees to the deliverables for the project, and that mechanisms are in place for addressing areas of project risk.

Deliverables of the planning phase

The planning phase deliverables provide the basis for making future tradeoff decisions. The following deliverables are produced during the planning phase:

- Functional specification
- Risk management plan
- Master project plan and master project schedule

What Is the Developing Phase?

During the developing phase, the project team creates the solution. This process includes creating the code that implements the solution and documenting the code. In addition to developing code, the team also develops the infrastructure for the solution.

Development process

The team performs the following key tasks during the developing phase:

- *Starting the development cycle.* Verification that all tasks identified during the envisioning and planning phases have been completed so that the team can begin developing the solution.

- *Creating a prototype application.* Verification of the concepts of the solution design in an environment that resembles the environment to which the solution will be eventually deployed. This environment is as similar as possible to the production environment. This task is completed before development begins.

- *Developing the solution components.* Development of the solution's core components and the extension of these components to the specific needs of the solution.

- *Building the solution.* A series of daily or frequent builds that culminate with major internal builds that signify points when the development team is delivering key features of the solution.

- *Closing the developing phase.* Completion of all features, and delivery of code and documentation. The solution is considered complete, and the team enters a milestone approval process.

Milestones of the developing phase

During the developing phase, the team creates a proof-of-concept application and then creates the solution. The interim milestones of the developing phase are as follows:

- *Proof-of-concept application complete.* The proof-of-concept application tests key elements of the solution in a test environment. The team leads the operations team and users through the solution to validate their requirements.

- *Internal builds complete.* Because a solution is developed in segments, it is a good practice to synchronize the solution segments at product level. You do this with the help of internal builds. The number and frequency of internal builds depends on the size and complexity of the project.

The developing phase culminates in the *scope complete* milestone. At this milestone, all features are complete and have gone through unit testing. The product is now ready for external testing and stabilization. Additionally, customers, users, operations and support personnel, and key project stakeholders can evaluate the product and identify any issues that must be addressed before the solution is shipped.

Deliverables of the developing phase

The deliverables of the developing phase include:

- Source code and executable files
- Installation scripts and configuration settings for deployment
- Finalized functional specification
- Performance support elements
- Test specifications and test cases

What Is the Stabilizing Phase?

During the stabilizing phase, the team performs integration, load, and beta testing on the solution. In addition, the team tests the deployment scenarios for the solution. The team focuses on identifying, prioritizing, and resolving issues so that the solution can be prepared for release. During this phase, the solution progresses from the state of all features being complete as defined in the functional specification for this version to the state of meeting the defined quality levels. In addition, the solution is ready for deployment to the business.

Stabilization process

The team performs the following key tasks during the stabilizing phase:

- *Testing the solution.* Implementation of test plans to validate the solution. Once the solution is considered stable, a pilot is conducted in a test environment. A rigorous test includes:
    - Component testing
    - Database testing
    - Infrastructure testing
    - Security testing
    - Integration testing
    - User acceptance and usability testing
    - Stress, capacity, and performance testing
    - Regression testing
    - Recording the number of bugs
- *Conducting the pilot.* Deployment of the solution in a staging area and testing of the solution with actual users and real usage scenarios.

Test tracking and reporting

Test tracking and reporting occurs at frequent intervals during the developing, testing, and stabilizing phases. During the stabilizing phase, reporting is dependent upon the issue and bug count. Regular communication of test status to the team and other key stakeholders ensures a well-informed team.

Milestones of the stabilizing phase

The interim milestones of the stabilizing phase are as follows:

- *Bug convergence.* A milestone of the stabilizing phase that marks the point at which the team makes measurable progress against the active issue and bug count. At bug convergence, the rate of bugs resolved exceeds the rate of bugs found. Because the bug rate will still rise and fall—even after it starts its overall decline—bug convergence usually manifests itself as a trend rather than a fixed point in time.

  After bug convergence, the number of bugs should continue to decrease until zero-bug release. Bug convergence informs the team that the end of the project is near.

- *Zero-bug release.* A milestone of the stabilizing phase that marks the point at which the issue and bug count has met the zero-defect metric for this point in the project.

- *Release candidates.* A series of milestones of the stabilizing phase that reflect incremental improvements in the reduction of the issue and bug count as compared to that of the zero-bug release milestone.

- *Golden release.* A milestone of the stabilizing phase that is identified by the combination of zero-defect and success criteria metrics.

The stabilizing phase culminates in the *release readiness* milestone. After the solution has been reviewed and approved, it is ready for full deployment in the production environment. The release readiness milestone occurs when the team has addressed all issues and has shipped the product. At the release readiness milestone, the responsibility for managing and supporting the solution is officially transferred from the project team to the operations and support teams.

Deliverables of the stabilizing phase

The deliverables of the stabilizing phase are as follows:

- Final release
- Release notes
- Performance support elements
- Test results and testing tools
- Source code and executable files
- Project documents
- Milestone review

What Is the Deploying Phase?

During this phase, the team deploys the solution technology and site components, stabilizes the deployment, transfers the project to operations and support, and obtains final customer approval of the project. After deployment, the team conducts a project review and a customer satisfaction survey. The deploying phase culminates in the *deployment complete* milestone.

Deployment process

The team performs the following key tasks during the deploying phase:

- *Completion of deployment and operations procedures.* Formal documentation of deployment and operational procedures to outline how the project team intends to perform deployment and transition tasks.
- *Deployment and stabilization.* Completion of the actual component and site deployments.
- *Project review.* Completion of post-project reviews with the customer and project team.

Note   Stabilizing activities might continue during this phase because the project components are transferred from a test environment to a production environment.

Milestones of the deploying phase

The interim milestones of the deploying phase are as follows:

- *Core components deployed.* Most infrastructure solutions include a number of components that provide the underlying structure for the entire solution. Though these components do not represent the solution from the perspective of the customer, successful deployment of sites depends on these components. Depending on the solution, the core technology might need to be deployed before or simultaneously with site deployments. To avoid delays, core components must be reviewed and approved for deployment while other parts of the solution are still being stabilized.
- *Site deployments complete.* At the completion of this milestone, all intended users must be able to access the solution. Lead developers for each site must confirm that their sites are operating. This milestone might not be applicable for projects that do not include client-side deployments.
- *Deployment stable.* At this milestone, the customer and team agree that the sites are operating satisfactorily. Some issues might arise with the various site deployments. These issues can be tracked and resolved.

Note   The customer might agree that the team has met its objectives before it can declare the solution to be in production and close the project. Making this agreement requires a stable solution and clearly stated success criteria. For the solution to be considered stable, appropriate operations and support systems must be implemented.

The period between the deployment stable milestone and the deployment complete milestone is sometimes referred to as a *quiet period*. Although the team is no longer active, team resources will respond to issues that are presented to them. Typical quiet periods last between 15 and 30 days. During this period, the team measures the effectiveness and performance of the solution and can estimate the maintenance effort required for continuing operations. The team can also work on the next release of the solution during this time.

- *Deployment complete*. This milestone is the culmination of the deploying phase. By this time, the deployed solution should be providing the expected business value to the customer.

It can be difficult to determine when a deployment is complete. Newly deployed systems often go through a continuous process of identifying and managing production support issues. The team can have a difficult time closing the project because of the ongoing issues that arise after deployment. Therefore, the team needs to clearly define a completion milestone for the deployment rather than attempting to reach a point of absolute finality.

Deliverables of the deploying phase

The deliverables of the deploying phase are as follows:

- Operation and support information systems
    - Procedures and processes
    - Knowledge base, reports, and logbooks
- Documentation repository for all versions of documents and code developed during the project
- A training plan
- Project completion report
    - Final versions of all project documents
    - Customer satisfaction data
    - Definition of next steps

Lesson 3: Introducing the Case Study— Adventure Works Cycles Application

This lesson introduces the scenario that is used to illustrate the concepts and procedures for designing applications that are based on the Microsoft .NET Framework. This scenario will be used in many of the forthcoming lessons.

After this lesson, you will be able to

■ Recognize the basic business requirements of the case study application.

Estimated lesson time: 10 minutes

The Adventure Works Cycles Case Scenario

The purpose of this case study is to enable you, the application architect, to understand the nature of business problems that you will need to solve. Adventure Works Cycles, a large, multinational manufacturing company, produces and distributes metal and composite bicycles to North American, European, and Asian commercial markets. While its base operation is located in Bothell, Washington, and employs 500 people, several regional sales teams are located throughout the company's market region.

In 2000, Adventure Works Cycles bought a small manufacturing plant, Wide World Importers, which is located in Mexico City, Mexico. Wide World Importers manufactures several critical subcomponents for the Adventure Works Cycles product line. These subcomponents are shipped to the Bothell location for final product assembly. In 2001, Wide World Importers became the sole manufacturer and distributor of the touring bicycle product group.

After a successful fiscal year, Adventure Works Cycles is looking to broaden its market share by focusing its sales efforts on the company's best customers, extending product availability through an external Web site, and reducing the cost of sales by reducing production costs.

What Are the Business Problems?

The business problems can be categorized according to the various departments— Sales, Human Resources (HR), Wide World Importers Acquisition, Purchasing, Information Systems, Production, System Administration, and Engineering.

Business problems in the Sales department

Sales representatives from regional sales offices have assigned sales territories in the United States, Canada, England, Australia, Germany, and France. Each regional office consists of several sales representatives and a team manager. In their daily sales activities, sales representatives use both laptops and Handheld PCs that run Microsoft® Windows CE.

A typical work day for a sales representative starts with the representative dialing in to the regional office and downloading current data such as inventory, product, and promotional information. During customer visits, the sales representative takes orders on the laptop or Handheld PC. At the end of each day, the sales representative sets up appointments for the following day or week, checks the appointments of other representatives in the area for possible collaboration, and updates the contact list. The sales representative dials back in to the regional office, sends updated information, and receives any new internal communications from the base office or regional office. The company currently uses Microsoft Outlook® for e-mail.

The sales teams have identified the following requirements that will enable them to perform their jobs better:

- *Customer segmentation and profiling.* The sales team needs to be able to extract valuable information from raw data available in the databases to answer questions such as the following:
  - What are the early warning signs of problems?
  - Who are the best customers across all product lines? With whom should the sales team focus its efforts for building long-term relationships?
  - What are customers' issues, categorized according to demographic groups (geographic location, revenue history, and so on)?
  - What products are the customers buying and at what rate?
- *Sales activity.*
  - The current discount policy allows sales representatives the discretion to discount a particular order up to 15 percent. Sales managers can increase their own discounts or customer discounts up to 20 percent. The product should allow employees to provide appropriate discounts to customers, depending on the employee's role.
  - To support sales activity throughout the world, the sales team needs international support, including the ability to have product information, especially dates and pricing, available in multiple languages and currency types.
- *Internal communication.* Each sales representative must receive customer and sales data pertinent only to that representative. Each team manager must receive relevant customer and appointment data along with detailed information for each sales representative on that manager's team. A manager must be able to assign customers to sales representatives based on their relationships with the customers, though usually customers are assigned by region.

- *Opportunity management.* Sales representatives need a method to store and access sales opportunity data and, when a sale is generated, to convert some or all of the information into a sales order without reentering information.
- *Decision support system.* The decision support system should provide the following features:
  - Allow marketing/sales staff to query and use customer data to generate standard reports; execute custom queries; obtain information related to promotion tracking, sales forecasting, and customer segmentation; and access third-party data sources and financial evaluation tools.
  - Present all customer activity in a unified way, including multiple contacts, conversations, and transactions.
  - Allow marketing personnel to initiate new promotions and programs on a multinational basis. Currently, sales representatives do not know how to associate these programs with specific areas for the best impact.
  - Identify, analyze, and share all aspects of customer relationships with individuals throughout multiple departments.

Business problems in the HR department

The current retention rate of Adventure Works Cycles employees is 90 percent for hourly employees and 75 percent for salaried employees. Management predicts that they will need to hire 35 percent more workers during the next fiscal year to replace departing employees and meet the projected increase in production. In addition, the acquisition of Wide World Importers has significantly increased the department's hiring and employee retention tasks because of the increase in employees and job candidates.

Management has determined that they need a solution to track both employee reviews and the resumes of prospective employees. In addition, they want to improve their ability to forecast the number of employees needed and to plan for changes in work compensation and benefits. The HR department requires the following features from the solution:

- *Resume and review management.* All resumes and reviews are stored in documents of different formats. A system is needed to provide:
  - Unified storage for all file types
  - Access to existing employee data (relational database tables) with links to reviews or resumes
  - Tools for converting all files types to documents that can be shared internally across departments
  - Ability to secure some areas of documents, such as salary information, from designated users
  - Ability to search resumes or reviews for keywords or phrases

- *Analysis and planning.* The HR department needs support for performing the following types of analysis:
    - Compensation and benefits analysis, including impact of international currency exchange rates
    - Planning to assess the required workforce
    - Payroll cost simulations and forecasting

Business problems in the Wide World Importers Acquisition department

Wide World Importers is located in Mexico City, Mexico. They manufacture several critical components used in the Adventure Works Cycles product line. Adventure Works Cycles recently purchased Wide World Importers in an effort to expand its infrastructure to support the expected growth of the company. Wide World Importers is considered a separate business unit from Adventure Works Cycles; however, it is imperative that some applications and data be shared between the two companies. The business problems associated with this department are as follows:

- *Data transfer.* Adventure Works Cycles cannot migrate and transfer data regularly because:
    - Wide World Importers does not have a high-speed data transfer utility for moving data from their local database to the three Microsoft SQL Server™ databases in Bothell.
    - Adventure Works Cycles has a centralized environment; it needs to enhance the scalability of its production database by transitioning to a distributed environment.
    - The data is currently not being transferred by means of a secure network connection.
- *Administration and support.* Wide World Importers has limited Information Systems (IS) support. Departments maintain their own workstations and the servers that support the Oracle database are monitored and maintained by two administrators and the IS manager. The company lacks many of the standardized processes used by Adventure Works Cycles in its daily operations management.

Business problems in the Purchasing department

Adventure Works Cycles currently uses several vendors to supply various components and raw materials for its product line. The Purchasing department has identified a major supplier who is interested in establishing an Electronic Data Interchange (EDI) with Adventure Works Cycles to transmit critical data and documents such as purchase orders, invoices, payments, and product specifications. Purchasing agents and accounting employees spend more than 50 percent of their time handling these major vendors. After the EDI solution is fully implemented, the Purchasing department manager anticipates a 30 percent increase in employee efficiency in these departments.

The Adventure Works Cycles application must provide the following features:

- The ability for Adventure Works Cycles and the vendors to transmit and receive a variety of data and file types, including structured and semi-structured data
- The ability for vendors to submit their data directly to the Microsoft SQL Server™ purchasing tables
- A Web-based system that provides secure information specific to each vendor
- The ability to automatically detect when the vendors have incoming files or other data ready for Adventure Works Cycles to receive

Business problems in the Information Systems department

The Adventure Works Cycles Internet site is being developed. Currently, customers can access basic product information, find the closest sales office, and request printed information. They cannot order products online or view the status of an existing order. The ability to search the current Web site for product information is limited to viewing products by category. To increase its customer base and provide additional functionality for existing customers, Adventure Works Cycles is expanding its Internet site to include the following features:

- Online product ordering for customers
- Online order-status checking
- Better search capabilities for product information
- Ability to access explicit sections of engineering product specifications
- Ability to view product information and pricing in international currency and character sets

In addition to the Internet site, Adventure Works Cycles has a small intranet Web site consisting of a home page and links to all department sites. Each department is responsible for maintaining its own site and notifying the IS department of any changes that need to be made to its links on the home page. The focus for the intranet site is to improve internal communication. Jose Lugo, Adventure Works Cycles' finance manager, says that it is difficult to get information from one department and supply it to other departments. The department managers want to route more file transactions and data access through the internal Web site. This intranet site must support the following features:

- The ability to search for information across departmental sites.
- The ability to change or update to internal information (pricing changes, customer complaints, and so on).
- The availability of product data to all departments. It must be visible and adaptable to multiple needs (sales, marketing, and engineering).

Business problems in the Production department

The Adventure Works Cycles product line consists of nine bicycle product groups. Each product contains one or more subcomponents, depending on the customer order. Currently, production receives a specification from the Engineering department and uses it to assemble the product. A product clerk enters all the specification information used by production. Certain basic product information is available to customers on the external Web site. However, customers do not have access to the entire product specification. The entire product specification is available to the sales staff from the internal site.

As products move through each assembly area, subcomponents and other value-added materials are added to the product until it reaches the final assembly area. Some of the problems associated with production workflow are as follows:

- *Scheduling and production.* To avoid delays in production, the team needs:
    - Easier access to manufacturing data, such as work orders and inventory levels, that is applicable to a specific assembly area.
    - The ability to analyze workflow data.
- *Inventory auditing.* Instead of manually auditing and updating the inventory system, the company wants to use barcode scanning by using a Handheld PC with the existing inventory audit application.

Business problems in the System Administration department

Full availability of Adventure Works Cycles' key systems has become a focus for the System Administration department. Complaints about the amount of system downtime have been increasing steadily.

The System Administration department does not have central control of database management functions. As a result, each database group is developing its own practices and procedures. This decentralized approach might not be an optimal use of resources. In addition, the IS staff has requested a better method of monitoring system resources across all operating systems.

The System Administration department at Adventure Works Cycles must provide the following functionality to address these business problems:

- Availability of services at all times to support Adventure Works Cycles' key systems
- Backup and recovery systems for all databases being used at Adventure Works Cycles, including data stored at World Wide Importers
- Monitoring of all resources across all operating systems

Business problems in the Engineering department

The Engineering department is responsible for designing the major components for all Adventure Works Cycles products. The team needs a system to manage the documentation needs of the department. Some of the requirements of this system are as follows:

- *Collaborative content management.* The department needs an automated system that allows them to control how drawings and specifications are reviewed, approved, and released to manufacturing for use.

- *Accessing and storage of multiple file types.* The department needs a consistent method for storing, retrieving, and archiving various files, such as computer-aided design (CAD) drawings and XML product specifications. This system must be linked to the tabular data used to track drawing and specification versions.

What Are the Requirements of the Adventure Works Cycles Application?

The Adventure Works Cycles application is a Web-based retail application. It is intended for both customers and other businesses, such as retail stores reselling Adventure Works Cycles products. In addition, the application needs to host one or more pages to allow potential job applicants to submit resumes to Adventure Works Cycles and retrieve and edit the resumes.

Business tasks

The Adventure Works Cycles application must support the following tasks:

- Customers must be able to place orders.
- Customers must be able to delete orders.
- Application system must be able to reject orders.
- Customers must be able to modify existing orders that are being processed.
- Customers and resellers must be able to review existing orders.
- Customers must be able to create new customer records.
- Customers must be able to edit customer information.
- Customers must be able to submit resumes for employment consideration.
- Customers must be able to retrieve and edit previously submitted resumes.

Note   Customers and resellers can access only their own information.

Web site requirements

The Internet Web site for Adventure Works Cycles must support the following features:

- Every page on the Web site must display a search option with appropriate search controls and a navigation bar on the left side.

- The customer must be able to search for products by using a part of a product description and a price range.

- The home page must display products that are on sale and special offers, and it must include a picture and description of each product.

- A Groups page must display a hierarchical list of links to groups of bicycle models or bicycle parts in a tree structure.

- A Product Details page must display information about a single product model. It must contain the product name and description, a large picture, and a price range. If the model is available in multiple sizes, multiple colors, or both, appropriate drop-down lists must be provided. When the customer selects a size or color, the other list is repopulated, and the price range narrows to the price of the specific product.

- A Current Order page must display the products a customer has ordered and the quantity of each product, and it must include unit and total prices. A customer must be able to change quantities or remove items from this page. A Continue Shopping button must take the customer back to the last instance of the Products page visited.

- A Customer Sign-in page must allow registered customers to sign in with their e-mail addresses and passwords. New customers must be able to register from this page. (Resellers will not use this page.)

- A Sign-in Information page must allow customers to input or change their e-mail addresses, passwords, and other personal information.

- An Address Maintenance page must allow customers to create, view, update, and delete billing and shipping addresses in their profiles.

- An Addresses Selection page must allow customers to select or remove billing and shipping addresses for an order.

- An Order Summary page must display an order, and it must include sales tax, shipping cost, and the details of reseller discounts. The customer must be able to change the quantities and remove items.

- An Arrange Payment page must allow customers to use credit cards that are on file in the database or to input new credit card information. Resellers must be able to select payment types and input purchase order numbers.

- An Order Confirmation page must display a summary of the submitted order, and it must include an order date, a confirmation number, and order status.

- An Order Status Lookup page must display a list of all orders entered by the signed-in customer. The customer must be able to select one of the orders so that it can be displayed in the Order Confirmation page.

- An Available Jobs page must allow customers to submit their resumes.

In the remaining chapters, you will learn how to design a solution that meets the requirements of the Adventure Works Cycles application.

Summary

- The MSF Process Model is a combination of the waterfall and spiral process models.
- The MSF Process Model is a milestone-based, iterative approach to developing solutions.
- The MSF Team Model specifies six roles for project teams that are involved in developing solutions: product management, program management, development, testing, release management, and user experience.
- You need to define the scope of a project by managing tradeoffs.
- MSF recommends an iterative approach to designing solutions.
- You implement iterations in a development life cycle by creating versioned releases and maintaining living documents.
- You create the vision/scope document during the envisioning phase of the MSF Process Model.
- You create functional specifications during the planning phase of the MSF Process Model.
- You create the solution during the developing phase of the MSF Process Model.
- You test the solution and conduct pilots during the stabilizing phase of the MSF Process Model.
- You deploy the solution in the production environment and submit the solution to the operations and support team during the deploying phase of the MSF Process Model.

Review

The following questions are intended to reinforce key information presented in this chapter. If you are unable to answer a question, review the lesson materials and try the question again. You can find answers to the questions in the appendix.

1. Describe the differences between the waterfall model and the spiral model, and describe how MSF uses both in the MSF Process Model.

2. In the MSF Team Model, who is responsible for the design process?

3. The tradeoff triangle describes the three types of tradeoffs that a project team and the customer can make. What is a fourth tradeoff that could be considered but that should never be compromised?

4. Using the following statement, complete the tradeoff matrix below.

   "Given a fixed feature set, we will choose resources and adjust the schedule as necessary."

	Fixed	Chosen	Adjustable
Resources			
Schedule			
Features			

5. Describe the purpose of performing daily builds in the MSF Process Model.

6. When you reach the release readiness milestone, what phase have you completed?

7. During which phase of the MSF Process Model is the initial risk assessment document created?

8. When are test cases established in the MSF Process Model?

9. List several types of tests that are performed during the stabilizing phase.

10. Why is it important to create a vision statement for the project during the envisioning phase?

11. What are some of the key tasks that are performed during the planning phase?

12. Describe the *quiet period* and the activities that occur during this period.

C H A P T E R 2

Gathering and Analyzing Information

About This Chapter

Gathering and analyzing information are steps that you perform throughout the Microsoft® Solutions Framework (MSF) Process Model. These lessons provide you with an overview of how to gather and analyze information. You will learn about the types of information that you need to gather, sources of information, and some techniques for gathering information. In addition, you will learn how to analyze all the gathered information and become familiar with some techniques for analyzing information.

Note This chapter presents information that is not specific to a particular phase in the MSF process but that is relevant to all phases. It is important to learn information gathering and analysis techniques before you start the process of envisioning and designing a solution.

Before You Begin

To complete the lessons in this chapter, you must

- Be familiar with the MSF Process Model.
- Have Microsoft Visio® 2000 Professional, for creating diagrams.

Lesson 1: Gathering Information

When gathering information, you need to be aware from the outset of the various types and characteristics of information to ensure that you gather the appropriate information. The purpose of this lesson is to introduce you to the various ways you can think about the information you need to gather about a business challenge. By taking a broad view of information, you can increase your chances of gathering all of the input you need to make an effective analysis.

After this lesson, you will be able to

- Identify the types of information that you should gather.
- Identify the techniques for gathering information.
- Identify various sources of information for gathering requirements.
- Create an information gathering strategy.

Estimated lesson time: 20 minutes

Categories of Information

An enterprise architecture is a representation of a business—a dynamic system—at a single point in time. The enterprise architecture for a business aligns information technology groups and processes with the goals of a business. To gather information about an enterprise architecture, use four descriptive categories from an enterprise architecture model to guide and classify the information you gather. The four categories are business, applications, operation, and technology.

Business

The *business* category describes how the business works. It describes the functions and the cross-functional activities that an organization performs. Information from this category also describes the business's high-level goals and objectives, products and services, financial structures, integrated business functions and processes, major organizational structures, and the interaction of these elements. It includes broad business strategies and plans for transforming the organization from its current state to its future state.

Application

The *application* category includes the services and functionality that can cross organizational boundaries and link users of different skills and functions to achieve common business objectives. Information in the application category describes the automated and non-automated services that support the business processes. It provides information on the interaction and interdependencies of the business's application systems.

Automated business services can include complete applications, utilities, productivity tools, components, and code modules that allow for the analysis of information or task functionality.

In an organization, identical tasks are often repeated multiple times by using different tools. As you gather information about processes in the organization, investigate the different applications used to conduct company activities. These existing applications or portions of these applications can provide core services for any new solution. It is more cost effective to reuse than to re-create these services. The information you gather will help to refine the business processes by indicating potential inefficiencies or redundancies.

The application category provides information about the current use of systems and services. You will also obtain indicators about future directions when you gather information from resources such as users and business documents.

Operations

The *operations* category describes what the organization needs to know to run its business processes and operations. This category includes standard data models, data management policies, and descriptions of the patterns of information consumption and production in the business.

You should identify the information's origin, ownership, and consumption. Tracking and analyzing its access and use patterns provides the basis for making data distribution, replication, and partitioning decisions, in addition to identifying what is needed to establish standards and guidelines for replication, repositories, and data warehousing. Often, the consumers of information are not adequately questioned to determine not only what information they need, but also what they do with the information when they have it.

The relationship between key business processes and the information required to perform these processes helps to set standards and guidelines for creating, retrieving, updating, and deleting information and data; for sharing critical documents and data; and for defining security levels and standards for access. Realize that not all information is centralized or easy to access by each person or system that needs the information. Often, the information most critical to a business resides on database servers, on the workstations that make up the active working environment of the business, and possibly in the heads of the employees (meaning that the information is not recorded anywhere).

Technology

The *technology* category defines the technical services needed to perform and support the business mission, including the topologies, development environments, application programming interfaces (APIs), security, network services, database management system (DBMS) services, technical specifications, hardware tiers, operating systems, and more.

This category also provides information about the standards and guidelines that a business uses for acquiring and deploying workstation and server tools, base applications, infrastructure services, network connectivity components, and platforms.

Technology provides the link between applications and information. Applications are created and based on different technologies. They use technology to access information, which is stored by using various storage technologies.

You can use information from the technology category to determine the standard interfaces, services, and application models to be used in development. This information can translate into development resources for the project teams, including component and code libraries, standards documents, and design guidelines. This information can also provide a basis for an application's design goals and constraints.

What Are the Techniques for Gathering Information?

There are six main techniques that you can use for gathering information:

- Shadowing
- Interviewing
- Focus groups
- Surveys
- User instruction
- Prototyping

Note   You might not use all of these techniques. You need to identify which techniques will work best for the specific source you are going to extract information from. In addition, you need not be an expert on all of the techniques. For implementing these techniques, you might need training or the help of an expert.

Shadowing

Shadowing is a technique in which you observe a user performing the tasks in the actual work environment and ask the user any questions related to the task. You typically follow the user as the user performs daily tasks. The information you obtain by using this technique is firsthand and in context. In addition, you understand the purpose of performing a specific task. To gather as much information as possible, you need to encourage the user to explain the reasons for performing a task in as much detail as possible.

Shadowing can be both passive and active. When performing *passive shadowing*, you observe the user and listen to any explanations that the user might provide. When performing *active shadowing*, you ask questions as the user explains events and activities. You might also be given the opportunity to perform some of the tasks, at the user's discretion.

Tip   Shadowing works well for tasks that are performed frequently. However, if a task is performed only occasionally, finding an opportunity to shadow someone for that specific task might be difficult.

Shadowing is a good way to get an idea of what a person does on a day-to-day basis. However, you might not be able to observe all the tasks during shadowing because more than likely the person will not, during that session, perform all the tasks he or she is assigned. For example, accounting people might create reports at the end of the month, developers might create status reports on a weekly basis, and management might schedule status meetings only biweekly.

In addition to the information that you would collect from the individual, you might collect relevant work artifacts, such as documents and screen shots of the current solution.

Note   In information gathering, an *artifact* is any item that is physically available in the business environment that describes an element or core business process. Artifacts are discussed in detail later in this lesson.

Examples of questions for shadowing

While gathering information by using the shadowing technique, you encourage the user to answer the following questions:

- How do users structure their work?
- What decisions do users make when starting or completing a task?
- How does the current implementation define the way users perform their jobs?
- How often does the system interfere with their jobs?
- How do interruptions affect users? Can users resume where they left off after being interrupted?
- With how many people does a specific user interact during a given activity?
- What modifications has the user made over time to make it easier to complete the task?
- Are there any variations in the steps that the user performs to complete the task? What are these variations, and under what conditions are the variations used?

In addition to learning how users perform their tasks, you can learn about the parts of the current solution and process that cause users to feel dissatisfied or frustrated.

During the shadowing process, look for answers to the following questions:

- How do users currently perform these tasks?
- How can the processes be made more efficient? Should any tasks that are performed manually be performed by an automated solution?
- Which related tasks might affect the design of the solution?
- What system features are needed to support the tasks?
- What are the performance criteria?
- How should the features of the solution be structured?
- How can the current system be improved?
- Which features of the current system are being used frequently, and which features are being used rarely?
- What do users like and dislike about the current system?
- How can training and support costs be reduced?
- What information about the users is not documented?
- What are the users' working environments?
- What are the characteristics and preferences of users?
- What are the concepts and terminology used by the users?
- What training has been provided to users?
- What training do users need?
- Have users been through training, or are they self-taught? How does the training or lack of training affect their ability to use the system and perform their tasks?

Note Ensure that you observe and question both the management and users. If there are external customers, include them in your observations.

Interviewing

While shadowing provides an effective means to discover what is currently being done in a business, it might not provide all the necessary information. Shadowing is not the best option for gathering information about tasks such as management-level activities; long-term activities that span weeks, months, or years; or processes that require little or no human intervention. An example of a process that requires no human intervention is the automatic bill-paying service provided by financial institutions. For gathering information about such activities and processes, you need to conduct interviews.

An *interview* is a one-on-one meeting between a member of the project team and a user or a stakeholder. The quality of the information a team gathers depends on the skills of both the interviewer and the interviewee. An interviewer who becomes an ally can learn a great deal about the difficulties and limitations of the current solution. Interviews provide the opportunity to ask a wide range of questions about topics that you cannot observe by means of shadowing.

Some important points to remember before conducting interviews include:

- Start with non-specific set of questions and encourage interviewees to think about all the tasks they perform and any information they can provide.
- Using the answers to the questions, ask interviewees to put the larger tasks they perform in order, and to break the larger tasks into smaller tasks.
- Specifically ask interviewees to identify information that is usually missing and alternative paths that can occur.
- Reiterate through the preceding steps several times and continue to ask interviewees what else might be involved.
- Ask interviewees for ideas that they have to improve the situation, but avoid assuming that those ideas are the correct solution.

Examples of questions for interviewing

While conducting an interview, structure questions carefully so that you do not ask misleading questions or questions that ask for more than one type of information. Some of the questions that you might ask during an interview are:

- What problems do you encounter while performing your tasks?
- What kind of help do you need when you work remotely?
- Do you have special needs that are not documented?
- What business policies help you or hinder you in performing your job?
- What individuals or documents provide essential information that you need to do your job?
- What other users or systems, such as third-party suppliers or support specialists, affect your work?

Focus groups

A *focus group* is a session in which individuals discuss a topic and provide feedback to a facilitator. Focus groups concentrate on group interviewing techniques. Use this method in cases in which there are more users than you can involve directly in the information gathering process. For the information gathered during a focus group to be useful, ensure that the participants of the focus group represent the users or stakeholders associated with the business. You should also ensure that you have appropriately defined the topic of the focus group and that you keep the group focused on this topic.

Focus groups allow you to gather detailed information about how an activity fits into the business as a whole. Individuals in a focus group can fill knowledge gaps for one another and provide a complete description of a business process.

Focus groups might not be successful if the participants are located in different geographical locations. Focus groups also might not work if the users that were identified to participate do not perform the same activity or do not have enough knowledge about the activity. Finally, focus groups are not successful if the facilitator is unable to direct the meeting and keep the discussion focused.

Surveys

Surveys consist of sets of questions that are created to gather information. Examples of surveys include user registration forms and customer feedback or satisfaction forms.

Creating survey questions can be a labor-intensive process. You need a trained professional for creating the survey questions and analyzing the results of the survey. You can use surveys to gather information and to identify further information gathering activities that you need.

One of the benefits of using surveys is that they enable users to respond anonymously. You can collect information that might be impossible to collect with any other technique. However, you might need to treat the responses to the survey with confidentiality to protect the respondents. You might want to modify or neutralize the language so that the identity of the person remains confidential. Surveys provide results that can be tabulated and easily interpreted.

Note   The results of a survey can be affected by user attitudes. Surveys are therefore very subjective.

Examples of information that can be collected by using surveys include:

- Organizational structures, policies, or practices that facilitate or interfere with tasks
- Frustrations with technical support structures or policies
- Special needs related to hardware or software
- Training issues, such as the effectiveness of current training programs, types of training programs that users like, and training programs that work best in the users' work environment

User instruction

When you use the *user instruction* technique, users actually train you on the tasks that they perform. This allows you to participate in the activity and view each step of the process from the user's perspective. You might also gain knowledge that an individual has learned over time and that is unavailable from artifacts or systems.

User instruction can be time consuming if the process you are investigating is long. This method could also be frustrating for the researcher if the user is not accustomed to teaching others. In addition, different users might perform the same task differently. Consequently, you should collect information from multiple users.

Planning   Identify the experts in different activities within the business. They might know shortcuts that overcome problems in a process. Experts can act as models for developing new processes or improving existing processes.

You can also use *help desks* at a business to gather information about the user experience. A help desk is a useful source because it provides a direct perspective on the problems experienced by users. Gathering information from help desk is one way of benefiting from user instructions.

By allowing users to teach you the tasks they perform, you can gather information to determine:

- User interface design
- Training needs for both current and future processes
- System performance criteria
- The impact of the physical environment on a task

Prototyping

Prototyping allows you to gather information by simulating the production environment. You can use several tools to collect information, such as a camera to monitor visual activity or a computer program to monitor keystrokes and mouse clicks. The tool that you select for prototyping depends on the type of information you want to collect.

Use prototypes when it is impossible to shadow a person in the normal work environment. The data that you collect by prototyping is typically empirical rather than responses from users. Therefore, you can easily validate this data. However, the cost of prototyping might be high.

Prototypes can help you to verify or document information from the user and business perspectives, including:

- Customer quality requirements
- Response-time requirements and goals
- Ease of use
- Integration of current technologies and applications
- User interface issues, such as the features that users want to see added to an application
- Verification of workflow processes

What Are the Sources of Information?

You have learned about the different types of information that you can gather in a business. This information can be found in various forms. The number and diversity of information sources depends on the size of the business. Some of the information sources are:

- Artifacts
- Systems
- People

Artifacts

An *artifact* in information gathering is an item that is physically available in the business environment and that describes an element or core business process. As in archeology, artifacts help us understand the current environment. They provide information about tasks, processes, business needs, and constraints. Examples of artifacts include training manuals, video recordings, regulatory requirements, earlier program files or tapes, help desk documentation, and financial reports.

You can easily identify some artifacts that are used in a business. For example, employees keep frequently used artifacts around their work areas. Other artifacts might be stored in file cabinets or on computer media and are therefore less visible. You might require access to proprietary artifacts to review all information thoroughly. Use discretion in handling artifacts that are directly or indirectly part of the intellectual property that allows a business to compete in the marketplace.

Individuals in a business typically develop their own artifacts. For example, a user might create an instruction sheet for an application or process, or outline how to accomplish a task in e-mail messages. These unofficial artifacts provide valuable information. They indicate not only what people do in their daily work, but also the type of support information that is lacking in the current solution and possibly why they need to perform these tasks. Sometimes these artifacts will be the only documentation you will find related to certain processes.

During a project, the project team creates artifacts such as project meeting notes, summaries of the information gathered within the business, and the vision document. Some artifacts, such as meeting notes, are used exclusively by the project team. However, the vision document is shared by both the project team and stakeholders.

Systems

Systems describe an element of the business that is performing an action. A specific system is a set of discrete processes that accomplish an action. A system might be composed of subsystems. A system can be a tangible process, such as an inventory tracking system, or an intangible process, such as the methods that a manager uses to identify and resolve problems within a department.

Systems can be complex because they can contain multiple subsystems and many categories of information. In addition, all the subsystems might not be readily apparent. For these reasons, you might need to budget additional time to understand a system completely. Systems indicate how a business conducts day-to-day activities.

Tip   It is a good practice to enlist the help of someone who is an expert on the system and have the expert lead you through the different processes that the system performs.

People

The people who are stakeholders in the business can be the source of valuable insights into the business, often providing information that is not documented anywhere. These stakeholders include executives, developers, managers, customers, and users. In cases where documentation is incomplete (or non-existent), people might be the only source for the information you need to learn about the business.

Before approaching people to gather information, take the time to identify the different roles that the people perform in the business. For example, the group of people who provide support and information to users to help them perform their tasks might provide insight into which areas cause the most difficulties for users. Long-term employees with experiences in multiple operations within the business can provide insight as to how different activities relate to each other. Also, if the business uses a third-party vendor for any of its processes, the vendor might have a unique perspective on the efficiency of the business and its processes.

Planning   Before talking to users, you should gain some experience with the systems that they use. Gaining this experience helps you avoid broad questions like "How do you use the system?" "What do you do throughout the day?" or "What is a workday like for you?"

How to Define the Information Gathering Strategy

When gathering information, you should define an information gathering strategy. Defining an information gathering strategy includes identifying the users, defining questions, and choosing an appropriate technique for gathering information.

When defining an information strategy, you need to keep in mind the following questions:

- What sources do you want to poll for information?
- What information do you need to collect?
- What techniques will you use to collect the information and to what sources will each technique be applied?
- How will you record the information you collect?
- What time frame will you use to collect the information?

The following are some of the guidelines that you can use to define an information strategy:

- *Use multiple information gathering techniques.* If you rely on only one information gathering technique, you might have an incomplete view of the business. By combining various techniques, you overcome any shortcomings associated with any one technique. For example, assume that a process occurs once per month in the accounting department of a business. If you shadow a user in the accounting department for a few days, you might miss important information about the process because the user might not perform the tasks for this process while you are shadowing. By complementing shadowing with a focus group or a follow-up interview, you can gather information about all the processes that occur in the accounting department.

- *Identify the most effective technique.* Weigh the advantages and disadvantages of each technique when you are developing your information gathering strategy. For example, you might need to collect information as quickly as possible to respond to an immediate business challenge. Surveys take time to plan, administer, and analyze. Instead, shadowing, interviews, or user instruction can help you gather information quickly.

- *Remember all perspectives, types of information, and information sources.* Regardless of the information gathering technique, remember that you need to gather information from both user and business perspectives. Explore as many sources of information as possible within the time you have to gather information.

- *Gather information from groups that use similar business processes.* Different groups in a business might be following similar processes and might have responded to similar business challenges. Information gathered from those groups might help the project team to look at the business challenge from a new perspective.

Lesson 2: Analyzing Information

In this lesson, you transition from the process of gathering information to the process of analyzing information. The processes of gathering and analyzing information are iterative. You gather some information and analyze it. As you review that information, you will undoubtedly discover that you have more questions. You will then formulate your questions and take them back to the appropriate sources for clarification. Having this new information will help you to continue analyzing the business. This form of collaboration will continue throughout the life cycle of the project, although most of the information gathering and analysis will occur at the beginning of the life cycle.

After this lesson, you will be able to

- Analyze enterprise architecture information.
- Describe use cases and usage scenarios.
- Create internal project documentation.

Estimated lesson time: 20 minutes

Enterprise Architecture Information

When you think you have gathered enough information from the customer, you will have a large amount of information that you need to review to determine what information is most relevant to the business challenge. You need to synthesize the information to create a detailed description of the current state of the business.

As you analyze the information you have gathered, verify that you have enough information to indicate the current state of the business and product requirements, including:

- Security needs.
- Support structures for the solution and their characteristics.
- Planned changes in the business that could affect the product design.
- Performance that users expect or that the business needs to remain competitive.
- Existing applications that will need to interact with the new product.
- How the existing business processes affect the solution.

As you synthesize and analyze the information, you can identify any gaps that exist in the information you collected, and, if necessary, gather additional information.

When the development team actually develops the final product, it will need to verify that the final product meets all the requirements that were established during the gathering and analyzing processes. The team will also need to document the effects that the new product might have on the existing environment in terms of new requirements for the business, such as support, maintenance, and extensibility issues. The new requirements must also adhere to the constraints that you documented during analysis.

High-Level Use Cases and Usage Scenarios

After you have synthesized the information, you can develop use cases and usage scenarios to document the business processes and business and user requirements in more detail. The use cases and usage scenarios that you develop will provide structure for the development team when it designs the solution. In addition, each use case and usage scenario will correspond to one or more requirements. This correspondence allows you to ensure that the requirements are being met.

Use cases

Use cases show the functionality of a system and how an individual interacts with the system to obtain value.

The purposes of use cases are to:

- Identify the business process and all activities from start to finish.
- Document the context and environmental issues.
- Establish a connection between business needs and user requirements.
- Describe needs and requirements in the context of use.
- Focus users and the development team.

Use cases provide the following benefits:

- Provide context for requirements
- Facilitate common understanding
- Provide the basis for usage scenarios
- Facilitate objectivity and consistency in evaluating user suggestions

Usage scenarios

Use cases describe the high-level interactions between an individual and a system. *Usage scenarios* provide additional information about the activities and task sequences that constitute a process. Together, use cases and usage scenarios provide a description of a workflow process.

You will learn how to create use cases and usage scenarios in Lesson 4.

Draft Requirements Document

After the team has gathered information from the customers, one of the steps in analysis is to create a draft requirements document. This document includes a preliminary list of requirements from the information that is gathered by the team. The main purpose of this document is to record any possible requirements and, in doing that, to ensure that no valuable information is lost. The information that you gather from different sources will include requirements and wants from the business and user perspectives. The requirements indicate what the product or solution needs to do to solve the business challenge as derived from the business and user perspectives. The wants indicate what stakeholders and users would like to see in the final product or solution.

The requirements listed in the draft requirements document are not refined and therefore can be a combination of requirements and wants. These requirements are refined further in later stages of envisioning and planning, when the team gathers more information from the customers.

You will learn more about identifying requirements, wants, and constraints in Chapter 4, "Creating the Conceptual Design."

Example of an interview

Following is an example of an interview from the Adventure Works Cycles scenario that was introduced in Chapter 1, "Introduction to Designing Business Solutions."

Summary of an interview with the territory sales manager

We had a great year in sales this year. Our jobs have been a lot easier since the company equipped us with laptop computers and PDAs. We have been doing some forecasting for the next year, and we are starting to see a slow decline in sales, particularly if we continue to operate like we have in the past. The sales department has established a number of goals for the new fiscal year. The top three goals are (a) focus on our best customers, (b) use sales staff time more effectively, and (c) manage sales opportunities better.

We don't have an easy way to analyze our customer base. Currently, customer data is stored in our systems, but there's no easy way to retrieve the data and allow us to view the data in different ways. To better identify our best customers and why they are our best customers, we need a way to access our data and to be able to analyze it in a meaningful way.

Another problem we've experienced in recent months is in presenting our products and achieving sales in our foreign markets. Currently, all the information on our computers is written in English only. We need to store multilingual and multiregional information in the database rather than depending on the sales force to translate the information.

Example of an interview *(continued)*

Our team needs to obtain the latest pricing information on a daily basis, and we should be doing this every day. Currently, the sales representative connects to the corporate network and downloads the new pricing list each day in the morning. However, the download process does not identify which prices have been modified for that individual sales representative. So the sales representative must download the entire list every morning. You can imagine how customers feel when they have negotiated a deal with us only to find out that the price was incorrect.

Another area that needs definite improvement is in our sales opportunities management. Employees are supposed to use our customer management system to plan, execute, and track sales and marketing strategy. In addition to that, sales representatives need to install a large application on their laptop computers and connect to the corporate network to use it. We want to be more mobile than that; we want to be able to access this information from a Web site. The information must be easy to access and meaningful for the sales representatives and the company; otherwise it doesn't help anyone. We want to achieve the following goals with the new system: Minimize the amount of technical knowledge that sales and marketing needs to access the data, and allow the staff to obtain standard reports, generate custom queries, track promotions, and view customer segmentation information. In addition, we want this system to be flexible enough so that we can add third-party data sources and financial evaluation tools. No matter who views a particular customer's information, that individual must get a clear, unified view of the customer and the customer's relationship with us.

Example of a use case diagram

Figure 2.1 shows a preliminary use case, which is based on the interview shown in the previous section.

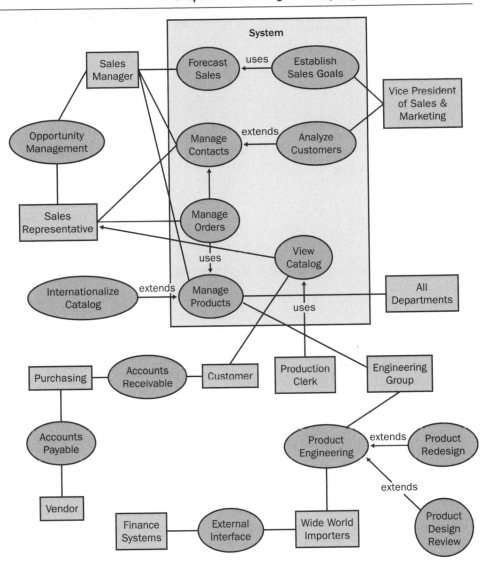

Figure 2.1.   Use case diagram

Example of a draft requirements document

Figure 2.2 contains a list of draft requirements that you might have identified from the interview and use case.

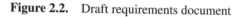

	A	B	C	D	E	F	G	H
1								
2		Req ID	Req desc	Priority	Source	UC ID	Current func	V-Next
3		1	can sync up with our online applications to record all the information collected throughout the day		Territory sales manager		x	
4		2	retrieve the customer data and allow us to view the data in different ways		Territory sales manager		x	
5		3	determine who our best customers are		Territory sales manager			

Figure 2.2.   Draft requirements document

As you analyze information, you will most likely find that you need to gather additional information. The number of iterations that you conduct depends on the business challenge, the complexity of the problem, and other factors, such as time limits imposed by stakeholders.

Figure 2.3 is an example of the draft requirements document with additional questions that you might ask your customers for clarification about specific requirements.

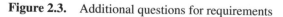

	A	B	C	D	E	F
1						
2		Req ID	Req desc	Priority	Source	Questions from this item:
3		1	can sync up with our online applications to record all the information collected throughout the day		Territory sales manager	What specific information is collected? What does "sync up" mean, with what? What specifically is done differently after "synching up"? What specific information is really necessary and on what timing during the day? Week?
4		2	retrieve the customer data and allow us to view the data in different ways		Territory sales manager	What specific ways do you view this customer data? What does "customer data" mean?
5		3	determine who our best customers are		Territory sales manager	How do you define best? Revenue, percentage of revenue, frequency, certain collections of products?

Figure 2.3.   Additional questions for requirements

Internal Project Team Documentation

After gathering information, as a part of analysis, the team creates several internal documents that are not typically provided to the customers. These documents—the actors catalog, business rules catalog, and glossary—are living documents and are refined during the course of project life cycle.

Actors catalog

The *actors catalog* contains information about all the actors that will be used in use cases. (An *actor* is an entity that interacts with the system.) The actors catalog contains the following information:

- Actor name
- Responsibility of the actor
- Source for this information

For example, in the Adventure Works Cycles scenario, a sales representative is an actor whose responsibilities include establishing contacts with customers within a geographic region, and acquiring knowledge about products and their specifications and information about all the customers. The source of this information is tracked in case you need to go back to the source for additional information or clarification.

Figure 2.4 is an example of an actors catalog.

	A	B	C	D	E
1					
2		Actor	Responsibilities	Source	Business Title
3		Sales Representative	Establish contact with customers	Sales Manager	
			Needs to know about the products and their		

Figure 2.4.   Actors catalog

Business rules catalog

The *business rules catalog* is a living document that lists the business rules for a solution. The business rules catalog is a predecessor for the requirements document. This document is created early in the design process, when the team gathers information. This document, like the actors catalog, is meant only for the team and is typically not provided to the customer.

The business rules catalog includes the following fields to document information about a business rule:

- Identification number for the business rule, for tracking and traceability
- Short title for the business rule
- Description of the business rule
- Authority (the source of the business rule)
- UC/BR (use case or business rule), which specifies either the use case to which the business rule might refer or another business rule to which the business rule relates
- Current functionality, which indicates the functionality related to the business rule in the current system

For example, a business rule identified during interviews and conversations with the sales manager in the Adventure Works Cycles scenario is that sales representatives can provide a discount of up to 10 percent to their customers. However, sales managers can approve and provide a discount of up to 20 percent to their customers.

Figure 2.5 is an example of a business rules catalog.

	B	C	D	E	F	G
1						
2	BR ID	Business Rule Title	Business Rule	Authority	UC/BR	Current func.
3	100	Discount	The Sales Representative can provide a discount of up to 10% only	Sales Manager	UC5.01	
4						
5						

Figure 2.5.   Business rules catalog

Glossary

When designing a business solution, the team will identify terms that need to be defined. The *glossary* contains a list of these terms and their meanings. The purpose of the glossary is to ensure that everyone is using the same terms and that everyone understands what those terms mean.

Lesson 3: Using Modeling Notations

You use models to describe business processes, to understand the current state of the business, and to model new processes that do not exist but that you plan to create in the future. Models help you depict business processes and their relationship with other processes. You also depict the tasks that comprise the process. In this lesson, you will learn about the benefits of models and the different types of modeling notations that you can use.

Note   This lesson assumes that you use Microsoft Visio® for Enterprise Architects for creating diagrams.

After this lesson, you will be able to

- List the benefits of modeling.
- Describe the role of Unified Modeling Language (UML) in conceptual design.
- Describe the purpose of various UML views.
- Describe the purpose of the various UML diagrams.
- Describe the role of Object Role Modeling (ORM) in conceptual design.
- Describe the relationship between UML views and the different phases of the MSF Process Model.

Estimated lesson time: 20 minutes

Benefits of Modeling

You use models to describe both the current and proposed solution to a business challenge. Some of the benefits of using models are:

- Models provide you with a common terminology that can describe both the current and proposed solutions.
- Models help to describe complex problems in a simpler structure and enable easy communication.
- Models enable consensus by helping the project team understand the business challenge, the business and user requirements, and the information that must be gathered.

As the business processes are modeled and adapted to reflect the requirements, you can build a model of the architecture that describes the final business solution. Two commonly used modeling notations are:

- Unified Modeling Language (UML)
- Object Role Modeling (ORM)

What Is UML?

UML is a standard modeling language that you use to model software systems of varying complexities. These systems can range from large corporate information systems to distributed Web-based systems.

UML was developed to provide users with a standard visual modeling language so that they can develop and exchange meaningful models. UML is independent of particular programming languages and development processes. You use UML to:

- Visualize a software system with well-defined symbols. A developer or application can unambiguously interpret a model written in UML by another developer.
- Specify the software system and help build precise, unambiguous, and complete models.
- Construct models of the software system that can correspond directly with a variety of programming languages.
- Document the models of the software system by expressing the requirements of the system during its development and deployment stages.

More Info   For additional information about UML, you might find the following references useful: *The Unified Modeling Language User Guide* by Grady Booch, Ivar Jacobson, and James Rumbaugh (Addison-Wesley, 1999) and *Use Case Driven Object Modeling with UML: A Practical Approach* by Doug Rosenberg with Kendall Scott (Addison-Wesley, 1999).

- It is a simple, extensible, and expressive visual modeling language.
- It consists of a set of notations and rules for modeling software systems of varying complexities.
- It provides the ability to create simple, well-documented, and easy to understand software models.
- UML is both language independent and platform independent.

What Are UML Views?

UML enables system engineers to create a standard blueprint of any system. UML provides a number of graphical tools that you can use to visualize and understand the system from different viewpoints. You can use diagrams to present multiple views of a system. Together, the multiple views of the system represent the model of the system.

You use models or views to depict the complexity of a software system. The various UML views depict several aspects of the software system. The views that are typically used are:

■ *The user view.* The user view represents the goals and objectives of the system from the viewpoint of the users and their requirements for the system. This view represents the part of the system with which the user interacts. The user view is also referred to as the *use-case view*.

■ *The structural view.* The structural view represents the static or idle state of the system. The structural view is also referred to as the *design view*.

■ *The behavioral view.* The behavioral view represents the dynamic or changing state of the system. The behavioral view is also referred to as the *process view*.

■ *The implementation view.* The implementation view represents the structure of the logical elements of the system.

■ *The environment view.* The environment view represents the distribution of the physical elements of the system. The environment of a system specifies the functionality of the system from the user's point of view. The environment view is also referred to as the *deployment view*.

What Are UML Diagrams?

The various UML views include diagrams that provide multiple perspectives of the solution being developed. You might not develop diagrams for every system you create, but you must understand the system views and the corresponding UML diagrams. Similarly, you might not use every diagram to model your system. You need to identify which models will best suit the needs of modeling the system successfully.

Use the following UML diagrams to depict various views of a system:

■ *Class diagrams.* A class diagram depicts various classes and their associations. Associations are depicted as bidirectional connections between classes.

■ *Object diagrams.* An object diagram depicts various objects in a system and their relationships with each other.

■ *Use case diagrams.* A use case diagram represents the functionality that is provided to external entities by the system.

■ *Component diagrams.* A component diagram represents the implementation view of a system. It represents various components of the system and their relationships, such as source code, object code, and execution code.

■ *Deployment diagram.* A deployment diagram represents the mapping of software components to the nodes of the physical implementation of a system.

- *Collaboration diagrams.* A collaboration diagram represents a set of classes and the messages sent and received by those classes.

- *Sequence diagrams.* A sequence diagram describes the interaction between classes. The interaction represents the order of messages that are exchanged between classes.

- *State diagrams.* A state diagram describes the behavior of a class when the external processes or entities access the class. It depicts the states and responses of a class while performing an action.

Note   You can use Visio to generate UML diagrams. Visio enables you to design and document your solution from the initial analysis and design stages to the final deployment of your system.

Relationship Between UML Views and the MSF Process Model Phases

You create different UML diagrams in different phases of the MSF Process Model. The software development life cycle is typically composed of the UML notations to depict various views of a system. For example, during the planning phase, you might use a set of diagrams to depict the proposed design for the solution. During the developing phase, you can use a different type of diagram to depict software components.

Figure 2.6 depicts the UML views and the diagrams associated with the views.

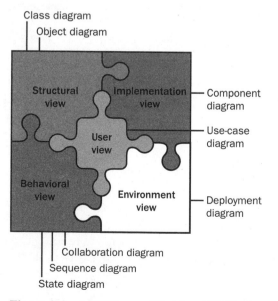

Figure 2.6.   MSF Process Model and UML views

Table 2.1 lists the UML views and the corresponding phases of the MSF Process Model.

Table 2.1.   UML Views and the MSF Process Model Phases

UML views	UML diagrams	Purpose	Create the diagram	Use the diagram
User view	Use case diagrams	To understand user requirements	Envisioning and planning phases	All phases
Structural view	Class diagrams, Object diagrams	To identify the basic components of the system	Planning phase	Developing and stabilizing phases
Behavioral view	Collaboration diagrams, Sequence diagrams, State diagrams	To identify the behavior of the system in various circumstances and conditions	Planning phase	Developing and stabilizing phases
Implementation view	Component diagrams	To know how the various structural blocks identified in structural view can be grouped and packaged	Planning phase	Developing and stabilizing phases
Environment view	Deployment diagrams	To know the physical and deployment aspects of the system	Planning phase	Developing and stabilizing phases

What Is ORM?

The *Object Role Modeling* (*ORM*) method is a fact-oriented method for analyzing information, in terms of objects and the roles they play, at the conceptual level. By using this methodology, you can document business rules and design databases to model complex, data-related business requirements.

You use ORM to model business requirements during the conceptual design stage of the planning phase. A benefit of the ORM method is in its conceptual approach to modeling. This approach helps to ensure the correctness, clarity, adaptability, and productivity of a solution by allowing you to describe the solution by using concepts and language that people can understand easily.

The quality of a solution depends on its design. To design a solution, you build a formal model of the application area. The application area is called the *universe of discourse* (UoD) in ORM. ORM uses a natural language and intuitive diagrams. You present information as elementary facts. An *elementary fact* asserts that an object has a property, or that one or more objects participate in a relationship.

Note   The associated language, FORML (Formal Object Role Modeling Language), is supported in Visio for Enterprise Architects.

More Info   For more information about modeling languages, see *Information Modeling and Relational Databases: From Conceptual Analysis to Logical Design* by Terry Halpin (Morgan Kaufmann Publishers, 2001).

ORM conceptual schema design procedure

The ORM *conceptual schema design procedure* (CSDP) focuses on the analysis and design of data. The conceptual schema specifies the information structure of the application: the *types of fact* that are of interest; *constraints* on these facts; and the *derivation rules* for deriving some facts from others. The CSDP consists of the following tasks:

- Analyzing external information and transforming it into elementary facts.
- Applying a population check to fact types. (All combined instances of an item in the UoD are known as that item's *population*.)
- Identifying primitive entity types in the conceptual model.
- Applying uniqueness constraints to the conceptual model.
- Applying mandatory role constraints to the conceptual model.
- Adding value constraints, set-comparison constraints, and subtype constraints to the conceptual model.
- Adding ring constraints to the conceptual model.

Analyze and transform external information into elementary facts

This is the most important stage of the CSDP. In this stage, the information required from the system is presented in natural language. Examples of such information include output reports and input forms of the required system. ORM models represent the set of all valid data use cases in the UoD.

Some of the important terms used in modeling are:

- *Instance*. An item of interest in the UoD.
- *Population*. The group of all combined instances of a given type of item of interest in the UoD is known as that item's *population*. In database terms, all rows in a table make up that table's population.
- *Set*. Any group of instances, but a set is not necessarily the same as a population. A set could be part of a population, or a combination of instances from more than one population. All populations are sets, but not all sets are populations.
- *Fact instance*. An individual observation of the relationship between two or more data values.
- *Fact type*. The set of fact instances that share the same object types and predicate relationships.

- *Object type.* The set of all possible instances of a given object.
- *Predicate.* A verb phrase that the domain expert uses to relate object types.

Consider the following example of a fact instance:

The author known as Hemingway wrote the book known by the title "A Farewell to Arms."

In this example, the author, Hemingway, and the book, *A Farewell to Arms*, are both data values, related by the action verb "write."

Table 2.2 contains another example. This table displays data used by a university to maintain details about its academic staff and academic departments.

Table 2.2.   Example of a table used to store data

Employee Number	Employee Name	Department	Room	Telephone Extension	Telephone Access
715	Adams, J	Computer Science	69-301	2345	Local
720	Bassli, S	Biochemistry	62-406	9642	Local
139	Canuto, S	Mathematics	67-301	1221	International
430	Culp, S	Computer Science	69-507	2911	International
503	D'Hers, T	Computer Science	69-507	2988	Local
651	Jones, B	Biochemistry	69-803	5003	Local

Each fact defines a relationship between two objects. Some of the elementary facts that can be stated from the above table are:

- The Instructor with Employee Number 715 has Employee Name "Adams, J."
- The Instructor with Employee Number 715 works for the Department named "Computer Science."
- The Instructor with Employee Number 715 occupies the Room 69-301.
- The Instructor with Employee Number 715 uses the Telephone Extension 2345.

The name of the Object Role Modeling method reflects the way it uses objects and roles. Objects are either values or entities. *Values* are character strings or numbers and are identified by constants such as "Adams, J" and 715. *Entities* are real-world objects that have descriptions, such as the Instructor with Employee Number 715.

You can combine facts. For example, two facts stated earlier can be combined as follows:

The Instructor with Employee Number 715 and Employee Name "Adams, J" works for the Department named "Computer Science."

Apply a population check to fact types

To apply a population check, you must enter a meaningful sample population into the model. *A meaningful sample population* represents instances of information in the UoD, and the real-world problem that the project team is trying to solve. The sample population can be from sources such as reports, charts, graphs, input screens, and forms. In the data maintained by the university about its academic staff and academic departments displayed earlier, each row in the table represents one fact instance. Each column in the table represents instances of an object type's role in the fact type.

Identify primitive entity types

To model business requirements, you must identify object types in the UoD. Object types can be classified as entity types and value types. Primitive entity types represent the most basic entity types in a UoD, and they are mutually exclusive and exhaustive. They are the lowest common denominator of a group of entity types. All primitive entity types are atomic and mutually exclusive:

- *Atomicity.* Primitive entity types are atomic because they cannot be broken down into other entity types or structures.
- *Mutual exclusivity.* The populations of two or more primitive entity types never overlap. A union of the members of two or more primitive entity types will never produce redundant instances.

  An example of a primitive entity type would be the combination of the Start-Time and StopTime object types into a new Time primitive entity type.

Consider the following fact types:

- Professor obtained Degree from University
- Senior Lecturer obtained Degree from University
- Lecturer obtained Degree from University

The common predicate in these fact types suggests that the entity types—Professor, Senior Lecturer, and Lecturer—can be combined to the single primitive entity type: Academic.

Apply uniqueness constraints

You should explicitly test and enforce uniqueness to ensure the strict use of elementary facts and to eliminate redundancy. A *uniqueness constraint* prevents duplication of role instances spanned by the constraint. A uniqueness constraint placed across all roles in a predicate effectively prevents the duplication of instances of the fact type. Uniqueness constraints are used to assert that entries in one or more roles occur *at most once*.

Some of the benefits of uniqueness constraints are that they:

- *Prevent fact redundancy*. Uniqueness constraints ensure that no fact instances are repeated.

- *Enforce internal uniqueness*. A uniqueness constraint on roles within a single predicate is an internal uniqueness constraint. An internal uniqueness constraint ensures that fact table entries for a role, or combination of roles within a single predicate, occur only once. All instances of a fact type must be unique for the fact type to be elementary. For example, the university academic staff is classified as professors, senior lecturers, or lecturers, and each instructor specializes in a research area. The internal uniqueness constraints on the fact types assert that each instructor has at most one rank, holds at most one specialization, works for at most one department, and has at most one employee name.

- *Enforce external uniqueness*. An external uniqueness constraint spans roles from two or more predicates and ensures that instances of the role combination occur only once. For example, the external uniqueness constraint stipulates that each department and employee name combination applies to, at most, one academic.

Apply mandatory role constraints

In a relationship, you might have to enforce the fact that every instance of an object type has information recorded. You accomplish this by placing constraints on the object type's population. A *mandatory role constraint* forces all instances of an object type to participate in a role.

Mandatory role constraints have the following characteristics:

- *Global nature*. Mandatory role constraints are global in nature, to the extent that they force the enumeration of the entire population of an object type. This constraint is important because it forces you to consider all instances for inclusion in all other roles in which an object type participates. For example, if you model a mandatory constraint on an employee's name and birth date, you must know both items for all employees.

- *Implied with functional dependency*. A role is functionally dependent on another if there is a many-to-one or a one-to-one relationship between the roles, and if the first role in the relationship always has a uniqueness constraint. For example, if it is mandatory that each father have a child, and that children are functionally dependent on their fathers, it is mandatory that all children have fathers.

Mandatory role constraints are expressed in FORML notation by the inclusion of the word "Each" in front of an object type. Consider the following example:

```
Each Person has Name.
```

In the FORML expression, the word "Each" indicates that the Person role in this fact type has a mandatory role constraint on it and that the name of each instance of the object type Person is known.

Add value constraints, set-comparison constraints, and subtype constraints

Constraints are used to limit populations. ORM provides several methods of limiting the domain of an object type. The domain of a population represents all of the possible values that exist in the population. It is not necessary to use each member of the domain.

For example, an object could be constrained to allow only a number between 1 and 5, or to allow only the names of the days of the week.

Value constraints

Limit the population of an object type to a specific domain of allowable values. The FORML expression of a value constraint follows the pattern of specifying the object type and then the phrase "The possible values of," followed by the object type and the word "are," followed by an enumerated list of values. The following FORML expression represents a value constraint on the Person object type that restricts the domain of the object type to Jeff, Maria, and Pierre.

```
Person(Name) is an entity object type.
Every Person is identified by one distinct Name.
The possible values of "Name" are: "Jeff", "Maria","Pierre".
```

Set constraints

Often, a relationship exists between the populations of two different fact types. ORM uses set constraints to capture these relationships. *Set constraints* limit the instances that can participate in a fact type. A set constraint is external and spans roles in two different fact types. By constraining the roles in two different fact types, you constrain the fact instances in each of the fact types. Set constraints restrict two populations in relation to each other. Some of the different types of set constraints are:

- *Set exclusion constraint.* Prevents instances in one set from appearing in another.

  ```
  No Employee that is paid some HourlyWage is paid some Salary.
  ```

- *Set equality constraint.* Forces all instances in one set to appear in another.

  ```
  Employee e is paid some Salary if and only if Employee e works as som
  e SalesManager.
  ```

- *Set subset constraint.* Limits instances in one set to those that are also in another.

  ```
  If Employee e works as some SalesManager then Employee e works as som
  e Salesperson.
  ```

Entity subtypes

You might need to control a subset of an object type's population differently from the entire population. This subset of the population might participate in different fact types. In addition, you must classify a subset of a group of objects into more specific groups to understand them or gather more useful information from them.

For example, the specialization of the population of the Vehicle object type might result in the object types GasVehicle and DieselVehicle. You could further specialize each of those as ConsumerVehicle and CommercialVehicle object types.

An *entity subtype* is an object type that is contained in another object type. Entity subtypes must be well defined in terms of relationships played by their supertypes. Entity subtypes with the same supertype might overlap. You must be able to identify entity subtypes and supertypes.

An object type's FORML expression is annotated to represent every entity subtype in which the object type participates, either as a parent or as a child. The following FORML expression represents the subtype relating to the Salesperson object type:

```
Salesperson is an entity object type.
Salesperson is primarily identified by the identification scheme of Empl
oyee.
Salesperson is a subtype of Employee /
  Employee is a supertype of Salesperson.
Employee is the primary supertype of Salesperson.
Subtype definition: The subset of Employee who is Salesperson.
Each Manager is a Salesperson but not every Salesperson is necessarily a
 Manager.
```

Add ring constraints to the conceptual model

An *object type* plays just one role in a fact type. When two roles in a fact type are played by the same object type, the path from the object type through the role pair and back to the object type forms a ring. For example, consider the following fact type: *Person voted for Person*. This has two roles—voting and being voted for. However, both roles can be played by the same object, such as PersonA voting for PersonA.

Ring constraints control the population of an object type's roles when the object type has two roles in a single fact type. Different types of ring constraints are:

- *Irreflexive.* An irreflexive (ir) ring constraint prevents an instance from being related to itself. The FORML expression for an irreflexive ring constraint is:

```
No Object is related to itself.
```

- *Symmetric.* The symmetric (sym) ring constraint ensures that a mirror image of every tuple exists in the fact type's population. In functional programming languages, a *tuple* is a data object containing two or more components. The FORML expression for a symmetric ring constraint is:

```
If Object o1 is related to Object o2
then Object o2 is related to Object o1.
```

- *Asymmetric.* An asymmetric (as) ring constraint ensures that no mirror images of any tuple exist in the fact type's population. The FORML expression for an asymmetric ring constraint is:

```
If Object o1 is related to Object o2
then it cannot be that
Object o2 is related to Object o1.
```

- *Antisymmetric.* An antisymmetric (ans) ring constraint ensures that no mirror images of any tuple exist in the fact type's population, and that no instance is related to itself. The FORML expression for an antisymmetric ring constraint is:

```
If Object o1 is related to Object o2
and o1 is not the same Object as o2, then it cannot be that
Object o2 is related to Object o1.
```

- *Intransitive.* An intransitive (it) ring constraint enforces hierarchical relationships between instances in a population. The FORML expression for an intransitive ring constraint is:

```
If Object o1 is related to Object o2
and Object o2 is related to Object o3
then it cannot be that
Object o1 is related to Object o3.
```

- *Acyclic.* An acyclic (ac) ring constraint prevents a path from looping back on itself through a chain of relationships. The FORML expression for an acyclic ring constraint is:

```
An Object cannot cycle back to itself through one or more application
s of the relationship:
Object is related to Object.
```

Lesson 4: Creating Use Cases and Usage Scenarios

Use cases and usage scenarios capture the functional requirements of a system. In this lesson, you will learn more about use cases and usage scenarios and how to create them.

After this lesson, you will be able to

- Create use cases.
- Describe usage scenarios.
- Create usage scenarios.
- Refine requirements from use cases and usage scenarios.

Estimated lesson time: 10 minutes

How to Create Use Cases

Use cases are functional descriptions of the transactions that are performed by the system when a user initiates an event or action. The use cases that you develop should represent the system processes, including all events that can occur in all possible situations.

Use cases consist of elements that are inside the system and are responsible for the functionality and behavior of the system. They are the actions that the system performs to generate the results that the users request. This model allows the project stakeholders to agree on the capabilities of the system and system boundary.

A use case diagram documents the following design activities:

- Identifying the system
- Identifying actors
- Defining the interactions between the actor and the system
- Determining the system boundary

Identifying the system

A *system* is a collection of subsystems that have a real-world purpose. For example, in a sales and marketing scenario, the order system might have a subsystem that determines applicable discounts for a customer invoice. When you develop use cases, you identify a single system or subsystem. A collection of use cases indicates the relationships among the subsystems that make up the system, in addition to the relationships between systems that interact with each other.

Identifying actors

The actor is an integral part of the use case. The use case represents the interactions between an actor and the system. An *actor* is an entity that interacts with the system to be built for the purpose of completing an event. An actor can be:

- A user of the system.
- An entity, such as another system or a database, that resides outside the system.

For example, in the Adventure Works Cycles scenario, some of the actors are sales representatives, sales managers, customers, and production clerks.

The roles played by actors explain the need and outcome of a use case. By focusing on the actors, the design team can concentrate on how the system will be used instead of how it will be developed or implemented. Focusing on the actors helps the team to refine and further define the boundaries of the system. Defining the actors also helps to identify potential business users that need to be involved in the use case modeling effort.

When looking for actors, ask the following questions:

- Who uses the system?
- Who starts the system?
- Who maintains the system?
- What other systems use this system?
- Who gets information from this system?
- Who provides information to the system?
- Does anything happen automatically at a preset time?
- Who or what initiates events with the system?
- Who or what interacts with the system to help the system respond to an event?
- Are there any reporting interfaces?
- Are there any system administrative interfaces?
- Will the system need to interact with any existing systems?
- Are any actors already defined for the system?
- Are there any other hardware or software devices that interact with the system and that should be modeled during analysis?
- If an event occurs in the system, does an external entity need to be informed of this event? Does the system need to query an external entity to help it perform a task?

Defining the interactions between the actor and the system

After you have identified the system and the actor, you need to describe the interaction between them. You need to create one use case for each interaction. Describe only those interactions that are important to the business challenge and the vision statement.

Determining the system boundary

One of the more difficult aspects of use case modeling is determining the exact boundary of the system to be built. People who are new to use case modeling might find it difficult to determine whether certain actors should be part of the system.

To define the boundary of the system, the team should try to answer the following questions:

- What happens to the use cases associated with that actor?
- Who or what interacts with those use cases now?
- What if you find new requirements? Will these requirements be a part of the system?
- Are these requirements necessary for this system?
- Are these requirements something this system would logically do?
- Can these requirements be handled by one of the current actors?
- Are these requirements something the customer/user would expect the system to do?

Figure 2.7 depicts an example of a diagram of a set of use cases.

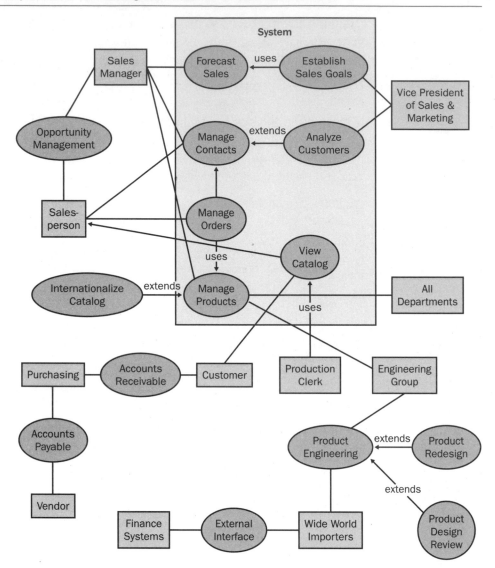

Figure 2.7.   Example of a diagram of a set of use cases

Typically, an actor is shown as a stick figure, a single use case is shown as an ellipse, and a set of cases are enclosed in a box, which represents a system.

What Are Usage Scenarios?

Use cases describe the high-level interactions between an actor and a system. The use cases grouped together describe a workflow process in detail. Usage scenarios provide additional information about the activities and task sequences that constitute a process. Usage scenarios document the sequence of tasks.

Usage scenarios describe in detail a particular instance of a use case. It takes many usage scenarios to document a use case completely. Whereas use cases are diagrams, usage scenarios are narratives.

Usage scenarios depict objects in a workflow process. Objects are something that are affected by the system, something that affects the system, or something that a system needs to be aware of to function properly. For example, objects in a training center include the customer, the training course, and the sales representative. Objects provide a view of the characteristics and behavior of elements in the problem domain that is addressed by the business challenge. In the conceptual design phase, you create usage scenarios that depict the objects in the problem domain.

In addition to objects, usage scenarios depict exceptions. *Exceptions* are atypical events or alternate task sequences to meet the use case. An example of an exception condition for entering information for a new customer into the training center contact system is when the system is down and the sales representative must use other means to take customer information.

Tips for handling exceptions in a system include:

- Ask "what if" to capture exceptions to the work task or step.
- Determine the relative probability of each exception.
- Discuss how the exception is currently handled and any alternative methods.
- Incorporate handling of high-probability exceptions into the design of the solution.

When you develop usage scenarios, you might identify a task that must be treated as a use case. For example, in the "Register customer for course" use case, you might determine that the task sequence "Process customer payment" is a high-level use case that is part of the workflow process and has several usage scenarios.

Consequently, each usage scenario for "Register customer for course" ends with "Entering course number." Then you create all relevant usage scenarios for the new "Process customer payment" use case.

You identify the use cases that correspond to the workflow process and then develop usage scenarios that describe the task sequences for each use case. From the usage scenarios, you can determine the current state requirements.

Why Create Current State Usage Scenarios?

After you identify a use case, you can determine the different usage scenarios that can occur for the use case. You then use the information that you gathered from users to describe the different usage scenarios possible for the use case. Creating a usage scenario helps you determine if you gathered the appropriate level of information. Gathering the required amount of information for describing the current state is part of the iterative aspect of gathering and analyzing information.

You can create scenarios for both the current and the future states of the business environment. The *current state scenario* depicts how business activities are currently conducted; the *future state scenario* presents the activities as the business wants them to be. For both states, the scenario emphasizes business processes, information, users, and tasks.

In some situations, full scenarios need be developed only for use cases that are known to have many exceptions or dependencies. This allows the project team to balance costs against the potential benefits. Use cases and scenarios should be developed iteratively, and can be discovered or continued during development work on the initial set of use cases.

Benefits

Although there are various ways to analyze current work processes, use cases and usage scenarios are especially effective in modeling the process. Creating use cases and scenarios provides the following benefits:

- By measuring productivity levels of the current system, the team can determine whether the new system has achieved usability goals.
- The team can identify the problems in the system and what works in the system.
- The team might discover that the problems perceived by users are different from the actual problems and their causes. The team can then concentrate on the real problems.

Creating a usage scenario

To create a usage scenario, you need to perform the following tasks:

- Determine the preconditions for the usage scenario, specifying information or conditions that must exist before a scenario can be executed.
- Identify the postconditions for the usage scenario, which identify the work or goal completed during the task sequence.
- Break the activity into discrete steps.
- Identify exceptions that might occur for any step. You might need to develop usage scenarios for these exceptions.
- Identify the requirement that this particular usage scenario addresses, for tracking and traceability.
- Identify the source for this usage scenario, for further discussion and clarification.

Following is an example of how you can derive a usage scenario from the Adventure Works Cycles use case:

Use case title: Customer requests product literature

Abbreviated title: Customer requests product literature

Use case ID: UC05.1

Requirements ID: 14.1

Description: Customer wants to obtain information for a product. The customer is able to view a copy online, print a copy, or request a hard copy to be delivered by mail.

Actors: Customer

Preconditions:

Customer has Internet access.

Customer has browsed to the Adventure Works Cycles Web site.

Customer has clicked **Browse Product Descriptions**.

Product information exists in the database, and the site is working properly.

Task sequence	Exceptions
Customer scrolls to desired product.	Product is not in current view.
Customer selects product by clicking on product graphic or details.	
Customer views basic product information (name, description, image, in-stock status, price, item number).	Any piece of data is not available.
Customer clicks **Need Complete Specification?**	
Customer views full product specification online (UC05.1.3).	Customer chooses printable version (UC05.1.2).
Customer clicks **Mail Me Full Brochure** (UC05.1.1).	Customer is not in database. Customer completes and saves profile.
	Customer is in database. Customer confirms address.
Customer clicks **Submit**.	Submit process fails.
Customer browses away from product specification.	

Postconditions: The request to receive the full specification by mail is complete and saved in the database.

Unresolved issues: How should saved requests best be queued for fulfillment?

If submit process fails three times, what process should be invoked?

Authority: Mike Danseglio

Modification history:

Date: November 6, 2002

Author: Heidi Steen

Description: Initial version

Note   Although this chapter teaches you how to create a detailed usage scenario, you would not create such a detailed usage scenario until the conceptual design phase. This example is used to teach you the technique of how to create a usage scenario.

How to Refine Requirements

As mentioned earlier, when you analyze information with use cases and usage scenarios or by using any other tool, you also refine the list of requirements. When you create more detailed use cases, you can differentiate between requirements, wants, and constraints, and also identify any hidden requirements from the gathered information. The requirements and wants will eventually define the features of the completed solution. At this stage, the team only describes, organizes, and prioritizes the requirements and wants. Later, in the process of developing the product, the development team will determine the features of the product.

Note   Refining requirements typically happens during the envisioning phase and the conceptual and logical design processes of a project life cycle. You create a first level of requirements during envisioning, and then further refine them to eventually derive the feature set and determine which requirements are in scope for this version of the product. Once you progress to physical design, any change in requirements will cause the project to re-iterate. Therefore, you should get an agreement from the customer about the requirements during the conceptual and logical design.

Requirements and wants

Requirements indicate the characteristics of the process that are essential for meeting the goals of the business. Wants are important but not essential to achieving the business goals or resolving the business challenge. Wants are based on the actual day-to-day experiences of people. However, they represent an ideal state of how people would like things to be in the business. As you discuss the requirements and wants with the customer, some wants might become requirements, and some requirements might become wants.

Constraints and assumptions

Constraints indicate the parameters to which the final business solution must adhere. They are aspects of the business environment that cannot or will not be changed. Often, thcsc constraints become design goals for the application. If constraints are not identified properly, the project team might design a product that cannot be deployed within the business.

Examples of possible constraints that you should document include:

- Budget limitations
- Characteristics of existing or supporting systems
- Network system architecture
- Security requirements
- Operating systems
- Planned upgrades in technologies
- Network bandwidth limitations
- Maintenance and support agreements and structures
- Knowledge level of development or support staff
- Learning limitations of users

Assumptions are identified as you talk to the customer and analyze the data you have gathered. Assumptions and constraints are very similar. An example of an assumption is "We will use Microsoft .NET as the basis of the new solution." In this case, the team is assuming that it will build the solution by using .NET.

A constraint prevents you from accomplishing something; an assumption is a piece of knowledge that you possess when beginning the project—it might be good or bad.

Hidden requirements

It is especially important to identify hidden requirements. Imagine completing the design and then learning about a merger your client will go through in the near future, meaning that you need to consider interacting with the systems of the acquired company. Your customers might feel the need to withhold this information, not realizing the impact to the project. Some examples of hidden requirements are:

- Interoperability with peer networks and the Internet
- No firewall to enable barrier-free connectivity
- Mergers, acquisitions, and other changes in the business constituency
- Meeting regulatory requirements that come into being after the project is in process
- Maintenance of the deployed system after the expiration of the stipulated period
- Personnel changes that might affect the project or the team

Activity: Gathering and Analyzing Information

In this activity, you use what you learned in the lessons to work through information gathering exercises.

Exercise 1: Preparing for an Interview

You will be interviewing the human resources manager at Adventure Works Cycles to gather information about their current system. To prepare, you want to develop a series of questions to ask during the interview. What questions would you formulate for the interview?

After you have completed your list, view the document named "Interview with the Human Resources Manager" in the \SolutionDocuments\Chapter02 folder on the CD to determine whether there are any other questions you would ask during the interview or in a subsequent interview with the human resources manager.

Some possible questions are:

- How many employees does human resources have to account for currently?
- How are the employees classified (full time versus part time versus contractors)?
- How many new employees does the company anticipate it will hire in the next fiscal year?
- What are the shortcomings of the current solution that you would like to see addressed in the new solution?
- Describe how the hiring process works today.
- Describe how the review process works today.
- Describe how the usage of benefits is analyzed today, and how the results of the analysis are used to make future decisions about benefits.
- How many different documents do you store for each employee? For each employment candidate?
- What categories do you use to manage employees and candidates (such as skills, levels, industry keywords, or specialities)?
- Are all documents currently in Microsoft Word format? If not, what other formats are they in?
- What are the various storage areas for your documents? (List all network drives and databases, including server names.)
- Who has the authority and ability to view, change, or enter employee and candidate records?

Exercise 2: Deriving Use Case Statements for the Sales Automation Project and for the Web Enhancement Project

Your team has completed most of the information gathering for the Adventure Works Cycles project. Using the interviews for the territory sales manager, the information services manager, the vice president of production, and the Web customer, and the shadowing report for the sales associate, derive as many use case statements as you can. Derive only the use case statements here. You will complete the full usage scenario in a later exercise. Develop use cases that follow the Actor-Action-Object format: An example of a use case statement would be "Sales Representative views product information."

Use Visio to create a UML use case diagram.

 To see one possible solution for this exercise, see the Visio document named C02Ex2_Answer.vsd in the \SolutionDocuments\Chapter02 folder on the CD.

Exercise 3: Developing Draft Requirements from Initial Information Gathering

You have started the initial gathering of information by talking to people in the Sales department, the network adminstrator, and the project sponsor. You also have a beginning collection of use cases. Identify phrases in the interviews or use cases that might eventually be requirements.

Use the Microsoft Excel document named C02Ex3.xls in the \SolutionDocuments \Chapter02 folder on the CD to record your work. Use the Original Tab to write down the actual phrases from the interview. To guide your work, three examples have been given in the Revised tab. To see one possible solution, see the document named C02Ex3_Answer.xls in the \SolutionDocuments\Chapter02 folder on the CD. The Original Tab contains the phrases from the interviews that are potential requirements. The Revised Tab shows revised phrases starting with the Sales Manager comments. The phrases have also been reorganized into related groups. This document also shows questions that could be derived from the first three potential requirement statements from the Sales Manager.

Exercise 4: Developing a Usage Scenario

You need to document the usage scenario for the use case "Customer requests product literature." You will first need to define the actor, the objects, and the system. You will then need to complete the precondition and postcondition. Next, complete the task sequence and note any exceptions. Use the information in the interview and shadowing documentation, in addition to your own experience with developing software and completing online purchases.

Use the Excel document named C02Ex4 in the \SolutionDocuments\Chapter02 folder on the CD to record your work. To see one possible solution for this exercise, see the document named C02Ex4_Answer in the same folder on the CD.

Summary

- Gathering and analyzing information are steps that you perform throughout the Microsoft Solutions Framework (MSF) Process Model.

- Gathering and analyzing are iterative collaboration processes between you and your customer.

- Some techniques for gathering are interviewing, shadowing, user instructions, and prototyping.

- Analysis involves creating use cases and usage scenarios, draft lists of requirements, actors catalogs, and business rules catalogs.

- Modeling represents another method of describing business processes. Models indicate relationships and behavior among business processes, in addition to the tasks that make up the processes.

- ORM is a fact-oriented method for analyzing information at the conceptual level.

- UML is a standard modeling language that you use to model software systems of varying complexity.

- UML views depict several aspects of a software system by using UML diagrams.

- UML diagrams depict various views of a system.

- Creating use cases involves:
  - Identifying the system
  - Identifying actors
  - Defining interactions between the system and the actors
  - Determining the system boundary

- Use cases describe the interactions between an actor and a system and are used to describe a workflow process.

- Usage scenarios provide information about the activities and task sequences that constitute a process.

- After you begin analysis, you need to eliminate redundancies to determine the information that is most important to the business and the business challenge.

- You need to distinguish between requirements and wants when you synthesize the information from both the business and user perspectives.

- Constraints indicate the parameters to which the final business solution must adhere and indicate the aspects of the business environment that cannot be changed.

Review

The following questions are intended to reinforce key information presented in this chapter. If you are unable to answer a question, review the lesson materials and try the question again. You can find answers to the questions in the appendix.

1. What is the difference between the interviewing and focus-group techniques of gathering information?

2. When should you use prototyping instead of shadowing to gather information?

3. How do you identify the most effective information gathering technique for a project?

4. What is the purpose of creating use cases?

5. What is an actors catalog?

6. What is ORM?

7. What is UML?

8. What are the purposes of the various UML views?

9. What is an actor in a use case?

10. What is the purpose of a usage scenario?

11. What are the steps in creating a usage scenario?

C H A P T E R   3

Envisioning the Solution

About This Chapter

The success of a project depends on the ability of the project team members and the customers to share a clear vision of the goals and objectives of the project. You define the vision of the project during the envisioning phase of the Microsoft® Solutions Framework (MSF) Process Model. In the following four lessons, you will learn about the envisioning phase and the roles and responsibilities of team members during this phase. You will also learn how to define the vision of the project and analyze risks associated with the project.

Before You Begin

To complete the lessons in this chapter, you must

- Understand the MSF Process Model.
- Understand techniques for gathering and analyzing information.

Lesson 1: The Envisioning Phase

The envisioning phase is the period during which the team, the customer, and the sponsors define the high-level business requirements and overall goals of a project. The main purpose is to ensure a common vision and reach consensus among the team members that the project is both valuable to the organization and likely to succeed. During envisioning, you should focus on creating clear definitions of the problem. The envisioning phase culminates in the vision/scope approved milestone.

After this lesson, you will be able to

- Describe the purpose of the envisioning phase.
- Describe the roles and responsibilities of team members during the envisioning phase.
- List the guidelines for setting up the project team.
- Describe the deliverables of the envisioning phase.

Estimated lesson time: 5 minutes

Purpose of Envisioning

The first phase of the MSF Process Model is envisioning. During this phase, the team creates an overview of the business problem to be solved and how that problem relates to the business, the customers, and the environment. This helps the team get a clear vision of what the team must accomplish for its customers. For a successful project, you need to know what the customer wants to achieve with the solution.

Figure 3.1 indicates how the envisioning phase fits into the overall MSF Process Model.

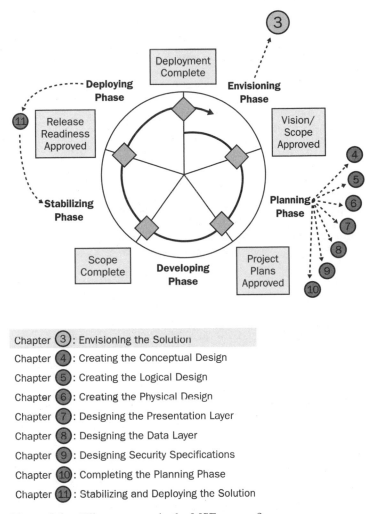

Figure 3.1.   Where are you in the MSF process?

For example, consider an organization that wants you to develop its Web site. "We need a Web site" is a good reason but not a good vision for the Web site project. To create the most effective solution, the team should identify the goals that the organization wants to achieve by building and deploying this Web site. In addition, the team needs to determine whether the Web site has any unique characteristics that the organization can take advantage of for maximum benefit. Does the organization want a complex site, or a site that supports a growing number of users? Perhaps the organization needs to plan for both complexity and scalability? The team should consider the intended market and expected volume of site visits. Another consideration for the team is the organization's brand and projection of image in the marketplace.

Envisioning serves many purposes. The team uses the envisioning phase to:

- Identify the goals and constraints of the project.
- Answer feasibility questions, gain approval from key stakeholders, and acquire a common set of expectations from everyone involved.
- Form the basis upon which team members build the solution later in the project.
- Define the scope of the project, which helps in the detailed planning effort of the next phase.
- Estimate the resources that are required to develop the solution.
- Identify and schedule the major milestones for the project.

Roles and Responsibilities of the Team Members

Although the project team works as a single unit to achieve the vision/scope approved milestone of the envisioning phase, each role has a specific focus during each phase of the project life cycle.

Figure 3.2 shows the roles for the project team during the envisioning phase.

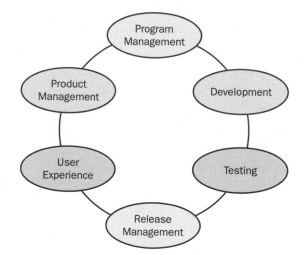

Figure 3.2.   The MSF Team Model

The MSF Team Model specifies six roles for a project in the envisioning phase:

- *Product management.* The responsibility of product management includes ensuring that the team addresses the customer requirements. The product management role collaborates with the program management role and drives the effort to establish a shared project vision. To accomplish this goal, product management studies and analyzes the business problem, business requirements, project vision, business goals, and user profiles.

- *Program management.* Program management establishes project design goals, defines success factors and metrics, articulates the solution concept, and sets up the project infrastructure.

- *Development.* The development team provides feedback to the team on the technical implications of developing the product and on the feasibility of the solution concept.

- *User experience.* The user experience team analyzes the performance needs and support issues of users and considers the product implications of meeting those needs.

- *Testing.* The testing team provides feedback to the team on the quality goal for the solution and specifies the actions that will be needed to achieve that level of quality. The testing team then applies decisions about the quality goal to testing strategies and acceptance criteria that will be used to measure quality.

- *Release management.* The release management team identifies what will be required to deploy the product, how the product will be deployed, when it will be deployed, and whether deployment will require additional infrastructure.

How to Form a Project Team

One of the tasks that you perform during the envisioning phase is setting up the team. It is important that the project team members are competent and can perform the tasks necessary for creating the solution. The task of forming a team brings together the skills that are essential for completing the project successfully. When identifying appropriate team members for a project, you need to consider the following for each member:

- *Knowledge.* Represents the information that an individual must possess to perform the job competently, such as knowledge of computer science fundamentals.

- *Skills.* Represent the behavior or abilities making up the competency and correspond to the skills of the team member, such as mathematical logic or artistic ability.

- *Performance level.* Represents the ability and the expected results from capable execution. For example, you might choose a person who meets deadlines consistently while meeting the quality requirements for the assigned task.

In addition to considering each individual's capabilities, there are some practical considerations to selecting team members. These include:

- Availability of the team members.
- Cost or project budget.
- Security clearance of the team members.

How to Prepare the Deliverables of the Envisioning Phase

Although there are interim milestones during the envisioning phase, such as formation of the core team, creation of the draft version of the vision/scope document, and creation of the draft version of the risk assessment document, there are three major deliverables of the envisioning phase. These are as follows:

- *Vision/scope document.* The vision/scope document describes the project goals and constraints. It outlines the product being developed, the needs it will meet, its features, and an initial schedule.

- *Project structure document.* The project structure document outlines the project organization structure and describes the project management process. It outlines who is responsible for each role in the MSF Team Model and identifies the team lead for each role.

- *Risk assessment document.* The risk assessment document provides an initial identification and analysis of risks associated with the project, along with mitigation and contingency plans to help the team in managing risks.

Depending on the extent of the project, additional deliverables for the envisioning phase can include:

- An initial list of testable features
- Preliminary requirements and use cases
- Preliminary architecture
- A graphical user interface (GUI) storyboard

In addition to the documents that are shared with the customers, the project team also develops the following documents for its internal use:

- An actors catalog
- A business rules catalog
- A glossary of terms

Note   You learned about these documents in Chapter 2, "Gathering and Analyzing Information."

Lesson 2: Creating a Vision/Scope Document

The final milestone of the envisioning phase is an approved vision/scope document. In this lesson, you learn how to create a vision/scope document for a project.

After this lesson, you will be able to

- Describe the contents of the vision/scope document.
- Create a problem statement.
- Create a vision statement.
- Create user profiles.
- Define the project scope.
- Create a solution concept.
- Identify project goals.
- Validate the vision/scope document.

Estimated lesson time: 20 minutes

What Is the Vision/Scope Document?

The vision/scope document is one of the final deliverables of the envisioning phase. This document contains the goals and constraints of a business solution. The vision/scope document represents the first agreement among everyone involved in the project. It guides the team to the high-level achievement of specific business goals. Initially, the team relies heavily on the vision/scope document to decide whether to go ahead with the project. After the project is approved, the team uses the vision/scope document to structure its planning efforts throughout the rest of the project.

To create the vision/scope document, the team conducts more interviews with customers and stakeholders, analyzes the high-level use case of the business to a lower level of detail, and identifies assumptions and constraints in the organization. Remember that you continue to gather and analyze information during all phases of the MSF process.

The vision/scope document must focus on understanding and defining the problem. The contents of the vision/scope document include the following:

- Problem statement
- Vision statement
- User profiles
- Scope of the project
- Solution concept
- Project goals
    - Business goals
    - Design goals
- Critical success factors
- Initial schedule

How to Create the Problem Statement

A *problem statement* is usually a short narrative describing the issues the business hopes to address with the project. It relates primarily to the current state of business activities. The more accurately the problem statement is defined, the more you are able to gauge its impact on the business needs of the organization.

Because the aim of any project is to solve a problem, the understanding of the problem determines the design of the solution. A problem statement outlines the business problem that the team is trying to solve. This statement must provide sufficient information about the business problem. A new team member can use the problem statement and the rest of the documentation to put the project into context.

Following are some examples of problem statements:

- Telephone operators cannot deal with the high number of calls because of the time it takes them to navigate through and interact with the current application.
- The organization needs to eliminate the ongoing costs associated with earlier versions of hardware and software.
- Users need clear directions from the system to resolve errors when they occur.
- We need to increase the number of online registrations by making our Web site easier to browse.

How to Create the Vision Statement

The purpose of the vision statement is to establish a common vision and reach consensus among the team members that the project is valuable to the organization and is likely to succeed. The vision statement also ensures agreement about the future of the project among the entire team.

Characteristics of a vision statement

A vision statement must be short enough to be remembered, clear enough to be understood, and strong enough to be motivational. A good vision statement has the following five characteristics:

- *Specific.* A vision statement should be specific and include the ideal state of the business problem so that the end result is meaningful.
- *Measurable.* By creating a vision statement that is measurable, the project team can determine the success of the project and whether it met the business goals.
- *Achievable.* Given the resources, the time frames, and the skills of the team members, the vision statement should be achievable. An achievable vision statement motivates the team to complete the project.
- *Relevant.* The vision statement should relate to the business problem being addressed. If the vision statement is not relevant, the project team might discover that they are trying to solve a business problem that does not exist, and the project might lose sponsorship.
- *Time-based.* The vision statement should clearly indicate the estimated time frame for the delivery of the solution.

Note The above qualities of the vision statement are also referred to as *SMART characteristics*, each letter of the acronym standing for one of the five characteristics.

Examples of vision statements

Consider an organization whose e-commerce Web site is experiencing much lower online sales than the Web sites of its competitors. In the envisioning phase of solving this business problem, you might use the following vision statement:

Before the end of the year, we will become the top revenue-producing company in the industry by increasing our online sales.

Consider another example. An online library has a huge catalog of books, magazines, articles, white papers, and journals. The library wants its subscribers to be able to track all items in the catalog that they want to be able to find again, regardless of which computer they used to access the Web site. A vision statement for such a project might be as follows:

During the current fiscal year, we will enable all our subscribers to create bookmarks to selected pages from our Web site for access from any computer or device the end user might use.

Note that both vision statements have all five SMART characteristics. Both vision statements are specific, measurable, achievable, relevant to the business problem, and have an estimated time of availability.

How to Create User Profiles

A business solution is used by a set of customers. Before getting much further into the design of the solution, it is important to understand the users for whom you are developing the solution. To capture a clear description of each user, the team creates user profiles. *User profiles* identify the users so that the team can assess the expectations, risks, goals, and constraints of the project.

When creating user profiles, take into account the following considerations:

- *Goals.* An end-user's goal would include a list of the things that the user expects to accomplish by interacting with the product.
- *Constraints.* It is important to understand factors that might affect a user's ability to use the solution, such as hardware and software. For example, for certain solutions, you might need to consider the operating systems that are in use by all kinds of users. There is no reason to design a solution for one specific operating system if the users are using several different operating systems in the organization.
- *Support issues.* User profiles also contain information about the problems that users might have had with similar products. This information will help you plan for support features that users might require while using the new product.
- *Global users.* Determine whether the solution will support various cultures and localization needs.
- *Geographical boundaries.* Describe user locations, including geographical and physical locations, the number of users at each site, and the bandwidth and usage of the network links between sites.
- *Information flow between users.* Describe the communication that occurs between users, including the types of communication, their importance, and the volume of data that flows between the various user communities.

- *User functions.* Describe the tasks that the user performs, such as "completes customer profile," and "edits customer order and details." This information will be developed into the use cases.

- *Organizational communication.* Some organizations have rigid hierarchical divisions that restrict how, why, and when individuals can communicate across the lines of hierarchy. In such a situation, you need to accommodate these restrictions. Document the composition and boundaries of the organizational hierarchy.

- *Decision-making policies.* Describe decision-making policies that directly influence the effective implementation of the proposed solution.

- *Additional factors.* You should also document the availability and usage of resources at each user location, and identify any additional factors, such as incompatible protocols, network operating systems, and applications that might affect the success of a geographically based solution.

How to Define the Scope

One of the critical factors in the success of a project is clearly defining the scope of the project. *Scope* defines what will and will not be included in a project. The scope uses the project vision as defined in the vision statement and incorporates the constraints imposed on the project by resources, time, and other limiting factors. The scope is defined by the features that the customer considers mandatory in the solution. The team must address these features in the first release of the solution. While defining the scope, the team might decide to wait until future releases of the project to incorporate functionality that is not directly related to the core features of the solution. The features that are considered out-of-scope should be documented in a next-version or future-project document.

To begin defining the scope of the project, you continue to develop the high-level use cases that you created for analyzing the business and recording high-level business requirements. For the purpose of defining the scope, you identify the areas in the use case that directly impact the business challenge and address the business. You might need to prioritize the business challenges and identify those that will be dealt with in future versions of the solution. You can typically draw a box around the relevant parts of the high-level use case and derive a new use case diagram that you will subsequently use in the project.

Figure 3.3 shows the use case diagram that represents a part of the business. The scope of the project is enclosed in a box.

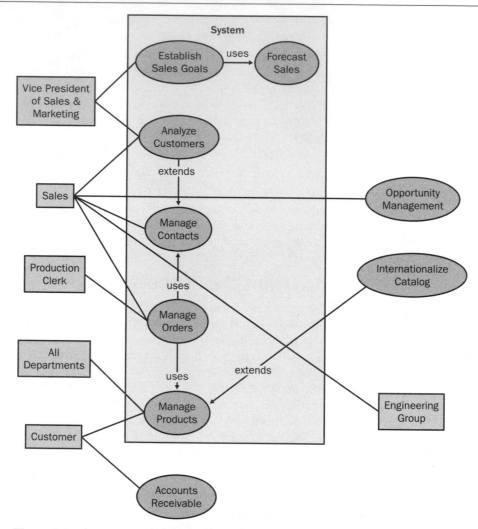

Figure 3.3.   Use case diagram showing the scope of the project

Figure 3.3 shows only the use cases that are now within the scope of the project. To understand what is not within the scope of the project, refer to the Microsoft Visio® document named AWC Use Cases in the \SolutionDocuments\Chapter03 folder on the companion CD.

Refining requirements

An important activity in defining the scope of a project is refining the requirements. Remember that you continue to analyze and refine requirements during both the envisioning and planning phases. During the envisioning phase, you analyze the gathered information and identify specific phrases that will lead to a requirement statement. You then work through those phrases to express the requirements in the language of "what the business needs and wants." You can also begin by collecting customer language directly from interviews and other sources. Consider the following high-level requirement:

The system must support localization to correspond to the end user's culture.

After refining this requirement during the envisioning phase, you have the following requirement:

The system must have procedures for globalization, localization, and accessibility.

The tradeoff triangle and priorities

Defining the scope means balancing the needs of a diverse set of end users and considering other priorities prescribed by the customer. Several variables might affect the potential success of the project, including costs, resources, schedule, functionality, and reliability. The key is to find the right balance between these variables.

The tradeoff triangle in Figure 3.4 shows the three most critical elements in setting the scope of a project. The tradeoff triangle dictates that resources, schedule, and features are three interconnected elements of any project, and that constraining or enhancing one or more of these elements requires tradeoffs.

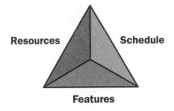

Figure 3.4.   The tradeoff triangle

Role of versioning

While defining the scope of the project, you identify the requirements that will be addressed by the various versions of the solution. During envisioning, you define which use cases and then which related candidate requirements will be handled by the solution.

The features of the solution correspond to requirements. The decision to include a feature of the solution depends on how the feature relates to the business problem selected in the first version of the use case and on how many users are affected by the feature. You should give highest priority to features that will affect the greatest number of users.

After identifying and prioritizing business problems, you can focus on the use cases related to the highest priority problem. With each version, focus on the set of features that addresses the most urgent problem and affects the maximum number of users. Eliminate the features that are required by smaller numbers of users and those that address other problems. This enables you to define the scope of the solution for each version and for the entire project.

More Info   Remember, the requirement statements develop into feature lists during the planning phase, near the end of logical design. Chapter 5, "Creating the Logical Design," describes the logical design stage.

Role of assumptions and constraints

The scope of the project is also affected by the assumptions and constraints made by the business and the customers. Typically, assumptions add to the constraints of the project. Examples of assumptions include:

- *We will use the Microsoft .NET Framework for development.*
- *We will use two development teams.*
- *We will have both OLAP and OLTP systems.*

Constraints indicate the parameters to which the final business solution must adhere. They are aspects of the business environment that cannot or will not be changed. Often, these constraints become design goals for the application. If constraints are not identified properly, the project team might design a product that cannot be deployed within the business.

Examples of possible constraints that you should document include:

- Budget limitations
- Characteristics of earlier supporting systems
- Network system architecture
- Security requirements
- Operating systems
- Planned upgrades to technologies
- Network bandwidth limitations
- Maintenance and support agreements and structures
- Knowledge level of development or support staff
- Learning limitations of users

List the constraints that affect the business challenge and the potential solution. The project team uses these constraints to design a solution that optimizes the requirements and conforms to the parameters established by the constraints.

Role of estimates

Depending on the assumptions and constraints of the project, you can provide estimates for developing the solution. Estimates include time, effort, and cost. You estimate the time it will take to build the solution, the resources required to build the solution, the cost of resources, and their effort.

In addition, you might want to add disclaimers and contractual details in the estimates section. This helps you clarify the extent of your responsibilities in the project.

Benefits of defining the scope

Some of the benefits of defining the scope of a project are as follows:

- The scope enables the team to focus on identifying the work that must be done.
- The scope enables the team to divide large and vague tasks into smaller and more specific tasks.
- The scope helps you specify the features that will be in each release of the solution.
- The scope includes defined feature sets and functions, which helps you to divide work among subcontractors or partners on the team.
- The scope clarifies what the team is and is not responsible for in the current deliverable.

Revising the scope

During the envisioning phase, the project variables start to become apparent. However, the team can more thoroughly understand the project variables with the help of a more detailed planning process. At this stage of the envisioning phase, the team is likely to know project variables only at a basic level. Defining and balancing the project variables is an iterative process. As analyzing, prototyping, and planning activities proceed, the team might need to revise the scope to:

- Incorporate a better understanding of user requirements.
- Incorporate a change in business requirements.
- Adjust the solution according to technical issues or risks.
- Make tradeoffs among the project variables, such as resources, schedule, and features, because project variables have changed.

How to Create the Solution Concept

The *solution concept* outlines the approach the team will take to meet the goals of the project and provides the basis for proceeding to the planning phase. After identifying the business problem and defining the vision and scope, the team creates the solution concept that explains in general terms how the team intends to meet the requirements of the project.

Figure 3.5 shows a sample solution concept for the scope identified for Adventure Works Cycles.

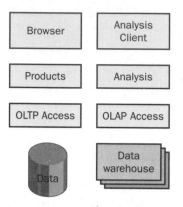

Figure 3.5.   Solution concept

Creating a business-oriented draft

The solution concept can serve as a business case. Because it focuses only on the concepts and not the details of the solution, it is not very technical. For the team to get approval and funding, the team should establish an executive sponsor who will use the vision/scope document to establish funding.

The solution concept includes a conceptual model of the system's software and hardware architectures. The solution concept is the proposed method of addressing the issues identified as being in scope. The team must evaluate the various options and select the one that is the best for its particular situation. A team can then narrow the range of solution concept options to a few alternatives.

For example, in the case of an e-commerce Web site, the choices might include building an e-commerce site internally from the very beginning, employing an outside company to build one, or purchasing a commercially available solution. Similar issues exist for hosting the e-commerce Web site: Should the site be hosted on local servers or should the company use a service provider?

Elements of the solution concept

After the team has evaluated its options, it chooses a solution concept that best meets its needs, resources, and the time frame available for implementation. The solution concept includes the following elements:

- Project success factors and acceptance criteria. These criteria include a checklist of requirements that must be satisfied before the solution goes into production.

- Initial approaches to developing and delivering the solution. These approaches include sample scenarios for the site and methods for implementing the solution, the number of users who will use the new solution, and a complete list of project deliverables that will make the new product operational.
- Initial description of functionality of the solution that will address the business problem.

Note   Creating user profiles and the solution concept need not be a linear process in solution design. These steps can be done in parallel.

How to Identify Project Goals

For a project to be successful, it is essential that you correctly identify the goals of the project. Project goals can be categorized as follows:

- Business goals
- Design goals

Business goals

Business goals represent what the customer wants to achieve with the solution. Business goals form the basis for determining the success criteria of the solution. The purpose of defining business goals is to clearly articulate the objectives for the project and to ensure that your solution supports those business requirements. The team needs to determine the best method for identifying the goals and agreeing on them.

Throughout the life of the project, the team makes tradeoffs among resources, schedule, and features. It is important that business goals are prioritized in a way that will allow the team to have a clear understanding about which ones the customer believes are most important, in case some of the goals cannot be achieved.

For an e-commerce project, business goals might include the following:

- Expand the company's geographic market beyond the current range of physical stores.
- Expand the company's demographic market to include younger consumers who have higher disposable incomes and who shop online with greater frequency than the current customer base.
- Shorten the time to sell products by using more efficient online sites.
- Integrate all suppliers worldwide by using a workflow process, and shorten the order placement and delivery cycle time.

Design goals

Design goals are similar to business goals in many ways. The difference is that *design goals* focus more on the attributes of the solution and less on what the solution will accomplish for the business. Design goals address not only what the team wants to accomplish but also what the team is *not* trying to accomplish with the solution. As with business goals, you need to prioritize design goals so that the team knows which goals must be accomplished, in case the project cannot achieve all of them.

Consider the case of an e-commerce Web site. Some of the design goals for the online shopping cart might include:

- Improve the user experience by reducing page-download wait times to 5 seconds or less.
- Limit dependency on connectivity with the server.
- Reduce the time and level of effort required for a user to complete the online registration.

For the server-side online library's server-side bookmark project, the design goals might include:

- The service and all supporting applications must be localized for users worldwide.
- The service must have an availability of 99.99 percent.
- The service cannot lose data.
- The service must permit access only by authorized users.

For designing the interface of a mobile application, some of the design goals might include:

- Users must be able to easily input and retrieve information.
- The application must be customized for the intended mobile device.

How to Validate the Vision/Scope Document

After creating an early version of the vision/scope document, the team reviews and modifies the document. The envisioning phase culminates in the *vision/scope approved* milestone. This milestone represents the point at which the project team and customer agree on the overall direction for the project, including the scope of the solution. This baseline version of the document is a project deliverable that is used in the subsequent phases of the project.

The vision/scope document is formally approved in a vision/scope meeting. The team validates the work done in the use cases, usage scenarios, and usage profiles with the appropriate stakeholders. (This validation is a process that will occur throughout the project.) By having the customer validate the completed work, the team prepares the customer to understand the tradeoffs that are made in defining the scope. The customer is also educated about the project and the team's approach, creating a feeling of involvement that can greatly reduce difficulties in consensus and in future feature discussions.

The vision/scope meeting ensures that the team and the customer arrive at a shared understanding regarding how the proposed solution will address the business challenge and how it is applicable to the current business scenario, given the scope that has been defined.

This meeting is a mechanism for the team to share ideas and achieve a shared vision with the customer. This meeting also enables the customers to understand that the team is listening to them and actively involved in the project. The team uses this meeting to decide whether the project should proceed. The available resources and the potential gains may not be worth the total cost of the project. This validation step allows the team to redefine either the project solution or the resources and constraints.

By approving the vision/scope document, the members of the project team, the customer, and the key stakeholders agree on the following:

- A broad understanding of the business needs that will be met by the solution
- The vision of the solution
- The design goals for the solution
- The risks that might be incurred by undertaking the project
- Project management's initial concept of the business solution
- The members of the project team
- The mechanism for managing the project

The complete vision/scope document for the Adventure Works Cycles case study is available in the \SolutionDocuments\Chapter03 folder on the companion CD. The Adventure Works Cycles team has defined the scope of version 1 of this project to include the sales order and analysis, contact management, and Web ordering processes. This leaves solutions for product tracking, human relations documentation, and vendor data for future versions or projects.

If any issues are discovered by the team that will cause significant changes in the scope or deliverables of the project, you might need to follow up with discussions or another vision/scope meeting.

Lesson 3: Creating the Project Structure Document

The project structure document is a key deliverable of the envisioning phase. This lesson describes the purpose of the project structure document and itemizes the major sections within the document.

After this lesson, you will be able to

- Describe the purpose of the project structure document.
- Describe the components of the project structure document.

Estimated lesson time: 5 minutes

What Is the Project Structure Document?

The project structure document defines the approach the team will take to organize and manage the project. It describes the team's administrative structure, standards and processes, and project resources and constraints. It serves as an essential reference for the project team members on how they will work together successfully.

The project structure document can be the formal documentation of the approach followed by each of the MSF team roles in the project. In addition, it documents the change management and configuration management approaches that will be implemented for the project. The level of detail in the project structure document depends on the project. If you expect a lot of changes during the later stages of the project, the project structure document should describe in detail how the team will handle the changes.

The change management section of the project structure document for a project named Scout is shown below. The two companies involved in the project used in this example are Adventure Works Cycles and Contoso, Ltd.

Change Management

The highest priority in Scout is the delivery of the first feature sets by the project completion date. (To be determined upon completion of the Project Master Plan. Estimated completion dates are September 1, 2003, for the Web site and November 15, 2003, for the sales automation project.) Therefore, change control procedures will be implemented as follows.

Change Control Process and Documentation Owners:

The program manager will be responsible for the change control process and documents. The application project manager for Adventure Works Cycles will be the primary decision maker in the change control process to manage changes requested by the customer.

Change Management   *(continued)*

Features by Version:

During planning, requirements gathering, and feature specification development, each feature will be identified as Critical V1.0, Want V1.0, Critical V2.0, Want V2.0, Critical V3.0, or Want V3.0.

Change Advisory Board:

The Scout Change Advisory Board is made up of members from Contoso, Ltd. (the development team and the program manager), and the Adventure Works Cycles team (project manager and developers), all of whom can make feature-set change requests. Other team members can take their feature set suggestions to any one of these individuals, who can then add the suggestions to the list for discussion at the next status meeting. If the individual deems the items critical, the individual can bring them up as critical issues and start the evaluation prior to the next status meeting.

Feature Evaluations:

The feature definition and its effect on the design, its effect on the solution, its value to version 1.0 (or any other version), and its risk will be evaluated by the team.

Feature Tradeoffs:

Features will be compared to other features, and any possible tradeoffs will be determined.

Resource Tradeoffs:

The tradeoff triangle will be reviewed and the appropriate element (resource or feature) will be added or deleted. (The schedule is fixed.)

Resolved Feature to Design:

After a feature is resolved as Critical V1.0, V2.0, or V3.0 or Want V1.0, V2.0, or V3.0 and resources are added or other features are deleted or reduced, the features enter the appropriate point in the design process. The budget and contract will be adjusted. (If Adventure Works Cycles decides that the schedule is worth adjusting for a feature, they can request the schedule change, and appropriate changes to the contract, design, budget, and schedule can be made.)

Change Cutoff:

Both companies agree that once the scope complete milestone is 70 percent complete, any new features will be introduced only on the V2.0 or V3.0 lists.

Team role and responsibility

Program management is responsible for facilitating the creation of the project structure document. The key inputs are supplied by the team members.

Components of the project structure

There are three primary components of the project structure document:

- Team and structure
- Project estimates
- Project schedules (early versions)

A project structure document is a tool for documenting the decisions made regarding the execution and management of the project, including:

- Team and customer roles and responsibilities
- Communication decisions
- Logistical decisions
- Change management decisions
- Progress assessment decisions

What Are Team and Customer Roles and Responsibilities?

The roles and responsibilities section of the project structure document lists the names of the people involved in the project and their contact information, such as telephone numbers and e-mail addresses. In addition, this section describes the decisions regarding responsibilities of various roles in the subsequent phases of the project.

Decisions during the planning phase

During the planning phase, the team needs to make decisions to answer the following questions:

- How will the project plans be developed?
- In creating the project plan, how will the team use the knowledge and experience gained from the reviews of other projects?
- Will the team have scheduled status meetings throughout the project?
- How often will customer reviews occur?
- How will the features be distributed among the various releases of the solution?
- Who will identify the risks associated with the project and define contingencies?
- What tools will be used to develop and track project plans?
- Will the team have review meetings during the planning phase? Who will attend the review meetings?

Decisions during the developing phase

During the developing phase, the team needs to make decisions to answer the following questions:

- With what groups, organizations, and third-party vendors will the team interact during the project? Who is responsible for creating and managing contracts with third-party vendors?

- What is the role and responsibility of each team lead in the development work?

- If different components in the solution are being developed by different teams, what are the roles and responsibilities of each of the component team leads in the project?

- Will each component team be assigned a help desk, a user experience team, and a testing team?

- What is the role of the executive staff in the project?

- What is the role of subcontractors, if required, in the project? Who will select subcontractors and monitor their work?

What Are Communication Decisions?

The communication decisions section of the project structure document specifies the communication processes that the team will follow during the project. These processes apply to communication within the team and with customers. The team makes decisions to answer the following questions:

- Who needs to be informed of the planning decisions?

- How will the customers, stakeholders, and team be informed of the planning decisions?

- What type of meetings will be held, where will they be held, and who will attend each type of meeting?

- Who will produce the agenda of the meetings?

- Who will facilitate the meetings?

- Who will prepare and distribute the minutes of meetings?

- Who must be informed of the project's progress, and how will they be informed?

Decisions regarding project files

Typically, a file is maintained for every project in an organization. This file contains information such as contracts, schedules, and plans. In the project structure document, the team decides what information will be maintained in the project files. Some of the decisions that must be made regarding the project file include:

- What information will be included in the project files, such as project specifications, schedules, plans, outstanding issues, contracts, and so on?

- Who will create and maintain the project files?

- Who can access the project files?

- Who will keep the project files after the project is complete, and for how long will they be kept?

Decisions regarding post-implementation reviews

Post-implementation reviews are an important part of a project. They help you evaluate whether the project was a success and identify the support you need to provide. Some of the decisions that must be made regarding post-implementation reviews include:

- When will the post-implementation review be conducted, and who will attend it?
- What subjects will be addressed during the post-implementation review?
- What information will be collected during the life cycle of the project to facilitate the post-implementation review? Who will collect this information?

What Are Logistical Decisions?

The logistical decisions section of the project structure document lists decisions made regarding the development of the solution. The team makes decisions to answer the following questions:

- What development practices will be used for the project? Some possibilities include:
  - Development methods such as product specification checks and a zero-defect checklist
  - Testing methods
  - Documentation methods
  - Marketing methods
- Who will define the content for the product specifications? Who will use the product specifications during the project, and how will they use the specifications?
- What are the tools that will be used to define the solution features?
- How will completion criteria for the product specifications be determined?
- Who will provide the team with any updates to the product specifications?
- What specifications will be provided to each of the third-party vendors working on the project? Who will create these specifications?
- How will zero-defect methods be defined and implemented for the project?
- Who will estimate the effort and time required for the project? What is the basis for this estimation (personal experience, post-implementation reviews, and so forth)?
- Who needs training in the technologies and skills supported by the solution, such as project management training? Who needs training on the solution during the planning phase?

What Are Change Management Decisions?

The change management decisions section of the project structure document covers the processes the team will follow to handle any changes in the project. Some of the decisions that are made regarding change management include:

- How will you define change on the project (for example, a change in schedule or an increase in project cost)?
- What is the release date? Who will determine the release date, and how will it be determined? What will the basis be for determining the release date?
- Who will define the change management process that will be used?
- How will proposed changes be identified and tracked? Who will track this information?
- How will you assess the impact of a change? How much deviation are you willing to accept before major rescheduling?

What Are Progress Assessment Decisions?

The progress assessment decisions section of the project structure document covers the processes the team will follow to track and evaluate the progress of the project. Some of the decisions that are made regarding progress assessment of the project include:

- How will the progress of the project be assessed? What information will be collected to measure progress?
- How will progress information for each task be obtained from team members? How often will this information be collected?
- How often will group schedules be updated? How often will the master project schedule be updated?
- Who will identify and assess the effect of each variance?
- Who will be involved in developing adaptive actions? Who will recommend and approve adaptive actions? How will you track the effectiveness of these actions?
- How will any outstanding issues be documented, tracked, and monitored?
- What criteria will be used to define exceptions for exception reporting? Who will be involved in assessing and resolving the exceptions?
- How will problems and issues be resolved between different teams? If a problem or issue cannot be resolved between teams, will the issue be escalated? If so, who will escalate it?

Lesson 4: Analyzing Risks

Risk is the possibility of a loss. The loss could be anything from the diminished quality of a solution to increased cost, missed deadlines, or project failure. MSF recommends that project risk be assessed continuously throughout a project. In this lesson, you will learn about analyzing risks and creating a risk document for the project.

After this lesson, you will be able to

- Describe the MSF risk management process.
- Identify the contents of a risk assessment document.
- Identify the risks for a project.

Estimated lesson time: 10 minutes

What Is the Risk Management Process?

Risks arise from uncertainty surrounding project decisions and outcomes. An essential aspect of developing a successful solution is controlling and mitigating the risks that are inherent in a project. Most individuals associate the concept of risk with the potential for loss in value, control, functionality, quality, or timeliness of completion of a project. However, project risks also include the failure to maximize gain in an opportunity and uncertainties in decision making that can lead to a missed business opportunity.

The MSF risk management process, as shown in Figure 3.6, is a proactive approach that the team practices continuously throughout the project. The team continually assesses what can go wrong and how to prevent or minimize any loss. MSF advocates tracking risk by using a formal risk assessment document and prioritizing risks.

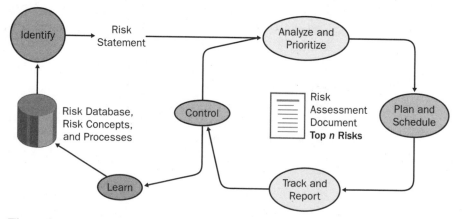

Figure 3.6.   MSF risk management process

The MSF risk management process defines six steps through which the team manages current risks, plans and executes risk management strategies, and documents knowledge for future projects. The six steps in the MSF risk management process are as follows:

1. *Risk identification* Identify the risks and make the team aware of potential problems.
2. *Risk analysis and prioritization* Convert the information and data about potential risks to information that the team can use to make decisions and prioritize resources for mitigating the risk.
3. *Risk planning and scheduling* Use the information developed in the risk analysis stage to formulate risk mitigation strategies, plans, and actions. Allocate time for risk planning in the project plan.
4. *Risk tracking and reporting* Monitor the status of specific risks and the progress of their specific mitigation plans. Report this progress to the team, customers, and key stakeholders.
5. *Risk control* Execute the risk mitigation plan and report the status of the risks to the team and customer.
6. *Risk learning* Document the lessons learned from the project so that the team and the organization can reuse this information.

Note The steps in risk management are logical steps; they do not need to be followed in chronological order. Teams often iterate through the identification, analysis, and planning steps as they develop experience on the project for a set of risks, and only periodically return to the learning step.

Contents of the Risk Assessment Document

During the envisioning phase, the team practices risk management by creating a risk assessment document, identifying and documenting all the known risks, and assessing them for probability of occurrence and impact.

The risk assessment document must contain the following items:

- *Risk statements*, which capture the nature of each risk
- *Risk probability*, which describes the likelihood of the occurrence of the risk
- *Risk severity*, which specifies the impact of the risk
- *Risk exposure*, which specifies the overall threat of the risk
- *Mitigation plans*, which describe the efforts for preventing or minimizing the risk
- *Contingency plans and triggers*, which specify the steps that you need to take when a risk occurs and when to take those steps
- *Risk ownership*, which specifies the name of the team member who is responsible for monitoring the risk on a regular basis

How to Create the Risk Assessment Document

The program manager creates the risk assessment document. The team might compare the risks associated with different solution concepts before documenting the solution concept.

For example, imagine that you are creating an e-commerce Web site. One option would be to create the site from the very beginning. However, this would require assembling and managing extensive development resources. You would also need a lot of time to complete the project. Another option would be to quickly move to the development process by using Microsoft Solution Accelerator for the Internet Storefront. The preconfigured source code, MSF project planning principles, and resource kit with reference documents and tools could help the team achieve its business goals. In addition, this would help mitigate the risks associated with building an e-commerce site from the beginning.

Calculating risks

When you create a risk assessment document, assign a numeric value to risk probability and impact. *Probability* measures the likelihood that a loss will occur; *impact* measures the severity of that loss, should it occur. Then calculate the exposure of each risk by multiplying the two numbers. This process allows you to compare risks and determine their relative severity and priority. For example, use a number between 1 and 4 to designate probability and impact for each risk, with 4 being the highest and 1 being the lowest. By multiplying the numbers representing probability and impact for a risk, you obtain an *exposure factor* between 1 and 16. This process allows you to identify and address the most severe risks first.

Important   You do not need to use the same numeric scale to assess both probability and impact. However, you must use a consistent scale to calculate the probability for every risk and its impact. If you can accurately calculate the financial loss that can be caused by each risk, you can express impact in financial terms. However, if you express the impact of some risks by using a number and others by using financial terms, you cannot compare the exposure of the different risks.

Creating a top 10 list

After creating the risk assessment document and ranking each risk according to its exposure, you can create a list of the top risks so that the team can focus on them. Often called a top 10 list, this list need not contain exactly 10 risks. The program manager should review the list frequently and update it according to the importance of the risks.

Risk exposure in an e-commerce project presents areas that are unique to the situation and that might be new to the team. Some possible risks to an e-commerce project include:

- Inexperience with Web site creation, deployment, and ongoing support
- Potential liabilities, such as image and brand damage for the company, if the site does not function correctly or suffers from availability issues
- Security risks, which include intrusion into the system by malicious users and theft of confidential customer data such as credit card numbers

Activity: Developing a Vision/Scope Document

In this activity, you will use what you learned in the lessons to work through the envisioning phase of a project. Each of the exercises is based on the following scenario.

Scenario

Adventure Works Cycles, a large, multinational manufacturing company, produces and distributes metal and composite bicycles to North American, European, and Asian commercial markets. Its base operation is located in Bothell, Washington, and employs 500 people; several regional sales teams are located throughout the company's market region.

Sales representatives from regional sales offices are responsible for assigned sales territories. Each regional office consists of several sales representatives and a team manager. In their daily sales activities, sales representatives use both laptops and Handheld PCs that run Microsoft Windows® CE.

A typical work day for a sales representative starts with the representative dialing in to the regional office and downloading current data such as inventory, product, and promotional information. During customer visits, the sales representative takes orders on the laptop or Handheld PC. At the end of the day, the sales representative sets up appointments for the following day or week, checks the appointments of other representatives in the area for possible collaboration, and updates the contact list. Finally, the sales representative dials back in to the regional office, sends updated information, and receives any new internal communications from the base office or regional office.

Currently, the sales teams at regional sales offices do not have an easy way to analyze the customer data. The customer data is stored in the systems, but there is no easy way to retrieve the data and allow the sales teams to request specific information. For example, the system does not provide a way to identify the best customers overall or the best customers of specific models. To better identify the best customers and to determine why they are the best customers, the company needs a way to access and analyze customer data in a meaningful way.

In recent months, the sales teams have been trying to present their products and achieve sales in the company's European and Asian markets. Currently, all the information they have in their systems is written in English. A sales representative working in the Hanover office has said that she actually translates the product information into German before she goes on her sales calls. She knows the language quite well, but there might be some technical terms that she might not translate correctly. Because of this translation process, inaccuracies might appear in the translated materials. The company therefore needs to store multilingual and multiregional information in the database rather than relying on the sales force to translate the information.

The sales team needs to obtain the latest pricing information on a daily basis. Currently, the sales representative connects to the corporate network and downloads the new pricing list each day in the morning. However, the download process does not identify which prices have been modified for that individual sales representative. So the sales representative is required to download the entire list every morning. Typically, sales representatives will find out that nothing pertaining to their area or product has changed, and the 20 minutes that it took to download the latest information were wasted.

This difficulty in downloading information to find out whether there are changes has had some unfortunate results. Most sales representatives have stopped downloading the pricing information on a daily basis. Because they have stopped downloading this information, sales representatives frequently miss changes that affect them. When sales representatives miss changes that affect them, they need to redo orders, recalculate pricing, and notify customers of the price changes. As a result, customers are unhappy when they find out that the prices offered to them were incorrect. Currently, the sales teams can override the system and sell products to customers at the prices that were initially negotiated. But this process has received criticism from the corporate base office because the company has lost money in recent months because of this approach.

Currently, the sales opportunities are managed by individual sales representatives and are not entered into the system. Each sales representative creates a Microsoft Word document and stores information such as contact name, address, telephone number, products the contact is interested in, date first contact was made, date last contact was made, and so on. In addition, the sales associate tracks "rules," which are statements that help the associate convert a sales opportunity into a sale. For example, a rule might be "Customer C will buy product P if (a) the price of product P is reduced by 5 percent or (b) product P comes with components X, Y, and Z as options."

The regional sales office employees are supposed to use the customer-management system to plan, execute, and track sales and marketing strategy. The problem with the system is that the customer management system is an older fourth-generation-language model, and getting anything even remotely meaningful out of it is very difficult. In addition, the sales associates are required to install a large application on their laptops and connect to the corporate network to use it.

The sales teams have identified the following requirements that will help them perform their jobs better:

- *Customer segmentation and profiling.* The sales team needs to be able to extract information from raw data available in the databases to answer questions such as the following:

  - What are the early warning signs of problems?

  - Who are the best customers across all product lines? On whom should the sales team focus its efforts for building long-term relationships?

  - What are customers' issues, categorized according to demographic groups?

  - Where are the best customers of Adventure Works Cycles?

  - What products are the customers buying and at what rate?

- *Sales activity.* To support sales activity throughout the world, the sales team needs international support, including Unicode characters, multiple languages, date and time data types, and multiple currency formats.

- *Internal communication.* Each sales representative must receive customer and sales data pertinent only to that representative. In addition, each team manager must receive relevant customer and appointment data along with detailed information for each sales representative on the team.

- *Opportunity management.* Sales representatives need a method to store and access sales opportunity data, and, when a sale is generated, to convert some or all of the information into a sales order without re-entering information.

- *Decision support system.* The decision support system should support the following tasks:

  - Allow marketing and sales staff with little technical knowledge to query and use customer data to generate standard reports; execute custom queries; obtain information related to promotion tracking, sales forecast, and customer segmentation; and access third-party data sources and financial evaluation tools.

  - Present a single unified view of the customer and the customer relationship.

  - Allow sales representatives to initiate new promotions and programs on a multinational basis. Currently, sales representatives do not know how to associate these programs with specific areas for the best impact.

  - Allow sales representatives to identify, analyze, and share all aspects of customer relationships with individuals in multiple departments.

Exercise 1: Writing Problem Statements

Read the sample scenario describing the Adventure Works Cycles Sales department, and write problem statements for the project described. Ensure that the problem statements you write outline the business problems and provide direction to the project team in the scenario.

Sample possible problem statements include the following:

Sales are lost because we cannot identify the best customer opportunities.

Product information can be incorrect because of manual translation of the product information by the sales representatives.

Sales representatives often work with incorrect price and product data, because of difficulty in downloading that information.

Sales representatives have to guess which customers to focus on and can end up spending their time less productively than possible.

Exercise 2: Writing a Vision Statement

Write a vision statement for the application described in the sample scenario.

Get the right information to each specific person when and where that person needs it, and increase sales totals for each representative over the next year.

Exercise 3: Developing Project Goals

From the scenario given, identify the project goals, including the business goals and the design goals.

Business goals include the following:

Increase sales over the next year by making the sales force more productive.

Focus on the best sales opportunities.

Improve sales tracking and marketing strategies.

Design goals include the following:

Improve sales activity throughout the world by providing international support.

Provide specific data pertinent only to a specific employee.

Summary

- Envisioning provides the team with a clear vision of what the team wants to accomplish for its customers.
- The members of a team must have the competencies and proficiencies required to perform the task for developing the solution.
- The scope of the project specifies what will and will not be included in the project.
- The deliverables of the envisioning phase include the vision/scope document, the risk assessment document, and the project structure document.
- The project team also develops documents such as the actors catalog, the business rule catalog, and a glossary of terms for its internal documentation.
- The vision/scope document includes information about the team and project structure, the problem statement, the vision statement, the scope of the project, the solution concept, user profiles, and project goals.
- The vision statement states the long-term solution that addresses the business problem.
- The problem statement specifies the problem that will be addressed by the solution.
- The scope of the project specifies what will and will not be included in the project.
- The scope of the project is affected by the assumptions, constraints, and estimates of the project.
- The solution concept specifies how the team intends to meet the goals of the project.
- User profiles identify all probable users of the solution and their expectations, goals, risks, and constraints.
- Business goals represent what the customer wants to accomplish with the solution.
- Design goals represent the attributes of the solution that the project team is going to develop.
- The project structure document includes information such the team's administrative structure, standards and processes, and project resources and constraints.
- The key components of the project structure document are:
  - Team and structure
  - Project estimates
  - Project schedules (early versions)

- A project structure document is a tool for documenting the decisions made regarding the execution and management of the project, including:
  - Team and customer roles and responsibilities
  - Communication decisions
  - Logistical decisions
  - Change management decisions
  - Progress assessment decisions
- The envisioning phase culminates with an approved vision/scope document.
- The team, key stakeholders, and customers indicate the completion of the envisioning phase by approving the vision/scope document.
- MSF advocates constant risk management throughout the life of the project.
- The MSF risk management process defines six steps through which the team manages current risks, plans and executes risk management strategies, and documents knowledge for the enterprise. The six steps are as follows:
  - Risk identification
  - Risk analysis and prioritization
  - Risk planning and scheduling
  - Risk tracking and reporting
  - Risk controlling
  - Risk learning
- During the envisioning phase, the team practices risk management by creating a risk assessment document. Contents of the risk assessment document include:
  - Risk statements
  - Risk probability
  - Risk severity
  - Risk exposure
  - Mitigation plans
  - Contingency plans and triggers
  - Risk ownership

Review

The following questions are intended to reinforce key information presented in this chapter. If you are unable to answer a question, review the lesson materials and try the question again. You can find answers to the questions in the appendix.

1. What is the purpose of envisioning?

2. What are the responsibilities of the various roles during the envisioning phase?

3. What are the outputs of the envisioning phase?

4. What is the purpose of specifying the project scope?

5. How does the envisioning phase end?

6. What kinds of change management decisions are recorded in the project structure document?

7. What is the difference between business goals and design goals?

8. What are the guidelines for creating user profiles?

9. What are the essential components of a risk assessment document?

10. What are the guidelines for assessing risks for a project?

C H A P T E R   4

Creating the Conceptual Design

About This Chapter

During the envisioning phase, the project team gathers enough information to start the project, which allows them to create the baseline vision/scope document. Near the end of the envisioning phase, the team moves on to the planning phase of the Microsoft® Solutions Framework (MSF) Process Model. During this phase, you ensure that the business problem to be addressed is fully understood so that you can design the solution that addresses the business problem. In addition, you plan how the solution will be developed and determine whether you have the resources to develop the solution.

During the planning phase, you create a collection of models and requirements documents. This collection of models and documents makes up the functional specification, or blueprint, of the solution. You begin working on the functional specification of the solution during the planning phase.

In this chapter, you will learn about the purpose of the planning phase and the three design processes that occur during the planning phase: conceptual, logical, and physical design. You will also learn about the purpose and benefits of functional specification. In addition, you will learn about the conceptual design process in detail.

Note There are many modeling techniques that you can use to model business processes and key activities in a business. This training kit primarily uses use cases and usage scenarios for modeling business processes.

Before You Begin

To complete the lessons in this chapter, you must

- Understand the MSF Process Model.
- Be able to create use cases, usage scenarios, and use case diagrams.
- Be familiar with the outputs of the envisioning phase, such as vision/scope, project structure, and risk analysis documents.
- Be able to distinguish between the different kinds of information: business, user, system, and operations.

Lesson 1: An Introduction to the Planning Phase

During the planning phase, the team defines the solution: what to build, how to build it, and who will build it. During this phase the team prepares the functional specification, works through the design process, and prepares work plans, cost estimates, and schedules for the various deliverables.

In this lesson, you will learn about the purpose of the planning phase and the responsibilities of the various MSF roles during the planning phase. In addition, you will learn about the key deliverables of this phase.

After this lesson, you will be able to

- Describe the purpose of the planning phase.
- Describe the three steps and interim roles of the planning phase.
- Describe the responsibilities of the various MSF roles during the planning phase.
- Identify the common deliverables of the planning phase.

Estimated lesson time: 5 minutes

What Is the Planning Phase?

Before you start learning more about the planning phase and its deliverables, it is important to understand where the planning phase fits in the overall MSF process.

Figure 4.1 illustrates how the planning phase fits into the MSF Process Model.

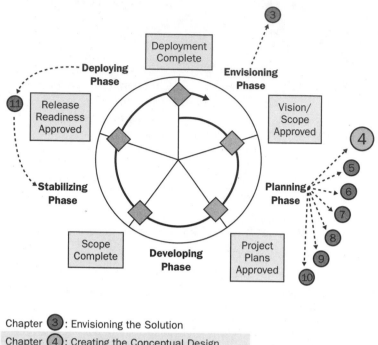

Figure 4.1.   Where are you in the MSF process?

Moving to the planning phase

During the envisioning phase, the team gathers enough information to determine the scope of the project. The planning phase can begin during the envisioning phase, whenever enough information has been gathered for the team to begin organizing and analyzing that information. During the planning phase, the team takes the work it has done during the envisioning phase and continues to elaborate on it and further organize and analyze it.

Figure 4.2 illustrates how the project team moves from the envisioning phase to the planning phase.

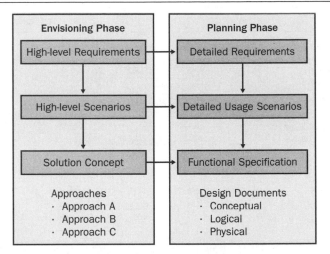

Figure 4.2.   Moving from the envisioning phase to the planning phase

Purpose of the planning phase

During the planning phase, the team continues with the work done during the envisioning phase, specifically the draft requirements, tasks and task sequences, and user profiles. The planning phase results in the architecture and design of the solution, the plans to accomplish developing and deploying the solution, and the schedules associated with tasks and resources. During the planning phase, the team works to articulate a clearer image of the solution. Although the planning process is intended to move the project forward, many teams get stuck in planning—in essence, they do too much planning. The key for the team is to know when it has enough information to move forward. Too little information is a risk, and too much information can cause a project team to stagnate.

The Three Design Processes: Conceptual, Logical, and Physical

There are three design processes in the planning phase: conceptual, logical, and physical design. These three processes are not parallel. Their starting and ending points are staggered. These processes are dependent on each other. Logical design is dependent on conceptual design, and physical design is dependent on logical design. Any changes to the conceptual design affect the logical design, leading to changes in the physical design.

Figure 4.3 illustrates the three processes within the planning phase.

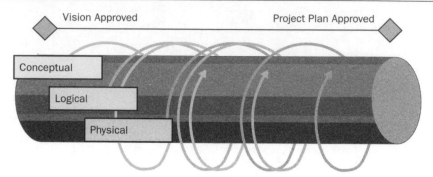

Figure 4.3. The planning phase of the MSF Process Model

Table 4.1 summarizes the design processes of the planning phase.

Table 4.1. **The Three Design Processes**

Type of design	Perspective	Purpose
Conceptual	View the problem from the perspective of the user and the business.	Defines the problem and solution in terms of usage scenarios.
Logical	View the solution from the perspective of the project team.	Defines the solution as a logical set of cooperating services.
Physical	View the solution from the perspective of the developers.	Defines the solution's services and technologies.

Note Conceptual design can be broken down further into conceptual design research, conceptual design analysis, and conceptual design optimization. This chapter focuses on the three steps of the conceptual design process.

Roles and Responsibilities in the Planning Phase

Although the project team works as a whole during the planning phase, each role on the team has a different responsibility during the planning phase:

- *Product management* ensures that the plan meets the customer needs. This role is responsible for refining requirements, analyzing the current business state, optimizing the solution concept, and creating the conceptual design.

- *Program management* ensures that the resources can accomplish the project plan. This role is responsible for the overall design, with an emphasis on logical design and the functional specification. The project management team creates the project plans and schedules and is responsible for completing the planning phase.

- *Development* ensures that the plan is technically feasible. This role is responsible for creating the logical and physical design of the solution and adding it to the functional specification. This team also determines the time and effort required for developing and stabilizing the solution.

- *Testing* ensures that the plan meets the requirements. This role is responsible for evaluating the design to determine whether features can be tested and for providing a plan and schedule for testing them.

- *Release management* evaluates the design for ease of deployment, management, and support. In addition, this role plans for and schedules deployment of the solution.

- *User experience* ensures that users will be able to use the product. This role is responsible for analyzing user needs and creating performance support strategies and for evaluating the completed design for usability. This role also estimates the time and effort required to develop user support systems and conduct usability testing for all user interface deliverables.

Milestones and Deliverables of the Planning Phase

The planning phase culminates in the project plan approved milestone, which is the point at which the project team, the customer, and project stakeholders agree on the project deliverables and that the plan meets the requirements and is likely to be successful. The final deliverables at this milestone of the planning phase are:

- *Functional specification (baseline).* The functional specification represents what the product will be, based on input from the entire team. You will learn about the functional specification in Lesson 2.

- *Master project plan (baseline).* The master project plan is a collection of plans that addresses tasks performed by each of the six team roles to achieve the functionality described in the functional specification. It documents the strategies by which the various teams intend to complete their work.

- *Master project schedule (baseline).* The schedule applies a time frame to the master plan. The master project schedule synchronizes project schedules across the teams. It includes the time frame in which the teams intend to complete their work. Aggregating the individual schedules gives the team an overall view of the project schedule and is the first step toward determining a fixed ship date.

- *Updated master risk assessment document.* The master risk assessment document that was developed during the envisioning phase is reviewed and updated regularly, but particularly at the milestones. It describes the risks associated with developing the solution. Typically, multiple risk assessments are sorted to identify the highest risks that must be addressed and aggregated to give an overall risk assessment.

All of these documents are living documents, evolving as the project progresses. Although these documents can be modified, any modifications to the documents must first be approved by a committee of users and stakeholders.

Figure 4.4 shows the deliverables of the planning phase.

Summary of Milestones and Deliverables

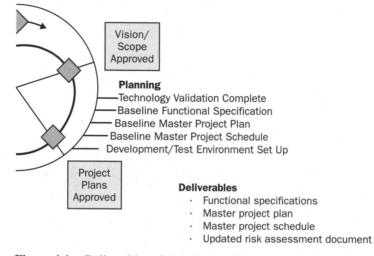

Figure 4.4.   Deliverables of the planning phase

Lesson 2: An Overview of the Functional Specification

During the planning phase, the focus of the project team begins to shift from problem definition to solution design. The planning phase of the MSF Process Model culminates in the project plan approved milestone. One of the primary deliverables at this milestone is the functional specification. The functional specification defines what will be built, how it will be built, and when it will be built. The project plan and schedule identify how the project will proceed and provide dates for various milestones in the project. In this lesson, you will learn about the goals and benefits of a functional specification. You will also learn about the risks of not creating a functional specification.

There is no finite beginning or ending point for the process of creating a functional specification. During the planning phase, each of the design processes—conceptual, logical, and physical—contributes different elements to the functional specification. With the completion of each task during the planning phase, the functional specification becomes more complete. The functional specification exists in a baseline version at the end of physical design and is updated throughout development as a best practice.

After this lesson, you will be able to

- Describe the purpose of a functional specification.
- Describe the goals and benefits of creating a functional specification.
- List the risks of not creating a functional specification.
- Describe the contents of a functional specification.

Estimated lesson time: 10 minutes

What Is a Functional Specification?

A *functional specification* is the virtual repository of project and design-related artifacts that are created during the planning phase of the MSF Process Model. The artifacts are a result of design activities during the conceptual design, logical design, and physical design processes of the planning phase. These artifacts can include Unified Modeling Language (UML) models such as use case diagrams, usage scenarios, candidate requirements (evolving), candidate features, and various information models.

> **More Info**   UML is a standard modeling language used to document projects that use object-oriented design. The following references provide more information about UML: *UML Distilled: A Brief Guide to the Standard Object Modeling Language, 2nd edition* by Martin Fowler and Kendall Scott (Addison-Wesley, 2000) and *Use Case Driven Object Modeling with UML: A Practical Approach* by Doug Rosenberg with Kendall Scott (Addison-Wesley, 1999).

It is important to remember that a functional specification is virtual in nature. Many of the conceptual, logical, and physical design artifacts are likely to be in electronic form and stored in the databases of various tools. The functional specification can manifest itself in different forms—electronic or paper; textual document or graphical; Microsoft Word document or Microsoft PowerPoint® presentation. Consequently, it is not easy to collate all these artifacts as a single physical document or deliverable. The functional specification is not just the work of one person or role but rather a joint effort by a number of roles on the team.

The functional specification describes the scope of the current version of the solution by listing which features will be a part of the solution. Excluded items should remain in the vision/scope document as potential features of a future version of the solution or as wants or items considered to be out of scope. The functional specification is used to record the decisions and agreements made regarding the functionality of the solution, its interface, design goals, and priorities.

You communicate the result of the design efforts of the team to the development team by using the functional specification. In addition to the development team, the testing team uses the functional specification to create test scripts, test plans, and data, and to test hardware requirements for the solution.

What Are the Goals of a Functional Specification?

Some of the goals of a functional specification are:

- *Consolidate a common understanding of the business and user requirements.* The features of a solution depend on the business and user requirements that the solution is going to address. For a small project, the number of requirements might be small and easily documented. For a large and complex project, the number and complexity of requirements increases. A functional specification helps the customer and the project team arrive at a common understanding of the requirements of the solution.

- *Break down the problem and modularize the solution logically.* For a complex project to be a success, it is important that the team identifies all parts of the problem clearly. Also, you need to break the solution into distinct, unambiguous parts. A functional specification helps you simplify a solution into logical parts and document them. It also helps the team make changes to the design early in the development process. Making changes to the solution at this stage is less risky and less expensive than making them later in the process.

- *Provide a framework to plan, schedule, and build the solution.* The functional specification provides the program manager with a basis for identifying the team's tasks and creating cost estimates and budgets for the entire project. In addition, the program manager can correctly estimate the resources and time required by the project, and create project plans and schedules. The testing team uses the functional specification to create test cases and test scenarios early in the project life cycle. The release management team uses the functional specification for deploying the solution and supporting the development and test environments.

- *Serve as a contract between the team and the customer for what will be delivered.* In most organizations and on most projects, the functional specification serves as a contract between the team and the customer; it is the written evidence of what is to be developed and delivered. A functional specification is not necessarily a legal document, but it can serve as one. If third-party teams or other organizations are involved in the project, the functional specification can serve as an addendum to a project work order.

What Are the Risks of Not Creating a Functional Specification?

Sometimes, constraints such as budget and time prevent the team from creating and using the functional specification. Although the team can proceed to the developing phase of the MSF Process Model without a functional specification, the risks of the project increase significantly. Some of the risks of not creating the functional specification are:

- The team might develop a solution that does not completely address the customer requirements.

- The team might be unable to clearly define customer expectations and share a common understanding with the customer. Consequently, the team might not know whether they are developing the required solution.

- The team might not have enough detail to validate and verify that the solution meets customer expectations and is of the required quality level.

- The project manager might be unable to estimate the budget and schedule of the project accurately. The information in the functional specification helps the team estimate the effort and skills necessary for developing the solution.

Figure 4.5 illustrates the risks of not using the functional specification for developing a solution.

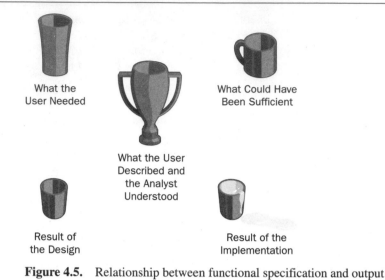

Figure 4.5. Relationship between functional specification and output

Elements of the Functional Specification

The possible elements of a functional specification are listed below. Each element might be a separate document.

- *Conceptual design summary.* This section provides a summary of the conceptual design of the solution and includes information such as solution overview and solution architecture. The following artifacts from the conceptual design are used in the functional specification:

  - Use cases

  - Usage scenarios

  - Context models such as screen shots of existing systems and photocopies of current user manuals

  These artifacts can exist in various forms. For example, context models can be in the form of screen shots of an existing system or photocopies of current user manuals or reports; use cases can be in a use case documentation database; and conceptual user interface (UI) prototypes can be in electronic form.

- *Logical design summary.* This section provides a summary of the logical design and includes information such as users, objects, and attributes. The following artifacts from the logical design phase are included in the functional specification:

  - Task and task-sequence models

  - Logical object and service models

  - Conceptual models of the proposed solution

- UI screen flows
- Logical database model
- System architecture

- *Physical design summary.* This section provides a summary of the physical design document and includes information from key sections of the document, such as the application and infrastructure sections. The following artifacts from the physical design phase are included in the functional specification:
    - Component packaging
    - Component distribution topology
    - Technology usage guidelines
    - Infrastructure architecture and design
    - Description of UI screens
    - Physical database model

- *Standards and processes.* This section includes information about the standards and processes that the team uses as guidelines for performing various tasks for the project. In addition, this section includes details of quality and performance metrics that will be used. These metrics are gathered during tests and help achieve the goals defined by the requirements.

Depending on the size and scope of the project, you can include the following sections in the functional specification. To avoid unsynchronized versions, it is recommended that you use references to documents that exist separately rather than reproducing information. For example, do not include information in the functional specification that already exists in the vision/scope document or the risk assessment document.

- *Project vision/scope summary.* This section summarizes the business opportunity, the solution concept, and the scope of the project as documented in the vision/scope document.

- *Project history.* The section describes the important events and decisions that have been made up to the current date and that have helped deliver the project to its current state. The historical information ensures that the project team and the customer have the same understanding of the project. This information also helps to ensure a thorough understanding of the project.

- *Functional specification summary.* This summary is often useful for customers and new team members. You create the first version of the summary after user requirements have been gathered and analyzed and the UI design has been created. In addition to references to the other documents that make up the entire functional specification, this section typically contains screen shots that illustrate the proposed functionality of the solution.

- *Requirements summary.* This section provides a summary of the user, system, operations, and business requirements document. The business requirements summary describes what the customer, users, and stakeholders think the solution must do. The user requirements summary includes usage scenarios and describes who will use the solution, when the solution will be used, and how the solution will be used. The systems requirements summary includes information such as systems and services dependencies. The operation requirements summary includes information such as the security, manageability, and supportability requirements of an organization.

- *Usage scenario and use case studies summary.* This section provides a summary of the contents of the usage scenarios document. This summary includes a brief statement of each of the key use cases that are included in the document.

- *Assumptions and dependencies.* This section lists the project-oriented assumptions and dependencies. An example of a dependency might be the set of technical skills that is required for developing the solution. An example of an assumption might be that the deployment platform for the solution is the Microsoft Windows® operating system. You also need to identify tests that will challenge and validate these assumptions.

- *Security strategy summary.* This section describes the security strategy that will influence the design of the solution. The physical design document contains the specific security details in a per-feature and per-component format. This section contains a synopsis of the security strategy, along with references to the security plan.

- *Installation and setup requirements summary.* This section is a summary of the environmental requirements for installing the solution. This information is derived from the installation section of the deployment plan of the solution. The physical design document contains details on how these requirements will be addressed.

- *Removal requirements summary.* This section describes how the solution should be removed from its environment. This should include a definition of what must be considered prior to removing the solution. In addition, this section also covers information about data that must be backed up before uninstalling the solution, to ensure safe recovery and rebuilding later.

- *Integration requirements summary.* This section contains a summary of integration and interoperability requirements and the project goals related to these requirements. It includes a summary of the migration plan. The physical design document contains information about how integration will be delivered.

- *Supportability summary.* This section provides a summary of the supportability requirements and the project goals related to these requirements. This information is contained in the operations plan and the support plan. The physical design document describes how supportability will be delivered in the solution.

- *Legal requirements summary.* This section provides a summary of any legal requirements that must be taken into account. Legal requirements are typically defined by the customer's corporate policies and by regulatory agencies governing the customer's industry.

- *Risk summary.* This section describes the risks that might affect development and delivery of the solution. Along with each risk, this section contains information about the calculated exposure to the risk and a mitigation plan.

- *References.* This section describes any internal or external resources that provide supplementary information to the functional specification.

- *Appendixes.* This section is a collection of the outputs of the design process that the team used to develop the functional specification. It includes additional conceptual design details such as field surveys and user profiles, and physical design details such as existing server and client configurations.

Lesson 3: An Overview of the Conceptual Design Process

The planning phase of the MSF Process Model involves three design processes: conceptual, logical, and physical. The conceptual design starts during the envisioning phase of the MSF Process Model and continues throughout the planning phase. Because the MSF design process is evolutionary as well as iterative, conceptual design serves as the foundation for both logical and physical design.

In this lesson, you will learn about the conceptual design process. You will also learn about the goals and benefits of conceptual design.

After this lesson, you will be able to

- Define conceptual design.
- Describe the goals of conceptual design.
- Describe the steps in conceptual design.
- Describe the research step of conceptual design.

Estimated lesson time: 10 minutes

What Is Conceptual Design?

Conceptual design is the process of gathering, analyzing, and prioritizing business and user perspectives of the problem and the solution, and then creating a high-level representation of the solution.

Developing requirements

During information gathering, draft requirements are captured. It is important that the project team understands the difference between the different categories of requirements: *user*, *system*, *operation*, and *business*. Draft requirements can be gathered from the initial interviews or from other information that has been gathered. They can then be developed into more-precise statements as the business problem is better understood by the team. These requirements, called the *candidate* requirements, are later transformed from the language of the user into the language of requirements.

Note You will learn more about transforming draft requirements to candidate requirements in Lesson 4.

Communicating requirements through modeling

To create an accurate and usable conceptual design of a solution, you need to set up an effective method of understanding and communicating the solution with all types of users. For this, you create models of the tasks covered by the scope of the solution. One way to model these tasks and their task sequences is to generate use cases and usage scenarios.

More Info   For more detailed information about writing use cases, you might find the following reference useful: *Writing Effective Use Cases* by Alistair Cockburn (Addison-Wesley, 2001).

Consider the example of a team that has been assigned to design an e-commerce Web site. To determine what the customer requires from the e-commerce Web site, the team asks the customer what lines of products will be sold on the site and how end users will use the site. To answer these questions, the customer must consider the product catalog and its maintenance, and the various activities that end users will perform on the site. The team can generate a set of tasks and describe them in use cases. For each activity that the customer describes, the architect creates a detailed usage scenario. Exceptions and alternatives that occur in an activity are also recorded in the usage scenario.

Conceptual design in the MSF Process Model

As defined by the MSF Process Model, conceptual design occurs during the planning phase. However, the project team might have begun conceptual design while drafting the vision document during the envisioning phase. After the team has established enough information to further gather and refine requirements, conceptual design can begin.

Figure 4.6 illustrates when the conceptual design occurs in the MSF Process Model.

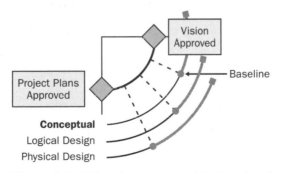

Figure 4.6.   When does conceptual design take place?

Remember that the design process is iterative. Consequently, the logical and physical designs might overlap with the conceptual design. These three design phases are not parallel; they have different starting points and baselines. Because of the iterative nature of the design process, conceptual design might be modified as a result of the logical and physical designs.

What Are the Goals of Conceptual Design?

Without a conceptual design, you might create a great solution to the wrong problem. Some of the goals of creating a conceptual design are:

- *Understanding the business problem to be solved.* Conceptual design involves understanding the problem to be solved and framing the future state of the process to the point of improving the business processes. It embodies a process for refining, documenting, and validating what the users and the business need from the solution.

- *Understanding the requirements of the business, the customer, and the end user.* Conceptual design helps the project team determine a project's needs in context, resulting in a view of the solution that focuses on both the process and the user. The view is not limited to a list of desirable functions; it also includes the broader context of business processes and activities.

- *Describing the target future state of the business.* Conceptual design also formalizes the target future state of the business activities. This future state becomes the basis for the next phases of the design process.

In conceptual design, the project team attempts to understand the context of the problem, records the business activities, and tries to portray their boundaries and their relationships. The entire functional specification is not created during conceptual design. However, the project team uses conceptual design to begin work on the functional specification.

Table 4.2 clarifies the scope of the conceptual design.

Table 4.2.   Scope of the Conceptual Design

Conceptual design is not	But it helps you to
The complete functional specification	Begin the functional specification
A definition of system components	Identify the parts of the business problem that will be addressed by the eventual components
A technology solution	Records the business activities and portray their boundaries and their relationships

What Are the Steps in Conceptual Design?

Conceptual design has the following three steps and associated baselines. Conceptual design is an iterative process and the steps are repeated as required.

1. *Research.* During this step, you perform the following tasks:
   - Obtaining answers to key questions
   - Identifying key business processes and activities
   - Prioritizing processes and activities
   - Validating, refining, and extending draft requirements, use cases, and usage scenarios created during the envisioning phase

2. *Analysis.* During this step, you perform the following tasks:
   - Reviewing the user and business research
   - Refining candidate requirements
   - Documenting and modeling the context, workflow, task sequence, and environmental relationships

3. *Optimization.* During this step, you perform the following tasks:

   - Optimizing the solution concept created during the envisioning phase
   - Validating and testing the improved business processes

   The optimization baseline leads to the baseline of the conceptual design.

Figure 4.7 illustrates the steps in the conceptual design.

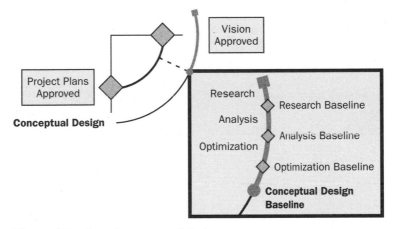

Figure 4.7.   Steps in conceptual design

During the research step of conceptual design, the team gathers more information to refine and validate data collected during the envisioning phase. Typically, the information gathered during the envisioning phase is high level and lacking in detail. During the first step of the conceptual design, the team needs to collect detailed information. For example, the team first identifies questions raised by the first iteration of information gathering; the team then continues to clarify the tasks, business processes, and workflow. As greater detail is discovered, the results are incorporated in the use cases and draft requirements.

More Info   You will learn about the analysis step of conceptual design in Lesson 4 and about the optimization step in Lesson 5.

Lesson 4: Building the Conceptual Design

After gathering detailed information about business and user requirements and business process, the team proceeds to the analysis step of conceptual design. At this step, the team analyzes the artifacts created during envisioning phase and elaborates and refines them.

In this lesson, you will learn how to use requirement restating to refine the information you have gathered. You will also learn how to categorize requirements and refine use cases and usage scenarios. In addition, you will learn how to make high-level architectural choices for the solution.

After this lesson, you will be able to

- Describe the analysis step of conceptual design.
- Restate requirements.
- Categorize requirements as user, system, operations, and business requirements.
- Refine use case diagrams.
- Select an appropriate application architecture for a solution.

Estimated lesson time: 20 minutes

What Is the Analysis Step in Conceptual Design?

In the analysis step of the conceptual design, you synthesize the information that you gathered in the research step and create detailed usage scenarios. The purpose of the analysis step is to:

- Review user and business processes and activities
- Document and model the context, workflow, task sequence, and environmental relationships of the business

Tasks in the analysis step

In the analysis step, you perform the following tasks:

- Synthesizing information
- Refining use case diagrams
- Selecting an appropriate application architecture for the solution
- Creating a conceptual model of the solution

Synthesizing information is the process of assimilating gathered data and interpreting the results. The team transforms the gathered data into meaningful information. To synthesize data, the project team performs the following tasks:

- Identify discrete pieces of information about what the user said and did.
- Record the detailed flow of the tasks that the user performed.
- Identify tools and pieces of information that were used.
- Identify exceptions and alternatives that occur while the user performs task.
- Model the relationship between business processes, business systems, and users.
- Model the current environment in which the user works and any possible changes to that environment.

Deliverables of the analysis step

Table 4.3 lists the key tasks and deliverables of the analysis step.

Table 4.3.   Tasks and Deliverables of Conceptual Design Analysis

Tasks	Deliverables

Synthesize gathered information	• Information models:
	    • Relationship between business processes, business systems, and users
	    • Workflow process
	    • Task sequence
	• Updated user profiles
	• Candidate requirements
	• Detailed use cases

Create usage scenarios	Current usage scenarios

How to Restate Requirements

When you restate requirements, keep the following criteria in mind:

- Requirements must be *well defined*. A well-defined requirement is a complete sentence and typically uses "shall," "may," "must," or "should."
- Requirements must be *concise*. Each requirement must address one item only.
- Requirements must be *testable*. Each requirement should have specific inputs resulting in known outputs.
- Requirements should be *organized in a hierarchy of related requirements*. You need to group related requirements together under a single high-level requirement to form feature sets.
- Requirements should be written in the language of the business and should not use jargon.

Table 4.4 shows potential requirement statements that the project team collected and formulated from the interview texts during the envisioning phase.

Table 4.4.   Draft Requirement Statements in the Envisioning Phase

Requirement ID	Requirement
1	Identify best customers by product and location (profit analysis and geographical analysis); these are the customers on which the sales team should focus.
2	Identify decreases in a customer's sales.
3	Identify best customers.
4	Identify top buyers.

During the analysis step of conceptual design, the team restates the requirements to ensure that each requirement is a concise, complete, and testable statement. While the team is refining requirements, they might also discover new requirements. Restated versions of the requirements are listed in Table 4.5, based on the requirements in Table 4.4. The restated requirements are now concise, complete, and testable. Multiple related requirements are organized in a logical hierarchy.

Table 4.5.   Restated Requirements

Requirement ID	Requirement
1.1	Must be able to analyze customer data
1.1.1	Must be able to analyze profit levels by product
1.1.2	Must be able to analyze profit levels by customer
1.1.3	Must be able to analyze profit levels by region
1.2	Must be able to sort (descending, ascending) customers
1.3.1	Must be able to sort (descending, ascending) customers by amount of sales
1.3.2	Must be able to sort (descending, ascending) customers by amount of sales of particular products
1.3.3	Must be able to sort (descending, ascending) customers by amount of sales in regions and amount of sales over a specified period of time
1.3.4	Must be able to sort (descending, ascending) customers by amount of sales over a specified period of time
1.4	Must be able to identify sales trends
1.4.1	Must be able to identify drop in sales
1.4.2	Must be able to identify drops in a customer's sales

Note   Remember that at each step you must validate requirements with the customer.

How to Categorize Requirements

After refining requirements, you categorize them as user, system, operations, and business requirements.

User requirements

User requirements define the non-functional aspect of the user's interaction with the solution. They help you determine the user interface and performance expectations of the solution in terms of its reliability, availability, and accessibility. In addition, they help you identify the training that the users will need to effectively use the solution. A successful solution satisfies both the organization's need for technology and the user's expectations for employing that technology.

Examples of user requirements

Some of the user requirements might be:

- Sales representatives should not need to type any name they previously typed during any single sales call.
- A cashier should be able to complete more than one transaction per minute.
- A customer should be able to complete the purchase of a product on the shopping Web site within five minutes.

System requirements

System requirements specify the atomic transactions and their sequence in the system, and help the project team define how the new solution will interact with the existing systems. The project team also identifies the critical dependencies with external systems that must be managed. Before developing a new solution, the project team must understand the current infrastructure in the organization. This helps the project team to design and develop a solution that can be deployed in the organization with the minimum negative impact.

Examples of system requirements

Some of the system requirements might be:

- All enterprise line-of-business applications supporting near-real-time user notifications must either implement the approved notification component or have received a waiver during final design review.
- The solution should not require a user credential other than the credentials passed from logging on to the corporate network.

Operations requirements

Operations requirements describe what the solution must deliver to maximize operability and improve service delivery with reduced downtime and risks. It addresses the following key elements of operations:

- Security
- Availability and reliability
- Manageability
- Scalability
- Supportability

Examples of operations requirements

Consider the example of a music store that wants to implement an e-commerce Web site. Some of the operations requirements for this site include:

- *Availability and reliability.* Customers should be able to access the site and use its resources at any time within stated service levels.
- *Scalability and flexibility.* The solution should be able to handle varying volumes of users and transactions. In addition, the site must be designed so that it can be modified and upgraded without affecting availability or performance. Both the infrastructure and business processes must be scalable and flexible.
- *Performance manageability.* The site design should include a system for managing the total system throughput and response time within stated service levels.
- *Strong security.* The data, services, and devices in the system must be protected from unauthorized access. The system should also provide authentication and secure transactions.
- *Administrative manageability.* The site should allow the administrators to perform their tasks both onsite and remotely.
- *Recoverability.* The site should be able to recover from critical failure without major impact, or within stated service levels.

Business requirements

Business requirements describe the organization's needs and expectations for the solution. Business requirements define what the solution must deliver to capitalize on a business opportunity or to meet business challenges. To identify business requirements, you need to consider the organization as a valid entity with its own set of needs from the solution. These requirements exist at the managerial decision-making level and provide the context in which the solution will operate.

Examples of business requirements

Some examples of business requirements might be:

- Call-center managers must be able to view the last, current, and average call times for each telephone operator.
- Cashiers can override an item's price to a specified amount without the supervisor's code.
- The solution must be designed, built, and deployed as quickly as possible.
- The solution must be able to interact and communicate with other business processes, applications, and data sources.

Consider a music store that wants to increase the sales of its CDs and DVDs and sell to a larger segment of the market. The organization has decided to implement an online shopping site. Some of the business requirements of this organization are:

- After the user submits an order, inventory must be marked "for fulfillment" and removed from "available" status.
- The application must provide a method of applying a discount to orders over a specified amount.

How to Refine Use Cases Diagrams

During the envisioning phase, the project team creates a use cases diagram that specifies all high-level use cases in the organization. The purpose of this use cases diagram is to list the key use cases in the system, to define of the scope of solution, and to provide a basis for the solution concept. To create a conceptual model of the design, you need to refine the use cases that are within the scope of the solution by using the information gathered during the research step of conceptual design.

To refine the use cases diagram, you perform the following tasks:

- Create subordinate use cases.
- Create usage scenarios for each subordinate use case.
- Validate each use case and usage scenario against the original interviews, against other documentation, and with the user.
- Refine requirements with the validated use cases and usage scenario information.

Creating subordinate use cases

To create subordinate use cases, you revisit each use case in the use cases diagram that is within the scope of the project. You then identify each task associated with the use case, and model them as subordinate use cases for the higher-level use case. You also identify all actors that perform the tasks and the relationship between the various tasks and actors.

Figure 4.8 illustrates a refined use cases diagram. This diagram shows many subordinate use cases for the Manage Orders use case.

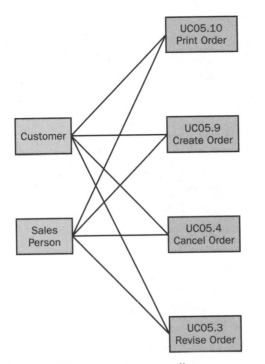

Figure 4.8.   Refined use case diagram

Usage scenarios for subordinate use cases

After creating subordinate use cases, you need to create usage scenarios for the new use cases. This step includes elaborating on the original usage scenario and adding a detailed scenario narrative; specifying the basic course; specifying an alternative course, if any; and describing the preconditions and postconditions.

The following is a sample usage scenario of a high-level use case included in the Adventure Works Cycles case study.

Use case title: Order Product Specifications

Abbreviated title: Order Product Specifications

Use case ID: UC 05.1

Requirements ID: 15.1

Intent: To provide full (not basic) product specification document to customer

Scenario narrative: While a customer is viewing an item in the catalog, the customer requests the product specifications.

Actors: Customer

Use case title: Order Product Specifications   *(continued)*

Preconditions: Customer is browsing through the product catalog.

Customer is viewing an item in the catalog.

Basic course:

1. Use case begins when a customer clicks Order Specifications for This Item
2. Customer selects the format of the specification.
3. Customer selects the shipping method.
4. Address is confirmed.
5. Use case ends when the order is complete, submitted, and ready to be fulfilled.

Alternative course:

Postconditions: Order is complete, submitted, and ready to be fulfilled. Customer is returned to last view in Browse Products.

Uses/extends: Customer Updates Profile, Customer Creates Profile, Submit Order

User implementation requests: None

Frequency: Occurs in 17 out of 100 sessions by Web customer.

Unresolved issues: None

Authority: Mike Danseglio

Modification history: Date: November 6, 2002

Author: Heidi Steen

Description: Initial version

One of the subordinate use cases for the Order Product Specifications use case is Order Product Specifications by Mail. The usage scenario for this subordinate use case is as follows.

Use case title: Order Product Specifications by Mail

Abbreviated title: Product Specifications by Mail

Use case ID: UC 05.1.1

Requirements ID: 15.1.1

Intent: Provide a means for a customer to receive the specification for a selected catalog item through the postal service.

Scenario narrative: A customer wants to receive a product specification through the postal service. The customer browses through the catalog (UC 05.1) and views the catalog item of interest. After choosing delivery by the postal service, the customer must specify a delivery address. If the customer has logged on with a valid account, the customer can select an address from a list of addresses on file. The customer can also specify an address in a form. After the request has been submitted, the customer receives a confirmation number for future reference.

Actors: Customer

Use case title: Order Product Specifications by Mail   *(continued)*

Preconditions:

- Customer is browsing through the product catalog.
- Customer is viewing an item in the catalog.

Basic Course:

1. Use case begins when a customer clicks Order Specifications for This Item
2. Customer selects the format of the specification, such as specification sheet or brochure.
3. Customer selects the shipping method, such as electronic, United States Postal Service, one-day delivery, or two-day delivery.
4. Address list from profile appears.
5. Customer chooses an address from a list of addresses.
6. Address is confirmed.
7. Customer submits the request.
8. Use case ends when the customer is given a confirmation number.

Alternative course:

1. Alternative course begins at 4.
2. 4a. Address does not exist in profile.
   4b. Go to Customer Updates Profile or Customer Creates Profile.
3. Use case resumes at 5.

Postconditions: Order is complete, submitted, and ready to be fulfilled. User is returned to last view in Browse Products.

Uses/extends: Extends UC 05.1, Order Product Specifications

User implementation requests: None

Frequency: Occurs in 17 out of 100 sessions by Web customer

Unresolved issues: None

Authority: Mike Danseglio

Modification history:

Date: December 6, 2002

Author: Heidi Steen

Description: Initial version

Validating use cases and usage scenarios

It is essential that the team validate the candidate requirements, use cases, and usage scenarios with users and other stakeholders. This step helps determine whether any steps in the process have not been documented. The features list is then developed based on the requirements. Revisions to the feature list are identified by elaborating on the use cases, and any additions are validated by the customer.

Remember that validation is an iterative process. It helps you identify gaps in requirements in addition to use cases and usage scenarios.

How to Select an Application Architecture

The key deliverable of the conceptual design is the conceptual model of the solution. To be able to create a conceptual model, you need to understand the services that the solution must provide.

Services in a solution

A *service* is defined as a unit of application logic that includes methods for implementing an operation, a function, or a transformation.

Services are mapped to actions and used to implement business rules, manipulate data, and enable actions such as adding, retrieving, viewing, and modifying data. Services are accessible across a network through a published interface that contains the interface specification. Customers are not concerned about how a service is implemented; they are concerned about the ability to perform the required actions.

Services can be either simple or complex. For example, services for creating, reading, updating, and deleting information are simple. You might also develop services to implement complex mathematical calculations.

The services that a solution typically provides are:

- *User services.* User services are units of application logic that provide the user interface in an application. The user services of an application manage the interaction between the application and its users. To design efficient user services, you need a thorough understanding of the users of the application, the tasks that they will perform, and the typical interactions they will have with the application to perform their activities.

- *Business services.* Business services are units of application logic that enforce business rules in the correct sequence. A business service hides the logic of implementing business rules and transforming data from the user services, other business services, and data services.

- *Data services.* Data services are units of application logic that provide the lowest visible level of detail for manipulating data. You use data services to implement business schema on the data store being used by the application. Data services are used to manage all kinds of data—static, structured, and dynamic. You use data services in all scenarios in which a user or business service needs to access or work with data.

- *System services.* System services are the units of application logic that provide functionality outside the business logic. Common system services include:
  - Backup services
  - Error handling services
  - Security services
  - Messaging services

Examples of services

Table 4.6 lists the various services in an order processing application.

Table 4.6.   Examples of Services

Services	Examples
User services	• Displaying the order service
	• Displaying the customer account service
	• Displaying product information service
Business services	• Order placing service
	• Updating customer account service
	• Retrieving product information service
	• Checking product inventory service
Data services	• Order information service
	• Customer account service
	• Product information service

Remember that you classify a service according to its function and not according to its location. The classification into user, business, or data service depends on what the service actually does, as opposed to where it is located. For example, a data service on the client workstation is still a data service.

Application architecture

You also need to know how the services are organized in the solution. The services are organized according to the application architecture. Application architecture consists of definitions, rules, and relationships that form the structure of an application. It shows how an application is structured but does not include implementation details. It focuses on the solution and not the technologies that will be used to implement the solution. To be able to develop a conceptual model of the solution, you need to select the application model and candidate application architecture that the solution will use.

The project team selects the architecture based on both the services that the solution must provide and users' expectations of the performance of the application. In addition, assumptions about the solution and constraints of the project affect the choice of the application architecture for the solution. Assumptions include the operating systems used in the system. Examples of constraints include budget, time, skills, and resources available for completing the project.

Some of the application architectures that are used are:

- Client/server architecture
- Layered architecture
- Stateless architecture
- Cache architecture
- Layered-client-cache-stateless-cache-server architecture

Client/server architecture

The *client/server architecture* is a two-tier approach that is based on a request-and-provide strategy. The client initiates a session with the server and controls the session, enlisting the server on demand. The client requests the server for one of its services. Upon receiving the request, the server performs the required operation and returns the result to the client.

The benefit of implementing this application architecture is that you can divide the processing required to accomplish a task between the two devices. The client can execute specialized processes and avoid overloading the server with processing requests.

However, one of the limitations of this architecture is that the clients depend heavily on the servers. If the client fails to communicate with the server, the client cannot perform even the most basic task. This is typical in solutions that must process a large number of requests. Such an application is not highly scalable.

Layered architecture

Layered architecture is an evolved version of the client/server architecture and is composed of hierarchical layers. The various services in the application are clearly positioned in specific layers in such a way that a service cannot communicate with other services except the ones in the adjacent layer. Layers encapsulate services and protect one service from another while providing a simplified set of interfaces for shared resources. User, business, and data services are examples of a layered architecture.

Benefits of layered architecture include improved system scalability and high security. You can balance services across available resources and various layers. In addition, layers allow you to implement security on well-defined boundaries with very little negative impact on communications between services within the system.

Layering adds overhead and latency that can negatively affect performance of the system as perceived by the user. You can mitigate the impact of this problem by adding shared caches to the system. However, this approach increases the complexity of the solution, the effort required to design and develop the solution, and the resources required to operate the solution.

Stateless architecture

Stateless architecture is a version of the client/server or layered architecture in which each client request contains all the information that is required by the server to understand and process the request. No information is stored on the client.

Some of the benefits of stateless systems are:

- *Improved visibility.* For example, a monitoring system does not need to read more than a single request to determine the full nature of the request
- *Reliability.* For example, the solution can easily recover from a partial failure
- *Scalability.* The resources used by the solution can be quickly released and easily pooled.

Note   A stateless environment places an additional burden on clients to manage their own state. Because a lot of information is passed to the server for every request, the load on the communication channels is also increased.

Cache architecture

Caching is another approach in which the application provides a means for processing some client requests without forwarding the request to another device. To implement this kind of application architecture, you need to identify what can and cannot be cached. You also need to define ways to manage the lifetime of items in the cache.

Because caching avoids transferring request and response data between clients and servers, the application and network performance are greatly improved. In addition, this approach provides a high degree of scalability by creating local storage for frequently requested resources that would otherwise be queued to access a shared repository.

However, caching reduces the reliability of the solution. For example, the cached data might be outdated and so might not match the information that would be received if the request were processed by the server.

Layered-client-cache-stateless-cache-server architecture

Layered-client-cache-stateless-cache-server architecture is the browser-based version of the Windows Distributed interNet Applications (DNA) architecture. It combines the layered-client-server, client-cache, and cached-stateless-server approaches by adding proxies throughout the system as necessary.

This architecture allows you to create highly flexible and scalable applications by distributing processing and remaining stateless on the server. You can scale up and scale out the solution without affecting the transactional integrity of the solution. In addition, this architecture ensures the manageability and flexibility of the solution.

The layered-client-cache-stateless-cache-server architecture is complex and precariously balanced. Any deviation from the implied implementation can quickly deteriorate its portability, network, and user perceived performance.

Example of a conceptual model

Figure 4.9 illustrates the conceptual model of the solution in the Adventure Works Cycles case study. Notice that the model has multiple layers and that the various services of the solution are located in the solution's three layers.

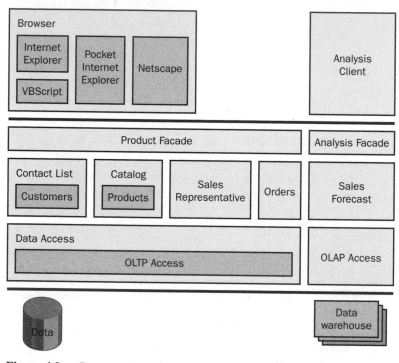

Figure 4.9.   Conceptual model of solution for Adventure Works Cycles

Lesson 5: Optimizing the Conceptual Design

The final step of conceptual design is optimization. During optimization, you begin designing the solution by evolving the solution concept as it will be in the final application.

Table 4.7 lists the tasks and deliverables of optimization.

Table 4.7.   Tasks and Deliverables of Conceptual Design Optimization

Task	Deliverable
Improve the process.	Description of problems addressed by solution.
Validate the design.	Validated future state of the solution.

In this lesson, you will learn how to optimize the process descriptions gathered during conceptual design. You will also learn how to evaluate the optimized processes and validate the conceptual design.

After this lesson, you will be able to

- Optimize processes.
- Evaluate optimized processes.
- Validate optimized processes.
- Validate the conceptual design.

Estimated time: 15 minutes

How to Optimize Processes

In addition to researching and analyzing current business processes, you determine which processes will be included in the solution and how the needs of those processes are met. The management or process owners, the users, and the project team must work together to arrive at a solution that focuses on both the processes and the users.

To design the future state, you examine the current state scenarios and eliminate inefficiencies, bottlenecks, and redundant effort. The future state is best designed by the project team and users together with the help of experts in business process reengineering.

Note   The project team and the business process reengineering team should design a target future state and redesign business processes only if these activities are included in the scope of the project.

Although many application development teams can do a great deal to design the future state, the involvement of business process reengineering experts is a best practice. To describe the future state, the team performs the following tasks:

- Envision the target future state.
    - Improve productivity of the current state.
    - Consider needs versus wants.
    - Balance business and user requirements.
    - Balance impact and technical feasibility.
- Redesign the current process to optimally support key business activities and processes, involving business process redesign experts as appropriate.
    - Optimize the entire process.
    - Integrate processes where possible.
    - Eliminate inefficiencies, bottlenecks, and redundancies.
- Build target future state usage scenarios that reflect the redesigned process.
- Validate future state scenarios with stakeholders.
- Iterate the redesign process as needed.

Instead of designing the future state from an analyst's perspective, redesign the solution from the users' perspective. You might find improvement opportunities in workflow activities, outdated or unproductive business policies, unchallenged bureaucracies, missed communication, and non-value-added roles that hinder and fragment the overall effectiveness of a business process. To identify the requirements from the user's perspective, keep in mind the following guidelines:

- Identify undesirable sequential activities, bottlenecks, and unnecessary steps in the process.
- Remove redundancies in the current environment.
- Integrate individual functional information systems into consolidated process-wide systems.
- Identify and remove all unnecessary paperwork.
- Determine the minimum performance level that must be achieved by a process. Try to design a process that achieves the same results with less effort.
- Reduce the wait time in a system by identifying steps that can be performed simultaneously instead of sequentially.
- Improve the system by providing users information such as feedback about performance to ensure that problems are resolved immediately.

Redesigning processes identified during design

The key objective of the project team, along with the business process reengineering experts, is to design an elegant solution that minimizes user effort as much as possible. There is no single method for redesigning a process effectively. The team can conduct brainstorming sessions that use various creativity techniques: metaphors, word and thought variation, creativity-barrier exploration, idea-generation exercises, open forum, and non-critical discussions. These ideas represent new approaches to the problem rather than detailed blueprints.

Key questions for the business process reengineers include:

- Where are the opportunities for user empowerment?
- Can certain decisions be delegated? If so, what is the impact of delegation on business activities?
- What can be done in software that is difficult to achieve in the physical world or on paper?
- What are the opportunities for automation or applying new technologies?

During the redesign process, explore multiple alternatives. It is important to encourage the creative process. Often, a problem has more than one solution.

A key principle in redesign is that every rule or assumption can be challenged. Also, you need to consider all elements of a process during redesign—inputs, outputs, performance levels, resources, control procedures, productivity, and timing. The following summary lists the key elements to consider when optimizing a process:

- Challenge rules and break assumptions that rules are unquestionable. For example, you can question a rule such as "In this company, all medical claim requests submitted by employees must be approved at the unit, departmental, and divisional levels."
- Align the process with performance goals. Think of performance in terms of meeting customer requirements and not just short-term profits.
- Design activities around products and services. The responsibilities of a user should be designed to meet the goals and objectives of the process and not be designed around a specific task.
- Replace bureaucracies and hierarchies with self-organized teams that work in parallel.
- Improve productivity by moving the focus from work fragmentations and task specialization toward task compression and integration.
- Determine where you can use technology to enable and support the redesigned process.
- Break the process into subprocesses and deal with each subprocess one process at a time.

Once the process is optimized and targeted as the goal, the focus shifts to redesigning the work. Redesigning work is based on what is necessary from a business standpoint, not what initially seems reasonable or accomplishable. The team needs to examine the conceptual model of the solution and reorganize it to make the process more efficient.

Also, the team might discover new use cases and need to incorporate them into the conceptual model. Based on the new use cases, several alternative process designs might be generated. Validate these alternatives with end users and business process experts by using techniques such as role playing. Based on the results of testing and validation, you can select an alternative for subsequent detailed design.

The process for redesigning work can be summarized as follows:

- Brainstorm for maximum ideas.
    - Use visualization.
    - Think creatively and break the rules.
    - Generate, evaluate, and challenge options.
- Supplement brainstorming with other techniques.
- Validate alternatives with end users and process experts.

How to Evaluate the Redesigned Process

You evaluate the redesigned process to determine whether there is any misunderstood or missing information about user requirements. You also confirm that no problems have occurred because of varying views of the solution among the team.

You also evaluate the cost and benefits of the solution in its current state. Many projects are canceled at this stage because evaluation indicates that the return on investment (ROI) of the new solution does not meet business criteria.

In addition, you need to determine the primary and secondary benefits. The specific benefits should be stated, and the stakeholders, including customers, should be identified.

Table 4.8 summarizes the evaluation criteria for most business solutions.

Table 4.8.   Evaluating Benefits and Costs of a Redesign

Evaluating benefits	Evaluating cost
Effectiveness and efficiency of whole and parts	Resources, work effort, and time
Beneficiaries of the solution	Operational costs of technical options and emerging technology
Organizational and cultural effects	Annual and recurring life-cycle costs
Potential revenue and savings	

How to Validate the Conceptual Design Model

After creating the conceptual design, validate it with users and other stakeholders. You can integrate validation directly into the process of evaluating user input. Validation enables you to get users' confirmation that the conceptual model and requirements represent their view of the business solution and that the solution addresses all use cases and usage scenarios.

You validate the conceptual design of the solution against the use cases, usage scenarios, business requirements, architecture, risks, available resources and time, and all other artifacts that you have developed. Users find it easier to validate a scenario because the scenario contains the context of the requirements.

The validation of the scenarios should also include a validation of the results from the prioritization activity. In other words, the priorities and volume of activity for the scenario should be verified. You get the conceptual design of the solution validated because validation:

- Reduces risk.
- Highlights missing information.
- Indicates diverging views and interpretations of the solution, especially between the business and users.
- Verifies the volume of activity.
- Assists in prioritization.
- Provides a baseline for proceeding to logical design.

The process for validating, testing, and redesigning can include the following steps:

1. Redesign the work.
2. Build a set of scenarios that support the work.
3. Build a prototype of the system.
4. Draw the user interface.
5. Obtain user and business feedback.
6. Repeat until users and the business are satisfied.

Repeat steps 5 and 6 as required.

Techniques for validating conceptual design

There are several techniques for validating scenarios. Some of those techniques include:

- *Walk through.* A facilitator guides users through the scenario and asks questions along the way to determine whether the users agree with individual actions and events.

- *Role playing.* A set of selected users executes multiple scenarios to evaluate the process and identify areas of refinement. This helps the team select one of the scenarios for detailed design.

- *Prototyping.* A prototype provides details of the process, process flow, organizational implications, and technology possibilities. Prototyping is an effective way to communicate the gathered and synthesized requirements to the user. You can create a prototype as an electronic application or in paper form as the functional specification summary. Prototypes should be reviewed and evaluated by the team and should allow management to decide about the final process design. The team also needs to prototype multiple user interfaces. Such prototypes are used to validate that the team has included appropriate information— not whether the dialog box looks right or whether the colors are correct.

Activity: Analyzing Requirements

In this activity, you will use what you learned in the lessons to work through the process of analyzing requirements.

Exercise 1: Refining Use Cases and Requirements

Open the Microsoft Visio® diagram named C04Ex1 in the \SolutionDocuments \Chapter04 folder on the CD. Look at the second tab: AWC Use Case - Ex1ToSolve.

1. What questions would you ask the customer's project staff to identify the subordinate use cases contained in Manage Orders?

    Questions you would ask might include:

    - What does it mean to manage orders?

    - What does the Sales Representative role do when managing orders? Name as many specific tasks as possible.

    - What does the Customer role do when managing orders? Name as many specific tasks as possible.

    - What are the differences between the tasks that the customer performs with orders and the tasks that the sales representative performs?

2. The customer gives you the following information:

    - Both the Customer and the Sales Representative roles need to create, print, change, and cancel orders by using the Web site and the devices the sales representative uses.

    - The Adventure Works Cycles project staff agree that a Help function is needed and that they want the user to be able to view a frequently asked questions (FAQ) section, get Help by means of a wizard, and have instant messaging (IM) sessions available.

    - The sales representative, but not the customer, can apply a discount to the order.

    Use this information and your requirements to enter the appropriate use cases on the third tab, Ch4 Manage Orders, in the Visio file. The Create Order and Revise Order use cases have been provided to give you a starting point.

To see one possible solution, see the C04Ex1_Answer document in the \Solution Documents\Chapter04 folder on the companion CD.

Exercise 2: Viewing a Conceptual Model Diagram

Open the Visio diagram named C04Ex2.vsd in the \SolutionDocuments\Chapter04 folder on the CD. Review the conceptual model. Open the requirements document C04Ex2.xls in the same folder. Review and revise the requirements statements and organize them into a loose hierarchy by using the conceptual model to guide you. For example, organize all requirements related to Revise Order together. Does the conceptual model allow the current requirements to be covered in the solution?

 To see one possible solution, see the C04Ex2_Answer.xls document in the \Solution Documents\Chapter04 folder on the companion CD.

Summary

- The planning phase results in the architecture and design of the solution, the plans to accomplish the development and deployment of the solution, and the schedules associated with tasks and resources.
- There are three design processes in the planning phase: conceptual, logical, and physical design.
- The program management team manages and is responsible for the planning phase.
- The key deliverables of the planning phase are:
  - The functional specification, which represents what the product will be, based on input from the entire team
  - The master project plan, which is a collection of plans for how each of the six team roles will perform their tasks to achieve the functionality described in the functional specification
  - The master project schedule, which specifies the time frame in which the teams intend to complete their work
  - The updated master risk assessment document, which describes the risks associated with creating the product
- A functional specification is the virtual repository of project and design-related artifacts that are created during the planning phase of the MSF Process Model.
- The goals of a functional specification are:
  - Consolidating a common understanding of the business and user requirements
  - Breaking the problem into logical modules
  - Providing a framework for planning, scheduling, and creating the solution
  - Serving as a contract between the team and customer about what will be delivered
- The functional specification consists of:
  - Conceptual design summary
  - Logical design summary
  - Physical design summary
  - Standards and processes used by the team
- Conceptual design is the process of gathering, analyzing, and prioritizing business and user perspectives of the problem and the solution, and then creating a preliminary version of the solution.

- The goals of creating a conceptual design are:
  - Determining the business problem to be solved
  - Determining the requirements of the business, the customer, and the end user
  - Describing the target future state of the business
- The process of conceptual design consists of three steps: research, analysis, and optimization.
- During the research step, the team gathers more information about the business requirements, the use cases, and the usage scenarios.
- The tasks performed during the analysis step are:
  - Synthesizing information
  - Refining the use cases diagram
  - Selecting an appropriate application architecture for the solution
  - Creating a conceptual model of the solution
- A business requirement must be:
  - Well defined
  - Concise
  - Testable
  - Grouped in a hierarchical manner
  - Written in a business language without jargon
- Business requirements can be categorized as:
  - User
  - System
  - Operations
  - Business
- To refine the use cases diagram, the project team:
  - Creates subordinate use cases
  - Creates usage scenarios for each subordinate use case
  - Validates each use case and usage scenario against refined requirements
- To create the conceptual design of the solution, you need to determine the services and the architecture of the solution.
- A solution can provide business, user, data, and system services.
- Application architecture consists of definitions, rules, and relationships that form the structure of an application.

- An application can be based on one of the following architectures:
    - Client/server architecture
    - Layered architecture
    - Stateless architecture
    - Cache architecture
    - Layered-client-cache-stateless-cache-server architecture
- During the optimization step of conceptual design, the team optimizes the solution and business processes and validates them against business requirements and use cases.
- To describe the future state of the system, the project team:
    - Envisions the target future state
    - Redesigns the current process to optimally support key business activities and processes
    - Builds target future state scenarios that reflect the redesigned process
    - Validates future state scenarios with stakeholders
    - Iterates the redesign process as needed
- To redesign a process, the project team:
    - Brainstorms for maximum number of ideas
    - Supplements brainstorming with other techniques
    - Validates alternatives with end users and process experts
- The project team validates the conceptual design of the solution against the use cases, usage scenarios, and business requirements.

Review

The following questions are intended to reinforce key information presented in this chapter. If you are unable to answer a question, review the lesson materials and try the question again. You can find answers to the questions in the appendix.

1. What is the purpose of the planning phase?

2. What is the difference between the responsibilities of the product management and project management roles during the planning phase?

3. What are the major deliverables of the planning phase?

4. How does a functional specification serve as a blueprint for the development team?

5. What are the goals of a functional specification?

6. What are the risks of not creating a functional specification?

7. What is the difference between the business and user requirements of the solution?

8. What are the benefits of creating a conceptual design?

9. A company plans to increase its sales by 15 percent during the next financial year by implementing an online shopping site. The company intends to provide its users a Web site that is fast, provides secure credit card processing, and is available at all times. Also, only registered users will be able to purchase products on the site. What are the user, system, operation, and business requirements for this site?

10. What are the goals of the analysis step of conceptual design?

11. What is the benefit of synthesizing information?

12. What are the tasks for creating the future state?

13. What are the benefits of validating the conceptual design?

14. What are the four service categories?

15. Study and categorize the following services.
    - Displaying the employee details service
    - Updating the employee details service
    - Employee information service
    - E-mail service

16. What are the characteristics of a refined business requirement?

17. How do you refine use cases during the analysis step of conceptual design?

18. What are the criteria for evaluating the cost of a solution?

C H A P T E R 5

Creating the Logical Design

About This Chapter

The planning phase consists of three levels of design—conceptual, logical, and physical. These design levels occur consecutively; however, they have overlapping start and end points. Therefore, the conceptual design process always starts before the logical design process, but conceptual design will be in process when the logical design process starts. Likewise, the logical design process always starts before the physical design process, but the logical design will be in process when the physical design process starts. Table 5.1 summarizes the design process in the planning phase.

Table 5.1.   The Three Design Processes

Type of design	Perspective	Purpose
Conceptual	View the problem from the perspective of the user and the business	Defines the problem and solution in terms of usage scenarios
Logical	View the solution from the perspective of the project team	Defines the solution as a logical set of cooperating objects and services
Physical	View the solution from the perspective of the developers	Defines the solution's services and technologies

In this chapter, you will learn about the logical design process of the planning phase. This chapter provides an overview of the purpose and benefits of logical design in addition to the team composition during this process. It describes how to create the logical design for a business solution and how to use tools and techniques for documenting the output. In addition, this chapter covers how to optimize the logical design.

Before You Begin

To complete the lessons in this chapter, you must

- Understand the Microsoft® Solutions Framework (MSF) Process Model.
- Be familiar with the outputs of the envisioning phase.
- Be familiar with the planning phase.
- Understand the three steps of conceptual design—research, analysis, and optimization.

Lesson 1: An Overview of Logical Design

In conceptual design, you describe the solution from the business and user perspectives. The next step is to describe the solution from the project team's perspective. This is done in the logical design process.

In this lesson, you will learn about the goals and purpose of logical design.

After this lesson, you will be able to

- Describe logical design.
- Describe the benefits of logical design.
- Describe the roles and responsibilities of team members during logical design.

Estimated lesson time: 10 minutes

What Is Logical Design?

Logical design is defined as the process of describing the solution in terms of its organization, its structure, and the interaction of its parts from the perspective of the project team. Logical design:

- Defines the constituent parts of a solution.
- Provides the framework that holds all parts of the solution together.
- Illustrates how the solution is put together and how it interacts with users and other solutions.

When creating a logical design, the team takes into account all the business, user, system, and operations requirements that identify the need for security, auditing, logging, scalability, state management, error handling, licensing, globalization, application architecture, and integration with other systems.

Planning   Because the MSF design process is evolutionary as well as iterative, logical design affects the physical design.

When does logical design take place?

When the project team begins to identify significant objects and entity attributes, it can start the logical design, so logical design can begin before conceptual design ends. The decision to start logical design is made on a case-by-case basis, depending on the project and the team. Figure 5.1 illustrates where the logical design fits within the MSF Process Model.

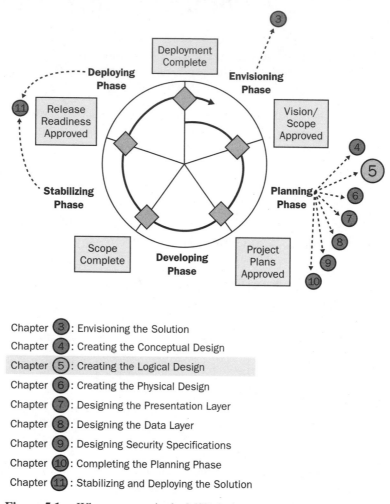

Figure 5.1.   Where are you in the MSF design process?

When project teams proceed from conceptual to logical design, their perspectives change. During conceptual design, the project team defines the business problem based on the data it has gathered from the business and user communities. During logical design, the project team defines the solution elements from its own perspective. The members of the team identify what the solution needs to do. Based on that information, they define the behavior and organization of the solution.

Note   Logical design helps the team further refine the requirements that were initially created during the envisioning phase and refined during the conceptual design process.

A good logical design depends on a good conceptual design. If the project team creates a good logical design, it should be easy for a new team member to look at the design, identify important parts of the solution, and understand how the parts work together to solve the business problem. Most often, the work on the logical design overlaps the work on the physical design.

Note   The project team optimizes the structure of the solution during the logical design and improves its operation during the physical design, thus leading to an iterative process between logical and physical design.

Logical design tasks

At a more detailed level, the logical design phase can be broken down into the following tasks:

- Logical design analysis, in which the team performs the following tasks:
    - Refining the list of candidate tools and technologies
    - Identifying business objects and services
    - Identifying important attributes and key relationships
- Logical design optimization, in which the team performs the following tasks:
    - Refining the logical design
    - Validating the logical design

Figure 5.2 illustrates the analysis and optimization tasks in logical design.

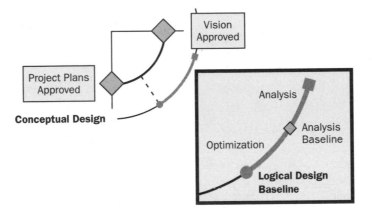

Figure 5.2.   Tasks in logical design process

During logical design, the team might encounter some new requirements or features that have not been discovered previously. At this point, the team needs to go back to the customer to verify that these requirements or features are valid, and learn what the customer wants to do with this discovery. Depending on the customer's answer, the scope of the project might change. If the project scope changes, revise the documentation and models that have been created to incorporate the new requirements or features.

The primary purpose of logical design

The primary focus of the logical design is to identify what the system must do and explain it by using a set of elements. Logical design enables you to:

- Specify the business needs that should be supported by technology. The logical design is not a technology solution; however, it helps the project team specify the business needs that the solution must support.
- Identify technology constraints and opportunities. Although the logical design is independent of the physical implementation, the project team can start to identify constraints and opportunities that might affect the selection and implementation of a technology.
- Identify the appropriate technologies to be implemented. The team must understand the solution completely before the team selects the technology for implementing the solution. The logical design is not optimized for a selected physical model, but it helps the project team identify the most appropriate technologies for implementing the solution. Candidate technologies can be identified during logical design if the logical design demonstrates a good match to the technologies.
- Identify the areas of logical design that must be adjusted to accommodate infrastructure, operational, and deployment issues. Logical design is not affected by technologies required to develop the components. However, the logical design affects the physical design, and the physical design depends on technologies. Therefore, if the customer requires a Web-based solution for example, the project team should be aware of the deployment constraints during the logical design process.

Outputs of logical design

The outputs of the logical design process are:

- A logical object model
- A high-level user interface design
- A logical data model

Note   The logical object model and the logical data model document similar information in different ways. For most projects, one model is sufficient to document the logical design. However some teams might want to create both models as a precursor to physical design, and then validate one model with the other.

Each type of output is described in detail in Lesson 3.

The outputs of the logical design serve as a foundation for the physical design. To understand clearly what happens in the logical design process, consider the analogy of designing a house. During conceptual design, the customer and the architect list the customer requirements, such as entertainment, sleeping, dining, storage, and utility needs. During logical design, the architect creates the floor plan and identifies structural features such as doors, windows, roof, patio, and rooms. The architect also creates a complete layout of the house. Similarly, the project team works with users and the business customer during conceptual design to determine the requirements. Based on these requirements, the project team identifies the components of the solution and devises an overall framework into which the components then fit.

What Are the Benefits of Logical Design?

Creating a logical design for a solution has several benefits, such as helping to create a strong link between the members of the team who have technical knowledge and those who do not. The following list itemizes several of the benefits of logical design.

- Logical design helps manage the complexity of the project by defining the structure of the solution, describing the parts of the solution, and describing how the parts interact to solve the problem. Many projects fail because they are too complex and are not well designed before their implementation. Complexity can cause confusion, resulting in a poor design of the solution. Logical design helps the team understand and manage the inherent complexity of business processes.

- Logical design reflects and supports the requirements of conceptual design by verifying that the design will address the business problem. Logical design helps the team discover errors and inconsistencies in the conceptual design, eliminate redundancy in the requirements, and identify potential reuse in the scenarios. These discoveries can be applied back into the conceptual design and measured against the requirements to ensure that the solution will solve the problem.

- Logical design serves as a point of contact for organizing cross-functional cooperation among multiple systems in the enterprise and provides a coherent view of the entire project. The team can analyze the logical design to identify areas of reuse and make the design more efficient and maintainable.

- Logical design is used as the starting point for the physical design. Because logical design is an object model, the project team can determine the location and attributes of the objects for their physical representation.

What Are the Responsibilities of Team Roles During Logical Design?

During logical design, each team has a different set of responsibilities. For example, the program management team is responsible for developing the functional specification, facilitating communication and negotiation with the team, and maintaining project schedule and reporting project status. This team takes the primary responsibility for completing the logical design.

Figure 5.3 highlights the responsibilities of the various roles during logical design.

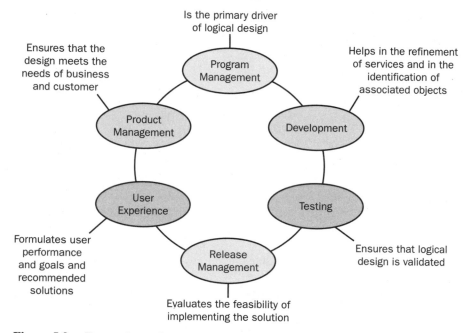

Figure 5.3.   Team roles and responsibilities

Table 5.2 summarizes the tasks that each team role performs during the logical design process.

Table 5.2.   Team Roles

Role	Primary task	Secondary task
Product management	Ensuring that the design meets the needs of the business and the customer	Managing customer expectations
Program management	Takes the primary responsibility for the logical design deliverables	Defining project plan, including resources, schedules, and risk assessments
Development	Identifying services and associated objects	Serving as technology consultants to evaluate and prototype technologies
Testing	Validating logical design models against conceptual design	Defining a high-level testing plan
User experience	Defining user performance goals and recommended solutions	Defining a high-level plan for user education
Release management	Evaluating the feasibility of implementing the solution	Defining infrastructure and deployment solutions

Lesson 2: Creating a Logical Design

During the analysis step of logical design, the team breaks the overall problem and its solution into smaller units called modules. A *module* is a logical unit used as an abstraction for the use cases and scenarios created in conceptual design. For each module, the team identifies objects, services, attributes, and relationships. The team also identifies candidate technologies for the solution during logical design.

In this lesson, you will learn how to identify candidate technologies for a business solution by considering the conceptual design, business objects, services, attributes of objects and services, and relationships between objects from use cases.

After this lesson, you will be able to

- Select candidate technologies.
- Identify candidate business objects from use cases.
- Identify services from use cases.
- Identify attributes from use cases.
- Identify relationships between objects from use cases.

Estimated lesson time: 20 minutes

How to Refine the List of Candidate Technologies in Logical Design

During conceptual design, the team begins to identify possible technologies that could be used to address parts of the solution. During logical design, the team further refines the list of candidate technologies already identified, while submitting additional candidate technologies to the list. In evaluating candidate technologies, the team addresses business considerations, enterprise architecture considerations, and technology considerations.

Business considerations

Some of the business considerations include:

- *Feasibility.* Determine whether the technology will actually meet the business needs and address the requirements.
- *Product cost.* Understand the complete product cost, which includes developer, server, and reseller licenses, and upgrade costs. The team also needs to consider costs for initial hardware and software, support, infrastructure, and training. A new product can be a short-term or long-term investment. A short-term

investment solves an immediate need temporarily, such as creating a small and simple client user interface until an intranet Web application is complete. Long-term investments are items that bring benefit for years, such as rewiring a workplace to support higher speed networks or purchasing leading-edge hardware for servers and workstations.

- *Experience.* Understand that the amount of experience users have with various technologies can have a large impact. Try to collect answers to questions such as "What experience is available in terms of training, consultation, and comfort level?"

- *Return on investment.* Each investment must correspond to a return on investment. Do not select a technology simply because it is new. The investment in new technologies should provide value to the business, such as an increase in revenue or a decrease in costs.

- *Maturity.* A mature product is accepted in the market, is well understood, is stable, and has knowledgeable support resources available.

- *Supportability.* When selecting a technology, it is important to realize that the technology will need to be supported along with the solution built. The team needs to consider the implications of providing required levels of support for the project and the enterprise.

Some other factors to consider when selecting candidate technologies are:

- Ease of deployment
- Competitive advantage
- Time needed to market the candidate technology
- Industry perception of the product
- Ability to integrate with existing systems

Enterprise architecture considerations

The application must fit within the goals and principles outlined by the enterprise architecture. In addition to looking at the existing enterprise architecture, the project team must consider any future plans for the enterprise architecture. For example, if the business is planning to use Microsoft Windows® Server 2003, align the selection of candidate technologies with this plan.

The enterprise architecture describes the current-state and future-state plans. The solution must fit within the constraints of the enterprise architecture. For example, a new technology such as streaming video might require enhanced networking capabilities. A new imaging system might require larger screens. Such changes require not only money to purchase new equipment, but also time to learn and implement the new technologies. If two technologies have an equivalent feature set, the best choice is the one that aligns more closely to the existing enterprise architecture.

The technology must work with the other systems within an organization. In addition, a communication interface must be defined so that other applications can easily interact with the new technology.

Technology considerations

Some of the technology considerations are:

- *Security*. Evaluate security considerations for a new solution in terms of authentication, access control, encryption, and auditing. Authentication and authorization are two separate steps in the process of granting users access to resources. *Authentication* determines whether an individual is who he or she claims to be; *authorization* permits the authenticated individual to perform permitted actions within the system. Security services also provide encryption to protect the information as it is transported or stored. *Auditing* creates a permanent record of actions that individuals are performing or attempting to perform within the system.

- *Services interaction standards*. Platforms and interaction standards are related. When the team selects a service interaction standard, it needs to evaluate cross-platform integration against power and performance. For example, the Microsoft .NET Framework simplifies application development in a distributed environment. Besides providing cross-language integration features, it reduces the performance problems of scripted or interpreted environments and provides a simplified model for component interaction.

- *Data access*. When selecting a data access service, consider performance, standardization, future direction, data access management, and the diversity of supported data stores. Candidate technologies for implementing a data access service might need to support industry standards. One of the requirements of data access services might be to allow the team to efficiently use the service regardless of the data store. Data access services should not force the development team to use a specific language or create a specific client interface. This independence from the requesting client allows the development team to use the most effective tools to process data, regardless of how the data is accessed.

- *Data storage*. Data storage systems are responsible for storing all of a business's information, such as employee, company, and customer information. When selecting a data store, evaluate multiple products. The decision should be based on the same structure and location of information. The location of the information is important. Data can be stored on a single computer, in a server farm, or distributed on client computers. The data storage location directly affects the performance of the application and how it is developed.

- *System services*. The project team should evaluate the system services that are required and identify the technologies that will provide those services. System services can also provide many high-availability services, such as fault tolerance and load balancing. In the past, many system services were programmed into each application, but many systems now offer system services independent of a specific application.

The following services are examples of system services:

- Transactional services provide the mechanisms and framework for a transaction-based application. In a transactional system, a sequence of steps can be grouped together as a single transaction. If any of the steps fails, the entire transaction fails and can be reversed or rolled back.

- Asynchronous communication services do not require immediate communication. These services provide a message-based form of execution. A requesting application can be guaranteed that a message will arrive at the remote system, but the requesting application is not dependent on a response within any given period.

- Messaging services are more than just electronic mail. They route information and deliver information that is not time dependent to many individuals. Queuing services are used to queue messages when the destination is not available. This allows the application to submit messages to a recipient regardless of the recipient's availability.

- *Development tools*. Development tools provide the ability to develop the various parts of an application, such as services and components. They provide integrated development environments, source code control, wizards, and code libraries. These tools can help decrease the time required to create applications. While evaluating development tools, the project team should consider several factors:

  - The first consideration is the skills of the developer. New tools require additional training and learning time for the development team and can affect schedule and resource constraints.

  - Specific project requirements might suggest a tool that requires team training or outsourcing to a third-party development team. Some development tools are easier to use than others. Consider the amount of time a particular development tool will require to implement a project. There is often a tradeoff involving the complexity of the development tool and the efficiency of the developed product. For example, assembly language can be used to develop an extremely fast application, but the development team would likely take much longer using assembly language than it would using a tool such as Microsoft Visual Basic® .NET.

  - Consider different languages for different tasks in the project. When choosing a development language, evaluate whether the language supports the design and implementation of loosely coupled components that can be replaced and upgraded as necessary. However, before implementing the use of different languages for different tasks, evaluate the current skills of the development team and the maintenance issues that might need to be addressed after the solution is deployed. For example, the .NET Framework programming model supports a range of programming languages. This also accelerates developer productivity because the developer can choose to develop in the development language of choice.

- Remember that the choice of development tools affects other technology decisions. For example, a specific operating system might be required for using the tool or for implementing solutions created by the tool. Microsoft ASP.NET provides a language-independent platform to create Web applications, but it is not platform independent. The applications must run on the Windows operating system.

- *Operating systems.* When selecting the operating system, the services that are provided by the operating system can significantly reduce the coding requirements of the application. Additionally, security and scalability needs can be met by the operating system. The choice of operating system might also depend on the types of devices, such as Handheld PCs, desktop computers, servers, and specialized devices particular to a specific industry.

Important   All technologies identified at this stage are documented in a technical specification section, which can be a part of any project document, such as a project plan or a functional specification document. This section is further refined during physical design when the team has identified the technologies that will be used to implement the solution.

How to Identify Candidate Business Objects

Objects are defined as the people or things described in the usage scenarios. Objects form the basis for services, attributes, and relationships.

Figure 5.4 shows the overall process of identifying objects, services, attributes, and relationships in the analysis step of logical design.

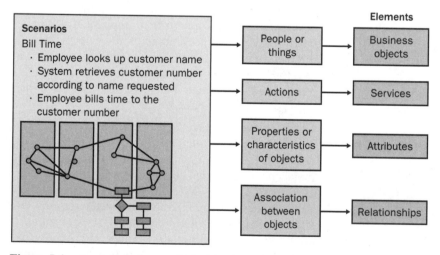

Figure 5.4.   Logical design analysis: identifying objects, services, attributes, and relationships

Identifying objects

You need to identify the business objects, or components, that will provide the functionality for the solution. Look at the usage scenarios you created during the conceptual design process to help you identify these objects. Figure 5.5 illustrates this process. When you have identified an object, you then need to identify the behaviors and attributes of the object in addition to its relationships with other objects.

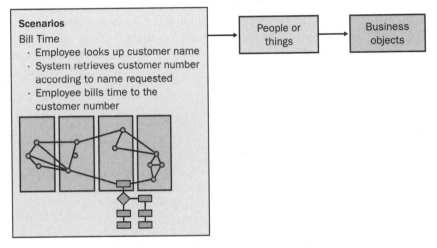

Figure 5.5.   Identifying business objects

Some usage scenarios might not explicitly contain objects, even though objects are necessary to perform the required business activities. The objects might be hidden within sentences, depending on how the usage scenario is written. Look for hidden references to structures, systems, devices, things, and events. To identify missing objects, think about the scenario in terms of required information and behavior that is not associated with an object.

Example of business objects

To clearly understand the concept of business objects, consider the following use cases:

- Employee completes a time sheet by recording the billable hours spent at work.
- Employee creates a contract with the customer.
- Employee reviews prior billings to the customer.
- Employee bills time to the customer number

After studying these use cases, you can identify the following business objects:

- *Employee.* Performs actions within the system.
- *Customer.* The recipient of actions performed by the employee.

- *Time sheet.* The means by which the employee identifies the amount of time spent on a project.
- *Contract.* The agreement between the employee and the customer.
- *Billings.* Invoices that the customer has received for work performed.
- *Customer number.* A means of identifying a specific customer in the system.

How to Identify Services

A *service* is a specific behavior that a business object must perform. It refers to an operation, a function, or a transformation that can be applied to or implemented by an object. You use services to implement business rules, manipulate data, and access information. A service can perform any activity that can be described by a set of rules.

Identifying services

To identify services for an object, examine the usage scenario again. To identify a service, determine what the object is supposed to do, the kind of data the object must maintain, and the actions that the object must perform. If an object maintains information, it also performs the operations on the information. Some examples of such actions that an object might perform include:

- Calculate total amount
- Determine the cost of shipping

Figure 5.6 illustrates identifying actions, and therefore services, from a usage scenario.

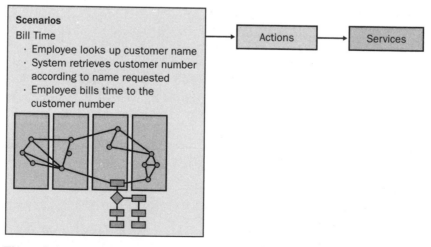

Figure 5.6.   Identifying services

Assign the service that you identify to the associated object. This object is either the recipient of the action or is responsible for performing the action in the usage scenario. If it is difficult to identify the correct object for assigning a service, examine all possibilities by a walkthrough of the scenario. A walkthrough of the scenario involves working step by step through every requirement.

State the capabilities and responsibilities of a service in terms as broad as possible. In addition, you need an unambiguous name to identify the service. If you cannot assign a clear name to the service, it indicates that the purpose of the service is not clearly understood and needs more work in the conceptual design.

Examples of services

Figure 5.7 contains examples of services that can be identified from the sample usage scenario.

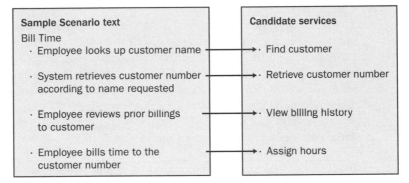

Figure 5.7.   Identifying services from a scenario

Consider the following usage scenarios:

- Employee looks up customer name. This usage scenario corresponds to the service *find customer* for the Employee business object.

- System retrieves customer name. This usage scenario corresponds to the service *retrieve customer number* for the Customer business object.

- Employee records billable hours on the time sheet. This usage scenario corresponds to the service *fill time sheets* for the Employee business object.

- Employee reviews prior billings to customer. This usage scenario corresponds to the service *view billing history* for the Employee business object.

- Employee bills time to the customer name. This usage scenario corresponds to the service *assign hours* for the Employee business object.

How to Identify Attributes

Attributes of an object are the definitions of data values that the object holds. Attributes are also known as *properties*. Each instance of an object maintains its own set of values. For example, for the Employee business object, one of the attributes is *given name*. In a particular instance, the value of the attribute *given name* is *John*. In another instance, the value of *given name* could be *Janet*. The set of values of an object's attributes at any given time is known as the *state of the object*.

Identifying attributes

To identify the attributes for an object, return to the usage scenario. Look for the words or phrases that further identify the object. For example, the length of a bridge, the name of a person, and the brand name and model of a computer indicate attributes.

The actual attributes of an object are often specified in greater detail than the information covered in usage scenarios. To identify the correct attributes, the project team uses its knowledge of the real world and experience in the problem domain. For example, the project team might derive the attribute *name* from a usage scenario. Based on their knowledge, the team members might modify this attribute to *given name* and *family name*. Often this level of detail is done during the physical design process. However, if sufficient information is available to start this process earlier, the team can start during the logical design.

Note   Although many attributes can be listed for an object, the project team should include only the relevant attributes. For example, the attributes *given name* and *family name* can be used for most solutions. However, attributes such as *height* and *weight* might only be relevant for, for example, a health care solution. To avoid the risk of omitting important attributes, document all the attributes at this stage of the design process. These attributes can be further refined at a later stage of analysis.

To identify the attributes of an object, the project team should consider each business object and attempt to answer the following questions:

- How is the object described in general and as part of this solution?
- How is the object described in the context of this solution's responsibilities?
- What information does the object contain?
- What information should the object maintain over time?
- What are the states in which the object can exist?

Each attribute is generally identified with an object. You need to clearly label each attribute to avoid confusion with other attributes. In addition, record the structure or type of the attribute, such as text or number.

Tip   In many cases, attributes are derived. The computation of such attributes should be recorded as a service of the object. After compiling the list of attributes, study all the attributes carefully. If some attributes are totally unrelated to the other attributes of a specific object, you might need to create a new business object.

Examples of attributes

Consider the following use cases in a usage scenario that describes the purchase order process.

- Customer has an account number, name, and address
- Customer must have an approved credit rating for work to be performed
- Depending on history, customer can request the last consultant that was on site

Based on these use cases, Table 5.3 identifies a business object with its attributes and associated values.

Table 5.3.   Example Object with Attributes and Values

Business object	Attributes	Values at one state
Customer	Account Number	10076
	Name	Contoso, Ltd.
	Address	123 East Main
	Credit	Approved
	Last Consultant	Greg Chapman

How to Identify Relationships

Relationships illustrate the way in which objects are linked to each other. Unified Modeling Language (UML) defines four types of relationships: dependency, generalizations, associations, and realizations.

- *Dependency.* A relationship between two objects in which a change to one object (independent) can affect the behavior or service of the other object (dependent). Use dependency when you want to show one object using another. For example, a water heater depends on pipes to carry hot water throughout a building. In UML diagrams, dependency between two logical objects is represented by a directional (that is, with an arrow) dashed line.

- *Association.* A structural relationship that describes a connection among objects. *Aggregation* is a special type of association that represents the relationship between a whole and its parts. For example, "Order contains details" is an example of an aggregation relationship. Typically in an aggregation relationship, the whole manages the lifetime of the parts. This form of relationship is called *composition*. Graphically, association is represented as a solid line. Aggregation is represented by a solid line with a hollow diamond on the end of the line that connects to the whole. Composition is represented in UML diagrams by a solid line with a filled-in diamond on the end of the line that connects to the whole.

- *Generalization.* A relationship between a general thing (called the parent) and the specialized or specific thing (called the child). For example, the Manager class is a specific type of the Employee class. A child inherits the properties of its parents, especially their attributes and operations. Generalization means that the child can substitute the parent object anywhere, but the opposite is not true. In UML diagrams, generalization is represented as a solid line with a hollow arrowhead pointing to the parent.

- *Realization.* A relationship between classes, in which one abstract class specifies a contract that another class needs to carry out. When you model, you find a lot of abstractions that represent things in the real world and things in your solution, such as a Customer class in a Web-based ordering system. Each of these abstractions can have multiple instances. In general, the modeling elements that can have instances are called *classes*. A class has structural and behavioral features. All instances of a class share the same behavior but can have different values for their attributes.

  Realization relationships exist between interfaces and the classes and components that realize these interfaces, and between use cases and collaborations. Graphically, generalization is represented as a cross between generalization and dependency relationship, with dashed lines and hollow arrowhead pointing to the parent.

Figure 5.8 illustrates the graphical representations of the four types of relationships.

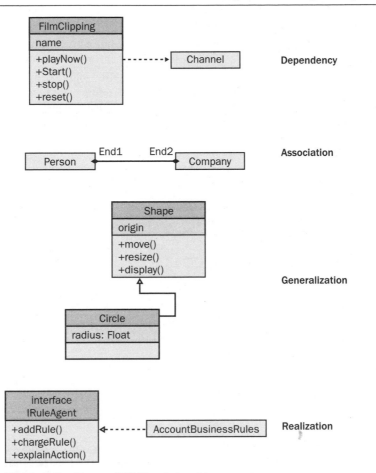

Figure 5.8.   Types of UML relationships

Figure 5.9 illustrates the two types of associations—the aggregation and composition relationships.

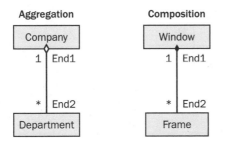

Figure 5.9.   Aggregation and composition relationships

Identifying relationships from use cases

To identify relationships from use cases, look at the usage scenario for information that describes physical location, directed action, communication, or ownership, or that indicates that a condition has been met. The project team reviews the scenario and determines which behaviors are associated with an object, and identifies relationships between two or more objects. Figure 5.10 illustrates how associations between objects indicate relationships.

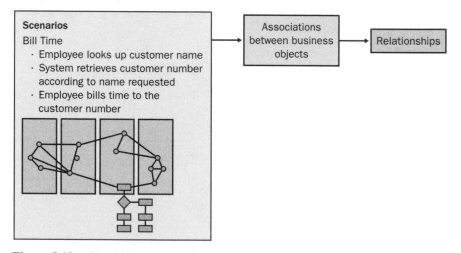

Figure 5.10.   Identifying relationships between objects

Examples of relationships

Relationships represent how the actions of an object or a system affect another object or system, especially if a known state exists between the two. Figure 5.11 illustrates that relationships must exist between objects for a company to produce meaningful work and data.

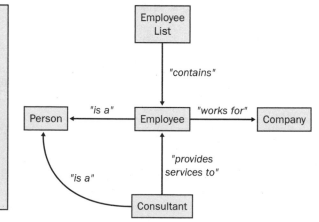

Figure 5.11.   Examples of relationships

Some relationships between the objects are:

- The consultant and the customer are related because they are both people.
- The consultant and the customer are related because they interact with each other.
- The consultant performs services for the company, and the company requires the services of the consultant.
- A company has one or more divisions.

Additional relationships might exist in the system. For example, the consultants bring revenue to the company, and the accountants manage the company's money.

Lesson 3: Documenting Logical Design Output

During logical design, the team creates several outputs that will help in developing the solution design. The outputs include the logical object model, the logical data model, and a high-level user interface (UI) design. There are several tools for documenting and diagramming these outputs. This lesson discusses how to create and document the outputs of logical design.

For more information about diagramming the logical design, see Chapter 2, "Gathering and Analyzing Information."

After this lesson, you will be able to
- Use CRC cards to depict interactions between objects.
- Use sequence diagrams to depict interaction between objects.
- Create a logical object model to describe relationships between objects.
- Create a high-level UI design.
- Create a high-level database design.

Estimated lesson time: 20 minutes

How to Model Relationships

You can use several methods to document logical design outputs. Two such techniques are Class-Responsibility-Collaboration (CRC) cards and sequence diagrams.

Note   You can use CRC cards and sequence diagrams in combination to validate the objects and their relationships that you have identified during analysis.

Class-Responsibility-Collaboration cards

A CRC card helps teams focus on high-level responsibilities of a class instead of detailed methods and attributes. Project teams use the CRC card to brainstorm the responsibilities of a class; identify the responsibilities of a class to identify its services. The CRC card indicates all the classes with which a class must interact and identifies the relationships between classes. To validate CRC cards, the team recreates the usage scenarios by using the CRC cards.

Example of a CRC card

Order	
Roles: To maintain order information	
Responsibilities	**Collaboration**
Determine whether items are in stock	Get current stock information from Order Line
Determine price	
Check for valid payment	Get address from Customer
Dispatch to delivery address	
Issues	
Where do we store the price information?	

Sequence diagrams

A *sequence diagram* shows the actors and objects that participate in an interaction along with a chronological list of the events they generate. A vertical line in a sequence diagram represents an object's lifetime. An arrow between the lifetimes of two objects represents a message, which is a form of communication between two objects that conveys that an activity will take place. The receipt of a message instance is normally considered an instance of an event. The order in which these messages occur is shown top to bottom on the page.

In a solution design, the overall flow of control and sequence of behavior can be difficult to understand. Sequence diagrams help you see the sequence clearly.

Figure 5.12 is a sequence diagram for the logical design of the Adventure Works Cycles scenario.

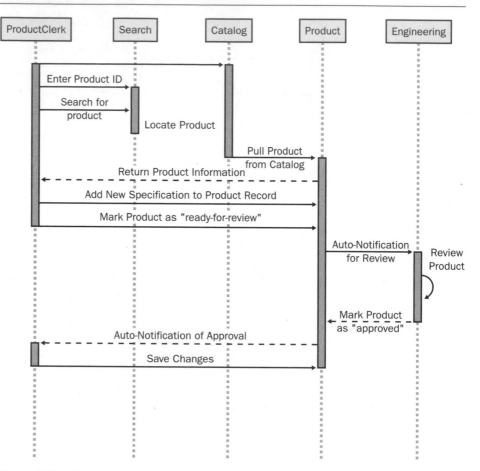

Figure 5.12.   Sequence diagram

How to Create the Logical Object Model

The primary output of the logical design process in solution design is the logical object model. The logical object model is created from the objects, services, attributes, and relationships that were created earlier in the logical design process.

Considerations for the logical object model

When creating the logical object model, it is important that you consider all the business and user requirements that are applicable to your scenario, such as security, globalization, localization, auditing and logging, error handling, integration with existing systems, and state management. It is also important to consider all the business constraints when creating a logical object model for a solution design.

Example of logical object model

Figure 5.13 is an example of the logical object model for the Adventure Works Cycles scenario. The object model takes into account the security and logging requirements identified during the conceptual design process.

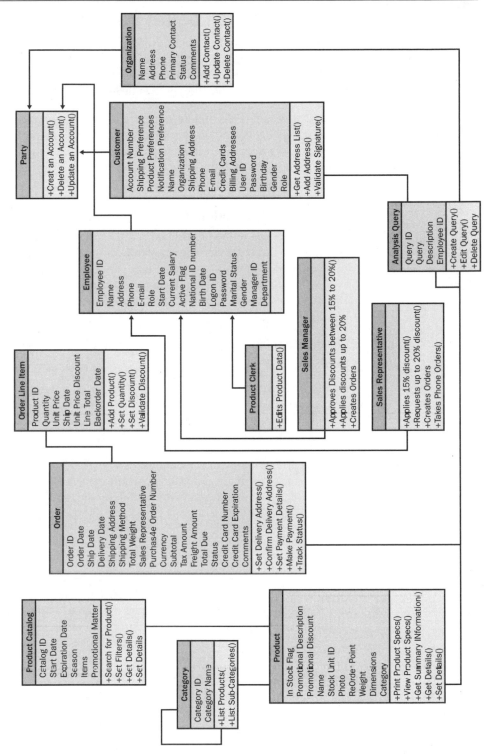

Figure 5.13.   Logical object model

How to Create a Logical Data Model

You can use either a logical object model or a logical data model to represent a logical design. However, a project team can create both models to represent a logical design in different ways. Both models might be necessary if one model represents a portion of the design more clearly than the other.

The logical design is the middle stage of the natural progression from conceptual design to physical design. When creating the logical data model, you convert the conceptual data needs identified during conceptual design into actual entities and relationships that will define how the data interacts. This information is then used to help model the physical design.

Identify entities and attributes

When you proceed to the logical stage of data design, one of your first tasks is to formulate entities from data requirements and other related information. An *entity* can be defined as any person, place, item, or concept that defines data or about which data will be collected and stored. An attribute is a characteristic that further defines and describes the properties of an instance of an entity. An entity can have multiple attributes.

Consider the following example, in which italicized words indicate possible candidates for entities:

"*Consultants* enter their *hours* onto a *time sheet* on a weekly basis. The time sheet is then forwarded to the *administrative assistant*, who types the *hours* into the invoicing program. The *administrative assistant* then sends *invoices* to the *customers* based on the *time* reported."

After identifying the entities, you must determine which of their attributes you want to gather. Attributes describe the solution's entities. For example, the attributes of a car might be its color, brand, model, and year of production.

When the physical design is implemented, the attributes might become the columns in the database tables.

Define tables

The objects that you identify in the analysis step of logical design are strong candidates for tables and might be transformed into tables in the database during physical design. Tables are meant for those objects about which you need to store information. For example, in a simple order processing system, objects such as customers, products, and catalog might be transformed into tables. In a more complicated system, objects might map to more than one table.

Define columns

The attributes of an object form the columns of the table associated with the object. For example, *given name*, *family name*, and *job title* can be the attributes (and therefore column names) for the Employee table. Each row in the table stores values for various fields for a specific instance of the object.

Define relationships

After identifying tables and their columns, you need to identify any association between tables. Such associations represent the relationship between objects. For example, a relationship exists between the objects Employee and Department— every Department has Employees and every Employee belongs to a Department. You can use cardinality and multiplicity to further define relationships.

Cardinality is an identifying property of a relationship. Cardinality allows you to specify the number of instances of an entity that are allowed on each side of a relationship. For example, one consultant can be assigned more than one project at a time. *Multiplicity* specifies the range of cardinalities an entity can assume.

You will learn more about defining object relationships in Chapter 8, "Designing the Data Layer."

Note   During logical design, if you have sufficient information to refine columns and define primary and foreign keys, you can create a logical data model that includes columns, primary keys, and foreign keys. However, this level of detail is typically recorded during the physical design process.

Figure 5.14 shows the logical database design that a team typically achieves during the logical design phase.

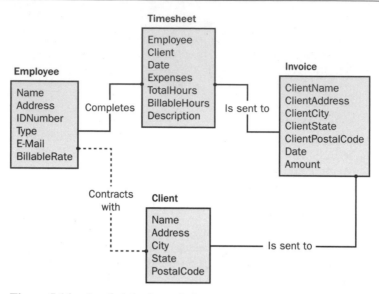

Figure 5.14.   Logical database design

How to Create a High-Level User Interface Design

Using the objects, services, attributes, and relationships identified during the analysis step of logical design, the team might decide to create a high-level user interface and database design. Creating a high-level user interface and database design enables the project team to describe the flow of processing that the end user will experience when the solution is ready for customers.

The list of objects and services gives the team an idea about the kind of functionality expected by the users. The team can use this information to design user interface elements such as buttons, text fields, and menu items.

Note   For most projects, a major portion of the user interface design is done during the physical design process. However, if the team members believe that they have sufficient information, they can create a high-level user interface design during the logical design process.

Consider the following usage scenario:

```
The Customer selects a Catalog to browse. The Categories and Products in
the
root of the selected catalog are displayed. The Customer can then select
a
Product to view its details or select a Category to view the Products and
subcategories in the selected category.
```

On the basis of this scenario, the team can create the following high-level design for the user interface:

■ Products Information page that displays information about products, such as product description, pricing, and availability
■ Customer Information page that displays information about the customer, such as registration and personal details

The scenario can be expanded to provide the customer with shopping features. Therefore, the user interface can also include the following:

■ Order Information, Check Out, and Order Status pages
■ A history of the previous transactions completed by the customer

Note   You will learn more about user interface design in Chapter 7, "Designing the Presentation Layer."

Lesson 4: Optimizing Logical Design

During the analysis step of logical design, the team analyzes the usage scenarios and defines the solution in terms of objects, services, attributes, and relationships between objects. After the analysis step, the team moves to the optimization step. In this step, the real challenge for the team is to refine and optimize the design by measuring it against the usage scenarios and requirements.

In this lesson, you will learn about refining the list of objects. You will also learn how to verify the business model and establish control in the logical design.

After this lesson, you will be able to

- Refine the list of objects identified during analysis.
- Verify the existing business model.
- Establish control in a logical design model.

Estimated lesson time: 15 minutes

How to Refine Objects

During the analysis step of logical design, the project team identifies objects. All objects might not be completely relevant to the solution. When the team refines objects, they determine whether the objects are relevant.

When refining objects, consider the following:

- If two objects express the same information or control the same activity, you might be able to combine them and give the combined object a more descriptive name.
- An object should be specific. Some candidate objects might be created by evaluating additional information from the scenarios. These objects are not necessarily incorrect, but they need to be made more tangible or real. In addition, you might want to examine these objects to determine whether they are within the scope of the project.
- If an attribute needs to exist independently in the solution, assign it as an object.
- You might need a new object to control or coordinate a set of services.
- You can also use services to refine the list of objects. For every service, identify the object on which the service acts.

How to Verify an Existing Logical Object Model

You can verify an existing logical object model by validating it against the set of requirements, by using individual object verification, and by the usage scenario walkthrough.

Validate against requirements

The most important task in optimizing and finalizing the logical design is to validate the logical object model against the existing set of requirements. Ensure that the logical object model documents each requirement that has been identified. If there are requirements that have not been documented, you need to fix the logical object model so that it addresses the missing requirements. After the logical object model captures all the requirements; you are ready to proceed to physical design.

Important   If the logical data model misses even a single requirement, it is considered incomplete.

Verify individual objects

In individual object verification, you identify an object's inputs and outputs and the capability or functionality that the object must provide. For any given input, you should be able to accurately predict the output and behavior and verify the independent parts of the object.

Individual object verification simplifies integration of systems because you can test the individual pieces of the system before integrating them into a single large product. If the constituent pieces have been verified and are correct, the project team can safely assemble the system.

Walk through the scenario

Although the individual object verification technique allows you to verify the independent aspects of a business object, the project team also needs to study how a set of objects solves the complex problems documented in the scenarios. A collection of objects that are interdependent in solving problems can be complex. You can verify the interdependence of objects by conducting a full walkthrough of the scenario, ensuring that all needs of the scenario are met by some combination of objects. Alternatively, you can implement role playing in the scenario. When using role playing, you assign individuals to represent objects and then walk through the scenarios. Role playing also exposes ambiguities that occur when various individuals have different interpretations of what a specific service must do.

By evaluating a scenario one step at a time, you can determine which services are required, and also the sequence in which the services are required in order to move the project team to a successful completion of the logical design. From the starting point of a usage scenario, determine all the objects from which the scenario needs services.

Any message sent between objects indicates a communication between those objects. To determine the type of communication, analyze the requests sent by each object and try to answer the following questions:

- Does the object have enough information to construct the request?
- Does the information content of the request come from either the object's internal data or from the request that triggered the operation?
- Does the object rely on the internal data of the supplier?
- Is information that is being passed from the consumer to the supplier linking the object to other parts of the system in an unintended way?

In addition, the project team should examine the input parameters of each request. You need to examine the input parameters and determine whether they provide context-sensitive information that the receiving object does not need. In addition, you need to identify any reliance on information regarding external context that can reduce the reusability of the object in other contexts. You can resolve these issues by shifting responsibilities between objects or by creating new objects.

For a walkthrough of a scenario, consider the following:

- Determine any dependencies of the operation on the existence or consistency of other business objects.
- Determine any consistency, sequencing, or concurrency issues. Is a sequential order of operation required in all or part of the transaction?
- Identify any critical timing. Is it critical to respond immediately, or can an activity be suspended?
- Consider any organizational issues, such as a transaction occurring in multiple functional areas.
- Look for business rules that are in more than one business object.
- Identify audit and control requirements. Identify who is accountable. Verify situations in which accountability is shared by two or more people.
- Estimate the frequency of an activity. How often does the activity occur? Is it uniform or periodic?
- Determine locations and cross-location dependencies.
- Determine whether the service that controls the transaction is dependent on services currently contained in other business objects.

How to Establish Control in Logical Design

Examining the object interactions for various scenarios illustrates that activities need to be performed in a specific sequence. One possible way to examine object interaction is by using state diagrams. Identifying the flow of control enables you to sequence object interactions. Control in logical design:

- Ensures the transactional integrity of a scenario
- Coordinates services across multiple objects
- Identifies cross-object interdependencies

For any activity to complete, specific ordering might be required. Multiple events might occur concurrently. Wait states that must be completed before continuing processing might exist for some services. Such issues determine the issues that the project team must consider during logical design to ensure that error-free actions are carried out at the right time and in the right order, relative to other activities in the system.

Control can be synchronous or asynchronous. *Synchronous control* refers to the situation in which object services are invoked and the calling object waits for control to be returned. In a synchronous scenario, control is transferred from the calling object to the called object, and the operation is executed immediately. The calling object is suspended until the called object completes its task. After the operation is completed, control is returned to the calling object.

In *asynchronous control*, a client can submit a request and then continue performing other tasks. The service will process the request and notify the client when processing completes. In this way, the client is not blocked from performing other, unrelated activities while the service is working on the client's request. The control of the overall process is not transferred from the calling object to the called object. This means that the called object must take responsibility for the integrity of its data resources that might be accessed simultaneously by multiple objects, and it must also maintain common resource coordination throughout the processing sequence.

Tip   In a distributed system, consider whether to create additional objects that handle the various aspects of control, sequencing, and dependency. You need to isolate dependencies and abstract those services that are likely to change frequently with changes in the business.

Control models

Figure 5.15 illustrates the two general models that are available for the control of objects.

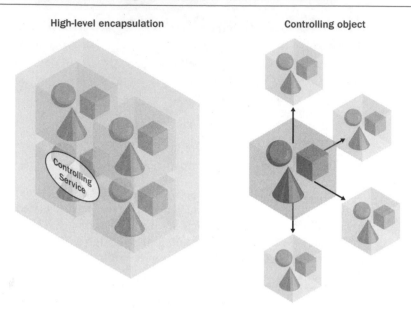

Figure 5.15.   Control models

The first model uses a high-level encapsulation of the objects to be controlled. The outer object has control and ownership of all of the logical resources required for the activity provided by the inner objects. Because the outer object contains everything that it needs to proceed with an activity, the design is simplified. This control and potential simplification results in a rigid structure for the activity.

For example, the inner objects can be used only by the other objects contained at the same level or by means of some service of the outer object. This can be thought of as a single-user model because only the single outer object can use the inner objects. The outer object is responsible for routing all incoming messages to the correct inner object.

The second model is more flexible, but it can be more difficult to design. In this model, you implement a controlling object at the same level as the resources that it needs to control. This model can be thought of as a multiple user model because the controlling object does not exclusively own the objects that it might be using. These objects can be used simultaneously by other parts of the system. The controlling object is not aware of any of these other potential interactions with the controlled objects. Maintaining the integrity of resources is more difficult in this model.

User interface in control

The two models of control—high-level encapsulation and controlling object—do not take into account the control that users have when they trigger events in objects. In interactive systems, the user interface places control with the users. In reality, however, most systems combine user control with control that is embedded in a set of controlling objects in the system.

Ultimately, joint control and dependency direct the sequence of events. Although you use objects to control transactions, users trigger the sequences of events.

Activity: Identifying Objects for the Logical Design

In this activity, you use what you learned in the lessons to identify objects for inclusion in the logical design.

Exercise 1: Identifying Objects from Use Cases

Following is a list of possible use cases for the company Web site project that Adventure Works Cycles is funding. Examine each use case and identify any objects that should be included in the logical design. You can find the answers to the questions in the appendix.

1. The shopping cart checks inventory to determine the availability of a particular product.

2. A new user creates an account in order to place orders.

3. A user adds a product to the shopping cart.

4. A user retrieves an order to check its status.

Exercise 2: Creating a Services Matrix

Open the files C05Ex2, Usage Scenario 06.1 View Catalog, Usage Scenario 06.1.1 Add Items in Catalog, and Usage Scenario 06.3.1 Edit Items in Catalog from the \SolutionDocuments\Chapter05 folder on the CD. Using the usage scenario documents, complete the service matrix in C05Ex2 for the Catalog Items business object. Be sure to identify the services, actors, responsibilities, and collaborations for each service, and to map each entry to one of the usage scenarios. To help you get started, an example of a service matrix has been provided in C05Ex2. One possible answer to this exercise can be found in C05Ex2_Answer in the \SolutionDocuments\Chapter05 folder on the CD.

Exercise 3: Creating a Sequence Diagram

Open the C05Ex3 Microsoft Visio® file from the \SolutionDocuments\Chapter05 folder on the CD, and click the Sequence Diagram tab. The page is blank. Assume that a customer has logged on to the online retail site for Adventure Works Cycles. Use the following use case to create a sequence diagram that shows the interaction between the objects. One possible answer to this exercise can be found in C05Ex3_Answer in the \SolutionDocuments\Chapter05 folder on the CD.

The customer opens a catalog, searches for items in the catalog, and adds an item to a new order.

Summary

- Logical design is defined as the process of describing the solution in terms of the organization, structure, syntax, and interaction of its parts from the perspective of the project team.
- The logical design phase consists of two overlapping steps:
    - Logical design analysis, during which the project team identifies business objects, services, attributes, and relationships between objects
    - Logical design optimization, during which the team verifies business objects and identifies implied business objects and scenarios
- The outputs of the logical design process are:
    - The logical object model, which is a set of objects with corresponding services, attributes, and relationships
    - A high-level user interface design
    - The logical data model
- Objects are the people or things described in the usage scenarios.
- A service is the behavior that a business object performs.
- Attributes are the definitions of data values that an object holds.
- Relationships illustrate the links between objects.
- A CRC card helps you focus on high-level responsibilities of a class instead of detailed methods and attributes. CRC cards also help identify relationships between different objects in the logical design.
- A sequence diagram shows the actors and objects that participate in an interaction and a chronologically arranged list of the events they generate.
- The list of objects and services helps the team to create a high-level user interface design of the solution.
- To create a database design, the team performs the following tasks:
    - Identify entities, attributes, and relationships
    - Define tables
    - Define columns
    - Define relationships
- To verify the design, validate the logical object model by comparing it to the existing requirements.
- To verify the design by using individual object verification, you identify an object's inputs and outputs and the capability or functionality that the object must provide.

- To verify the design by walkthrough of the usage scenario, you evaluate a scenario one step at a time and determine which services are required and the sequence in which they are required.
- Control enables you to sequence object interactions.
- Synchronous control refers to the situation in which object services are invoked and the calling object waits for control to be returned.
- Asynchronous control refers to the situation in which object services are invoked and the calling object continues to perform unrelated tasks until the service notifies the calling object of the results of the operation.
- In the high-level encapsulation method of control, the outer object has control and ownership of all of the logical resources required for the activity provided by the inner objects.
- In the controlling object method of control, a controlling object is defined at the same level as the resources that it needs to control.

Review

The following questions are intended to reinforce key information presented in this chapter. If you are unable to answer a question, review the lesson materials and try the question again. You can find answers to the questions in the appendix.

1. What are the two steps of logical design?

2. What are the outputs of the logical design?

3. Should you focus on technological issues during logical design?

4. What are the benefits of logical design?

5. How do you identify services in a usage scenario?

6. How do you identify attributes in a usage scenario?

7. What is a sequence diagram?

8. How do you design the tables and columns in a data store for a solution?

9. What is the purpose of refining the list of objects?

10. How do you verify the design by using individual object verification?

11. What is the purpose of control in logical design?

12. You are creating the logical design of a solution for a customer, and you discover a scenario that was not discovered in your previous analysis. What should you do with this new information?

13. What is the responsibility of the testing role during logical design?

C H A P T E R 6

Creating the Physical Design

About This Chapter

Along with conceptual and logical design, the project team creates a physical design of the solution during the planning phase. In this introduction to physical design, you will learn about the purpose of physical design, and the tasks and deliverables involved in completing the physical design. You will also learn about the four steps in creating a physical design: research, analysis, rationalization, and implementation.

More Info   As with the conceptual and logical designs, the outputs of the physical design step are documented in the functional specification, which is one of the outputs of the planning phase. You can learn more about the functional specification in Chapter 4, "Creating the Conceptual Design," and Chapter 10, "Completing the Planning Phase."

You will learn about creating the physical design for the presentation layer in Chapter 7, "Designing the Presentation Layer," and for the data layer in Chapter 8, "Designing the Data Layer."

Before You Begin

To complete the lessons in this chapter, you must

- Understand the Microsoft® Solutions Framework (MSF) Process Model.
- Be familiar with the outputs of the envisioning phase and the three steps of conceptual design: research, analysis, and optimization.
- Be familiar with the logical design phase in MSF.

Lesson 1: An Overview of Physical Design

Physical design is the last step in the planning phase of the MSF Process Model. The project team proceeds to physical design after all members agree that they have enough information from the logical design to begin physical design. During physical design, the team applies technology considerations and constraints to the conceptual and logical designs. Because the physical design evolves from the conceptual and logical designs, its success depends on the accuracy of the previous two designs. The reliance of physical design on the conceptual and logical designs ensures that the team will be able to complete a physical design that meets the business and user requirements.

Note   To review the three design processes in the planning phase, refer to Table 5.1 in Chapter 5, "Creating the Logical Design."

In this lesson, you will learn about the purpose and goals of physical design. You will learn about the various steps that the team performs during physical design. You will also learn about the responsibilities of the various roles in physical design. In addition, this lesson covers the deliverables of physical design.

After this lesson, you will be able to

- Describe physical design.
- Describe the goals of physical design.
- List the steps in physical design.
- Describe the responsibilities of various team roles during physical design.
- List the deliverables of physical design.
- Describe the purpose and deliverables of the research step.

Estimated lesson time: 15 minutes

What Is Physical Design?

Physical design is the third design activity in the planning phase of the MSF Process Model. Physical design is the process of describing components, services, and technologies of the solution from the perspective of development requirements. Physical design defines the parts of the solution that will be developed, how they will be developed, and how they will interact with each other. Figure 6.1 illustrates where the physical design fits within the MSF Process Model.

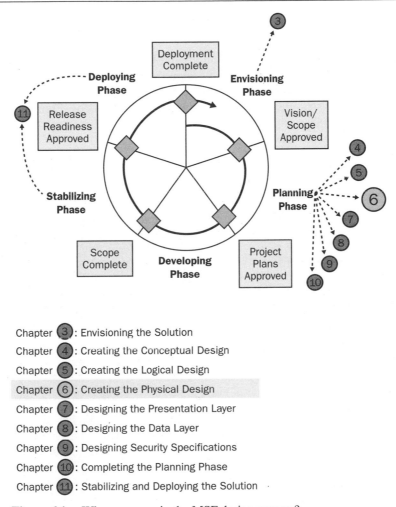

Figure 6.1.   Where are you in the MSF design process?

While working on the physical design, the team creates designs based on prior designs and refines the architecture of the solution that has been created up to this time. These designs apply real-world technology constraints to the logical model, including development tools and the deployment environment of the solution. In addition, the team tries to develop a solution that addresses design considerations such as security, availability, scalability, manageability, and performance. The team tries to achieve these goals in a manner that is appropriate to the project and its requirements.

The inputs to the physical design are all of the artifacts that have been created up to this time. This includes the logical object model, a high-level user interface design, and a logical data model generated during logical design. Artifacts such as the project plan might get minor updates and are referred to in setting the deadlines for the milestones of physical design.

During the physical design, the project team reduces the gap between the logical design of the solution and the implementation by defining the solution in terms of implementation details. The purposes of the conceptual design and logical design processes are to understand the business and its requirements and to design a solution that meets those requirements. The physical design process primarily addresses how to implement this design.

At the end of the physical design, the team delivers specifications for a set of components, Microsoft .NET assemblies, binaries, and link libraries; details of the user interface for the solution; the database schema; database objects such as triggers, indexes, and stored procedures; and details of any reports that will be used by the solution.

Figure 6.2 shows the purpose of the physical design process.

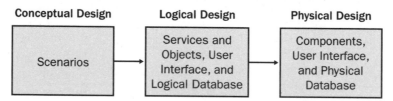

Figure 6.2.   What is physical design?

Consider the analogy of designing and building a house. In logical design, you determine requirements such as overall electrical capacity, levels of light, and plumbing fixtures required by the house. In physical design, you select the appliances that you will use, the electrical requirements for each device and the corresponding wiring, and circuit specifications.

To proceed from logical design to physical design, the team uses the layered services-based architecture.

Note   You can learn more about application architectures in Chapter 4, "Creating the Conceptual Design."

Scope of the physical design

Table 6.1 explains the scope of physical design.

Table 6.1.   Scope of the Physical Design

Physical design is not	But enables you to
Coding	• Create detailed component specifications for development • Determine where components should be located
Technology deployment	Identify technologies that can be used for developing the solution

During physical design, the project team develops the component specifications and deployment topology with which the development team will work to create the solution. The development team takes the target topology into consideration while building the solution.

Remember that in physical design you are still designing the solution and not developing a version of the solution that can be released and deployed.

Difference between logical and physical designs

Whereas during logical design the team views the problem from the perspective of the project team, during physical design the team views the problem from the perspective of the development team. During the logical design, the team documents the activities, constraints, and assumptions of the business. During the physical design, the team defines a solution addressing the constraints of the selected development technologies and deployment environment. In this sense, physical design views the design from a more technical viewpoint.

Basically, physical design is a refinement of the logical design that leads to the implementation of the design to create the solution.

What Are the Goals of Physical Design?

The project team creates the physical design with the following goals:

- *Identifying appropriate technologies for development.* During physical design, the project team evaluates technologies and determines the technologies that can be best used to develop the solution.

- *Transforming the logical design into physical design models.* During physical design, the team uses the outputs of logical design to produce a flexible specification based on components. This specification describes the application from the development team's perspective. The team describes the solution in just enough detail to allow the development team to begin creating the solution according to the requirements.

- *Providing a baseline for the development process.* In addition to creating models and strategies, the team defines the development roles, responsibilities, and processes.
- *Defining when the project plan approved milestone has been achieved.* The team reaches this milestone when the baseline physical design is complete. At the project plan approved milestone, the team re-assesses risk, updates priorities, and finishes estimates for resources and schedule.

What Are the Responsibilities of Team Roles During Physical Design?

During physical design, each team role has a different set of responsibilities. Table 6.2 summarizes the tasks for each team role during physical design.

Table 6.2.   Roles and Responsibilities in Physical Design

Role	Primary task	Secondary task
Product management	Managing customer expectations and creating the communications plan	Preparing for solution deployment
Program management	Managing the physical design process and creating the functional specification	Defining project plan, including resources, schedules, and risk assessments
Development	Creating the physical design deliverables: design models, development plans and schedules, and development estimates	Evaluating technologies, building prototypes if necessary, and preparing for the development environment
Testing	Evaluating and validating the functionality and consistency of the physical design against the usage scenarios	Defining detailed testing plans and preparing the testing and quality assurance (QA) environment
User experience	Evaluating physical design against user requirements and designing help solutions	Defining user education plan
Release management	Evaluating the infrastructure implications of the physical design	Defining infrastructure and operations requirements and deployment solutions

What Are the Deliverables of Physical Design?

At the end of the physical design phase, the project team has enough completed design documentation for the development team to begin creating the solution.

Specific documentation can vary from solution to solution. Some of the deliverables at the end of physical design include:

- *Class diagrams* of the solution.
- *Component models, sequence diagrams, or activity diagrams* of the solution.
- *Database schema* of the solution.
- *Baseline deployment model* that provides:
  - The network topology, which indicates hardware locations and interconnections.
  - The data and component topology, which indicates the locations of solution components, services, and data storage in relation to the network topology.
- *Component specifications* that include the internal structure of components and component interfaces.
- *Packaging and distribution strategy* that identifies the services to be packaged together in a component and specifies how the components will be distributed across the network topology. It might also include a preliminary deployment plan.
- *Programming model* that identifies implementation choices; choices in object state and connection modes; and guidelines for threading, error handling, security choices, and code documentation.

What Are the Steps in Physical Design?

Physical design is the last stage of the planning phase. The planning phase ends when the team reaches the project plan approved milestone. The project team completes the physical design before reaching this milestone.

Figure 6.3 shows the physical design in relationship to the conceptual and logical designs in the planning phase.

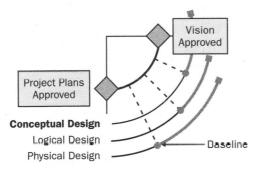

Figure 6.3.   When does physical design take place?

Figure 6.4 shows the four steps of physical design and their associated baselines.

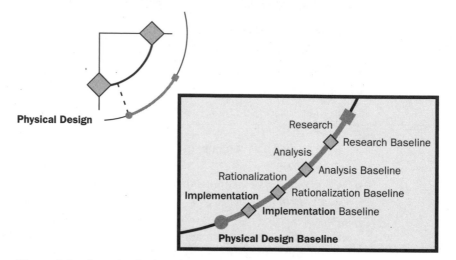

Physical Design

Research
Research Baseline
Analysis
Analysis Baseline
Rationalization
Rationalization Baseline
Implementation
Rationalization Baseline
Implementation Baseline
Physical Design Baseline

Figure 6.4.   Steps in physical design

The four steps in physical design are:

- *Research*, during which the team performs the following tasks:
  - Determining physical constraints and requirements
  - Identifying any infrastructure changes or concerns
- *Analysis*, during which the team performs the following tasks:
  - Developing a preliminary deployment model
  - Selecting technologies that will be used to develop the solution
- *Rationalization*, during which the team performs the following tasks:
  - Determining a packaging and deployment strategy
  - Packaging components and services
  - Distributing components across the network topology
- *Implementation*, during which the team performs the following tasks:
  - Determining a programming model
  - Specifying component interfaces, attributes, and services

Note   The implementation baseline leads into the baseline of the physical design.

What Is the Research Step in Physical Design?

During the physical design phase, the team focuses on creating technical solutions based on the logical design. To derive these technical solutions, the team must consider constraints such as the enterprise architecture, the business process, and the infrastructure. In addition, the team needs to consider the architectural and performance requirements of the solution, such as security, availability, scalability, and manageability. For example, perhaps the solution must be able to handle a specified number of transactions per second. During the research step of physical design, the team identifies these constraints and requirements.

Deliverables of the research step

The deliverables of the research step of physical design describe the current infrastructure of the business and provide the foundation for the analysis, rationalization, and specification steps of physical design. The deliverables of the research baseline include:

- Current network topology
- Current data topology
- Current component topology
- Physical application requirements
- Updated risk assessment and mitigation plans

Identifying physical requirements and constraints

Throughout the design process, you gather and analyze information about the requirements and constraints of the business. During physical design, you focus on the physical requirements and constraints that affect the development of the solution.

You gather physical requirements from sources such as the current business environment and the enterprise architecture. Some typical physical requirements of a solution are:

- Performance
- Cost and benefit
- Ease of use
- Deployability
- Supportability
- Reliability
- Reusability

Some typical physical constraints of a solution are:

- Budget
- Schedule
- Network topology
- Data topology
- Component topology
- Technology guidelines
- Security

Resolving conflicts between requirements and constraints

Often the requirements and constraints conflict with each other. By identifying these conflicts early in the design and addressing them, you can reduce potential problems early. If a problem occurs, you have a plan for mitigating it. For example, an application might require 100 megabits per second (Mbps) of bandwidth on the network, whereas the existing network infrastructure can support only 10 Mbps.

To resolve the conflict, you typically perform the following tasks:

- Identify the requirements that are absolutely necessary for the project. Identify conflicts among requirements and also analyze the impact of any constraints. Make as many tradeoff choices as possible before development begins.
- Identify the areas in the infrastructure where the requirements might conflict with the constraints.
- Analyze the gaps between the requirements and constraints and determine whether you need to make some kind of choice to resolve the conflict. For example, you might choose to upgrade the network to support 100-Mbps speeds. You must make these choices early in the design phase to avoid creating a solution that cannot be implemented.
- Brainstorm solutions with all groups associated with the project—business, users, project team, and development team.

You can address the gaps between requirements and constraints in the following ways:

- *Accept the gap without doing anything.* This implies that the gap is acceptable for the initial release of the solution. Clearly describe the consequences of accepting the gap. In addition, all stakeholders must reach a consensus that this is the appropriate choice.
- *Identify a way to work around the gap.* Working around the gap might not be the optimal solution in the long term. However, it may be necessary because of constraints such as limited project resources.
- *Defer addressing the requirement until later stages of the project.* The project team can decide to address a requirement in later stages of the project. The team can modify constraints by providing a business case for the change and identifying the impact of the change.

Lesson 2: Physical Design Analysis

During the analysis step of physical design, the team creates and refines the physical design models by using the logical design documentation. In addition, as in each phase, the team refines artifacts that are related both to the design and specifications (UML models, requirements, and use cases) in addition to those related to the project (risk documents, project plans and schedules, and the actors catalog). Physical design involves selecting candidate technologies for the implementation, based on the application requirements. After selecting the probable technologies, the team creates a preliminary deployment model.

In this lesson, you will learn how to refine Unified Modeling Language (UML) models. You will also learn how to select candidate technologies and create a preliminary deployment model.

After this lesson, you will be able to

- Refine logical design UML models.
- Create a preliminary deployment model.

Estimated lesson time: 10 minutes

How to Refine UML Models

At the end of the logical design, the team has UML models for objects, services, attributes, and relationships in the solution. Typically, the team uses the artifacts that best capture their intent and decisions to manage the complex parts of the project. This includes the following set of deliverables:

- Objects and services inventory
- Class diagrams
- Sequence diagrams
- Activity diagrams
- Component diagrams

During physical design, the team refines these models.

Objects and services inventory

In the analysis step of the physical design, examine the services inventory for the following tasks:

- Categorizing services based on the MSF services-based application model:
  - User services
  - Business services
  - Data services
  - System services
- Identifying hidden services

  The team tries to identify services that were not apparent during the logical design, such as system services or specific technical services for transforming data. Remember that each hidden service must be synchronized with development goals by validating it against requirements.

Class diagrams

Class diagrams are used in logical design to represent the static structure of the application object model. During physical design, the team performs the following tasks to refine UML class diagrams:

- Transforming logical objects into class definitions, including their interfaces.
- Identifying objects that were not apparent during logical design, such as services-based objects (also known as common services).
- Consolidating logical objects if necessary.
- Categorizing objects into a services-based model:
  - The *logical boundary objects* are potential user services.
  - The *logical control objects* are potential business services.
  - The *logical entity objects* are potential data services.

  There might be exceptions for these recommendations. Therefore, the team must carefully examine all relevant factors before making decisions.
- Refining the methods by focusing on parameters, considering the use of overloads, combining or dividing methods, and identifying how to handle passing values.
- Refining the attributes. Minimize the public attributes as much as possible for applications based on stateless server architecture. During physical design, the team focuses on internal protected attributes, which will be used by derived objects.

Figure 6.5 shows the class diagram for the Order components.

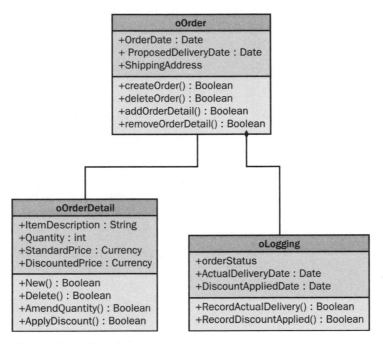

Figure 6.5.   Class diagram

Sequence diagrams

Sequence diagrams represent the interaction between objects and the dynamic aspect of the object model. They are usually used to clarify complex class relationships that might not be easily understood by reviewing the static methods and attributes of a group of classes. In the physical design, the team performs the following tasks:

- Updating classes based on the refined physical design classes
- Refining the sequence diagram to include interactions between the classes or services based on physical constraints or technology requirements
- Identifying additional messages (methods) that are triggered by the new physical classes

Figure 6.6 shows the sequence diagram for the Product and Catalog objects.

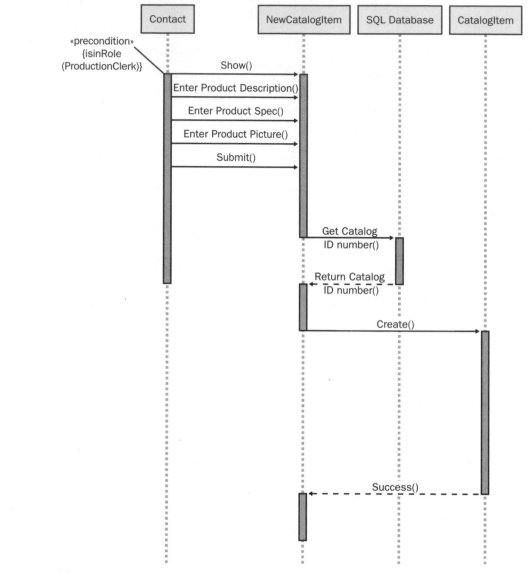

Figure 6.6.   Sequence diagram

Activity diagrams

Activity diagrams are used to represent the state transition and flow of an application. You can use activity diagrams instead of sequence diagrams and vice versa. In the physical design, the project refines activity diagrams to:

- Include physical platform and technology requirements.
- Identify potential workflow processes.

Component diagrams

Component diagrams are used to represent the dependencies between components or component packages. As with sequence and activity diagrams, they are typically used in more complex situations. In the physical design, the project team might create component diagrams to:

- Clarify dependencies between components.
- Further define packaging decisions.

Figure 6.7 illustrates the component diagram for the Order process.

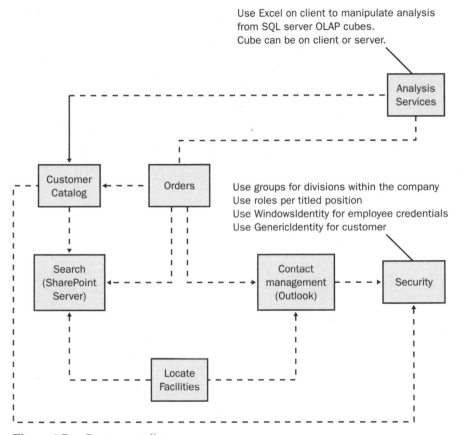

Figure 6.7. Component diagram

How to Create a Preliminary Deployment Model

Taking artifacts such as the application architecture, the team structure, the project schedule, the requirements, the risks assessment document, and candidate technologies into consideration, the team can draft a *preliminary deployment model*. The preliminary deployment model includes network, data, and component topologies.

This model enables the project team and other stakeholders to review the design. Remember that during physical design the team proposes topologies for solutions that have not been selected yet.

Network topology

The network topology is an infrastructure map that indicates hardware locations and interconnections. The map shows workstations and servers and describes their functions. Additionally, the topology shows the network infrastructure that connects the computers.

Figure 6.8 illustrates a sample network topology for a solution.

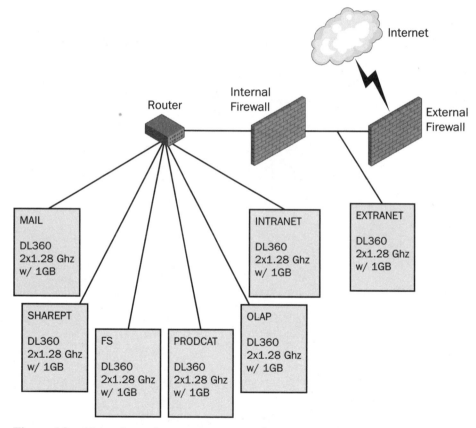

Figure 6.8.   Network topology

On the CD   The figure shows a sample network topology. For the complete network topology for the Adventure Works Cycles case study, refer to AWC - Network in the \SolutionDocuments\Chapter06 folder on the companion CD.

Component and Data Topology

The component and data topology is a map that indicates the locations of packages, components, and their services in relation to the network topology, in addition to data store locations. The map shows the physical distribution of the components and their locations across the various service layers. The current-state version should already exist if the team is not working on a completely new solution. You can add any new components and services required by the application at this time.

Figure 6.9 illustrates a sample component and data topology for Adventure Works Cycles.

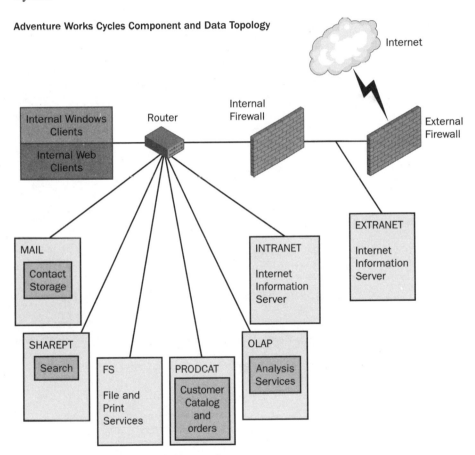

Figure 6.9.   Component and data topology

On the CD   The figure shows a sample component and data topology. For the complete component and data topology for the Adventure Works Cycles case study, refer to AWC Component Topology in the \SolutionDocuments\Chapter06 folder on the companion CD.

Lesson 3: Physical Design Rationalization

After selecting candidate technologies, the project team proceeds to the rationalization step of physical design. In this step, the project team designs services-based components for services-based applications and develops a distribution strategy for those components.

In this lesson, you will learn about the deliverables of the rationalization step. You will also learn how to develop strategies for distributing and packaging the services that have been designed. In addition, you will learn the effect of coupling and cohesion on the packaging strategy. You will also create a component topology and validate and refine the topology.

After this lesson, you will be able to

- Identify the deliverables of the rationalization baseline.
- Create distribution and packaging strategies.
- Describe cohesion and coupling.
- Transform services into components.
- Distribute preliminary components into layers.
- Create a deployment model.
- Validate and refine distribution and packaging.

Estimated lesson time: 10 minutes

What Are the Deliverables of Rationalization?

The rationalization step results in several deliverables. These deliverables describe the technologies, strategies, and topologies that you have designed for the solution.

The deliverables of the rationalization baseline include:

- A distribution and packaging strategy
- Services-based preliminary components
- Deployment models:
    - Future network topology
    - Future data topology
    - Future component topology
- A baseline deployment model

How to Create Distribution and Packaging Strategies

The *rationalization* step is an iterative process during which the project team tries to design an optimal solution. One of the goals of the rationalization step is the distribution of services and the packaging of those services into components.

The *distribution strategy* is a rationale for determining where the services will be located in the solution architecture. Distribution is services-based and not component-based.

The *packaging strategy* is a rationale for determining which services go into each component. You might have multiple strategies in a single solution. For example, a common practice is to divide the business services into business objects (commonly called a business facade layer) without incorporating the business rules directly in the class interfaces. This practice allows the team to create a business rules layer that incorporates most of the business rules (limiting discounts by authorization, for example). The business rules layer can then be changed and redeployed without modifying the business objects. Creating this layer limits the changes to interfaces that communicate with these objects. This strategy can be decided in advance.

To determine an appropriate overall distribution and packaging strategy, you must consider state management and performance of the solution.

State management

State management is the process by which the solution maintains state and page information over multiple requests for the same or different pages. Some methods of managing state in a Web-based solution are:

- *Hold state on client.* You can hold state on the client by using objects that retain values between multiple requests for the same information.
- *Structured Query Language (SQL) query strings.* A query string is information appended to the end of a page's URL, such as product number and its category ID.
- *Cookies.* A cookie is a small amount of data stored either in a text file on the client's file system or in memory in the client browser session.
- *Application state.* Application state is a global storage mechanism accessible from all pages in the Web application. You use it to store information that is required between server round trips and between pages.
- *Session state.* Session state is similar to application state but is limited to the current browser session. If different users are using the solution, each user has a different session state. In addition, if a user leaves the solution and returns later, the user will have a different session state.

Design considerations

Some of the design considerations include:

- *Scalability.* Scalability involves the ability to quickly and easily extend the solution to handle more transactions or more users.
- *Performance.* Performance of a system includes the response time of the system and the speed with which a system performs application tasks.
- *Manageability.* Manageability of a system includes the ease with which the system can be managed on all levels.
- *Reuse.* Reuse addresses the ease with which components can be reused by other applications.
- *Business context.* Business context involves separate business functions such as accounting or sales.
- *Granularity.* Granularity involves the number of services and objects packaged in a single component.

While defining a strategy for distributing and packaging the services of the business solution, the team must consider the solution and its physical requirements and constraints.

When using multiple strategies, the team should strive for a balance between the various requirements and constraints of the solution. For example, the team might decide to choose a strategy focusing primarily on the performance needs of the application. This might affect the scalability of the solution. In such a scenario, the team must decide how to handle this tradeoff.

What Are Cohesion and Coupling?

One of the features of a good component plan is high cohesion and loose coupling. *Cohesion* is the relationship among different internal elements of a component. *Coupling* is the relationship of a component with other components.

Cohesion

A component whose services are closely related is said to have high cohesion. The reliability of a component is directly dependent on the close relation between its services. Cohesion can be both beneficial and detrimental, depending on the cause of the cohesion. Cohesion can be:

- *Functional.* A unit performs only one task. This is the strongest type of cohesion.
- *Sequential.* A unit contains operations that must be performed in a specific order and that must share the same data.

- *Communicational.* Operations in a unit use the same data but are not related in any other way. This type of cohesion minimizes communication overhead in the application.
- *Temporal.* Operations are combined because they are all performed simultaneously.

Not all cohesion is beneficial. Other types of cohesion can result in a solution that is poorly organized and difficult to understand, debug, and modify. Ineffective types of cohesion include the following:

- *Procedural.* Operations are grouped together because they are executed in a specific order. Unlike sequential cohesion, the operations do not share data.
- *Coincidental.* Operations are grouped without any apparent interrelationship.

Coupling

Coupling can be tight or loose. When a component is tightly coupled, the component depends heavily on external components to accomplish its function. When a component is loosely coupled, the component is not dependent or is less dependent on external components.

Typically, the looser the link that binds components to each other, the easier it is for the developer to use individual components without causing problems. A component should depend as little as possible on other components. If a dependency exists, the connection between the dependent components must be as clear as possible so that you can easily define interfaces. Another reason to represent the dependencies clearly in design is to ensure that future decisions do not cause a series of failures in the design.

How to Package Components

The primary focus of the physical design rationalization is distributing and packaging services. In the first step of this process, you package the services into layers: user, business, and data.

To begin the process of distribution, identify the high-level services in the physical object model and break them into their individual, layer-based services.

For each business object, group the resulting low-level services into three layers: the user services layer, the business services layer, and the data services layer.

Figure 6.10 illustrates the three service layers.

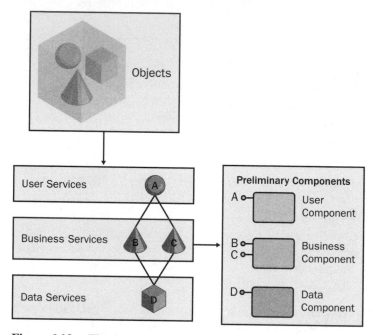

Figure 6.10.   The three service layers

How to Distribute Preliminary Components

After packaging services into components, you distribute the components across the network topology and create a component topology. To start the distribution process, the team identifies categories of services—user, business, and data—for each node in the network topology. These categories serve as the baseline for distribution. The distribution strategy evolves as the design is validated against the solution requirements.

Figure 6.11 illustrates the three layers of services and the corresponding components in a sample application.

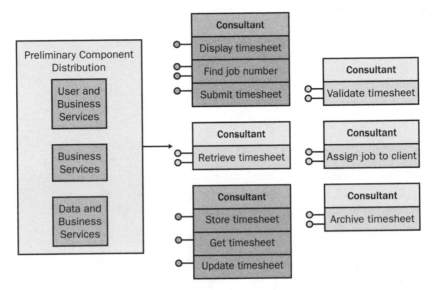

Figure 6.11.   Distributing preliminary components

To help with the distribution of layers, use the following guidelines:

- Distribute user services to the Web servers or to the client computers.
- Distribute business services to application servers or Web servers.
- Distribute data services to the data locations identified in the data topology, including database servers or other locations where the data services will reside.
- After identifying where service layers will reside, distribute the preliminary components into their indicated service layers. This represents the initial component topology that will evolve throughout the rationalization process.

Figure 6.12 illustrates the logical partitioning of the three service layers in the component model of a generic order processing system.

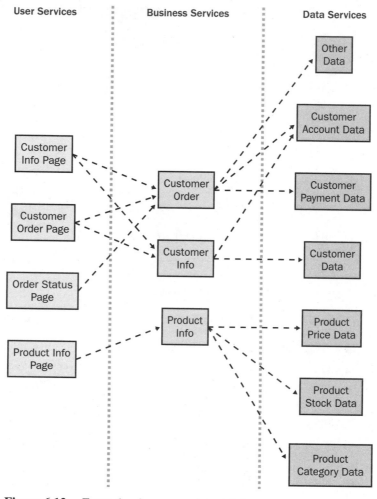

Figure 6.12.   Example of a component model

Note   The illustration shows a sample logical partitioning of the three service layers.

How to Create a Deployment Model

The deployment model shows the mapping of the application and its services to the actual server topology. The purpose of the deployment model is to allow the development team and the release management team to design and plan the server topology and configuration.

Figure 6.13 shows an example of a deployment model.

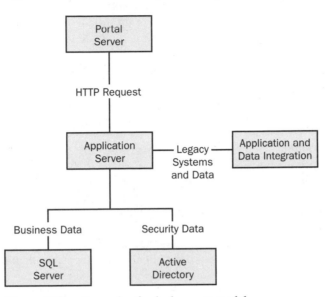

Figure 6.13.   Example of a deployment model

There are five sets of servers:

- Application servers that host Web applications and components
- Database servers that host business databases
- Portal servers that handle all portal functionality, including all HTTP requests from the application servers
- Directory or security servers that manage security data, such as enhanced employee data
- Application and data integration servers that support the optional Microsoft BizTalk Server and the Microsoft Host Integration Server

How to Validate and Refine Distribution and Packaging

After creating the component and deployment models, the project team validates and refines these models.

Validating component and deployment models

During the physical design, the team should validate the component topology against the strategies and requirements of the solution. Validation occurs on an ongoing basis. This enables the team to iterate the design as required.

The project team arrives at an optimal solution by iterating through the process of validation and testing, and by using prototypes to test and tune the packaging and distribution of the components. The team should stop iterating through the solution when only marginal improvements can be made to the solution.

Refining component and deployment models

The key to refining the component topology is to work with services, not components. To evolve the component topology, undo the preliminary component packaging and redistribute the services to meet the needs of the solution.

For example, a requirement states that users must be able to scroll through an entire list without interruption. For best performance, the project team might choose to distribute some of the data services on the client.

After the services have been redistributed, you need to repackage the services. At each location, package the services according to the strategies identified earlier. For example, if ease of deployment is the main goal, the project team might choose to have only one component on the client computer rather than many small components.

Tip   Always take the concepts of cohesion and coupling into consideration when repackaging and redistributing. High cohesion and loose coupling are the ideal, but that ideal might not be practical given the requirements of the solution.

Lesson 4: Physical Design Implementation

During the implementation step of physical design, the team specifies the programming model that the development team will use, the interfaces for each component, and the internal structure of each component. The deliverables of physical design implementation include a programming model; component specifications for interfaces, attributes, and services; and a baseline component specification. The level of detail for each of these deliverables depends on the level of interaction between project management and the development team.

In this lesson, you will learn about the implementation step of physical design. You will learn about the programming model. You will also learn how to specify component interfaces and define the internal structure of components. In addition, you will learn about designing the user interface (UI) and database models.

After this lesson, you will be able to

- Describe the programming model.
- List the guidelines for designing component interfaces.
- Create the internal structure of a component.
- Describe the physical UI model.
- Describe the database model.

Estimated lesson time: 10 minutes

What Is the Programming Model?

Because physical design presents the solution from the developer's perspective, the project team should provide the developers with specifications for component design and technology selection. Component specification provides the development team with enough detail to develop the components of the solution. The specification includes interfaces and the scope of various services and attributes of components. The specification is directly related to the programming model selected for implementation.

A programming model describes how components will be structured. It is based on the goals of the solution and the technologies being implemented.

Purpose of the programming model

The programming model describes how the development team can use the selected technologies. It consists of the programming specifications or standards that will be followed during implementation of the project. The programming model sets specific guidelines to provide consistent component implementation and to increase the maintainability of the components.

The standards prescribed by a programming model might vary for different aspects and service layers of an application. Physical design standards reflect the implementation of the guidelines prescribed by the architecture. If the team decides to implement a stateless server and a stateful client, all attributes are eliminated from class definitions in the physical design. The stateful client might use disconnected .NET datasets as the preferred means of transferring subsets of information to the client.

Design considerations for the programming model

There are several aspects of the programming model that you should consider, including the following:

- *Implementation technologies.* Implementation technologies consist of the programming languages, application programming interfaces (APIs), servers and server technologies, and other technologies that are required for implementing a solution. To efficiently use these technologies, you must use a specific programming model. For example, COM+ 2.0 requires single-entrant, single-threaded, in-process components.

- *Stateful versus stateless objects.* The state that an object maintains can directly affect its performance, scalability, and implementation complexity. Stateful objects retain information that was used in one or more client calls; stateless objects do not maintain transaction-related information. When creating stateful objects, especially in Web-based solutions, the team must determine where and how the state will be maintained; in contrast, stateless objects typically send and receive all necessary information when the objects are invoked or when objects complete the transaction.

- *In-process versus out-of-process function calls.* In-process components perform all execution within a single process, thus eliminating marshalling overhead and increasing performance. Out-of-process components perform their tasks in a process that is separate from that of the invoking client, thus incurring marshalling overhead and degrading performance.

- *Cohesion and coupling.* Cohesive components are closely related to other objects with regards to their functionality. Coupling refers to the strength of component interconnections and interactions. In determining how to apply these principles to a programming model, you should design highly cohesive components and loosely coupled objects. If an object is highly cohesive, its methods and properties are tightly related, and the objects within a component are related. Loosely coupled objects are not highly dependent on the interface, state, or the status of other objects. The communication between loosely coupled objects is implemented by means of messages.

- *Connected versus connectionless modes.* In distributed component environments, various components participating in the service must have real-time, live connections to each other to function properly. If these real-time connections are severed, the components involved in the interaction fail. Because real-time components must typically be run in connected mode, components written to run in a connectionless environment must be able to reestablish connections as required.

- *Synchronous versus asynchronous programming models.* A synchronous programming model blocks the calling component from proceeding with other work until the called interface has completed the requested service and returned control to the calling component. An asynchronous programming model allows components to send messages to other components and then continue functioning without waiting for an immediate reply. A component designed to use an asynchronous programming model is more difficult to program, although technologies such as COM+ Queued Components greatly simplify asynchronous programming. A component that uses an asynchronous programming model lends itself to more scalability because individual components are not blocked and do not need to wait for another process to complete before proceeding.

- *Threading model.* Choosing the threading model for a component is a difficult task because the appropriate model depends on the function of the component. A component that performs extensive input and output (I/O) processing might support free threading to provide maximum response to clients by allowing interface calls during I/O latency. In addition, an object that interacts with the user might support apartment threading to synchronize incoming Component Object Model (COM) calls with its window operations.

- *Error handling.* Because no component performs perfectly or within a perfect environment, components need an error-handling strategy. Certain programming and deployment model decisions constrain the number of error-handling options available. For example, an error message written to a log file on the client might be difficult to retrieve and pass to someone trying to identify system-wide problems.

- *Security.* Security for components and services can be addressed in four basic ways:
  - Component-based security is at the method level, interface level, or component level.
  - Database-based security is handled after data is involved.
  - User context–based security is an interactive method, using system security, or a fixed security within the application.
  - Role-based security involves groups, such as a general manager group.

- *Distribution.* Carefully consider the method for distributing the application. Remember that three logical layers do not necessarily translate into three physically distributed tiers. For example, some business services tend to reside on the client, so you should use as many physical tiers as are required to meet the needs of your application and the enterprise's business goals, possibly even distributing all components to a single location.

Although not a part of the programming model itself, the skills and experience of the technical people who will implement the programming model are an important consideration.

Note   Typically, there is not just one programming model for all components. An application might use many programming models, depending on the requirements of the various components.

How to Specify Component Interfaces

After describing the programming model, the project team defines how the components will interact. This interaction is documented by the component's interfaces, which describe how to access their services and attributes. An interface can represent one or more services. The interface provides a means for requesting a service to perform an operation and a means for receiving information about the resulting attributes. The external structures of the component are outlined in the component interfaces. A component interface:

- Represents the supplier and consumer relationship between components
- Is a means to access the underlying services
- Represents a set of related methods that are a part of a service
- Includes underlying object attributes for a stateful component

The specification of a component interface typically includes all of the ways a component can be accessed and examples of how the component can be used for each means of access. This specification is complete only when the development team finishes creating the component.

When you create component interfaces, remember that:

- A published interface is considered as permanent as possible.
- A modification of an existing interface should be published either as a new component or as a new interface.
- The data types of published attributes must be supported by the service interface consumer.

The only way to access the underlying services within a component is to use the component's published interface. A poorly defined interface can negatively affect other parts of the solution.

Most programming languages allow developers to use Interface Definition Language (IDL) interface definitions when coding components. These definitions help to ensure consistency and change control when multiple developers are coding components.

Each implementation language varies in the syntax and complexity required to define a component's interface. Languages such as Microsoft Visual Basic® often hide much of the interface complexities from developers, whereas languages such as Microsoft Visual C++® provide more control and access to the interfaces. This added control increases coding complexity. Remember that the physical design remains the same, regardless of the implementation language. During physical design, the team can provide a fully-qualified method signature in pseudocode, IDL, or the selected programming language. However, the development team will convert these specifications to a concrete implementation with the selected tools, languages, and technologies during the developing phase.

The Physical Design UI Model

The presentation layer enables users to interact with a system. It provides a communication mechanism between the user and the business services layer of the system. There are two types of users: human users who require an interface through which they can interact with the system, and other computer systems. Although other computer systems do not require a user interface, they require an intermediary to the system with which they will interact. Typically, this intermediary is the user services layer or a Web services interface that facilitates communication between the two layers.

Note   A user interface provides a visual means for humans to interact with systems. User services provide the navigation, validation, and error-processing logic.

To design the user interface and user services layer, the project team uses the outputs of the conceptual design. These outputs include:

- Solution requirements and constraints
- Future-state usage scenarios
- Workflow models
- User profiles
- Task descriptions
- User terminology and concepts

More Info   You will learn more about user interface design in Chapter 7, "Designing the Presentation Layer."

The Physical Design Database Model

During logical design, the database team explores different ways in which the information needs of the conceptual design can be structured in a logical model for a database. The primitive definition for a database is simply an organized collection of data values.

During physical design, the database team must consider:

- Physical database constraints, such as memory and disk size
- Performance tuning considerations, such as deadlock detection, indexing, and hot spots
- Primary keys and foreign keys
- Trigger design
- Stored procedure guidelines
- Application object model considerations
- Indexing specifications
- Partitioning data
- Data migration from the previous database systems
- Operational considerations, such as cluster failover, backup process, and update process

---

More Info   You will learn more about database design in Chapter 8, "Designing the Data Layer."

Activity: Working on the Physical Design

In this activity, you use what you learned in the lessons to create a class model and then create a component model diagram.

Exercise 1: Creating a Class Model

Open the C06Ex1 Microsoft Visio® file from the \SolutionDocuments\Chapter06\ folder on the compact disc, and examine the logical design. Using these diagrams, design a physical class model that is derived from the Catalog, CatalogItem, ManageCatalogItems, and Search objects. You might need to delete or add objects or their attributes and operations. You can see one possible answer to this exercise in C06Ex1_Answer, which is located in the \SolutionDocuments\Chapter06 folder on the CD.

Following are some of the possible discoveries and decisions that have been made in C06Ex1_Answer.

The ManageCatalogItems logical object functionality can best be handled by the Catalog object's operations: addCatalogItem, removeCatalogItem, countSelected-Items, and so on, so it has been deleted from the diagram.

The customer needs to be able to select items for purchase from the catalog while still browsing the catalog. The group of selected items might change in many ways before it is submitted as an order. To meet these needs, a new object is added to the design: the ShoppingCart object.

Exercise 2: Creating a Component Model Diagram

Open the C06Ex2 Visio file from the \SolutionDocuments\Chapter06\ folder on the CD, and then click the Component Model tab. The page is blank. Create a component model for the objects identified in Exercise 1, "Creating a Class Model." Assume the following:

- Sales representatives maintain customer contact information in Microsoft Outlook®.

- Information about Web customers are maintained in a Microsoft SQL Server™ database and managed by using an authorization component.

You can see one possible answer to this exercise in C06Ex2_Answer, which is located in the \SolutionDocuments\Chapter06 folder on the CD.

Summary

- During physical design, the project team defines the services and technologies that will be provided by the solution.
- Physical design is defined as the process of describing the components, services, and technologies of the solution from the perspective of the development team.
- The goals of physical design are:
  - Transforming the logical design into specifications for a set of components
  - Providing a baseline for implementing the design
  - Identifying appropriate technologies for development
  - Creating a structural view of the solution from the perspective of the development team
- There are four steps in physical design: research, analysis, rationalization, and implementation.
- The new deliverables of physical design include:
  - Class diagrams
  - Sequence diagrams
  - Baseline deployment model
  - Programming model
  - Component specifications
- The deliverables of the research baseline include:
  - Current network topology
  - Current data topology
  - Current component topology
  - Physical application requirements
  - Risk assessment and mitigation plan
- During the research step of physical design, the project team identifies the requirements and constraints of the solution and tries to reduce the gap between the two.
- During the analysis step of physical design, the project team refines the UML model created during the logical design, which includes an objects and services inventory, class diagrams, sequence diagrams, and activity diagrams.
- During the analysis step of physical design, the project team creates a preliminary deployment model that includes network, data, and component topologies.
- The network topology is an infrastructure map that indicates hardware locations and interconnections.

- The data topology is a map that indicates data store locations in relation to the network topology.
- The component topology is a map that indicates the locations of components and their services in relation to the network topology.
- The deliverables of the rationalization step include:
    - Distribution and packaging strategy
    - Services-based preliminary components
    - Deployment models
    - Baseline deployment model
- The distribution strategy is a rationale for determining where services will be located in the solution architecture. Distribution is services-based, not component-based.
- The packaging strategy is a rationale for determining which services will go into each component. You might have multiple strategies in a single solution.
- Cohesion is the relationship among various internal elements of a component.
- Coupling is the relationship of a component with other components.
- To distribute services, identify the high-level services in the business object model, and break them into their individual, layer-based services.
- To package services, group the low-level services into three components: the user services component, the business services component, and the data services component.
- The deployment model links the application and its services to the actual server topology.
- The team must validate the component topology against the strategies and requirements of the solution.
- To refine the component and deployment model, the team must undo the preliminary component packaging and redistribute the services to meet the needs of the solution.
- During the implementation step of physical design, the team specifies the programming model that the development team will use, the interfaces for each component, and the internal structure of each component.
- A programming model describes how components will be structured based on the goals of the solution and the technologies being implemented.
- A component's interface describes how to access its services and attributes.
- The presentation layer enables users to interact with a business system and provides a communication mechanism between the user and the business services layer of the system.

Review

The following questions are intended to reinforce key information presented in this chapter. If you are unable to answer a question, review the lesson materials and try the question again. You can find answers to the questions in the appendix.

1. What are the goals of physical design?

2. What is the difference between conceptual, logical, and physical designs?

3. What does the development team do during physical design?

4. What does the deployment model include?

5. What does the project team do during the research step of physical design?

6. How does the project team handle the gap between requirements and constraints?

7. During the analysis step of physical design, how does the project team use the list of objects and services created during logical design?

8. How does the project team refine the class diagrams during the analysis step of physical design?

9. How do you select the candidate technologies for the solution?

10. What is the difference between the network topology and the data topology of the deployment model?

11. What is the difference between the distribution strategy and the packaging strategy?

12. What is the difference between cohesion and coupling?

13. What is the purpose of a programming model?

14. What is a component interface?

15. What are the various types of users of the user services layer of an application?

C H A P T E R   7

Designing the Presentation Layer

About This Chapter

You have learned the process of designing a business solution, focusing on the envisioning phase and planning phase, which includes the conceptual, logical, and physical design processes. However, the design of any system that will be used by users is not complete without a way for users to interact with that system. User interaction takes place by means of the application's *presentation layer*. You design the user interface of an application during the physical design process.

Figure 7.1 illustrates where the design of the presentation layer fits into the MSF Process Model.

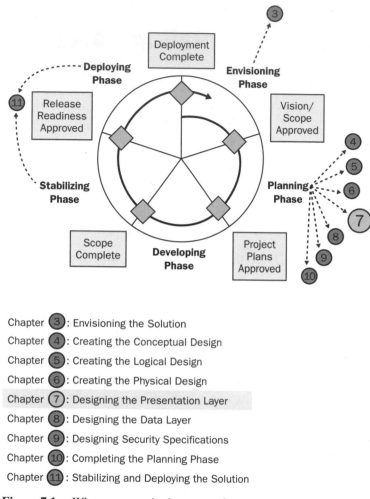

Chapter ③: Envisioning the Solution

Chapter ④: Creating the Conceptual Design

Chapter ⑤: Creating the Logical Design

Chapter ⑥: Creating the Physical Design

Chapter ⑦: Designing the Presentation Layer

Chapter ⑧: Designing the Data Layer

Chapter ⑨: Designing Security Specifications

Chapter ⑩: Completing the Planning Phase

Chapter ⑪: Stabilizing and Deploying the Solution

Figure 7.1. Where are you in the process?

In this chapter, you will learn about designing the presentation layer of an application. You will also learn about the two pieces of the presentation layer—the user interface (UI) components and the user process components—and how to design them.

Before You Begin

To complete the lessons in this chapter, you must

- Understand the MSF Process Model.
- Be familiar with the MSF design process.

Lesson 1: Basics of User Interface Design

In this lesson, you will learn about the basics of user interface design, including the various types of user interfaces, the goals of the user interface design process, and the characteristics of a good user interface design.

After this lesson, you will be able to

- Explain the functions of user interface components.
- Determine the guidelines for user interface design.
- Identify some metaphors and elements that can be used in user interface design.
- Distinguish between a well-designed and poorly designed user interface.

Estimated lesson time: 20 minutes

What Is the Presentation Layer?

The *presentation layer* is the part of the business application that provides a communication mechanism between the user and the business service layer of the system.

Elements of the presentation layer

Simple presentation layers contain *user interface components* that are hosted in a graphical user interface (GUI) such as Microsoft Windows® Forms or Microsoft ASP.NET Web Forms. For more complex user interactions, you can design *user process components* to orchestrate the UI elements and control the user interaction, as shown in Figure 7.2.

User process components are especially useful when there is a specific process that must be followed and access to that process varies depending on the user. For example, a retail application might require two user interfaces: one for the e-commerce Web site that customers use, and another for the Windows Forms–based applications that the sales representatives use. Both types of users perform similar tasks by using these user interfaces. Both user interfaces must provide the ability to view the available products, add products to a shopping cart, and specify payment details as part of a checkout process. This process can be abstracted in a separate user process component to make the application easier to maintain.

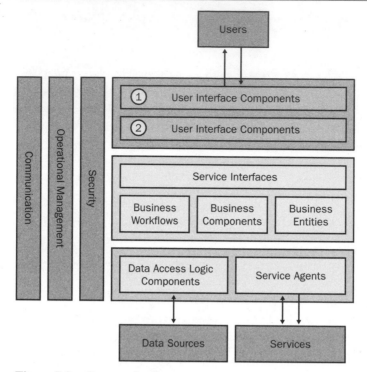

Figure 7.2.   Presentation layer

Inputs to the presentation layer design

The information that you researched, analyzed, and optimized during the envisioning and planning phases is the input for the design of the presentation layer. This information includes:

- Solution requirements and constraints
- Usage scenarios
- Workflow models
- User profiles
- Task descriptions

What Is a User Interface Component?

The first area of the presentation layer that you will learn about is the user interface. In some ways, this interface could be considered the most important part of the business application because, to most users, it *is* the application. A well-designed user interface helps to ensure the success and acceptance of a business application.

User interface components manage interaction with the user. They display data to the user, acquire data from the user, interpret events that are caused by user actions, change the state of the user interface, and help users view progress in their tasks.

User interface components perform view or control roles, or both, in the Model-View-Controller (MVC) pattern. The MVC pattern divides an application, or even an application's interface, into three parts: the model (application object), the view (representation to the user), and the controller (user control).

Tip   Separation of model, view, and controller provides greater flexibility and possibility for reuse.

A component plays a view role when it displays data to users. Control functions are called when the user performs an action that changes the state of the related business data in the user interface process. A control function is a method that performs an action based on the user interface component that the user acted on, and the data that was provided at the time the action was initiated.

What Are the Functions of the User Interface Components?

User interface components display data to users, acquire and validate data from user input, and interpret user actions that indicate the user wants to perform an operation on the data. Additionally, the user interface should filter the available actions to let users perform only the operations that are appropriate at a certain point in time.

User interface components perform the following functions:

- Acquire data from users and assist in its entry by providing visual cues (such as ToolTips), validation, and the appropriate controls for the task.
- Capture events from the user and call controller functions to notify the user interface components to change the way they display data, either by initiating an action on the current user process or by changing the data of the current user process.
- Restrict the types of input a user can enter. For example, the Age field might limit user entries to whole numeric values.
- Perform data entry validation, for example, by restricting the range of values that can be entered in a particular field, or by ensuring that mandatory data is entered.
- Perform simple mapping and transformations of the information provided by the user controls to values needed by the underlying components to do their work. For example, a user interface component might display a product name but pass the product ID to underlying components.

- Perform formatting of values (such as formatting dates appropriately).

- Perform any localization work on the rendered data, for example, using resource strings to display column headers in a grid in the appropriate language for the user's locale.

- Provide the user with status information, for example, by indicating when an application is working in disconnected or connected mode.

- Customize the appearance of an application based on user preferences or the kind of client device used.

Note   In addition to the listed functions, user interface components also help manage the flow of actions needed to perform a task, control resource usage, group information to aid user understanding, convert tabular data into graphical form to help users interpret it, and support local caching for performance improvements.

Guidelines for User Interface Design

Designing a user interface that provides a good user experience requires knowledge and understanding of the users' needs and workflow. You accumulate this information during the envisioning and planning phases.

Guidelines

The design of the interface must implement the users' tasks in a way that is intuitive to the user. This goal is accomplished by including users in all stages of the design of the user interface. Prototyping, beta testing, and early adoption programs are methods for involving the user during the design and implementation of the UI.

The success or failure of an application might depend on the user interface. If users have difficulty using the interface, they see their difficulties as a failure of the application. Designing and developing a user interface that truly meets the needs of users involves asking user-focused questions and incorporating the answers in your design.

Designer's questions

Some design questions to consider include:

- How are users going to interact with the system?
- Does the interface represent the concepts and terminologies of the users?
- Are appropriate metaphors used in the design of the user interface?
- Do the users have the control that they require to override automated processes when needed?
- Can users easily find the features required to complete common tasks?
- Is the workflow correct and complete?
- Does the interface optimize the workflow of the users?

- Can users easily access help for specific problems?
- Are users able to customize the UI to meet their particular needs?
- Are there alternative ways to perform a specific task in case a problem arises, for example, if a mouse gets disconnected from the computer?

What Features Does a Well-Designed Interface Include?

Users judge an application by its interface. If the interface fails to provide a good experience to the users, the overall effort of application development is wasted. However, do not compromise functionality to make the application interface user-friendly. Getting users to accept an interface requires that the users' needs and workflow be taken as a primary consideration during its design and development. You want to ensure that the UI is accessible by all users, including users with physical, visual, or auditory disabilities.

The following features help make an interface effective.

- *Intuitive design.* Design the interface so that a user can intuitively understand how to use it. An intuitive design helps a user become familiar with the interface more quickly. The interface should guide the user's interactions with the application. To make an effective interface, label controls appropriately and make Help context-sensitive.

- *Optimum screen space utilization.* Determine the content of the interface by planning the amount of information that is displayed and the amount of input required from the user. When possible, place all related information and input controls on the same screen. Sometimes, there is too much information for one screen. In such cases, provide tabbed panes or child windows. You could also provide a wizard that guides a user through the data input process.

- *Appearance.* You can use factors, such as the frequency and length of time that a user will interact with a specific piece of the interface, to determine the appearance of the interface.

  For example, when you design Windows-based applications for data entry, do not use bright colors because bright colors strain the eyes. Also, refrain from using colors to indicate specific things, such as red for error messages, because the user might change the color settings because of accessibility or cultural requirements.

  You can, however, use bright colors for Web-based interfaces to make them attractive. For example, when designing confirmation and status pages, you might use bright colors to attract the user's attention to the information. Users tend to spend more time on data input screens than they do on confirmation and status screens. Following accepted guidelines and standards, such as those in the article *Official Guidelines for User Interface Developers and Designers* on MSDN® (*http://msdn.microsoft.com/library/en-us/dnwue/html/welcome.asp*), will help you succeed in designing a usable user interface.

More Info   For more information about designing user interfaces for applications that run on the Windows operating system, see *Microsoft Windows User Experience* (Microsoft Press, 1999).

- *Ease of navigation.* Because different users prefer different ways of accessing components on an interface, design the components so they are easily accessible by using the TAB key, the arrow keys, and other keyboard shortcuts, in addition to the mouse. Sometimes, as in the preceding data entry example, faster navigation is more important than guided navigation. When designing keyboard shortcuts into the UI, associate the shortcut keys with the action being performed. For example, if you are creating a shortcut that will fill in default data for a product description, a shortcut such as CTRL+ALT+D might be more intuitive than CTRL+ALT+P.

- *Controlled navigation.* Although it is important for an interface to provide easy navigation, it is also important to maintain the order in which the components can be accessed. For example, in interfaces that are designed for the purpose of data entry and modifications, you might require that the values be entered in a specific order. However, be wary of taking away the user's feeling of control over the input process.

  One of the key benefits of Windows-based applications is that they typically do not constrain a user to an input sequence, so users have more control. You should also consider adding *breadcrumb trail navigation* functionality to the interface. This type of navigation shows the path the user has navigated to get to the current position. To see an example of a Web site that uses the breadcrumb trail navigation functionality, see the article *The Developing Phase*, on MSDN, at *http://msdn.microsoft.com/library/en-us/dnsolac/html/m05_develphase1.asp*.

- *Populating default value.* If the interface includes fields that always take default values, it is better to provide the default values automatically, therefore avoiding the user having to enter anything whenever possible.

- *Input validation.* It is important to validate the user input before the application processes the input. You need to determine when validation should occur. For example, determine whether validation should occur every time the user moves the focus from one input field to another, or whether it should occur when the user submits the inputs. Sometimes both approaches can be required if there are data dependencies between fields.

- *Menus, toolbars, and Help.* Design the interface to provide access to all of the application's functionality by means of menus and toolbars. In addition, a Help feature should provide complete information about what a user can do with the application.

Note   Although menus and toolbars are the primary methods for input, most frequently used features of an application should also have alternative methods of access, such as keyboard shortcuts, in case the primary input device becomes unusable.

- *Efficient event handling.* The event-handling code that you write for the components of the interface controls the interaction of the user with the interface. It is important that the execution of such code does not cause the user to wait a long time for the application to respond.

Lesson 2: Designing the User Interface

Now that you have learned the basics of designing a user interface, the next step is to learn about the process. In this lesson, you will learn about the process of designing a user interface, and about the deliverables of this process.

After this lesson, you will be able to

- Create an initial user interface design.
- Distinguish between a high-fidelity and a low-fidelity design.
- Design user assistance for an application.
- Select an appropriate user interface model for an application.
- Identify the technology options and considerations for a client environment.
- Validate a user interface design.
- Identify the deliverables of the user interface design process.

Estimated lesson time: 35 minutes

How to Create an Initial User Interface Design

The first part of designing a user interface is creating an initial design that the users can review. This initial design can be either low fidelity (for example, created with a pencil on paper) or high fidelity (for example, a prototype created with a tool such as Microsoft Visual Basic®), as shown in Figure 7.3.

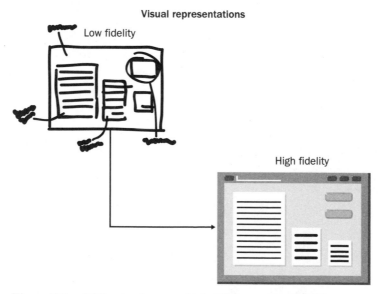

Figure 7.3. Difference between high fidelity and low fidelity

A *low-fidelity design* shows the main structure and features of the UI and illustrates the navigation path. This type of design is useful for brainstorming sessions where you will receive immediate feedback. It provides one way to quickly identify design problems and explore alternative designs.

A *high-fidelity design* provides detailed information about screen layout and interface elements. This type of design is often based on a low-fidelity design. Compared to a low-fidelity design, a high-fidelity design is relatively quick to implement and adjust.

In addition, you can create a *navigation map* for the user interface. A navigation map shows which component is called for each UI event. To keep the focus on the workflow, do not yet include field validation or error processing.

By involving the users early in the design process and keeping them involved throughout the design process, you mitigate the risk of design flaws and increase the likelihood of designing an interface that the users will find acceptable.

Planning   Consider providing a low-fidelity representation, rather than a prototype, to the users. When the initial design is being created, it is better to create a low-fidelity design. Later, when the design is more complete, you can create prototypes to give a detailed representation of the design to the customers. This approach reinforces that what they are reviewing is truly a design and that they can have an influence on the final version.

These initial designs should use the elements that were agreed upon with the users. They should also incorporate the terminology and concepts of the users. The glossary that you create during the envisioning and planning phases serves as a good starting point for the terminology. However, for a better understanding of the terminologies and concepts, you need to talk to the users.

How to Provide User Assistance

User assistance is frequently neglected, or poorly implemented, in computer applications. There are several options available for providing user assistance in applications.

Online Help

Online Help refers to any help that is immediately available upon user request while the user is interacting with the system. This assistance can be installed with the application, located on a CD, or located on an intranet or the Internet. Online Help is an important part of all applications and provides an effective way to answer user queries.

Online Help can be either context-sensitive or in a reference format. *Context-sensitive* Help provides information about a specific field or area of the UI. Other Help formats allow the user to read the Help contents in a specific order (by topic or an alphabetized list) or to search for information.

Tip   When designing your Help system, try to include topics that provide answers to task-oriented questions. Task-oriented Help is most useful for less-experienced users.

ToolTips

A *ToolTip* is a small label that is displayed when a user moves the mouse over a control or an option in the user interface. The label provides a description of the function of the control. ToolTips are normally used in conjunction with toolbars, but they also work well in many other parts of the interface.

Tip   As with other parts of the interface, ensure that the text clearly conveys the intended message to the user.

Status displays

Status displays are a useful way to provide instructions or messages that might not fit easily into a ToolTip. To provide status displays, you can use a status bar control or a label control.

Wizards

A *wizard* is a user assistance device that guides the user step-by-step through a procedure. Wizards are mostly used to provide task-specific assistance. They help a user complete a difficult task that would otherwise require a lot of time to learn and accomplish. Wizards are also used to provide advanced information to a user who has enough experience with basic steps but wants additional or advanced information.

Accessibility aids

Accessibility aids are specialized programs and devices that help people with disabilities use applications more effectively. There are many types of aids. Some examples include:

- Screen enlargers that enlarge portions of the screen
- Screen-reading software that presents graphics and text as speech
- Speech recognition systems that provide input by using your voice instead of the keyboard or mouse

When designing accessible applications, you should follow certain guidelines. Some examples of accessibility guidelines include:

- Applications must be compatible with specific system color, size, font, sound, and input settings.

  This guideline provides a consistent user interface across all applications on the user's system.

- Applications must provide keyboard access to all features.

  This guideline allows the user to interact with the application without requiring a pointing device, such as a mouse.

- Applications must not convey information by sound alone.

  This guideline requires that applications that convey information by sound must provide additional means of expressing this information, such as on-screen messages.

More Info   For more information about the guidelines for designing accessible applications, see the MSDN Library (*http://msdn.microsoft.com*), and the Microsoft Accessibility Web site at *http://www.microsoft.com/enable*.

How to Select a User Interface Model

When designing an application, it is important to select the best user interface model because the user interface can affect deployment, how users interact and relate to the data, and how the state is maintained while the application is interacting with the user. Some of the common user interface implementation models and technologies include:

- Windows-based user interfaces
- Web-based user interfaces
- Mobile device user interfaces
- Document-based user interfaces

Windows desktop user interfaces

Windows-based user interfaces are used when you need to provide users with disconnected or offline capabilities and rich user interactions. Windows user interfaces provide a wide range of state management and persistence options, and local processing power. There are three main categories of standalone user interfaces:

- *Full-featured workstation/Tablet PC user interfaces created with Windows Forms.* These UIs involve creating an application with Windows Forms and Windows controls. In these applications, the application provides all or most of the data rendering functionality. These UIs give the developer total control over the user experience and the appearance and functionality of the application.

- *Embedded HTML.* You can implement the entire user interface by using Windows Forms, or you can use additional embedded Hypertext Markup Language (HTML) in your Windows-based applications. Embedded HTML provides greater run-time flexibility (because the HTML can be loaded from external resources or even a database in connected scenarios) and user customization. Extra coding is necessary to load the HTML, display it, and connect the events from the control with your application functions.

> **Important**   Careful planning is needed to ensure that malicious scripts cannot be introduced through the embedded HTML.

- *Application add-ins.* For some applications, the use cases developed during the planning phases might suggest that the user interface of the application could be better implemented as an add-in for other applications, such as Microsoft Office, AutoDesk AutoCAD software, customer relationship management (CRM) solutions, engineering tools, and so on. In such cases, the developers can use all the data access and display logic of the host application and just provide their business-specific code to gather the data and work with their business logic.
- *Remote access.* By using programs such as Windows XP Remote Desktop Connection and Windows Terminal Services, remote users can access remote computers and run applications on them remotely. The only information passed between the client computer and the remote user is the user interface. All other functionality, such as data validation and computations done by the CPU, is performed on the remote computer.

Web-based user interfaces

In Microsoft .NET, you develop Web-based user interfaces with ASP.NET. ASP.NET provides a rich environment in which you can create complex Web-based interfaces that support the following features:

- Consistent development environment
- User interface data binding
- Component-based UIs with controls
- Integrated .NET security model
- Rich caching and state management options
- Availability, performance, and scalability of Web processing

Mobile device user interfaces

Mobile devices such as handheld computers, Wireless Application Protocol (WAP) phones, and Handheld PCs are becoming increasingly popular, and building user interfaces for a mobile device has several challenges.

A user interface for a mobile device needs to be able to display information on a much smaller screen than other common applications, and must offer acceptable usability for the devices being targeted. Because user interaction can be difficult on mobile devices, design your mobile user interfaces with minimal data input requirements. A common strategy is to allow users to pre-register data by means of a workstation-based client, and then select the data when using a mobile client. For example, an e-commerce application might allow users to register credit card details by means of a Web site so that a pre-registered credit card can be selected from a list when orders are placed from a mobile device, thus avoiding the requirement to enter full credit card details by using a mobile phone keypad.

Document-based user interfaces

In some applications, you might benefit from having users enter or view data in document form. Document-based user interfaces include:

- *Showing data.* The application allows users to view their data in a document, such as showing customer data as a Microsoft Word form, a sales report as a Microsoft Excel worksheet, or a project timeline as a Microsoft Project Gantt chart.
- *Gathering data.* You can allow sales representatives to complete Word forms with customer information, allow accountants to enter data into Excel worksheets, or let designers enter design data with Microsoft Visio®.

How to Select the Client Environment

The selection of a client environment for the user interface of a business application is determined by how the user will be using the application, in addition to how the user will be connected to the systems that support the application.

When users are on a local area network (LAN) or a high-speed wide area network (WAN), the main choice of client is a feature-rich environment known as a *rich client*. For these users, the communication speed between their computers and the system they are accessing is not a primary issue. This type of client also has the greatest number of options for development and implementation. Additionally, the processing of the application can easily be distributed between the servers and the clients.

Another choice of clients is the *thin client*. However, thin clients, such as Web browsers and remote desktop connections, are most frequently used for remote or distributed users, or users with slower connections such as a dial-up modem. These users are frequently concerned with communication speed and require a user interface that sends the minimum amount of information possible over their connections. These users might benefit from a rich client if the business requires functionality that is not available otherwise.

You should take the following factors into account when deciding whether to create a thin-client or a rich-client application.

Note   This choice between thin and rich clients is also known as the choice between reach clients and rich clients.

- *Client devices.* An application that must be used on a wide variety of client devices is ideally suited to being a thin-client application. If the application must run on Windows-based computers but must also run on computers and are not running Windows, or on PDAs, telephones, or interactive televisions, the application will typically be a thin client.

  You must use special care in these situations when using heterogeneous systems because the client might have limitations. For example, a browser might be unable to host ActiveX® controls, or it might not have a Java Virtual Machine. When an application can be hosted in an unknown browser, the ASP.NET server controls can be used because the server will determine the browser's capabilities and render the controls accordingly. If mobile devices are to be targeted, Mobile Internet Controls must be used for the same reason.

- *Graphics.* If an application makes heavy use of highly dynamic graphics, such as computer-aided design (CAD) or video applications, then you need to use a rich client.

  If an application is not heavily graphical and it can avoid using animations and other cosmetic graphical effects, it can work well as a thin client. Dynamic HTML can be used to provide some localized effects, but doing so increases the size of each page. The features that you use depend on the capabilities of the browser that you are targeting.

- *Interaction.* If an application is highly interactive and provides the user with a rich experience, it is best suited to being a rich client. Highly interactive applications are those that present a dynamic user interface that changes frequently based on user input (for example, a word processor, a game, or a CAD application), allows drag-and-drop operations, performs immediate inter-control validations, and so on.

- *Network bandwidth.* A thin-client application generally uses much more network bandwidth than a locally hosted rich client. This is especially true if the interface uses Web server controls because many mouse clicks result in a round trip to the Web server. This is also true for Terminal Services clients and remote desktop connections because, in the case of remote clients, user interface rendering and responses need to travel across the network. Therefore, if network bandwidth is an issue, a rich client is the preferred choice.

- *Disconnected client.* If the client must be able to operate while disconnected from the corporate network, then you use a rich client. This would include applications used by mobile personnel, or by personnel working from customer locations.

- *CPU-intensive operations.* If users need to perform operations that require a lot of CPU-intensive work (for example, CAD and graphics applications), these operations should occur on the end-user's computer; otherwise the operations could quickly overload the server. CPU-intensive applications are best suited to a rich-client environment.

- *Database locking.* If the application requires a high degree of concurrency control, a rich client is essential. For example, if an application must use pessimistic locking, it cannot be a thin client because the locks are released after each page has been processed.

- *Local resources.* If an application needs access to local resources, such as files (storage), the registry (configuration), databases (storage), or any other local devices, a rich client might be more suitable.

- *Security.* In a highly secure environment, a thin-client application has the following benefits:
  - Privileged operations can be confined to the server.
  - Code that could be misused by a malicious user is kept away from workstation computers (as long as active content is avoided).
  - The workstation can be locked down.
  - Sensitive data is not stored outside the data center.

The following advantages apply to rich-client applications hosted by Terminal Services:

- Authorization: user-based and code access security-based
- Authentication
- Secure communication and state management
- Auditing

How to Create a User Interface Prototype

After you have made the design decisions for the user interface, you are ready to create a user interface prototype from the gathered interviews, requirements document, use cases, usage scenarios, and activity diagrams created during the planning phase.

Example usage scenario

To learn how to create a user interface prototype, consider the example of the Adventure Works Cycles scenario. The following is a usage scenario that was created based on the use cases defined during early stages of planning for sales representatives and sales managers.

Adventure Works Cycles Usage Scenario

Use case title: UC 05.5.1 Apply Discount to Product

Abbreviated title: Apply Discount to Product

Use case ID: UC 05.5.1

Requirements ID: 2.1.1, 2.1.2, 2.1.3

Description: A sales representative is creating an order for a specific customer. The representative wants to offer the customer a discount on one or more products in the order. This affects the total order price, and it is the recalculated price that the customer will then pay. Sales managers can also apply discounts to orders.

Sales representatives are currently authorized to apply a discount of up to 15 percent without approval. Sales managers can apply a discount of up to 20 percent.

Actors: Sales Representative, Sales Manager

Preconditions:

- Actor has access rights to view customer and sales data
- An order is in the process of being created

Task sequence	*Exceptions*
1. Actor chooses to apply a discount to an order	Product is not in current view
2. Application requests which order is to be discounted	
3. Actor selects the order to be discounted	Any piece of data is not available
4. Application presents order information (including any existing discounts) and requests discount amount	
5. Actor enters discount amount	
6. Application validates discount amount and presents order information with updated total price	• If discount amount is over a certain threshold, system reports this fact • Use case continues at Step 5 of main path to enable actor to re-enter discount amount
7. Information is passed to a method of delivery	

Postconditions:

Uses/Extends:

1. EXTENDS UC 05.5 Apply Discount to Order

Unresolved issues:

Sales Managers have authority to supply a higher level of discount than sales representatives. This is captured in extended use case UC 5.5.1.1.

Authority: Mike Danseglio

Modification history:

Date: December 19, 2002

Author: Yan Li

Description: Initial version

> **Tip**   When designing the user interface, keep in mind the preconditions, the basic course, the alternative courses, and the extensions specified in the usage scenarios. All these factors need to be addressed by the UI.

Example requirements

Following are some of the requirements that were identified and refined during the planning phase for Adventure Works Cycles:

- Sales representative should be allowed to search the site for information across all products or within a specific catalog.
- Sales representative should be allowed to view the categories of the product.
- Sales representative should be allowed to view product details such as pricing and information about promotions.
- Sales representative should be allowed to view product specifications.
- Additional navigation links should appear on the page. These links include Home, About Adventure Works Cycles, Track Orders, Shipping Rates and Policies, Contact Us, and a copyright notice.
- Sales representative should be allowed to view the customer reviews about the product.
- Sales representative should be allowed to provide discounts of up to 15 percent to the customers.
- Sales representative can provide discounts from 16 through 20 percent to the customers with prior approval from a sales manager.
- Sales manager should be allowed to search the site for information across all products or within a specific catalog.
- Sales manager should be able to view the categories of the product.
- Sales manager should be able to view product details such as pricing and information about promotions.
- Sales manager should be able to view product specifications.

- Sales manager should be able to view the customer reviews about the product.
- Sales manager should be able to provide discounts of up to 20 percent to the customers.
- Sales manager can approve discounts of up to 20 percent to the customers.

You need to address the above requirements when you design the user interface for Adventure Works Cycles Web site.

Example UI prototypes

Figure 7.4 is an example of a UI prototype that was created to address the requirements derived from use cases and usage scenarios. This prototype shows the information that a sales representative needs on the product information page.

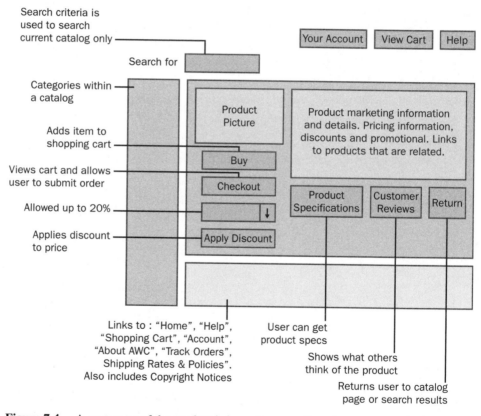

Figure 7.4. A prototype of the product information page for sales representatives

Figure 7.5 is another example of a UI prototype. This prototype shows the information that a sales manager needs on the product information page.

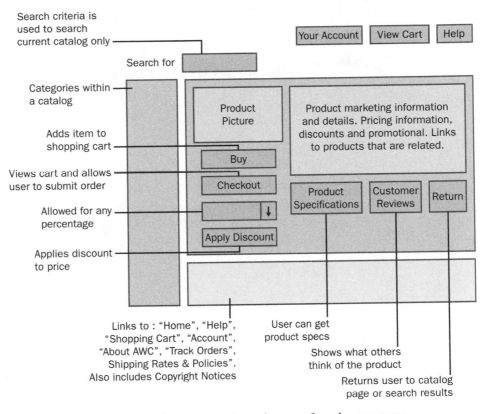

Figure 7.5. A prototype of the product information page for sales managers

How to Validate User Interface Design

As part of the design process, validate that the user interface is addressing the requirements of the users.

After you create the UI prototypes, you need to map the UI back to the requirements, use cases, usage scenarios, and logical design. Ensure that all the requirements are addressed by the user interface. If a requirement has not been addressed in the user interface, you need to address it and incorporate that in the design before you present the prototypes to the customers.

The navigation and flow are validated to ensure that the flow is as expected. The maps should be compared to the future-state usage scenarios to confirm that the user interface is able to handle the scenarios.

The final step of the validation process is to review the design with the users and obtain their agreement that it satisfies their requirements.

The next step is to create prototypes of limited functionality so that the user interface can be validated in usability tests.

What Are the Deliverables of the UI Design Process?

Like all the other processes of designing a business solution, the UI design process has deliverables:

- The project team, customer, and users should have an agreement on the guidelines for the design, including the elements that are being used in the application. The guidelines, and an identification of common interface elements, should be documented for the development team.

- The design should include descriptions of how the interface will provide appropriate feedback (such as progress bars) and user assistance (such as ToolTips) to the user.

- The design produced should be testable by storyboarding and by comparing it against the future-state usage scenarios.

Lesson 3: Designing User Process Components

User interaction with your application might follow a predictable process. For example, the Adventure Works Cycles Web site might require users to enter product details, view the total price, enter payment details, and finally enter delivery address information. This process involves displaying and accepting input from a number of user interface elements, and the state for the process (the products that have been ordered, the credit card details, and so on) must be maintained between each transition from one step in the process to another. To help coordinate the user process and handle the state management required when displaying multiple user interface pages or forms, you can create user process components.

In this lesson, you will learn about the functions of user process components and how to design them.

After this lesson, you will be able to

- Explain the function of user process components.
- Separate the user interface from user processes.
- Design user processes.

Estimated lesson time: 20 minutes

Functions of User Process Components

Separating the user interaction functionality into user interface and user process components provides the following advantages:

- Long-running user interaction state is more easily persisted, allowing a user session to be abandoned and resumed, possibly even using a different user interface. For example, a customer could add some items to a shopping cart by using the Web-based user interface, and then later call a sales representative to complete the order.
- The same user process can be reused by multiple user interfaces. For example, in the retail application, the same user process could be used to add a product to a shopping cart from both the Web-based user interface and the Windows Forms–based application.

Figure 7.6 shows how the user interface and user process can be abstracted from one another.

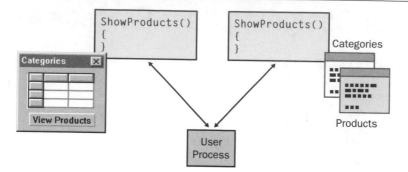

Figure 7.6.   User interfaces and user process components

User process components are typically implemented as classes that expose methods that can be called by user interfaces. Each method encapsulates the logic necessary to perform a specific action in the user process. The user interface creates an instance of the user process component and uses it to transition through the steps of the process.

User process components coordinate the display of user interface elements. They are abstracted from the data rendering and acquisition functionality provided in the user interface components. You should design them with globalization in mind, to allow for localization to be implemented in the user interface. For example, you should endeavor to use culture-neutral data formats and use Unicode string formats internally to make it easier to consume the user process components from a localized user interface.

User process components:

- Provide a simple way to combine user interface elements into user interaction flows without requiring you to redevelop data flow and control logic.
- Separate the conceptual user interaction flow from the implementation or device in which it occurs.
- Encapsulate how exceptions can affect the user process flow.
- Keep track of the current state of the user interaction.
- Keep internal data related to application business logic and their internal state, persisting the data as required.

How to Separate a User Process from the User Interface

Before you design a user process component, separate user process components from user interface components. It is important to determine what functions can be done by the user interface and what needs to be handled by the user process components.

To separate a user process from the user interface, perform the following tasks:

1. Identify the business process or processes that the user process will help to accomplish. Identify how the user sees this as a task. You can usually do this by consulting the sequence diagrams, use cases, and usage scenarios that you created as part of your requirements analysis.
2. Identify the data needed by the business processes. The user process will need to be able to work with this data when necessary.
3. Identify additional state you will need to maintain throughout the user activity to assist rendering and data capture in the user interface.
4. Design the visual flow of the user process and the way that each user interface element receives or gives control flow.

Note Implementing a user interaction with user process components is not a trivial task. Before committing to this approach, you should carefully evaluate whether your application requires the level of orchestration and abstraction provided by user process components.

What Are the Guidelines for Designing User Processes?

Use the following guidelines when designing user processes for an application:

- Decide whether you need to manage user processes as separate components from the user interface components. Separate user processes are generally only needed in applications with a high number of user interface dialog boxes, or in applications in which the user processes might be subject to customization and might benefit from a add-in approach.
- Choose where to store the state of the user process:
  - If the process is running in a connected fashion, store interim state for long-running processes in a central Microsoft SQL Server™ database; in disconnected scenarios, store it in local XML files, isolated storage, or local Microsoft SQL Server 2000 Desktop Engine (MSDE) databases. On Handheld PC devices, you can store state in a Microsoft SQL Server CE database.
  - If the process is not long-running and does not need to be recovered in case of a problem, you should persist the state in memory. For user interfaces created for rich clients, you might want to keep the state in memory. For Web applications, you can choose to store the user process state in the Session object of ASP.NET. If you are running in a server farm, you should store the session in a central state server or a SQL Server database. A server farm is a grouping of several Web servers used for load balancing. When you implement a Web site on a server farm, the processing load is distributed across different Web servers. ASP.NET will remove unnecessary SQL Server–stored session to prevent the buildup of unwanted data.

- Design your user process components so that they are serializable. This will help you implement any persistence scheme.

- Include exception handling in user process components, and propagate exceptions to the user interface. Exceptions that are thrown by the user process components should be caught by user interface components.

Activity: Creating the User Interface

In this activity, you use what you learned in the lessons to work through the process of creating a user interface.

You have been assigned the task of creating a prototype of the product information management tool. The product clerks will use this tool to manage products for the online shopping application. The prototype should be designed in Microsoft PowerPoint®. The requirements for the management tool are as follows:

- The tool should allow the clerk to look up products by supplying a product identification number or by searching the product database. For searching, clerks should be allowed to specify the catalog in which they want to search, or search for the product across all catalogs.

- The information for each product should be broken down into separate sections, such as name, description, part number, catalog, pricing, entry date, expiration data, last modified date, pictures, specifications, promotions, and discount. Rather than displaying all this information on a single screen, the clerk should be allowed to select the type of information and work with that specific data.

- When the clerk wants to add a new product, a new product record must be created and a new product ID must be supplied. The clerk fills in each section of information for the product. Some sections might be optional while others are mandatory. After all the information has been entered, the clerk must explicitly save the new information to the database.

- When the clerk wants to edit an existing product, the clerk must look up the product in the database, explicitly indicate that changes will be made to the information, select each section of information to change, and make the changes. After all the changes have been made, the clerk must explicitly save the changes to the database.

- For each section of information, the clerk should be allowed to cancel edits. This should cancel the edits on only that section of data. For example, if the clerk makes changes to the description of a product and then makes changes to the promotional information for the product, the clerk can cancel the changes to the promotional information without affecting the changes made to the description of the product.

- For each product record that has been added or changed, the user should be allowed to cancel all the entries and changes made since the user last saved the product record.

- When clerks want to delete an existing product, they must look up the product in the database, explicitly indicate that the record will be deleted, and confirm that the record should be deleted. The record is deleted from the database by changing its expiration date to a date that occurred in the past.

Be sure to point out the functionality that can be accessed on the page and what each area of the user interface provides to the user. After you have designed the user interface, compare it to the preceding requirements. To see one possible solution to this exercise, open C07Ex1_Answer.ppt, which is located in the \Solution-Documents\Chapter07\ folder on the CD.

Summary

- Design of any application is not complete without a way for users to interact with the system. User interaction takes place through the application's presentation layer. The presentation layer is the part of the application that provides a communication mechanism between the user and the business service layer of the system.

- The most simple presentation layers contain user interface components, such as Windows Forms or ASP.NET Web Forms. For more complex user interactions, you can design user process components to orchestrate the user interface elements and control the user interaction.

- User interface components display data to users, acquire and validate data from user input, and interpret user gestures that indicate the user wants to perform an operation on the data. Additionally, the user interface should filter the available actions to let users perform only the operations that are appropriate at a certain point in time.

- The features of a good user interface include:
  - Intuitive design
  - Optimum screen space utilization
  - Ease of navigation
  - Controlled navigation
  - Input validation
  - Menus, toolbars, and Help
  - Efficient event handling

- There are several types of user interface models:
  - Windows desktop user interfaces
  - Web-based user interfaces
  - Mobile device user interfaces
  - Document-based user interfaces

- User assistance in an application can be provided by using any or all of the following options:
  - Online Help
  - ToolTips
  - Status displays
  - Wizards
  - Accessibility aids

- User process components are typically implemented as .NET classes that expose methods that can be called by user interfaces. User process components coordinate the display of user interface elements. They are abstracted from the data rendering and acquisition functionality provided in the user interface components.

Review

The following questions are intended to reinforce key information presented in this chapter. If you are unable to answer a question, review the lesson materials and try the question again. You can find answers to the questions in the appendix.

1. What is the function of the presentation layer in the business application architecture?

2. What are the features of a good user interface?

3. What are the differences between a high-fidelity and low-fidelity design?

4. What are some of the options that application developers can use to design user assistance for an application?

5. What are the various types of user interface models, and when should you use them?

6. Describe the difference between a user interface component and a user process component. Describe a situation in which you would use a user process component.

7. How do you separate user interface from user process?

8. Your design calls for the use of Windows Terminal Services. What kind of user interface will you create to implement this design?

9. During the envisioning and planning phases, you determined that the users of the solution will be using a wide variety of hardware, will be located at various remote locations, and will not all have access to the company's intranet. What type of client lends itself to these constraints?

10. After your design of the user interface is complete, what are some of the ways you can validate the design before implementing it?

C H A P T E R   8

Designing the Data Layer

About This Chapter

During the planning phase of the Microsoft® Solutions Framework (MSF) Process Model, the project team designs the data layer of the solution, along with the presentation and business layers. In this chapter, you will learn about designing the data layer for a solution. You will also learn about optimizing data access and implementing data validation in the solution.

Before You Begin

To complete the lessons in this chapter, you must

- Be familiar with the various phases of the MSF Process Model.
- Understand the envisioning phase of the MSF Process Model.
- Understand the tasks and deliverables of the conceptual and logical design processes of the planning phase.
- Understand how to design the presentation layer and business layer of a solution in the physical design process.

Lesson 1: Designing the Data Store

The *data layer* of a solution consists of a data store and data services. The *data store* is typically a database in which data is organized and stored. In this lesson, you will learn about data models and how data is structured in various data models. You will learn how to identify entities and attributes in a data model. You will also learn how to derive tables and columns for a data store and implement relationships among various entities.

After this lesson, you will be able to

- Describe a database schema.
- Identify entities and attributes.
- Identify tables and columns for a data store.
- Implement relationships.

Estimated lesson time: 20 minutes

What Is a Database Schema?

Throughout the planning phase, the project team focuses on analyzing requirements and designing the solution that meets those requirements. Therefore, in addition to identifying the features of the solution, the project team analyzes the data requirements of the solution and specifies how data will be structured, stored, accessed, and validated in the solution.

Research and analysis of data requirements begins during the conceptual design process. These requirements help determine what actually needs to be stored and processed by the business solution. During logical design, the project team derives a set of data entities from sources that include the logical object model, usage scenarios, and data artifacts such as data schema, triggers, constraints, and topology from any existing data store. During physical design, the team defines tables, relationships, field data types, indexes, and procedures to create a database schema, and finalizes data services. In addition, the team plans how to provide for data migration, backup and recovery, and failover support.

Definition of database schema

A *database* is defined as a collection of data values that are organized in a specific manner. A *database schema* specifies how data is organized in a database. During the physical design process, the members of the project team create a database schema so that they can focus on what must be built before they focus on how to build it.

During the logical design process, the team describes the entities and attributes that will be stored in the database, and how the users will access, manipulate, and browse through the data. During the physical design, the team creates the database schema that provides specifications for creating, reading, updating, and deleting data that is used in a solution.

When the team begins to design the database schema, the schema has a close relationship with the logical object model. The schema defines the main entities of interest to the problem, the attributes of those entities, and the relationships between entities. Most data modeling techniques define an entity as an abstraction of something in the real world. You learned to derive entities and attributes of those entities while defining the object model for a solution.

Note   The final production schema might not resemble the logical object model.

Figure 8.1 shows part of the database schema for the Adventure Works Cycles system.

Typically, database objects are modeled in an entity relationship (ER) diagram. The ER diagram consists of entities, attributes, and relationships. It provides a high-level logical view of the data. In an ER model, all data is viewed as stating facts about entities and relationships.

Note   You will learn more about entities, attributes, and relationships in the subsequent topics in this chapter.

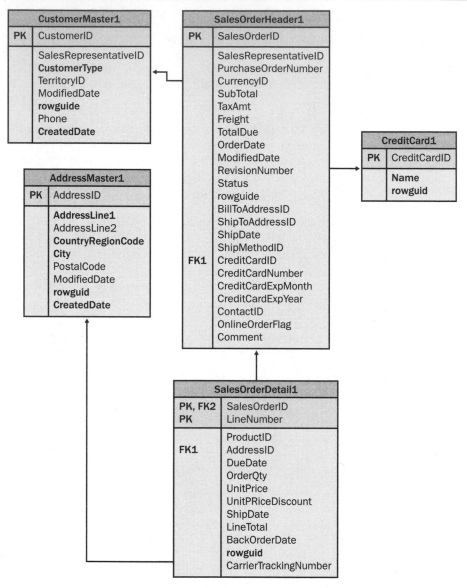

Figure 8.1.   Partial database schema for the Adventure Works Cycles system

Types of physical data models

In addition to defining the logical database design, you must select a technology for physically storing data. The physical data model of a *database management system* (DBMS) defines the internal structure that the DBMS uses to keep track of data. The structure reflects the types of database tables that you can create, as well as the speed of access and versatility of the database. The various types of physical data models that commonly exist are:

- *Flat-file.* A flat-file database stores all data in a single file as a set of rows and columns. There is no relationship between multiple flat-file databases because each database exists without knowledge of any other database. They can provide fast updates and retrieval because they support an indexing method called the *indexed sequential access method* (ISAM). Legacy mainframe databases, as well as smaller PC-based databases, implement ISAM storage technology.

- *Hierarchical.* Hierarchical databases store a wide range of information in a variety of formats. Therefore, they are extensible and flexible. You use this type of database when information storage requirements vary greatly. An example of a hierarchical database is Microsoft Exchange, which can store varying types of information in a format that facilitates messaging and collaboration applications that require many types of information to be encapsulated in messages.

- *Relational.* In a relational model database, data is stored in multiple tables and columns. Relational databases combine the advantages of both flat-file and hierarchical databases by providing good performance and flexibility of storage. The relational model tends to be the most popular because tables can be linked together with unique values. It is important to understand, however, that the other models are still in use and that developers who are working in enterprise environments will likely need to interface with one of these other types of databases at some time. The relational model focuses on storing data, retrieving data, and maintaining data integrity. Related items of data can be retrieved efficiently by using Structured Query Language (SQL), regardless of whether the items are stored in one table or in many tables. Data integrity is maintained by applying rules and constraints.

- *Object-oriented.* In an object-oriented database, database objects appear as programming language objects, in one or more existing programming languages. The *object-oriented database management system* (ODBMS) extends the language with transparently persistent data, concurrency control, data recovery, associative queries, and other database capabilities. You use an ODBMS if you need to store complex data and require high performance. Complex data is characterized by lack of natural, unique identification, many-to-many relationships, and frequent use of type codes as used in relational models.

At Adventure Works Cycles, the data storage technology currently being used is Microsoft SQL Server 7.0. After looking at the long-term requirements for data storage, the project team chose Microsoft SQL Server 9.0 for this solution. The completed application will convert the existing data store to allow for several improvements. Therefore, the physical model selected for the Adventure Works Cycles system is the relational model. The physical model reflects the target implementation environment.

How to Identify Entities and Attributes

In the logical design process, the project team analyzes use cases and usage scenarios to identify entities and attributes. These entities and attributes form the basis for logical design and are used in the physical design process to model the physical design of the solution. The logical design helps ensure that the data design for the solution represents and maps to the conceptual requirements. However, the actual structures that are used to store the data are optimized for the environment in which the physical data model will be implemented.

Guidelines for deriving entities

When identifying entities for the purpose of logical data design, keep in mind that entities are:

- Objects about which information will be stored. Some examples of entities are Product, Order, and Customer.

- The starting point for the logical data design. The identification of these entities is the first step in the design of a database.

- The equivalent of rows in one or more database tables. An instance of an entity corresponds to a row of a table.

Consider the following use cases:

```
Employee creates a contract with the client.
Employee reviews prior billings to the client.
```

Based on these use cases, you identify the following objects:

- *Employee.* The employee performs actions within the system.
- *Client.* Client is the recipient of actions that are performed by the employee.
- *Contract.* The agreement between the employee and the client.
- *Billings.* Invoices that the client has received for work performed.

In addition to being objects in the object model of the solution, the preceding entities are used in the logical data design. The database for the solution must store information for every instance of the Employee, Client, Contract, and Billings entities that are within the scope of the solution. Remember that the entity description helps determine relationships between the entities.

Characteristics of attributes

After identifying the entities, you must determine the attributes that you want to capture in the database. Attributes have the following characteristics:

- Attributes describe a solution entity. For example, the attributes of a car can include its color, make, model, and year of production. Although size is a characteristic of a car, it is not related to the solution and is not included as an attribute.

- Attributes exist only when attached to an entity. For example, the attribute of color does not describe anything tangible unless the color is applied to an object.

- Attributes define the columns in database tables. When the physical design is implemented, the attributes become the columns in the database tables. They are fully described by type, length, and any applicable relationships.

For example, the entity Client has the attributes account number, name, and address. You must store this information for each instance of the Client entity.

How to Identify Tables and Columns

During physical design, the outputs of logical design are used to produce components, user interface specifications, and physical database design. The entities, attributes, and constraints derived during logical design are mapped to tables, fields, relationships, and constraints in a database. This database physically represents the logical model.

Definition of tables

Tables are the physical representation of entities in a relational database. Tables can store a wide variety of data. A table can contain names, addresses, pictures, audio files, video files, Microsoft Word documents, and so on. Because of this flexibility, a database can be used to store not only simple text data, but also the knowledge base of a business, no matter what form that knowledge takes. A database represents the relationships between various data items.

The data in a table is stored in *rows*, or records. Each record must be unique. Records in a relational database can be manipulated by using Extensible Markup Language (XML). XML can be used to transmit data between databases, and different enterprises, without aligning the table structures of the two communicating databases.

A traditional method of manipulating relational data is by using the American National Standards Institute (ANSI) standard relational database language, which is referred to as SQL. SQL is an English-like language that abstracts the operations that are performed on a database into easily readable statements, such as Insert, Update, and Delete. Most databases adhere to the ANSI SQL standard, although the version and enhancements that are used vary from product to product.

Tip   Tables can be linked to other tables within the same database file. This capability allows one type of data to be joined to another type and allows data normalization.

Definition of columns

The data in each record is stored in *columns*, or fields, that are specified from the attributes of the table's defining entity. Each field contains one distinct item of data, such as a customer name.

Example of tables and columns

Consider the Adventure Works Cycles system. One of the entities in the system, *SalesOrderDetail,* maintains details about an order placed by a customer. The attributes of this entity include SalesOrderID, ProductID, AddressID, UnitPrice, and DueDate. Corresponding to this entity and its attributes, the Adventure Works Cycles database includes a table named SalesOrderDetail that contains the following columns: SalesOrderID, ProductID, AddressID, UnitPrice, and DueDate.

Purpose of data types

Data types specify the kind of data that is stored in a field. Every field within a database must have a data type. The data type allows you, and the database engine itself, to verify that a value entered in a field is valid for the information that the field represents. Remember that a valid data type does not ensure valid data. For example, an integer data type field can store numeric data. According to the business rules, the field values can range from 1 through 20. If a user inputs 25, the value is a valid entry by type but it is not valid data.

The data types that are allowed for a given field depend on the data types that are supported by the hosting DBMS. When defining your tables, choose data types that will optimize performance, conserve disk space, and allow for growth. Most DBMSs support two major classifications of data types:

- *System-supplied data types.* Every DBMS contains its own data types. Examples of system-supplied types are *Integer, Character*, and *Binary*. Some DBMSs contain variations of these types as well as additional types.

- *User-defined data types.* Some DBMSs allow you to define your own data types based on the system-supplied types. For example, in Microsoft SQL Server, you can define a state data type with a length of 2 that is based on the character data type. Defining this data type helps maintain conformity across all tables that include a state field. In every table, any field of state data type would be consistent and identical.

Table 8.1 shows a set of common data types, each of which is a variation on a generic character, number, or binary data type.

Table 8.1. Common Data Types

Data type	Description
Binary	Fixed or variable length binary data
String	Fixed or variable length character data
Date	Date and time data
Float	Floating point numeric data (from -1.79E+308 through 1.79E+308 in Microsoft SQL Server 2000)
Decimal	Fixed precision and scale numeric data (from $-10^{38} + 1$ through $10^{38} - 1$ in SQL Server 2000)

Table 8.1.   Common Data Types   *(continued)*

Data type	Description
Integer	Integer (whole number) data. Different DBMSs have different variations with upper limits at 255, 32,767, or 2,147,483,647
(Long) Integer	Integer value of longer ranges than the Integer type listed above
Monetary	Currency values with fixed scale
(Double) Float	Float value with double-precision data range over regular Float data type

Data types also specify how data is displayed. For example, fields of the Float, Money, and Integer data types all store numeric data. However, each type of data is stored, calculated, and displayed in a different format. Because their data is stored in different formats, different data types consume different amounts of storage space.

Note   The double variants of a data type can store a number that is twice as large or store a fraction to more decimal places, but they typically use twice as much storage space.

During physical design, you must consider the requirements of each data object and choose the smallest possible data type that will accommodate every possible value for that object or attribute. Each data storage technology—including Microsoft SQL Server, Oracle Database, Sybase Adaptive Server Enterprise, IBM DB2 and Informix, and the NCR Teradata Warehouse—defines its own data types.

Table 8.2 illustrates the columns and their data types, using SQL data types, of the ProductMaster table in the Adventure Works Cycles database.

Table 8.2.   ProductMaster Table

Columns	Data type	Allow nulls
ProductID	uniqueidentifier	Not allowed
Name	text	Not allowed
ProductNumber	text(25)	Allowed
DiscontinuedFlag	bit	Allowed
MakeFlag	bit	Not Allowed
StandardCost	money	Allowed
FinishedGoodsFlag	bit	Not Allowed
Color	text(15)	Allowed
CreatedDate	datetime	Not Allowed
ModifiedDate	datetime	Allowed
SafetyStockLevel	smallint	Allowed
ReorderPoint	smallint	Allowed

Table 8.2.   ProductMaster Table   *(continued)*

Columns	Data type	Allow nulls
ListPrice	money	Allowed
Size	text(50)	Allowed
SizeUnitMeasureCode	char(3)	Allowed
ProductPhotoID	int	Allowed
rowguid	LongBinary	Allowed
WeightUnitMeasureCode	char(3)	Allowed
Weight	float	Allowed
DaysToManufacture	int	Allowed
ProductLine	char(2)	Allowed
DealerPrice	money	Allowed
Class	char(2)	Allowed
Style	char(2)	Allowed
ProductDescriptionID	int	Allowed
ProductSubCategoryID	smallint	Allowed
ProductModelID	int	Allowed

Types of keys

Keys are an important part of a relational database. Keys uniquely identify each instance of an entity within the data model. Keys also provide the mechanism for tying entities together.

A relational database might use several types of keys:

- *Primary keys* that uniquely identify each row of data in a table. To assign the primary key of a table, identify the attribute that is unique for each instance of the entity. For example, SalesOrderID is unique for each order and is the primary key for the SalesOrderHeader table. In some cases, you might need to create a new attribute to accomplish this. Most DBMSs provide several mechanisms for creating primary keys, including auto-generation of unique identifiers and the ability to create *composite keys*, which enforces uniqueness across two columns, such as SalesOrderID and LineNumber in the SalesOrderDetail table).

Note   Another frequent practice is to use *smart keys*, in which the key has some relation to the domain data—for example, using BLDG001 to identify records in a table storing building information.

- *Foreign keys* that link two tables. For example, ProductID is a foreign key in the SalesOrderDetail table. The attribute ProductID is the primary key in the ProductMaster table and links the SalesOrderDetail and ProductMaster tables. This allows the SalesOrderDetail table to refer to a product by its unique ID, thereby avoiding redundant product data such as name and description in the two tables.

On the CD   For the complete database schema of the Adventure Works Cycles database, refer to Adventure Works Cycles Data Schema.vsd in the \SolutionDocuments\Chapter08 folder on the CD.

How to Implement Relationships

Various relationships can exist between database tables. Just as the entities and attributes that are identified during logical design are represented as tables and columns in physical design, the relationships that are identified during logical design must be represented in the database during physical design.

In the physical database design, you represent relationships between entities by adding the keys from one entity table to other entity tables so that the entities are bound together by the common key value.

A relationship can represent one of the following multiplicities:

- One-to-one relationship
- One-to-many relationship
- Many-to-many relationship

One-to-one relationship

In a *one-to-one relationship*, an instance of one entity is directly related to the corresponding instance of the other entity. For example, every department can have only one faculty member as the head of the department. In addition, a faculty member can be the head of only one department. If both entities are required for the relationship, the entities and their relationship can be represented in one of three ways:

- *As one table*. You can combine two entities into one table and use the primary keys as a composite key of the combined tables. The advantage of combining the entities into one table is that you do not need to maintain separate tables. This technique eliminates the need for query parsers to deal with a join condition. It also uses space storage more efficiently. The disadvantage is that if the relationship changes some time in the future, reversing this design decision might be costly.

- *As two tables.* You can keep each entity in its own table and add the primary key of one entity as a foreign key of the other entity. Often, there is an implied parent-child relationship between entities. In such situations, you should add the primary key of the parent entity as a foreign key in the child entity because the child entity needs the parent entity to exist. This arrangement forces the database to allow only unique entries in each key field and helps to ensure that each instance of one entity can relate to only one instance of the other entity.

- *As multiple tables.* If the relationship between the entities is optional and the parent entity can exist without a related instance of the child entity, you should create a separate table for each entity and use foreign keys to implement the relationship. For example, consider an organization that assigns cars to employees and provides insurance policies for both the driver and the car. There might be a situation when no car is assigned to an employee or a car has no assigned driver. In addition, the insurance policy might not exist as yet. Therefore, the relationship between the three entities is optional. You can use three tables and create a join table containing all three keys or implement two foreign keys in each table.

Figure 8.2 illustrates the one-to-one relationship between two tables.

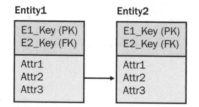

Figure 8.2. One-to-one relationship

One-to-many relationship

The physical design of a *one-to-many relationship* requires that you define tables for a parent entity such as Customer and a child entity such as Order, where many child entities can exist for each parent entity. It requires the use of foreign keys in the child entity that determines the existence of the relationship. Enforcing the relationship involves confirming that the foreign key is a valid parent entity.

Note   A one-to-many relationship is used frequently in data design because it tends to use storage space efficiently.

Figure 8.3 illustrates the one-to-many relationship between two tables.

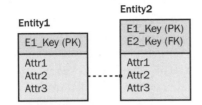

Figure 8.3. One-to-many relationship

Many-to-many relationships

Most relational database systems, including SQL Server, cannot directly represent a *many-to-many relationship*, except by using denormalization. (You will learn more about normalization in Lesson 2.) Many DBMSs work around this problem by using a new table, called a *join table*, to hold information that maintains the relationship between the entities.

In Figure 8.4, the Employee and Client entities have a many-to-many relationship. A single Employee can contract with many Clients, and a single Client can have contracts with many Employees. Because this relationship cannot be expressed directly, each entity's primary key is used as a foreign key in a separate Contracts table. This foreign key pair uniquely identifies the relationship between the Employee table and the Client table.

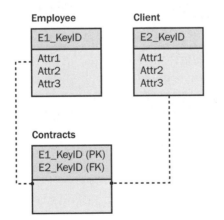

Figure 8.4. Many-to-many relationship

Lesson 2: Optimizing Data Access

The goal of optimization is to minimize the response time for each query and to maximize the throughput of the entire database server by minimizing network traffic, disk I/O, and processor time. This goal is achieved by understanding the application's requirements, the logical and physical structure of the data, and the trade-offs between conflicting uses of the database, such as a large number of write-intensive insertions and heavy read-intensive queries.

In this lesson, you will learn about the guidelines for optimizing data access. You will also learn about optimizing data access by indexing, partitioning, normalizing, and denormalizing data.

After this lesson, you will be able to

- List the best practices for optimizing data access.
- Describe the impact of indexing data.
- Describe the purpose of partitioning data.
- Describe the purpose of normalizing data.

Estimated lesson time: 10 minutes

What Are the Best Practices for Optimizing Data Access?

Performance issues should be considered throughout the development cycle and not at the end when the system is implemented. Data access performance affects the overall performance of the application. You can achieve significant performance improvements by optimizing both application and database design from the beginning.

Optimize the application

When you design an application that accesses a database, consider the following coding guidelines:

- Minimize roundtrip requests for result sets.
- Minimize the amount of data involved in a result set.
- Reduce concurrency (multiple users editing the same record) and resolve conflicts efficiently.
- Carefully evaluate the tradeoffs between managing data results on the client or on the server, especially for Web-based applications.

Stress test the application

The only way you can understand the behavior of your application is to run it under a moderate load with a test tool such as the Microsoft Web Application Stress tool, and then execute the application. You cannot adequately determine where bottlenecks exist in your application unless you test it under load. It is usually a better practice to stress test your application than it is to stress test your users.

Use transactions wisely

Transactions should be short-lived and incorporate only what is required. Distributed transactions require significant overhead that can adversely impact application performance. As such, they should be used only when necessary.

Communicate effectively across boundaries

Any cross-boundary communication that occurs between applications or processes adversely impacts performance. You can minimize this impact by minimizing the number of transitions that occur. For example, it is more efficient to call a method requiring six input parameters than it is to set six properties and then call the method. This design pattern promotes the use of a stateless business logic layer.

Optimize the database

The most commonly used techniques to optimize data access include:

- Indexing data
- Partitioning data
- Normalizing data

Note   You will learn about these techniques in detail in the next few topics in this lesson.

To remove bottlenecks while accessing and writing to the database, you can perform the following steps:

- Identify potential indexes, but do not index excessively.
- If using Microsoft SQL Server, use SQL Server Profiler and Index Tuning Wizard.
- Monitor total processor usage; desired range is 75 to 80 percent processor time.
- Analyze query plans by using Query Analyzer to optimize queries.
- Use stored procedures to maximize performance.
- Normalize data that is written frequently.
- Denormalize data that is read frequently.

How to Index Data

You need to optimize a system for both accessing and updating data. Indexing is one of the most commonly used techniques for optimizing data access. An *index* is an ordered list of rows in a table that a DBMS can use to accelerate lookup operations.

Purpose of an index

An index is structured like a tree and maintains a sorted list of a specific set of data. Queries performed on indexed data are much faster and more efficient than queries on data that is not indexed. Rather than scanning an entire table each time a value is needed, the DBMS can use the index to quickly lead the query to the direct location of the required data because the index records the location of the data in the table.

Benefits of indexing

Some of the benefits of indexing include:

- *Faster data access.* Indexes in databases are similar to indexes in books. In a book, an index allows you to find information quickly without reading the entire book. In a database, an index allows the DBMS to find data in a table without scanning the entire table.

- *Data integrity.* Some DBMSs allow indexes to ensure the uniqueness of each record of a table.

Types of indexes

To optimize retrieval of data, you can use two types of indexes:

- *Clustered.* A clustered index physically reorders the rows of data in the table to match the order of the index. It is a very high-performance index for read operations. A clustered index is usually defined as a table's primary index. (Most DBMSs allow only one clustered index per table.) For example, the SalesOrderDetail table uses the columns SalesOrderID and LineNumber as the clustered index. One limitation of clustered indexes is that they can slow down writes because rows might be physically rearranged frequently.

- *Nonclustered.* A nonclustered index simply maintains a small table of index information about a column or group of columns. A table can have many non-clustered indexes.

How to Partition Data

Often, the number of records stored in a table increases to a level at which data optimization techniques can no longer help improve data access speed. In such a situation, you must partition the tables. You can implement horizontal or vertical partitioning of large data tables to increase processing speed.

Horizontal partitioning

In *horizontal partitioning*, you divide a table containing many rows into multiple tables containing the same columns. However, each table contains a subset of the data. For example, one table might contain all customer names with last names beginning with the letters A through M, and another table contains all customer names with last names beginning with the letters N through Z.

Vertical partitioning

In *vertical partitioning*, you divide a table containing many columns into multiple tables containing rows with equivalent unique identifiers. For example, one table might contain read-only data, whereas the other table contains updateable data. In a large data environment, partitioning can extend across several database servers to further distribute the workload.

How to Normalize Data

Normalization is the process of progressively refining a logical model to eliminate duplicate data from a database. Normalization usually involves dividing a database into two or more tables and defining relationships among these tables.

Database theorists have evolved standards of increasingly restrictive constraints, or *normal forms*, on the layout of databases. Applying these normal forms results in a normalized database. These standards have generated at least five commonly accepted normal form levels, each progressively more restrictive on data duplication than the preceding one.

Tip   Typically, you work toward achieving the third normal form because it is a compromise between too little normalization and too much.

Benefits of normalization

Normalized databases typically include more tables with fewer columns than non-normalized databases. Normalizing a database accomplishes the following:

- Minimized duplication of information

  A normalized database contains less duplicate information than a non-normalized database. For example, you need to store timesheet and invoice information in a database. Storing timesheet information in the Invoice table would eventually cause this table to include a large amount of redundant data, such as employee, job, task, and client information. Normalizing the database results in separate, related tables for timesheets and invoices, thus avoiding duplication.

- Reduced data inconsistencies

  Normalization reduces data inconsistencies by maintaining table relationships. For example, if a client's telephone number is stored in multiple tables or in multiple records within the same table, and the number changes, the telephone number might not be changed in all locations. If a client's telephone number is stored only once in one table, there is minimal chance of data inconsistency.

- Faster data modification, including insertions, updates, and deletions

  Normalization speeds up the data modification process in a database. For example, removing client names and address information from the Invoice table results in less data to track and manipulate when working with an invoice. The removed data is not lost because it still exists in the Client table. Additionally, reducing duplicated information improves performance during updates because fewer values must be modified in the tables.

Note   Normalization can reduce performance for write operations due to locking conflicts and the potential of increased row sizes after the write.

The first normal form

The first step in normalizing a database is to ensure that the tables are in first normal form. To accomplish this step, the tables must adhere to the following criteria:

- Tables must be two-dimensional and have data organized as columns and rows. Entities specified in the logical data model are transformed into database tables represented in a two-dimensional table, similar to a spreadsheet.
- Each cell must contain one value.
- Each column must have a single meaning. For example, you cannot have a dual-purpose column such as Order Date/Delivery Date.

Figure 8.5 shows the Timesheet table, which was not originally in first normal form. The original Timesheet table had no unique identifier and not all of its attributes were singularly tied to one piece of information. Also, each column in the Timesheet table could have multiple meanings. In the first normal form, the Employee attribute can be divided into two distinct attributes: EmployeeFirstName and EmployeeLastName.

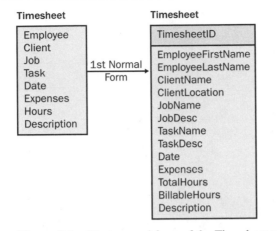

Figure 8.5.   First normal form of the Timesheet table

The second normal form

The second normal form is a bridge process that eventually leads to the third normal form. To move a data design to second normal form, you must look at several instances of an entity and move any redundant data within an entity's attributes to a separate table.

- Eliminate redundant data within an entity.
- Move attributes that depend on only part of a multivalue key to a separate table.
- Consolidate information when possible.

Figure 8.6 shows the Timesheet table. If a client moves to a different city, the client database must be updated, as well as every timesheet that references that client. The solution is to remove the client information from the Timesheet table and replace the information in the Timesheet table with a ClientID foreign key that corresponds to the ClientID primary key of the Clients table. The Timesheet table can then find the client's name and address by means of the foreign key relationship. When the address of a client changes, the change is recorded in the Client table only. Similarly, the second normal form replaces the employee information with an EmployeeID foreign key that links the timesheet to the individual employee who enters information into the timesheet. The second normal form also eliminates any other duplicate information. The JobName and JobDesc attributes have been replaced with a single attribute, JobDesc, because the job description would likely contain the job name. This logic also applies to the TaskName and TaskDesc attributes.

Timesheet

TimesheetID
EmployeeFirstName EmployeeLastName ClientName ClientLocation JobName JobDesc TaskName TaskDesc Date Expenses TotalHours BillableHours Description

2nd Normal Form →

Timesheet

TimesheetID
EmployeeID *ClientID* JobDesc Date Expenses TotalHours BillableHours Description

Figure 8.6. Second normal form of the Timesheet table

The third normal form

Third normal form is the level to which most design teams strive to normalize their data designs. Third normal form eliminates any columns that do not depend on a key value for their existence. Any data not directly related to the entity is generally moved to another table. Third normal form is generally the final form that you should implement.

- Eliminate any columns that do not depend on a key value for their existence.
- Generally, move any data not directly related to the entity to another table.
- Reduce or eliminate update and deletion anomalies.
- Verify that no redundant data remains.

Third normal form helps to avoid update and deletion anomalies because all data can be reached by means of foreign key values, and redundant data within each table no longer exists. This level of normalization greatly increases database robustness and generates a more optimized design.

Figure 8.7 shows the Timesheet entity that has been normalized to third normal form. All attributes that do not depend on the primary key have been moved into separate tables, and foreign keys now take the place of unrelated data. This form, like second normal form, further eliminates update and deletion anomalies because all data can be directly referenced from one point, instead of residing in multiple tables within the database.

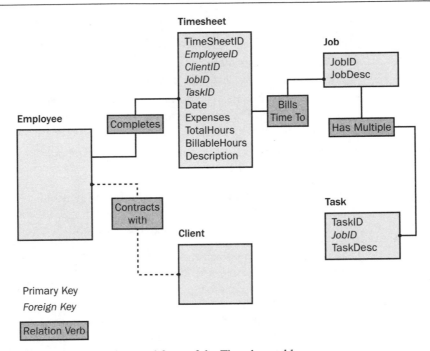

Figure 8.7.   Third normal form of the Timesheet table

Denormalization of Tables

Optimizing the physical data design for updates is a common practice. In many systems, data changes frequently, and having a system optimized for this activity is important.

A database design that is based solely on normalization rules produces a large number of narrow tables. This design technique reduces data redundancy and decreases the number of pages on disk that are required to store the data. However, complex joins are required to retrieve data.

Denormalization is the process of reversing normalization to generate tables with more fields that require fewer joins. Depending on the type of queries and updates that are being performed on the database, denormalization can dramatically increase its overall performance. For this reason, denormalization is a common optimization technique even though some DBMS systems include an optimizer that enables joins to be performed efficiently.

When deciding whether to use denormalization as an optimization technique, keep the following issues in mind:

- The data becomes more redundant. Related data is moved into one table to increase query performance and reduce disk access times.

- The number of tables is reduced, which makes query programming and administration easier. The disadvantage is that the data is located in fewer places, thus creating tables with more fields and possibly duplicating data across tables.

- Data that appears in more than one place can get out of synchronization if it is updated in one table and not others.

Although there are tradeoffs between a highly normalized physical data design and an intelligently denormalized design, a strategy of selective and intelligent denormalization most often results in the greatest performance gains.

Data that is over-normalized can cause performance issues in certain types of applications and can adversely affect read and write operations. Normalizing the ER model is a major step in creating the logical database design. The goal of normalization is to ensure that there is only one way to know a fact. It eliminates redundancy in the data and ensures that the correct business rules are recorded. The logical database design is implementation-independent—without details of a specific DBMS. However, for this discussion, a relational model is assumed.

During physical design, the database team must consider the following:

- Physical database constraints, such as memory and disk size.
- Performance tuning considerations, such as deadlock detection, indexing, and hot spots.
- Primary keys and foreign keys.
- Design of triggers.
- Stored procedures guidelines.
- Normalization. Although the third normal form is often appropriate, evaluate fourth and fifth normal forms if justified by the target data.
- Application object model considerations. Some tables that do not appear in the logical data model might be required to support the application.
- Data migration from any legacy database systems.
- Quality of existing data.
- Operational considerations, such as cluster/failover, backup process, and update/deployment process.

Lesson 3: Implementing Data Validation

In addition to the performance of the database, you need to ensure the quality of the data stored by the database. This means that the database implements data integrity and stores valid data that conforms to the business rules.

In this lesson, you will learn about data integrity requirements of the solution. You will also learn how to identify business rules and implement them in the database and the business layer.

After this lesson, you will be able to

- Define data integrity.
- Identify data integrity requirements.
- Identify business rules.
- Implement business rules in a database.
- Implement business rules as components.

Estimated lesson time: 15 minutes

What Is Data Integrity?

Data integrity refers to the consistency and accuracy of data. An important step in database planning is deciding how to ensure this integrity. You can implement three types of data integrity in a database: domain, entity, and referential.

Domain integrity

Domain integrity specifies a set of valid data values for a column and determines whether null values are to be allowed. You can enforce domain integrity by implementing validity checking and restricting the data type, format, or range of possible values that are allowed in a column. For example, you must store discount rates. According to business rules, the discount rate must be between 2 percent and 18 percent. In addition, the discount rate cannot be zero because it causes errors in calculations.

Entity integrity

Entity integrity requires that each row in a table has a unique identifier, known as the *primary key value*. Whether the primary key value can be changed, or whether an entire row can be deleted, depends on the level of referential integrity that is required between the primary key of the table and the foreign keys of any other tables. For example, a customer record must have a primary key. If there is a business need for the key to be changed, such as a merger, or for the record to be inactivated but not deleted, the business rules determine your choices in entity and referential integrity.

When used together, domain and entity integrity help to ensure that each entity in a physical design maintains consistency. When planning for databases in your design, you must consider consistency among entities and data validity within the entities as important additional aspects of data integrity.

Referential integrity

The domain and entity integrity categories suffice for enforcing data integrity in a single table. However, many databases contain multiple tables with parent and child entities and are related. When both entities in a relationship must exist and must have a valid link with one another, *referential integrity* ensures that these conditions are met. Referential integrity ensures that the relationships between the primary keys (in the parent entity's table) and foreign keys (in the child entity's table) are always maintained.

As a result of the restrictions that referential integrity imposes on tables, it is important that you consider what to do when a primary key must be updated or deleted. If the primary key value in the parent entity is changed or deleted, the instance of that entity is modified. Consequently, all child entities that referenced the parent entity must be modified as appropriate. By cascading through all related child tables and updating or deleting data as necessary, the database can maintain referential integrity.

Data validation

It is important to have valid data. Domain, entity, and referential integrity ensure that data exists where necessary and that entities follow a basic set of rules for existence. None of these data integrity categories, however, can determine whether the data is valid. You can ensure that the data is correct by checking it using the following methods:

- *Range checking* involves making sure that the data's value is within a set of limits determined by the functional specification.
- *Data format checking* involves making sure that the data conforms to a set of format specifications, such as currency formatting, telephone number formatting, or length-of-character strings.
- *Data type checking* involves making sure that the data belongs to the proper data type and that an invalid data type is not used to represent the data when it is written to the database.

To ensure that queries return correct information, you must make sure that the information being stored is valid. You can validate data in two ways:

- *Client-side checks* can ensure that invalid data is not posted to a database. These checks can be coded in many ways, including in scripts, in the user interface controls, as part of an executable program, or as part of a Web page. For example, if a field on a Web page denotes a monetary value, validation controls on the page can ensure that the information in that field is the proper data type and format.
- *Server-side checks*, which are executed by the DBMS engine, can be implemented with field data types, default values, and constraints. These checks can also ensure that invalid data is not stored in the database.

The methods or combination of methods that you use depends on the objectives and requirements of the solution. Although more difficult to maintain than server-side checks, client-side checks can help decrease the processing load on the DBMS server. Server-side checks might present a bottleneck if the server has to validate many client requests. Remember that a strong test process is needed to verify that the business rules have been correctly implemented while maintaining a high quality of user experience.

How to Identify Data Integrity Requirements

Identifying data integrity requirements helps ensure that all logical and physical requirements for a solution are met and that the physical design supports the full intent of your specification.

When attempting to identify the data integrity requirements of a solution, you must start with the data requirements specified during the solution's design. When you examine the data requirements, identify areas within the requirements in which uniqueness, or limits and constraints, has been specified or deemed necessary to help ensure that entities can exist and be implemented correctly.

If limits and constraints are specified, you must determine whether the limits and constraints are bound to an entity or to a relationship between entities. Consider the following examples:

- You need to determine whether a particular task can exist without a related job number. If it cannot exist without a job number, you must implement a data integrity requirement to ensure that no instance of that task is created without a corresponding job number.
- A consultant must submit a weekly timesheet for a client. No timesheet can duplicate another timesheet, and no two timesheets can represent the same time or work performed by a consultant. Therefore, a data integrity requirement exists for guaranteeing the uniqueness of timesheet information. Each timesheet within the database must be represented by a unique attribute or a combination of unique attributes.

Finally, you must implement referential integrity requirements to ensure that all relationships are maintained. For example, if a customer wants to be removed from the database, a referential integrity requirement must ensure that the customer cannot be deleted as long as payment has not been received for any outstanding invoices.

How to Identify Business Rules

Business rules form a foundation for encapsulating logic from the data requirements into the solution. Business rules represent logic specified within a solution.

The data development team already identified many of the business rules for the solution while identifying requirements. The team must reexamine the solution's data requirements for the criteria that the data integrity rules must satisfy. The team should also review any existing process documentation, use cases, and usage scenarios to identify the data-centric processes that are currently being executed and the processes that must be executed in the future.

While identifying business rules, consider the following criteria:

- *Conditions that must be satisfied for data to be considered valid.* For example, issues that you might consider when determining applicable business rules include whether a product can be shipped to a customer if no payment has been received.

- *Conditions that must be avoided.* For example, issues you might consider include whether product pricing can drop below certain levels or whether inventory levels for products can drop below zero.

- *Sequences in which events must occur.* For example, you must determine what to do when an inventory product drops below zero or when payment for an order is received.

You can implement business rules and data integrity requirements by using the following methods:

- *Directly in the database.* Most DBMSs provide automated processes that can be bound to tables and columns to enforce business rules and data integrity requirements.

- *Programmatically within or outside the database.* You can code business rules and data integrity requirements into client applications, create components that can be deployed on application servers, or use programming logic and languages that are part of the database engine.

The primary distinction between these two methods is that the former involves rules that are automatically processed by the database engine, whereas the latter involves rules that must be called or invoked by an application's logic.

Determining where to implement rules is often based on the nature of the required programming logic. Most relational database engines now execute automatic methods that incorporate simple and commonly required application logic. This logic applies to specific business rule tasks and resides in a single location. It is also easily updated and efficient to execute. If more complex logic is required, it can be implemented as application code that can reside in any of the three service layers: user, business, or data.

How to Implement Business Rules in a Database

If you choose to implement business rules directly in the database, the DBMS performs much of the work for you by using its automatic and built-in checks.

Within the database engine, business rules and data integrity requirements can be enforced through a set of criteria that data must either meet or not meet. Usually, most of the data integrity requirements are implemented by using the automatic controls and properties of the database engine. This automatic control involves the specification, or declaration, of the criteria at the time an object (such as a field, table, index, or key) is created.

Database features for implementing business rules

Enforcing data integrity through built-in database features has some distinct benefits: integrity is enforced automatically, and the criteria do not have to be maintained or updated unless they change. You can use the following database features to enforce data integrity:

- *Data types*. Setting appropriate data types for the fields in a database ensures that incorrect types of data cannot be added to the table. For example, if a data type of Date is specified, the database rejects any string or numeric value that is not in a date format. Data types ensure that the format of the data is valid, but it cannot ensure that the value is valid.

- *Default values*. Default values specify the values to be used for a field when the values have not been explicitly supplied in INSERT statements. By using default values in your table definitions, you can ensure that a field value is valid even when a user does not explicitly supply it.

- *Data validation rules*. Data validation rules encapsulate logic for specifying data values that are acceptable in a table's fields. They can specify the length of a field, an input mask, or a range of valid values. For example, you can use data validation rules for making simple comparisons.

- *Keys*. Most database engines can automatically monitor referential integrity between tables. The primary and foreign key relationships from the physical model directly correspond to the database engine's key settings. These key settings automatically enforce referential integrity between linked tables.

- *Triggers*. Triggers are sets of programmatic statements that are explicitly defined for a particular table. When a specific action (such as an insert, update, or delete) occurs in that table, the trigger causes the statements to automatically run. For example, a trigger can verify data in other tables or perform an automatic update to a different table.

Programmatic implementation of business rules

The team's analysis will determine that certain business rules are best implemented in the business layer and others in the data layer. You can implement business rules programmatically in the data layer by using the following methods:

- *Stored procedures*. Stored procedures are named collections of SQL statements that are stored on the DBMS. They are precompiled, eliminating the need for the query analyzer to parse the statement every time the stored procedure is called. By using stored procedures, you can write one piece of code that performs an action, store it, and call it repeatedly as necessary.

  Stored procedures are useful for controlling changes to a table. For example, instead of granting a user update rights to a specific table, you can allow updates to the table only through stored procedures. You can then determine whether the modifications are valid and then either disregard or apply the change.

  The flow of a process can also be handled through the use of stored procedures. For example, you can change or reorder several tables by using a stored procedure. You can also use stored procedures to perform administrative tasks.

- *Scripts*.   Typically, you write a script in a database to automate a process that is either impractical or inefficiently handled by the DBMS engine. For example, you might write a script that maintains a database by importing a series of mainframe downloads, re-indexing the database, and then copying a report file to another file server.

The script logic can be written in any of several languages. Each script executes outside the memory space of the DBMS and might perform more tasks than simply manipulating data. Scripts are generally used in a command-line environment or as part of a batch process that performs other tasks.

How to Implement Data Validation in Components

In a multitier application, a data service acts as an intermediary between the application's business services and its data store. Therefore, if there are any changes to the data store, the application's business services do not need to be changed. Data services perform basic tasks such as creating, retrieving, updating, and deleting data. Data services are also used to manipulate data within the database and to implement data integrity. You can design and develop components to implement data services in an application.

Components are executable collections of code that reside on a server or within another program. Components are similar to scripts, but allow for tighter integration with development environments, database engines, and custom code.

You can enforce data integrity through logic that is encapsulated in a component and is called or invoked as needed. The criteria for the logic are determined by the business rules, including any additional data integrity requirements that have been identified for the solution.

Typically, components are deployed on application servers, on a separate computer. Some of the benefits of deploying components on application servers include:

- *Easier maintenance.* Because the code is stored in only one or a few locations, it is much easier to maintain than if it were included in the application itself. The increased cost of an application server might be offset by the maintainability of the system. Any necessary changes can be made on only one or a few computers, as opposed to possibly thousands of clients.
- *Scalability.* As the load on the system increases, additional application servers can be added to distribute the load.

Implementing business rules by using components can increase the overall cost of the solution. The added cost is associated not only with the hardware and software of the computers serving as the application server, but also in the development costs of creating and maintaining the code that will serve the data access requests.

Activity: Creating a Data Schema

In this activity, you use what you learned in the lesson to create a data schema.

Exercise 1: Creating a Data Schema

This exercise builds on the Adventure Works Cycles scenario. Customers of Adventure Works Cycles use the Sales Order form to order products. Some of the considerations for order processing are:

- The customer provides a purchase order number to start an order.
- An order can be revised.
- Discounts are applied per item in an order.

You need to design a data schema for capturing all information in the Sales Order form. The data schema should include:

- One or more tables that store order-related data
- Primary and foreign keys
- Data types for all columns
- Indexes
- Fields needed for data or business requirements

To get started with this exercise, use the data schema that is provided on the P08 Schema Starter tab in the file C08Ex1.vsd in the \SolutionDocuments\Chapter08 folder on the CD. To view the Sales Order form, open the file C08Ex1.doc in the \SolutionDocuments\Chapter08 folder on the CD.

You can view one of the probable solutions to this exercise in the file C08Ex1_ShortAnswer.vsd in the \SolutionDocuments\Chapter08 folder on the CD. You can also design a detailed data schema as illustrated in the file C08Ex1_LongAnswer.vsd in the \SolutionDocuments\Chapter08 folder on the CD. To view the data schema for the complete Adventure Works Cycles system, open the file Adventure Works Cycles Data Schema.vsd in the \SolutionDocs\Chapter08 folder on the CD.

Summary

- In the planning phase, the project team analyzes the data requirements of the solution and specifies how data will be structured, stored, accessed, and validated in the solution.
- A database schema reflects the entities of the problem, attributes of the entities, and the relationships between entities.
- The physical data model of a DBMS defines the internal structure that the DBMS uses to keep track of data.
- The three physical data models that are typically used are flat files, the hierarchical model, and the relational model.
- The entities and attributes that are derived during logical design are mapped to tables, fields, and relationships in a database.
- Tables are the physical representation of entities in a relational database.
- Columns are the physical representation of attributes in a relational database.
- Data types specify the kind of data that is stored in a field and how the data is displayed.
- Keys uniquely identify each instance of an entity within the data model.
- Primary keys uniquely identify each row of data in a table.
- Foreign keys link two tables in a database.
- Relationships between entities are represented by adding the keys of one entity table to other entity tables.
- To optimize the performance of a database, you need to:
  - Optimize your database.
  - Stress test the application.
  - Use transactions wisely.
  - Communicate effectively across borders.
- An index is an ordered list of rows in a table that a DBMS can use to accelerate lookup operations.
- You can optimize processing speed of huge tables by partitioning data, either vertically or horizontally.
- In horizontal partitioning, you segment a table containing a large number of rows into multiple tables containing the same columns.
- In vertical partitioning, you segment a table containing a large number of columns into multiple tables containing rows with equivalent unique identifiers.
- Normalization is the process of progressively refining a logical model to eliminate duplicate data and wasted space from a database.

- Normalization results in reduced data inconsistencies and faster data modification.

- Denormalization is the process of reversing normalization to generate tables with more fields that require fewer joins, which can improve query processing.

- Data integrity refers to the consistency and accuracy of data.

- Domain integrity specifies a set of legitimate data values for a column and determines whether null values are to be allowed.

- Entity integrity requires that each row in a table has a unique identifier, known as the primary key value.

- Referential integrity ensures that the relationships between the primary keys (in the parent entity's table) and foreign keys (in the child entity's table) are always maintained.

- Identifying data integrity requirements helps ensure that all logical and physical requirements for a solution are met and that the physical design supports the full intent of your specification.

- Identifying business rules includes identifying conditions that must be met, conditions that must be avoided, and sequences in which events must occur.

- You can implement business rules in a database by using the built-in checks of the DBMS engine, such as data types, data validation rules, default values, keys, and triggers.

- You can implement business rules in a database programmatically by using stored procedures and scripts.

- You can implement business rules by using components that are deployed on application servers.

Review

The following questions are intended to reinforce key information presented in this chapter. If you are unable to answer a question, review the lesson materials and try the question again. You can find answers to the questions in the appendix.

1. How is the data model designed during the planning phase?

2. What is the purpose of the database schema?

3. What are the characteristics of attributes?

4. What is the purpose of specifying data types in a database?

5. How do most DBMSs support a many-to-many relationship?

6. How do you optimize transactions for good system performance?

7. What is the impact of indexing on data access?

8. What is the difference between horizontal and vertical partitioning?

9. What are the benefits of normalization?

10. What is denormalization?

11. What are the three types of data integrity that can be enforced in a database?

12. How do you identify data integrity requirements?

13. What are the criteria for identifying business rules?

14. How do keys implement referential integrity?

15. What are the benefits of using components to implement business rules?

C H A P T E R 9

Designing Security Specifications

About This Chapter

In this chapter, you will learn how to design security in an application. Designing security features and policies is one of the most important aspects of application development. As the amount of money that is spent on securing corporate networks increases, so do the losses that are accrued by businesses in terms of stolen intellectual property, system downtime, lost productivity, damage to reputation, and lost consumer confidence. It is possible, however, to defend your business applications in this hostile environment by adding the appropriate authentication and authorization schemes, ensuring data integrity with encryption, and performing data validation.

Before You Begin

To complete the lessons in this chapter, you must have

- A general understanding of Microsoft® technologies.
- Familiarity with security concepts.

Lesson 1: Overview of Security in Application Development

You can secure your application by employing several security mechanisms, such as firewalls, proxies, secure channels, and authentication schemes. However, all it takes for a security breach to occur is for an attacker to find one weakness in your system. In this lesson, you will learn about some common security weaknesses in applications and how some malicious users exploit these security weaknesses. You will also learn about some drawbacks of the traditional security models. You will then learn about some important principles of secure coding.

After this lesson, you will be able to

- Identify some of the common security vulnerabilities of applications.
- Identify some of the drawbacks of traditional security models.
- Explain some of the security principles for designing secure applications.
- Define some security terms.

Estimated lesson time: 15 minutes

Common Types of Security Vulnerabilities

Malicious attackers use various methods to exploit system vulnerabilities to achieve their goals. Vulnerabilities are weak points or loopholes in security that an attacker exploits to gain access to an organization's network or to resources on the network. Some vulnerabilities, such as weak passwords, are not the result of application or software development design decisions. However, it is important for an organization to be aware of such security weaknesses to better protect its systems. Common vulnerabilities of applications include:

- *Weak passwords.* A weak password might give an attacker access not only to a computer, but to the entire network to which the computer is connected.
- *Misconfigured software.* Often the manner in which software is configured makes the system vulnerable. If services are configured to use the local system account or are given more permissions than required, attackers can exploit the services to gain access to the system and perform malicious actions on the system.
- *Social engineering,* A common form of discovering passwords that generally occurs when users are not aware of security issues and can be deceived into revealing their passwords. For example, an attacker posing as a help desk administrator might persuade a user to reveal his or her password under the pretext of performing an administrative task.

- *Internet connections.* The default installation of Internet Information Services (IIS) version 5.0 often enables more services and ports than are necessary for the operation of a specific application. These additional services and ports provide more opportunities for potential attacks. For example, modem connections bypass firewalls that protect networks from outside intruders. If an intruder can identify the modem telephone number and password, the intruder can connect to any computer on the network.

- *Unencrypted data transfer.* If the data sent between a server and the users is in clear text, there is a possibility that the data can be intercepted, read, and altered during transmission by an attacker.

- *Buffer overrun.* Malicious users probe applications looking for ways to trigger a buffer overrun because they can use a buffer overrun to cause an application or an operating system to crash. They can then find more security weaknesses by reading error messages.

- *SQL injection.* SQL injection occurs when developers dynamically build SQL statements by using user input. The attacker can modify the SQL statement and make it perform operations that were not intended.

- *Secrets in code.* Many security problems are created when a malicious user is able to find secrets that are embedded in code, such as passwords and encryption keys.

More Info   For more information about security issues, refer to the *Microsoft Windows Security Resource Kit* (Microsoft Press, 2003).

Drawbacks of Traditional Security Models

Traditional security models do not adequately meet the security challenges presented by the networked computing environment. Most traditional security models restrict access to resources based on the identity of the user who is running the code. There is no specific mechanism in this model to restrict resources based on the identity of the code.

Security that is based on user identity is circumvented if a trusted user unknowingly runs malicious code. A trusted user can inadvertently launch malicious code by:

- Opening an e-mail attachment.
- Running a script that is embedded on a Web page.
- Opening a file that was downloaded from the Internet.

Principles for Creating Security Strategies

To design a secure application, you should be familiar with the following principles of security and employ them when creating security strategies:

- *Rely on tested and proven security systems.* Whenever possible, you should rely on tested and proven security systems rather than creating your own custom solution. Use industry-proven algorithms, techniques, platform-supplied infrastructure, and vendor-tested and supported technologies. If you decide to develop a custom security infrastructure, validate your approach and techniques with expert auditing and security review organizations before and after implementing them.

- *Never trust external input.* You should validate all data that is entered by users or submitted by other services.

- *Assume that external systems are not secure.* If your application receives unencrypted sensitive data from an external system, assume that the information is compromised.

- *Apply the principle of least privilege.* Do not enable more attributes on service accounts than those minimally needed by the application. Access resources with accounts that have the minimal permissions required.

- *Reduce available components and data.* Risk will increase with the number of components and amount of data you have made available through the application, so you should make available only the functionality that you expect others to use.

- *Default to a secure mode.* Do not enable services, account rights, and technologies that you do not explicitly need. When you deploy the application on client or server computers, its default configuration should be secure.

- *Do not rely on security by obscurity.* Encrypting data implies having keys and a proven encryption algorithm. Secure data storage will prevent access under all circumstances. Mixing up strings, storing information in unexpected file paths, and so on, is not security.

- *Follow STRIDE principles.* Each letter in the STRIDE acronym specifies a different category of security threat: spoofing identity, tampering, repudiation, information disclosure, denial of service, and elevation of privilege. These are classes of security vulnerabilities a system needs to protect itself against.

More Info   For more information about security practices, see *Writing Secure Code* by Michael Howard and David LeBlanc (Microsoft Press, 2002).

Lesson 2: Planning for Application Security

Before you start planning for security features in an application, you must understand the kinds of threats an application is likely to encounter so that you can specify and develop the appropriate security features. Planning for security in applications involves the following tasks:

- *Identify the threats to the application (Threat modeling).* This is the most important task in planning for security. Without first identifying the threats, the security policies cannot be determined. When assessing threats to your application, gather the following information:
    - What are the assets of the organization that need to be protected?
    - What are the threats to each of the assets?
- *Create a security policy to prevent or minimize the threat.* After most of the threats are identified, you need to categorize these threats and define a strategy for each type of threat. You will learn more about mitigation techniques later in this lesson.

    You can use various techniques to identify and categorize threats. One commonly used technique of identifying threats is STRIDE. In this lesson, you will learn about threat modeling with STRIDE.

After this lesson, you will be able to

- Identify the security tasks performed during various stages of the Microsoft Solutions Framework (MSF) design process.
- Explain threat modeling.
- Create a threat model.
- Use the threat model to respond to a threat.

Estimated lesson time: 15 minutes

Security in the Application Development Process

Application security fails most often because security is not planned from the very beginning of product design. If you wait to think about security until the late phases of development, security will be less effective and development and maintenance costs will be higher.

The planning and implementation of security features should persist throughout product development. Table 9.1 shows each phase in the MSF Process Model and the corresponding security initiative.

Table 9.1.   Security Initiatives and the MSF Process Model

Phase	Security initiative
Envisioning	Gather security requirements. The team talks to the customers and stakeholders to learn about sensitive data and operations, privileges each user needs, and how the application currently manages these security requirements. From this information, security requirements are established and listed in the requirements document.
Planning	Create a threat model, discussed in the What Is the STRIDE Threat Model? section, to anticipate security threats. In the functional specification, propose security features that mitigate each identified risk.
Developing	Implement security features as identified in the functional specification.
Stabilizing	Conduct security testing. Revise the threat model if new information about threats is uncovered by research, testing, and customer feedback.
Deploying	Monitor security threats to an application.

After the solution is released to the customer, security and any attacks to the solution are monitored to ensure that the product remains secure. If any breaches occur, the problem is resolved and the circumstances are noted for the next version of the product.

What Is the STRIDE Threat Model?

The STRIDE threat model is a technique used for identifying and categorizing threats to an application. Each letter in the STRIDE acronym specifies a different category of security threat: spoofing identity, tampering, repudiation, information disclosure, denial of service, and elevation of privilege. Most security threats combine more than one element of the STRIDE model:

- **Spoofing identity**   A malicious user poses as a trusted entity. For example, a malicious user might obtain the password of a trusted user to gain access to restricted materials or to send an e-mail message that appears to come from a trusted source.

Note   IP spoofing is a special case of spoofing identity. It happens when a malicious user inserts a false Internet Protocol (IP) address into an Internet transmission so that the transmission appears to originate from a trusted source. In this way, the malicious user can gain unauthorized access to a computer system.

- **Tampering**   A user gains unauthorized access to a computer and then changes its operation, configuration, or data. Tampering can be either malicious or accidental. For example, accidental tampering can occur when users inadvertently delete files on a network or change a database that they should not have permission to change.

- **Repudiation**   A system administrator or security agent is unable to prove that a user—malicious or otherwise—has performed some action. For example, a malicious user can repudiate having attacked a system because the system did not adequately log events leading to the attack.

- **Information disclosure**   An unauthorized user views private data, such as a file that contains a credit card number and expiration date.

- **Denial of service**   Any attack that attempts to shut down or prevent access to a computing resource. Denial-of-service (DoS) attacks can cause:

  - An application or the operating system to stop functioning

  - The CPU to engage in long, pointless calculations

  - System memory to be consumed so that the functioning of applications and the operating system is impaired

  - Network bandwidth reduction

- **Elevation of privilege**   A user gains access to greater privileges than the administrator intended, creating the opportunity for a malicious user to launch attacks of every other category of security threat.

How to Create a Threat Model

Creating a threat model is a first step in building a secure application. This process involves the following tasks:

1. Arrange for a brainstorming meeting.

   Invite experienced developers and members of every MSF role to the brainstorming session to identify potential threats.

2. List all the possible threats.

   During the brainstorming meeting, provide participants with a proposed list of features and describe the architecture of the product. Instruct the participants to think of threats that might occur between application components and to connections between your application and other systems.

3. Apply the STRIDE security categories.

   After you create an initial listing of possible security threats, use the STRIDE threat model to categorize the threats.

4. Create notes.

For each security threat, your group should create a note that includes the following information:

- Type of threat
- Impact of the attack to the organization in terms of cost and effort
- The technique that will be used by the attacker to carry out the threat
- The likelihood of the attack taking place
- Possible techniques to mitigate this attack

5. Conduct research.

Inevitably, factual and technical questions will be raised during the brainstorming process. If you conduct your meeting in a facility that can access the Internet, you might be able to resolve research questions during the meeting.

6. Rank the risk of each threat.

Assign each threat a risk rank by dividing the criticality of the threat by its chance of occurrence.

Example

Figure 9.1 depicts a Web-based expense report application. You will create a threat model for this application.

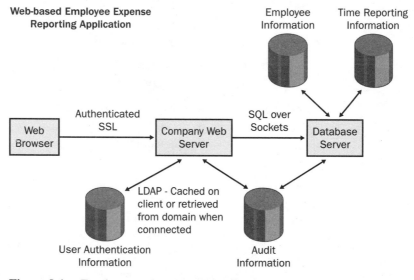

Figure 9.1. Employee expense report application

Threats and their categories

Table 9.2 lists possible threats to the expense report application that were identified during a brainstorming meeting. It also lists their categorization based on the STRIDE model.

Table 9.2.   Threats to the Expense Report Application.

Threat	Category
The time reporting and employee information databases are vulnerable to direct access, which could allow unauthorized users to view and modify confidential data such as historical data.	T, I
The database server can become unavailable if it is flooded with Transmission Control Protocol/Internet Protocol (TCP/IP) packets.	D
Audit logs can be viewed, modified, and deleted by unauthorized users or applications.	T, R
Lightweight Directory Access Protocol (LDAP) authentication packets can be intercepted and viewed. Based on the information in each packet, the perpetrator might be able to figure out how to impersonate another user on the system. For example, the perpetrator might be a computer operator but might be able to act as the chief financial officer.	S, I, E
The data that is exchanged between the Web browser and the Web server is vulnerable to being viewed by an unauthorized user. This might compromise sensitive information such as passwords, employee IDs, employee information, salary information, and time reporting information.	T, I
The Web server can be become unavailable. If the Web server is shut down, an unauthorized server can be installed in its place, therefore compromising information that is sent from the browser.	S, T, I, D, E
The Web pages that are rendered to the browser might be altered to include viruses and worms. If the browser displays the Web page, the virus or worm can be invoked and possibly damage the user's machine.	T, D

How to Use a Threat Model

After you have identified the threats, you must decide how to respond to each threat identified in the threat modeling exercise. You can respond to a threat in several ways:

- *Inform users about the threat.* If a security weakness is created when the user performs some action, it can be appropriate to warn the user. For example, in Microsoft Windows XP, users who choose the option that displays protected operating system files are warned that doing so poses a risk to those files. In this case, the threat of tampering results primarily from enabling the user to access and potentially damage operating system files.

- *Remove features.* If you know of a feature that will introduce a significant security risk, and the risk cannot be mitigated effectively, consider whether the feature is worth including in the final version of the product.
- *Identify a mitigation technique.* If you must include a feature that introduces a security risk, you must choose a technique that mitigates the risk. There are several techniques for mitigating threats.

Incorporating Mitigation Techniques

Mitigation techniques can be divided into two categories, general techniques and techniques for the STRIDE model. Table 9.3 describes some of the general mitigation techniques used for resolving threats.

Table 9.3. Mitigation Techniques

Technique	Description
Authentication and authorization	Authentication is the process by which an entity verifies that another entity is who or what it claims to be. Authorization is the process of determining access to resources.
Secure communication	You must ensure that communication between the tiers of your application is secure to avoid attacks in which data is tampered with while it is being transmitted or is being stored in a queue. For secure communication use: *Secure Sockets Layer (SSL).* SSL is used to establish an encrypted communication channel between client and server. *IPSec.* IPSec can be used to secure the data sent between two computers; for example, an application server and a database server. *Virtual private networks (VPNs).* A VPN lets you establish a point-to-point IP transport over the Internet (or other networks).
Quality of service(QoS)	Implements profiling on the messages that are sent to your system.
Throttling	Limits the number of messages sent to your system. If there is no control over the rate at which messages are sent, a target can be inundated with more messages than it can handle.
Auditing	The process of collecting information about user activities and important events and storing the information for analysis at a later stage. Auditing is also commonly known as *logging*. Windows event logs allow your applications to record information about important events. You can use these records to audit access to your system and troubleshoot problems.

Table 9.3.   Mitigation Techniques   *(continued)*

Technique	Description
Filtering	The process of intercepting and evaluating messages sent to your system.
Least privilege	Provides users with the minimum level of privilege that will allow their work to be completed, and no more.

Table 9.4 includes a partial list of threat mitigation techniques as applied to various STRIDE threats.

Table 9.4.   Mitigation Techniques for STRIDE Threats

Mitigation technique	Type of threat
Authentication	S, D
Protect secrets	S, I
Audit trails	R
Do not store secrets	S, I
Privacy protocols	I
Authorization	T, I, D
Hashes	T
Message authentication codes	T
Digital signatures	T, R
Tamper-resistant protocols	T, R
Time stamps	R
Filtering	D
Throttling	D
Quality of service	D
Run with least privilege	E

More Info   For more information about threat modeling and mitigation technologies for some common threats, see *Writing Secure Code* by Michael Howard and David LeBlanc (Microsoft Press, 2002).

Lesson 3: Using .NET Framework Security Features

This lesson describes the important security features in the .NET Framework.

More Info   For more information about creating secure Microsoft ASP.NET applications, see the article "Building Secure ASP.NET Applications: Authentication, Authorization, and Secure Communication" under .NET Security on the MSDN® Web site (*http://msdn.microsoft.com*).

After this lesson, you will be able to

- Define type safety verification.
- Define code signing.
- Define encryption and data signing.
- Define code-access security.
- Define role-based security.
- Define isolated storage.
- Explain the security features of .NET Web technologies.

Estimated lesson time: 20 minutes

What Is Type Safety Verification?

Type safety verification plays a crucial role in assembly isolation and security enforcement.

Definition of type-safe code

Any code that accesses only the memory it is authorized to access is called type-safe code. For example, type-safe code does not access values from the private fields of another object.

Code that is not type-safe can cause security threats to an application. For example, unsafe code might access and alter native (unmanaged) code and perform malicious operations. Because the code is unsafe, the runtime is unable to prevent the code from accessing the native code. However, when code is type-safe, the security enforcement mechanism of the runtime ensures that it does not access native code unless it has permission to do so. Before it can run, all code that is not type-safe must have been granted a security permission with the *SkipVerification* member. This permission is granted only to code that is trusted at a very high level.

Definition of type safety verification

During just-in-time (JIT) compilation, Microsoft intermediate language (MSIL) code is compiled into native machine code. As this process occurs, a default verification process examines the metadata and MSIL code of a method to verify that they are well formed and type-safe.

Type-safe components can run in the same process even if they are trusted at different levels. For code that is verifiably type-safe, the runtime can rely on the following statements being true:

■ A reference to a type is compatible with the type being referenced.

■ Only appropriately defined operations are invoked on an object.

■ Methods are called by means of defined interfaces so that security checks cannot be bypassed.

These restrictions provide assurances that security restrictions on code can be enforced reliably. Also, multiple instances of different type-safe assemblies can run safely in the same process, because they are guaranteed not to interfere with each other's memory.

What Is Code Signing?

To make any source reliable for software download, you need to consider the following:

■ *Ensure authenticity.* Ensures that users know the origin of the code and helps to prevent malicious users from impersonating the identity of a publisher.

■ *Ensure integrity.* Verifies that the code has not been changed by unauthorized sources since it was published.

Definition of code signing

Signing code with a strong name defines the unique identity of code and guarantees that code has not been compromised. Code signing is the process of providing a set of code with credentials that authenticate the publisher of the code. The credentials of the code can be verified prior to installing and running the code.

Code signing in the .NET Framework

.NET Framework code signing relies on strong name signatures. The .NET Framework also supports Authenticode® digital certificates and signatures.

What Is Encryption and Data Signing?

Data signing and encryption are processes that are used to protect data contents from being discovered and to verify that data has not been compromised.

Definition of encryption and decryption

Encryption is the process of disguising data before it is sent or stored. Before it is encrypted, the content is referred to as *plaintext*. Data that has undergone encryption is called *ciphertext*. A plaintext message that is converted to ciphertext is completely unreadable. *Decryption* is the process of unscrambling ciphertext into readable plaintext. The processes of encrypting and decrypting data rely on the techniques of hashing and signing data.

Definition of cryptographic hashing

Hashing is the process of matching data of any length to a fixed-length byte sequence. The fixed-length byte sequence is called a *hash*. A hash is obtained by applying a mathematical function, called a hashing algorithm, to an arbitrary amount of data. Cryptographic hashes that are created with the cryptography functions of the .NET Framework approach statistical uniqueness; a different two-byte sequence does not hash to the same value.

Definition of signed data

Signed data is a standards-based data type. Signed data consists of any type of content plus encrypted hashes of the content for zero or more signers. The hashes are used to confirm the identity of a data signer and to confirm that the message has not been modified since it was signed.

What Is Code-Access Security?

Windows operating system security ensures that unauthorized users are not allowed access to the computer system. However, Windows operating systems security alone cannot ensure against the possibility of authorized users downloading and running malicious code.

Definition of code-access security

The .NET Framework provides code-access security to help protect computer systems from malicious or faulty code and to provide a way to allow mobile code to run safely.

Code-access security allows code to be trusted to varying degrees, depending on the code's origin, code's evidence (such as its strong name signature), and on other aspects of the code's identity. For example, code that is downloaded from your organization's intranet and published by your organization might be trusted to a greater degree than code that is downloaded from the Internet and published by an unknown entity.

Requesting level of privilege required

The .NET Framework allows you to include features in your application that request a specific level of security privilege from the operating system. This request specifies the level of privilege your application:

- Requires to run
- Can make use of but is not required for the application to run
- Does not need and should be expressly excluded from ever being granted permission to access

What Is Role-Based Security?

Role-based security relates mostly to the spoofing identity security threat by preventing unauthorized users from performing operations that they are not authorized to perform. Role-based security allows code to verify the identity and role membership of the user.

Tip   The .NET Framework includes classes to identify Windows users and groups, in addition to classes to help implement role-based security for other authentication schemes.

Figure 9.2 depicts the role-based security model.

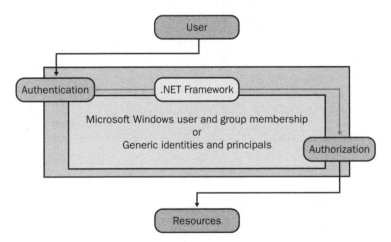

Figure 9.2.   Role-based security

Authentication

Authentication is the process of discovering and verifying the identity of a user by examining the user's credentials and then validating those credentials against some authority. A variety of authentication mechanisms are used, some of which can be used with .NET Framework role-based security.

Examples of commonly used authentication mechanisms include the operating system, Passport, and application-defined mechanisms, such as NTLM and Kerberos version 5 authentication.

Authorization

Authorization is the process of determining whether a user is allowed to perform a requested action. Authorization occurs after authentication and uses information about a user's identity and roles to determine what resources that user can access. You can use .NET Framework role-based security to implement authorization.

What Is Isolated Storage?

A common requirement of applications is to store data, such as user preference information or application state, on the client.

One challenge to storing data successfully is the possibility that the storage location will be accessed or corrupted, either intentionally or unintentionally. Without a standard system in place to manage these problems, developing improvised techniques that minimize storage conflicts can be complex and the results can be unreliable. Therefore, it is important to protect your data by providing isolated storage.

Isolated storage allows developers to use an isolated virtual file system on the client to save data. When using isolated storage, applications save data to a unique data compartment that is associated with some aspect of the code's identity, such as its Web site, publisher, or signature.

The data compartment is an abstraction, not a specific storage location. It consists of one or more isolated storage files, called *stores*. The actual directory location of the data is contained in a store. To the developer, the location of the actual data is transparent. A quota can be used to limit the amount of isolated storage that an assembly uses.

Access permission to a store can be based on identity of:

- User
- Assembly
- Application

Security Features of .NET Technologies

.NET Web applications implement one or more of the logical services by using technologies such as Microsoft ASP.NET, Enterprise Services, XML Web services, remoting, Microsoft ADO.NET, and Microsoft SQL Server. To create effective security strategies, you need to understand how to fine-tune the various security features within each product and technology area, and how to make them work together.

ASP.NET security

ASP.NET provides a useful tool for application developers to use to create Web pages. When a Web site records a user's credit card information, the file or database that stores such information must be secured from public access. ASP.NET, in conjunction with IIS, can authenticate user credentials such as names and passwords by using any of the following means of authentication:

- Windows: basic, digest, or integrated Windows authentication (NTLM or Kerberos)
- Passport authentication
- Forms
- Client certificates

ASP.NET implements authentication by means of authentication providers. ASP.NET supports the following authentication providers:

- *Forms authentication.* A system by which unauthenticated requests are redirected to a Hypertext Markup Language (HTML) form by using HTTP client-side redirection. The user provides credentials and submits the form. If the application authenticates the request, the system issues a cookie that contains the credentials, or a key for reacquiring the identity.
- *Passport authentication.* A centralized authentication service provided by Microsoft that offers a single logon and core profile services for member sites.
- *Windows authentication.* A system used by ASP.NET in conjunction with IIS authentication. Authentication is performed by IIS in one of three ways: basic, digest, or integrated Windows authentication. When IIS authentication is complete, ASP.NET uses the authenticated identity to authorize access.

More Info   For more information about ASP.NET security, see "ASP.NET Security" under the section "Building Secure ASP.NET Applications" on the MSDN Web site (*http://msdn.microsoft.com*).

Enterprises Services security

Traditional COM+ services such as distributed transactions, just-in-time activation, object pooling, and concurrency management are available to .NET components. In the .NET environment, such services are referred to as Enterprise Services.

The authentication, authorization, and secure communication features supported by Enterprise Services applications are shown in Figure 9.3. The client application shown in Figure 9.3 is an ASP.NET Web application.

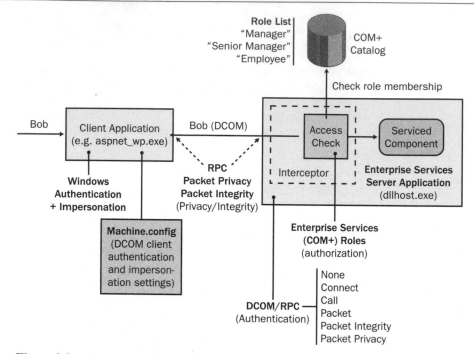

Figure 9.3. Enterprise Services role-based security architecture

---

More Info   For more information about Enterprise Services security, see "Enterprise Services Security" under the section "Building Secure ASP.NET Applications" on the MSDN Web site (*http://msdn.microsoft.com*).

Web services security

Web services enable the exchange of data and the remote invocation of application logic by using SOAP-based message exchanges to move data through firewalls and between heterogeneous systems. Web service security can be used at three levels:

- Platform/transport-level (point-to-point) security
- Application-level (custom) security
- Message-level (end-to-end) security

More Info   For more information about Web services security, see "Web Services Security" under the section "Building Secure ASP.NET Applications" on the MSDN Web site (*http://msdn.microsoft.com*).

.NET remoting security

.NET remoting allows you to access remote and distributed objects across process and machine boundaries. Remoting does not have its own security model. Authentication and authorization between the client and server is performed by the channel and host process.

ADO.NET and SQL Server

ADO.NET provides data access services. It is designed for distributed Web applications, and supports disconnected scenarios. When you build Web-based applications, it is essential that you use a secure approach to accessing and storing data. ADO.NET and SQL Server provide several security features that can be used to ensure secure data access.

Figure 9.4 shows the remote application tier model together with the set of security services provided by the various technologies.

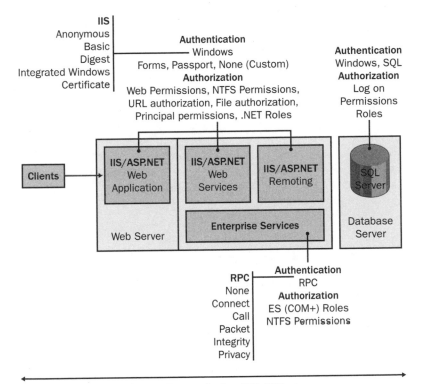

Figure 9.4.   Security architecture

Table 9.5 summarizes the authentication, authorization, and secure communications features provided by .NET technologies.

Table 9.5.   Security Features and .NET Technologies

Technology	Authentication	Authorization	Secure communication
ASP.NET	• None (custom) • Windows • Forms • Passport	• File authorization • URL authorization • Principal permissions • .NET roles	
Web services	• Windows • None (custom) • Message-level authentication	• File authorization • URL authorization • Principal permissions • .NET roles	• SSL and message-level encryption
Remoting	• Windows	• File authorization • URL authorization • Principal permissions • .NET roles	• SSL and message-level encryption
Enterprise Services	• Windows	• Enterprise Services (COM+) roles • NTFS permissions	• Remote Procedure Call (RPC) Encryption
SQL Server	• Windows (Kerberos/NTLM) • SQL authentication	• Server logons • Database logons • Fixed database roles • User-defined roles • Application roles • Object permissions	• SSL

Lesson 4: Designing Authorization, Authentication, and Auditing Strategies

Designing an authorization and authentication strategy for an application is a challenging task. Proper authorization and authentication design during the early phases of your application development helps to mitigate many serious security risks. In many cases, you will also need to implement auditing functionality to track user and business activity in the application for security purposes.

In this lesson, you will learn the general process for designing authorization and authentication strategies. You will then learn how to design authorization, authentication, and auditing for the application tiers.

After this lesson, you will be able to

- Identify the process of designing authorization and authentication strategies.
- Design authorization strategies for user interface and user process components.
- Design authorization strategies for business components and data access components.
- Design authentication strategies for user interface and user process components.
- Design authentication strategies for data access components.
- Design auditing strategies.

Estimated lesson time: 25 minutes

How to Design Authorization and Authentication Strategies

To design authentication and authorization strategies for your application, you need to perform the following steps:

1. Identify resources.
2. Select an authorization strategy.
3. Select the identities used for resource access.
4. Consider whether identity should flow through the system.
5. Select an authentication approach.
6. Decide how to flow identity through the system.

Identify resources

Identify the resources that the application provides to the clients. Examples of resources include:

- Web server resources such as Web pages, Web services, and static resources (HTML pages and images)
- Database resources such as per-user data or application-wide data
- Network resources such as remote file system resources and data from directory stores such as Active Directory®

Select an authorization strategy

The two basic authorization strategies are:

- *Role based.* Users are associated with roles; if a user is authorized to perform the requested operation, the application uses fixed identities with which to access resources.
- *Resource based.* Individual resources are secured by using Windows access control lists (ACLs). The application impersonates the caller prior to accessing resources, which allows the operating system to perform standard access checks.

Choose the identities used for resource access

Choose the identity or identities that should be used to access resources across the layers of your application.

- *Original caller's identity.* Assumes an impersonation or delegation model in which the original caller identity can be obtained and then flowed through each layer of your system. The delegation factor is a key criterion used to determine your authentication mechanism.
- *Process identity.* This is the default case. Local resource access and down-stream calls are made using the current process identity. The feasibility of this approach depends on the boundary being crossed, because the process identity must be recognized by the destination system.
- *Service account.* Uses a fixed service account. For example, for database access this might be a fixed user name and password presented by the component connecting to the database. When a fixed Windows identity is required, use an Enterprise Services server application.
- *Custom identity.* When you do not have Windows accounts to work with, you can construct your own identities that can contain details that relate to your own specific security context. These could include role lists, unique identifiers, or any other type of custom information.

Consider identity flow

To support per-user authorization, auditing, and per-user data retrieval, you might need to flow the original caller's identity through various application tiers and across multiple computer boundaries. For example, if a back-end resource manager needs to perform per-caller authorization, the caller's identity must be passed to that resource manager.

Based on resource manager authorization requirements and the auditing requirements of your system, identify which identities need to be passed through your application.

Select an authentication approach

Two key factors that influence the choice of the authentication approach are the nature of your application's user base (the types of browsers they are using and whether they have Windows accounts), and your application's impersonation/delegation and auditing requirements.

You have a variety of options for authentication in your .NET-connected Web applications. For example, you can choose to use one of the supported IIS authentication mechanisms, or you might decide to perform authentication in your application code. Consider some or all of the following factors when choosing an authentication method:

- Server and client operating systems
- The client browser type
- The number of users, and the location and type of the user name and password database
- Deployment considerations, such as whether your application is Internet- or intranet-based and whether it is located behind a firewall
- The application type, such as whether the application is an interactive Web site or a non-interactive Web service
- Sensitivity of the data you are protecting
- Performance and scalability factors
- Application authorization requirements, such as making your application available to all users, or restricting certain areas to registered users and other areas to administrators only

Some of the ASP.NET and IIS authentication types include:

- Forms
- Passport
- Integrated Windows (Kerberos or NTLM)
- Basic
- Digest

Decide how to flow identity

You can flow identity (to provide security context) at the application level or you can flow identity and security context at the operating system level. To flow identity at the application level, use method and stored procedure parameters. Application identity flow supports:

- Per-user data retrieval using trusted query parameters, as shown in the following code:

```
SELECT x,y FROM SomeTable WHERE username='jane'
```

- Custom auditing within any application tier

Operating system identity flow supports:

- Platform level auditing (for example, Windows auditing and SQL Server auditing)
- Per-user authorization based on Windows identities

To flow identity at the operating system level, you can use the impersonation/delegation model. In some circumstances, you can use Kerberos delegation, while in cases where the environment does not support Kerberos, you might need to use other approaches, such as using Basic authentication. With Basic authentication, the user's credentials are available to the server application and can be used to access downstream network resources.

How to Design Authorization Strategies for User Interface Components

User interface components show data to users and gather data from them. You perform authorization at this level if you want to hide specific data fields from the user, show specific data fields to the user, or enable or disable controls for user input.

Authorization for user interface components

If the user is not supposed to see a certain piece of information, the most secure option is to avoid passing that piece of information to the presentation components in the first place.

It is common to perform some level of personalization of the user interface or menu so that users can see only the panes, Web elements, or menu entries that they can act on depending on their roles. A user interface .exe file usually starts the application. You should set code-access permissions on the user interface assemblies if you do not want to let it (or the local components it calls) access sensitive resources such as files.

Planning   Consider the security context in which the presentation components of the application will run, and test them in an appropriately restricted environment.

Authorization in user process components

User process components manage data and control flow between user processes. You should perform authorization at this level if you need to:

- Control whether a user can start a user interface interaction process at all.
- Add and remove steps or full user interface components in a user interaction flow based on who is executing it. For example, each sales representative might see data for only the appropriate region, so there is no need to present a step to choose the region of a sales report.

User process components are typically consumed only from user interface components. You can use code-access security to restrict who is calling them. You can also use code-access security to restrict how user process components interact with each other. This approach is especially important in portal scenarios when it is critical that a user process implemented as an add-in cannot gather unauthorized information from other user processes and elements.

How to Design Authorization Strategies for Business Components

Like the other tiers of an application, you can set authorization for business components. Use the following guidelines when setting authorization:

- Try to make the business process authorization independent of user context, especially if you plan to use many communication mechanisms as queues and Web services.
- Use role-based security as much as possible rather than relying on user accounts. Roll-based security provides better scalability, eases administration, and avoids problems with user names that support many canonical representations. You can define roles for serviced components in an Enterprise Services–based application, or you can use Windows groups or custom roles for .NET components that are not running in Enterprise Services.

How to Design Authorization Strategies for Data Access Components

Data access components are the last components that expose business functionality before your application data. You need to perform authorization at this level if you need to share the data access components with developers of business processes that you do not fully trust and if you want to protect access to powerful functions made available by the data stores.

To perform authorization, you can use Enterprise Services roles and .NET *PrincipalPermission* attributes, if you are using Windows authentication. Use .NET roles and attributes if you are not using a Windows security context.

If you are flowing the same user context into your data store, you can use the database's authorization functionality, for example, granting or revoking access to stored procedures.

Because data access components are typically called only by other application components, they are a good candidate for restricting callers to the necessary set of assemblies—usually a combination of assemblies with components of the user interface layer, business process components, and business entities (if present).

How to Design Authentication Strategies for User Interface Components

User interface components need to authenticate the user if the application needs to perform authorization, auditing, or personalization.

Authentication for Web-based UI

A wide range of authentication mechanisms are available for Web-based user interfaces (UIs). To choose the right one for your scenario, see Figure 9.5.

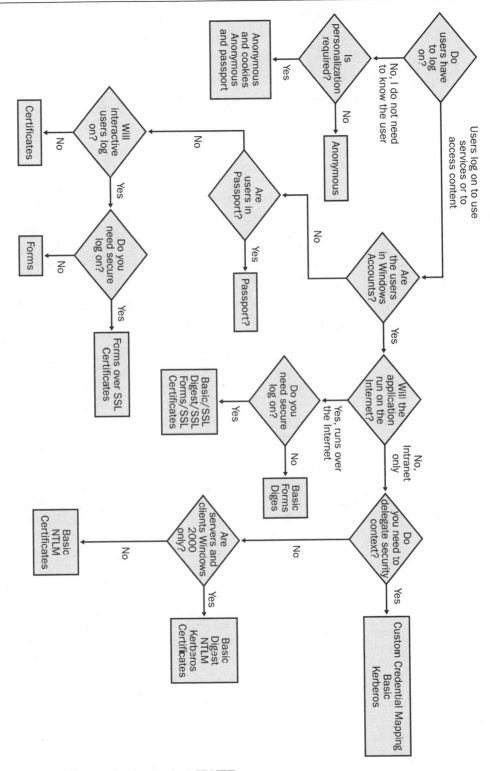

Figure 9.5. Authentication in ASP.NET

Authentication for Windows-based UI

Windows-based user interfaces usually either rely on a custom authentication mechanism (in which the application prompts for a user name and password), or they authenticate users by using their Windows logons.

Authentication for user process components

User process components do not perform authentication; they rely on the security context set at application start.

The user process components should run in the same user context as the user interface itself, so that all authentication tasks are delegated to the user interface or even the rendering infrastructure. For example, in ASP.NET, any request to an ASPX page results in IIS requesting authentication credentials or ASP.NET redirecting the user to a forms-based authentication page. This operation is handled transparently to any user process layer and does not interrupt state flow, even when an authenticated session expires and needs to be reestablished.

How to Design Authentication Strategies for Data Access Components

Data access components are designed to be used by other components in the application or service. They are not usually meant to be called from scripts or other applications, so you can design them to rely on the security context set by the caller or the authentication mechanism of your remoting strategy. Data access components can authenticate with the database in two main ways: using service accounts and impersonating the caller.

Service accounts

Use one or a limited set of service accounts that represent roles or user type. In most cases, it will be just one service account, but you can use more if you need more control over authorization. For example, in the order processing application you could access your database as "TheOrderApplication," or log on selectively as "OrderProcessingManager" or "OrderProcessingClerk," depending on the role of the caller identity.

Use service accounts when:

- You connect to the underlying data source from an environment in which impersonation of the initial caller is unavailable (for example, Microsoft BizTalk® Server).
- You have very limited change control over the accounts that can log on to the other system, for example, when logging on to a relational database management system, which is strictly managed by the database administrator.

■ The data store you are accessing has a different authentication mechanism than the rest of your application, for example, when you are logging on to a Web service across the Internet.

Do not use service accounts when:

■ You do not have a secure way of storing and maintaining service credentials.
■ You need to access the data store with specific user resources because of security policies, for example, when you need access to data or objects in SQL Server on behalf of users.
■ The data store audits activities, and these audits need to correspond to individual users.

Impersonating the caller

You are impersonating the caller when you access a data store with a set of accounts that correspond one-to-one with your application user base. For example, if Jane logs on to your application, and your data access components access a database, you are impersonating Jane if you log on to this database with Jane's credentials.

You need caller impersonation when:

■ The data store performs authorization based on the logged on user.
■ The data store needs to audit the activities of each individual end user.

How to Design Auditing Strategies

To audit your business activities, you need a secure storage location. In fact, auditing can be thought of as secure logging. If you are implementing your own auditing solution, you must ensure that audit entries are tamperproof or at least tamper-evident (achieved with digital signatures) and that storage location is secured (for example, either connection strings cannot be changed or storage files cannot be replaced, or both). Your auditing mechanism can use document signing, platform authentication, and code-access security to ensure that spurious entries cannot be logged by malicious code.

Auditing in user interface and user process components

The activity that occurs in user interface components is not usually audited. Activities that are audited at the user interface include global events such as logon, logoff, password changes, and all security exceptions in general.

Because user process components represent user activities, which can be stopped, abandoned, and so on, it is not common to audit them. As always, you might want to audit security-related exceptions.

Auditing in business process components

Auditing is most often performed for business processes. You will want to know who performed key business activities and when the activities occurred.

If you are auditing within the context of a transaction to a transactional resource manager such as SQL Server, you will want to have a new transaction started by your auditing component so that the failures in the original transaction tree do not roll back the audit entry.

Auditing in data access components

Data access components are the closest custom business logic layer to the data store. The data layer is a good location for implementing auditing.

The data access components in your application will usually invoke stored procedures that actually do the data-intensive work, so you might want to also audit inside the data base management system (RDBMS).

More Info   For information about how to implement auditing in SQL Server, see "Auditing SQL Server Activity" in the SQL Server 2000 SDK on the MSDN Web site (*http://msdn.microsoft.com*).

Activity: Threat Modeling and Mitigation

In this activity, you use what you learned in the lessons to work through threat modeling exercises.

Exercise 1: Identifying Potential Threats

The sales staff at Adventure Works Cycles can create orders for their customers in two ways. The first way allows the sales staff to use the public Web site in a manner similar to how the customers place orders. However, the sales staff will need to provide their credentials, which will allow discounts to be applied to the order. The second way is accomplished by means of the Handheld PCs and laptop computers that each sales representative has and a Windows Forms application that is installed on each laptop. The sales representative creates the order either on the Handheld PC or the laptop and obtains the customer's signature by means of the Handheld PC. Later, the sales representative can connect to the network and upload the order to the order entry application.

Both ways of creating orders can be subject to a number of security threats. Open the C09Ex1.ppt file in the \SolutionDocuments\Chapter09 folder on the CD and examine the high-level architecture diagram for the Windows Forms application. Using the STRIDE threat model, identify some of the security threats to the application.

One possible answer to this exercise can be found in C09Ex1_Answer.ppt in the \SolutionDocuments\Chapter09 folder on the CD.

Exercise 2: Applying Mitigation Technologies

Using the possible threats you identified in Exercise 1, list some technologies that would help to mitigate these threats.

One possible answer to this exercise can be found in C09Ex2_Answer.ppt in the \SolutionDocuments\Chapter09 folder on the CD.

Summary

- Common types of security vulnerabilities include:
    - Weak passwords
    - Misconfigured software
    - Social engineering
    - Internet connections
    - Unencrypted data transfer
    - Buffer overrun
    - SQL injection
    - Secrets in code
- Principles for building security strategies include:
    - Rely on tested and proven security systems.
    - Never trust external input.
    - Assume that external systems are non-secure.
    - Apply the principle of least privilege.
    - Reduce available components and data.
    - Default to a secure mode.
    - Do not rely on security by obscurity.
    - Follow STRIDE principles.
- The STRIDE model is a threat model. Each letter in the STRIDE acronym specifies a different category of security threat: spoofing identity, tampering, repudiation, information disclosure, denial of service, and elevation of privilege.
- The steps to create a threat model are:
    - Arrange for a brainstorming meeting.
    - Apply the STRIDE security categories.
    - List all possible threats.
    - Create notes.
    - Research.
    - Rank the risk of each threat.
- The important security features of .NET Framework include:
    - Type safety verification
    - Code signing
    - Encryption and data signing
    - Code-access security
    - Role-based security
    - Isolated storage

- To design an authentication and authorization strategy for your application, you need to perform the following steps:
  - Identify resources.
  - Select an authorization strategy.
  - Select the identities used for resource access.
  - Consider identity flow.
  - Select an authentication approach.
  - Decide how to flow identity.

Review

The following questions are intended to reinforce key information presented in this chapter. If you are unable to answer a question, review the lesson materials and try the question again. You can find answers to the questions in the appendix.

1. What are some of the drawbacks of traditional security models?

2. What are some of the principles of secure coding?

3. Which of the following statements about buffer overruns is true? (Select all that apply.)

   ■ Type safety verification was designed to eliminate buffer overruns.

   ■ A buffer overrun can cause an application to stop responding or to malfunction.

   ■ A buffer overrun can be exploited by a malicious user to run arbitrary code.

   ■ The error message that results from a buffer overrun can pose a security threat.

4. During which MSF phase should the threat model be created?

   ■ Planning

   ■ Developing

   ■ Stabilizing

5. What is the STRIDE model?

6. Read the following security attack scenario, and then decide which elements of the STRIDE model are implicit in the attack.

   Carl sees that Bob has left his workstation unattended and unlocked. Carl sits down at Bob's workstation and opens Bob's e-mail application. Carl, pretending to be Bob, sends an e-mail message to Alice. Carl quits the e-mail client and then walks away unobserved.

7. What is code-access security?

8. What is role-based security?

9. Which are the authentication providers supported by ASP.NET?

10. What are the three types of security provided by Web services?

11. What are the steps for designing an authorization and authentication strategy for an application?

C H A P T E R   1 0

Completing the Planning Phase

About This Chapter

The planning phase encompasses the greater part of the architecture and design of a solution. It also results in plans to accomplish the development and deployment of the solution, and the schedules associated with tasks and resources. These plans help the project team to work on the subsequent phases of the project.

In this chapter, you will learn about the tasks and plans that the project team works on to complete the planning phase of the project.

Before You Begin

To complete the lessons in this chapter, you must

- Understand the MSF Process Model.
- Be able to create use cases, usage scenarios, and use case diagrams.
- Be familiar with the outputs of the envisioning phase, such as vision/scope, project structure, and risk analysis documents.
- Be familiar with tasks and outputs of the three design processes of the planning phase—conceptual, logical, and physical design.

Lesson 1: Incorporating Design Considerations

During the planning phase, several elements affect and shape the design of the application. Some of these elements might be non-negotiable and finite resources, such as time, money, and workforce. Other elements, such as available technologies, knowledge, and skills, are dynamic and vary throughout the development life cycle. While these elements influence the design of an application to some extent, the business problem dictates the capabilities the application must have for a satisfactory solution.

In this lesson, you will learn about the capabilities and considerations that might be addressed by a solution. You will learn about design considerations such as scalability, availability, reliability, performance, interoperability, and globalization and localization. You will also learn the techniques for incorporating these design considerations into a solution.

After this lesson, you will be able to

- Design a solution for scalability.
- Design a solution for availability.
- Design a solution for reliability.
- Design a solution for performance.
- Design a solution for interoperability.
- Design localization and globalization specifications for a solution.

Estimated lesson time: 25 minutes

How to Design for Scalability

Scalability is defined as the capability to increase resources to produce an increase in the service capacity. In a scalable application, you can add resources to manage additional demands without modifying the application itself.

A scalable application requires a balance between the software and hardware used to implement the application. You might add resources to either software or hardware to increase the scalability of the application. Adding these resources might produce a benefit; however, it could also have a negative or null effect, with the application showing no significant increase in service capacity. For example, you might implement load balancing in an application. This will help only minimally if the application has been written to make synchronous method calls or to retrieve lengthy datasets in response to a user's request.

Common approaches

The two most common approaches to scalability are:

- *Scaling up*. Refers to achieving scalability by improving the existing server's processing hardware. Scaling up includes adding more memory, more or faster processors, or migrating the application to a more powerful computer. The primary goal of scaling up an application is to increase the hardware resources available to the application. Typically, you can scale up an application without changing the source code. In addition, the administrative effort does not change drastically. However, the benefit of scaling up tapers off eventually until the actual maximum processing capability of the machine is reached.

Figure 10.1 illustrates the effect scaling up has on the service capacity of an application.

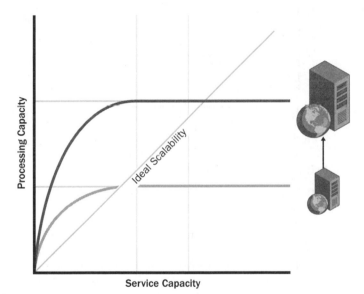

Figure 10.1.   Scaling up an application

- *Scaling out*. Refers to distributing the processing load across more than one server. Although scaling out is achieved by using multiple computers, the collection of computers continues to act as the original device configuration from the end-user perspective. Again, the balance between software and hardware is important. The application should be able to execute without needing information about the server on which it is executing. This concept is called *location transparency*. Scaling out also increases the fault tolerance of the application.

Figure 10.2 illustrates the effect scaling out has on the service capacity of an application.

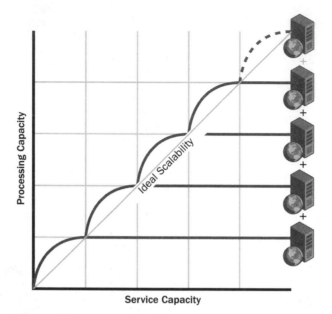

Figure 10.2.   Scaling out an application

Designing for scalability

Good design is the foundation of a highly scalable application. The planning phase has the greatest impact on the scalability of an application.

Figure 10.3 illustrates the role of design, code tuning, product tuning, and hardware tuning in the scalability of an application. Design has more impact on the scalability of an application than the other three factors. As you move up the pyramid, the impact of various factors decreases. The pyramid illustrates that effective design adds more scalability to an application than increased hardware resources.

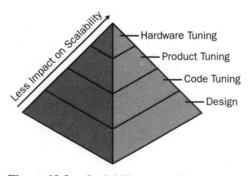

Figure 10.3.   Scalability pyramid

To design for scalability, use the following guidelines:

- *Design processes such that they do not wait.* A process should never wait longer than necessary. A process can be categorized as *synchronous* or *asynchronous*. A synchronous process waits for another process to complete before it continues. Such processes must wait for another process to succeed or fail completely before performing another operation. Applications that implement synchronous processes encounter bottlenecks for resources. These bottlenecks affect both the performance and the scalability of the application. One way to achieve scalability is to implement asynchronous processes. In applications that have asynchronous processes, long-running operations can be queued for completion later by a separate process.

- *Design processes so that processes do not compete for resources.* One of the biggest causes of scalability problems is competition for resources such as memory, processor cycles, bandwidth, or database connections. Plan your resource usage to minimize these problems:

  - Sequence resource usage to use the most plentiful resources first and the least plentiful resources last.

  - Acquire resources as late as possible. The shorter the amount of time a process uses a resource, the sooner the resource becomes available to another process.

- *Design processes for commutability.* Two or more operations are called *commutative* if they can execute in any order and still obtain the same result. Typically, operations that do not involve transactions are commutative. For example, a busy e-commerce site that continuously updates the inventory of its products might experience contention for record locks. To prevent this, each inventory increment and decrement could become a record in a separate inventory transaction table. Periodically, the database could add the rows of this table for each product and then update the product records with the net change in inventory.

- *Design components for interchangeability.* An interchangeable component is designed to release its resources, move into a pool managed by a resource manager, and be re-initialized for use by a new client. Design the component so that no client-specific state persists from client to client. In addition, the component should support aggregation and not be bound to a specific thread. Resource pooling schemes such as COM+ component pooling and Open Database Connectivity (ODBC) connection pooling use interchangeable resources. For example, you can use the Component Services Administration tool to enable object pooling, set minimum and maximum pool size, and create timeout settings. For more information, refer to *Improving Performance with Object Pooling* in the Platform SDK: COM+ (Component Services documentation in MSDN).

- *Partition resources and activities.* Minimize relationships between resources and activities by partitioning them. This helps you avoid the risk of bottlenecks. Partitioning activities can also ease the load on critical resources such as the processor and bandwidth. For example, using Secure Sockets Layer (SSL) to provide a secure connection results in significant overhead. Therefore, you might decide to use SSL only for pages that require a high level of security and use dedicated Web servers to handle SSL sessions. You can also partition resources and activities by creating many small components rather than a few large components, and by limiting cross-device communication. However, partitioning can make a system more complex. Dividing resources that have dependencies can add significant overheads to an operation.

How to Design for Availability

Though all applications are available at least some of the time, Web-based applications and mission-critical enterprise applications must provide services at all times. If your enterprise application needs to work 24 hours a day, 7 days a week, you need to design for high availability. Advances in hardware and software have increased the quality of high-availability applications.

Definition of availability

Availability is a measure of how often the application is available to handle service requests as compared to the planned run time. Availability also takes into account repair time because an application that is being repaired is not available for use.

Note   Availability does not address business continuation issues such as backups and alternative sites.

Table 10.1 shows the measurements used for calculating availability.

Table 10.1.   Measurement Types for Calculating Availability

Name	Calculation	Definition
Mean Time Between Failure (MTBF)	Hours / Failure Count	Average length of time the application runs before failing
Mean Time To Recovery (MTTR)	Repair Hours / Failure Count	Average length of time needed to repair and restore service after a failure

The formula for calculating availability is:

```
Availability = (MTBF / (MTBF + MTTR)) × 100
```

For example, the typical availability requirement for the Adventure Works Cycles application is that the site is available 24 hours a day, 7 days a week. If you assume 1000 continuous hours as a checkpoint, two 1-hour failures during this time period results in availability of:

```
((1000 / 2) / ((1000 / 2) + 1)) × 100 = (500 / 501) × 100 = .998 × 100 =
99.8%.
```

A popular way to describe availability is by the *nines*, for example, three nines for 99.9 percent availability. However, the implication of measuring by nines is often misunderstood. You need to do the arithmetic to discover that three nines (99.9 percent availability) represent about 8.5 hours of service outage in a single year. The next level, four nines (99.99 percent), represents about 1 hour of service outage in a year. Five nines (99.999 percent) represent about 5 minutes of outage per year.

Planning availability levels

To determine the level of availability that is appropriate for your application, you need to answer a few questions, such as:

- Who are the customers of the application? What are their expectations from the application?
- How much downtime is acceptable?
- Do internal company processes depend on the service?
- What is the schedule and budget for developing the application?

Techniques for availability

Designing for availability includes anticipating, detecting, and resolving hardware or software failures before they result in service errors, faults, or data corruption, thereby minimizing downtime. To ensure availability, provide multiple routes to application services and data. Use only tested, proven processes (both automated and people-based) that support the application throughout its life cycle.

In addition to unplanned downtime, planned downtime must be reduced. Planned downtime can include maintenance changes, operating system upgrades, backups, or any other activity that temporarily removes the application from service.

Availability of an application also depends on its reliability. For a highly available and reliable application, you need a reliable foundation: good application design, rigorous testing, and certification. Some of the techniques used for designing for availability include:

- *Reduce planned downtime.* To avoid planned downtime, use *rolling upgrades*. For example, to update a component on a clustered server, you can move the server's resource groups to another server, take the server offline, update the component, and then bring the server online. Meanwhile, the other servers handle the workload, and the application experiences no downtime. You can use this strategy in an application that scales out.

- *Reduce unplanned downtime with clustering.* Clustering is a technology for creating high-availability applications. A cluster consists of multiple computers that are physically networked and logically connected using cluster software. By using clustering, a multiple server Web site can withstand failures with no interruption in service. When the active server fails, the workload is automatically moved to a passive server, current client processes are switched over, and the failed application service is restarted automatically. If a resource fails, customers connected to that server cluster might experience a slight delay, but the service will be completed. Cluster software can provide failover support for applications, file and print services, databases, and messaging systems that have been designed as cluster-aware and assigned to a cluster.

- *Use network load balancing.* Network load balancing (NLB) is used to distribute traffic evenly across available servers. NLB also helps increase the availability of an application: if a server fails, you can use NLB to redefine the cluster and direct traffic to the other servers. NLB is especially beneficial for e-commerce applications that link external clients with transactions to data servers. As client traffic increases, you can scale out the Web server farm by adding up to 32 servers in a single cluster. NLB automatically detects server failures and redirects client traffic to the remaining servers, all the time maintaining continuous, unbroken client service.

- *Use redundant array of independent disks (RAID) for data stores.* RAID uses multiple hard disks to store data in multiple places. If a disk fails, the application is transferred to a mirrored data image and the application continues running. The failed disk can be replaced without stopping the application.

- *Isolate mission-critical applications.* An application is constantly performing tasks and requesting resources such as network communications, data access, or process threads. Each of these resource requests can affect the performance and availability of applications sharing the same resources. If an application shares these services on the same servers, the workload and throughput characteristics for these servers might change unfavorably. It is recommended that mission-critical applications use dedicated infrastructures and private networks.

- *Use queuing.* Queuing enables your application to communicate with other applications by sending and receiving asynchronous messages. Queuing guarantees message delivery; it does not matter whether the necessary connectivity currently exists (with mobile applications, for example). Queuing removes a failure point from the application. Queuing is also a solution for managing peak workloads that can require a lot of hardware. In addition, by increasing the number of routes for successful message delivery, an application can increase the chances for successful and immediate message completion.

How to Design for Reliability

The reliability of an application refers to the ability of the application to provide accurate results. Reliability and availability are closely related. While availability measures the capacity to handle all requests and to recover from a failure with the least loss of access to the application, reliability measures how long the application can execute and produce expected results without failing. Users bypass unreliable Web sites, resulting in lost revenue and reduced future sales. In addition, the expense of repairing corrupted data increases the cost of application failure. Unreliable systems are also difficult to maintain or improve because the failure points are typically hidden throughout the system.

Reasons for application failure

An application is a collection of hardware, operating system services, software components, and human processes that together provide pre-specified business services. Reliability of the entire application depends on the reliability of the individual components. Because all components in a system are related, failure of one component can affect the reliability of other components.

Application failures can occur for many reasons:

- Erroneous code
- Inadequate testing
- Change management problems
- Operational errors
- Lack of ongoing monitoring and analysis
- Lack of quality software engineering processes
- Interaction with external services or applications
- Changing operating conditions, such as usage level or workload changes
- Unusual events, such as security failures and broadcast storms
- Hardware failures (disks, controllers, network devices, servers, power supplies, memory, and CPUs)
- Environmental problems (power, cooling, fire, flood, dust, and natural disasters)

Designing for reliability

To design for reliability, you need to examine the application's expected usage pattern, create a reliability profile, and create a solution that meets the profile. You must examine how a particular service is provided, evaluate failure scenarios, and design preferred alternatives. In addition, you need to consider the application's interactions with other applications.

It is difficult to identify reliability problems and solutions for a system that has not been developed. However, you can begin by analyzing the currently running applications in the organization. Such analysis reveals the failure frequency and distribution, root causes, and possible improvements for existing systems. You can use this information to design a reliable solution.

A reliable solution ensures error-free data input, data transformations, state management, and non-corrupting recovery from any failure conditions. Creating a high-reliability application depends on the entire software development lifecycle, from the planning phase, through development and testing, to deployment and stabilizing. The following tasks can help you create a reliable application:

- Putting reliability requirements in the specification
- Using a good architectural infrastructure
- Including management information in the application
- Using redundancy
- Using quality development tools
- Using reliability checks that are provided by the application
- Implementing error handling
- Reducing the application's functionality instead of completely failing the application

How to Design for Performance

An application's performance is defined by metrics such as transaction throughput and resource utilization. A user might define an application's performance in terms of its response time.

Performance goals and metrics

Before designing for performance, you need to determine performance goals of the application and metrics for measuring performance. To determine performance goals, you need to answer questions such as:

- *What is the business goal?* For example, if the business goal of the solution is to handle more orders each week, you could begin with the expected increase in revenue and convert the figure into a performance goal for each functional area.

- *What is the critical functionality of the solution?* Identifying critical features allows you to prioritize the system design. You might decide to degrade the performance of a low priority feature to maintain or increase the performance of a higher priority feature.

- *What are the features required by different sets of users?* You can create profiles according to the various expectations of the organization and the end users of the solution. Because of varying expectations, the performance requirements of the application can differ. You need to determine the relationship between each functional area and performance goal. For example, the database stores all information about orders placed by the customer. From the customer's perspective, the application should quickly update the database. The organization expects the solution to store valid data quickly. Therefore, the performance goal of the solution is to ensure fast inserts and updates to the database. Creating profiles helps in partitioning and developing accurate tests for the solution.

Note   For the purposes of testing, the performance goal must be expressed in a way that is measurable in your testing routines. You need to identify performance metrics for the application. For example, the performance goal of fast inserts and updates to a database can be measured in terms of transactions per second.

Designing for performance

You must define performance requirements before the team proceeds to the developing phase. To define a good performance requirement, you must identify project constraints, determine services that the application will perform, and specify the load on the application.

- *Identifying constraints.* Constraints in the project include budget, schedule, infrastructure, and the choice of development tools or technologies. For example, you might need to deploy an application by a specific date. You might also need to use a specific development tool because the team has expertise in that tool only. You might not be able to design and develop applications that are processor intensive because the client computers do not have adequate hardware. You need to design an application so that it meets its performance goals within the limitations of the constraints. Instead of changing some aspects of a project to improve performance, you can modify aspects of the project that are not constrained to determine how you can improve performance. For example, can the team be trained so that they can create components by using a different tool? Can data access be improved by changing the data access technology?

- *Determining features.* The features of an application correspond to use cases and usage scenarios. You can identify the usage scenarios that affect the performance of the application and, for each such scenario, specify what the user does and what the application does in response, including how databases and other system services are accessed. In addition, you need to determine how often each feature will be used. This information can help you create tests for measuring performance that resemble actual usage of the application as closely as possible.

- *Specifying the load.* You can specify the load of an application as the number of clients that will use the application. In addition, you can examine how the load might vary over time. For example, the number of requests for an e-commerce site will be higher during certain times of year. You can use the load to define the performance metrics of the application.

How to Design for Interoperability

Typically, medium and large organizations have heterogeneous computing environments. For example, many organizations deploy distributed *n*-tier client/server applications that require access to data or transactions on existing systems. In addition, your application might need to interact with applications that have been developed using proprietary or third-party software.

Reasons for interoperability

You need to design for interoperability because interoperability:

- *Reduces operational cost and complexity.* Customers can continue to work in mixed environments for the foreseeable future. The ability for different systems to operate in the same environment together reduces the cost of developing and supporting a heterogeneous infrastructure.

- *Enables optimal deployments.* Customers might have business requirements that can be delivered with specific applications and platforms. An interoperable application enables the organization to continue using the diverse applications that address its specific requirements.

- *Uses existing investments.* Typically, customers have a large and diverse range of systems installed in their environments and move to a new platform gradually. Therefore, new applications must be able to interact with previous applications. In addition, existing applications might be made Web-aware and need to allow access from an intranet or the Internet to systems hosted on environments such as an IBM mainframe. This extends the functionality of existing applications and protects the investments that the organizations have made.

Designing for interoperability

To integrate heterogeneous applications, you need to consider the following types of interoperability:

- *Network interoperability.* Refers to the ability of multiple vendor systems to communicate with each other without having to use common protocols. In the past, applications might have been designed for predefined protocols such as Transmission Control Protocol/Internet Protocol (TCP/IP), Internetwork Packet Exchange /Sequenced Package Exchange (IPX/SPX), or Systems Network Architecture (SNA). Implementing technologies or standards such as Hypertext Transfer Protocol (HTTP), Extensible Markup Language (XML), SOAP, Web Services Description Language (WSDL), and XML Web services to make use of the Internet can make your applications independent of programming language, platform, and device.

- *Data interoperability.* Refers to the ability of applications to access and use data stored in both structured and unstructured storage systems such as databases, file systems, and e-mail stores. Enterprise applications often require the sharing of data between disparate data sources and multiple applications. Published data exchange standards, such as cascading style sheets, ODBC, and XML, allow data access to both Windows-based and non-Windows-based data sources.

- *Applications interoperability.* Refers to the infrastructure required to ensure interoperability between new *n*-tier applications and existing applications, business logic, and data. As you create new *n*-tier applications, they will need to work with a wide variety of existing applications. One of the methods of enabling application interoperability is by using Common Language Specification (CLS). CLS is a standard that is currently met by more than twenty different languages to allow the interoperability of services created in any CLS-compliant language.

You can enable interoperability in Microsoft .NET-connected applications to access and use traditional Active Server Pages (ASP) and Component Object Model (COM) applications that you are not yet ready to migrate to .NET–connected solutions. In addition, XML was specifically created to allow applications to exchange data easily and without conversion code that would need to be created for each instance or type of data exchange.

- *Management interoperability.* Refers to the tasks of user account management, performance monitoring, and tuning for heterogeneous applications in the organization.

How to Design for Globalization and Localization

Globalization and localization are processes that you use for developing world-ready applications. During the planning phase, you need to clearly identify and document globalization and localization requirements so that the design of the application can address these requirements.

Note   In the Microsoft .NET Framework, three namespaces have been provided to make your application easy to globalize and localize. They are the System.Globalization namespace, the System.Resources namespace, and the System.Text namespace.

Definition of globalization

Globalization is the process of designing and developing an application that can operate in multiple cultures and locales. Globalization involves:

- Identifying the cultures and locales that must be supported
- Designing features that support those cultures and locales
- Writing code that executes properly in all the supported cultures and locales

Globalization enables you to create applications that can accept, display, and output information in different language scripts that are appropriate for various geographical areas. To globalize these functions, you use the concept of cultures and locales. A culture and locale is a set of rules and a set of data that are specific to a given language and geographical area. These rules and data include information about:

- Character classification
- Date and time formatting
- Numeric, currency, weight, and measure conventions
- Sorting rules

Definition of localization

Localization is the process of adapting a globalized application to a specific culture and locale, using separate resources for each culture that is to be globalized. A resource file contains culture-specific user interface items that are provided to an application as a text file, a *.resx* file, or a *.resources* file. An application prepared for localization has two conceptual blocks: the *data block* and the *code block*. The data block (usually contained in resource files) contains all user-interface string resources. The code block contains the application code that is applicable for all cultures and locales and accesses the correct resource file for the culture currently selected in the operating system.

To create a localized version of the application, you change the data block and combine it with the code block, which essentially remains the same. You need to have a basic understanding of relevant character sets commonly used in modern software development and the issues associated with them. Although all computers store text as numbers, different systems can store the same text by using different numbers.

To successfully create a localized version of an application, ensure that:

- The code block is separate from the data block.
- The application code can read data accurately, regardless of the culture and locale.

Issues in globalization and localization

Some of the issues that you need to consider while planning for globalization and localization are:

- *Language issues.* Language issues are the result of differences in how languages around the world differ in display, alphabets, grammar, and syntactical rules. For example, various languages are read and written left-to-right, right-to-left, or top-to-bottom.
- *Formatting issues.* Formatting issues are the primary source of discrepancies when working with applications originally written for another language, culture, and locale. During globalization and localization, you need to pay attention to factors such as addresses, currency types, dates, paper sizes, telephone numbers, time formats, and units of measure. Developers can use the National Language Support (NLS) application programming interfaces (APIs) in Microsoft® Windows® or the System.Globalization namespace to handle most of these issues automatically.
- *String-related issues.* Strings are the text displayed in the various elements in an application's user interface, such as message boxes, dialog boxes, title bars, status bars, and menus. For example, message boxes typically concatenate strings of standard text and context-specific texts. In different languages, the concatenated string might not be grammatically correct.

- *User interface issues.* You should pay special attention to the design of the following user interface (UI) components:

  - *Messages.* The length of messages might differ in different languages.

  - *Menus and dialog boxes.* Menus and dialog boxes might become larger as a result of localization.

  - *Icons and bitmaps.* Icons and bitmaps must use symbols that are internationally accepted and convey the same meaning, regardless of the culture or locale.

  - *Access and shortcut keys.* The keyboards used in the different locales might not have the same characters and keys. You need to ensure that access keys and shortcut keys are supported in the keyboards used in the destination locales.

  - *UI controls.* UI controls should not be hidden or used as a parts of strings.

Best practices for globalization and localization

The following best practices provide a checklist of the issues associated with developing world-ready software.

- *Technical issues.*

  - Use Unicode as your character-encoding standard to represent text. All applications process data, whether text or numerical. Different cultures and locales might use different data encoding techniques. *Unicode* is a 16-bit international character-encoding standard that covers values for more than 45,000 characters. It allows each character in all the required cultures and locales to be represented uniquely.

  - Implement a multilingual user interface. If you design the user interface to open in the default UI language, and offer the option to change to other languages, users who speak different languages can quickly switch to the preferred interface.

  - Examine Windows messages that indicate changes in the input language, and use that information to check spelling, select fonts, and so on.

  - Detect the culture that your application uses to handle dates, currencies, and numeric differences and change it to correspond to the culture that application supports. In the .NET Framework, *culture* refers to the user's language, which can be combined with that user's location. By specifying a culture, it is possible to use a set of common preferences for certain information, such as strings, date formats, and number formats, that corresponds to the user's language and location conventions.

- *Cultural and political issues.* Examples of cultural and political issues include disputes related to maps, which can induce governments to prevent distribution in specific regions. These issues do not prevent the application from running. However, they can create negative feelings about the application and customers might seek alternatives from other companies. To avoid such issues:
    - Avoid slang expressions, colloquialisms, and obscure phrasing in all text.
    - Avoid images in bitmaps and icons that are ethnocentric or offensive in other cultures and locales.
    - Avoid maps that include controversial regional or national boundaries.
- *User interface issues.*
    - Store all user interface elements in resource files, message files, or a private database so that they are separate from the program source code.
    - Place only those strings that require localization in resource files. Leave non-localized strings as string constants in the source code.
    - Use the same resource identifiers throughout the life of the project. Changing identifiers makes it difficult to update localized resources from one version of the application to another.
    - If the same string is used in multiple contexts, make multiple copies of the string. The same string might have different translations in different contexts.
    - Allocate text buffers dynamically because text size might change when text is translated.
    - Be aware that dialog boxes might expand because of localization.
    - Avoid text in bitmaps and icons.
    - Do not create a text message dynamically at run time.
    - Avoid composing text that uses multiple insertion parameters in a format string.
    - If localizing to a Middle Eastern language such as Arabic or Hebrew, use the right-to-left layout APIs to lay out text in the application from right to left.
    - Test localized applications on all language variants of the operating system.

Lesson 2: Planning for Administrative Features

Administrative features are an important part of a solution. In this lesson, you will learn how to design and plan administrative features such as monitoring, data migration, and the licensing specifications of a solution.

After this lesson, you will be able to

- Plan for monitoring in a solution.
- Plan for data migration.
- Create licensing specifications.

Estimated lesson time: 10 minutes

How to Plan for Monitoring

Application monitoring is used to ensure that the application is functioning correctly and performing at an optimal level. Automated monitoring enables identification of failure conditions and potential problems. Monitoring helps to reduce the time needed to recover from failures.

Typically, application monitoring is the responsibility of administrators and operators within the operations team. It is critical for an operations team to establish guidelines and procedures for application monitoring. Communicating these procedures to the development team allows both teams to work together to log and monitor information that can assist problem discovery and problem diagnosis. This process is ongoing and requires revision; both the operations and development teams should strive to continually refine monitoring processes.

Error logging is closely related to monitoring and is a development function. You should design an appropriate strategy for error management at an early stage during the design phase. The development team must communicate with the operations team to inform them of the types of error logs generated by the application. The operations team must inform the development team of the various mechanisms that are available for monitoring errors. Together, both teams must decide on the appropriate logging mechanisms and then develop and monitor applications accordingly.

The monitoring plan

The monitoring plan defines the process by which the operational environment will monitor the solution. It describes what will be monitored, how it will be monitored, and how the results of monitoring will be reported and used. Organizations use automated procedures to monitor many aspects of a solution.

The plan provides details of the monitoring process, which will be incorporated into the functional specification. Once incorporated into the functional specification, the monitoring process (manual and automated) is included in the solution design. Monitoring ensures that operators are made aware that a failure has occurred so that they can initiate procedures to restore service. Additionally, some organizations monitor their servers' performance characteristics to identify usage trends. This process allows organizations to identify the conditions that contribute to system failure and to take action to prevent those conditions from occurring.

Elements of the monitoring plan

Some of the key sections of the monitoring plan are:

- *Resource threshold monitoring.* Identifies the solution resources that will be monitored. This section also includes the threshold values of each of the resources. A threshold value might be, for example, when processor usage increases to more than 80 percent.

- *Performance monitoring.* Defines the performance metrics to be gathered for the performance of the solution and the individual components of the solution. This section indicates the events that will be recorded and monitored, their frequency of occurrence, start and end times, and success and failure status. For example, you can record the logon attempts made by users, and the number of repeated failed logon attempts by the same user.

- *Trend analysis.* Defines the analysis that will take place on the data collected during performance monitoring. You can use this information for predicting the performance of the application under varying situations. For example, you can predict the number of users for various parts of the day and determine how the application will perform under varying loads.

- *Detecting failures.* Describes how the development, operations, and maintenance teams will use the functional specification and user acceptance criteria to detect failure incidents. You use the functional specification to determine the success criteria for the solution. This information is also included in the user acceptance criteria. For example, if shoppers must be able to browse items and select them from a list, and the list does not display any items, the event is marked as a failure.

- *Error detection.* Describes the processes, methods, and tools teams will use to detect and diagnose solution errors. These errors are typically identified and resolved by the development, operations, and maintenance teams without the knowledge of the users.

- *Event logs.* Describes the logs that will provide a system for capturing and reviewing significant application and system events. For example, you can use Microsoft SQL Server™ logs for an application that uses a SQL Server database.

- *Notifications.* Describes how the operations team will be notified when monitoring and exception trapping has detected solution failures. Notification methods can include pagers and e-mail.

- *Tools.* Describes the tools teams can use to detect, diagnose, and correct errors and to improve a solution's performance. The team can use tools such as Microsoft Systems Management Server and System Monitor.

How to Plan for Data Migration

When data from earlier or existing sources is identified as a part of the new solution, data migration becomes a critical element. Without well-tested migration paths, new solutions can fail because earlier components can introduce risks that were never accounted for during planning. If data from earlier systems cannot be migrated successfully to the new solution, the new solution cannot be deployed and a return on investment cannot begin.

The migration plan describes the migration from existing systems or applications to the new solution. Migration is often more important in infrastructure deployment than it is in application development projects, but application development projects usually include some sort of migration.

The migration plan includes the following sections:

- *Migration strategies.* Describes the strategy or strategies that will guide the migration process. These strategies do not need to be mutually exclusive but can describe different pieces of the overall migration. Strategy can be organized around releases (related to the business or to development or technology maturity) or organized around solution components. These strategies also need to take into account moving earlier systems into the new solution environment. You might have multiple migration strategy sections if you need to migrate both business objects and data.

- *Tools.* Identifies the tools that will be used to support the migration strategy. These tools can include conversion tools, installation tools, testing tools, and training tools.

- *Migration guidelines.* Describes the guidelines that must be followed within the environment, such as how migrated data will be validated or in what order data must be migrated.

- *Migration process.* Describes how the migration will be conducted. It includes the preparatory activities in addition to the migration stages necessary to complete the migration process.

- *Test environment.* Describes the test environment that replicates the production environment. This includes all environmental attributes that must be in place.

- *Rollback plan.* Describes how a customer can roll back to the prior configuration if problems occur during migration.

How to Create Licensing Specifications

It is a good practice to determine purchasing requirements early in the project for both hardware and software that will be required by the solution. Purchasing specifications developed early in the process ensure that there is sufficient time for the approval process and that vendors have sufficient time to deliver hardware so as not to affect the schedule. An important part of purchasing specifications is licensing specifications.

You need to provide licensing specifications for both the developing and deploying phases. During the developing phase, the team will work with selected technologies and software products. You must ensure that you have sufficient licenses of the required products.

Depending on the type of solution and the number of users who will use the solution, you need to specify the number of licenses of any software that might be used.

For example, if your application can be deployed only on Windows XP, you need the appropriate number of Windows XP licenses for all users to install and run the application.

Lesson 3: Planning for Future Phases

The MSF Process Model consists of five phases: envisioning, planning, developing, stabilizing, and deploying. During the planning phase, you plan what will be developed, how it will be developed, and who will develop it. You also create plans for the activities that must be performed in the subsequent phases.

In this lesson, you will learn to plan for tasks in the subsequent phases of the project.

After this lesson, you will be able to

- Create plans for the developing phase.
- Create plans for the stabilizing phase.
- Create plans for the deploying phase.

Estimated lesson time: 5 minutes

How to Plan for the Developing Phase

Before the team actually begins developing the solution, it is important to verify that the infrastructure of the development and test environments is ready. The test environment should ideally represent the production environment, but the team must balance the level of representation with the associated costs. It is important to maintain separation between the production environment and the development and test environments to prevent occurrences in development and test from affecting live production systems.

The development plan

During the planning phase, the project team creates a master project plan and a master project schedule. In addition, the team can create a development plan and a development schedule. The development plan describes the solution development process used for the project, in addition to the tasks necessary to create and assemble the components of the solution. This plan complements the functional specification that provides the technical details of what will be developed. The plan also provides consistent guidelines and processes to the teams creating the solution.

Having the development process documented indicates that the team has discussed and agreed on a consistent structure and direction to be used during the development process. This documentation allows developers to focus on creating the solution. Development guidelines and standards promote meaningful communication among the various teams, because they will use a common approach and common processes. The guidelines and standards also facilitate reuse among different groups and minimize the dependency upon one individual or group.

The development role in the MSF Team Model creates the development plan and the development schedule. The focus of the development role during this process is to consider how key aspects of the development process should be undertaken.

Elements of the development plan

Some of the key sections of the development plan are:

- *Development objectives.* Defines the primary drivers that were used to create the development approach and the key objectives of that approach.

- *Overall delivery strategy.* Describes the overall approach to delivering the solution. Examples of delivery strategy include staged delivery, depth-first, breadth-first, and features then performance.

- *Tradeoff approach.* Defines the approach for making design and implementation of tradeoff decisions. For example, you might agree to trade features for schedule improvements or to trade features for performance.

- *Key design goals.* Identifies the key design goals and the priority of each goal. Examples of design goals include interoperability and security.

- *Development and build environment.* Describes the development and build environment and how it will be managed. Include information on items such as source code control tools, design tool requirements, operating systems, or other software installed.

- *Guidelines and standards.* Lists and provides references to all standards and guidelines to be used for the project.

- *Versioning and source control.* Describes how versioning and source control will be managed. This section includes identification of the specific tools that will be used and how developers are expected to use them.

- *Build process.* Describes the incremental and iterative approach for developing code and for builds of hardware and software components. It also describes how the build process will be implemented and how often it will be implemented.

- *Components.* Provides a high-level description of the set of solution components and how they will be developed.

- *Configuration and development management tools.* Identifies all the development tools the team will use during the project. This includes tools for all steps in the project: development, testing, documentation, support, operations, and deployment.

- *Design patterns.* Identifies the design patterns or templates that the team will use for this project and their sources. The team can acquire design patterns from both external and internal sources or create new design patterns.

- *Development team training.* Identifies the training necessary to ensure that the development team will successfully develop the solution.

- *Development team support.* Identifies the various types of support the development team will require, the sources of that support, the amount of support of each type that the team will require, and the estimated schedule for support.

How to Plan for the Stabilizing Phase

During the stabilizing phase, the testing team conducts tests on a solution whose features are complete. Testing during this phase emphasizes usage and operation under realistic environmental conditions. The team focuses on resolving and prioritizing bugs and preparing the solution for release.

During the planning phase, the team typically creates the following plans that will be used during the stabilizing phase:

- The test plan
- The pilot plan

The test plan

The test plan describes the strategy and approach used to plan, organize, and manage the project's testing activities. It identifies testing objectives, methodologies and tools, expected results, responsibilities, and resource requirements. This document is the primary plan for the testing team. A test plan ensures that the testing process will be conducted in a thorough and organized manner and will enable the team to determine the stability of the solution. A continuous understanding of the solution's status builds confidence in team members and stakeholders as the solution is developed and stabilized.

The testing role in the MSF Team Model is responsible for creating the test plan. This team is also responsible for setting the quality expectations and incorporating them into the testing plan.

The test plan breaks the testing process into different elements, including:

- Code component testing
- Database testing
- Infrastructure testing
- Security testing
- Integration testing
- User acceptance and usability testing
- Stress, capacity, and performance testing
- Regression testing

Elements of the test plan

The key sections of a test plan are:

- *Test approach and assumptions.* Describes at a high level the approach, activities, and techniques to be followed in testing the solution. If different approaches are required for the solution's various components, you need to specify which components will be tested by each approach.

- *Major test responsibilities.* Identifies the teams and individuals who will manage and implement the testing process.

- *Features and functionality to test.* Identifies at a high level all features and functionality that will be tested.

- *Expected results of tests.* Describes the results that should be demonstrated by the tests. This information includes expectations of both the solution team and the testers. This section also defines whether the results must be exactly as anticipated or whether a range of results is acceptable.

- *Deliverables.* Describes the materials that must be made available or created to conduct the tests and that will be developed from the tests to describe test results.

- *Testing procedures and walkthrough.* Describes the steps the testing team will perform to ensure quality tests.

- *Tracking and reporting status.* Defines the information that test team members will communicate during the testing process. This section defines the specific test status information that will be created and distributed. This information normally includes status information for each test case and the probability of completing the test cycle on schedule.

- *Bug reporting tools and methods.* Describes the overall bug reporting strategy and methodology. This section also defines what will qualify as a bug in the code, product features, and documentation.

- *Schedules.* Identifies the major test cycles, tasks, milestones, and deliverables. This section also describes who is responsible for each test cycle and its tasks. In addition, it identifies the expected start and completion date for each test cycle and the tasks within that cycle.

For the test plan for the Adventure Works Cycles case study, refer to the AWC Test Plan document in the \SolutionDocuments\Chapter10 folder on the companion CD.

Note Testing is covered in detail in Chapter 11, "Stabilizing and Deploying the Solution."

The pilot plan

The pilot plan describes how the team will move the candidate release version of the solution to a staging area and test it. The goal of the pilot is to simulate the equipment, software, and components that the solution will use when it is active.

This plan also identifies how issues discovered during the pilot will be solved. The pilot plan includes details about how to evaluate the pilot; the results of the evaluation will facilitate a decision whether to move the solution to production.

Project teams often conduct one or more pilots to prove the feasibility of solution approaches, to experiment with different solutions, and to obtain user feedback and acceptance on proposed solutions. Pilot solutions implement only those subsets or segments of requirements or the functional specification that are necessary to validate the solution.

Note Some projects might not conduct a pilot.

The pilot plan provides the means to validate the business requirements and the technical specification prior to deploying the solution into production. Planning the details of the pilot ensures that the participating project teams identify their roles and responsibilities and resource requirements specific to pilot development, testing, and deployment activities.

Note You can learn more about creating pilot plans in Chapter 11, "Stabilizing and Deploying the Solution."

How to Plan for the Deploying Phase

During the deploying phase, the team deploys the solution technology and components, stabilizes the deployment, transitions the project to operations and support, and obtains final customer approval of the project.

The deployment plan

During the planning phase, the team typically creates the deployment plan. The deployment plan describes the factors necessary for a relatively problem-free deployment and transition to ongoing operations. It includes the processes of preparing, installing, training, stabilizing, and transferring the solution to operations. These processes include details of installation scenarios, monitoring for stability, and verifying the soundness of the new solution. This plan guides the implementation of the solution into production. This plan also provides detailed deployment guidelines and helps drive the solution's deploying phase. Deployment is the beginning of the realization of business value for a given solution. A detailed and verified deployment plan accelerates value realization for both the customer and the project team.

The release management role of the MSF Team Model is responsible for designing and implementing the solution's deployment plan. Release management is also responsible for specifying the solution infrastructure and ensuring that the solution continues to run as expected after it has been deployed.

Elements of the deployment plan

Some of the key sections of the deployment plan are:

- *Deployment scope.* Describes the solution architecture and scale of deployment.
- *Seats.* Describes the magnitude of the deployment in terms of sites, number of workstations, countries and regions, and other relevant size factors.
- *Components.* Lists and describes the components to be deployed and any critical dependencies among them.
- *Architecture.* Describes the solution's architecture and how it might affect deployment.
- *Deployment schedule.* Identifies the critical dates and anticipated schedule for the deploying phase.
- *Installation.* Defines how the overall deployment will occur.
- *Deployment resources.* Identifies the workforce that will be needed to complete the deployment and the sources of the personnel.
- *Solution support.* Describes how the users will be supported during the deployment.
- *Help desk.* Describes the support provided to users and applications by the help desk team, including support for direct user questions and application issues, and also in-depth support for new or difficult issues.
- *Desktop.* Describes any changes in current workstation application support that might be required during deployment.
- *Servers.* Describes any changes in current server support that might be required during deployment.
- *Telecommunications.* Describes any changes in current telecommunication support that might be required during deployment.
- *Coordination of training.* Describes how end-user and support staff training is coordinated with the deployment schedule.
- *Site installation process.* Describes the four phases of site installation: preparing, installing, training, and stabilizing.

Lesson 4: Creating the Technical Specification

To begin creating the solution, the development team uses the technical specification document. In this lesson, you will learn about technical specification and the components of a technical specification document.

After this lesson, you will be able to

■ Describe the purpose of technical specification.

■ List the elements of a technical specification document.

Estimated lesson time: 5 minutes

What Is the Technical Specification?

The technical specification is a set of reference documents that usually include the artifacts of physical design, such as class specifications, component models, metrics, and network and component topologies. During the developing phase, the developers use the technical specification to scope and define their work products. The technical specification includes interface definitions, registry entries, bytes required to install, dynamic-link library (DLL) and assembly names, strong names, keys, and all identified elements that will affect deployment. When elements of the solution are completed during development, the technical specification is updated to ensure that it documents the solution.

Elements of a Technical Specification Document

The sections of a technical specification include:

■ *Architecture overview.* Describes the architecture that will be implemented by the solution.

■ *Object model.* Describes the object model of the solution. This section includes a description of all objects in the solution and their functionality.

■ *Interfaces.* Contains the code and details of methods of each interface in the solution.

■ *Code flow.* Describes the operation of each method in the solution.

■ *Error codes.* Describes the error codes used for error handling in the solution.

■ *Error logging.* Describes how various errors will be handled and logged in the solution.

■ *Configuration.* Describes how the solution will be registered on the destination computer. This section includes registry keys and their settings.

- *Supporting documentation.* Lists the documents that describe the solution, such as the functional specification, and their locations.

- *Issues.* Describes any known issues with the solution. Typically, the probable date of resolution for each is also specified in this section.

For the technical specification for the Adventure Works Cycles case study, refer to AWC Technical Specification.doc in the \SolutionDocuments\Chapter10 folder on the companion CD. This is a draft version of the technical specification document, as it would look prior to the developing phase. This document is updated throughout the developing phase.

Activity: Reviewing a Test Plan and Technical Specification

In this activity, you use what you learned in the lessons to work through a review of a test plan and a technical specification.

Exercise 1: Reviewing a Test Plan

Open the document named AWC Test Plan.doc in the \SolutionDocuments\Chapter10 folder on the companion CD.

1. Review the test plan and then list three ways that use cases and usage scenarios are used in the testing process for AdventureWorks Cycles.

2. How will bugs be approved and documented for action for the solution?

3. Which user accounts must be configured on the test environment servers?

4. Why is the following threat important to list under threats to testing?

   Availability of sales staff for testing. The test team should be overseen by at least one sales representative. Mitigation: Gain prior agreement from the vice president of sales for two sales representatives to be assigned to test the application.

Exercise 2: Reviewing a Technical Specification

Open the document named AWC Technical Specification.doc in the \SolutionDocuments\Chapter10 folder on the companion CD. Answer the following questions:

1. What are the parameters for the *addOrderDetail* method?

2. Will two types of client interfaces be available in the application?

3. Why is the Interfaces section still to be determined?

Summary

- Scalability is defined as the capability to increase resources to yield a linear increase in service capacity.
- You can either scale up or scale out an application.
- Guidelines for scaling include:
  - Design processes so that they do not wait
  - Design processes so that they do not fight for resources
  - Design processes for commutability
  - Design components for interchangeability
  - Partition resources and activities
- Availability is a measure of how often an application is available for use.
- To decide the availability level of an application, you need to answer the following questions:
  - Who are the customers and what are their expectations?
  - How much downtime is acceptable?
  - Do internal company processes depend on the application?
  - What are the schedule and budget for developing the application?
- Guidelines for designing for availability of a solution include:
  - Reduce planned downtime
  - Reduce unplanned downtime by using clustering
  - Use network load balancing
  - Use RAID for data stores
  - Isolate mission-critical applications
  - Use queuing
- The process of designing for reliability involves reviewing the application's expected usage pattern, specifying the required reliability profile, and engineering the software architecture with the intention of meeting the profile.

- To create a good reliability design, you need to perform the following tasks:
  - Put reliability requirements in the specification.
  - Use a good architectural infrastructure.
  - Include management information in the application.
  - Use redundancy.
  - Use quality development tools.
  - Use reliability checks that are provided by the application.
  - Use consistent error handling.
  - Reduce the application's functionality instead of completely failing the application.
- An application's performance is defined by key application metrics, such as transaction throughput and resource utilization.
- To determine performance goals, you need to answer questions such as the following:
  - What is the business goal?
  - What is the critical functionality of the solution?
  - What are the features required by different sets of users?
- To integrate heterogeneous applications, you need to consider the following types of interoperability:
  - Network interoperability, which provides the core foundation for interoperability between systems
  - Data interoperability, which delivers the ability for users and applications to access and query information stored in both structured and unstructured storage engines
  - Applications interoperability, which provides the key infrastructure required to ensure interoperability between new and existing applications
  - Management interoperability, which focuses on reducing the burden of administration of multiple systems, including user accounts management
- Globalization is the process of designing and developing a software product that functions in multiple cultures and locales.
- Localization is the process of adapting a globalized application to a particular culture and locale.
- Application monitoring is used to ensure that the application is functioning correctly and performing at the optimal level.
- The monitoring plan describes what will be monitored, how the application will be monitored, and how the results of monitoring will be reported and used.

- The migration plan describes the migration from existing systems or applications to the new solution.
- You need to provide licensing specifications for both the developing and deploying phases.
- The development plan describes the solution development process used for the project.
- The test plan describes the strategy and approach used to plan, organize, and manage the project's testing activities, and identifies testing objectives, methodologies and tools, expected results, responsibilities, and resource requirements.
- The pilot plan describes elements of the solution that will be delivered as a pilot and provides the details necessary to conduct the pilot successfully.
- The deployment plan describes the factors necessary for a smooth deployment and transition to ongoing operations and includes the processes of preparing, installing, training, stabilizing, and transferring the solution to operations.
- The technical specification is a set of reference documents that usually include the artifacts of physical design, such as class specifications, component models, metrics, and network and component topologies.

Review

The following questions are intended to reinforce key information presented in this chapter. If you are unable to answer a question, review the lesson materials and try the question again. You can find answers to the questions in the appendix.

1. How do you scale up an application?

2. What do you need to take into consideration while designing for scalability?

3. What do you need to take into consideration while designing for availability?

4. How does clustering enhance the availability of an application?

5. How do you reduce planned downtime of an application?

6. Why is reliability an important design consideration for an application?

7. How do you design for reliability of an application?

8. How do you define a performance requirement?

9. Why do you need to design for interoperability?

10. How do you prepare an application for globalization?

11. What is the purpose of a monitoring plan?

12. What is the purpose of the migration strategies section of the migration plan?

13. Why do you need to provide licensing specifications for both the development and the deployment phase?

14. What is the purpose of the development plan?

15. What is the purpose of the test plan?

16. Who creates the deployment plan?

17. What is a technical specification?

C H A P T E R   1 1

Stabilizing and Deploying the Solution

About This Chapter

After the development phase of a project is complete, the project enters its stabilizing and deploying phases. The goal of the stabilizing phase of the Microsoft® Solutions Framework (MSF) Process Model is to improve the quality of the solution to meet the acceptance criteria for release to production. During the deploying phase, the solution is deployed to the production environment.

Before You Begin

To complete the lessons in this chapter, you must have

- General understanding of Microsoft technologies.
- Understanding of the MSF process and its phases.

Lesson 1: The MSF Stabilizing Phase

During the stabilizing phase, testing is conducted on a solution whose features are complete. Testing starts early in the MSF process with activities such as defining the success criteria and the testing approach during the envisioning phase, and creating a testing plan during the planning phase. However, it is during the stabilizing phase that the Testing team completes the tasks and creates the deliverables that move the feature-complete build to a state in which the defined quality level is reached and the solution is ready for full production deployment.

Testing during this phase emphasizes usage and operation under realistic environmental conditions. The team focuses on resolving and prioritizing bugs and preparing the solution for release.

The two main tasks in the stabilizing phase are:

- *Testing the solution.* The team implements the test plans that were created during the planning phase, which were enhanced and tested during the development phase.
- *Conducting the pilot.* The team moves a solution pilot from development to a staging area to test the solution with actual users and real scenarios. The pilot is conducted before the deploying phase is begun.

After this lesson, you will be able to

- Explain the deliverables of the MSF stabilizing phase.
- Explain the interim milestones of the MSF stabilizing phase.
- Explain the team roles and responsibilities during the stabilizing phase.

Estimated lesson time: 15 minutes

MSF Stabilizing Phase Deliverables

The goal of the MSF stabilizing phase is to improve the quality of a solution and to stabilize it for release to production. During this phase, the team conducts testing on a feature-complete solution. The testing in this phase also includes testing the accuracy of supporting documentation, training, and other non-code elements.

The following are the deliverables of the stabilizing phase:

- Pilot review
- Release-ready versions of:
  - Source code and executables
  - Scripts and installation documentation
  - End-user Help and training materials
  - Operations documentation
  - Release notes
- Testing and bug reports
- Project documents

MSF Phase Interim Milestones

In addition to the deliverables, the stabilizing phase has interim milestones. The interim milestones of the stabilizing phase are:

- Bug convergence
- Zero-bug bounce
- Release candidates
- Golden release

Bug convergence

Bug convergence is the point at which the team makes visible progress against the active bug count. It is the point at which the rate of bugs that are resolved exceeds the rate of bugs that are found.

Figure 11.1 illustrates bug convergence.

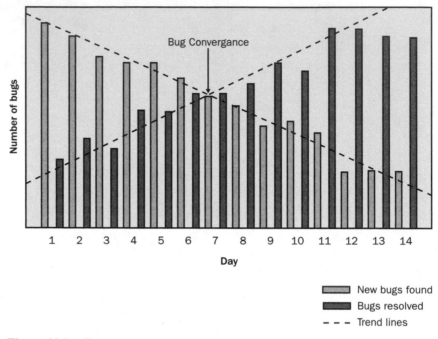

Figure 11.1.   Bug convergence

Because the bug rate will still vary—even after it starts its overall decline—bug convergence usually manifests itself as a trend rather than a fixed point in time. After bug convergence, the number of bugs should continue to decrease until zero-bug release.

Zero-bug bounce

Zero-bug bounce (ZBB) is the point in the project when development resolves all the bugs raised by Testing and there are no active bugs—for the moment. Figure 11.2 illustrates ZBB.

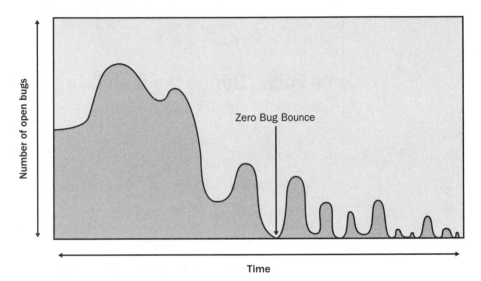

Figure 11.2.   Zero-bug bounce

After zero-bug bounce, the bug peaks should become noticeably smaller and should continue to decrease until the product is stable enough to release.

Careful bug prioritization is vital because every bug that is fixed creates the risk of creating a new bug, or regression issue. Achieving zero-bug bounce is a clear sign that the team is in the final stage as it progresses toward a stable product.

Note   New bugs will certainly be found after this milestone is reached. But it does mark the first time that the team can honestly report that there are no active bugs—even if it is only for the moment—and it focuses the team on working to stay at that point.

Release candidates

After the first achievement of zero-bug bounce, a series of *release candidates* are prepared for release to the pilot group. Each of these releases is marked as an interim milestone. The release candidates are made available to a preselected group of users so they can test it. The users provide feedback to the project team, and the project team in turn continues to improve the product and resolve bugs that appear during the pilot. As each new release candidate is built, there should be fewer bugs to report, prioritize, and resolve. Each release candidate indicates that the team is nearing the end of deployment.

Golden release

Golden release is the release of the product to production. Golden release is a milestone in the stabilizing phase, which is identified by the combination of *zero-defect* and *success criteria* metrics. At golden release, the team must select the release candidate that they will release to production. The team uses the testing data that is measured against the zero-defect and success criteria metrics and the tradeoff triangle to make this selection.

Team Focus During the Stabilizing Phase

Each team role has a specific focus and responsibilities during stabilization. The primary team roles that drive the stabilizing phase are testing and release management. Table 11.1 describes the roles and responsibilities of each team during the stabilizing phase.

Table 11.1. Stabilizing Phase Roles and Responsibilities

Role	Focus
Product management	Communications plan execution; production launch planning
Program management	Project tracking; bug priority
Development	Bug resolution; code optimization
User experience	Stabilization of user performance materials, training materials, user assistance materials
Testing	Testing; bug reporting and status; configuration testing
Release management	Pilot setup and support; deployment planning; operations and support training

Lesson 2: Testing and Piloting for Stabilization

The testing process is designed to identify and address potential solution issues prior to deployment. Testing certifies that the solution components meet the project plan's goals for schedule and quality. It should also verify that the solution components meet the agreed-upon feature set.

The development team designs, documents, and writes code that is tested through unit testing and daily builds. This team tracks development progress against a project schedule, resolves reported bugs, and documents testing results.

The testing team designs and documents test specifications and test cases, writes automated scripts, and runs acceptance tests on components that are submitted for formal testing. This team assesses and reports on overall solution quality and feature completeness, and certifies when the solution features, functions, and components meet the project goals.

After this lesson, you will be able to

- Identify the best practices of testing.
- Explain the types of testing in the MSF process.
- Explain the testing terms.
- Explain the issue and bug tracking process.
- Identify some of the tasks involved in testing.
- Explain the process of conducting a pilot.
- Close the stabilizing phase.

Estimated lesson time: 40 minutes

Testing Best Practices

There are some testing best practices that the testing team should consider implementing when testing a solution.

Success criteria

Judging whether a project has been successful is almost impossible without something to measure the project's results against. The creation of *success criteria* involves defining conditions under which the proposed solution will achieve its goals. Success criteria are sometimes referred to as *key performance indicators*.

Note   Although defined here, success criteria for a project needs to be established during the envisioning and planning phases.

Zero-defect mindset

Zero-defect mindset means that the project team commits to producing the highest quality product possible. Each team member is individually responsible for helping achieve the desired level of quality. The zero-defect mindset does not mean that the deployed solution must be perfect with literally no defects; rather, it specifies a predetermined quality bar for the deliverables.

Testing Types

MSF defines two types of testing: coverage testing and usage testing.

Coverage testing

Coverage testing is low-level technical testing. For example, when a developer writes a section of code or a subject matter expert creates an automated unattended installation, he or she typically performs low-level testing to ensure that the solution meets the functional specification. In MSF, this type of testing is called coverage testing; in Microsoft product groups, it is also referred to as *prefix testing*.

Of course, if developers or subject matter experts are the only groups to perform coverage testing, risk is increased. Their closeness to the work and the pressures to deliver a finished product make it difficult for them to identify all issues and bugs in the solution. This is where *external coverage testing* can help. External coverage testing is low-level testing that is performed by a tester other than a developer or subject matter expert. Often this external coverage testing is automated to promote consistency and speed.

A typical strategy that is used for performing the coverage testing role is to use the *buddy tester* principle. Buddy testing involves using developers who are not working directly on the creation of a particular code segment, and employing them to perform coverage testing on their colleague's code. This strategy works well because the skills that are required by coverage testers are on the same level as the skills that are required for development.

Usage testing

Usage testing is high-level testing that is often performed by potential users of the solution or subsets of this group. This type of testing is very important because it ensures that issues and bugs that are related to user performance enhancement are captured and addressed. Automated scripts and check lists are a best practice in this area because they provide repeatability and prescriptive direction to the usage tester, which will improve accuracy.

Testing Terms

Before you learn more about testing a solution, it is important to be familiar with some basic testing terms.

Check-in tests

Check-in testing ensures that tested code is behaving acceptably. This type of testing is performed by developers or testers before the code is checked in to the change control system. Check-in testing can be thought of as the aggregation of all internal coverage tests that are performed by developers before the code is checked in to the change control system.

Unit tests

A unit test is a form of developer-performed internal *coverage testing* or *prefix testing* that takes advantage of automated testing. The philosophy behind unit testing is to perform testing on isolated features (one small piece at a time).

Functional tests

Functional tests are normally specified by the users of the solution and are created by the testing team. These tests are often automated tests and are normally conducted by the testing team. They focus on testing end-to-end functionality rather than isolated features.

Build verification tests

The objective of build verification testing is to identify errors during the build process. It can be thought of as the identification of compilation errors, as opposed to run-time errors, of all solution components. This type of testing can be performed by both developers and testers. For some projects, a specific team might perform these tests.

Regression tests

Regression testing is the process of repeating identical actions or steps that were performed using an earlier build of a product on a new build or version of the product. The goal of this process is to determine the following:

- Is the problem you previously reported still present?
- Has the problem been completely resolved?
- Did the resolution cause other or related problems?

Configuration tests

Most software-based solutions can be installed and configured in many different ways. The aim of configuration testing is to conduct solution tests in each of the possible solution configurations. Each of these configurations has the potential to affect the behavior of the solution and might result in the identification of new issues or bugs.

Compatibility tests

Often there is a requirement for the solution under development to integrate and interoperate with existing systems or software solutions. This form of testing focuses on integration or interoperability of the solution under development with existing systems.

This type of test often involves groups that are external to the project team. The external team must be identified as early as possible so its involvement can be planned for. Also, performing these tests in a completely isolated environment might not be possible.

Stress tests

Stress tests, also known as *load tests,* are specifically designed to identify issues or bugs that might present themselves when the solution under development is highly stressed. By stressing the solution, which most commonly entails loading the solution beyond the level that it was designed to handle, new issues or bugs might be seen.

Performance tests

Performance testing focuses on predicted performance improvements by the solution under development. These tests are often performed in conjunction with stress or loading tests. For example, if a design goal of the solution under development is to increase e-mail message throughput by 15 percent, tests would be devised to measure this predicted increase.

Documentation and Help file tests

This form of testing focuses on testing all developed support documents or systems. The documents and Help files are compared with the solution to discover any discrepancies. For example, testers might look for incorrect instructions, outdated text and screen shots, typographic errors, and so on.

Alpha and beta tests

In the MSF testing discipline, *alpha code* broadly refers to all code produced in the developing phase of the MSF Process Model, whereas *beta code* is all code tested in the stabilizing phase. Therefore, during the developing phase of the MSF Process Model tests are performed on alpha code, whereas during the stabilizing phase of the MSF Process Model tests are performed on beta code.

Parallel testing

Parallel testing is a common usage testing strategy. Parallel usage testing is testing both the current solution and the new solution, under development, side-by-side at the same time. The advantage of parallel usage testing is that it provides a quick check on expected solution behavior. For example, data is entered into the current solution and behaviors are observed. Then, the same data is entered into the new solution and its behavior is observed. These two observed behaviors can then be compared and used as usage testing data.

Planning   Parallel testing can be automated to quickly help validate the results without involving production users. However, the disadvantage of parallel testing is that if parallel testing cannot be automated, it doubles the work load of production users.

How to Categorize and Track Bugs

It is impossible to release a high quality solution to production without data from an issue or bug tracking system. Without a bug tracking system, the team cannot judge whether the zero-defect criteria have been met.

Categorization process

The MSF issue or bug categorization process builds on the risk categorization system of the MSF risk management process. In the MSF risk categorization system, team members are asked to estimate risk probability and impact, and these two variables are multiplied together to derive the risk exposure value, which is used in turn to prioritize these risks.

The issue or bug categorization prioritization system is a similar system. A risk is something that has not yet occurred, so probability of occurrence and impact of the risk to the project are appropriate variables to estimate. However, issues or bugs are things that have happened or exist now. The important variables to an individual issue or a bug are:

- *Repeatability.* A variable that measures how repeatable the issue or bug is. Repeatability is the percentage of the time the issue or bug manifests itself. Is the issue or bug 100 percent repeatable, or can it be reproduced only 10 percent of the time? Note that zero is not a valid metric here because it would mean the issue or bug is never repeatable.

- *Visibility.* A variable that measures the situation or environment that must be established before the issue or bug manifests itself. For example, if the issue or bug occurs only when the user holds down the Shift key while right-clicking the mouse and viewing the File menu, the percentage of obscurity is high. A highly obscure issue or bug is not very visible and therefore not as compelling as a highly visible issue or bug.

- *Severity.* A variable that measures how much impact the issue or bug will produce in the solution, in the code, or to the users. For example, when an issue or bug occurs, does it crash the operating system or application, or does it cause one pixel of color to change on a menu bar? To be able to assign severity, the project team needs to define a list of problematic situations, with associated severity. For example, if the system crashes with loss of data and no workaround, it is severity 10; if it crashes with loss of data but with a workaround, it could be severity 9.

These three variables are estimated and assigned to each issue or bug by the project team and are used to derive the issue or bug priority. Table 11.2 describes the symmetrical scales to assign a value to each variable.

Table 11.2.   Variables for Categorizing Bugs

Variable	Scale
Repeatability	A percentage in the range of 10% (integer value '0.1') through 100% (integer value '1'), where 100% indicates that the issue or bug is reproducible on every test run.
Visibility	A percentage in the range of 10% (integer value '0.1') through 100% (integer value '1'), where 10% indicates that the issue or bug is visible under only the most obscure conditions. Issues or bugs that manifest themselves in environments with simple conditions are said to be highly visible.
Severity	An integer in the range of 1 through 10, where classification 10 issues or bugs present the most impact to the solution or code.

The priority of a bug can be calculated by using the following formula:

```
(Repeatability + Visibility) * Severity = Priority
```

Table 11.3 provides an example of this priority calculation displayed in a matrix.

Table 11.3.   Bug Prioritization Matrix

Description	Repeatability	Visibility	Severity	Priority	Submitted By	Assigned To
Description	1	1	10	20.0	Name	Name
Description	0.9	0.9	9	16.2	Name	Name
Description	0.8	0.8	8	12.8	Name	Name
Description	0.7	0.7	7	9.8	Name	Name
Description	0.6	0.6	6	7.2	Name	Name
Description	0.5	0.5	5	5.0	Name	Name
Description	0.4	0.4	4	3.2	Name	Name

Issue or bug tracking process

The bug tracking process, shown in Figure 11.3, is driven by the development and testing roles.

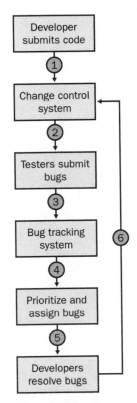

Figure 11.3.   Issue or bug tracking process

The steps in the bug tracking process are:

1. Developers develop code, perform internal coverage testing, and then check this code into the change control system.

2. Testers perform the daily or periodic build and external coverage testing on all submitted code.

3. Testers submit issues or bugs into the issue or bug tracking system, entering issue or bug descriptions and Repeatability, Severity, and Visibility variables.

4. The development and test leads conduct a Prioritization or Issue/Bug Prioritizing meeting and:

    ■ Calculate the priority of each issue or bug. This task is referred to in the MSF Testing Method as *Issue/Bug Prioritizing.*

    ■ Assign issues or bugs that exceed the zero-defect criteria to developers for correction.

    ■ Retire issues or bugs from a previous cycle of the sub-process that were corrected.

5. Assigned developers resolve or correct issue or bug.

6. Developers perform internal coverage testing and then check this code into the change control system.

This is a continuous process that starts again when developers develop code and check it into the change control system.

Testing Tasks

Two important tasks in the MSF Testing Method are *code reviews* and *development environment construction*. These two project tasks are very important to the successful implementation of the MSF Testing Method.

Code reviews

The MSF Testing Method defines three types of code reviews:

- *Comprehensive.* A comprehensive code review is a formal review in which the developer is asked to present or walk through his or her code with the rest of the development team.

- *Casual.* A casual code review is a peer-based review that is conducted by other developers from the direct development team. This is a particularly good strategy to mentor junior developers.

- *Independent.* An independent code review is a review that is conducted by a third-party organization with the goal of providing a fresh set of eyes to review the code.

Testing environment construction

Before any development and therefore testing work can proceed, it is important that a development and testing environment is designed and built. This environment must be separated from the production environment and be capable of accommodating both development and testing requirements. Typical testing requirements are:

- *Build hardware* to enable the testers to perform the daily and periodic builds.

- *Automate testing* to facilitate the automation of as many test functions as possible.

- *Create change control systems*; these systems must be in place and accessible to the testers.

- *Create issue or bug tracking systems*; these systems must be in place and accessible to the testers.

How to Conduct a Pilot

A *pilot* is a test of the solution in the production environment, and a trial of the solution by installers, systems support staff, and end users. The primary purposes of a pilot are to demonstrate that the design works in the production environment as expected and that it meets the organization's business requirements. A secondary purpose is to give the deployment team a chance to practice and refine the deployment process.

A pilot tests the solution under live conditions and takes various forms depending on the type of project.

- In an enterprise, a pilot can consist of a group of users or a set of servers in a data center.
- In Web development, a pilot can take the form of hosting site files on staging servers or folders that are live on the Internet, only with a test Web address.
- Commercial software vendors, such as Microsoft, often release products to a special group of early adopters prior to final release.

These various forms of piloting have one element in common—the tests occur in a live production environment. The pilot is not complete until the team ensures that the proposed solution is viable in the production environment and every component of the solution is ready for deployment.

Process

The pilot is the last major step before full-scale deployment of the solution. Prior to the pilot, integration testing must be completed in the test lab environment.

The pilot provides an opportunity for users to provide feedback about how features work. This feedback must be used to resolve any issues or to create a contingency plan. The feedback can help the team determine the level of support they are likely to need after full deployment. Some of the feedback can also contribute to the next version of the product.

Important   Ultimately, the pilot leads to a decision either to proceed with a full deployment or to delay deployment so you can resolve problems that could jeopardize deployment.

The pilot process is iterative. It starts with planning tasks, such as creating a pilot plan and preparing users and sites, and then moves to implementing the pilot, evaluating the results, fixing problems, and deploying another version until reaching the scope and quality that indicate the readiness for a full deployment.

Figure 11.4 illustrates the primary steps for planning and conducting a pilot.

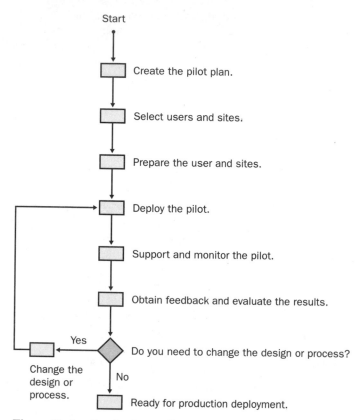

Figure 11.4.   Conducting a pilot

Preparing for the pilot

A pilot deployment needs to be rehearsed to minimize the risk of disruption for the pilot group. At this stage, the development team is performing last-minute checks and ensuring that nothing has changed since pre-production testing. The following tasks need to be completed before starting the pilot:

- The development team and the pilot participants must clearly identify and agree on the success criteria of the pilot. The criteria should map back to the success criteria for the development effort.

- A support structure and issue-resolution process must be in place. This process might require that support staff be trained. The procedures used for issue resolution during a pilot can vary significantly from those used during deployment and when in full production.

- To identify any issues and confirm that the deployment process will work, it is necessary to implement a trial run or a rehearsal of all the elements of the deployment.

- It is necessary to obtain customer approval of the pilot plan. Work on the pilot plan starts early during the planning phase so that the communication channels are in place and the participants are prepared by the time the test team is ready to deploy the pilot.

Tip   The pilot sets the tone for the full deployment, so it is important that the plan is developed carefully and communicated effectively to the participants, and that the results are evaluated thoroughly.

A recommended pilot plan includes the following:

- Scope and objectives
- Participating users, locations, and contact information
- Training plan for pilot users
- Support plan for the pilot
- Communication plan for the pilot
- Known risks and contingency plans
- Rollback plan
- Schedule for deploying and conducting the pilot

Implementing the pilot

Avoid the mistake of making pilot testing too easy. As much as possible, try every use case and scenario that will arise in production, including operations tasks, by including various use cases and scenarios in the rollout group. It is also recommended that you intentionally cause the pilot to fail so that you can test rollback procedures, disaster recovery, and business continuity planning.

Evaluating the results

At the end of the pilot, its success is evaluated and the next step is recommended. The project team then needs to decide whether to continue the project beyond the pilot. To help with the evaluation and recommendation, analyze information from a variety of sources. For example, obtain information from:

- Web site feedback forms
- Sessions with business managers
- Problem reports
- End-user surveys
- Observations of the IT project team
- Solution and operating system logs

It is important to obtain information about both the design and the deployment processes. Review what worked and what did not work so that it is possible to revise and refine the plan. Example of information to be gathered includes:

- Training required for using the solution
- Rollout process
- Support required for the solution
- Communications
- Problems encountered
- Suggestions for improvements

The feedback is used to validate that the delivered design meets the design specification, as well as the business requirements. The pilot is then evaluated to answer the following questions:

- Did the pilot meet the success criteria you defined before the pilot began?
- If metrics were established to measure your success, how did the pilot measure up?

After the data is evaluated, the team must make a decision. The team can select one of following strategies:

- *Stagger forward.* Prepare another release candidate and release it to the original group and then to additional groups in serial fashion. The release to more than one group might have been part of the original plan or might have been a contingency triggered by an unacceptable first pilot.
- *Roll back.* Return the pilot group to their pre-pilot state.
- *Suspend the pilot.* Put the solution on hold or cancel it.
- *Patch and continue.* Fix the build that the pilot is running and continue.
- *Proceed to deployment phase.* Move forward to deploy the pilot build to the full live production environment.

Outputs of conducting a pilot

As cycles of the pilot tests are completed, the team prepares reports detailing each lesson learned and how new information or issues are resolved. The following can result from performing the pilot testing:

- The identification of additional risks
- The identification of frequently asked questions for training purposes
- The identification of user errors for training and documentation purposes
- The ability to secure buy-in and support from pilot users
- Documentation of concerns and issue resolutions
- Updates to documentation—particularly Help files and deployment plans
- Determination of whether all success criteria were met

How to Close the Stabilizing Phase

Closing the stabilizing phase requires completing a milestone approval process. The team needs to document the results of the different tasks it has performed in this phase to submit the project to management for approval.

The stabilizing phase culminates in the *release readiness approved* milestone. This milestone occurs when the team has addressed all outstanding issues and has released the solution and made it available for full deployment. This milestone is the opportunity for customers and users, operations and support personnel, and key project stakeholders to evaluate the solution and identify any remaining issues they need to address before beginning the transition to deployment and, ultimately, release.

After all of the stabilization tasks are complete, the team must formally agree that the project has reached the milestone of release readiness. As the team progresses from the release milestone to the next phase of deploying, responsibility for on-going management and support of the solution officially transfers from the project team to the operations and support teams. By agreeing, team members signify that they are satisfied with the work that is performed in their areas of responsibility.

Project teams usually mark the completion of a milestone with a formal sign-off. Key stakeholders, typically representatives of each team role and any important customer representatives who are not on the project team, signal their approval of the milestone by signing or initialing a document stating that the milestone is complete. The sign-off document becomes a project deliverable and is archived for future reference.

Lesson 3: The MSF Deploying Phase

At the end of the stabilizing phase, the *release readiness approved* milestone indicates the solution's readiness for deployment into the production environment.

During the deploying phase, the team deploys the solution technology and components, stabilizes the deployment, moves the project to operations and support, and obtains final customer approval of the project. After the deployment, the team conducts a project review and a customer satisfaction survey. Stabilizing activities might continue during this period as the project components are transferred from a test or staging environment to a production environment.

After this lesson, you will be able to

- Describe the dynamics of the team composition during deployment.
- Explain the goal, milestones, and deliverables of the MSF deploying phase.

Estimated lesson time: 15 minutes

MSF Deploying Phase Milestones and Deliverables

The main deploying tasks include preparing for deployment and then deploying the solution. After deployment, stabilization, and transfer to operations, the project team conducts a project review.

The deploying phase culminates in the *deployment complete* milestone. Deliverables during this phase are:

- Operations and support information systems
- Procedures and processes
- Knowledge base, reports, and logbooks
- Repository of all versions of documents, configurations, scripts, and code
- Project closeout report
    - Project documents
    - Customer survey
    - Next steps

Team Focus During the Deploying Phase

After completing the stabilizing phase, the project team can migrate to the deploying phase in a variety of ways. One deployment option is to use the organization's operations team to handle the actual deployment. If the operations team manages the entire deployment, representatives from the development team usually remain on the project for a period of time after going live to mitigate potential problems during the transfer of ownership. Another option is to combine members from each group and create a separate deployment team. The release management role is responsible for coordinating the required activities that ensure a successful deployment.

Table 11.4 lists the focus and responsibility areas of each team role during deploying.

Table 11.4.   Deploying Phase Roles and Responsibilities

Role	Responsibility
Product management	Customer feedback, assessment, sign-off
Program management	Solution/scope comparison; stabilization management
Development	Problem resolution; escalation support
User experience	Training; training schedule management
Testing	Performance testing; problem identification, definition, resolution, and reporting
Release management	Site deployment management; change approval

Deployment Scenarios

Some of the solution scenarios for deployment include Web applications and services, client/server applications, packaged applications, enterprise infrastructure, and mobile applications.

The MSF process model works regardless of the type of project you are trying to deploy. However, the complexity and length of the deploying phase varies depending on what you are deploying. For example, a Web application can be deployed with ease and minimal impact to physical locations, geographies, and workstations, whereas an infrastructure project that involves rolling out workstations is a longer and more complicated process. It is essential to make sure the team's solution scenario for deployment is appropriate for the project type.

In addition to the solution scenarios, it is necessary to consider the types of hardware and operating system requirements when deploying a solution. A solution needs a different type of solution scenario depending on whether it is to be deployed to a datacenter, to a group of enterprise servers, or to mobile devices. Some of the hardware and operating system requirements for solution scenarios include:

- Enterprise servers
- Datacenter (Internet, department, global)
- Web services
- Clients (desktop, mobile)

Lesson 4: Deploying to a Production Environment

This lesson focuses on the considerations that are involved in deploying a solution to a production environment and the steps that are taken in the deployment.

After this lesson, you will be able to

- Explain how to plan for deployment.
- Distinguish between core and site-specific components.
- Deploy core components.
- Deploy site-specific components.
- Explain how to prepare for the transition to operations.
- Describe the steps for deploying the solution to a production environment.
- Explain the closeout activities for the deploying phase.

Estimated lesson time: 30 minutes

How to Plan for Deployment

During development and especially as the stabilizing phase nears completion, the release management lead assigns deployment tasks to staff members. These individuals review the project status and test results, and update the deployment plan, which is initially created during the planning phase. The team creates task-based procedures that help ensure a successful deployment.

Staging and production environments

To be ready for deployment, the physical infrastructure, system software, and application software are tested, installed, and configured in their respective environments.

Documentation

The project team and operations representatives revisit and update the following documentation:

- *Deployment diagrams* that are created during the planning phase.
- A *test plan* that includes coverage for areas that are exposed in real use. The operation team needs to update the test plans that were created during the planning phase.
- A *security plan* that the operations team uses to ensure that all personnel are aware of the security standards and rules to which the project adheres.

- *A backup plan* that will prevent the loss of data. During the planning phase, the team creates a plan for processes that the team will use for file and data backups to prevent loss of data. This is updated when planning for deployment.

- *A plan for analyzing system performance and site usage.* The operations team is responsible for the site's daily maintenance and routine care.

- *A plan for log handling* and other administrative tasks.

- *A disaster recovery plan.* During the planning phase, the team creates a disaster recovery plan that establishes what the team expects to happen to the solution, its equipment, personnel, and data should a crisis occur. During the planning process for deployment, the team will review the document and validate and update its contents.

- *A business contingency plan.* During the planning phase, the team creates a business contingency plan, establishing what will happen if the business activities halt. When planning for deployment, the team reviews and validates the contents of the business contingency plan.

- *Training information.* The team must ensure that support personnel who will maintain or update the solution are properly trained, and that proper channels or regulations are provided in the event of a disaster.

Deployment plan review

The deployment plan is created during the planning phase and revised throughout the development process. However, when planning for deployment, the release manager might need to make changes to the deployment plan because of changes made to the solution during development and stabilization. The release manager must review and revise the deployment plan and confirm that the team has accomplished the following tasks:

- The deployment strategy is reviewed and approved.

- Setup, installation, configuration, test, operation, and support procedures are available, reviewed, and approved.

- Deployment procedures are documented, reviewed, and approved.

- Hardware and software components are available and tested.

- The deployment team has clearly defined roles, and the assigned personnel are trained and available.

- There is a plan and ample resources for ownership transfer to the operations team.

Customer sign-off

The solution's key stakeholders review the collateral documentation and solution and confirm that the solution is ready for deployment. The project team prepares an affidavit reiterating that the key stakeholders have reviewed the solution and the accompanying collateral documentation, and that they find the solution to be final and acceptable in the current state.

Core Components vs. Site-Specific Components

For efficient deployment of solutions, it is important to group components as core components and site-specific components.

Core components

Core components are components located at a central location that enable interoperability of the overall solution. Core components are usually the enabling technology of the enterprise solution. Examples of core components are:

- Domain controllers
- Network routers
- Database servers
- Mail routers
- Remote access servers

Site-specific components

Components that are located at individual locations and enable users to access and use the solution are called site-specific components. Examples of site-specific components are:

- Local routers
- File print servers
- Client applications, such as Microsoft Office XP

In most cases, core components must be deployed before site-specific components are deployed. For example, when Microsoft Exchange Server is deployed, the core backbone, which supports all sites, must be in place first, and only then can the site components be deployed.

How to Deploy Core Components

Deploying core components involves selecting an appropriate deployment strategy and then performing the deployment. Selecting a deployment strategy requires a thorough understanding of both the solution and the needs of the customer.

A core component is often shared by multiple locations; it is a critical or enabling part of the overall solution. For virtually any solution, you must deploy some core components before users can use the solution. When considering how to deploy a solution, it is necessary to identify those components that are not functionally vital to the overall solution and to decide on an effective strategy for deploying them. For many projects, the cost of deploying all core components first is excessive and unnecessary.

Tip   Devices that are functionally redundant and exist only to provide capacity usually do not need to be installed before deploying to the sites.

You can use two main strategies for deploying core components:

- *Serial.* All core components are deployed prior to any site deployments. This approach has less risk and is adequate for short deployments and small environments.
- *Parallel.* Core components are deployed as needed in parallel to support each site deployment. This is a more cost-effective approach for larger environments or for deployments that will extend over a longer period.

Depending on the solution scenario, the core technology might need to be deployed before or in parallel with site deployments.

How to Deploy Site-Specific Components

Site deployment represents a process within a process. It involves the execution of a well-thought-out plan for installing the solution. Figure 11.5 depicts the process of deploying site-specific components.

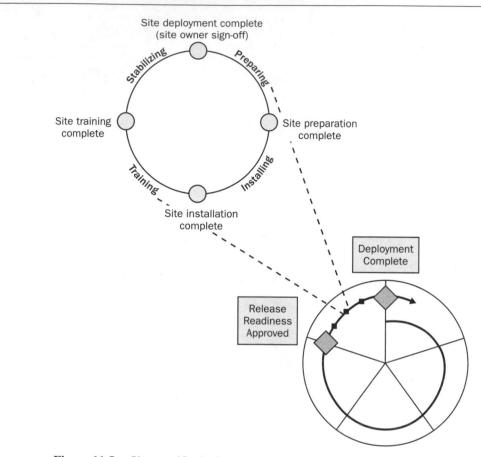

Figure 11.5.   Site-specific deployment process

Sites can be deployed serially by fewer teams or in parallel by more teams. Parallel site deployment requires more coordination and provides less opportunity to deal with the ramp-up of usage. However, a more serialized deployment can introduce confusion to the users, especially when the new solution must coexist with an existing system.

Site deployment also involves the use of the system by users in a production environment. The team must take steps to ensure that the necessary operations and support infrastructures exist for these users as they gain access to the system. Site deployment involves four phases:

- Preparing the site deployment
- Installing the site deployment
- Training during site deployment
- Stabilizing the site deployment

Preparing for the site deployment

Preparing for site deployment involves three distinct activities: taking inventories, scheduling, and informing. A coordinator often performs these activities off-site. The coordinator validates all the deployment information collected during planning, creates a final schedule for the actual site deployment, and informs the team about when the deployment will occur. This phase is performed to validate the information about the site to make sure that nothing significant has changed since the site survey was performed during the planning phase. It is also used to verify that all required equipment for the deployment has been delivered to the site.

Installing the site deployment

To minimize disruption and confusion about the process, the team does not install the solution until all preparations are made. In some cases, last-minute issues that are uncovered during the preparatory phase might indicate the need to revisit the site after the issues are resolved.

Note   In some cases, the team might choose to delay activation until the solution is stable and users have undergone training.

During installation, the following tasks are performed:

- Installing or upgrading required hardware or software
- Validating that the installed systems function as expected
- Activating the system for user access

During deployment, the team should have a support mechanism in place in case it encounters problems. Generally, developers and testers on the core project team should be ready to support the site deployment team.

Training during site deployment

It is the responsibility of the deployment team to ensure that all users receive suitable training. During the planning phase, the project team developed a training plan that prescribes the appropriate level and type of training for all users. Training can be delivered before, during, or after installation.

Use the following guidelines for training during site deployment:

- Deliver appropriate training to each user
- Vary training based on user background and experience
- Include a variety of media as defined in the training plan
- Train local support staff

Avoid the temptation to employ a one-size-fits-all strategy. If the training strategy requires all users to undergo the same training process, novice users will be forced to learn too quickly, and more experienced users will feel held back. Consider alternatives to the traditional courseware approach to training, such as coaching sessions and a mentoring program.

Stabilizing the site deployment

Stabilization is an important part of the site deployment process. It is never a good idea to install a solution and then simply walk away from the deployment. It is the responsibility of the deployment team to remain with the project until the team is comfortable putting it into production. For this to occur, the team must focus on the success criteria, obtain the customer's approval, and collect user feedback to ensure satisfaction and evolve the site deployment process. Each site deployment should go through the sign-off process. During the planning phase, a person at the site should have been designated to have the authority to sign off on the site deployment.

What Is the Quiet Period?

The quiet period begins when deployments are complete. During the quiet period, the team begins transferring responsibility to operations and support. A quiet period of 15 to 30 days is needed to generate statistically useful data. The quiet period also serves as a baseline for the service-level agreement.

The operations plan and acceptance criteria established by the project team during the planning phase define service levels for the solution. These levels serve as a baseline for the service-level agreement (SLA), which operations begins monitoring when responsibility is transferred to them.

A service-level agreement is defined as an agreement between the service provider and the customer that defines the responsibilities of all participating parties and that binds the service provider to provide a particular service of a specific agreed-upon quality and quantity. It constrains the demands that customers can place on the service to those limits that are defined by the agreement.

How to Transfer the Project to Operations and Support

Disengaging from the project includes transferring operations and support functions to permanent staff. In many cases, the resources to manage the new systems already exist. In other cases, it might be necessary to design new support systems.

Some of the tasks that need to be performed during transferring the project to operations and support include:

- *Activate report systems.* Ensure that you transfer call volume and issue resolution to the help desk. Transfer system faults, corrective actions, and trend analysis to operations.
- *Publish knowledge base.* The knowledge base provides easy access to corrective knowledge and can be used by support teams and users.
- *Validate operations.* Before disengaging from the project, verify that the operations are being performed.

Note   It is very important for the project team to transition responsibility for the deployment to a support group at the customer's company. If the project team cannot transition the responsibility, the project team will become the support group. The customer will continue to rely on the project team for help with questions and support issues.

Closeout Activities

After deployment is complete and ownership and responsibility have been transferred to operations and support, the team performs closeout activities for the project.

When the team has obtained customer sign-off, the project is officially complete, and the team has reached the deployment complete milestone. The following are the closeout activities:

- *Survey customer satisfaction.* The customer satisfaction survey provides an important opportunity for the team to receive feedback from the customer. It is a necessary component of the closeout report and represents validation of the entire project. At a minimum, the persons who are surveyed should include project sponsors and key stakeholders.
- *Prepare closeout report.* The closeout report is the final physical deliverable of the deployment. It includes final versions of all the major deliverables: the vision/scope document, the functional specification, and so on.

  Typically, the closeout report also includes a summary of information solicited from the customers and users and a summary of the known next steps. Essentially, the closeout report answers the question, "Where do we go from here?"

- *Conduct project review.* Typically, the team conducts two types of project reviews: team and customer. Most technology projects end with a meeting, or *project review*, in which team members review the project and identify areas that could be improved in future projects.

  The project review is an opportunity for the entire team to reflect on the process and outcomes of the implementation. The team documents this reflection as action items in the next project plan.

  Important In addition, customer reviews are conducted with sponsors and key stakeholders to determine customer satisfaction levels, outstanding issues, and next steps.

- *Obtain customer approval.* Upon project closeout, the product manager obtains the final sign-off from the customer, signaling the customer's approval of the solution and permission to disengage from the project.

Activity: Prioritizing Bugs

In this activity, you use what you learned in the lessons to assign and prioritize bugs.

The project testing team has been testing the E-Commerce Web application and has identified a number of bugs. The following is a list of the identified bugs without any priority assigned to them:

- In 12 out of 75 tests, the browser stopped responding when the user submitted an order. The order status on the server showed that it was submitted, but the user never received a confirmation or an order number in these instances.

- If a sales representative applies a discount that is greater than 15 percent, the system accepts it without approval from a manager.

- When the user is viewing the order confirmation page and he or she clicks Keep Shopping, the account logon page appears. This seems to occur only for users whose user names are longer than 8 characters. In the test database, this equates to 20 users out of 172.

- When the customer logs on, the background of the Help page changes from white to off-white.

- In 50 tests, the Track Orders page twice displayed order details for the wrong order.

- Performing a load test of 1000 simultaneous users showed a degradation of 18 percent in performance. Average number of users to simultaneously access the E-Commerce Web site in production is estimated to be 300.

- The copyright notice does not appear on the Order Confirmation page.

- In 130 tests, the home page failed to load 6 times. Performing a refresh successfully loaded the home page.

- Every time the home page appears, the View Cart button is missing. This happens even after something is placed in the cart.

- In 40 tests, there were 2 instances in which the sales manager was unable to apply a discount that was greater than 15 percent to an order. In all 40 tests, the same sales manager account was used, but different products were added to the orders.

- In 8 out of 50 tests, error HTTP 404 - File Not Found occurred when the user clicked Keep Shopping on the Order Confirmation page.

- The list of catalogs does not appear when viewing product details for bicycle helmets.

- If the sales manager is viewing product details and he or she presses the Enter key, the Help topics home page appears in the browser.

- In 25 tests, the Order Confirmation page failed to appear 3 times.

- In 25 tests, the Track Orders page failed to show the order details 16 times.

- Every time the production clerk attempts to connect to the administration site over SSL, the following error message appears: "The page cannot be displayed. The page you are looking for is currently unavailable. The Web site might be experiencing technical difficulties, or you may need to adjust your browser settings." The production clerk cannot access the data to manage the online catalog.

Estimate the repeatability, visibility, and severity of each of the preceding bugs. You might have to guess at some of the values based on the amount of information you have available. Then, using the formula discussed in the chapter, compute the priority of each of the bugs.

Open the C11Ex1.doc file in the \SolutionDocuments\Chapter11 folder on the companion CD to complete this exercise. One possible answer to this exercise can be found in C11Ex1_Answer.doc in the \SolutionDocuments\Chapter11 folder.

Summary

- The purpose of the stabilizing phase is to reduce the risks of releasing the solution to production.
- A successful stabilizing phase requires that the team make the transition from a mindset focused on building features to one focused on getting the solution to a known state of quality.
- The goals of the deploying phase are:
    - Place the solution into a production environment.
    - Facilitate the smooth transfer of the solution from the project team to the operations team.
    - Secure customer approval that the project is complete.
- Steps in the site deployment process are preparing, installing, training, and obtaining sign-off.
- The project team can disengage from the project only after sign-off from the customer.
- Deliverables of the deploying phase are operations and support information systems, repository of all versions of documentation and code, and project closeout reports.

Review

The following questions are intended to reinforce key information presented in this chapter. If you are unable to answer a question, review the lesson materials and try the question again. You can find answers to the questions in the appendix.

1. What are some of the specific goals of the stabilizing phase?

2. How does ongoing analysis of bug convergence provide warning signs about the stability of the project?

3. Why is zero-bug bounce a positive indicator for the project?

4. What is a release candidate, and what are some of its features?

5. What is a pilot, and what are its goals?

6. Why should pilot testing not be too easy?

7. What are the deliverables of the deploying phase?

8. Which person or group is the best candidate to deploy the solution?

9. What are some examples of core components? What are some examples of site components?

10. What is the quiet period, and what are some of its features?

11. What type of documents result from completing closeout activities?

12. Which MSF role handles the final sign-off from the customer?

13. What are the two types of project reviews that MSF advocates at the end of the deployment phase?

A P P E N D I X   A

Questions and Answers

Chapter 1   Introduction to Designing Business Solutions
Review

Page 35

1. Describe the differences between the waterfall model and the spiral model, and describe how MSF uses both in the MSF Process Model.

The waterfall model is based on milestones. For a milestone to be achieved, all the tasks related to that phase must be completed. The next phase of development cannot be started until the milestone from the previous phase is completed. The clearly identifiable milestones of this model make it is easy to monitor the progress of the project and the schedule, and to assign responsibilities and accountability to the appropriate resources. The waterfall model is more applicable to projects that have clearly defined requirements and are not liable to modifications in the future.

The spiral model was created with the intention of being able to refine the product requirements and project estimates on a regular basis. Each time the project goes through an iteration of the spiral model, the development team can assess the project and plan for the next iteration. However, because the spiral model has no clear checkpoints, monitoring the progress of the project is difficult. The spiral model is suited best for rapid development of small projects.

The MSF Process Model incorporates the milestone approach of the waterfall model with the iterative approach of the spiral model. By using the process model, the development team takes an iterative approach to building a solution, while tracking the progress of each iteration by using milestones.

Page 35

2. In the MSF Team Model, who is responsible for the design process?

The program management role is responsible for the design process.

Page 35

3. The tradeoff triangle describes the three types of tradeoffs that a project team and the customer can make. What is a fourth tradeoff that could be considered but that should never be compromised?

Quality is another tradeoff that could be considered in addition to features, resources, and schedule. However, quality should be the last tradeoff to be compromised because of the poor results that would ensue.

Page 35   **4. Using the following statement, complete the tradeoff matrix below.**

"Given a fixed feature set, we will choose resources and adjust the schedule as necessary."

	Fixed	Chosen	Adjustable
Resources		X	
Schedule			X
Features	X		

Page 35   **5. Describe the purpose of performing daily builds in the MSF Process Model.**

Daily builds allow the development team and the customer to understand the current state of the project and to measure the stability of the project on a frequent basis. Daily builds can be applied to both software development projects and hardware infrastructure projects.

Page 36   **6. When you reach the release readiness milestone, what phase have you completed?**

The stabilizing phase is complete when the project team reaches the release readiness milestone and the solution has been validated by the project team and the customer.

Page 36   **7. During which phase of the MSF Process Model is the initial risk assessment document created?**

During the envisioning phase, risk assessment begins and a risk assessment document is created. However, risk assessment is an ongoing process that occurs throughout the duration of the project. Therefore, the risk assessment document will continue to undergo changes and updates while the project progresses. In addition, as the project progresses, risk mitigation plans are created as a part of risk assessment.

Page 36   **8. When are test cases established in the MSF Process Model?**

The majority of work on test cases is performed during the developing phase. However, the testing role is involved in the project from the very beginning.

Page 36   **9. List several types of tests that are performed during the stabilizing phase.**

Following is a list of the types of tests that will be conducted during the stabilizing phase:
- Component testing
- Database testing
- Infrastructure testing
- Security testing
- Integration testing
- User acceptance and usability testing
- Stress, capacity, and performance testing
- Regression testing
- Recording the number of bugs

Page 36   **10. Why is it important to create a vision statement for the project during the envisioning phase?**

The vision statement communicates the direction for guiding the team toward its business goals. Everyone on the project team must agree to and support the vision of the solution. This agreement and support is fundamental to the success of the project. If members of the team do not agree with the vision statement, the success of the project is at risk.

Page 36   **11. What are some of the key tasks that are performed during the planning phase?**

- Creation of the functional specification
- Creation of the development, testing, and staging environments
- Development of the project plans
- Creation of the project schedule
- Development of the solution design and architecture

Page 36   **12. Describe the *quiet period* and the activities that occur during this period.**

The quiet period is the time between the deployment stable interim milestone and the deployment complete interim milestone of the deploying phase. During this period, the effectiveness and performance of the solution are measured. The results of this activity lead to an estimate of the effort needed to maintain the solution for continued operations.

Chapter 2   Gathering and Analyzing Information Review

Page 82   **1. What is the difference between the interviewing and focus-group techniques of gathering information?**

An interview is a one-on-one meeting between a member of the project team and a user or stakeholder. The interviewer asks the user or stakeholder questions related to work and processes.

A focus group is a form of group interview, in which a group of individuals discuss a process or an activity in the presence of a facilitator. The group of individuals represents all the relevant users and stakeholders of the process. You should use focus groups when many people must be interviewed in a short period. In addition, the various people in a focus group can help each other fill any information gaps.

Page 82

2. When should you use for prototyping instead of shadowing to gather information?

Shadowing is the process of gathering information by observing a user performing day-to-day tasks in the actual work environment. You can ask the user questions related to the work. However, some activities cannot be understood by watching. You might need to document the actions that the user performed, such as keystrokes. In such a situation, you must use prototyping.

Page 82

3. How do you identify the most effective information gathering technique for a project?

To identify the most effective information gathering technique, you consider the advantages and disadvantages of each technique. You identify the type of information to be collected and the amount of time you have to collect the information. If you want to gather information quickly, use interviewing or focus groups instead of surveys.

Page 82

4. What is the purpose of creating use cases?

You create use cases to:

- Identify the business process and all activities from start to finish.
- Document the context and environmental issues.
- Document relationship between business needs and user requirements.
- Describe needs and requirements in the context of use.
- Focus users and the development team.

Page 82

5. What is an actors catalog?

The actors catalog contains a list of actors used in the use cases. It contains information such as actor name, actor responsibilities, and the sources from which the actor was identified.

Page 82

6. What is ORM?

ORM is a modeling language that allows to you to present information as elementary facts. An elementary fact asserts that an object has a property and that one or more objects participate in a relationship. ORM expresses the model in terms of natural concepts, like objects and roles. ORM is based on the assumption that objects play roles in real life.

Page 83

7. What is UML?

UML is a simple, extensible, and expressive visual modeling language. It is a set of notations and rules for modeling software systems of varying complexities. UML enables the creation of simple, well-documented, and easy-to-understand software models.

Page 83

8. What are the purposes of the various UML views?

The five UML views are:

- The user view, which represents the goals and objectives of the system from the viewpoint of various users and their requirements from the system.

- The structural view, which represents the static or idle state of the system.
- The behavioral view, which represents the dynamic state of the system.
- The implementation view, which represents the distribution of the logical elements of the system.
- The environment view, which represents the distribution of the physical elements of the system.

Page 83   **9.   What is an actor in a use case?**

An actor is an entity that interacts with the system to be built for the purpose of completing an event. An actor can be:

- A user of the system.
- An entity, such as another system or a database, that resides outside the system.

Page 83   **10.   What is the purpose of a usage scenario?**

A usage scenario describes in detail a particular instance of a use case. You need to create many usage scenarios to completely describe a use case.

Page 83   **11.   What are the steps in creating a usage scenario?**

To create a usage scenario, you perform the following steps:

- Determine the preconditions for the usage scenario, specifying information that must exist before a scenario can be executed.
- Identify the postconditions for the usage scenario, which describe what must be accomplished upon completion of the usage scenario.
- Break the activity into discrete steps.
- Identify exceptions that might occur for any step. You might need to develop usage scenarios for these exceptions.
- Identify the requirement that this particular usage scenario addresses, for tracking and traceability.

Chapter 3   Envisioning the Solution
Review

Page 120   **1.   What is the purpose of envisioning?**

The overall purpose of envisioning is to develop a common vision of the goals of the solution and share it with the customers. Specifically, some of the purposes served by envisioning are as follows:

- Achieving an early understanding of the goals and constraints of the project among the customers and the team
- Analyzing the feasibility of the solution and gaining approval from key stakeholders
- Defining the scope of the project
- Estimating the resources that are required to complete the project
- Identifying the major milestones for the project

Page 120   **2.   What are the responsibilities of the various roles during the envisioning phase?**

Responsibilities of the various roles are as follows:

- The product management role is responsible for ensuring that the customer requirements are addressed by the project team.

- The program management role is responsible for developing the project design goals and solution concept.

- The development role is responsible for providing the technical implications of the proposed solution and the feasibility of the solution concept.

- The user experience role is responsible for analyzing the performance needs and support issues of the end users of the solution.

- The testing role is responsible for defining the quality requirements of the solution and how the specified level of quality can be achieved.

- The release management role is responsible for identifying all that is required for deploying the solution.

Page 120   **3.   What are the outputs of the envisioning phase?**

The key outputs of the envisioning phase are as follows:

- The vision/scope document, which describes the goals and constraints of the project

- The project structure document, which describes the organization of the team and the standards used by the team for documentation

- The risk assessment document, which lists the risks associated with the project, their impact, and corresponding mitigation plans

Page 120   **4.   What is the purpose of specifying the project scope?**

You create the project scope to specify what the project will and will not accomplish. Therefore, you identify the features that the customer considers essential in the solution and focus on successfully including them in the solution. To accomplish this, you need to analyze all project variables and make the appropriate tradeoffs. Some of the benefits of defining the scope of the project are that scope enables the team to focus on the work that must be done. Defining the scope also helps the team to clearly identify all tasks in the project.

Page 120   **5.   How does the envisioning phase end?**

The envisioning phase ends at the vision/scope approved milestone. This milestone involves a meeting and follow-up conversations in which key stakeholders, customers, and representatives of each role in the team approve the vision/scope document to indicate that they have a formal agreement about the goals and objectives of the project and solution. They "sign off" on this document to indicate that all parties believe the team can proceed with the project.

Page 120   **6.   What kinds of change management decisions are recorded in the project structure document?**

In the change management section of the project structure document, you record the processes that the team will follow to handle changes in the project. Some of the decisions that are made include:

- How will you define change on the project?
- What is the release date? Who will determine the release date, and how will it be determined? What will the basis be for determining the release date?
- Who will define the change management process that will be used?
- How will proposed changes be identified and tracked? Who will track this information?
- How will you assess the impact of a change? How much deviation are you willing to accept before major rescheduling?

Page 120   **7.   What is the difference between business goals and design goals?**

Business goals use business language to describe what the customer wants to change in the business by using the solution. Design goals represent the attributes of the solution that the project team is going to develop. The project team uses the design goals to illustrate what they want to accomplish with the solution.

Page 121   **8.   What are the guidelines for creating user profiles?**

While creating user profiles, remember the following:

- Identify the goals and expectations of the users of the solution.
- Identify the factors that might affect the ability of the user to use the solution.
- To help provide required support, identify problems that users might have had with similar products or solutions and methods.
- Determine whether the solution will be used globally.
- Identify the number of users at each location where the solution will be implemented, the infrastructure at each location, and the network bandwidth available at each location.
- Identify how the information flows between users of the solution. Identify the volume and importance of the communication.
- Analyze the hierarchical structure of the organization and its implications on information flow between different levels of the hierarchy.
- Analyze the scope of user functions.
- Analyze policies that might affect the implementation of the solution.

Page 121   **9.   What are the essential components of a risk assessment document?**

A risk document must contain the following:

- Risk statements, which capture the nature of the risk
- Risk probability, which describes the likelihood of the occurrence of the risk
- Risk severity, which specifies the impact of the risk
- Risk exposure, which specifies the overall threat of the risk
- Mitigation plans, which describe the efforts for preventing or minimizing the risk
- Contingency plans and triggers, which specify the steps that you need to take when a risk occurs and when to take those steps
- Risk ownership, which specifies the team member who is responsible for monitoring the risk

Page 121   **10.   What are the guidelines for assessing risks for a project?**

You must use a consistent scale to calculate the probability for every risk and its impact. If you express the impact of some risks by using a number and others by using financial terms, you cannot compare the exposure of the different risks. In addition, you need to rank the risks according to their exposure. Review this list frequently during the life of the project and update the list according to the importance of the risks.

Chapter 4   Creating the Conceptual Design
Review

Page 168   **1.   What is the purpose of the planning phase?**

The purpose of the planning phase is to achieve a detailed and validated understanding of the problem to be solved and to define a solution that addresses the problem. This is the solution that is most likely to be successful given the assumptions and constraints as understood by the team.

Page 168   **2.   What is the difference between the responsibilities of the product management and project management roles during the planning phase?**

During the planning phase, product management represents the users and ensures that the product addresses their needs. Project management ensures that the solution is created to specifications defined by the product manager.

Page 168   **3.   What are the major deliverables of the planning phase?**

The major deliverables of the planning phase are:

- The functional specification, which describes what will be built and how it will be built.
- The master project plan document, which presents how the solution will be built by the various teams involved in the project.

- The master project schedule, which specifies the time frame during which the project team will build and deploy the solution.
- The updated master risk assessment document, which lists the risks associated with the project and their mitigation plans.

Page 168   **4.   How does a functional specification serve as a blueprint for the development team?**

The functional specification identifies what the solution is going to be. This enables the development team to formulate development strategies and estimate the time and effort required to develop the solution.

Page 168   **5.   What are the goals of a functional specification?**

The goals of a functional specification are:

- Consolidating a common understanding of the business and user requirements.
- Articulating a logical way to break down a problem and modularize the solution.
- Providing a framework to plan, schedule, and develop the solution on time.
- Serving as a contract between the team and the customer about what will be delivered.

Page 168   **6.   What are the risks of not creating a functional specification?**

Some of the risks of not creating a functional specification are:

- The solution might not address the customer requirements.
- The project manager might not correctly estimate the time and effort required to complete the project.
- The team might be unable to define customer expectations clearly or share a common understanding of the solution with the customer.
- The team might not have enough information to validate that the solution meets the customer requirements.

Page 168   **7.   What is the difference between the business and user requirements of the solution?**

The business requirements of the solution are specified by the customer. These requirements focus on meeting the business goals and objectives.

The user requirements are provided by the end user of the solution and focus on using the solution to effectively perform day-to-day tasks.

Page 169   **8.   What are the benefits of creating a conceptual design?**

The conceptual design helps you:

- Develop part of the functional specification.
- Develop an effective user interface.
- Determine how different components work together in a solution.
- Design a solution that addresses both business and user needs.

Page 169   **9.** **A company plans to increase its sales by 15 percent during the next financial year by implementing an online shopping site. The company intends to provide its users a Web site that is fast, provides secure credit card processing, and is available at all times. Also, only registered users will be able to purchase products on the site. What are the user, system, operation, and business requirements for this site?**

The requirements for this site are:

- Business requirement: A Web site that improves the annual sales by 15 percent.
- User requirements:
  - Users can complete their purchases in five minutes.
  - Users can access only their own credit card details.
- System requirement: Only registered users will be able to purchase products on the site.
- Operation requirement: The users must be able to access the site at all times.

Page 169   **10.** **What are the goals of the analysis step of conceptual design?**

The goals of the analysis step are to:

- Review the user and business processes and activities.
- Create scenarios to illustrate context, workflow, task sequence, and environmental relationships in the business.

Page 169   **11.** **What is the benefit of synthesizing information?**

When you synthesize information, you present the information to the entire team and receive their perspectives about user requirements and solutions. You also ensure that all team members have a common understanding of user requirements and expectations.

Page 169   **12.** **What are the tasks for creating the future state?**

To create future state usage, the team performs the following tasks:

- Envision the desired future state.
- Redesign the current process to optimally support key business activities and processes.
- Create accurate target future state scenarios.
- Validate future state scenarios by using iteration.

Page 169   **13.** **What are the benefits of validating the conceptual design?**

Some of the benefits of validation include:

- Reducing risk.
- Highlighting missing information.
- Indicating diverging views and interpretations of the solution, especially between the business and users.
- Verifying the volume of activity.

- Assisting in prioritization.
- Providing a baseline for proceeding to logical design.

Page 169   **14.   What are the four service categories?**

The four service categories are:

- User services that provide the user interface in an application
- Business services that enforce business rules in the correct sequence
- Data services that provide the lowest visible level of detail for manipulating data
- System services that provide functionality outside the business logic

Page 170   **15.   Study and categorize the following services.**

- Displaying the employee details service
- Updating the employee details service
- Employee information service
- E-mail service

The categorized services are:

- Displaying the employee details service: User service
- Updating the employee details service: Business service
- Employee information service: Data service
- E-mail service: System service

Page 170   **16.   What are the characteristics of a refined business requirement?**

A business requirement must be:

- Well defined.
- Concise.
- Testable.
- Grouped in a hierarchical manner.
- Written in business language without jargon.

Page 170   **17.   How do you refine use cases during the analysis step of conceptual design?**

To refine the use cases diagram, you perform the following tasks:

- Create subordinate use cases.
- Create usage scenarios for each subordinate use case.
- Validate each use case and usage scenario against refined requirements.

Page 170   **18.   What are the criteria for evaluating the cost of a solution?**

The criteria are:

- Resources, work effort, and time
- Operational costs of technical options and emerging technologies
- Annual and recurring life cycle costs

Chapter 5   Creating the Logical Design
Activity

Page 208   **1.** **The shopping cart checks inventory to determine the availability of a particular product.**

Objects include shopping cart, inventory, and product.

Page 208   **2.** **A new user creates an account in order to place orders.**

Objects include user, account, and orders.

Page 208   **3.** **A user adds a product to the shopping cart.**

Objects include user, product, and shopping cart.

Page 208   **4.** **A user retrieves an order to check its status.**

Objects include user and order.

Chapter 5   Creating the Logical Design
Review

Page 212   **1.** **What are the two steps of logical design?**

- Analysis, during which you identify objects, services, attributes, and relationships
- Optimization, during which you refine the object list, verify the design, and implement control

Page 212   **2.** **What are the outputs of the logical design?**

- The logical object model, which is a set of objects with corresponding services, attributes, and relationships
- A high-level user interface design
- The logical data model

Page 212   **3.** **Should you focus on technological issues during logical design?**

Though logical design is considered to be technology independent, it is a good practice to consider physical constraints and opportunities during logical design to validate that the design can be implemented. Experienced teams and designers typically use the optimization step of logical design to identify the technology constraints to create a pseudophysical design. Logical design is the basis for evaluating the feasibility of the physical design and deciding implementation alternatives.

Page 212   **4.** **What are the benefits of logical design?**

- Logical design reduces the complexity of the solution.
- Logical design reflects and supports the requirements of conceptual design.
- Logical design provides a view of the solution as a single unit.
- Logical design acts as a point of contact for organizing cross-functional cooperation among multiple systems.
- Logical design acts as a starting point for the physical design.

Page 212   **5.   How do you identify services in a usage scenario?**

To identify services, examine a usage scenario to determine what the object is supposed to do, the kind of data the object must maintain, and the actions that the object must perform. If an object maintains information, it also performs the operations on the information.

Page 212   **6.   How do you identify attributes in a usage scenario?**

In a usage scenario, look for the words or phrases that further identify the object.

Page 212   **7.   What is a sequence diagram?**

A sequence diagram shows the actors and objects that participate in an interaction and the events they generate, arranged chronologically. It also identifies object dependencies in the system.

Page 213   **8.   How do you design the tables and columns in a data store for a solution?**

Each object that maintains data corresponds to a table in the data store. The attributes of the object form the columns in the table. Each row in the table stores values for various fields for a specific instance of the object.

Page 213   **9.   What is the purpose of refining the list of objects?**

You need to refine the list of objects because:

- Two objects might express the same information or control the same activity.
- Nouns in usage scenarios might be key attributes of another object.
- You might need a new object to control or coordinate a set of services.

Page 213   **10.   How do you verify the design by using individual object verification?**

In individual object verification, you identify an object's inputs and outputs and the capability or functionality that the object must provide. For any given input, you should be able to accurately predict the output and behavior and verify the independent parts of the object.

Page 213   **11.   What is the purpose of control in logical design?**

Control enables you to sequence objects. Control in logical design:

- Ensures transactional integrity of a scenario.
- Coordinates services across multiple objects.
- Identifies cross-object interdependencies.

Page 213   **12.   You are creating the logical design of a solution for a customer, and you discover a scenario that was not discovered in your previous analysis. What should you do with this new information?**

First, you should review all your current documentation to verify that the new information is not covered in your analysis. If the new information does not exist in your analysis, determine the effect of including functionality based on this new information in this version of the solution. Also determine the effect of omitting functionality based on the new information from this version. Once you have this information, you should notify the customer of the situation and work together to determine the best way to manage the new information. Be aware that the scope of the project might change depending on what you do with the new information.

Page 213 **13. What is the responsibility of the testing role during logical design?**

The testing role is primarily responsible for validating the logical design by measuring it against the conceptual design to validate that the logical design will cover the requirements. In addition, the testing role begins to define a high-level test plan.

Chapter 6   Creating the Physical Design
Review

Page 250 **1. What are the goals of physical design?**

The goals of physical design are:

- Transforming the logical design to specifications for a set of components
- Providing a baseline for implementing the design
- Identifying appropriate technologies for development
- Creating a structural view of the solution from the perspective of the development team

Page 250 **2. What is the difference between conceptual, logical, and physical designs?**

During conceptual design, the project team describes the solution from the perspective of the business and user communities. During logical design, the project team describes the solution from its own perspective. During physical design, the project team describes the solution from the perspective of the development team.

Page 250 **3. What does the development team do during physical design?**

During physical design, the development team evaluates technologies, creates prototypes, and prepares for development.

Page 250 **4. What does the deployment model include?**

The deployment model consists of:

- The network topology, which indicates hardware locations and inter-connections.
- The data topology, which indicates data store locations in relation to the network topology.
- The component topology, which indicates the locations of components and their services in relation to the network topology.

Page 250 **5. What does the project team do during the research step of physical design?**

During the research step, the team considers constraints such as enterprise architecture, business process, and infrastructure. In addition, the team identifies the requirements of the solution in terms of performance, availability, and scalability. The team then analyzes the differences between the requirements and constraints.

Page 250   **6.   How does the project team handle the gap between requirements and constraints?**

To handle the gap between requirements and constraints, the project team:

- Identifies the areas in the infrastructure where the requirements might conflict with the constraints.
- Analyzes the gaps between the requirements and the constraints and determines whether they need to make choices to resolve conflicts.
- Identifies the requirements that are absolutely necessary for the project.
- Brainstorms solutions with all groups associated with the project.

Page 250   **7.   During the analysis step of physical design, how does the project team use the list of objects and services created during logical design?**

The project team uses the list by:

- Categorizing services as user services, business services, data services, and system services
- Identifying hidden services

Page 251   **8.   How does the project team refine the class diagrams during the analysis step of physical design?**

The project team refines the class diagrams by:

- Identifying objects that were not apparent during logical design
- Consolidating logical objects
- Categorizing objects into a services-based model
- Refining the methods by focusing on parameters
- Refining the attributes

Page 251   **9.   How do you select the candidate technologies for the solution?**

In evaluating and selecting candidate technologies for the solution, you address business considerations, enterprise architecture considerations, and technology considerations.

Page 251   **10.   What is the difference between the network topology and the data topology of the deployment model?**

The network topology is an infrastructure map that indicates hardware locations and interconnections. The data topology is a map that indicates data store locations in relation to the network topology.

Page 251   **11.   What is the difference between the distribution strategy and the packaging strategy?**

The distribution strategy is a rationale for determining where the services will be located in the solution architecture. Distribution is services-based and not component-based.

The packaging strategy is a rationale for determining which services will reside in each component. You might have multiple strategies in a single solution.

Page 251   **12. What is the difference between cohesion and coupling?**

Cohesion is the relationship among various internal elements of a component. Coupling is the relationship of a component with other components. A component should be tightly cohesive but loosely coupled.

Page 251   **13. What is the purpose of a programming model?**

The programming model:

- Describes how the development team can use the selected technologies.
- Specifies standards that will be followed during the implementation of the project.
- Sets specific guidelines to provide consistent component implementation.

Page 251   **14. What is a component interface?**

A component interface:

- Is a contract that represents the supplier and consumer relationship between components
- Is a means to access the underlying services
- Represents one or more services
- Includes underlying object attributes

Page 251   **15. What are the various types of users of the user services layer of an application?**

There are two types of users of the user services layer of an application: human users who require an interface through which they can interact with the system, and other computer systems. A user interface provides visual means for humans to interact with systems. User services provide the navigation, validation, and error-processing logic.

Chapter 7   Designing the Presentation Layer
Review

Page 283   **1. What is the function of the presentation layer in the business application architecture?**

The presentation layer is the part of the business application that provides a communication mechanism between the user and the business service layer of the application. The presentation layer contains the components that are required to enable user interaction with the application. The most simple presentation layers contain user interface components, such as Windows Forms or ASP.NET Web Forms. For more complex user interactions, you can design user process components.

Page 283   **2. What are the features of a good user interface?**

Some of the features of a good user interface design include:

- Intuitive design
- Optimum screen space utilization
- Ease of navigation

- Controlled navigation
- Input validation
- Menus, toolbars, and Help
- Efficient event handling

Page 283   **3.   What are the differences between a high-fidelity and low-fidelity design?**

- Low-fidelity designs show main features, structure, and navigation; high-fidelity designs show the detailed screen layouts and interface elements.
- Low-fidelity designs allow you to quickly and easily explore alternative designs; high-fidelity designs, although quick to implement and change, require a computer and software.
- Low-fidelity designs are great for brainstorming and quick feedback; high-fidelity designs are typically developed from a low-fidelity design.

Page 283   **4.   What are some of the options that application developers can use to design user assistance for an application?**

Some of the options for designing user assistance in applications include:

- Online Help
- ToolTips
- Wizards
- Status displays
- Accessibility aids

Page 283   **5.   What are the various types of user interface models, and when should you use them?**

- *Windows desktop user interfaces* are used when you need to provide disconnected or offline capabilities or rich user interaction, and maybe even integration with the user interfaces of other applications.
- *Web-based user interfaces* allow for standards-based user interfaces across many devices and platforms. Therefore, you should use Web-based user interfaces when an application must be used on a wide variety of client devices.
- *Mobile device user interfaces* need to be able to display information on a much smaller screen than other common applications and must offer acceptable usability for the devices being targeted.
- *Document-based user interfaces* are used in some applications so that users can enter or view data in document form in the productivity tools they commonly use.

Page 283   **6.   Describe the difference between a user interface component and a user process component. Describe a situation in which you would use a user process component.**

A user interface component makes up the interface to the application that the user will be interacting with. A user process component encapsulates a specific process that a user might perform while interacting with the application. An example of a user process component is the user logon process. A user might be able to log on by means of a Web browser or a Windows-based application. The interfaces will be different, but the process of logging on can be the same. Abstracting the process of logging on away from the interface promotes reuse and consistency within the application.

Page 284   7.   **How do you separate user interface from user process?**

To separate user interface from user process, perform the following steps:

a.   Identify the business process or processes that the user interface process will help to accomplish. Identify how the user sees this as a task. (You can usually do this by consulting the sequence diagrams that you created as part of your requirements analysis.)

b.   Identify the data needed by the business processes. The user process will need to be able to submit this data when necessary.

c.   Identify additional state you will need to maintain throughout the user activity to assist rendering and data capture in the user interface.

d.   Design the visual flow of the user process and the way that each user interface element receives or gives control flow.

Page 284   8.   **Your design calls for the use of Windows Terminal Services. What kind of user interface will you create to implement this design?**

The remote computer will contain a Windows Forms user interface. The local computers will simply use Remote Desktop as a thin client to access the remote computer.

Page 284   9.   **During the envisioning and planning phases, you determined that the users of the solution will be using a wide variety of hardware, will be located at various remote locations, and will not all have access to the company's intranet. What type of client lends itself to these constraints?**

A Web-based client would be most appropriate. Because the users will not have a consistent hardware configuration, and because some might not have access to the company intranet, a secure Web-based solution would be appropriate.

Page 284   10.   **After your design of the user interface is complete, what are some of the ways you can validate the design before implementing it?**

The design of the UI will be derived from interviews with the users, the requirements that the customer has identified and approved, and the various use cases, usage scenarios, and activity diagrams that you created during the conceptual and logical design processes. After the user interface design is complete, you compare it to each of the sources to ensure that the user interface meets all the requirements.

Chapter 8   Designing the Data Layer
Review

Page 317   1.   **How is the data model designed during the planning phase?**

During the conceptual design process, the team researches and analyzes data requirements. These requirements help determine what actually must be stored and processed by the business solution. During logical design, the project team derives a set of data entities that are derived from the data requirements. At this stage, the team defines the relationships between various entities and creates a database schema.

Page 317

2. What is the purpose of the database schema?

A database schema specifies how data is organized in a database. In the logical design process, the members of the project team create a database schema so that they can focus on what must be built before they focus on how to build it.

Page 317

3. What are the characteristics of attributes?

The characteristics are:

- Attributes describe an entity.
- Attributes must be attached to the entity that they most closely describe.
- Attributes define the columns in database tables.

Page 317

4. What is the purpose of specifying data types in a database?

Specifying data types in a database fulfills the following purpose:

- Data types specify how data will be stored in a database.
- Data types specify how data will be formatted.
- Data types help enforce data validation.
- Appropriate data type choices optimize data storage.

Page 317

5. How do most DBMSs support a many-to-many relationship?

Most DBMSs support a many-to-many relationship by using a join table to hold information that maintains the relationship between the entities.

Page 317

6. How do you optimize transactions for good system performance?

The transaction should be short-lived, incorporate only what is required, and should not be distributed.

Page 317

7. What is the impact of indexing on data access?

Queries performed on indexed data are much faster and more efficient than queries performed on data that is not indexed. Rather than scanning an entire table each time a value is needed, the DBMS can use the index to quickly lead the query directly to the location of the required data because the index records the location of the data in the table.

Page 318

8. What is the difference between horizontal and vertical partitioning?

In horizontal partitioning, you segment a table containing a large number of rows into multiple tables containing the same columns. In vertical partitioning, you segment a table containing a large number of columns into multiple tables containing rows with equivalent unique identifiers.

Page 318

9.   What are the benefits of normalization?

- Minimized duplication of information
- Reduced data inconsistencies
- Reduction of empty fields (improved storage)

Page 318

10.   What is denormalization?

Denormalization is the process of reversing normalization to generate tables with more fields that require fewer joins.

Page 318

11.   What are the three types of data integrity that can be enforced in a database?

The following three types of data integrity can be enforced in a database:

- Domain integrity specifies a set of legitimate data values for a column and determines whether null values are to be allowed.
- Entity integrity requires that each row in a table has a unique identifier, known as the primary key value.
- Referential integrity ensures that the relationships between the primary keys (in the parent entity's table) and foreign keys (in the child entity's table) are always maintained.

Page 318

12.   How do you identify data integrity requirements?

To identify data integrity requirements:

- Examine data requirements for uniqueness or limits and constraints that might be specified to ensure that entities can exist and be implemented correctly.
- If limits and constraints have been specified, determine whether the limits and constraints are bound to an entity or to a relationship between entities.
- Implement referential integrity requirements to ensure that all relationships are maintained.

Page 318

13.   What are the criteria for identifying business rules?

The criteria for identifying business rules are:

- Identify conditions that must be satisfied for data to be considered valid.
- Identify conditions that must be avoided.
- Identify sequences in which events must occur.

Page 318

14.   How do keys implement referential integrity?

Primary and foreign key relationships from the physical model directly correspond to the database engine's key settings. These key settings automatically enforce referential integrity between linked tables.

Page 318

15.   What are the benefits of using components to implement business rules?

The benefits are:

- Easier maintenance because the code is stored in only one or a few locations and can be easily updated
- Scalability because additional application servers can be added to distribute the increased processing load

Chapter 9   Designing Security Specifications
Review

Page 352   **1.   What are some of the drawbacks of traditional security models?**

Some of the drawbacks of traditional security models include:

- They are based on user identity and not on code identity.
- They are highly prone to virus and worm attacks.

Page 352   **2.   What are some of the principles of secure coding?**

The following are some of the principles of secure coding:

- Rely on tested and proven security systems.
- Never trust external input.
- Assume that external systems are insecure.
- Apply the principle of least privilege.
- Reduce available components and data.
- Default to a secure mode.
- Do not rely on security by obscurity.
- Follow STRIDE principles.

Page 352   **3.   Which of the following statements about buffer overruns is true? (Select all that apply.)**

- **Type safety verification was designed to eliminate buffer overruns.**
- **A buffer overrun can cause an application to stop responding or to malfunction.**
- **A buffer overrun can be exploited by a malicious user to run arbitrary code.**
- **The error message that results from a buffer overrun can pose a security threat.**

All of these statements are true.

Page 352   **4.   During which MSF phase should the threat model be created?**

- **Planning**
- **Developing**
- **Stabilizing**

The threat model is created during the planning phase.

Page 352   **5.   What is the STRIDE model?**

The STRIDE model is a threat model that allows application designers to predict and evaluate potential threats to an application. Each letter in the STRIDE acronym specifies a different category of security threat: spoofing identity, tampering, repudiation, information disclosure, denial of service, and elevation of privilege.

Page 353   **6.   Read the following security attack scenario, and then decide which elements of the STRIDE model are implicit in the attack.**

Carl sees that Bob has left his workstation unattended and unlocked. Carl sits down at Bob's workstation and opens Bob's e-mail application. Carl, pretending to be Bob, sends an e-mail message to Alice. Carl quits the e-mail client and then walks away unobserved.

Four types of attacks—spoofing identity, tampering, repudiation, and elevation of privilege—are possible in the above scenario.

Page 353   **7.   What is code-access security?**

The .NET Framework provides code-access security to help protect computer systems from malicious code and to provide a way to allow mobile code to run safely. Code-access security allows code to be trusted to varying degrees, depending on the code's origin and on other aspects of the code's identity.

Page 353   **8.   What is role-based security?**

Role-based security applies mostly to the spoofing identity security threat by preventing unauthorized users from performing operations that they are not authorized to perform. Role-based security allows code to check the identity and role membership of the user. The .NET Framework includes classes to check Windows users and groups, in addition to classes to help implement role-based security for other authentication schemes.

Page 353   **9.   Which are the authentication providers supported by ASP.NET?**

ASP.NET supports three authentication providers: forms, Microsoft Passport, and Windows.

Page 353   **10.   What are the three types of security provided by Web services?**

The three types of security are:

- Platform/transport-level (point-to-point) security
- Application-level (custom) security
- Message-level (end-to-end) security

Page 353   **11.   What are the steps for designing an authorization and authentication strategy for an application?**

To design an authorization and authentication strategy for an application, you perform the following steps:

a.   Identify resources.

b.   Select an authorization strategy.

c.   Select the identities used for resource access.

d.   Consider identity flow.

e.   Select an authentication approach.

f.   Decide how to flow identity.

Chapter 10   Completing the Planning Phase
Activity, Exercise 1

Page 383   1.   **Review the test plan and then list three ways that use cases and usage scenarios are used in the testing process for Adventure Works Cycles.**

Adventure Works Cycles uses use cases and usage scenarios in the following ways:

- Use cases and usage scenarios define the actions to be tested for user functionality.
- Use cases and usage scenarios define the actions to be tested for adminstrative functionality.
- Use cases and usage scenarios will be used to write the specific test script scenarios.

Page 383   2.   **How will bugs be approved and documented for action for the solution?**

Change requests will be issued for bugs meeting the change criteria.

Page 383   3.   **Which user accounts must be configured on the test environment servers?**

- Network Administrator
- Sales Representative 1
- Sales Representative 2
- Sales Manager
- Web Customer 1
- Web Customer 2
- Reseller
- Production Clerk

Page 383   4.   **Why is the following threat important to list under threats to testing?**

Availability of sales staff for testing. The test team should be overseen by at least one sales representative. Mitigation: Gain prior agreement from the vice president of sales for two sales representatives to be assigned to test the application.

Because the bulk of the functionality is defined by usage scenarios with a sales representative as at least one of the actors, this requirement will greatly increase the validity of the testing. It will also ensure approval from the sales staff (provided the two selected representatives feel that their input is responded to by means of change requests). It can also provide the benefit of creating two representatives that are able to be very productive in the training and implementation of the application.

Chapter 10   Completing the Planning Phase
Activity, Exercise 2

Page 384   1.   **What are the parameters for the *addOrderDetail* method?**

The parameters are: ProductID and Quantity.

Page 384   2.   **Will two types of client interfaces be available in the application?**

Yes, Windows Forms and Web Forms.

Page 384   3.   **Why is the Interfaces section still to be determined?**

The interfaces cannot be documented until they are developed and validated. Although pseudocode could be written, it should not be left permanently in the technical specification, but replaced with the code when it is developed.

Chapter 10   Completing the Planning Phase
Review

Page 388   1.   **How do you scale up an application?**

You scale up an application by adding more memory, more or faster processors, or by migrating the application to a single more powerful machine.

Page 388   2.   **What do you need to take into consideration while designing for scalability?**

- Design processes so that they do not wait.
- Design processes so that they do not fight for resources.
- Design processes for commutability.
- Design components for interchangeability.
- Partition resources and activities.

Page 388   3.   **What do you need to take into consideration while designing for availability?**

Designing for availability includes anticipating, detecting, and resolving hardware or software failures before they result in service errors, event faults, or data corruption, thereby minimizing downtime.

Page 388   4.   **How does clustering enhance the availability of an application?**

Clustering allows two or more independent servers to behave as a single system. In the event of a failure of a component such as a CPU, motherboard, storage adapter, network card, or application component, the workload is moved to another server, current client processes are switched over, and the failed application service is automatically restarted, with no apparent downtime. When a hardware or software resource fails, customers connected to that server cluster might experience a slight delay, but the service will be completed.

Page 388   5.   **How do you reduce planned downtime of an application?**

One of the best ways to avoid planned downtime is by using rolling upgrades. For example, assume that you need to update a component on a clustered server. You can move the server's resource groups to another server, take the server offline for maintenance, perform the upgrade, and then bring the server online. During the maintenance, the other servers handle the workload and the application experiences no downtime.

Page 388   **6.   Why is reliability an important design consideration for an application?**

- Unreliable systems are very costly. Users bypass unreliable Web sites, resulting in lost revenue and reduced future sales.
- The expense of repairing corrupted data increases the loss due to application failure.
- Unreliable systems are difficult to maintain or improve because the failure points are typically hidden throughout the system.

Page 389   **7.   How do you design for reliability of an application?**

To design for reliability of an application, you need to perform the following tasks:

- Document reliability requirements in the specification.
- Use a good architectural infrastructure.
- Include management information in the application.
- Use redundancy.
- Use quality development tools.
- Use reliability checks that are provided by the application.
- Use consistent error handling.
- Reduce the application's functionality instead of completely failing the application.

Page 389   **8.   How do you define a performance requirement?**

To define a good performance requirement, you must identify project constraints, determine services that the application will perform, and specify the load on the application.

Page 389   **9.   Why do you need to design for interoperability?**

- Reduces operational cost and complexity
- Enables optimal deployments
- Uses existing investments

Page 389   **10.   How do you prepare an application for globalization?**

- Identify the cultures and locales that must be supported.
- Design features that support those cultures and locales.
- Write code that functions equally well in all the supported cultures and locales.

Page 389   **11.   What is the purpose of a monitoring plan?**

A monitoring plan describes what will be monitored, how the application will be monitored, and how the results of monitoring will be reported and used. Customers use automated procedures to monitor many aspects of a solution.

Page 389   **12.   What is the purpose of the migration strategies section of the migration plan?**

The migration strategies section describes the strategy or strategies that will guide the migration process. These strategies do not need to be mutually exclusive but can describe different parts of the overall migration. Strategy could be organized around releases (related to the business or to development or technology maturity) or organized around solution components. These strategies also need to take into account the migration of earlier systems into the new solution environment. You might have multiple migration strategy sections if you need to migrate both business objects and data.

Page 389   **13.   Why do you need to provide licensing specifications for both the development and the deployment phase?**

- During the developing phase, the team will work with selected technologies and software products. You must ensure that there are sufficient licenses for the required products.

- For the developing phase, you need to specify the number of licenses needed for any software that might be used. The number of licenses needed depends on the type of solution and the number of users who will use the solution.

Page 389   **14.   What is the purpose of the development plan?**

The development plan describes the solution development process used for the project. This plan provides consistent guidelines and processes to the teams creating the solution. Having the development process documented indicates that the team has discussed and agreed on a consistent structure and direction to be used during the development process. It also facilitates reuse among different groups and minimizes the dependency upon one individual or group.

Page 389   **15.   What is the purpose of the test plan?**

The test plan describes the strategy and approach used to plan, organize, and manage the project's testing activities. It identifies testing objectives, methodologies and tools, expected results, responsibilities, and resource requirements. This document is the primary plan for the testing team. A test plan ensures that the testing process will be conducted in a thorough and organized manner and will enable the team to determine the stability of the solution.

Page 389   **16.   Who creates the deployment plan?**

The release management role of the MSF Team Model is responsible for designing and implementing the solution's deployment plan. Release management is also responsible for specifying the solution infrastructure and ensuring that the solution continues to run as expected after it has been deployed.

Page 389   **17.   What is a technical specification?**

The technical specification is a set of reference documents that usually includes the artifacts of physical design, such as class specifications, component models, metrics, and network and component topologies. During the developing phase, the technical specification becomes the method for documenting the actual implementation of the developed solution.

Chapter 11   Stabilizing and Deploying the Solution Review

Page 424   **1. What are some of the specific goals of the stabilizing phase?**

The goals of the stabilizing phase include:

- Improve solution quality
- Address outstanding issues to prepare for release
- Make the transition from building features to focusing on quality
- Stabilize the solution
- Prepare for release

Page 424   **2. How does ongoing analysis of bug convergence provide warning signs about the stability of the project?**

If the numbers of reported and fixed bugs are not converging over time, the team is reporting as many new bugs as it is fixing. Solution stability is no closer than it was on the first day of the project. The team must treat this lack of convergence as a serious issue and resolve it quickly.

Page 424   **3. Why is zero-bug bounce a positive indicator for the project?**

Zero-bug bounce indicates that development has caught up with the backlog of active bugs needing resolution. It indicates that the quality of the build is improving.

Page 424   **4. What is a release candidate, and what are some of its features?**

After the first achievement of zero-bug bounce, a series of release candidates are prepared for release to the pilot group. Each of these releases is marked as an interim milestone. The purpose of the release candidate is to make the product available to a preselected group of users to test it. The users provide feedback to the project team, and the project team in turn continues to improve the product and resolve bugs that appear during the pilot.

Page 424   **5. What is a pilot, and what are its goals?**

A pilot is a test of the solution under live conditions, such as a subset of production servers, a subset of users in a users group, or a trial period for the entire production environment (with the ability to roll back). The goal of a pilot is to take the next step in the ongoing stabilization process and reduce the risks associated with deployment.

Page 424   **6. Why should pilot testing not be too easy?**

A pilot should test every case and situation that will arise in production, including operations tasks. A pilot that is too easy will not reveal enough information to select the strategy for moving forward. Intentional crashes of the pilot should be included to test rollback procedures, disaster recovery, and business continuity planning. The results of a rigorous pilot that is completed by proactive users will tell the team whether it should stagger forward, roll back, suspend the pilot, patch and continue, or proceed to the deployment phase (the ultimate goal of the pilot).

Page 424   **7.   What are the deliverables of the deploying phase?**

The deliverables of the deploying phase are: operations and support information systems, including procedures and processes, knowledge base, reports, and logbooks; a repository of all versions of documents, load sets, configurations, scripts, and code; and a project closeout report, including project documents and customer surveys.

Page 425   **8.   Which person or group is the best candidate to deploy the solution?**

This varies with the organization and the project. Sometimes the project team is the best candidate, and sometimes a specific deployment feature team should assume the responsibility. In some cases, an outside group should handle deployment. Ultimately, it is most important to develop a solid deployment plan and provide it to the person or group that is able to deliver a solid deployment.

Page 425   **9.   What are some examples of core components? What are some examples of site components?**

Core components are such things as domain controllers, mail routers, remote access servers, and database servers. Site components include such things as local routers and file print servers.

Page 425   **10.   What is the quiet period, and what are some of its features?**

The quiet period begins when deployments are complete and the team begins transferring responsibilities to operations and support. The quiet period generally lasts from 15 to 30 days.

Page 425   **11.   What type of documents result from completing closeout activities?**

Closeout activities usually produce a customer satisfaction survey, a closeout report (including formal project closure, final deliverable versions, a customer survey result compilation, and a summary of next steps), a project review document, and a customer sign-off document.

Page 425   **12.   Which MSF role handles the final sign-off from the customer?**

Product management typically obtains final sign-off from the customer for release of the solution. This signals the customer's approval of the solution and permission to disengage from the project.

Page 425   **13.   What are the two types of project reviews that MSF advocates at the end of the deployment phase?**

Two types of project reviews are team reviews and customer reviews. In a team review, the core team assesses what it did well and what could have been improved. In a customer review, the team discusses with sponsors and stakeholders the project's outstanding issues, the level of quality and customer satisfaction, and the next steps following the project.

Glossary

A

accessibility aids Specialized programs and devices that help people with disabilities use applications more effectively.

activity diagram A UML diagram used to represent the state transition and flow of an application.

actor An entity in a use case that interacts with the system to be developed for the purpose of completing an event.

actors catalog An artifact that contains information about all the actors that will be used in use cases. See also *artifact*.

aggregation A special type of association that represents the relationship between a whole and its parts.

alpha code All code produced during the developing phase of the MSF Process Model. See also *beta code*.

analyzing risk The process of converting risk data into information that can be used to make risk decisions.

application architecture A set of definitions, rules, and relationships that form the structure of an application.

applications interoperability The infrastructure required to ensure interoperability between new *n*-tier applications and existing applications, business logic, and data.

architecture A design and plan for building something. Also the style of that plan or design. See also *application architecture*.

artifact An item that is physically available in the business environment and that describes an element or core business process.

association A structural relationship that describes a connection among objects.

asynchronous communication services Services that provide a message-based form of execution in which the requesting application is not dependent on a response within any given period of time.

asynchronous control The situation in which a client can submit a request and then continue performing other tasks.

attributes The names of data values that an object holds. Also known as *properties*.

authentication The process of positively identifying the clients of your application. Clients might include end users, services, processes, or computers.

authorization The process of defining what authenticated clients are allowed to see and do within the application.

availability A measure of how often an application is available to handle service requests as compared to the planned run time.

B

behavioral view A UML view that represents the dynamic or changing state of a system.

beta code All code tested during the stabilizing phase of the MSF Process Model. See also *alpha code*.

buddy testing A type of testing that involves developers who are not working directly on the creation of a particular code segment, employing them to perform coverage testing on their colleague's code.

buffer overrun A type of error that occurs when more data is written to a buffer than the buffer was programmed to contain.

bug Any issue arising from the use of the product.

bug convergence The point at which the team makes visible progress towards minimizing the active bug count.

build verification testing A type of testing used to identify errors during the build process. It can be thought of as the identification of compilation errors, as opposed to run-time errors, of all solution components.

business goals Goals representing what the customer wants to achieve with the solution. Business goals form the basis for determining the success criteria of the solution.

business requirements Requirements defining what the solution must deliver to capitalize on a business opportunity or to meet business challenges.

business rules catalog An artifact in internal team documentation that lists the business rules for a solution. This is a living document.

business services Units of application logic that enforce business rules in the correct sequence.

C

cache architecture A version of the client/server architecture in which the application provides a means for processing some client requests without forwarding the requests to another device.

check-in testing A type of testing performed by developers or testers before the code is checked into the change control system. This testing is performed to ensure that tested code is behaving correctly.

class diagram A UML diagram that depicts various classes and their associations.

Class-Responsibility-Collaboration (CRC card) A modeling tool that indicates all the classes with which a class must interact and identifies the relationships between classes.

client/server architecture A two-tier architecture that is based on a request-and-provide strategy. The client initiates a session with the server and controls the session, enlisting the server on demand.

clustered index A type of index that physically reorders the rows of data in a table to match the order of the index.

clustering A technology for creating high-availability applications. A cluster consists of multiple computers that are physically networked and logically connected by cluster software.

code signing The process of providing a set of code with credentials that authenticate the publisher of the code.

code-access security A technique that allows code to be trusted to varying degrees, depending on the code's origin and on other aspects of the code's identity.

cohesion The relationship among different internal elements of a component.

collaboration diagram A UML diagram that represents a set of classes and the messages sent and received by those classes.

commutative processes Two or more operations that can execute in any order and still obtain the same result.

compatibility testing A type of testing that focuses on the integration or interoperability of the solution under development with existing systems.

component and data topology A map that indicates the locations of packages, components, and their services in relation to the network topology. It also indicates data store locations.

component diagram A UML diagram that represents the implementation view of a system. This diagram is used to represent the dependencies between components or component packages.

conceptual design The first design process of the planning phase, during which the project team views the problem from the perspective of the users and business requirements and defines the problem and solution in terms of usage scenarios.

conceptual schema design procedure (CSDP) A methodology in ORM that focuses on the analysis and design of data. The conceptual schema specifies the information structure of the application, including the types of facts that are of interest, any constraints on these facts, and the rules for deriving some facts from others.

configuration testing A type of testing used to conduct solution tests in each of the possible solution configurations.

constraints Parameters to which the final business solution must adhere. They are aspects of the business environment that cannot or will not be changed.

coupling The relationship of a component with other components.

coverage testing Low-level technical testing.

CRC card See *Class-Responsibility-Collaboration.*

CSDP See *conceptual schema design procedure.*

customer One or more individuals who expect to gain business value from a solution.

D

data integrity The consistency and accuracy of data.

data interoperability The ability for applications to access and use data stored in both structured and unstructured storage systems such as databases, file systems, and e-mail stores.

data services Units of application logic that provide the lowest visible level of detail for manipulating data.

data type A definition used to specify the kind of data that is stored in a field.

database A collection of data values that are organized in a specific manner.

database schema A description that specifies how data is organized in a database.

delegation An extended form of impersonation that allows a server process that is performing work on behalf of a client to access resources on a remote computer. See also *impersonation.*

denial of service (DoS) Any attack that attempts to shut down or prevent access to a computing resource.

denormalization The process of reversing normalization to generate tables with more fields that require fewer joins.

dependency A relationship between two objects in which a change to one object (independent) can affect the behavior or service of the other object (dependent).

deploying phase The final phase of the MSF Process Model. During this phase, the team deploys the solution technology and site components, stabilizes the deployment, transfers the project to operations and support, and obtains final customer approval of the project.

deployment diagram A UML diagram that represents the mapping of software components to the nodes of the physical implementation of a system.

deployment model A model that represents the mapping of the application and its services to the actual server topology.

deployment view See *environment view*.

design goals A type of project goal. These goals focus on the attributes of the solution.

design view See *structural view*.

developing phase The third phase of the MSF Process Model. During this phase, the project team creates the solution, creates the code to implement the solution, documents the code, and develops the infrastructure for the solution. The developing phase culminates in the *scope complete* milestone.

development An MSF Team Model role that is responsible for developing the solution according to the specifications provided by the program management role.

distribution strategy A rationale for determining where services will be located in the solution architecture.

documentation and Help file tests A type of testing that focuses on testing all developed support documents or systems. The documents and Help files are compared with the solution to discover any discrepancies.

domain integrity A type of data integrity used to specify a set of valid data values for a column and determine whether null values are to be allowed.

DoS See *denial of service*.

E

elementary fact Refers to the fact that an object has a property, or that one or more objects participate in a relationship.

elevation of privilege An attack in which a malicious user gains access to greater privileges than the administrator intended, creating the opportunity for the user to launch attacks of every other category of security threat.

encryption The process of disguising data before it is sent or stored.

end user One or more individuals or systems that interact directly with a solution.

entity integrity A type of data integrity that requires each row in a table to have a unique identifier, known as the primary key value. See *primary keys*.

environment view A UML view that represents the distribution of the physical elements of a system. Also known as the deployment view.

envisioning phase The first phase of the MSF Process Model, during which the project team is assembled and comes to agreement with the customer on the project vision and scope. The envisioning phase culminates in the *vision-approved* milestone.

F

fact instance An individual observation about the relationship between two or more data values.

fact type The set of fact instances that share the same object types and predicate relationships.

flat-file database A type of data store in which all data in a single file is stored as a set of rows and columns.

focus group An information-gathering technique in which individuals discuss a topic and provide feedback to a facilitator.

foreign keys Keys used to link two tables.

forms authentication A system by which unauthenticated requests are redirected to a Hypertext Markup Language (HTML) form by means of Hypertext Transfer Protocol (HTTP) client-side redirection.

functional specification A virtual repository of project and design-related artifacts that are created during the planning phase of the MSF Process Model.

functional tests Tests that are specified by the users of the solution and created by the testing team.

G

generalization A relationship between a general thing (called the parent) and a specialized or specific thing (called the child).

globalization The process of designing and developing an application that can operate in multiple cultures and locales.

glossary One of the artifacts in internal team documentation that contains a list of terms used in artifacts and their meanings.

granularity A measure of the number of services and objects packaged in a single component.

H

hashing The process of matching data of any length to a fixed-length byte sequence.

hierarchical database A database that stores a wide range of information in a variety of formats.

high-fidelity design A design that provides detailed information about screen layout and interface elements.

horizontal partitioning A method of partitioning tables in which a table containing many rows is divided into multiple tables containing the same columns.

I

identity A characteristic of a user or service that can uniquely identify the user or service.

impersonation A technique used by a server application to access resources on behalf of a client application.

implementation view A UML view that represents the structure of the logical elements of a system.

index An ordered list of rows in a table that a database management system (DBMS) can use to accelerate lookup operations.

information disclosure A security error in which an unauthorized user views private data, such as a file that contains a credit card number and expiration date.

instance An item of interest in the universe of discourse.

interchangeable component A component that is designed to release its resources, move into a pool managed by a resource manager, and be re-initialized for use by a new client application.

interface A means for requesting that a service perform an operation and a means for receiving information about the resulting attributes.

interim milestone A point in time that signals a transition within a phase and helps to divide large projects into manageable pieces. See also *milestone*.

interviewing An information gathering technique that involves a one-on-one meeting between a member of the project team and a user or stakeholder.

K

key A value used to uniquely identify each instance of an entity.

L

layered architecture A version of the client/server architecture in which various services in the application are clearly positioned in specific layers.

layered-client-cache-stateless-cache-server architecture A version of the client/server architecture that combines the layered-client-server, client-cache, and cached-stateless-server approaches by adding proxies throughout the system as necessary.

living documents Documents that are used and updated throughout the life cycle of the project.

localization The process of adapting a globalized application to a specific culture and locale, using separate resources for each culture.

logical design A process in the planning phase during which the solution is described in terms of its organization, its structure, and the interaction of its parts from the perspective of the project team.

low-fidelity design A design that shows the main structure and features of the user interface (UI) and illustrates the navigation path.

M

manageability The ease with which a system can be managed on all levels.

management interoperability The tasks of user account management, performance monitoring, and tuning for heterogeneous applications.

master project plan A collection of plans that addresses tasks performed by each of the six MSF team roles to achieve the functionality described in the functional specification.

master project schedule The schedule that applies a time frame to the master plan. The master project schedule synchronizes project schedules across the teams. It includes the time frame in which the teams intend to complete their work.

master risk assessment document A document used to describe the risks associated with developing the solution. The master risk assessment document that is developed during the envisioning phase is reviewed and updated regularly, but particularly at the milestones.

meaningful sample population Instances of information in the UoD, and the real-world problem that the project team is trying to solve.

messaging service A type of service used to route information and deliver information that is not time-dependent to many individuals.

Microsoft Solutions Framework (MSF) A structure developed by Microsoft that is a set of models, principles, and guidelines for planning, building, and managing business solutions.

milestone A point at which the team assesses progress and makes mid-course corrections. Milestones are review and synchronization points, not completion points.

mitigating risk The practice of predicting risks and then taking steps to eliminate them from a proposed course of action.

MSF See *Microsoft Solutions Framework.*

MSF Process Model A phase-based, milestone-driven, and iterative model that describes a generalized sequence of activities for building and deploying enterprise solutions. The MSF Process Model combines the waterfall model's milestone-based planning, and the resulting predictability, with the spiral model's beneficial feedback and creativity.

MSF readiness management process A process to help teams develop the knowledge, skills, and abilities (KSAs) needed to create and manage projects and solutions.

MSF risk management process A discipline that advocates proactive risk management, continuous risk assessment, and decision making throughout the project life cycle.

N

navigation map A map in user interface (UI) design that shows which component is called for each UI event.

network interoperability The ability of multiple vendor systems to communicate with each other without having to use common protocols.

network load balancing (NLB) A technique used to distribute traffic evenly across available servers.

network topology An infrastructure map that indicates hardware locations and interconnections.

NLB See *network load balancing*.

nonclustered index A type of index that maintains a small table of index information about a column or group of columns.

normalization The process of progressively refining a logical model to eliminate duplicate data from a database.

O

object diagram A UML diagram that depicts various objects in a system and their relationships with each other.

Object Role Modeling (ORM) A rich modeling methodology that allows you to analyze information at the conceptual level and model complex fact-driven, data-related business requirements.

object type The set of all possible instances of a given object.

object-oriented database A data storage system in which database objects appear as programming language objects in one or more existing programming languages.

objects People or things described in usage scenarios.

Online Help Refers to any help that is immediately available upon user request while the user is interacting with the system.

operations requirement A type of requirement that the solution must deliver to maximize operability and improve service delivery with reduced downtime and risks.

operations team The organization responsible for the ongoing operation of the solution after delivery.

ORM See *Object Role Modeling*.

P

packaging strategy A rationale for determining which services go into each component.

parallel testing A common usage testing strategy in which both the current solution and the solution under development are tested side-by-side at the same time.

Passport authentication A centralized authentication service provided by Microsoft that offers a single logon and core profile services for member sites.

performance testing A type of testing that focuses on predicted performance improvements to the solution under development.

physical design The final design process of the planning phase. During this process, components, services, and technologies of the solution are described from the perspective of development requirements.

pilot A test of a solution in the production environment, and a trial of the solution by installers, systems support staff, and end users.

pilot plan A plan that describes how the team will move the candidate release version of a solution to a staging area and test it.

planning phase The second phase of the MSF Process Model, during which the team determines what to develop and plans how to create the solution. The team prepares the functional specification, creates a design of the solution, and prepares work plans, cost estimates, and schedules for the various deliverables. This phase culminates with the *project plan approved* milestone.

population The group of all combined instances of a given type of item of interest in the UoD.

preliminary deployment model A model that includes network, data, and component topologies and enables the project team and other stakeholders to review the design.

primary keys Keys that uniquely identify each row of data in a table.

problem statement A short narrative describing the issues the business hopes to address with the project. It relates primarily to the current state of business activities.

process A collection of activities that yield a result, product, or service; usually a continuous operation.

process model A model that guides the order of project activities and represents the life cycle of a project.

process view See *behavioral view*.

product management An MSF Team Model role that is responsible for managing customer communications and expectations. During the design phase, product management gathers customer requirements and ensures that business needs are met. Product management also works on project communication plans such as briefings to the customers, marketing to users, demonstrations, and product launches.

program management An MSF Team Model role that is responsible for the development process and for delivering the solution to the customer within the project constraints.

programming model A model that describes how the development team can use the specific technologies and that sets guidelines for providing consistent component implementation and increasing the maintainability of the components.

project sponsor One or more individuals responsible for initiating and approving the project and its result.

project structure document A document that defines the approach a team will use to organize and manage a project. It describes the team's administrative structure, standards and processes, and project resources and constraints.

project tradeoff matrix A tool that helps identify the project features that are considered essential, the features that are not essential but that would be good to include, and the features that can be eliminated or added to the next version to accommodate the other two variables.

prototyping A technique in which information is gathered by simulating the production environment. Prototyping is a validation technique in which a prototype is used to provide details of processes, process flow, organizational implications, and technology possibilities.

R

realization A relationship, between classes, in which one abstract class specifies a contract that another class needs to carry out.

regression testing The process of repeating identical actions or steps that were performed using an earlier build of a product on a new build or version of the product.

relational model database A database in which data is stored in multiple tables and columns.

relationships A description of how objects are linked to each other.

release management An MSF Team Model role that is responsible for defect-free deployment and operations of the solution. Release management validates the infrastructure implications of the solution to ensure that it can be deployed and supported.

release readiness milestone The major milestone at the end of the stabilizing phase that represents the point at which the team has addressed all outstanding issues and releases the product.

reliability The ability of the application to provide accurate results.

repeatability A variable that measures how repeatable an issue or bug is. Repeatability is the percentage in which the issue or bug manifests itself. It is expressed as a percentage in the range of 10 percent (integer value 0.1) through 100 percent (integer value 1), where 100 percent indicates that the issue or bug is reproducible on every test run.

repudiation A situation in which a system administrator or security agent is unable to prove that a user—malicious or otherwise—has performed some action.

risk The possibility of loss or injury; a problem that might occur.

risk probability The likelihood that a risk will occur.

risk source Where a risk might originate.

role playing A validation technique in which a set of selected users performs multiple versions of a process to evaluate it and identify areas of potential refinement.

S

scalability The capability to increase resources to produce an increase in the service capacity.

scaling out Distributing the processing load across more than one server.

scaling up Achieving scalability by improving the existing server's processing hardware.

scope A guideline used to define what will and will not be included in a project. The scope corresponds to the project vision as defined in the vision statement and incorporates the constraints imposed on the project by resources, time, and other limiting factors.

secure communications A generic term used to describe the process of ensuring that messages remain private and unaltered as they cross networks.

security context A generic term used to refer to the collection of security settings that affect the security-related behavior of a process or thread.

sequence diagram A UML diagram that describes the interaction between classes. A sequence diagram shows the actors and objects that participate in an interaction, and a chronological list of the events they generate.

service A specific behavior that a business object must perform.

set Any group of instances. A set is not necessarily the same as a population. It can be part of a population, or a combination of instances from more than one population.

severity A variable that measures how much impact an issue or bug will have on a solution, on code, or on users. Severity is an integer in the range of 1 through 10, where classification 10 issues or bugs present the most impact.

shadowing An information gathering technique in which you observe a user performing tasks in the actual work environment and ask the user any questions you have related to the task.

signed data A standards-based data type that consists of any type of content combined with encrypted hashes of the content for zero or more signers.

solution concept A description of the approach the team will take to meet the goals of the project. Provides the basis for proceeding to the planning phase.

spiral model An iterative process model in which the stages of application development are characterized as inception, elaboration, construction, and transition. Each stage has five activity phases: requirements, design, implementation, deployment, and management. The spiral model's process is a continual cycle through the stages of development, with each stage requiring multiple cycles through the five phases.

spoofing identity An attack involving a malicious user posing as a trusted entity.

SQL injection A type of security error that can occur when developers dynamically build Structured Query Language (SQL) statements by using user input.

stabilizing phase The last of four distinct phases of the MSF Process Model. During this phase, all team efforts are directed toward addressing all issues derived from feedback. No new development occurs during this phase. The stabilizing phase culminates in the *release readiness* milestone.

state diagram A UML diagram that describes how a class behaves when external processes or entities access the class.

state management A process by which the solution maintains state and page information over multiple requests for the same or different pages.

stateless architecture A version of the client/server architecture in which each client request contains all the information that is required by the server to process the request. No information is stored on the server.

stored procedures Named collections of SQL statements that are stored on the DBMS. They are precompiled, eliminating the need for the query analyzer to parse the statement every time the stored procedure is called.

stress test A type of test specifically designed to identify issues or bugs that might present themselves when the solution under development is operating under extreme conditions.

STRIDE threat model A technique used for identifying and categorizing threats to an application. Each letter in the STRIDE acronym specifies a different category of security threat: spoofing identity, tampering, repudiation, information disclosure, denial of service, and elevation of privilege.

structural view A UML view that represents the static or idle state of the system. Also known as the design view.

surveys An information gathering technique in which sets of questions are created and administered to specific sets of users.

synchronous control The situation in which object services are invoked and the calling object waits for control to be returned.

system requirement A type of requirement that specifies the atomic transactions and their sequence in a system. System requirements help the project team define how the new solution will interact with existing systems.

system services Units of application logic that provide functionality outside the business logic.

T

tampering An attack in which a user gains unauthorized access to a computer and then changes its operation, configuration, or data.

technical specification A set of reference documents that usually includes the artifacts of physical design, such as class specifications, component models, metrics, and network and component topologies.

test plan A plan that describes the strategy and approach used to plan, organize, and manage a project's testing activities.

testing An MSF Team Model role that is responsible for identifying and addressing all product quality issues and approving the solution for release. This role evaluates and validates design functionality and consistency with project vision and scope.

top ten risk list An identification of the ten top priority risks, taken from the risk assessment document.

tradeoff triangle A tool that shows that any change to any one component represented in the tradeoff triangle implies that a corresponding change might need to be made to other components. The tradeoff triangle helps to explain the constraints and present the options for tradeoffs.

transactional service A type of service that provides the mechanism and environment for a transaction-based application.

type-safe code Any code that accesses only the memory it is authorized to access.

U

UML See *Unified Modeling Language*.

Unified Modeling Language (UML) A standard modeling language that is used to model software systems of varying complexity.

unit test A type of developer-performed internal coverage testing that takes advantage of automated testing.

universe of discourse (UoD) An application area in ORM that you create to design a solution.

UoD See *universe of discourse*.

usage scenario Specifies the activity performed by a particular type of user and provides additional information about the activities and task sequences that constitute a process.

usage testing A type of high-level testing that is often performed by potential users of a solution or by subsets of this group.

use case A description of high-level interactions between an individual and a system. A use case specifies the sequence of steps that a user will perform in a usage scenario.

use case diagram A UML diagram that represents the functionality that is provided to external entities by a system.

user experience An MSF Team Model role that is responsible for analyzing the performance needs and support issues of users and for considering the product implications of meeting those needs.

user instruction An information gathering technique in which users train the project team on the tasks that they perform.

user interface components Components that manage interaction with the user, display data to the user, acquire data from the user, interpret events that are caused by user actions, change the state of the user interface, and help users view progress in their tasks.

user profile A document that specifies the various users of the solution and their roles and responsibilities.

user requirement A type of requirement that defines the nonfunctional aspect of a user's interaction with a solution.

user services Units of application logic that provide the user interface in an application. The user services of an application manage the interaction between the application and its users.

user view A UML view that represents the part of the system with which the user interacts.

V

vertical partitioning A method of partitioning tables in which a table containing many columns is divided into multiple tables containing rows with equivalent unique identifiers.

visibility A variable that measures the situation or environment that must be established before an issue or bug manifests itself. Visibility is a percentage in the range of 10 percent (integer value 0.1) through 100 percent (integer value 1), where 10 percent indicates that the issue or bug is visible under only the most obscure conditions. Issues or bugs that manifest themselves in environments with under common conditions are said to be highly visible.

vision statement A short, concise statement used to establish a common vision and reach consensus among team members that a project is valuable to the organization and is likely to succeed.

vision/scope meeting A meeting during which the team and the customer arrive at a shared understanding regarding how the proposed solution will address the business challenge and how it is applicable to the current business scenario, given the scope that has been defined.

W

walkthrough A validation technique in which a facilitator guides users through a scenario and asks questions to determine whether the users agree with the description of individual actions and events.

waterfall model A linear process model that has the following well-defined development steps: system requirements, software requirements, analysis, program design, coding, system test, and operations. This process model has fixed transition and assessment points. All tasks for a particular step must be completed before proceeding to the next step.

Windows authentication A system used by Microsoft ASP.NET in conjunction with Internet Information Services (IIS) authentication.

wizard A user assistance device that guides users step by step through a procedure.

Z

ZBB See *zero-bug bounce*.

zero-bug bounce (ZBB) The point in the project when development resolves all the bugs raised by testing and there are no active bugs. More bugs might be logged after this point.

zero-defect mindset The goal for project teams in which the team commits to producing the highest quality product possible.

Index

A

E

O

P

At Microsoft Press, we use tools to illustrate our books for software developers and IT professionals. Tools very simply and powerfully symbolize human inventiveness. They're a metaphor for people extending their capabilities, precision, and reach. From simple calipers and pliers to digital micrometers and lasers, these stylized illustrations give each book a visual identity, and a personality to the series. With tools and knowledge, there's no limit to creativity and innovation. Our tagline says it all: *the tools you need to put technology to work.*

Learn how to develop software at your own pace with the proven *Microsoft* STEP BY STEP method!

Microsoft® Visual Basic® .NET Step by Step
ISBN: 0-7356-1374-5
U.S.A. $39.99
Canada $57.99

Web Database Development Step by Step .NET Edition
ISBN: 0-7356-1637-X
U.S.A. $39.99
Canada $57.99

Microsoft Visual C#™ .NET Step by Step
ISBN: 0-7356-1289-7
U.S.A. $39.99
Canada $57.99

Microsoft Visual C++® .NET Step by Step
ISBN: 0-7356-1567-5
U.S.A. $39.99
Canada $57.99

Learn core programming skills with these hands-on, tutorial-based guides—all of them designed to walk any developer through the fundamentals of Microsoft's programming languages. Work through every lesson to complete the full course, or do just the lessons you want to learn exactly the skills you need. Either way, you receive professional development training at your own pace, with real-world examples and practice files to help you master core skills with the world's most popular programming languages and technologies. Throughout, you'll find insightful tips and expert explanations for rapid application development, increased productivity, and more powerful results.

Microsoft Press has other STEP BY STEP titles to help you master core programming skills:

Microsoft ASP.NET Step by Step
ISBN: 0-7356-1287-0

Microsoft ADO.NET Step by Step
ISBN: 0-7356-1236-6

Microsoft .NET XML Web Services Step by Step
ISBN: 0-7356-1720-1

OOP with Microsoft Visual Basic .NET and Microsoft Visual C# Step by Step
ISBN: 0-7356-1568-3

XML Step by Step, Second Edition
ISBN: 0-7356-1465-2

Microsoft Visual Basic 6.0 Professional Step by Step, Second Edition
ISBN: 0-7356-1883-6

Microsoft Excel 2002 Visual Basic for Applications Step by Step
ISBN: 0-7356-1359-1

Microsoft Access 2002 Visual Basic for Applications Step by Step
ISBN: 0-7356-1358-3

To learn more about the full line of Microsoft Press® products for developers, please visit us at:

microsoft.com/mspress/developer

Learn how to *build dynamic, scalable Web applications* with ASP.NET!

Designing Microsoft® ASP.NET Applications
ISBN 0-7356-1348-6

Get expert guidance on how to use the powerful new functionality of ASP.NET! ASP.NET, the next generation of Active Server Pages, provides a new programming model based on the Microsoft .NET Framework for writing Web applications. Learn about ASP.NET development—with reusable code samples in languages such as Microsoft Visual Basic® .NET and Microsoft Visual C#™—in DESIGNING MICROSOFT ASP.NET APPLICATIONS. This book provides an in-depth look at how to create ASP.NET applications and how they work under the covers. You'll learn how to create Web Forms and reusable components, and how to develop XML Web services. You'll also learn how to create database-enabled ASP.NET applications that use XML (Extensible Markup Language) and ADO.NET (the next generation of Microsoft ActiveX® Data Objects).

Building Web Solutions with ASP.NET and ADO.NET
ISBN 0-7356-1578-0

Take your Web programming skills to the next level. Most Web applications follow a simple "3F" pattern: fetch, format, and forward to the browser. With this in-depth guide, you'll take your ASP.NET and ADO.NET skills to the next level and learn key techniques to develop more functional Web applications. Discover how to build applications for ad hoc and effective Web reporting, applications that work disconnected from the data source and use XML to communicate with non-.NET systems, and general-purpose applications that take advantage of the data abstraction of ADO.NET. Along the way, you'll learn how to take advantage of code reusability, user controls, code-behind, custom Web controls, and other timesaving techniques employed by ASP.NET experts.

Microsoft ASP.NET Step by Step
ISBN 0-7356-1287-0

Master ASP.NET with the proven Microsoft STEP BY STEP learning method. Get a solid handle on this revolutionary new programming framework and its underlying technologies with this accessible, modular primer. You'll quickly learn how to put together the basic building blocks to get working in ASP.NET and find examples drawn from the real-world challenges that both beginning and experienced developers face every day. Easy-to-grasp instructions help you understand fundamental tools and technologies such as the common language runtime, Web Forms, XML Web services, and the Microsoft .NET Framework. Throughout the book, you'll find insightful tips about best practices to follow while using ASP.NET to create scalable, high-performance Web applications.

Microsoft Press has many other titles to help you put development tools and technologies to work
To learn more about the full line of Microsoft Press® products for developers, please visit:

microsoft.com/mspress/developer

Get a **Free**
e-mail newsletter, updates,
special offers, links to related books,
and more when you
register on line!

Register your Microsoft Press® title on our Web site and you'll get a FREE subscription to our e-mail newsletter, *Microsoft Press Book Connections*. You'll find out about newly released and upcoming books and learning tools, online events, software downloads, special offers and coupons for Microsoft Press customers, and information about major Microsoft® product releases. You can also read useful additional information about all the titles we publish, such as detailed book descriptions, tables of contents and indexes, sample chapters, links to related books and book series, author biographies, and reviews by other customers.

Registration is easy. Just visit this Web page and fill in your information:

http://www.microsoft.com/mspress/register

Microsoft

Proof of Purchase

Use this page as proof of purchase if participating in a promotion or rebate offer on this title. Proof of purchase must be used in conjunction with other proof(s) of payment such as your dated sales receipt—see offer details.

MCSD Self-Paced Training Kit: Analyzing Requirements and Defining Microsoft® .NET Solution Architectures, Exam 70-300
0-7356-1894-1

CUSTOMER NAME

Microsoft Press, PO Box 97017, Redmond, WA 98073-9830

MICROSOFT LICENSE AGREEMENT
Book Companion CD

IMPORTANT—READ CAREFULLY: This Microsoft End-User License Agreement ("EULA") is a legal agreement between you (either an individual or an entity) and Microsoft Corporation for the Microsoft product identified above, which includes computer software and may include associated media, printed materials, and "online" or electronic documentation ("SOFTWARE PRODUCT"). Any component included within the SOFTWARE PRODUCT that is accompanied by a separate End-User License Agreement shall be governed by such agreement and not the terms set forth below. By installing, copying, or otherwise using the SOFTWARE PRODUCT, you agree to be bound by the terms of this EULA. If you do not agree to the terms of this EULA, you are not authorized to install, copy, or otherwise use the SOFTWARE PRODUCT; you may, however, return the SOFTWARE PRODUCT, along with all printed materials and other items that form a part of the Microsoft product that includes the SOFTWARE PRODUCT, to the place you obtained them for a full refund.

SOFTWARE PRODUCT LICENSE

The SOFTWARE PRODUCT is protected by United States copyright laws and international copyright treaties, as well as other intellectual property laws and treaties. The SOFTWARE PRODUCT is licensed, not sold.

1. **GRANT OF LICENSE.** This EULA grants you the following rights:

   a. **Software Product.** You may install and use one copy of the SOFTWARE PRODUCT on a single computer. The primary user of the computer on which the SOFTWARE PRODUCT is installed may make a second copy for his or her exclusive use on a portable computer.

   b. **Storage/Network Use.** You may also store or install a copy of the SOFTWARE PRODUCT on a storage device, such as a network server, used only to install or run the SOFTWARE PRODUCT on your other computers over an internal network; however, you must acquire and dedicate a license for each separate computer on which the SOFTWARE PRODUCT is installed or run from the storage device. A license for the SOFTWARE PRODUCT may not be shared or used concurrently on different computers.

   c. **License Pak.** If you have acquired this EULA in a Microsoft License Pak, you may make the number of additional copies of the computer software portion of the SOFTWARE PRODUCT authorized on the printed copy of this EULA, and you may use each copy in the manner specified above. You are also entitled to make a corresponding number of secondary copies for portable computer use as specified above.

   d. **Sample Code.** Solely with respect to portions, if any, of the SOFTWARE PRODUCT that are identified within the SOFTWARE PRODUCT as sample code (the "SAMPLE CODE"):

      i. **Use and Modification.** Microsoft grants you the right to use and modify the source code version of the SAMPLE CODE, *provided* you comply with subsection (d)(iii) below. You may not distribute the SAMPLE CODE, or any modified version of the SAMPLE CODE, in source code form.

      ii. **Redistributable Files.** Provided you comply with subsection (d)(iii) below, Microsoft grants you a nonexclusive, royalty-free right to reproduce and distribute the object code version of the SAMPLE CODE and of any modified SAMPLE CODE, other than SAMPLE CODE, or any modified version thereof, designated as not redistributable in the Readme file that forms a part of the SOFTWARE PRODUCT (the "Non-Redistributable Sample Code"). All SAMPLE CODE other than the Non-Redistributable Sample Code is collectively referred to as the "REDISTRIBUTABLES."

      iii. **Redistribution Requirements.** If you redistribute the REDISTRIBUTABLES, you agree to: (i) distribute the REDISTRIBUTABLES in object code form only in conjunction with and as a part of your software application product; (ii) not use Microsoft's name, logo, or trademarks to market your software application product; (iii) include a valid copyright notice on your software application product; (iv) indemnify, hold harmless, and defend Microsoft from and against any claims or lawsuits, including attorney's fees, that arise or result from the use or distribution of your software application product; and (v) not permit further distribution of the REDISTRIBUTABLES by your end user. Contact Microsoft for the applicable royalties due and other licensing terms for all other uses and/or distribution of the REDISTRIBUTABLES.

2. **DESCRIPTION OF OTHER RIGHTS AND LIMITATIONS.**

   - **Limitations on Reverse Engineering, Decompilation, and Disassembly.** You may not reverse engineer, decompile, or disassemble the SOFTWARE PRODUCT, except and only to the extent that such activity is expressly permitted by applicable law notwithstanding this limitation.

   - **Separation of Components.** The SOFTWARE PRODUCT is licensed as a single product. Its component parts may not be separated for use on more than one computer.

   - **Rental.** You may not rent, lease, or lend the SOFTWARE PRODUCT.

- **Support Services.** Microsoft may, but is not obligated to, provide you with support services related to the SOFTWARE PRODUCT ("Support Services"). Use of Support Services is governed by the Microsoft policies and programs described in the user manual, in "online" documentation, and/or in other Microsoft-provided materials. Any supplemental software code provided to you as part of the Support Services shall be considered part of the SOFTWARE PRODUCT and subject to the terms and conditions of this EULA. With respect to technical information you provide to Microsoft as part of the Support Services, Microsoft may use such information for its business purposes, including for product support and development. Microsoft will not utilize such technical information in a form that personally identifies you.

- **Software Transfer.** You may permanently transfer all of your rights under this EULA, provided you retain no copies, you transfer all of the SOFTWARE PRODUCT (including all component parts, the media and printed materials, any upgrades, this EULA, and, if applicable, the Certificate of Authenticity), **and** the recipient agrees to the terms of this EULA.

- **Termination.** Without prejudice to any other rights, Microsoft may terminate this EULA if you fail to comply with the terms and conditions of this EULA. In such event, you must destroy all copies of the SOFTWARE PRODUCT and all of its component parts.

3. **COPYRIGHT.** All title and copyrights in and to the SOFTWARE PRODUCT (including but not limited to any images, photographs, animations, video, audio, music, text, SAMPLE CODE, REDISTRIBUTABLES, and "applets" incorporated into the SOFTWARE PRODUCT) and any copies of the SOFTWARE PRODUCT are owned by Microsoft or its suppliers. The SOFTWARE PRODUCT is protected by copyright laws and international treaty provisions. Therefore, you must treat the SOFTWARE PRODUCT like any other copyrighted material **except** that you may install the SOFTWARE PRODUCT on a single computer provided you keep the original solely for backup or archival purposes. You may not copy the printed materials accompanying the SOFTWARE PRODUCT.

4. **U.S. GOVERNMENT RESTRICTED RIGHTS.** The SOFTWARE PRODUCT and documentation are provided with RESTRICTED RIGHTS. Use, duplication, or disclosure by the Government is subject to restrictions as set forth in subparagraph (c)(1)(ii) of the Rights in Technical Data and Computer Software clause at DFARS 252.227-7013 or subparagraphs (c)(1) and (2) of the Commercial Computer Software—Restricted Rights at 48 CFR 52.227-19, as applicable. Manufacturer is Microsoft Corporation/One Microsoft Way/Redmond, WA 98052-6399.

5. **EXPORT RESTRICTIONS.** You agree that you will not export or re-export the SOFTWARE PRODUCT, any part thereof, or any process or service that is the direct product of the SOFTWARE PRODUCT (the foregoing collectively referred to as the "Restricted Components"), to any country, person, entity, or end user subject to U.S. export restrictions. You specifically agree not to export or re-export any of the Restricted Components (i) to any country to which the U.S. has embargoed or restricted the export of goods or services, which currently include, but are not necessarily limited to, Cuba, Iran, Iraq, Libya, North Korea, Sudan, and Syria, or to any national of any such country, wherever located, who intends to transmit or transport the Restricted Components back to such country; (ii) to any end user who you know or have reason to know will utilize the Restricted Components in the design, development, or production of nuclear, chemical, or biological weapons; or (iii) to any end user who has been prohibited from participating in U.S. export transactions by any federal agency of the U.S. government. You warrant and represent that neither the BXA nor any other U.S. federal agency has suspended, revoked, or denied your export privileges.

DISCLAIMER OF WARRANTY

NO WARRANTIES OR CONDITIONS. MICROSOFT EXPRESSLY DISCLAIMS ANY WARRANTY OR CONDITION FOR THE SOFTWARE PRODUCT. THE SOFTWARE PRODUCT AND ANY RELATED DOCUMENTATION ARE PROVIDED "AS IS" WITHOUT WARRANTY OR CONDITION OF ANY KIND, EITHER EXPRESS OR IMPLIED, INCLUDING, WITHOUT LIMITATION, THE IMPLIED WARRANTIES OF MERCHANTABILITY, FITNESS FOR A PARTICULAR PURPOSE, OR NONINFRINGEMENT. THE ENTIRE RISK ARISING OUT OF USE OR PERFORMANCE OF THE SOFTWARE PRODUCT REMAINS WITH YOU.

LIMITATION OF LIABILITY. TO THE MAXIMUM EXTENT PERMITTED BY APPLICABLE LAW, IN NO EVENT SHALL MICROSOFT OR ITS SUPPLIERS BE LIABLE FOR ANY SPECIAL, INCIDENTAL, INDIRECT, OR CONSEQUENTIAL DAMAGES WHATSOEVER (INCLUDING, WITHOUT LIMITATION, DAMAGES FOR LOSS OF BUSINESS PROFITS, BUSINESS INTERRUPTION, LOSS OF BUSINESS INFORMATION, OR ANY OTHER PECUNIARY LOSS) ARISING OUT OF THE USE OF OR INABILITY TO USE THE SOFTWARE PRODUCT OR THE PROVISION OF OR FAILURE TO PROVIDE SUPPORT SERVICES, EVEN IF MICROSOFT HAS BEEN ADVISED OF THE POSSIBILITY OF SUCH DAMAGES. IN ANY CASE, MICROSOFT'S ENTIRE LIABILITY UNDER ANY PROVISION OF THIS EULA SHALL BE LIMITED TO THE GREATER OF THE AMOUNT ACTUALLY PAID BY YOU FOR THE SOFTWARE PRODUCT OR US$5.00; PROVIDED, HOWEVER, IF YOU HAVE ENTERED INTO A MICROSOFT SUPPORT SERVICES AGREEMENT, MICROSOFT'S ENTIRE LIABILITY REGARDING SUPPORT SERVICES SHALL BE GOVERNED BY THE TERMS OF THAT AGREEMENT. BECAUSE SOME STATES AND JURISDICTIONS DO NOT ALLOW THE EXCLUSION OR LIMITATION OF LIABILITY, THE ABOVE LIMITATION MAY NOT APPLY TO YOU.

MISCELLANEOUS

This EULA is governed by the laws of the State of Washington USA, except and only to the extent that applicable law mandates governing law of a different jurisdiction.

Should you have any questions concerning this EULA, or if you desire to contact Microsoft for any reason, please contact the Microsoft subsidiary serving your country, or write: Microsoft Sales Information Center/One Microsoft Way/Redmond, WA 98052-6399.

System Requirements

To get the most out of this training kit and the Supplemental Course Materials CD-ROM, you will need a computer equipped with the following minimum configuration:

- Pentium II, 266 MHz or faster
- 128 MB RAM
- 4-GB hard drive
- CD-ROM drive
- Microsoft Mouse or compatible pointing device
- Microsoft Windows 2000 Professional with Service Pack 3 or Microsoft Windows XP Professional
- Microsoft Office 2000 Professional with Service Pack 3 or later
- Microsoft Visio 2000 Professional or later

Test with Pearson VUE–
and save 15%!

Get certified

You invested in your future with the purchase of this book. Now, demonstrate your proficiency with Microsoft® .NET and get the industry recognition your skills deserve. A Microsoft certification validates your technical expertise and increases your credibility in the marketplace.

- Microsoft Certified Solution Developer (MCSD) for Microsoft .NET is the only certification that targets advanced developers who analyze and design leading-edge enterprise solutions using Microsoft .NET architecture, tools, and technologies.

- MCSD for Microsoft .NET reliably validates your ability to lead successful software development projects.

- As you earn the MCSD credential, you will cultivate your skills at envisioning and planning solutions and increase your opportunities.

Test with Pearson VUE

Pearson VUE, a Microsoft authorized test delivery provider since 1998, has teamed with Microsoft Press for a special, limited-time offer. Use this voucher to save 15% on one MCSD exam fee at any Pearson VUE™ Authorized Test Center!*

Redeem your discount voucher

Uncover your discount voucher code on the back of this page, and go to **www.pearsonvue.com/mspress** to register for the Microsoft MCSD Exam 70-300.

VOUCHER

Microsoft CERTIFIED
Exam Provider

PEARSON
VUE

eVoucher good for 15% OFF one
Microsoft MCSD Exam: 70-300

Register online only at
www.pearsonvue.com/mspress

See back
for discount code.

Expires June 30, 2004

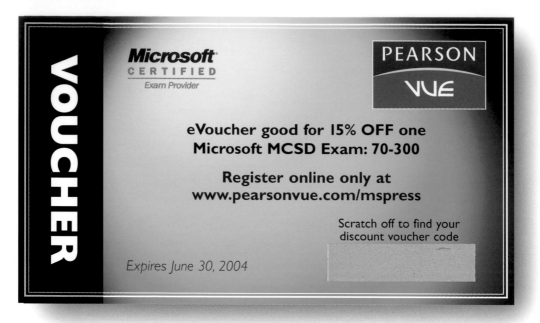

VOUCHER

Microsoft
CERTIFIED
Exam Provider

PEARSON
VUE

eVoucher good for 15% OFF one
Microsoft MCSD Exam: 70-300

Register online only at
www.pearsonvue.com/mspress

Scratch off to find your
discount voucher code

Expires June 30, 2004

Schedule your exam online only at
www.pearsonvue.com/mspress

When you test with Pearson VUE, you get state-of-the-art testing technology and world-class service, resulting in an enhanced testing experience.

Convenient – choose from over 3,300 quality Pearson VUE test centers in more than 130 countries

Easy – real-time access to Web-based exam scheduling means you have 24 x 7 control over your exam schedule

Reliable – your exam will be ready when you expect it, and your exam results will be quickly and accurately reported to Microsoft

Secure – Only Pearson VUE has a Web Digital Embosser that helps protect your certification

For the location of a Pearson VUE test center near you, visit www.pearsonvue.com/mspress

Promotion Terms and Conditions:
• Voucher discount must be redeemed online at **www.pearsonvue.com/mspress**
• Exam must be taken at a Pearson VUE Authorized Center
• Voucher is available only in the English language version of these books
• Discounted exam must be taken on or before June 30, 2004
• Discounted exam registration must be made online at **www.pearsonvue.com**
• Promotion is limited to one discounted exam per candidate for each book purchased
• 15% discount is valid only on Microsoft MCSD Exam 70-300

Voucher Terms and Conditions
• Expired voucher has no value
• Voucher may not be redeemed for cash or credit
• Voucher may not be transferred or sold

Part No. X09-49339

0-7356-1894-1